HJ454857

'Sissel-Jo Gazan has demonstrated that her acclaimed mystery, *The Dinosaur Feather* was no fluke ... The domestic intrigues of Marie and her relatives, and of Soren and Anna, prove as engrossing as the criminal conspiracies at hand'

Wall Street Journal, top ten mysteries of 2015

'*The Dinosaur Feather*, Sissel-Jo Gazan's acclaimed debut, proved that scientific controversy could feature in crime fiction ... This is a terrific novel, involving bitter rivalries among scientists'

Sunday Times

'Smart and compelling ... A high-end thriller for readers of Jo Nesbø and of John le Carré's *The Constant Gardener*'

Booklist

'Excellent ... draws the reader into the fiercely competitive, high-stakes world of medical research ... The action builds to a thrilling denouement'

Publishers Weekly

'A formidable mystery ... Among the latest crop of Scandinavian thriller writers, Gazan combines the broad scope of Jo Nesbø with the ability to focus as closely and remorselessly as Karin Fossum'

Kirkus

'From Denmark to West Africa, Gazan takes readers on a roller-coaster ride ... Less graphic than Stieg Larsson's Millennium trilogy but just as compelling, Gazan's novel breathes fresh life into the packed Scan

rnal

Sissel-Jo Gazan is a biology graduate from the University of Copenhagen. *The Dinosaur Feather* was her breakthrough novel, having sold in twelve countries and named the Danish Novel of the Decade. Its follow-up is *The Arc of the Swallow*. She lives in Berlin.

THE ARC OF THE SWALLOW

SISSEL-JO GAZAN

Translated from the Danish
by Charlotte Barslund

riverrun

First published in Denmark as *Svalens Graf* in 2013
First published in Great Britain in 2014 by Quercus
This paperback edition published in Great Britain in 2016 by riverrun
An imprint of

Quercus Publishing Ltd
Carmelite House
50 Victoria Embankment
London EC4Y 0DZ

An Hachette UK company

© Sissel-Jo Gazan 2013
Translation © Charlotte Barslund 2014

A CIP catalogue record for this book is available
from the British Library.

PB ISBN 978 0 85738 772 1
EBOOK ISBN 978 0 85738 243 6

10 9 8 7 6 5 4 3 2 1

Typeset by CC Book Production

Printed and bound in Great Britain by Clays Ltd, St Ives plc

This novel is pure fiction. The author's representation of some aspects of science is thus an artistic interpretation of the subject.

CHAPTER 1

It was Thursday, 18 March 2010, and still dark on Skovvej in Humlebæk. Deputy Chief Superintendent Søren Marhauge was woken up by his girlfriend, Anna, talking to him. She was sitting, fully dressed, on the edge of their bed with her bag slung across her chest and her short, dark hair in damp disarray as if she had just stepped out of the shower.

'Eh?' he grunted, still half asleep.

The night before they had both been reading in bed, but Anna had switched off her light first. Søren had assumed that she must be asleep until her eyes snapped open and she announced that his light was bothering her. He had switched it off ostentatiously and a foul mood had descended on the bedroom. From then on Søren's irritation had kept him wide awake while Anna had lain so still that it was obvious she was not asleep either.

Finally he had said, 'Did you have to sound quite so pissed off?' Whereupon Anna had launched into an angry tirade. He hadn't bothered listening properly to what she had said. A few minutes later, he had pulled off the duvet, grabbed her wrist and stuck his tongue between her legs. That was how their arguments usually ended.

He must have fallen asleep straight afterwards, dammit. They never had time to savour their stellar moments.

'I couldn't sleep,' Anna said, in the morning darkness. 'Please would you take Lily to nursery today? The deadline for my funding application is in two weeks and I can't get it out of my mind. I want to go to the faculty and write it up. Is that OK? I'll cycle to the station and catch the train. Please would you also pick Lily up, cook dinner and put her to bed? I know it's my turn, only I'd really like to be able to work late, with Anders T., if need be. So that we can crack that application. Do you mind?'

'Don't you ever draw breath?' Søren muttered, and pulled the duvet over his head. 'But, yes, I'll take Lily to nursery. And pick her up. And cook dinner. And everything else.'

'Thank you.' Anna quickly hugged him through the duvet. 'See you tonight. It'll be late.'

Shortly afterwards he heard the front door slam.

Across the passage Anna's daughter, Lily, was asleep in her natural-history bedroom. She had pictures of animals on the walls and, on the shelves, Plexiglas boxes with her findings: seven spotted eggshells, four feathers, thirty-two brown pine cones, moss dried out around the edges, piles of various leaves, a scrap of fur she had felt sorry for and three small rodent skeletons that were her prized possessions and displayed on cotton wool. When she grew up, Lily wanted to be a biologist, just like her mother.

Lily was five years old and the apple of Søren's eye. In the evening her soft, tiny hand would stroke the velvety patch at the top of his ears while he read aloud to her from natural-history books for children. With her other hand, she would point to the illustrations and explain to him how to tell the seagulls apart.

Lily and Søren had lived in the same house for a year now and everything in the garden was rosy. When he fetched her from nursery, Søren could pick out the colour of her snowsuit in a sea of other snowsuits at a distance of thirty metres. The children would flock around his legs when he opened the gate and he would reach down into the crowd, lift her up and she would hug him as hard as she could. 'My Søren,' she would say, as if he had rescued her from a frothing sea.

Lily called Søren Søren. After all, he wasn't her real dad: that was another man. Who was an idiot.

'You're jealous,' Anna would invariably remark, when Thomas, Lily's biological father, came to fetch Lily. Søren had stopped trying to deny it. Thomas was a doctor at Karolinska University Hospital in Stockholm and would say, 'Hello, hello,' when he turned up, as if visiting Lily was merely an extension of his rounds. What Anna had ever seen in him was beyond Søren. She had told Søren about her previous relationship and how Thomas, shortly after Lily's first Christmas, had dropped the happy-family project like a rotten plum and moved to Sweden, but Søren had never learned exactly what had gone wrong. Anna had only said that Thomas had got cold feet. It turned out family life wasn't his thing after all.

For a long time after Søren and Anna had got together, Thomas had not been a part of their life and Søren had been overjoyed. Several of his colleagues at Bellahøj Police Station had stepfamilies and they said it could be tricky. Not only in practical terms when it came to planning holidays, but also emotionally. Whose rules applied and who was in charge? And when new children arrived, the situation became extra complicated. Søren used to think he had been lucky with his package. When he had met Anna, Lily had been barely three; she hadn't seen her father for the last two years and winning her heart had been easy. However, shortly after Anna and Lily had moved into Søren's house in Humlebæk, Thomas was back on the scene. He was still living in Stockholm, now with his new wife and their baby, and would visit Copenhagen every three months where he would spend a long Saturday with Lily.

A very long Saturday.

Every time Thomas pulled up in front of the house, Søren would go outside and make small talk while Anna helped Lily get dressed. Lily would then, ignoring Søren, make a beeline for Thomas, shouting, 'Hi, Daddy,' and although Søren had noticed that Thomas never featured in Lily's drawings, he still had to bite his tongue as she dashed right past him with her SpongeBob SquarePants rucksack on her back and her greasy cuddly toy, Bloppen, dangling from her right hand and threw herself into the arms of her *real* dad. Søren never looked at Thomas when Lily hugged him; instead, he would stare at the hunched profile of the beech trees at the bottom of the garden where the woods began. Even so, he knew that Thomas was gloating.

Until recently Søren had been the youngest superintendent in Danish police history, but then he was promoted and became the youngest but most frustrated deputy chief superintendent in Danish police history. He was still working for

Copenhagen Police at the Violent Crimes Unit at Bellahøj Police Station, but with an extra rhombus on his lapel, a bigger office and a pile of paperwork with which now, only six months into his promotion, he was thoroughly fed up. The first few months he had swum in the fast lane to catch up with the workload, but now he had admitted to himself that it could not be done and had begun to slow down. Perhaps a little more than he should. He still spent a lot of time in his office and worked longer hours than he needed to on the days it was Anna's turn to pick Lily up, but his mind had started to wander. He would think about Anna and stare out of the window. He would look at the photograph of Lily on his desk and at the drawing on the wall she had done for him.

He Googled a recipe for pork meatloaf and decided that, from now on, he would cook only dishes inspired by the animal kingdom when he and Lily had dinner alone: mock turtle soup, bird's nest soup, butterfly cakes, spaghetti worms with tomato sauce. Internal reports, budget compliance meetings, job interviews and salary negotiations held no attraction for him. What made it all worse was that he had feared this was exactly what promotion would mean: drowning in a sea of mind-numbing paperwork. But Henrik Tejsner, his friend and junior colleague, had assured him that a higher rank would bring more freedom. And now that Søren had Lily, he wanted greater flexibility at work.

But it just wasn't true.

All Søren had got more of was trivial problems. For example, before Christmas he had wasted six weeks on the officially required procedure to get to the bottom of an incident where one officer had accused another of making racist comments in the lavatories during a staff party, and as soon as that case had been resolved, Søren had been told to draft a circular clarifying management guidelines for the use of private mobile telephones during working hours. He had wanted to scream. And, to top it all, someone had recently managed to nick eighty grams of confiscated cocaine from the evidence room in the basement under Bellahøj Police Station, which meant that Søren was forced to spend three long weeks investigating internal security measures, supervised by a surly civil servant from the National Police Force. But any number of people could have nicked that bag. The cleaners, an outsider, the police commissioner himself – what did Søren know? Well, one thing he did know was that he was desperate to be working an investigation hands-on again; he longed to knit backwards.

Besides, Søren suspected Henrik of having talked up the job of deputy chief superintendent purely so that Henrik himself would be considered for superintendent if Søren was promoted. And that was exactly what had happened. Three weeks after Søren's promotion, Henrik had been appointed superintendent at the Violent Crimes Unit.

Søren had met Anna during his investigation of 'the campus murders', as the media had dubbed the bizarre killings, first, of Anna's supervisor at the Institute of Biology and then, shortly afterwards, her best friend Johannes. Søren had fallen head over heels in love with her and not cared that it was unprofessional. Unfortunately, his feelings didn't appear to have been reciprocated in the slightest. When everyone of interest had been interviewed, the police report filed and the trial finished, Søren had risked emailing Anna, tentatively suggesting dinner. She had replied with an email consisting of just two letters:

No.

He had stared at the screen in amazement and concluded that she had a rare talent for antagonism. The only problem was that he couldn't stop thinking about her. After another three weeks, and Henrik's advice to 'forget about that drama queen', he decided to lay siege to her. He started inventing all sorts of excuses, both plausible and implausible, to see her. At lunchtime he would turn up with sandwiches at the Museum of Natural History where Anna was now a PhD student. 'I've already eaten,' she would say suspiciously, as he munched away and tried to keep the conversation going by asking her about her research. He invited her to the cinema every day for a week and received seven refusals. He started doing his shopping at the Kvickly supermarket on Falkoner Allé, and when he bumped into Anna and Lily, he would exclaim, 'Fancy meeting you here!' and would then insist on giving them a lift home afterwards. But it was no use: Anna's frostiness didn't thaw. So Søren ratcheted up the charm another notch. When they ran into each other in Kvickly for the fourth time that week, and Søren made no attempt to hide that he had been standing behind a shelf of tinned food spying on them for some time, Anna gave him a resigned look, said, 'Anyone would think you'd taken a second job as a shelf stacker,' and agreed to go to the cinema with him – once. She had held up her hand and shown him one finger.

Three cinema trips later they kissed on St Hans Torv and the following weekend they went to bed. Søren was delirious with happiness. He had never had sex like this before. Anna lunged at him, and when she had come, she rolled away from him, panting, demanding to be left alone. Søren was quite content to be put out to pasture for a while because, though the act itself had been too fierce and strange for intimacy, it beat peeping at her from behind a supermarket shelf. But after a couple of weeks, he began to long for her to open up and let him in.

It happened very suddenly. One night she didn't roll away from him. Søren lay completely still for fear of breaking the spell and realised that Anna was listening carefully to his heart. She did that five dates in a row before she raised her hand and put it on his chest.

'What is this?' she said, in a low voice. 'Just a bit of fun or are you serious? Because I can't bear . . . to be that unhappy again.' It was just as well that it was dark so that no one could see the huge smile on Søren's face.

'Anna, I'm very much in love with you,' he said.

Just over two years had passed since then. Anna had bought a half-share in his house in Humlebæk, they had written wills in favour of each other, and Søren had named Anna as his beneficiary on his pension. Everyone would look at their life and say, 'So, you won her over in the end, eh, Søren Marhauge?'

But Søren himself wasn't quite so sure.

Anna was married to her academic career and would go off to the university at the drop of a hat. When she talked about

her research, her eyes came alive. The biomechanics of vertebrates reached parts of Anna that Søren couldn't. When she
was at home, she tended to lie on the floor drawing pictures
with Lily while they listened to audio books or she would read
on the sofa or bake a cake. She was physically there, but she
wasn't present, at least not to him. He was starting to doubt
that she really loved him.

The very thought was terrifying.

Lily was still so young. If he and Anna broke up, Lily would
forget him while he would never be able to forget her. And
the thought of Anna with another man . . . Anders T., for
example. Anna's fellow PhD student was in his late twenties
and had an irritatingly casual manner, as if he had just parked
his surfboard on the beach while he carried out some important research before trekking around Annapurna in a ripped
T-shirt. Søren couldn't think of a more ridiculous sport for a
Dane than surfing.

'Well, he does spend a lot of time in Australia, actually,'
Anna had informed him.

To begin with, Søren had loved the way Anna threw herself
into anything she did. She would lose herself completely in a
book and, on the rare occasions that she ventured into the
kitchen, she would go all out to cook some ambitious French
dish that took hours, only to chuck the whole thing into the
bin because some aspect of it had failed. Anna did everything
at breakneck speed. In her he recognised himself as he used
to be. Back when he, too, had been married to his work and
his relationship with his ex-girlfriend, Vibe, had been a
pleasing backdrop rather than taking centre stage in his life.

Søren was starting to realise that he was most definitely not the centre of Anna's life. At the same time, he had stopped being quite so immersed in being a police officer, or at least in being a deputy chief superintendent. All he cared about was Anna and Lily. It troubled him.

Anna and he argued a lot. Frequently. Too frequently. They didn't argue when Lily was awake, but there was constant high-voltage tension between them and it could explode in a split second. In the kitchen, when Lily was watching children's television in the living room, Anna would snap at him because it was getting late. Søren had never hit a woman. He had barely had an argument with one. But Anna could rile him: when she started sulking and looked highly combustible, he couldn't stop himself striking a metaphorical match and flicking it in her direction. An arsonist could not have hoped for greater success. Anna would spin around when he baited her, her eyes blazing with rage, and he would be overcome by a strong urge to put in her place. What he did do was grab her and half turn her towards him. 'Bloody well relax, will you? There's no need to get so pissed off over a little thing like that,' he would hiss in her ear, so that Lily wouldn't hear.

Anna would respond by unbuttoning her jeans and he would unzip his and enter her deeply, it took only ten seconds, and it was vitally important that they did not drown the adventures of Bamse and Kylling on the telly, so Søren had to keep all the noise in his head. Nothing more was said. As they buttoned themselves up afterwards, they looked at each other, placated.

The earth was smouldering.

Then, for a little while, the mood would be lighter. Anna

would pour him a glass of wine, stroke his neck and call Lily, who would march into the kitchen with her doll's pram and Ib, her furry caterpillar, and announce that she was hungry. They would eat and Ib would join them at the table in his jam-jar next to Lily's plate. Søren could still smell Anna when he raised his fork to his mouth, and he had no idea what the hell was going on.

Søren never discussed Anna with anyone. He hadn't discussed his ex-girlfriend, Vibe, with anyone either, not even when their relationship was breaking down and they had split up. Henrik always chided him for it. Henrik himself had been married for twenty years to Jeanette and, after a rocky patch when Henrik had had an affair, they had ironed out their differences; as a result, Søren now received regular updates on how 'bloody brilliant it is that Jeanette has started having Brazilians' and 'The woman wants new tits now, would you believe it?' Henrik had whispered the latter and looked terribly pleased with himself. Last year he had even announced that there was 'an afterthought in the oven', even though he and his wife already had two teenage girls who drove him crazy.

'Why don't we ever swap stories about the *wimmin* in our lives?' Henrik asked, with a big, macho grin. But since Søren had already heard all the stories about Jeanette there were to know, he knew that Henrik was really asking why Søren never volunteered information about his relationship with Anna.

'Anna is an ocean,' Søren tried, one day, when he was still seething from last night's row with her.

Henrik had looked at him for a long time, then said, 'An ocean? What the hell are you on about, mate?'

Henrik had nicknamed Anna 'Tiger Pussy', and Søren knew that if he ever tried to explain his comparison Henrik would curl his hands into two claws, paw the air and say, 'Miaow, those bitches!'

But Anna wasn't a bitch. She was a force of nature.

Whenever Søren watched Thomas walk down the flagstone path holding Lily's hand, he knew perfectly well why Thomas had dropped the Anna-and-Lily project. It took the courage of a lion to be with Anna, and Thomas was fundamentally a lightweight who could not cope with Anna's sparring.

'Don't waste your breath, sweetheart,' Anna would say, and hug him from behind as Søren gazed at the flagstone path in front of their house.

'But I'm her dad,' he mumbled.

'Being a dad isn't about being a sperm donor,' Anna replied, 'but about the next eighteen years. Of course you're Lily's dad.'

Søren had made this his one condition from the start of their relationship. Anna could date him as casually, as bizarrely as she wanted to and they could spend the night together when Lily was with Anna's parents, but if he was to stay over when Lily was at home, different rules would apply. If he was to get to know Lily, there could be no restrictions. He wanted the right to love Lily, and she should have the right to risk loving him. It meant that if he and Anna were to go their separate ways, Søren would still be in Lily's life.

A few months later, when Anna and Lily had moved in with him, Søren had fenced off the pond at the bottom of the garden that bordered the forest, fixed a padlock on the tool shed and put up jungle wallpaper in the bedroom that was to be Lily's. He unscrewed the sign saying 'Marhauge' on the front door and replaced it with a new one.

'Nor and Marhauge,' Anna said contentedly. 'It sounds like a karate chop. Highly effective.'

On the morning of 18 March, Søren was sitting in his office at Bellahøj Police Station waiting impatiently for information from the Institute of Forensic Medicine. The medical examiner, Bøje Knudsen, had promised to get back to him on Monday, but now it was Thursday. Søren knew Bøje was hard to track down – the man didn't even carry a mobile phone – but he was usually quick to respond to emails. Now he was unresponsive on all channels and Søren knew why. A series of violent rapes in the Kødbyen district demanded all police resources. The victims were young female students, and one of them had turned out to be the goddaughter of the justice secretary, so the assaults received considerable attention from both politicians and the media. When one of the girls had died from her injuries over the weekend, the case had gone viral, and Station City in central Copenhagen had requested assistance from Bellahøj. Which they had got, of course. Everyone was rushed off their feet. But Søren was still stuck with an unfinished case involving a ninety-two-year-old woman who had been beaten up in her home by burglars looking for jewellery; she had since died in hospital. They had arrested the burglars and the case was straightforward. But the woman's family called the police every day to find out when her body would be released for burial. What could Søren tell them? That Bøje was too busy to sign a piece of paper? It was unlike Bøje to treat ordinary Danes so insensitively. He hated snobbery. It had been one of the main reasons why he had opted for demotion, as he put it, and had quit his job as state pathologist last year and gone back to being a bog-standard medical examiner.

'All I want,' Bøje had said, when Søren had asked him, 'is to wield my scalpel like I used to, where all bodies are equal. It's back to basics for me.'

Søren had envied him, but it seemed that Bøje was just as snowed under now as when he had been the state pathologist. Søren decided that, unless Bøje called him very soon, he would have to swing by the Institute of Forensic Medicine himself.

Watching a hopeless morning briefing, in which Henrik had issued a frantic mess of contradictory orders as he distributed that day's assignments, had done nothing to improve Søren's mood. Henrik was stressed and clearly not just because he had had to lend officers to Station City. His forehead was glistening, he was irritable and, rather than spread calm and show leadership of his investigation team, he exuded anxiety. Henrik was actually a good police officer. He didn't deliver big, insightful breakthroughs, but he was a solid team player and particularly handy in any situation that required some muscle. His language could make even a sailor blush and on the street he had ice in his veins. But promoting him to management had been a mistake.

After the campus murders, Henrik and Søren's friendship had temporarily changed for the better. It had become serious, more forbearing, more Søren. But the respect Søren had developed for Henrik was dwindling, not least because Henrik was constantly sniping at him. When Søren was a superintendent, he had become famous all over Denmark for his investigative method of knitting backwards, a private metaphor that Søren had accidentally used in an interview in the *Politiken* newspaper. The expression had subsequently come into common use. Søren based his starting point on the impenetrability of the mystery, he had explained to the journalist, then worked his way backwards by unravelling what he saw. Eventually he would find himself back at the beginning and, in most cases, would know the identity of the killer. Since then he had come across the term in the newspapers several times. Young officers at the police academy were even taught the method, and he was proud of that, obviously. But it had also led to pranks at the station; for example, someone had recently stuck two crossed jumbo knitting needles on Søren's office door. No offence had been intended, but Henrik regarded these innocent jokes as his *carte blanche* for constant teasing.

'Time to put away your crochet hooks and other outdated investigative methods,' he had quipped that very morning, 'and knuckle down, boys and girls.'

Fortunately no one had thought it was funny.

Outside work, however, Henrik was nowhere near as cocky. Six months earlier, when he had been promoted to superintendent, he had started ringing Søren at all hours to discuss a rape case in north-west Copenhagen. The victim was a girl of the same age as Henrik's younger daughter, who had been beaten so badly that she was now in a coma. The police had the rapist's DNA, but as his profile was not in the DNA register and there was very little other evidence, the investigation was at a standstill. It was a hard case to take on as your first, especially because the media were following it closely. Henrik called Søren day and night to ask for advice. When the girl died shortly afterwards, the media went crazy. 'Sometimes that's just how it is,' Søren assured Henrik. 'You've done everything you can so now you have to move on and ignore the media frenzy. It won't last.' Søren told himself that his words had had some effect, but Henrik kept calling him. 'Hi, it's only me, Henrik,' had long since become a standing joke in Søren's house. Henrik was only calling to find out what Søren would have done about this and what Søren thought about that, and if Søren really had fallen foul of journalists all the time. And, as for the amount of paperwork, it was ridiculous. *You might have warned me that life as a superintendent is a chronic state of stress. Just get on with it? Easy for you to say. Being senior management is a cushy number.* 'But what can I do about it?' Henrik had said, sounding as if he felt sorry for himself when he called on Monday evening. He had been asked to send four of his twelve officers to Station City to assist.

'While those amateurs are slacking at Station City and getting on the front page of *Ekstra Bladet*, I spend my whole day in front of a computer,' Henrik complained. 'Anyone would think I was a secretary, not a superintendent.'

'Sometimes it's just the way it is, Henrik. Some weeks it's slow and steady, then all the criminals decide to strike at once, all hell breaks loose and your feet don't touch the ground. It's part of the job.'

'I haven't slept for four bloody nights,' Henrik said. 'When I finally get to bed, I can't shut my brain down.'

But the next morning Henrik had shouted something sarcastic to Søren across the room when he turned up for work and their relationship had soured again.

Now the corridors at the back of Bellahøj Police Station

where the Violent Crimes Unit was located had fallen silent. While Søren waited for the call from the Institute of Forensic Medicine, he drew a pie chart of his family life. He picked Lily up from nursery three times a week, no later than four o'clock so Anna could work late at the Institute of Biology, and he looked after her every Saturday when Anna would cycle to the university initially just for a couple of hours, but invariably she came back at seven in the evening. That made 19.5 hours a week. Then there was the one hour he had with Lily every morning, which made it 24.5 hours a week in total, plus sundry times when Anna would leave early or call home to let him know she would be late. He then started calculating how many hours he was with Anna. They rarely went to bed before midnight and, if he deducted putting Lily to bed, laundry and clearing up after dinner, that made it 3.5 hours a day, less the time they were in the same house, but doing different things; it meant that 'net time with Anna', as he wrote, equalled 12.5 hours per week. He stared at the number. Where was Anna during all those other hours? At the faculty, of course, where she was writing her PhD in 'Terrestrial Movement and Biomechanics in Mammals and Dinosaurs', which Søren had taught himself to reel off whenever someone asked him what his girlfriend did. But where exactly was she when she was there? Away with the fairies in her own head, completely immersed in her subject, lost to the world. Passionately lost to the world. Sitting next to Anders T. and his bulging biceps, one of which was tattooed with the poncy motto 'carpe diem' because, well, it would be, wouldn't it?

And then there was Søren. With his greying temples and budding spare tyre. If he didn't pull himself together soon, he would be summoned to Chief Superintendent Jørgensen's office and asked to explain himself. *What do you think you're doing, Søren?* Søren caught himself fantasising about the scenario. Finally he would have the chance to say it out loud: *I don't want to be senior management. I want to move down the ranks, please. I want to be a police officer again.*

When Bøje finally called, it took him less than five minutes to give the green light to the old lady's family. The body could be released. Bøje sounded pressured and hung up before Søren had had time to moan about the slow response time. The telephone rang again immediately. This time it was Henrik.

'Tell me, did you drop your mobile down the bog? I've called you eight times. I want you to know it's the last time I share a car with that tosser,' he ranted.

It was Søren's job to pair off the officers, and that morning he had put Henrik with one of the unit's older men, Per Molstrup, partly to wind Henrik up because Molstrup wasn't the sharpest knife in the drawer. Søren could hear Molstrup chuckle in the background.

'He's eaten pickled onions.' Molstrup laughed even louder.

'Anything else? I'm rather busy.'

'Yeah, right,' Henrik said. 'He says he's rather busy,' Henrik announced to Molstrup in a stage whisper. Søren was about to hang up.

'We're outside the Institute of Biology and—' Henrik said.

'What are you doing there?' Søren managed, before all his internal organs crashed onto the floor. 'Has something happened to Anna?'

The telephone crackled.

'With Anna? No, no. Hey, relax, I'd never give you bad news about Tiger Pussy with that moron in the car.'

Søren heaved a deep sigh of relief. 'Right. Then what is it?'

'We received a call. There's a professor hanging in an office up in . . .' Henrik read aloud from a piece of paper. 'The Department of Immunology at the Institute of Biology, Stairwell Four. Where the hell is that? Do you know where it is? We're parked outside the stairwell to Anna's department, Stairwell One, and we're lost. And don't tell me to look for the ambulance because it's parked right in front of me and they can't find it either. Can't you get Anna to ride to our rescue? It's what she usually does.'

Søren typed a text message to Anna. *Please look out of your window,* he wrote. To Henrik he said, 'Can you give me some more information?'

'I don't know very much. Merethe Hermansen, the department secretary, called the emergency services, and all I know is that a student found him hanging from a hook in the ceiling . . . Oh, I can see Tiger Pussy now. Always present whenever someone kicks the bucket around here. Got to go.' Before Søren had time to say anything, Henrik had hung up.

Søren shot up from his chair. Henrik, that waste of space, had just called Søren, his boss, to ask for directions.

A plate of Danish pastries had been set out in the briefing room earlier and it was still there, but one flashback to Anders T.'s biceps convinced Søren to leave its contents alone. The coffee in the Thermos flask was lukewarm, but he poured himself a cup anyway and accidentally added two heaped teaspoons of salt and had stirred them in before he spat out the vile concoction on the floor in front of the whiteboard. Bollocks! He stopped at the washroom on his way back to his office and rinsed his mouth.

Henrik had tricked Søren into accepting the promotion to deputy chief superintendent so that he could take over Søren's old job as superintendent. That was bad enough. But that Henrik called his boss because he was lost only to hang up on him the second Anna appeared had pushed Søren over the edge. He was sure that Henrik had already ogled Anna's bottom three times and delivered just as many smutty remarks. Henrik had lost all sense of boundaries. What the hell was the matter with him?

Søren sat down in his office and tried to focus on his paperwork. Two hours later he threw in the towel, got up and stood fuming in front of the window. Then he grabbed his jacket, went down to the basement car park of the station and headed for the University of Copenhagen. He had had enough of being the butt of everyone's jokes, especially Henrik's.

Søren's parents had died in a car crash when he was five years old. All his adult life he had believed that he had been on holiday with his maternal grandparents when it happened. That was what he had been told. It was not until the investigation into the campus murders two years ago that he had learned the truth: that he had also been in the car when his father overlooked a give-way sign and drove straight into a truck; that Søren had been trapped in the back of the car for more than an hour with his dead parents until the Falck emergency services had managed to free him.

'What a lot of boxes of unresolved crap we hide in our

mental basement, eh?' Anna had said, one day, when they were discussing the past. Her remark had hit a nerve. What was the point of knowing? Given the choice, wouldn't he have preferred to live out the rest of his life in blissful ignorance of the traumatic circumstances of his parents' death? What difference did it make that he now knew the macabre details? Knowing wasn't going to bring them back. He told himself that he had been more happy-go-lucky before old wounds had been reopened. The ability to put a lid on certain memories was a good one, he had said to Anna, mostly to provoke her. To his astonishment, Anna had agreed with him.

'No matter how illogical it sounds,' she mused, 'in a modern society where everyone is in therapy to straighten out their thinking, there has to be some evolutionary advantage in the ability to suppress, because otherwise that ability would have been deselected long ago. But, even so, I still believe it does us good to clear out our mental basements.'

Anna, too, had stumbled upon big secrets in her own family during the investigation of the campus murders, but she seemed resolved and at peace now. She got on well with her parents and saw them regularly; she had plenty of energy for her research and at night she slept like a log, even those nights when Søren was lying wide awake and deep in thought by her side. His maternal grandparents, who had looked after him since the death of his parents, had died, so he would never know why they had chosen to hide the circumstances of his parents' death from him. It made no sense because in every other respect they were intelligent and honest people. In the months after Søren had learned that he had been trapped in the wrecked car with his dead parents, he had half-heartedly tried to investigate the case. Like some pathetic TV detective, he had shaken his grandparents' books one after the other in the hope of finding a secret letter with a fanciful explanation. He had carefully examined the boxes in the loft of his grandparents' house in Snerlevej in Vangede before he had rented it out. He had used his police status to access the National Register of Persons – he had even trawled meticulously through the Marhauge family records – but he hadn't found anything. Finally he had reached the conclusion that he, too, was resolved and at peace.

'Are you sure?' Anna had asked.

'Yes,' he had replied. 'Quite sure.'

It took Søren only three minutes to drive from Bellahøj Police Station to the Institute of Biology because he switched on his siren and carved through the yielding traffic, having made up his mind to give Henrik a bollocking and show him how proper police work was done. He parked in front of the building, where a crowd of onlookers was still rubbernecking, watching the ambulance and Henrik's highly conspicuous patrol car. Søren had to ask one of the onlookers for directions and was told that all he had to do was 'just enter through that door, go up to the third floor, across the walkway, down to the second floor and there go through the first door on your right, but not the one which is the entrance to the Museum of Zoology, but the door opposite, and then Kristian Storm's office is at the far end of the corridor.' Søren had thanked him and sworn under his breath. Despite the labyrinthine architecture of the Institute of Biology, rumours appeared to spread faster here than in a hairdresser's salon.

Søren raced up the stairs, his whole being filled with the certain knowledge that, deputy chief superintendent or not, there was no way he was going back to a desk job.

When Søren entered the Department of Immunology, he spotted the red and white police cordon immediately and walked briskly down the main corridor towards what he surmised must be the entrance to the late professor's office. Where were his fellow police officers? Along the way he passed an open door and nodded briefly to a man sitting behind a desk. *Thor Albert Larsen*, Søren read on a sign. He also noticed a couple of young people on chairs around Larsen's desk, all very subdued.

When Søren reached the cordoned-off office, he stopped outside the doorway, aware that he must not enter the scene before he had donned protective clothing. To his huge surprise there were only two people inside, a crime-scene officer, Lars Hviid, in protective clothing and holding a camera, and Henrik, who was standing with his back to him, wearing shoe covers and a mask, but without the compulsory overalls.

'We'll put it down as an unexplained death,' Henrik was thinking out loud, 'but, if you ask me, there's bugger all to explain, wouldn't you say?' Lars Hviid nodded. He was relatively new to Bellahøj and even at the job interview Søren had thought he looked wet behind the ears, though his CV listed his date of birth as 1983. He was gazing at Henrik with boundless admiration and Henrik lapped it up.

'Now, if you ask me, our nerd killed himself,' Henrik said. 'And what removes the last bit of doubt, little Hviid? He left a note.' Henrik took an evidence bag from a box of other bagged items and waved it in the air, like a teacher. At that moment, Hviid spotted Søren and his gaze started to wander.

'And what happens to the computer now?' Henrik carried on. 'Come on, little Hviid, you know the answer . . . Hello?' Henrik followed Lars Hviid's distracted gaze and discovered Søren.

'Hi, Søren,' he said, taken aback. 'What the hell are you doing here?'

'Why aren't you wearing protective clothing?' Søren said. 'And where is the body?'

'The body was taken to the Institute of Forensic Medicine forty-five minutes ago. But what are you doing here?' Henrik said again.

'Forty-five minutes ago?' Søren thundered. 'How the hell did you manage to finish investigating the scene that quickly? Has the medical examiner been?'

'What the hell do you think?' Henrik pouted. 'Do you take us for complete amateurs?'

'Yes,' was all Søren said.

Later that day Søren was summoned to Chief Superintendent Jørgensen's office. Henrik was already in there and looked daggers at him. Since leaving the Institute of Biology, he had called Søren's mobile four times. Eventually Søren had switched it off.

'First, the case. Brief summary, please,' Jørgensen said, and nodded to Henrik, who cleared his throat. Søren was famous across the police force for being unsurpassable in the important discipline of producing a brief summary. On the day Henrik had been promoted to superintendent, he had had a beer or two too many and declared that he intended to wipe the floor with Søren in every discipline, especially the brief summary. Søren smiled sweetly at him and Henrik cleared his throat again.

'The deceased is a man in his mid-sixties, and we have had it confirmed that he's professor of immunology Kristian Storm, who has been employed by the University of Copenhagen since 1982. The deceased was found hanging from a noose attached to a light fitting in the ceiling, and on his desk we found a note where he confesses to scientific dishonesty and asks for forgiveness. In addition, there was a framed photograph smashed on the floor, which we have had confirmed is a picture of Storm and his two protégés. CSO Lars Hviid's initial assessment is that Storm had been dead for between fourteen and fifteen hours, so he died some time between nineteen thirty and twenty thirty yesterday, Wednesday, the seventeenth of March, but we'll have it confirmed once Bøje Knudsen has had a look at the body. Based on preliminary interviews with Kristian Storm's colleagues, the picture we have of the professor is as follows: he had an international reputation in his field and was notorious for his controversial views, but within the university itself he was respected for his dedication and his support of his students. However, I had an interesting conversation with a lecturer, Thor Albert Larsen, today. He has worked with Storm for many years, and he told me that Storm had recently been accused of scientific dishonesty, and that the case is currently being investigated by . . . eh,' Henrik glanced at a note in his hand, 'the DCSD, which is the acronym for the Danish Committees on Scientific Dishonesty. It's about some research results that

Storm and one of his students published last September. The accusations were made anonymously.' Henrik took another look at his note. 'Thor Albert Larsen has absolutely no doubt that these accusations were eating away at Storm and that it would be a huge blow for him to be found guilty. So Storm might have looked like a success from the outside, popular and respected and all that, but the truth was that he was facing career bankruptcy on a major scale. The note we found confirms Thor Albert Larsen's theory. It's one long spiel about how he has let down his colleagues and that he hopes his students can forgive him. Thor also told me that Storm's father committed suicide back in the 1980s, so it seems to run in the family. Besides, Steen has already got back to me regarding Storm's computer. It usually takes him a couple of days to plough his way through the entire hard disk, but this one was blank. Storm personally wiped everything there was on it at twenty oh two on Wednesday evening. To be honest, I think this is an open and shut case: Kristian Storm committed suicide.'

'Have you spoken to Storm's students?' Søren asked. 'Have you spoken to his support staff?'

'You're not the only one who went to the Police Academy. Yes, I spoke to the ones I thought might be relevant. But, come on, there's got to be a limit to how many police resources we can waste on a straightforward case like this.'

'Good work, Tejsner,' Jørgensen said, sounding satisfied. 'And you're right. Our resources must be targeted appropriately. We don't have too many of them. How many days do you need?'

'Three, max,' Henrik said. 'I still need to talk to Trine Rønn, who found Kristian Storm. She was so shocked she had to be seen by the trauma team. I'll call her tomorrow. As soon as Bøje pulls his finger out and takes a look at the body, I'll write my report, and that'll be the end of that. So, Tuesday morning at the latest.'

'Monday morning,' Jørgensen said. 'Two days should do it unless something crops up, but then you'll need to come and see me, understand?'

Henrik nodded. Søren was fuming. All that was left was for Henrik to place a shiny red apple on Jørgensen's desk.

'Good,' Jørgensen said, looking over the rim of his glasses, first at Søren and then at Henrik. 'Next. I hear there's trouble in the playground. What kind?'

'Several hours after we had arrived at the Department of Immunology, Søren marched in,' Henrik quickly interjected. 'But why? I had the situation under control. Everything had been documented and sealed, we had put Storm's note in an evidence bag and we had sent the body to the Institute of Forensic Medicine ages ago. Søren is my superior and has the right to view any scene I work, but I don't enjoy having strips torn off me in front of my staff. And just try to imagine what would have happened if I had stormed in six months ago and disturbed the master himself at work. Jesus Christ.' Henrik slapped his thigh.

Jørgensen nodded at length and then he looked at Søren. 'What do you have to say?'

'I quit.'

'What?' Henrik and Jørgensen both stared at Søren.

'Shut up. Of course you're not quitting,' Henrik said.

'Yes, I am,' Søren declared. 'I'm fed up with paper-pushing. I'm fed up with human-resources responsibility. I'm fed up with endless reports and planning interesting work for other people. Turning up at the university today was a mistake. I apologise.' Søren glared at Henrik. 'But you should see it as a sign that our working relationship is messed up. I'm a police officer, not some sort of . . . skivvy, who has nothing better to do than Google maps for you.'

'Oh, Søren, get a grip . . .' Henrik flung out his arms, but Søren had already opened the door and nodded to Jørgensen.

Somewhere down the corridor he heard Jørgensen say, 'Easy now, Tejsner, give the man a chance to cool down,' and Søren had to suppress a sudden urge to spin around and tell his boss to fuck off.

Two hours later Søren had signed his letter of resignation, cleared his office of personal belongings, filled a cardboard box with various papers, copied the unfinished reports on a USB stick and left it in Jørgensen's pigeonhole, along with his warrant card. He had put two half-dead pot plants on his secretary Linda's desk and handed in his service weapon to Human Resources. He looked at his watch. It was quarter past three, the perfect time for collecting Lily.

Outside the police station Søren stopped in his tracks. The spring had been chilly. Now the temperature could generously be described as into double digits and the sun had come out.

As he walked from the car park to the nursery, Søren looked forward to the precious moment when Lily would notice him. When she dropped whatever she had in her hands and threw her arms around his neck. A thousand tiny, wonderful, dirty outdoor smells in his nostrils, a tiny breath, Lily. She was not outside in the playground today as she normally was, so he went inside. The nursery teacher in Lily's unit looked surprised. Lily had developed a temperature and Anna had picked her up at two o'clock. They had rung him first because, according to their records, he was due to pick her up, but he had not replied.

Søren looked at his mobile as he walked back to his car. Shit. He'd forgotten he'd switched it off to avoid Henrik's calls. When he turned it on there were six unanswered calls and one text message from Anna:

Don't know where you are, but one of us has to pick Lily up because Kålormen called to say she is ill. If I don't hear from you in fifteen minutes, I'll get her. But hey, cool if you could call, right? There is that small matter of my application, you know . . .

She didn't sound pissed off, but Søren knew that, at best, she was mildly irritated.

He let himself into the house in Humlebæk and Lily came racing out into the hall. She did not seem particularly ill, a touch warm at the most, but she had a fine mesh of pale pink spots on her cheeks, upper body and arms.

'I got measles and I'm infectious,' she announced proudly. Søren knelt down, rubbed his nose against the rash and said that, since she had such fine-looking dots, he wanted some too.

'I can't go back to nursery until they're all gone,' Lily said smugly.

Anna was sitting on the sofa in the living room, working away with her laptop. Lily had been watching a movie.

'Sorry,' Søren said, and kissed Anna's forehead. 'My mobile was turned off.'

'It's fine,' she said. 'I was just surprised because we agreed only this morning that you would pick her up today. Never mind. It turns out Lily has . . . German measles. It's just rotten timing because Anders T. and I have to finish that application.' Suddenly she gave Søren a quizzical look. 'I had to show Henrik the way to the Department of Immunology earlier today. Is it true that Kristian Storm killed himself?'

Søren perched on the edge of the sofa and Lily immediately climbed onto his lap and started snuggling. He was keen to pump Anna for information about Storm, but not in front of Lily. 'Oh, Lily,' he said casually. 'I've been missing Ib so much today.'

'No, you haven't.' Lily giggled.

'Oh, yes, I have. Why don't you go and get the little creepy-crawly so I can give him a big hug?'

'You can't hug a caterpillar or you'll squash him,' she said, but she jumped down from his lap and sprinted to her room. When she was out of earshot, they were free to speak. Anna knew Kristian Storm well.

'He lectured on several occasions when I did my master's,' she said. 'He was inspirational. He was also a bit of a celebrity, if you can use that term for a scientist. He had a long list of publications and an army of . . . dedicated disciples, I guess you could call them. Thor Albert Larsen, for example, the youngest ever lecturer at the University of Copenhagen. He was eighteen when he started reading biology, twenty when he began assisting Storm at the Department of Immunology, and later he wrote his master's thesis and PhD with Storm as his supervisor and was eventually appointed the youngest lecturer at the Department of Immunology. Kristian Storm is known for hatching top scientists, but also to be interested only in his own research. I guess he was quite discriminating, especially when it came to his work in Africa. He would act as supervisor only for students who were interested in the same subject area as he was. Hey, I've actually just read a big feature on him, in *Weekendavisen*. Not this weekend but last, I think it was. Have you thrown out the papers yet?' Søren got up and started sifting through the contents of the wicker basket next to the wood-burner.

'He was heavily involved in a vaccine research project in West Africa and was practically commuting between Copenhagen and Guinea . . . Guinea something or other.' She grabbed the laptop and briefly glanced at the screen. 'Guinea-Bissau, and the research project is called . . . the Belem Health Project, after the district in the city where the research station is based. Storm would appear to have fallen out with half the world's immunologists following his allegation that some of the vaccines recommended by the World Health Organization aren't entirely without their problems. He even goes so far as to claim that they kill lots of children. He was one of those firebrands who think they can save Africa. Have you found the newspaper?' Søren shook his head and Anna changed the subject.

'Phew, when I stood there this morning, I had a flashback to the day I found Helland dead. And to add to the insanity of it all, I even know the woman who found Storm! Trine Rønn.

We studied terrestrial ecology together. She must be in total shock. People have spoken of nothing else all day. Anders T. and I didn't manage to write a single line of our application. People kept coming into our office wanting to talk about what had happened. And in the middle of it all, the nursery rang and I tried to get hold of you.'

At that moment Lily returned with tears streaming down her cheeks. 'Ib is gone,' she sobbed. 'But I don't understand how it happened. The lid is still on, but he really has gone!' Lily held up the jam-jar to Søren, who peered closely between the apple leaves for the psychedelic green caterpillar. He shook the jar gently.

'He hasn't gone, sweetheart,' he reassured her. 'He's here. He has pupated to his chrysalis stage.'

'Pupated?'

'Pupated. Your mother will explain it to you.' Søren scooped Lily up, placed her on the sofa next to Anna and left to hang up his jacket in the hallway. In the doorway he turned and said, 'By the way, we don't need to organise someone to look after Lily until she's better. You can go to the faculty whenever you like. I'll take care of her.' Anna looked like a question mark, but when Søren added, 'I've just quit my job,' her expression turned into an exclamation point.

When Lily had been put to bed that evening, Søren walked through the living room and heaved a sigh at the chaos of toys, magazines, reference books and clothing. He did not have the energy to tidy up, but flopped onto the sofa. Anna had returned to the university after speaking to Anders T. on her mobile.

'I'll only be a couple of hours,' she'd said to Søren before she left. 'I'll be back before eleven.' She had left her laptop on the sofa, and when Søren moved it to make himself more comfortable, he woke it up from its hibernation. Anna had several websites open. She would appear to have been reading about infectious diseases on Kristian Storm's homepage, www.belem.org.

The more frequently you are exposed to an infection, the more ill the disease will make you. This explains why the rate of infection is much higher in low-income countries than in industrialised countries because in low-income countries many people, especially children, sleep close to each other in very little space.

This was news to Søren. He had always believed that you became just as ill regardless of whether you were exposed to one bug or ten thousand. Suddenly he understood the point of vaccinating whole populations. He had heard the term 'herd immunity' before, but had never quite understood what it meant. Now the penny dropped. If the aim was to vaccinate the whole population so that it became immune, then even unvaccinated individuals gained a potential advantage because there would be fewer people to infect them and, in the long run, it meant that the disease would disappear. Genius. Wanting to know more, Søren read an article about recent outbreaks of otherwise eradicated diseases. It often happened in urban, educated environments in the Western world where some modern parents made a personal decision not to have their children vaccinated. Never before had it crossed Søren's mind: the magnitude of responsibility towards our fellow human beings, embodied in tiny needle pricks.

Anna had also Googled 'forgotten the MMR vaccine', Søren could see, but appeared to have found only useless hits. Moreover, she had visited the homepage of Statens Serum Institute, one of Denmark's largest research institutions in the health sector, to read up on German measles.

German measles is caused by infection with the Rubella virus. However, after the introduction of the MMR vaccine programme, German measles has been almost eradicated in Denmark.

Really? Then how had Lily caught it?

Søren could see that Anna had Googled images of 'German measles and rash' and by comparing the severity of the rashes he calculated that Lily was only mildly ill. He could conclude, with his new-found knowledge, that she had been exposed to the infection for a short period. Perhaps because she went to a nursery where the children spent so much time outdoors. When Lily had started at Kålormen Nursery, Søren had read on its homepage that children who were allowed to run around in the fresh air were less likely to fall ill than others. Now he understood why. When you spent most of your day hanging upside-down from a branch, there were fewer opportunities to swap germs.

Søren was overcome by a sudden urge to sneak a peek at Anna's inbox and quickly slammed shut the laptop.

At that moment Henrik called. Søren stared at the display and considered letting the call go to voicemail, but before he knew it, he had answered it.

'What the hell happened today?' Henrik demanded. 'You weren't serious, were you? Come on, mate, don't be such a—'

'I couldn't be more serious. I've handed in my resignation to Jørgensen,' Søren said.

'Yeah, yeah, I know all that. As does everyone at Bella. But you're not serious? Are you?'

'Yes,' was all Søren said.

'Only I really love my new job, Søren. Jeanette really loves that I got it, as well.'

'I'm not out to steal your job, Henrik. Relax. Besides, the union would give Jørgensen hell. I signed my new employment contract ages ago, as did you. We're not swapping football cards here.'

'And just imagine if Henrik Tejsner actually deserved his promotion,' Henrik snapped.

'You're a good police officer, Henrik,' Søren replied amicably. 'But you're a lousy manager. You're meant to lead your team.' Not treat them as your personal cheerleaders, he thought, but didn't say.

There was silence at the other end. Søren was about to say goodbye when Henrik said, 'I've just spoken to that Trine Rønn woman, the one who found Kristian Storm. She won't hear a word about suicide and doesn't care that we have a note and a motive. She totally lost it and demanded that "the police investigate this properly, all the evidence, every detail". What a drama queen.'

'You visited her?' Søren asked.

'Nah, I rang her from my comfortable chair. Resources, you know. You heard Jørgensen.' Henrik chuckled. 'But you'd agree with me, wouldn't you? Claiming that this death is something other than a suicide is over the top, right?'

Søren mulled it over. 'Well,' he said at length, 'if I were you I would probably visit her . . . and try to form an impression of who Kristian Storm was, both as a human being and as a scientist. Anna has told me that opinions about him were divided. On the one hand, people were queuing up for him to supervise their masters and PhDs, while on the other hand, he had a reputation for being quite obsessed with promoting his own area of research and probably wasn't universally popular among his colleagues, at home or abroad. Personally I would cast my eye over that contradiction and possibly also check up on his father's suicide. But let it simmer a day or two. If nothing else comes up, I, too, would file the case as suicide.'

Henrik made small affirmative noises. 'It was good to talk to you,' he then said. 'I'll call you soon, right? And please reconsider your decision. You can take the man out of the police force, but you can't take the police force out of the man, or however the saying goes . . . You've given Jørgensen at least another ten new grey hairs, mate.'

'I'm good with it,' Søren said. 'I've got other stuff I'd like some time to think over.'

'Is everything all right with you and Tiger Pussy?'

'Fine. Everything's fine.'

'Oh, by the way, there was something else I wanted to tell you . . . I attended another suicide this morning. Out in Vangede . . .'

At that moment a bleary-eyed Lily appeared in the doorway and Søren could see that she had wet herself. He remembered he had forgotten to put on her night-time nappy.

'Listen, got to run. Lily's woken up and—'

'Right. Time for you to breastfeed, ha-ha,' Henrik said.

Dickhead.

When Søren woke up the next morning, Lily was fast asleep next to him in the double bed. Anna was nowhere to be seen. Søren put his hand on Lily's forehead and could feel a light, quivering heat coming from her skin. He pulled off the duvet so she would not overheat and wandered down to the living room where he found Anna asleep on the sofa. She awoke with a start when he stepped on a toy on his way to the kitchen.

'Hiya.' She yawned.

'When did you get back?' he asked, while he made coffee.

'Not until one o'clock.' Anna had followed him and was standing in the doorway with one of the duvets from the guest bedroom wrapped around her. 'It dragged on. Something happened ...' Søren's heart started pounding. He had known something was bound to happen sooner or later. He knew Anders T.'s type. Anna came into the kitchen and pinched the cup of coffee he had just made for himself.

'I'll tell you about it,' she said calmly, 'but first I just need to know if you were serious when you said you'd quit your job.'

'Yes, I was.' Søren was standing with his back to her.

'But why?'

'I've always loved my work, Anna. I've always been my job. Until now. Now driving to Bellahøj makes no sense,' he said, without turning. 'I should never have agreed to that promotion. I've become a pseudo police officer. But it's not just that. It's—'

'I knew a desk job wouldn't suit you,' Anna said. 'I knew it!' Suddenly she was standing right behind him and Søren could feel her arms around him.

'Søren, I have to talk to you about something,' she said, and Søren closed his eyes.

'Trine Rønn, the woman who found Storm dead, called me last night and said she needed to talk to me. As I was at the faculty, I said, "Why don't you pop over?" but she said she was afraid. So I met her at a bar in Blågårdsgade. That's why I got home so late. She's in deep shock, Søren. Her hands were shaking and she was totally out of it. She needed to talk to someone who knew what it was like, she said. She wanted to know when the shock would start to wear off. So at first we just talked about her finding Storm. But then she suddenly said she was convinced that Storm didn't kill himself.'

'Perhaps Trine didn't know him as well as she thought she did.' Søren turned to Anna and hugged her with relief.

Anna wriggled to free herself. 'Søren, a box of documents from Storm's office has gone missing. It's his research from Guinea-Bissau, and Trine says that there's a Nobel Prize in that box. It's the most significant discovery within immunology since the invention of vaccination in the late seventeen hundreds, nothing less. Trine says that Storm had just returned from Guinea-Bissau with the most recent records of five years' work. It makes no sense for him to kill himself now when the finishing line's in sight. He was about to make a major scientific breakthrough.'

'She needs to tell that to Henrik or whoever ends up interviewing her,' he pre-empted her. 'When did Anders T. go home last night? Did you finish your application?'

'Don't change the subject,' Anna said. 'Trine did tell Henrik. Or, rather, yesterday, when the police reopened Storm's office, she went there to rescue the box and keep it safe, but it was gone. She called Henrik immediately to ask if the police had seized it and to draw their attention to how valuable it is. But Henrik said he hadn't taken any box. Besides, she wasn't interviewed properly. Trine is adamant that Kristian Storm was murdered, Søren. Henrik would appear to have hinted yesterday that the police regard the DCSD's charge against Storm as his motive to kill himself, but Trine says that's nonsense. Storm couldn't give a toss what other scientists thought about him. As in a Greek Orthodox toss, Trine says.'

'OK, that's a lot of conclusions in one go,' Søren said.

'Trine knew Storm really well, Søren! They worked closely together, especially in the last few months because Storm's regular assistant is on sick leave. Trine has been on maternity leave and out of the loop, but she's been back in the department since Christmas. Don't you think that she would have noticed just a little bit if Storm had intended to kill himself? And where is the box?'

At that point, Lily appeared in the doorway and Anna fell silent.

'Please can I watch cartoons?' she said.

'All right,' Søren said, over his shoulder to Anna. 'I'll look into it. Only I don't know how far I'll get without my badge. Come on then, munchkin, let's find you some cartoons.' He picked Lily up and carried her into the living room.

'Have you lost your badge?' Lily said, sounding anxious. She had been told countless times that she must never play with it because Søren would be told off by a man called Jørgensen if he lost it.

'I washed it by accident last night,' Søren said. 'With your wet PJs.'

'Then what happened?'

'It shrank and got very small.'

'So can I have it for my Sylvanian Family?' Lily wanted to know.

'I'll think about it,' Søren said.

It was well past noon that Friday before Anna drove to the faculty to meet Anders T., while Søren and Lily made themselves comfortable at opposite ends of the sofa and watched *My Neighbour Totoro*. Lily's temperature was not particularly high and she had a healthy appetite for crusty rolls with a thick layer of chocolate spread. Just before two o'clock Søren woke up to the credits and left to have a shower. When he had got dressed, he went to see Lily, who had started drawing.

'We're not really that ill, are we?' he said.

'I'm very ill,' Lily stated firmly.

'Too ill to go to the Natural History Museum and eat hot dogs afterwards?'

Lily pursed her lips while she gave the matter her full consideration. 'No,' she said. 'I'm not too ill for that. But what happens if Mum sees us?'

'She won't,' Søren assured her. 'Don't forget, she works in a completely different building. Besides, it's good for budding biologists to visit the Museum of Natural History as often as possible. Think of all the things you'll learn.'

It was Søren and Lily's umpteenth visit to the Museum of Natural History. First they touched the glacier that stuck out from the wall. Then they inspected all of Lily's favourite displays, ate French hotdogs in the café and finished off in the Evolution Room where an anxious-looking Lily kept her distance from the two human skeletons.

'Are they real?' she whispered, while Søren assured her yet again that they were plastic. Finally they took the lift down to the ground floor where they browsed in the museum shop while Søren surreptitiously made a mental note of all the doors he could see. One led to the lavatories and on another it said, 'University of Copenhagen, no public access'. While Lily admired all the colourful toys and knickknacks, Søren carefully pressed down the handle. It might be out of bounds to the public, but the door was not locked.

'Please may I have this one?' Lily asked, holding up a clear rubber ball with a poisonous green frog inside it to Søren.

'Yes, you may,' Søren said, and together they went to pay.

'And this one as well?' Lily was pushing her luck and had grabbed a random soft toy, which happened to be a squashy, full-size python.

'No, not that one.'

'OK,' Lily said, putting back the snake. They paid for the ball.

'Come on, we're off to the loo,' Søren said, dragging Lily towards the lavatories.

'But I don't need the loo,' Lily protested in a loud voice.

'Oh yes you do. You should always go when you have the chance,' Søren said, his voice just as loud.

'Oh, really,' Lily said, even louder.

The shop assistant, who had kept a sporadic eye on them over her half-rimmed glasses, now looked down at some papers on her counter. And, quick as a flash, Søren scooped Lily up and went through the unlocked door.

'Why are we here?' Lily said, sounding cross, and Søren whispered, 'Ssh, we're here to catch a thief.'

'A thief?' Lily exclaimed.

Søren glanced back at the door to the museum, but no one had come rushing after them. 'Yes,' he said, 'a thief who has stolen a box belonging to your mum's friend, which he brought back all the way from Africa. Come on, it's not dangerous – it's an awfully big adventure.'

Suddenly Lily looked very sly.

They got lost as always. Søren carried Lily through the long, deserted corridors, past tables covered with boxes of bones, books in classroom sets, cardboard sheets with herbaria, and stuffed animals, and Søren felt Lily dig her fingers into his back. A couple of times they heard a conversation through an open door and the moment they bumped into a human being – a young woman carrying a stuffed heron – Søren immediately asked for directions to the Department of Immunology.

'You need to go up two floors,' she said. 'The stairs are over there.'

'My mum knows everything about dinosaurs,' Lily said to the woman, and Søren quickly moved on. 'Why are you carrying me?'

Søren set Lily down and they walked on hand in hand.

At long last they reached the Department of Immunology. Here there were no stuffed animals or yellowing posters of water lilies and diving ducks, but modern laboratories laid out like pearls on a string, stainless-steel trolleys and a vaguely sinister atmosphere. Søren made his way to Storm's office.

He and Lily stopped to look at the many cards and flowers placed outside the door to Storm's office and Søren got a lump in his throat. *A great loss for us and for Africa*, he read on one card, *Thank you for everything, Storm*, on another. On a large, colourful bouquet, there was a small, silver-rimmed card that read, *In respect, in grief, from your colleagues at Stanford University*, and next to it someone had placed an African mask and lit tea lights. More flowers, more cards.

'Oh, doesn't that look nice?' Lily said.

Søren knocked on Thor Albert Larsen's half-open door, hoping that Thor would recognise him from yesterday and not ask to see his warrant card. 'Enter,' a voice called. Thor was on the telephone, but made a friendly gesture to indicate that Søren should wait. He ended his call and shook hands with both Søren and Lily.

'Today is my day off and I'm taking my daughter to the museum,' Søren lied. 'But when you're investigating a case, you're never really off duty – it's probably just like being a scientist.'

Thor asked Søren and Lily to sit down on a small seating arrangement in the corner of his office. He was pale, but composed. 'I did think about taking today off,' he said, glancing at Lily and the pale red rash on her face. 'I'm very upset, I must admit. But it wouldn't be in Storm's spirit to slack. "To research, to conquer" was his motto. Besides, it's just as well that I'm here. Colleagues from all over the world have heard about his death and the phone hasn't stopped ringing. Now, what can I do for you? I spoke to your colleague this morning, Henrik Tejsner, who is heading the investigation, and he said that the police have filed the case as suicide.' Suddenly he looked suspicious.

'It's correct that Kristian Storm killed himself,' Søren said, muttering curses under his breath. 'But, even so, I wanted a better understanding of the case. Please could you give me a list of Storm's students and anybody else employed here in the department? There are some loose ends we'd like to tie up.' Søren smiled again.

'Yes, of course.' Thor sat down behind his desk and looked at his screen. 'He had many students,' he added. 'I myself was one of them – once.'

'Was he a good supervisor?' Søren asked.

'Yes,' Thor replied, without hesitation. 'It's quite a few years ago now. I finished my PhD in 2005 and started working in the department the following year. But I still remember my three PhD years as the time when I gained my proper foothold as a scientist. No one can motivate a student like Storm. He'll keep pushing you . . . He would keep pushing you, home in on details, and he wouldn't let go until you'd had it up to here, but at the same time he could zoom out like no other scientist I have met and understand complex relationships. He was a true . . . mentor. I can't think of a single one of Storm's students who hasn't done exceptionally well, though it cost them blood, sweat and tears along the way.' Thor smiled and added, 'Except Marie, of course, but it wasn't her fault that she never managed to start her PhD.'

'Marie?'

'Oh, that has nothing to do with Storm. Marie Skov was one of Storm's master's students last year. The two of them in the same lab . . . sparks flew! But then Marie fell ill, that was all I meant. Her PhD proposal had already been approved and the funding was in place, but God knows if she'll ever get to finish it. By the way, it was Marie's lab figures that triggered the dishonesty case against Storm.' Thor got up and fetched a printout.

'Here's the list. Everyone's names, phone numbers and email addresses.' Again Thor looked sceptical. 'I'd actually promised to email it to Henrik Tejsner yesterday, but he didn't say anything about it when he called me this morning, so I presumed that it was no longer needed now that you have closed the case. But perhaps you could give it to him?'

'I'll do that,' Søren said lightly, and took the paper.

'We're looking for a stolen box,' Lily suddenly proclaimed and Søren spluttered.

'Why don't you go out into the corridor and try out your new bouncy ball?' he suggested to her. 'I bet it can jump all the way up to the ceiling if you whack it really hard against the floor.' Lily was already out of the door and soon afterwards they heard *boing-boing* noises.

'Are you surprised that Kristian Storm killed himself?' Søren asked.

Thor thought about it. 'Yes and no,' he said at last. 'When Trine found him yesterday, I quite simply refused to believe it. I had been chatting to him in the senior common room the day before and he appeared just as dedicated and diligent as usual. So initially it seemed absurd that he would have taken his own life. Since then I've thought of little else, of course, and last night I concluded that it does make sense after all. I no longer saw Storm outside work and I don't know anyone else who did. Marie Skov, perhaps, but like I said, she's on sick leave and hasn't seen him for a long time. Storm and I ran the Department of Immunology together and we were a good team, but we were not friends. So even if he had been depressed, he would not necessarily have confided in me. And, to tell you the truth, I wouldn't have wanted Storm's life. Despite what you may have heard, most scientists have a life outside their research. But not Storm. He worked twenty-four/seven, and when he finally did do anything social, it was with his students. It's dangerous to identify too closely with your profession.' Thor looked gravely at Søren. 'We've seen it before when we've had to make cuts. People suddenly realise they have nothing left if their work is taken away from them, and some choose to end their own life. And perhaps being accused of scientific dishonesty is even worse. It's bad enough that all activity has to stop while the DCSD review the research that has been called into question – and while that happens, it's practically impossible to be considered for grants or have any scientific papers published. But even if you're ultimately cleared, the accusation tends to stick. Everyone in science knows that. Storm *was* his research, and the fear of being found guilty of scientific dishonesty must have been extremely distressing . . .' Thor looked speculatively at Søren '. . . especially if he knew deep down that he had fiddled the figures.'

'Do you have any reason to believe that?'

'No.' Thor hesitated slightly. 'Not really. Storm was a fine scientist, very conscientious, highly critical, and he rose above the personal rivalries and desire for prestige that drive many scientists, myself included, I must admit. Seen from that perspective, he wasn't an obvious candidate to massage data. Saying that, Storm had become very fanatical about his Africa project in recent years, in fact so much so that the head of the institute commented on it when, yet again, I ended up presenting our annual accounts rather than Storm because he was in Africa – as usual. I didn't mind, so that wasn't the problem . . . but I was starting to notice it. How Storm slowly but surely put all his eggs into one basket, and that's always risky. Then there were the lab results, which Storm and Marie published in connection with her master's dissertation . . .' Thor hesitated again. 'They were just too good to be true . . . and their conclusion questioned the premise of every single WHO vaccination programme.'

'How?' Søren asked, with genuine interest.

Thor thought about it. 'Storm discovered that some of the vaccines which the WHO recommends worldwide are associated with a number of negative side effects as well as protecting against specific diseases. Most of the vaccines boost the immune systems of the people vaccinated so they develop increased resistance to diseases in general. But one of the vaccines appears to weaken the immune system. The former is good, the latter is catastrophic, and the overall observation is revolutionary. *If* it's true . . . So while I was pleased for Storm when he published the results, I was also sceptical.'

'You thought he might have cheated.'

Thor shrugged his shoulders. 'Storm obviously wanted Marie Skov's results to back up his observations from Guinea-Bissau. So "cheating" is too strong a word. But perhaps he misinterpreted them and hoped he would get away with it.'

'He misinterpreted them on purpose?'

'I'll leave it up to the DCSD to decide that,' Thor said.

'One of Storm's students insists that Storm "couldn't give a toss" about what other scientists thought of his research. That doesn't sound like a man who could be shamed by an accusation of scientific dishonesty or a possible verdict against him?'

Thor shook his head slowly. 'I'm aware of that. It's Trine, isn't it? She refuses to accept that it was suicide. She rang me to rant and rave only this morning. And I do understand that it's difficult to come to terms with it. Like I said, I reacted in exactly the same way at first. With disbelief. But Trine has been on maternity leave for more than a year – no, longer because she went on sick leave at the very start of her pregnancy and she's only just returned. She hadn't seen just how obsessed with his Africa project Storm had become. Nor did Trine know that Storm's father also killed himself. A not irrelevant detail. I told her about it when she called me today.'

'How did you know that Storm's father killed himself?' Søren asked.

'From Storm himself,' Thor said. 'I've known about it for many years, ever since I wrote my master's, I think. A long time ago there was a rumour at the institute that a museum professor had skimmed his department for money, and when Storm overheard me and another student talk about it, he rebuked us. His own father, who was a famous professor of medicine, had been the victim of that kind of damaging gossip, he told us, and even though he was eventually cleared, his reputation never recovered and he ended up taking his own life. Storm was clearly still affected by it, and, well, we know from psychological studies that suicide often recurs in families.'

Søren watched Thor for a moment. Then he stuck out his hand and thanked him for his help.

'You're welcome,' Thor said. 'And please don't hesitate to contact me, if you have any further thoughts. I'm here if you need me.' He stretched out his arms.

Outside in the corridor, a poisonous green frog jumped right into Søren's face.

'Oops, sorry,' Lily said, and Søren threw her over his shoulder, like a sack of potatoes, and carried her out of the university.

Oh, yeah, totally undercover.

CHAPTER 2

Marie Skov still had a photograph of herself, her brother and sisters taken in the back garden of their childhood home at nineteen Snerlevej. In the foreground, her baby sister Lea sat on her nappy-clad bottom while big sister Julie, with braces on her teeth, stood at the back. In the centre of the picture, standing in front of a blue paddling pool, Marie was holding the hand of her twin brother, Mads. Each of them had a kazoo in their free hand; they had different shades of brown hair, but the same bright blue toddlers' eyes. Marie thought it was funny how much the children looked like the adults they had grown into. Julie was very tall, Lea very cute, and Marie already looked ordinary, even then.

The photograph was one of the few to survive Marie's mother's frenzied attack with a pair of scissors when Mads died. The fever had come on suddenly and the doctors had assured Marie's parents, Frank and Joan, that it was not their fault. There was nothing they could have done; it was a very aggressive form of meningitis. Even so, Joan had cut up all their photographs and screamed over and over that she would never forgive herself. This was not something Marie could remember. Julie had told her. Julie was six years older than

Marie and seven years older than Lea and she could remember everything. It was Julie who had given Marie the photograph.

'Here,' she had said, as she put it on the desk in front of her. Marie had been about ten at the time. 'Dad wanted you to have it. But promise you won't show it to Mum, Marissen?' she added. 'It'll only make her sad.'

Marie had promised.

Before Joan had had her children, she had been an art student at Kunstakademiet and had been predicted a great future. She was a weaver and inspired by female expressionists, whose paintings from the early twentieth century she reinterpreted in vast tapestry wall-hangings. They were best suited to large exhibition halls and public spaces with high ceilings, and she sold several. Once the children were born, she took a job as an art teacher at Dyssegårdsskolen in Vangede, but carried on weaving in her spare time, smaller pieces that Frank would sell locally for quite respectable sums. When Mads died, Joan had gone on sick leave but lost her job shortly afterwards. The loom was left to gather dust and Frank had had to drop out of his civil-engineering degree course. Even though they could live cheaply in the house on Snerlevej, which they had inherited from Joan's parents, and even though their firstborn daughter, Julie, was a great help around the house, they could not make ends meet. Having to quit his studies was a big loss of face for Frank, who had promised his father he would make something of himself. Frank's father had worn himself out working at a canned-food factory and had taken to drinking. When he was on his deathbed, he had regretted his wasted life. 'Do you want smoker's lungs like mine?' he had rattled.

'Rotten teeth? A fatty liver?' Frank had sworn to his father that he would not squander his talents. His father had died soon afterwards.

Frank was forced to take work on a building site where he was soon promoted to foreman because he was good with his hands. But he loathed his boss, an unskilled oik, who was younger than Frank but had had the construction firm handed to him on a plate by his father, all ready for him to take over; Merry Christmas, son. The boss could not stand Frank either; he always frowned when he inspected his work and would order Frank to carry out practically impossible jobs on his own. Frank felt like punching the man's nose into his brain, but instead he trailed a coin along the side of his car one day when he hobbled home from work, having put his back out after his boss had told him to move a large pile of bricks.

When Frank arrived home, Julie would have his dinner ready as usual. She was twelve years old now and starting to get fat. This irritated Frank. Joan had lost her looks – grief had made her ugly – and he almost couldn't bear to look at her. She couldn't manage anything, these days; it was as if she had lost her mind when Mads died. That was why Julie had to cook all their meals.

Frank was seething with anger at his boss. His back would hurt all weekend and he would not be able to work on his new shed. The old shed had burned down and his tools had been rusting under some tarpaulin in the garden ever since. God only knew if he would ever have time to finish it.

Lea and Marie were in their pyjamas and circling his legs, like starving pigeons. Frank asked the girls if they had remembered to clean their teeth. Straight away they opened their mouths as wide as they could and Frank inspected them. He did not want his kids to have rotten teeth. Some people never bothered with the little things, yet it was those details that defined social divisions in Denmark. Otherwise how would his kids be able to change social class as he himself had done? He dismissed the idea of 'social heritage'. Frank had come from nothing, and when he was a boy, no one had cared about his teeth. His father would work, come home, watch telly or go to the pub, and his mother would sit in front of the telly or work night shifts. Frank and his brothers and sisters ate whatever they could find in the cupboard or they would make eggnog from five eggs and half a cup of sugar. But Frank had promised his father to be somebody. Once Joan went back to work and started behaving normally again, he intended to resume his studies. Until then he had to settle for being the best-looking and most overqualified builder in Copenhagen. He shaved every day, he had got himself dentures in Sweden, his clothes were impeccable, never expensive but immaculate, and he took an interest in the children's teeth, their education and manners. He tidied up the front garden, he cleaned the windows until they shone and he disciplined their dog, Bertha, with a firm hand. None of the neighbours should be able to criticise his family.

Lea opened her mouth even wider and pushed in front of Marie. 'Aaaaah,' she said, getting on Frank's nerves. He went into the living room to watch the telly.

The summer when Marie started school, Joan rediscovered her creativity and wove a wall-hanging that Frank managed to sell to Helsingør Town Hall.

'And it was luck rather than design, let me tell you,' he said to Joan, when he came home after having delivered it and slammed down four thousand kroner on the dining table in front of her. 'Do you think you could try weaving something a little less glum? Otherwise we'll run out of customers. Normal town halls want joy in their corridors, not hysterical women with snakes in their hair.'

'But it was inspired by Caravaggio's painting of Medusa,' Joan objected. 'Caravaggio invented the chiaroscuro technique – he revolutionised painting. It's about light and shade.'

'That's all well and good,' Frank said, 'but I'm telling you, a little colour wouldn't go amiss.'

But Joan started making clay figures instead. Tiny creatures with tortured faces.

'How about making some angels with wings?' Frank asked. By this time, he had been sacked from the building site and hoped to sell the figurines at various markets. But Joan refused, so Frank had to drop his market-stall plans; besides, people could buy much nicer ceramics in IKEA for next to nothing.

'Never mind, it's the process that matters,' Joan said to the children, when Frank was out of earshot. 'The product means nothing.'

Joan carried the figurines out into the garden and arranged them on the sooty spot where Frank's old shed used to be. Marie, Lea and Julie stood in the living-room window happily watching their mother. She carefully adjusted the figurines so eventually they made up a witches' circle of rugged ceramics. Then she straightened up and waved to her girls.

'Mum's having a good day,' Julie said, and smiled.

Every day Julie and Marie walked home from Dyssegårds-skolen together and Julie always carried Marie's satchel. When Julie went into the sixth form, she continued to pick up Marie from the after-school club and carry her satchel. Lea was too young to go to school yet and was looked after by one of their neighbours, a woman called Tove.

The walk home from school was Marie and Julie's special time, Julie said, as they skipped along. Sister time, Julie called it. 'We're two peas in a pod,' she used to say. Marie didn't know what that meant. When they came home, Julie had to take Bertha for a walk. Bertha had been a Christmas present from Frank, who'd thought he had bought a cocker spaniel, but in less than six months Bertha had turned into a fully grown St Bernard.

The girls loved Bertha and only Joan complained about her size. Couldn't they have got a small dog instead, one that would fit in her handbag? Frank said that a big family like theirs needed a big dog, though he conceded he had not thought Bertha would be quite that big. When Frank was at home, he would train Bertha and assiduously picked up her poo from the garden, but he was not home all that much.

While Julie walked Bertha, Joan and Marie would have a pretend tea party. Joan would perch on the edge of the sofa, and no one could hold an imaginary teacup in such a refined manner as Joan. She cooed over Marie and would kiss and hug her when she wasn't sipping her invisible cup. 'Where is Countess/Princess/Empress Lea?' she would ask. Marie would pretend that Joan's spiky hair was a queen's crown and she would reply that Her Royal Highness/Countess/Princess/Duchess Lea was visiting Tove. 'Oh, yes,' Joan would say. Then Joan would want to hear all about her day at school. Joan remembered everyone at Dyssegårdsskolen. 'Does Mr Nielsen still carry that massive bag around?' she would ask Marie, and 'How is Sune? Is he still making trouble during lunch?' Marie would answer all her questions. Then Joan would ask if she wanted her to read aloud from a Donald Duck comic, and Marie would say, 'Yes, please,' and carefully snuggle up to her mother. Sometimes, without warning, Joan would burst into tears and press Marie to her chest so hard that Marie could barely breathe. When Julie came home with Bertha, it was time for a quick snack; 'Hurry, hurry into the kitchen,' Julie would say. While Julie wrapped a blanket around Joan and gave her some water, Marie would eat lard and salt sandwiches cut into soldiers in the kitchen. It was her favourite snack and Julie made it for her every day.

'Mum is missing Mads a bit today,' Julie said lightly, when she came out into the kitchen to Marie and softly closed the door to the living room. 'You never recover from the loss of a child.'

'Or a brother?' Marie asked, with her mouth full of lard and bread.

Every day at five o'clock they would pick up Lea from Tove's house and Marie could not wait to see her baby sister. She asked why they didn't pick Lea up earlier so she could join in the tea party with Mum. 'No,' Julie said, 'not until five o'clock.' Marie would then get the buggy from the garage because Lea refused to walk the hundred metres home. Julie said that a four-year-old was quite simply too old to be pushed, but Marie just swerved the buggy from side to side in large curves, so Lea would laugh and stop behaving like a spoiled brat.

The list of things Lea would not do was a very long one. Eat up, for example, even though Julie made her sit at the table for hours. Or have her hair washed, even though Julie put Lea's beloved dolly on a tall shelf out of her reach. Or come home with them from Tove's house.

Marie, however, was a logical child and could not see the point of these battles. She just fetched the buggy and pushed it at racing speed to make Lea laugh.

Sometimes Frank would come back so late from wherever he had been that Marie and Lea were already in their bunk beds, Lea at the top and Marie at the bottom. Lea had threatened to cut the hair off all Marie's dolls unless she got the top bunk, and Marie had caved in immediately. Frank would stumble on the runner on the stairs when he came home late. In the middle of the night, he would impress upon them the importance of getting a good education because working as an unskilled labourer was hell when you were intelligent and overqualified, especially if your boss was a moron. Lea asked him what a moron was, but Frank told her not to worry about it. Frank smelt of cigarettes when he came home late and occasionally of something sweet. When he inspected their teeth, Marie would hold her breath. Lea, however, just said, 'You stink, Daddy,' and Marie would curl all ten toes under her duvet.

Every evening Frank would ask Marie, 'What kind of day has the best Marissen in the world had? Is she just as clever now as she was this morning, I wonder?'

'A little cleverer, I think,' Marie would reply happily. She was in her first year at school and her teacher had already remarked that she was very able.

'I knew it,' Frank said proudly, when Julie repeated the conversation she had had with Marie's teacher. Frank had forgotten Marie's parents' evening and had failed to come home in time, so Julie had cycled to school on her own.

Sometimes Frank would nibble Lea's feet if they stuck out from under her duvet. Then Lea would squirm with laughter and call out, 'Again, again!'

On a good evening Frank would then say, 'Only if my little Loopy-Lou has been a good girl. Have you?'

And Lea would reply, 'Yes!', even though it was a lie. But Frank would often bite her too hard and he got annoyed when Lea screamed.

Marie felt sorry for Lea when Frank got cross with her. Julie was forever saying to Marie, 'You're the apple of Daddy's eye and my little treasure, and Mummy's big, lovely girl.' But she never said anything nice to Lea, so one day Marie gave Lea all her shiny stickers.

'Are you sure?' Lea asked, and dried her eyes on her sleeve.

Marie nodded. 'You can even have the ones with the glitter puppies. Here you go.'

If only Lea liked going to school, Marie thought. Frank was brilliant at helping with homework – if you could be bothered to do your homework, that was, and Lea unfortunately could not. Doing homework with Frank was one of Marie's favourite activities. 'Sharpen your pencils, Marissen,' Frank would say, 'and I'll be with you in a moment,' and when he came up to Marie's room, he would always bring tea and chocolate biscuits, and he knew the answers to everything and had really nice handwriting when he wrote numbers. You had to be good at maths if you wanted to be an engineer, Frank explained.

But Lea didn't want to be an engineer – she wanted to be a rock star or a model – and it made no difference that Marie told her to try doing her homework with Frank.

Lea, however, did like drawing and every now and then Joan and Lea would draw together. They would both slip into an electric silence when they drew and Marie loved sitting in the kitchen, pretending to be reading a book, but secretly watching her mother and sister, who were lost in a world of their own at the dining table.

'And up at the castle,' Lea explained, making sweeping movements on her paper, 'there are dragons as well. You can see in their tummies how many princesses they have eaten. That one has eaten eight.'

Joan studied Lea's drawing for a long time. 'I really like your figures, Lea,' she said at length. 'They're simple, but you use clear lines and shapes. You're telling a story.'

Lea beamed from ear to ear and Marie loved seeing Lea so happy.

Marie also loved Julie's stories about the old days.

'We were very happy,' Julie would say dreamily, as she patted the sofa seat next to her. She would get Marie and Lea a bowl of sweets each, Dracula lollipops, Jenka bubble gum and liquorice humbugs and pull their small backsides very close to hers.

'Mum and Dad would throw these amazing garden parties,' Julie told them, 'with Chinese paper lanterns, home-made salads in big, ceramic bowls, bread that you tore chunks off so shards of glittering, coarse salt would fall to the ground, and they would run an extension cable through the basement window so they could play records under the open sky. And nobody ever complained about Mum and Dad's parties,' Julie continued, 'because they invited all the neighbours.'

Julie had been five years old when Joan discovered that she was pregnant with twins.

When Frank had come home from university that day, Joan pointed to two eggs she had managed to balance on a crack in the coffee table. Frank's face had been one big question mark at first, but then he spotted four tiny socks on a chair, and on the stairs eight dummies had been lined up. Upstairs, on their double bed, Joan had placed a large paper heart and, at the centre of the heart, she had written that they were expecting twins. At this point, Julie jumped out of the laundry basket and Frank hugged them both.

Joan got pregnant with Lea when the twins, Mads and Marie, were only three months old. It came as something of a surprise. Still, if any family was going to have lots of children, surely it should be theirs?

They owned a big house.

Joan regained her figure the day after each birth.

Frank was a modern patriarch.

They were good Social Democrats, but not the dull kind.

'Even the summers were longer in those days,' Julie said, looking gravely at her sisters.

'No, I'm telling you the truth,' she would insist, when Lea refused to believe her. 'The Chinese lanterns were prettier, the friends were funnier, the sun was out more and the problems were smaller.'

Marie couldn't remember anything from before Mads had died. She couldn't even remember Mads. Even so, she loved Julie's stories. Lea was less impressed. 'I don't believe that,' she would say, when Julie told her something, and when she turned ten, she could no longer be overawed by coloured lanterns, which you could buy for only ninety-eight øre in Søstrene Grene. When Marie showed her the photograph from the garden, she would narrow one eye and say, 'Alright, the kid looks cute, but how do we even know he's our brother?'

'Surely you can tell,' Marie said.

'I don't see it,' Lea said.

When Lea became a teenager, she was completely done with Julie's rose-tinted stories and recounted them in her own words: 'When Mads died, everything turned to shit, big fat piles of St Bernard shit. Joan should have been offered counselling, but she was simply wrapped in a blanket, put on the sofa and given a lump of clay to channel all her talent into. Frank was so crushed by his broken academic dreams that he had to drink beer every day. And there was never any food in the house – oh, no, wait, there were tins of spag bol, which we would eat for days in a row, and we were covered with layers of dirt because no one ever bothered to wash us.'

'That's not true,' Julie said, hurt. 'We always had food and I washed you every single day. And Mum loved washing you at the weekends – don't you remember? She even made her own bath oils, which she would put in your bath. We lived in a nice house – and why don't you ever call Dad "Dad" and Mum "Mum"? And we were lucky that we were allowed a dog! No one in my class at school had a dog,' she said, and added, 'Being angry when you're a teenager is normal, Lea, but now you're just exaggerating.'

'Exaggerating? Our brother died and Dad gave us a dog.

Great move, Frank. Right until "someone" ran it over on Sner-levej in the dark. Splat and it was a goner,' Lea said, in a loud voice.

'You're mean,' Julie hissed, and slapped Lea across the face. Marie could see how much it stung because Lea's eyes welled up. She had had a snakebite piercing the day before and had just cleaned it with hydrogen peroxide. Now she touched her lip gingerly.

If you ignored her facial piercings, which, as well as the two steel fangs, also included a tongue bar and a nose ring, Lea was beautiful. Her hair was long and dark, and she towered in the landscape on her platform boots. As she jumped to her feet and stormed out in a huff, she was at least as tall as Julie, but she weighed less than half as much.

'Did Dad really run Bertha over?' Marie asked Julie.

'No, of course he didn't. Sometimes you can be so naïve, Marie! Lea's always making things up,' Julie said.

Lea no longer lived at home. No one told Lea what to do, these days, least of all Julie, who was now married with children of her own. Julie dressed in long skirts and woolly roll-neck jumpers to hide the weight she had gained during her pregnancies. She had trained to be a nurse and had met her husband, Michael, during her initial practical training at Bispebjerg Hospital, where he worked as a porter.

'Michael is an oaf,' Frank always said, and Marie privately agreed with him. Julie and Michael had had two daughters in quick succession, Emma and Camilla, and that was just the way it was, Julie said.

'On your gravestone, it'll say, "She poured oil on troubled waters,"' Lea had once remarked to Julie, who had promptly retorted, 'Yes, and on yours it'll say, "She made a big deal out of nothing."'

Lea snorted and said that was the biggest pile of crap she had ever heard, but for once Julie simply shrugged.

Frank had been pleased when Julie started training to be a nurse. 'Nursing is honest work,' he said proudly. But then Julie met Michael, fell pregnant and quit her studies. Now she was working as a home carer, and Frank appeared not to have forgiven her. Maybe that explained why he constantly got at Julie, which encouraged Michael to join in. At family dinners and at Christmas, their treatment of Julie bordered on bullying as Michael and Frank egged each other on. Marie hated it, but never said anything because she had spoken up once and Julie had instantly given her 'the look' and later pulled her aside in the kitchen.

'There's no need for you to get involved. They don't really mean it, Marie,' she'd said lightly. 'It's quite enough that Lea flies off the handle over nothing. Let it go.'

Marie accepted the situation and she had to agree with Julie: Lea really did have a special talent for conflict escalation.

One evening Lea turned up at Snerlevej to fetch some clothes from her old room while Julie, Michael and their children were there. Frank had threatened to take Lea's belongings to the skip, but her room was still untouched. It bothered Julie. 'You're spoiling her, Dad,' she had said. 'She'll never learn that actions have consequences.' But Frank just muttered that he'd get round to doing it soon and reminded Marie of what a softie he was. They sat down for dinner. Four minutes later Michael and Lea were having a row because Lea had referred to Julie as Michael's lucky catch and Michael as Julie's big mistake.

'Stop arguing,' Joan said, but no one listened.

Sobbing, Julie ran out into the kitchen; Marie got up and followed her.

From there they could hear Michael get himself worked up over something and it turned out that Lea had pulled down her trousers and mooned at him. Camilla and Emma were about two and four at the time, and Michael shouted that there was no bloody way he would put up with this in front of his kids and followed it up with a lot of swearing. Ah, well, everything's relative, Marie thought, convinced that Michael's fruity vocabulary was ultimately more traumatising for his young daughters than the sight of their aunt's bare buttocks. Marie wondered why no one ever laughed at Michael. Or at Lea, for that matter. She thought they were both being ridiculous. But no one ever joked in the Skov family, and nothing was taken lightly. She wondered why. It was tempting to take Michael down a peg, tease Frank about his double standards, pull Julie's leg affectionately when she became a little too prim, and Lea's, too, when she became ultra-provocative. Michael carried on whingeing until Frank told him to shut up, and Joan finally managed to break through the inferno: 'I told you to stop arguing,' she said again.

'Why does Lea do it?' Julie wept in the kitchen and Marie put her arms around her sister's large body. 'Why does she always have to trample on other people?'

Marie didn't know how to reply. If she had to be honest, she had often felt like mooning Michael herself, but she never had, obviously.

'Lea was born a megalomaniac,' Julie sobbed, 'and that's why she thinks she can walk all over us.'

When they returned to the dining room, Frank and Michael had gone and the children were watching television in the living room. Lea was sitting at the dining table holding Joan's hand.

When Marie had started at medical school, Frank could barely contain his excitement. That summer Lea was 'God knows where', as he put it, so Marie was on the receiving end of his undivided attention. Marie was ambivalent about the experience. She wished the ground would open up and swallow her when Frank boasted to people that she was going to be a doctor and that she had inherited her academic talent from him, but it was lovely when he put his hands on her shoulders and called her 'Dr Marissen'.

'Medical school isn't for losers, Marie,' he lectured her one evening, as the conclusion to a lengthy monologue about how she had to hold her head up high and be confident. 'A good doctor believes in herself. How do you think it'll look when you're doing rounds? Patients need to see authority when you enter a ward. It's no good you sneaking along the wall, whispering to Mrs Jensen that she needs a new heart valve, is it?'

Marie almost burst out laughing at the scenario, but Frank looked very serious.

'When I was studying engineering . . .' he began.

That night Marie couldn't sleep. Although she didn't always recognise herself when Frank or Julie chided her for being quiet, there was some truth in what Frank had said. In the sixth form, her written exams had gone brilliantly, but her orals had been disastrous: she had received an irritatingly low six in history, for instance, which had dragged down her average. It wasn't that she didn't know her subject. She knew it inside out. But the moment she sat face to face with her teacher and the external examiner, the words refused to come out.

Marie met Jesper Just during freshers' week at medical school. He was organising the event and it was now four years since he had been subjected to the introductory fun and games, along with other various types of hazing by which new students were initiated.

'Medical school isn't for losers,' Jesper had announced, when he had introduced himself to the first years.

When Jesper and Marie had started dating, Marie worried that Frank would take an instant dislike to her boyfriend. Jesper drove an environmentally hazardous gas-guzzler, as Frank referred to cars like Jesper's pearl-white Range Rover deluxe, and, to top it all, he had been 'born with a silver spoon up his arse'. Frank himself had grafted for everything he had, not least his odd-job business, which he had started some years earlier, and his VW Transporter was purely a working vehicle. No one with a Copenhagen postcode needed a cross-country 4x4 for reasons other than showing off, and Frank didn't like show-offs – indeed he didn't as a rule like anyone who had been born rich.

But fortunately he approved of Jesper and made no attempt to hide that he was terribly excited at the thought of husband-and-wife doctors in the family.

Jesper was Marie's first real boyfriend and her sexual initiation. He was absolutely mad about her. He licked her all the way from the tip of her toes to the hollow under her ear and bit her nipples a little too hard. He adored her breasts and complimented her on being slim while still curvaceous. But he also loved her sweetness, he said. Her shy manner and her bright mind. He stressed that he could never be with an uneducated girl, and what did Marie think about the old proverb that behind every strong man was a strong woman? Eh, yes, Marie thought that sounded just fine, and Jesper nuzzled his face happily between her breasts.

'We'll be the perfect couple,' he whispered into her sweater.

They got married, and when Marie discovered she was pregnant, they took that in their stride. Jesper had graduated, was about to start work and would therefore be able to support his family. When Anton was born, Frank's joy knew no bounds.

'He's a lovely little lad,' he whispered, as he kept curling and uncurling Anton's tiny fingers. 'Can you see who he looks like, eh, Joan?' Joan nodded, incapable of speech because she was on the verge of tears. She wove a wonderful tapestry wall-hanging for Anton's room, her first in years. At the centre of it there was a big red sun, and beneath the sun a naked baby boy was kicking his arms and legs in the air. Above the sun was an angel with wings of soft white angora that Joan had worked over with a brush and the angel held its protective hands above the baby, like a heavenly umbrella.

With Anton's arrival, Marie had started to worry about Frank's obvious favouring of him at the expense of Julie and her children. Frank and Joan had never shown much interest in Julie's girls, but Julie had said that was fine. Not all parents were born grandparents, she had said. Now Frank would lie on the floor, tickling the baby and rolling balls to Anton for a whole hour. No one could make Anton laugh like Frank did.

Marie asked Julie if she was OK with it, but Julie brushed it aside.

'Really, Marie, don't upset yourself with such nonsense. I'm just delighted that Dad loves Anton. Look how happy he is. Some men find women a little difficult and God knows that Dad has been lumbered with enough crazy women to last him a lifetime. He probably needed a boy in the family and I'm happy for you. Stop worrying this instant.'

Julie gave her sister a hug and Marie breathed a sigh of relief.

Frank was so excited about his role as grandfather that he instigated a new tradition: family lunch at Snerlevej every Sunday. He built a brick barbecue in the garden, laid a terrace and bought garden furniture; he even got round to painting the new shed. He would grill steaks, drink red wine and tell everybody what a looker Joan had been when she was young.

Anton had transformed his grandfather.

Lea hardly ever turned up at these events and, if Marie was honest, it was a relief to avoid all the drama.

When Marie failed her end-of-year oral exam in medicine for the third time and had to tell Frank during a Sunday lunch that she was quitting medicine, he banged his fists so hard on the table that his plate of rissoles danced. The tears started rolling down Marie's cheeks. She knew the syllabus back to front and could not explain why her mind had gone blank.

'Marie will switch to biology,' Jesper said. 'She can transfer most of her credits and there are plenty of opportunities for her as a biologist. So just calm down, will you?' He looked sternly at Frank, who shut up and flipped the cap off another beer.

'Bloody hell,' he mumbled, and swigged from the bottle. 'I'd never have thought that of you, Marissen.'

Lea, who happened to be there to pick up her birth certificate, belched loudly and proceeded to declare that surely a degree was a degree and that, as far as Lea knew, Frank had yet to complete his education and should therefore back off. Lea would turn twenty soon and a thin chain hung from her left nostril to her left ear, her hair was dyed pitch black, she had a silver bar in her tongue, which she clicked, and five visible tattoos. One was a demonic-looking child that covered most of her upper arm. A few weeks ago she had told Frank and Joan that she had started training as a beauty therapist, and even though Frank thought training in the area of 'beauty idiocy' was ridiculous, Marie could still detect his relief that Lea was getting herself some kind of education at last.

'Please don't start arguing,' said Joan, and Frank, who had half got up from his chair, restricted himself to sending his youngest daughter an evil stare.

A smiling Julie circulated a dish. 'Yummy, this is delicious,' she said. Marie passed the dish on. Jesper winked to her. He loved putting Frank in his place.

The biology course had a different tempo from that for medicine. When studying medicine, Marie had mostly been trying to keep up with Jesper, but now she had her own subject area and the time to master it. Even Frank limited himself to saying, 'I hope you're not going to let me down, Marissen,' roughly once every three months, and Marie assured him that she would not.

Almost from the start of her coursework she developed a

special interest in the immune system. Millions of white blood cells attacked bacteria and viruses and, in a complicated genetic interchange, determined a person's state of health and longevity. Marie thought it was wildly exciting. In her fourth term she took a course in epidemiology with the famous professor of immunology and infectious diseases Kristian Storm. Her fascination knew no bounds. She learned about the Black Death that had killed almost half the population of Europe in the late Middle Ages, and about the cholera bacterium, which was regarded as the fifth most dangerous bacterium in the world. She learned about the Spanish flu that had claimed the lives of five million people across the world only a hundred years ago, and gazed tenderly at Anton, who was practically never ill. The vaccine was without a doubt the most amazing invention in the history of medicine, she thought. Benjamin Jesty must have been the bravest farmer in the world. It was he who in the eighteenth century had vaccinated his wife and two sons with pus from a cow that had died from cowpox. Jesty had noticed that the local milkmaids never fell ill from smallpox and he had wondered if this was because they had already been infected with a milder version of the disease from the cows they milked. *Vacca* was the Latin word for 'cow' and thus the word *vaccine* was invented. Marie thought it was mindboggling and could not imagine how Jesty had dared to use his own family as guinea pigs. He must have been truly convinced of his cause. Or truly desperate.

Later the vaccine was systematised by Edward Anthony Jenner. That was the first vaccine and it was live. Later still, inactive vaccines were added. However, it was the live vaccine that made the biggest impression on Marie. The thought of allowing yourself to be infected with a weakened version of death in order to develop resistance filled her with terror and awe in equal measures.

After the epidemiology course, Marie attended all of Kristian Storm's lectures, and as time passed, she grew increasingly impressed by him. Storm would alternate his courses of lectures with writing papers and visiting Guinea-Bissau in West Africa. Here he headed the research station, the Belem Health Project, which monitored demographically 190,000 inhabitants in the former Portuguese colony. What was the child mortality rate among children who were breastfed compared to children who were not? What effect did newly introduced vaccines have on the population's survival rate? Did impregnated mosquito nets help reduce the number of malaria cases? Storm and his local assistants would walk from hut to hut to interview every single family member about the state of their health. The result was a unique database.

With the database as his starting point, Storm had developed controversial views about infection. For example, he discovered that the longer a person was exposed to infection, the sicker they would become. The world of science got terribly agitated about his claims. One single bacterium or one single virus surely made the infected person just as ill as a thousand.

No, Storm said, referring to his database. Children who were briefly infected outside the home became much less ill than their siblings with whom they would share a bed night after night while the bacterium or virus worked its way through the whole family. The loudest outcry came when Storm argued that getting infected by someone of the opposite sex was worse. Absolute nonsense, said Storm's critics. 'Well, then, just take a look at my data,' Storm said calmly.

Marie was spellbound by his confidence and courage.

Kristian Storm was primarily an immunologist, but he was also obsessed with responsible research.

'And good research is almost a lost discipline in Denmark,' he had said at a lecture where Marie had filled sixteen pages with notes. 'Modern research is driven by money. No scientist can carry out research without a grant, and as it is almost exclusively the number of papers published in highly regarded journals which determine whether or not a scientist is awarded that grant, the main research aim of the modern scientist is thus to produce grant-generating papers. But do you think that these highly regarded journals are interested in publishing the outcome of failed experiments? Of course they're not. The result is that modern scientists carry out less risky research. And this is a death blow to the discipline of research, trust me, because if no one is prepared to risk a leap of faith, how will we ever learn anything new? It might not matter all that much right now, perhaps not even in five years' time, but one day it will be very clear – also to those blasted politicians – that we have ruined Denmark's fine research tradition. I sincerely hope,' he said, looking intently across the lecture hall, 'that you'll become good scientists! Real scientists. Driven by curiosity alone, not by competition and commercial interests.'

It was at the same lecture that Marie was introduced for the first time to Storm's ideas about *free research* and *strategic research*. Free research was classic research, Storm explained, where the scientist strives to acquire new knowledge without knowing in advance how that knowledge should be applied. Within free research it was acceptable, yes, almost the point, that the scientist could freely explore their area of interest and be permitted to make mistakes because as long as the *fumbling phase*, as Storm called it and everyone laughed, was insightful, it offered a unique opportunity to discover something of genius. The vaccine, penicillin and X-rays: these three fundamental discoveries were all arrived at by a fortuitous coincidence. Two steps forwards, three back, and suddenly a flash of insight.

Strategic research, however, allowed no room for that kind of intelligent meandering, Storm explained, and there was no doubt what kind of research Storm preferred and carried out himself. He called free research 'the door to the cathedral of truth' and Marie's mouth got dry just tasting the word. A place where you could work undisturbed, seek answers to the big questions of natural science and get as close to the truth as possible.

'Until now strategic research has mainly been a matter for industry. But in recent years, where ignorant politicians have demanded a shorter route between research and invoicing, it has started to infect the universities as well, regrettably,' he continued, while Marie scribbled furiously on her notepad. Storm was angry with politicians and outraged on behalf of Denmark as a research nation. It was a policy that looked attractive in the short term because industrial productivity would rise, but in the long run it was an admission of failure.

'Politicians don't like investing in free research so they call it "investing risk capital" or, in plain Danish, throwing money down the drain. And, yes, free research might cost more, but at the same time it's our only opportunity for new break-throughs and revolutionary results. If Denmark is to participate in international, elite research, we need to return to *free* research; so, mark my words: let your work be driven by curiosity. Be nerds. Focus your attention on what looks weird and doesn't fit with your expectations. Ask the difficult questions. Look under every stone.'

After the fifth term, the students had to write their bachelor dissertations and Marie heard herself say that her subject would be immunology and that Kristian Storm would be her supervisor. She was with a group of fellow students at the August Krogh Institute in a break between two lectures and everyone who heard her raised an impressed eyebrow.

Marie ran to the Ladies and locked herself into a cubicle. What had she been thinking? Everybody wanted Kristian Storm as their supervisor. He was the most high-profile scientist at the Institute of Biology and the main reason that the Department of Immunology was still a crucible of modern international research at a time when other departments were closing. How could she have said something like that? Kristian Storm didn't even know who she was.

It was not until Christmas that Marie braced herself and wrote an email to Storm; within a few hours she received a response, telling her to turn up at the institute the following day at ten o'clock, bringing her subject reports and exam results.

That night she was unable to sleep.

'What are you so scared of?' Jesper grunted, annoyed when Marie turned over for the umpteenth time. 'Go to sleep.'

'I wonder why you're so nervous,' Kristian Storm observed amicably when their conversation had been going for five minutes. His sparse grey hair stuck out as if he had just been asleep, but he was wearing a gaudy shirt that had been ironed for the occasion. His gaze was weatherworn and insistent. Marie was ashamed that her nerves showed so clearly. Storm flicked through the report from her first year and waited patiently for her to reply, but Marie was lost for words.

'Low marks in all your oral tests,' he then said, 'and top marks in all your written ones?'

Marie gulped. 'Yes, I . . . eh.'

'Aha,' Storm declared and looked at her across the half-rim of his spectacles. 'Performance anxiety. That won't get you very far.'

Marie left with her tail between her legs. She was pathetically grateful that he had at least been kind. However, by the time she got home, Storm had already emailed her. He had agreed to supervise her dissertation.

Marie started to frequent the Department of Immunology at the Institute of Biology, Universitetsparken 15, Jagtvej, more often. The department consisted of Storm, its head, and his former PhD student Thor Albert Larsen, some thirty years his junior, as his deputy. They were supported by a handful of temporary appointments whose research was financed by a patchwork of fixed-term grants. Storm and Thor also shared the supervision of five PhD students and nine master's students. While Marie completed her third-year undergraduate courses, Storm gradually included her in his laboratory work, let her co-write several of his more general publications about clinical immunology and taught her to think like a scientist.

'Hmm, you're somewhat rusty,' Storm said, when he tried to gauge her opinion about something and she had no idea what to say, 'but you'll pick it up, of that I have no doubt. Have you never learned to debate? Didn't you ever disagree in your family?'

'Not officially,' Marie said timidly. 'When I was a child it was best just to agree with my dad. Anything for a quiet life.'

'Well, you can forget all about that,' Storm said firmly. 'You can have peace when you're dead. And I tell you, if you don't know yourself what you think, you'll never be able to convince anyone else.'

Marie lapped it all up. Storm always listened attentively to what she said and quoted her so often that she started to believe in the validity of her ideas.

They also laughed a lot in each other's company. That was almost the best thing about Storm. He was filled with infectious laughter.

At night Marie would fall asleep the second her head hit the pillow, happy and exhausted, before Jesper had even brushed his teeth. When she finally woke up in the morning, he would complain in a surly tone that not even an elephant could have roused her.

'But what about a tyrannosaurus?' said Anton, who had climbed up on their double bed.

'Definitely a tyrannosaurus,' Marie said, and started tickling him. 'Everybody knows that they make an awful lot of noise.'

Anton squealed with delight and Jesper could not help smiling.

The only cloud in Marie's clear blue sky was Thor Albert Larsen. He seemed almost hostile, she thought, and if they happened to pass each other in the corridor, he would barely acknowledge her. Storm never commented on his obviously rude behaviour and, to begin with, Marie found it baffling. In time she realised that Storm was above such pettiness. He never spoke ill of anyone and he never indulged in gossip.

'It's probably because of what happened to his father,' Marie overheard one of the master's students say to the department's lab technician in the senior common room where she was sitting with her sandwiches.

'You see,' the postgraduate continued, when the lab assistant looked blank, 'when my father studied medicine in the 1980s, Storm's father, Birger Storm, was professor of medicine at the Faculty of Health Science and a highly respected scientist in internal medicine. One day, out of the blue, a female colleague accused him of sexual harassment. I believe it was one of the first really big sexual-harassment cases and the media was all over it. Birger Storm was forced to take leave while the allegation was investigated because students would walk out during his lectures. It wasn't until he was cleared in court that he dared return to the university, only to discover that mud has a tendency to stick. He killed himself shortly afterwards.'

'No!' Marie exclaimed. The lab assistant and the postgraduate student both looked at her.

'Yes,' the postgraduate said, 'so no wonder Storm is completely allergic to intrigues. I would be too.'

Marie was overcome by the urge to go straight to Storm's office and tell him how awful she thought it was that his father had killed himself.

CHAPTER 3

Kristian Storm, professor of immunology, was wrapping up a telephone conversation with a colleague in France when Marie Skov knocked tentatively on his half-open door and popped her head into his office. 'Sorry, I just wanted to . . .' she said, before she realised that Storm was on the phone, but he quickly waved her inside. 'Two minutes,' he mouthed, and Marie sat down on a small sofa just inside the door. Her timing was perfect: Storm wanted to talk to her about an important matter.

While the Frenchman was reaching the conclusion to his lengthy monologue, Storm reminisced about his first meeting with Marie. She had turned up at his office, practically tripping over her own toes to such an extent it was almost comical. She looked like a ruffled baby swallow, Storm had thought. His best protégés were always students who were not yet ready to fly solo, those who found it the most natural thing in the world to hide their light under a bushel because they did not know yet what else to do. They listened to him, they could be moulded and they needed Storm. Privately Storm called them his swallows and only his father would have understood why. As a child, Storm had found a baby swallow on the ground, still damp from the yolk sac, bald and lost. He was convinced that his scientist father would tell him to let nature take its course and ignore the baby bird. But Storm's father had found a large leaf and carefully scooped the baby bird back into the nest under the gutter from where it had fallen.

'Swallows are tough,' he had said to his son. 'Just you wait and see.'

Three weeks later the garden had been filled with fearlessly diving swallows, and Storm had searched the grass along the wall in vain and even double-checked the bin, but could find no trace of the baby bird.

'Oh, you won't find it,' Storm's father had said. 'It's up there.' He pointed towards a boomerang in the sky. Ever since then Storm had loved swallows.

When Storm had finally concluded his conversation with the Frenchman, he watched Marie for a moment. She had got up and was studying the photographs on his wall, which was covered with framed pictures and postcards from ex-students from around the world. There were also diplomas and newspaper cuttings and wooden African masks decorated with beads. His life. Storm got up and positioned himself next to Marie, who was taking a close interest in an old black-and-white photograph.

'That's me and my father, Birger Storm,' Storm said, pointing to the picture. 'My mother died when I was very young, but my father decided to bring me up himself, without a nanny. If you knew how many times I slept on a mattress on the floor in his office when he had just started working at the Faculty of Medicine! You could say my choice of career is the result of a work-related injury.' He chuckled to himself. 'My father died thirty years ago. He was the victim of a conspiracy. But I gather you've already heard.' Storm watched Marie, and when she nodded, he wanted to know more. 'What have you heard?'

'That he was falsely accused of sexual harassment,' Marie said honestly, 'and that he killed himself, even though he was cleared.'

Storm nodded slowly and returned to the photographs on the wall. 'Ah,' he said, pointing to another picture. 'This shack is the research station for the Belem Health Project in Bissau. My passion these last five years. I'm well aware that it looks like a pimped-up woodshed, but great science is happening behind its flimsy planks, trust me.' He laughed.

'That's Silas Henckel, isn't it?' Marie said, gesturing to the next photograph. 'I recognise him, even though I don't think I ever met him.'

Storm got a lump in his throat. The photograph had been taken two years ago and he was standing between two of his PhD students: Tim Salomon, who would soon become the first Guinean PhD student at the Belem Health Project, and Silas Henckel, who had drowned in a terrible accident in 2007.

Marie misinterpreted his silence. 'I'm sorry, I didn't mean to upset you,' she interjected.

'You haven't, but it's hard for me. Because in a way it was my fault that Silas died.'

'Your fault?'

'Never force a workaholic to take a vacation,' Storm said. 'I meant well, obviously. It was early December and Silas had just returned to Bissau after a lengthy trip to an impassable area of south-eastern Guinea-Bissau between the two Dulombi-Boe national parks, which border Guinea. Unfortunately, there was something very wrong with his figures so I sent him back to do them again. He was very unhappy, and when he had gone, I started to feel bad about it. It would be Christmas soon and, even though Silas was the toughest student I've ever had, I was sure that he didn't fancy spending Christmas in the bush. So I gave him a two-week holiday at a resort in Gambia as a Christmas present. There wasn't time for him to repeat the survey of the entire area before Christmas anyway, so a break in slightly more comfortable surroundings was perfect. So went my thinking. I booked it, paid for it and ordered him to go. "You've earned it," I wrote.

'I myself went to Skagen to celebrate Christmas with some friends and didn't return to the department until the twenty-eighth of December. I discovered numerous emails in my inbox and messages from Bissau on my answering-machine. While in Gambia, Silas had gone out with local mangrove fishermen and fallen overboard. He got caught in some fishing net and drowned. Naturally I flew to Africa straight away.'

For a moment, Storm stared vacantly into the air, then he shook his head.

'After bringing his coffin back, I found a message from Silas on my answering-machine. I had never got further with replaying my messages after Christmas than the news about Silas, but there were others and one of them was from him. He had called on a poor-quality line from the resort, thanked me for the enforced holiday, wished me a merry Christmas and asked me to call him back urgently.'

'I really am very sorry,' Marie said.

'The other guy is Tim Salomon,' Storm said, pointing to a young African man. 'Fortunately, he is very much alive and you'll meet him soon. Tim is my success story. The child of an unemployed widow in Bissau, he was doomed to a life in the cashew plantations – that's how most Guineans support themselves – but his teacher had spotted his potential and put him up for a full scholarship at Kingston University in London. Tim even completed a master's in biology before he returned to Bissau. That was where I was lucky enough to meet him and he started working for me, first as an interpreter but he soon became my right-hand man, assistant and friend. Apart from having a brilliant mind, his great advantage is that he's a native Guinean. Tim's father was a missionary and he was brought up as a Christian, but even so, he knows better than anyone else how to treat the various ethnic groups without treading on anyone's toes.

'Silas's death hit Tim hard, and everything ground to a halt for several months. But now it's back up and running, I'm glad to say. I look forward to you meeting him.

'And here we have Thor, the little pen-pusher, just look at him!' Storm pointed to another picture. Marie looked at the photograph, which showed a group of men gathered around an iron pot on an earthen floor. Apart from Thor, Marie recognised Silas and Tim; the rest appeared to be locals, all busy eating the grey and brown contents of the communal pot.

'Thor came to Guinea-Bissau once and it was a total disaster. He couldn't keep his socks white, he couldn't sleep at night because of the mosquitoes whining around outside the mosquito net. One evening he forgot that you risk getting infected with parasites if you brush your teeth in tap water, and when he remembered, he flipped out completely. That day proved to be the final straw.' Storm tapped his finger on the glass. 'We were in a village to collect data and the local tribal leader invited us for lunch. And this is how they do it. Rice and fish in a communal pot and one spoon for each. When Thor realised he wasn't going to get his own plate, I simply had to take that photo. We all thought it was hilarious.'

Storm howled with laughter, and when Marie joined in, he laughed even louder.

'By the way,' he said, when they had calmed down, 'I've been meaning to tell you something. Don't mind Thor. He has a grudge against every potential academic rival, and it has been like this since he was my student almost eight years ago, with a doctorate in between. But he's all right.'

Storm squeezed Marie's arm and went back to his desk. 'Please would you sit down for a moment,' he said, indicating the visitor's chair. 'I want to talk to you about something important. About your master's. It's time.'

Marie looked so terrified that Storm couldn't help winding her up by putting on a very stern face. Marie's debilitating insecurity often masked her intelligence. She was in fact extremely bright and on top of that she was great company. Storm could not remember ever working with a student with whom he was as much in tune as he was with Marie. Even when they worked at opposite ends of the laboratory and hours passed without them speaking, there was a special atmosphere. In the last few months, they had even started joking with each other, and Storm had realised Marie was not timid at all. On the contrary, her sense of humour was so subtle and dry that it might take Storm several moments before he twigged her allusion and could share the joke. All in all, Marie was a gift from Heaven, both for him and for his research project. And he told himself that Marie felt the same.

'So, what are your thoughts about your master's dissertation?' Storm asked.

Marie looked worried. 'I would really like to write it here, in this department. I really would,' she then said. 'And I hope it won't be a problem that I can't travel to Guinea-Bissau.'

'You can't travel to Guinea-Bissau?' Storm said, feigning surprise.

'Jesper has started training to be an orthopaedic consultant,' Marie said. 'Don't you remember me telling you? He's working ever so hard and I can't go to Africa because who would look after Anton? Jesper can't take time off. I was hoping it wouldn't be a problem. But I . . .' She fell silent.

'Oh,' Storm said. 'Never mind. I'm sure Thor won't mind acting as your supervisor back here at home.'

For an instant Marie seemed deeply disappointed, then she narrowed her eyes and gave him a sly look. 'You're teasing me,' she said.

Storm grinned from ear to ear. 'Marie,' he said, 'do you really think it would even cross my mind to dump my best student in the last twenty-five years on Thor Albert Larsen? You must be out of your mind. If you want to stay with the Department of Immunology, if you have the guts to specialise within this contentious field, I'd like to supervise your dissertation myself.'

For a moment Marie seemed about to cry. 'I'd really like that,' she then said, almost lost for words. 'I mean, thank you, I would absolutely love it. Thank you so much.'

In the weeks before Marie started work on her dissertation, Storm briefed her thoroughly about the Belem Health Project and his research in Guinea-Bissau. Marie was busy with her finals and Storm had plenty to do, but whenever the opportunity arose, they would meet at two o'clock in Storm's office where he would explain the background for his research, while Marie listened and took notes.

'How had it all begun?' Marie wanted to know.

'With one single unplanned observation,' Storm said.

In 2004 Storm was sent to Guinea-Bissau by SIDA, the Swedish International Development Co-operation Agency, with a brief to discover the reasons for and find ways to lower the extremely high child mortality rate in the small West African country. With him Storm had brought the Swedish nutrition expert Olof Bengtsson from the University of Lund, and a team of local assistants, including Tim. During three visits between 2004 and 2006 Storm and Bengtsson gathered data on 28,000 children under five, who lived in the four big suburbs of Bissau. They created a medical record for each child that covered every aspect of its development, health and the nature and date of any vaccines it had received. It was a gargantuan task, which resulted in the first systematic monitoring of children in the history of Guinea-Bissau.

One of the first discoveries made by Storm and Bengtsson was the low rate of vaccination cover. Alarmingly few children were vaccinated, a situation that needed to be addressed as quickly as possible. Storm and Bengtsson alerted the WHO to their findings, and by the following year enough new health clinics had opened and enough campaigns had been run in

Bissau and surrounding areas for the proportion of children being vaccinated to have risen dramatically.

In 2006, when Storm and Bengtsson were finalising the processing of their data, they made a surprise discovery. They had spent most of their week crunching statistics on their measles and TB data and late one night, shortly before their return home, they were discussing the graphs they had printed out and spread across the floor.

Storm was the first to see it.

As they would have expected, mortality had dropped among the children who had been vaccinated against measles and tuberculosis, but the extent by which it had fallen was much greater than they had anticipated.

The two scientists stared at the figures and scratched their heads.

Bengtsson started re-evaluating their survey method, but broke off to ask Storm whether he was planning to return to Africa next year if SIDA extended the funding. Absolutely, Storm had replied. Storm had never believed in overseas aid, but felt that their work had a purpose. They were laying down the basic structure for a public health-care system, and when the SIDA money ran out, they could hand over important data to the Guineans. Bengtsson nodded slowly. Personally, he had doubts whether he would continue. First, he was about to land an exciting new job, he revealed, and second, he had been taken aback by how deeply the poverty affected him. He had young children of his own and found it hard to watch babies die from diseases that would have been treatable if only they had been born on another continent.

Bengtsson got up to fetch two cold Cristal beers from the

fridge and Storm looked at the chart of diseases that most commonly claimed the lives of children in Guinea-Bissau. Malaria was, not surprisingly, a major culprit, but respiratory diseases and diarrhoea were high on the list of most frequent killers of young children. Storm could hear Bengtsson open the fridge in the research station's kitchen, then the pop of bottle caps and finally his footsteps across the hallway. Then the lights flickered and he was plunged into darkness.

Bengtsson swore.

The generator kicked in a moment later and the lights came back on. Storm stared at the printouts. What the hell was that? He quickly rearranged a few sheets of paper and pushed others aside and, like an obstinate 3D picture, it suddenly came into focus.

'"Bloody hell, Bengtsson," I said,' Storm continued. '"Just take a look at this." We didn't sleep that night. Or the next, for that matter. I'll never forget it, Marie.'

'What did you see?' Marie said, holding her breath. All the time Storm had been talking, her notepad had lain untouched in her lap.

'We realised why the mortality rate had fallen so disproportionately among children who had been vaccinated against TB and measles since the time we had alerted the WHO to the low vaccination cover. Not surprisingly, the children were much less likely to die from TB or measles against which they were now protected, but they were also less likely to die from other illnesses, such as malaria, respiratory diseases and diarrhoea. It was weird, but no matter how we examined the figures, the picture was the same: vaccinated children were less likely to die, and not just from the diseases they had been vaccinated against but from *all* diseases. Finally we agreed that it could mean only one thing: the TB and measles vaccines had an as-yet-unrecorded strengthening effect on the immune system to such an extent that overall mortality rate was halved.'

'*Halved!*'

Storm banged his fist on his desk. 'Right, that's enough for today,' he said, and glanced at his watch. He was delighted at how disappointed Marie looked when she picked up her bag and left.

Bengtsson and Storm had discussed the phenomenon all night, Storm told Marie, when she was back in his office a few days later, notepad on her lap. What the hell did it mean? While Storm ran the data through the statistics program once more, just to be on the safe side, Bengtsson finalised their statistics on the DTP vaccine, another standard immunisation in the WHO's global vaccination programme. This vaccine protected against diphtheria, tetanus and pertussis, also known as whooping cough.

'Same results here!' Storm yelled excitedly to Bengtsson, from his end of the room when he had double-checked the TB and measles vaccines and printed out the exact same graph a second time. 'What about the DTP?'

'Nothing. No positive correlation,' Bengtsson called, from the other end of the room and showed Storm a negative graph. 'Quite the opposite.'

'But these,' Storm said, flicking his fingers on his pile of graphs, 'they speak their own clear language!'

The WHO had to be alerted immediately, but how? From a

research point of view it was problematic that their observation was a by-product of work carried out to resolve a different issue because it meant they had not followed the appropriate protocol for this new discovery, which was alpha and omega for the validity of a scientific observation.

'And that's exactly why I hate strategic research,' he interjected, and Marie nodded.

Dawn had arrived before Bengtsson and Storm had decided their next move. For better or worse, the WHO was a conservative organisation. It could not simply change its global and deeply embedded vaccination programme on the basis of one set of new observations, but then again, their data was so significant that they must contact the WHO without delay. Finally they agreed that their position would be stronger if their approach was backed up by a well-established aid organisation such as SIDA. It did not matter that SIDA would end up taking the credit for their observation. This was about human lives, not personal promotion.

Back in Denmark, Storm had immediately set to work on writing the report to SIDA, and in a fairly extensive footnote, he accounted for their accidental observation. He called it *The Non-specific Positive Effects of Vaccines* and his tentative conclusion was that something in the TB and measles vaccines appeared to strengthen the immune system so much that anyone vaccinated did not just develop immunity towards those particular diseases but higher resistance towards diseases in general.

Storm emailed his report to Sweden, and when Bengtsson had added his comments, he sent it to SIDA's headquarters in Stockholm.

It was two weeks before the start of term; Storm's full-time and project staff were starting to return to the Department of Immunology and the place was buzzing. There were meetings, final adjustments to syllabuses, lecture-hall bookings and intense master's dissertation and PhD supervision work for Storm to carry out because he had been abroad. Even so, the discovery in Guinea-Bissau was constantly on his mind.

What if it was really true that certain vaccines boosted the immune system? What did that mean? Surely that the working of the immune system was fundamentally different from what people had thought until now. That a specific vaccine did not just protect against a specific disease but against a broad spectrum of diseases. As if the immune system was intelligent, Storm realised, and could apply information to other situations. Like the brain. An adaptive immune system!

It was mindboggling.

In the midst of that hectic autumn, Storm wrote a brief article about his initial thoughts on the adaptive immune system. He sent it to the university's intranet newsletter, Uni-Net, and had not in his wildest dreams imagined that it would lead to anything other than a few grunts from his peers, who were all busy with the new term.

'But, Marie,' Storm said, 'I'm telling you, they went crazy.'

To his surprise, the most bilious reaction came from Storm's own ranks in the shape of his former PhD student Stig Heller, who was now working at the Karolinska Institute in Stockholm. Heller had clearly reached for his red pen as soon as he read Storm's piece on Uni-Net because only two days later he uploaded a lengthy rant in which he demolished line by line Storm's rather cautiously expressed views about the possibility of an adaptive immune system. The whole thing was codswallop, Heller wrote. It was one thing to challenge the boundaries of classic research – Heller did not have a problem with that – but Storm's ideas about the adaptive immune system 'didn't fall far short of creationist non-science and other flat-Earth theories'.

'Heller and I batted the ball back and forth a bit,' Storm said, with a smile, 'but in the end I just lost interest because it was clear that Heller, the sourpuss, only cared about inflating his own ego. I should mention that he had just been passed over for the lecturer post here in the department, which went to Thor Albert Larsen, so it wasn't hard to work out why Heller had a major grudge against me, the department and my whole area of research. Quite unfairly, I hasten to add, because I had expressed a preference for Heller, but our human resources committee felt our research profiles were too similar so they picked Thor instead. Now, of course, I couldn't say any of that to Heller and, besides, I had more important things to do than mollify a petulant child. Do you happen to know Stig Heller?' Storm asked Marie.

Marie shook her head.

'Once he was one of my golden boys, bright as a button and deeply committed until he made an inexplicable U-turn. Anyway, back to the matter in hand,' Storm said. 'I emailed two valued colleagues in Ghana and Haiti who had also gathered vaccination data using the same method as we had in Guinea-Bissau and asked for insight into their measles and TB immunisation and mortality rates. They responded quickly and I got a shock when I saw their figures. When I had fed all the data to the statistics program and printed out the graphs, their results were identical to the ones I had from Guinea-Bissau. In Ghana and on Haiti, overall mortality had halved among the children who had been vaccinated against measles and TB. It meant that the phenomenon in Guinea-Bissau could no longer be considered a one-off.

'Then I noticed I had overlooked an attachment to the email from my Haitian colleague. "Records_DTP" was the file name and when I opened it, my colleague had written "Sending this as well. Didn't know if DTP is also of interest?" at the top of the page.

'And, no, I wasn't really interested in the DTP data. Bengtsson and I had already looked at the figures in Guinea-Bissau and the vaccine against diphtheria, tetanus and whooping cough would not appear to have the same positive side effect as the measles and TB vaccines. Even so, I opened the document and my jaw dropped. Because what was it Bengtsson had said?'

'Quite the opposite,' Marie answered straight away.

'Exactly! I immediately opened our files with the raw DTP records from Guinea-Bissau and found the graph Bengtsson had prepared on the basis of those figures. Then I entered all the DTP figures from Ghana and Haiti into the statistics program and saved everything in a folder, which I named "Quite the opposite". I hit print and practically sprinted down the corridor to the printer room – I tell you, Marie, my heart was pounding.

'All three graphs were negative. In Guinea-Bissau, in Ghana and on Haiti, DTP-vaccinated children had twice the mortality rate of unvaccinated ones. They no longer died from diphtheria, tetanus or whooping cough, so the vaccine worked as it was intended to, but they died from all sorts of other things:

diarrhoea, pneumonia, malaria and simple fever. And they were dropping like flies.'

Storm had rung Bengtsson in Lund in a state of agitation.

'I sensed his reluctance right away,' Storm told Marie. 'In Bissau he had been raring to go, but now he was . . . dragging his heels. At first I couldn't understand it. Our theory was that vaccines had certain non-specific, positive effects, but now it would appear that one vaccine might be harmful, and I told him that we had to act. I would write a follow-up note to SIDA immediately and alert them to the negative correlation, which we had initially overlooked, but I wondered if we shouldn't contact the WHO directly rather than wait for SIDA. What did Bengtsson think? If the DTP vaccine killed children, time was of the essence! Bengtsson asked me if I had any idea what I was saying, the implications of my discovery. "But it's what the data tell us, not my personal opinion," I stressed. Even so, he said. The outcome would be the same: the WHO, health authority to the whole world, had blood on its hands. Thousands of dead children in Guinea-Bissau and possibly hundreds of thousands across the globe! "Is that really what you're claiming?" he asked. At this point I got seriously hacked off. "Bengtsson," I said to him, "you're only guilty when you do something wrong intentionally. And the WHO isn't killing children in Africa on purpose, that goes without saying. This has nothing to do with me wanting to point the finger. It's about research. About what our numbers prove. We must do something. Now!"'

Then Bengtsson announced he had got the job he had mentioned when we were in Africa. It wasn't official yet, but he would shortly be leaving his post as a lecturer at the University of Lund and start work with Pons, the new Swedish research facility.

'And that's when I despaired, Marie,' Storm said. 'Have you heard about Pons?'

Marie thought the name rang a bell.

'Do you know who Göran Sandö is?' Storm then asked her. Yes, of course Marie knew who he was. World-famous Swedish consultant epidemiologist and a member of the Nobel Committee. Something of an *enfant terrible*, if the rumours were to be believed, and with his dark, curly hair, he had also made an impression on many women.

'Sandö is my highly treasured, favourite aversion,' Storm said. 'He's a brilliant scientist and orator and the top boss of Pons. Pons is a research hybrid set up to bridge the gap between the classical virtues of the university and industry's ever-growing focus on profit. It's affiliated to the University of Lund, where it's based, and half the group's funding comes from the Swedish Exchequer, while the other half comes from private investors. So you can see why Pons most certainly isn't my cup of tea. However, I rather like Sandö. In his own cashmere-clad fashion, his self-promotion is actually quite refreshing. Even so, Sandö represents everything about modern research that I object to. His own achievements take centre stage, he's blatantly ambitious, there's a short distance between research and invoicing, and the whole thing is wrapped up in a lot of waffle about doing it for "the greater good of science", though we all know that politicians hold a loaded gun to the head of science. Bengtsson insisted that his decision to withdraw had nothing to do with the fact that he was now working for Sandö. He just felt we would be making a serious accusation and we were basing it solely on a series of observational studies, which were begging to be demolished. He had no desire to be hung out to dry for lack of professionalism, he said, or, worse, being accused of scientific fraud.

"'Quite honestly, Storm," he said to me, "the WHO has used the DTP vaccine for twenty years. How come no one has noticed that the vaccine is a lethal injection?"

"'Yes, why do you think that is, Bengtsson?"

"'What we were doing in Guinea-Bissau was front-line research," I continued. "For one brilliant moment, your humdrum research career made sense and now you worry about being accused of scientific fraud? We saw something and we have a duty to act on it! When did morality and ethics disappear from science, eh, Bengtsson?"

'I think I might have been shouting at him at that point,' Storm said, and smiled cheerfully at Marie.

Bengtsson withdrew from the project, and three days later, SIDA's reaction to the report and the follow-up note, which Storm had composed and forwarded to them, arrived. SIDA *always* welcomed new scientific observations, but as a publicly financed body it had a duty to report to the research committees at the University of Stockholm and must comply with fundamental conditions for scientific responsibility and accountability. As a result, SIDA could under no circumstances support research that had completely exceeded its original remit, and where the scientists had failed to submit a change of hypothesis that went so far beyond the original protocol for their planned research.

'It was pretty much at this point,' Storm said to Marie, 'that

I hurled my pencil holder at the wall. I've never read such spineless, rhetorical drivel.'

'Once I had calmed down, I wrote to the WHO,' Storm continued, the next day, and hit some keys on his computer. 'Hang on, let me just bring up my letter. Here it is. I describe my observations in detail and refer to identical observations on Haiti and in Ghana. I wrote everything with all due caveats and took care to stress the weaknesses of the study. "Unplanned observation",' he read aloud. '"Absence of preceding hypothesis and protocol. Incomplete data collection. The observational nature of the study."

'"There is no doubt that it would have been preferable,"' Storm read on, '"for my study not to have had these weaknesses. However, it is not ethical to use blind testing with placebos when studying living human beings, least of all when it concerns vaccinations, which have been global policy for many years. After all, we cannot suddenly make vaccination in a population a lottery when the accepted view is that vaccination is the right choice. *Ergo*,"' Storm concluded his reading aloud, '"in this precarious situation we are forced to let the figures in a regrettably solely observational study decide that the phenomenon should be examined more closely without delay, and funds should be allocated for extended studies in Guinea-Bissau immediately."'

'Good letter,' Marie said.

'Yes, that's what I thought,' Storm said. 'I also enclosed the text for an article I had written for *Science* about my observations, then sent the whole thing to the WHO's headquarters in Geneva. I emailed the article to *Science*. Very soon afterwards, I received a reply from Terrence Wilson, editor-in-chief of *Science*. He was extremely excited and wanted to publish my article in volume 315, the following January, 2007. He even wrote that he had asked a professor of theoretical science from the Sorbonne to write a general article about major scientific breakthroughs in violation of scientific convention and thus believed he had warded off potential criticism of the lack of protocol. "I do see the problem,"' Storm quoted Wilson, '"but then again, I believe it would be deeply unethical not to act on those observations immediately."'

'Deeply unethical. Of course, I couldn't agree more,' Storm said to Marie.

The days passed and Storm had heard nothing from the WHO. Two weeks later he began to lose patience. In the middle of it all, Terrence Wilson from *Science* called and said there was a small problem. In principle, he was still interested in the article, but he had subsequently received two other articles related to the same topic and needed a little extra time to explore any impact these new articles might have on Storm's contribution. Initially it meant *Science* would have to postpone publication indefinitely. Storm asked where the new articles had come from, but Wilson refused to divulge that information. Storm had hung up in anger.

In the weeks that had followed, Storm tried contacting the WHO on a daily basis, but without success. Eventually he had to turn his attention to lectures, departmental meetings and student supervision, but he decided that if he had not heard from the WHO before the upcoming autumn half-term, he would fly to Geneva and go to the WHO's headquarters himself.

Two days before the autumn half-term, Storm received a cutting from an article that had just been published in the *Bulletin of the World Health Organization*, the WHO's own periodical. The article totally pulled the rug from under Storm's feet. The headline read: 'Scientist's criticism of DTP unfounded.' It was a well-written and pithy article, which reviewed the history of the DTP vaccine and its benefits, and concluded that the criticism which had recently been levelled at this particular vaccine had no basis in fact, but that the WHO, 'in order to eliminate any doubts, had immediately initiated further analysis of the DTP vaccine'. Gobsmacked, Storm reviewed the article's literature list to see if there were other articles concerned with non-specific vaccine effects or if the author of the article in the *Bulletin of the World Health Organization* had had the cheek to refer to Storm's as yet unpublished article. Storm had included his *Science* article in his letter to the WHO for information only.

The author of the article in the *Bulletin of the World Health Organization* was Paul Smith, and Storm Googled him. He was the head of WET, the WHO's epidemiology task force, and had written several articles about the DTP vaccine. However, Storm could not find a single article that questioned the effect of the vaccine in developing countries, neither in Smith's literature list nor in PubMed, the scientific-article database, which he trawled through for the umpteenth time. An enraged Storm called the WHO's main switchboard. After being transferred half a dozen times, he finally got hold of the editor-in-chief of the *Bulletin of the World Health Organization*.

'Paul Smith has no right to refer to an article, *my* article or *my* figures, that I have yet to publish,' Storm thundered, and the editor-in-chief said that he believed Smith was referring to other scientists' criticism of the DTP vaccine, not Storm's.

'Which other scientists?' Storm demanded. 'Which articles, which periodicals, and when were they published?'

The editor did not know that because he had been away on business, but he would discuss it with a colleague and get back to Storm.

'Which he obviously never did,' Storm said to Marie.

The next day Storm received an email directly from Paul Smith, who thanked him for getting in touch regarding the non-specific effects of the vaccine. He wanted Storm to be aware that 'the WHO took his letter very seriously' and had instantly allocated money from their contingency funds to further investigations. However, they would not be inviting Storm to participate in this work; Smith did not mention his underhand references to Storm's article.

Storm had been sitting crestfallen behind his desk when Terrence Wilson from *Science* emailed him with the *coup de grâce*. He was unable to print Storm's article after all, he wrote, because he had now received no less than three articles that proved that the DTP vaccine was quite safe. Wilson stressed that it had not been an easy decision, as Storm's figures really were very persuasive, but because they were the accidental result of an observational study, and there was therefore no way of knowing exactly what could have influenced them, *Science* had decided that Storm's article was too risky. However, he would very much like to hear from Storm again, if he could produce figures from a planned study that confirmed the negative effects of DTP.

That same week, the *Bulletin of the World Health Organization* published a two-page spread on vaccine criticism in general and firmly rejected all accusations. In the week that followed, the article was quoted in thirty-seven electronic peer-reviewed journals, then mentioned in forty-five newspapers and magazines across the world. Storm even found a note in the Danish newspaper *Information*, to which he had been a loyal subscriber for more than thirty years, saying, 'Accusation against the WHO's vaccination programme dismissed.'

When Storm saw it, he banged his head against the desk.

'I was knocked out for a week,' Storm told Marie. 'But then I clicked the heels of my ergonomic sandals and contacted the Danish National Research Foundation and – wouldn't you know it? – they granted me two million kroner for further analysis in Guinea-Bissau. Furthermore, they contacted Paul Smith from the WHO's epidemiology task force and invited him and a number of other VIPs, me included, to a meeting in Copenhagen.

'The only fly in the ointment was that the date of the meeting wasn't until nine months later, the fifteenth of July 2007.

'It was regrettable, the Danish National Research Foundation said. They had done everything they could, but that was the first available date in Paul Smith's diary.'

When Storm had ended the call, he was fuming. It was inconceivable that a Danish child would be allowed to die from an approved vaccine without tabloids such as *Ekstra Bladet* immediately clearing the front page, and the switchboard at the Patient Complaint Agency being inundated with calls. Inconceivable. His figures cried out to heaven that children in Guinea-Bissau were dying like flies from the DTP vaccine and the only thing the WHO could be bothered to do was turn up for a wishy-washy professional-user meeting nine months hence? At this point Storm got up, walked up two floors, knocked on the head of the institute's door and requested a leave of absence.

Storm used his grant from the Danish National Research Foundation to establish the Belem Health Project in the Belem area of the town of Bissau; it was a research station devoted exclusively to the study of non-specific effects of vaccines. Tim Salomon was hired as the project's first local PhD student, and on 1 January 2007, Storm and Silas Henckel flew to Bissau.

Slowly but surely Storm extended the population survey to large parts of Guinea-Bissau. He despatched teams of students and local helpers to rural areas, and for many months it was hard toil with little to show for it. They had a minimum six-month wait before they could survey vaccinated children again and they had to wait a whole year before they could draw any serious conclusions from a nationwide set of data. Storm had never worked so hard in his life. In addition to supervising his students in Bissau and Copenhagen, he wasted an irritating amount of time applying for new grants. The two million kroner from the Danish National Research Foundation was spent, and when Storm had had new applications turned down twice in a row, he sold his house in Frederiksberg, which he had inherited from his father, and put 1.5 million kroner of his own money into Belem.

Shortly afterwards, however, he got the good news that the Belem Health Project had been affiliated to Statens Serum

Institute and endowed with a small but ongoing grant of half a million Danish kroner per year. The Belem Health Project moved into bigger premises in Bissau and Storm extended his leave of absence from the University of Copenhagen for another six months.

In July 2007, a few weeks before Storm was due to return to Denmark to attend the Danish National Research Foundation's meeting with Paul Smith and the other big shots, he was finally in possession of all the surveys from the rural areas. He, Tim and Silas were rushed off their feet trying to analyse the latest figures. On the last night, Storm stuck the sheets up on the wall as the data was processed and silence spread across the room. He stood in front of a wall filled with graphs and, for a moment, could not bear to look up at them. Then he heard Silas exclaim, 'Holy shit.'

Storm looked up.

On every single graph the DTP vaccine was associated with increased mortality.

'My presentation in Copenhagen ended up lasting four hours,' Storm told Marie. 'The guest list had crept up to fifteen and I was bombarded with questions. It was a once-in-a-lifetime experience. At that moment I truly believed I had finally got through to them. Even Paul Smith was listening. After my presentation we immediately agreed to have an immunology workshop at the London School of Hygiene and Tropical Medicine in January the following year, and an American professor invited me to give three lectures at the University of California in Berkeley. It was almost surreal. The year before I had been on the rack because no one took me seriously, and now here

I was with the whole assembly as putty in my hands. Or so I thought. Because, do you know what happened? Sweet FA. The attendees went on their merry way and it was business as usual. The WHO still hasn't revised the historical data on which their global vaccination programme is based. They haven't reviewed the DTP vaccine, and they haven't allocated as much as one euro for a fresh evaluation of the obvious benefits of the TB and measles vaccines. The truth finally dawned on me at the workshop at the London School of Hygiene and Tropical Medicine last autumn. It was a total waste of time. Three days of pointless discussion of the methodology problems associated with observational studies, which left none of us any the wiser. One of the participants, the American immunologist Peter Bennett, even got up during one of my talks and exclaimed that our figures were "the worst crap he had ever laid eyes on". Even though his outburst triggered a sea of heartfelt protests, we were in serious trouble. Bennett is a Nobel Prize winner for medicine and an extremely influential man, and there was a large number of medical journalists present. The incident was mentioned in several periodicals and they made it sound as if our observations were far too vague and that our theory about non-specific effects was merely a whim.'

Storm paused and took a deep breath.

'And that's where we are now, Marie. It's 2009 and the WHO runs the same vaccination programmes it always did. I publish on the subject regularly, as I have done all along, but sadly in shorter articles in less prestigious periodicals. I can't get published in any peer review journals, even though I now have the support of several colleagues across the world. None of that matters one jot as long as the WHO remains to be convinced. The WHO has the final say. Only they and they alone can review the vaccination programmes. My goal is a big feature in *Science*. The fine gentlemen in Geneva might be able to ignore one mad Dane, but if I can get through to a leading journal such as *Science*, then they'll be forced to listen. One article that explains everything. The complete data from Guinea-Bissau, which I hope to have ready for Christmas, supported by convincing animal studies performed in the best possible laboratory by the best possible people.' Storm looked gravely at Marie before he said, 'And that's where you come into the picture.'

At last he fell silent and he watched Marie closely.

For a moment she sat quietly and said nothing, then she stuck out a resolute hand to him. As they shook, he had the strong sense that they were sealing a deal. He could not have been better pleased.

CHAPTER 4

Soon afterwards Marie began the laboratory experiment that was to form the core of her master's dissertation. She ordered seventy-two rats from the Serum Institute's animal unit, which arrived at the Department of Immunology on the same day that she also received three disease strains in sealed containers. She injected eighteen rats with the BCG vaccine against TB, also known as the Calmette vaccine. She went on to vaccinate the rats against measles before she tagged their tails so that she could tell them apart. Then she distributed thirty-six rats into three separate Plexiglas cages with six vaccinated and six unvaccinated animals in each. In cage number one, she infected the rats with malaria, in cage number two, with pneumococcal disease, and in cage number three, with E. coli.

Afterwards, she injected eighteen of the remaining thirty-six rats with DTP, the vaccine against diphtheria, tetanus and whooping cough, distributed the animals into three cages, again with six vaccinated and six unvaccinated in each, and infected them with the relevant disease strains.

Then she began observing them. Every day she would tend the rats, remove any dead ones and carefully note the results in her log.

It was a major undertaking and she found it hard going. Jesper was working shifts at the orthopaedic surgical ward at Rigshospitalet and stressed repeatedly that he needed his home life to run smoothly, so Marie grafted night and day to keep on top of everything. Nevertheless Jesper grew increasingly irritated that the house was a mess, at the absence of clean socks for him in the morning, and Anton declared on numerous occasions that he refused to eat pasta with shop-bought pesto ever again.

When Marie eventually finished her experiment, she processed her results statistically and was ready to present them to Storm. They had booked Lecture Hall A for the presentation and Storm sat in the third row, looking expectantly at Marie while she hooked up her laptop to the PowerPoint projector. She had butterflies in her tummy, thinking about her results, and she was utterly exhausted. This was her big break.

She opened her presentation by explaining the TB and measles experiments and carefully described the premise for her experiment, how she had vaccinated and infected the rats and finally how she had analysed the results statistically. Marie's three graphs showed clearly that, whether or not the animals had been infected with malaria, E. coli or pneumococcal disease, the mortality among vaccinated rats was significantly lower than among the unvaccinated. It was clear that the TB and measles vaccines did more good than 'merely' protect against tuberculosis and measles.

'And now we get to the DTP vaccine,' Marie said. 'And take a look at this . . .'

Marie clicked and her results came up.

'In this experiment, the mortality rate among unvaccinated

rats is the same as in the previous one,' she said, pointing first to one graph, then another. 'However, where before mortality was significantly lower for vaccinated animals than for unvaccinated ones, here it's the exact opposite. In fact, mortality has risen with a factor as much as 1.75. So while the DTP vaccine protects against diphtheria, tetanus and whooping cough, it has a negative impact on the immune system so that vaccinated animals become less resistant to other infections, such as malaria, E.coli or pneumococcal disease, than unvaccinated animals.'

Marie paused for breath.

'Sixty thousand children in Guinea-Bissau are given the DTP vaccine every year. Now, let's pretend for a moment that we can draw an exact parallel between the rat experiment and the effect on humans, and let's assume that the child mortality rate after the DTP vaccine is between eight and ten per cent. This means that the DTP vaccine is responsible for at least a couple of thousand extra deaths a year and please remember we're talking only about Guinea-Bissau.'

Marie tried to gauge Storm's reaction, but his facial expression had not changed since she had started her presentation.

'In developing countries,' Marie continued, 'every year more than one hundred million children are vaccinated with DTP on the recommendation of the WHO. If we are right, it means that the WHO's vaccination recommendation kills hundreds of thousands of children annually.'

Marie fell silent and Storm put his hands on the desk in front of him. They were different from her father's, she noticed. They were not soft, but were worn only by paper. Then he got up and walked down to the lectern where Marie was standing. He put his arms around her. He smelt of pipe tobacco, cardigan and board games, and Marie stood very still because she had never imagined he would smell like this. Then Storm held her at arms' length. 'Marie,' he said, much moved. 'You really *are* a scientist.'

Marie defended her master's on 24 September 2009 and got top marks for her dissertation. That evening she and Jesper celebrated her new accolade with an expensive dinner at his favourite restaurant in Frederiksberg, but the mood was strained and Marie had no appetite. Besides, she was due at the Department of Immunology at nine o'clock the following morning, so when Jesper made to pour more wine, she put her hand across her glass.

'I thought we'd finished with you being so busy. That you could start taking some time off. You promised.'

'I'll take next week off,' Marie assured him. 'Definitely. I'm incredibly tired, but Storm is going to Guinea-Bissau on Monday and he'll be away for months. We need to finalise my PhD application before he leaves.'

Jesper summoned the waiter irritably and asked for the bill.

When Marie entered Storm's office the next morning, he leaped up from his chair. 'At last, there you are!' he exclaimed. 'I have great news, Miss MSc. Terrence Wilson, editor-in-chief of *Science*, has emailed me. He's seen your lab results and he's seriously impressed. If I finish compiling my data, he promises to print my article!'

Storm's databank now consisted of two years' monitoring of 190,000 people in total. More than enough to draw conclusions, except that the Dulombi-Boe area was still giving them trouble. Since Silas's death, Storm and his team had surveyed the area twice, but this did not improve their figures one jot. On the contrary. At their last survey the child mortality rate had plummeted even further and was now at 0.15 per cent, which made the impassable and impoverished region between the two national parks in Guinea-Bissau one of the places in the world with the lowest child mortality rate. Something had to have gone wrong and it damaged the credibility of the article, especially now when Marie's impressive lab figures had proved irrefutably that the DTP vaccine was suspect.

'But,' Storm said happily, 'nothing can stop us now.'

Marie smiled feebly. 'Are you sure surveying that huge area again won't be too much for you?' she asked. Storm was sixty-five years old and she did not like the thought of him sleeping in the back of the car for several months, without telephone and Internet access.

'Pah, I'll be all right,' Storm said. 'And once I've got the new medical records, I won't let them out of my sight, even if it means I have to sleep with them under my pillow. And you,' Storm added sternly, 'make sure you rest. The whole of October, nothing less. In November, you can start systemising our data, research all existing material pertaining to critical vaccine research and ideally brainstorm everything you read. Have everything ready for when I, hopefully, come back with the icing on the cake.'

'When do you think that will be?'

'After New Year at the earliest. I'll have to wait and see how it goes. I'll arrive at Bissau towards the end of the rainy season and, to begin with, I'll want to spend some weeks sorting out

Belem with Tim Salomon. We need to install a new pump at the station and we have also been allocated two rooms at a nearby health clinic where we're going to set up an office, plus I need to settle in two new Guinean PhD students, now that Tim has almost completed his doctorate. So I reckon it'll be . . . Actually, I don't really know. But I promise to send you as many status reports as possible. And you'll let me know the moment you hear back from the PhD committee, won't you?'

'Deal,' Marie said.

When Storm had gone abroad and Marie had submitted her PhD proposal, she fell into a post-master's slump. She crashed on her sofa with no energy for anything.

Jesper grew more distant and irritable.

For more than eight years they had had regular sex and, right from the start, Jesper had made it clear to Marie that he would never be able to go without. A man had needs. 'Of course,' Marie had said. She liked sex but, truth be told, she liked the ten minutes afterwards better, when Jesper would draw on her back with his fingers. The drawing depicted a futuristic car, which had won him first prize in an art competition when he was ten years old and it was incredibly detailed. Several months had gone by since Jesper had drawn a car.

A week after her master's exam Marie was enjoying a kip on the sofa when she was suddenly woken up by Julie.

'Marie, you need to pull yourself together, for Jesper's sake. I hear you've been lying on that sofa all week. And what with Jesper being a doctor and all his responsibilities, he has to know he can count on you. Now that you've finished your master's, I don't think you have an excuse to just lie here the whole time. Have you even had a shower?'

Marie sat up. She felt dazed. 'Did Jesper tell you to say that to me?' she asked, still half asleep.

'No, of course not,' Julie said. 'But I've got eyes. You used to be the happiest couple in the world. Since you started your . . . Since you have . . . And Jesper says you go on about that professor of yours all the time. As if he were some kind of god. It's too much.'

'So Jesper *has* been talking to you?'

'No, he hasn't. I just want the two of you to be OK. For everything to be normal. But of course we talk. We talk every time he helps me with Mum's medication. Now, why don't you jump in the shower? I'll take Anton home with me tonight for a sleepover so Jesper and you can have some couple time, yes?'

When Julie had left with Anton, Marie dutifully put a bottle of wine in the fridge and took a shower.

At seven o'clock Jesper came home with sushi. Afterwards they had sex, but for once Marie could not ignore the way he kept flicking her left nipple as he lay on top of her. It didn't feel nice.

'Turn over and I'll draw the car,' Jesper said, when he had come, but instead of turning over, Marie went out into the bathroom. She splashed cold water on her face and watched her own reflection in the mirror.

The happiest couple in the world?

It was touching that Julie wanted Marie and Jesper to be happy.

But what if they weren't?

The next day they were invited to a birthday dinner at Sner-levej. Joan was turning fifty-seven, and when Marie and Anton arrived, Lea was in the kitchen, busy assembling a layer cake. A surprised Marie hugged her younger sister. She could not remember the last time Lea had turned up for a family get-together. Lea told her she had got a job as a nail technician in the spa in Magasin department store.

'How about you, sis?'

'I've just got my master's in biology,' Marie said.

'Cool,' Lea said. 'You always were the Einstein of the family.'

When Lea had set the cake aside to chill and disappeared into the living room, Marie stayed in the kitchen, saddened at the distance between them. As children they had stuck together like glue; Marie still loved her sister very much and secretly admired her for her wild nature, the way she constantly rained on Frank's parade, the long fringe that flopped over her eyes, even her tattoos, which Jesper found tasteless.

The mood during dinner was downbeat. It did not seem that Joan wanted to be celebrated, but even so Frank kept toasting her and wishing her a happy birthday, as if this was the best birthday party ever, and Julie loyally raised her glass to keep him company. Jesper turned up after a long shift at the hospital, but his kiss on Marie's cheek felt like rubber. Marie wanted to ask him what had happened to his affection for her, where was that place inside him where cautious, ambitious, diligent and now, unfortunately, exhausted Marie lived. 'Nowhere, Marie,' he would probably say and look at her. 'There's no place for you until you wash my socks.'

Julie's elder daughter, Camilla, knocked over her glass and

promptly burst into tears, but Julie said it was nothing to cry about. Michael was busy saving the world, especially his own little corner of it. 'You should help by teaching them Danish self-sufficiency, not give the Pakis everything on a plate,' he said, but Jesper replied that he couldn't be bothered to discuss politics at that level.

'The Danes,' Frank slurred, 'think they're too good to work in an abattoir or a building site or clean hospitals. They think they're too good for honest work while the immigrants put their backs into it.' Michael would have no truck with that because immigrants were the biggest expenditure in Danish history, with their insistence on prayer rooms, halal food, interpreters and demand for female doctors when their women needed their working parts checked out. So, bloody right they should take the shitty jobs.

Suddenly Marie noticed that Joan was crying. For once Lea had not argued back during dinner and Marie saw that she was holding their mother's hand. Julie asked if anyone fancied dessert and Frank knocked over his chair as he tried to get up.

In the car on their way home, Marie asked Jesper what they had just witnessed, but he looked at her with blank incomprehension. He thought things were not much different from what they usually were.

'But Dad was pissed out of his mind,' Marie insisted.

Jesper replied, 'Marie, your dad has been pissed out of his mind for every family dinner I've been to since we met eight years ago.'

'Mum was crying,' Marie persisted.

'You forgot to sign Anton up for swimming,' Jesper said, as

he indicated to turn into Ingeborgvej. 'The form has been on the fridge door for a month.'

'Mum was in tears,' Marie repeated.

'Right. Then again, turning fifty-seven is a big deal. You're not young any more and you have to come to terms with how you've lived your life,' Jesper said, and parked outside their house. 'But do think you could sign him up, Marie? Now that you're not doing anything anyway.'

Anton had fallen asleep in the back and Jesper carried him inside. Marie stayed in the car.

She had seen her family under a sharp white light.

And her breast was still sore where Jesper had pinched it.

On Tuesday, 8 October, Marie went to see her doctor. When her name was called out in the waiting room, her heart sank. What could she say? *I'm so tired I can't even tie my own shoelaces. The truth is my husband and I aren't happy. I'm more ambitious than our marriage can bear. I haven't heard from Storm since he left. Something is wrong with my family, but I can't work out what it is. I've changed.*

The doctor looked kindly at Marie.

'I think I've got something here,' Marie said, pointing to her heart.

The doctor asked her to take off her top and bra and spent a long time examining her left breast. At length he said, 'Yes, I can feel something. We need to get it checked out. It's probably nothing, but I'll refer you to the breast clinic at Rigshospitalet.'

For a moment Marie was confused. Could he really feel the discord?

On 19 October Marie had a mastectomy; the whole of her left breast was removed. The lump was three centimetres, but the cancer had not spread to the lymph nodes in her armpit. The consultant, Mr Guldborg, was a friend of Jesper's father and he made sure that she was seen immediately. Marie emailed Storm and seeing her news in writing felt simply insane.

Dear Storm,

On 16 October I received a letter from the PhD committee informing me that my PhD funding has been approved. Sadly I have also been operated on for breast cancer.

Love, Marie

He replied five weeks later. He had just returned to Bissau for a brief stay after several weeks in a rural area with no Internet coverage. He was halfway through the survey, he wrote, and so far it had gone really well. He also wrote that Marie's email was the worst he had ever received. Marie wrote back that she intended to start her research as early as possible in the New Year. She had had her first session of chemo and the only side effect so far had been the loss of her hair. Storm replied that that was good news and he was looking forward to making plans for her future when he came back to Denmark the following spring. Count me in, Marie replied. Of course, Storm wrote back.

But after her third chemo session, the side effects hit her really hard. Two hours after Marie had had the injection at the hospital, she began vomiting. 'I'm afraid it's very common for side effects to appear later,' Mr Guldborg said, when Jesper called Rigshospitalet. 'She'll just have to put up with it.'

Marie was as bald as an egg and weighed about as much as a roebuck. When she developed anaemia, she was hospitalised and given blood. During her stay she had the most vivid dreams and two dreams in particular kept repeating in a confusing loop. In the first she was about to meet with the doctors at the Oncology Unit, while Storm waited impatiently for her outside. His hair stuck out and Marie had the strangest feeling that she could reach out and touch him.

'Are you properly prepared?' Storm asked.

'Not really,' Marie replied.

'Take notes,' Storm said. 'I'll wait for you here. And when you're done, we'll go through your notes together. And, Marie?'

'Yes?'

'Stop being so bloody patient or you'll die. Be a scientist. Question everything. Ask the questions they least expect you to ask. We have the tools to interpret their answers. I'll help you.'

In her dream Marie kept records as if her life literally depended on it. She made columns so she could compare the doctors' predictions and prognoses and she put a big red tick next to any obvious discrepancies. If the doctors stated something or drew a conclusion and she noticed that they had failed to back it up with evidence, she put an exclamation mark in the margin. Her notes looked indecipherable, but Storm would help her to understand them. He had promised.

However, when Marie returned to the bench where Storm had been sitting, her arms filled with densely written notes, he had gone. She called out to him, she pleaded, she dropped her notes, but he did not come. When she gathered up her papers, she felt a shiver down her spine. Her notes consisted of only one sentence repeated over and over: *You are alone.*

The other dream was about her twin brother, Mads, who had died when they were three and a half years old. He called out to her and she called out to him, as if they were pulling at opposite ends of a sound. Mads was the stronger and Marie started stumbling towards him. At this point she always woke up, bathed in sweat. One night she found a nurse bent over her. 'You cried out for someone called Mads. Do you need anything?' Dazed, Marie explained that she had been dreaming, and the nurse turned over her duvet and dressed her in a clean hospital gown. When she had left, Marie was unable to go back to sleep.

She would have to pull harder than Mads had or she would die.

Storm was still in Guinea-Bissau and she rarely heard from him.

Several doctors came to see her every day. Consultants, senior house officers, junior doctors and medical students.

She lay in her bed, like a mouth organ in a moulded box.

'When can I go home?' she asked.

'We just need to get your blood-cell count up a bit, Marie,' one of them said. 'Then you can go home. Possibly this Friday.'

'Am I going to die?' she asked, when Mr Guldborg came by on his rounds.

'I don't indulge in that kind of speculation,' he replied.

'But am I?'

'We're doing everything we can to help you,' he replied.

'What does that mean?' Marie asked Jesper, when he visited her. '*We're doing everything we can to help you.* It means I'm going to die, doesn't it? Have they said anything to you?' The tears rolled down her cheeks. Jesper shook his head and massaged Marie's hands, which were swollen and disgusting.

'Anton has made a friend. Her name is Ida,' he told her. 'She lives at number three. He didn't want to come here today,' he added apologetically.

The last time Anton had visited, Marie had patted her sheet and said, 'Climb up here, darling,' but Anton had stayed where he was and wet himself.

'I miss him so much,' she whispered.

She started feeling better towards the middle of February. Her blood-cell count had been stabilised and her chemo was adjusted so it no longer made her quite so ill. Lea had visited her in hospital and presented her with a bright yellow scarf, which Marie tied around her head, surprised by how well the colour suited her. She took a taxi home to Hellerup and knew perfectly well what the driver must be thinking. When he pulled up outside the house and Anton came to greet her, Marie followed the driver's gaze, which rested on Jesper, behind Anton in the open front door. Poor guy, his expression said. He looks so worried. Let's hope for his sake, yes, also for the sake of the little one, that it'll be quick. Marie didn't tip him.

As promised, Storm called her as soon as he was back in Denmark. He had lots of news for her, he said eagerly, but wanted to start with the most important. Marie was certain that he meant her health, but Storm's mind was still in Africa.

'I'm ninety-nine per cent sure that somebody fiddled our figures, Marie. That's the reason the Dulombi-Boe area looked so good,' he said. 'In our records, sixty-five children were listed as living, even though they had been dead for years.'

'How is that possible?' Marie said in disbelief.

'The penny dropped in a tiny village west of Xitole. I visited to survey a five-year-old child, Marylyn, who had been included in the study back in 2004. When I finally found the hut where her parents lived, they were most unhappy to see me. Their child had died, you see. Now, of course it's not unusual for a child to die between visits, so I asked gently about the state of the child's health up until her death so that I could finish her medical record. Whereupon the mother started screaming and shouting that she had already explained everything to him, the other *branco*. To Silas. People came running from the other huts and I was practically lynched. Even the village elder turned up to scold me, and it wasn't until I had managed to talk him down that I realised what had happened. Marylyn was already dead when Silas visited the year before to check the figures and he had upset her parents by asking about her. "But how long has she been dead?" I asked. Four years. Four years! So can you explain to me, Marie Skov, just how the same child has been registered as living in our study all this time? Once I had spotted the first error, they all stared back at me. I went through every single medical record with a fine-tooth comb and discovered that seventy of them looked as if they had been tampered with. The paper was slightly fuzzy as if someone had rubbed it with an eraser. Of the seventy suspicious-looking medical records, only five belonged to children who were still alive. The rest had died long ago. That was the reason Silas tried calling me that Christmas. That was the urgent matter he wanted to discuss with me. He, too, had spotted it. No wonder those figures looked too good to be true.'

'But who could have done it?' Marie asked.

'Someone who doesn't want the harmful side effects of the DTP vaccine to see the light of day. There can't be any other explanation. The question is just who and why. The World Health Organization? I refuse to believe that. They are ultra-conservative and cautious, scared to lose authority, far too chicken to admit that they base their practice on inaccurate data, et cetera, et cetera. But they're definitely not saboteurs. So who is it? Someone utterly callous, it has to be. Someone who makes so much money by interfering with our research that they don't care how many people they end up killing. But who? As I'm sure you can imagine, I've thought of little else in the last few weeks. It's a fact that the sabotage must have happened somewhere between Xitole and Bissau. On *both* occasions. The first time, after the original survey, the medical records arrived at Bissau in four different cars with eight different drivers, of whom four no longer work for us and two are dead. Besides, they were nine days late arriving because of a monsoon and the car got stuck. This is Africa we're talking about. In 2007 Silas sent the data he had managed to collect before Christmas to Bissau with Tim. I've checked with Tim, of course. He says that he put the box with the medical records in the back of the car, as he always did. And I would have done the same. Nobody expects sabotage. But I knew something was up! In fact, I'm almost in a good mood because of it! This time I kept the medical records with me at all times, even when I went to the loo. No one has tampered with them, I'm absolutely sure of it. I still need to run statistics on the new figures, but I'll eat my old waders if that result doesn't turn out to be significant. It's nothing short of perfection that you have been awarded your PhD grant, my girl,' he interjected. 'Nothing short of perfection. Oh, I've completely forgotten to congratulate you on that. Congratulations! Do excuse me, I'm just rabbiting. Are you ready, do you think? When do you think you can start? How are you, anyway? How is your recovery going?'

'I'll need a little longer,' Marie whispered. 'A few months possibly. I haven't been feeling too good. I mean, it's a bit better now that the doctors have adjusted my chemo after I really hit rock bottom. But it'll still be a couple of weeks before I even finish my treatment, so . . .'

There was silence at the other end. Marie sat with her eyes closed and the phone pressed to her cheek.

'Oh,' Storm said. 'I'm really sorry to hear that.'

A tear trickled down Marie's cheek and, for a moment, she was incapable of speech.

'What was the other news you wanted me to know about?' she then said.

'Are you crying?' Storm asked her gently.

'No,' Marie said stubbornly.

'It would be all right if you were,' Storm said.

'I know,' Marie said.

Storm cleared his throat. 'The other thing I wanted to tell you is that your master's dissertation has been referred to the DCSD, the Danish Committees on Scientific Dishonesty. Or, more accurately, *I*'ve been reported to the DCSD for scientific dishonesty because I supervised and approved your dissertation and am thus partly responsible for you getting your MSc.'

'Oh, no.' Marie was horrified. 'What does that mean?'

'Sweet FA,' Storm said harshly. 'Because we won't let it. We know that we didn't cheat. Let's look on the bright side: it means another four people will read your dissertation.' Storm laughed. 'The only irritating thing is it can take up to six months before the DCSD clear us and in the meantime we'll have to live with the suspicion. When I lost my father, I made a decision, Marie. When you know your conscience is clear, you just have to let idiotic accusations bounce off you. What matters is being able to look at yourself in the mirror every morning. Keeping your side of the street clean.'

'But who is accusing us?' Marie said feebly.

'The accusation has been made anonymously,' Storm said. 'But it wouldn't surprise me if it turns out to be Stig Heller. Years ago we were as thick as thieves. Do you remember me telling you that he went berserk over my little article on Uni-Net? Heller is tragically conservative, even though he's only in his early forties. Incidentally, it's just been announced that he's joined the Nobel Committee. Fancy that. Do you know something? I think I'll give him a call and ask if he was the one who reported us. Hah, he'd like that, the sourpuss!'

'But what can we do?' Marie said miserably.

'Keep your head cool and your gunpowder dry. I'll send you some reading material in the next few days so you can get yourself fighting fit.'

Marie found it really rather difficult to share Storm's enthusiasm. Scientific dishonesty. It sounded sloppy and she did not like it one bit.

'By the way, do you want me to ask the PhD committee to hold off paying your grant?' Storm asked cautiously. 'You might need some extra time at the other end.'

Marie agreed.

'A month or something? How long do you plan on being ill?'

Now Marie couldn't help laughing. 'Well, you see, I don't have much experience with cancer . . .' she said ironically.

'In that case, we'll make it six weeks,' Storm said unperturbed. 'But not a minute more. I need you.'

When Storm had hung up, Marie sat looking out at the garden for a long time.

She admired Storm for wanting to save every child on the planet, but right now she just wanted to concentrate on her own survival.

Just two days later a parcel arrived from Storm, stuffed full of journals, copies of various articles, a big feature on Storm from *Weekendavisen* with the headline 'The stubborn man'. He had also sent her general information about the Danish Committees on Scientific Dishonesty and an article on the DCSD's most sensational case so far: the scientific dishonesty accusation against Bjørn Lomborg. *Read it, more to follow*, Storm had scribbled.

Marie started by skimming the article, which was critical of Lomborg. In 2002 he had been appointed director of the Environmental Assessment Institute and was reported to the DCSD the same year. In 2003 the accusations against him were upheld, but Lomborg was never penalised. The DCSD found that although he was guilty of dishonest research he had not intended to be dishonest, and as intentional dishonesty had to be proved beyond reasonable doubt, Lomborg could not be punished. On the other hand, neither was he ever acquitted or cleared.

Interesting, isn't it? Storm had noted in the margin in red pen. *If you do something without intending to, they can't punish you!*

A week later another parcel arrived from Storm. Three articles from American and German periodicals and the most recent issue of the *Journal of Epidemiology*, which even Storm had yet to read. The following week more magazines arrived, all with Post-it notes stuck in places where Storm had come across something interesting. Marie's heart sank as she flicked through the magazines, wondering how she would ever manage to read them all, when a bag of sugared almonds suddenly dropped into her lap. *Here's hoping they'll help the reading material go down more easily,* Storm had written. Four days later another bundle of articles arrived and two days after that yet another. This time Marie just ate the sugared almonds.

Being the perfect big sister that she was, Julie helped care for Marie after her chemo sessions. Thankfully, Marie had stopped vomiting, but she still felt wiped out. From the sofa she would watch Anton and Julie do jigsaw puzzles and bake muffins, and when Anton wanted to watch a movie, Julie would softly close the door to the TV room, then perch on the edge of the sofa like Marie's confidante. They spoke about Anton starting school after the summer holidays and about Marie and Jesper's garden, which would probably be left to grow wild this year, but so what? It was during a moment of such intimacy that Marie told Julie she suspected Jesper had met someone.

'Of course he hasn't!' Julie sounded outraged. 'He would never dream of doing that to you.' She got up and put on the kettle to make more tea.

'But he has stopped punishing me,' Marie said. 'He's kind.'

'How can you say a thing like that?' Julie was angry.

'He couldn't care less that we no longer have sex, Julie. I don't mind that very much because I can't say I feel terribly attractive, bald as I am and all dried up inside. But I wonder how Jesper manages. We no longer sleep in the same bed. I've been in the guest bedroom ever since my operation because I lie awake half the night and that disturbs Jesper. We've never had any intimacy other than sex, Julie. Now we have ... nothing.'

'But it would be madness to expect sex from your wife when she's as ill as you are,' Julie said indignantly.

'Has Michael ever been unfaithful to you?' Marie asked spontaneously.

'No, of course not!' Julie got red spots on her cheeks.

'How do you know? Have you ever asked him?'

'I know that he hasn't, Marie.'

'Do you think Dad has ever been unfaithful to Mum?'

'Marie! What's wrong with you?'

'My thoughts won't stop churning. I've nothing better to do,' Marie said.

'Then stop it right now,' Julie said, stroking Marie's cheek. 'Nothing good ever comes from worrying.'

Anton came in from the TV room and said he was thirsty. Marie watched while Julie poured water into a glass and buttered him a bread roll. She imagined that it was now Julie's head that was whirling. She felt hot so she took off her yellow headscarf and put it on the dining table, and when Anton had finished his bread roll, he rushed over, wanting to examine Marie's bald head.

'Do you think it's a good idea for him to see you bald?' Julie whispered, when Anton had gone back to watch the rest of the film.

'But bald is what I am,' Marie stated.

A few days later, Frank made an unannounced visit. He brought her a bunch of flowers and said that Joan sent her love. Marie hugged him, and before she could stop herself, she blurted out, 'Tell me, have you been drinking?'

'What the hell are you saying?' Frank said. 'It's two o'clock in the afternoon.'

'Oh, OK,' Marie quickly back-pedalled. 'I didn't mean it like that. I just thought . . .'

Frank lost his rag. 'You have some nerve accusing us of all sorts of things we haven't done. One moment you're saying Jesper's having an affair, the next it's Michael. I hear you've even insinuated that I cheated on your mother. And now I'm a drunk, is that it? You're seriously ill, Marie, but you need to . . . think about Anton. It's bad enough if that boy is going to lose his mother, but if he has to live in a house full of mad accusations, no wonder he wets himself. And put your scarf on,' he said irritably.

Dumbstruck, Marie poured boiling water into the cafetière and went upstairs to fetch her headscarf from the bathroom. No one in the family liked the sight of Marie's naked scalp, except Anton, who thought it was softer than a horse's muzzle. Marie gasped for air and could not decide whether it was the stairs or the unfairness that had knocked the wind out of her. Anton had only wet himself that one time at the hospital and Marie had not told anyone. That could mean only one thing. Jesper had told tales. *Again.*

When Marie came downstairs, Frank had already pushed down the plunger and poured himself a cup of weak coffee. When he had drunk half of it, he said, 'Anyway, I'd better be going.'

'But I'll see you on Sunday, won't I?' Marie said.

'Listen, sweetheart. Your mum and I have talked about it, and we're going to put our Sunday lunches on hold. Is that all right? Only until you're feeling a bit better.' Frank gave Marie a quick peck on the cheek and again she caught a whiff of the simultaneously sharp and fermented smell that lingered on his skin.

'Sure, but I'm actually doing quite well. In fact, I'd like to get out a bit . . .' Marie objected.

'Your mum has also been a bit under the weather . . .'

'If you say so,' Marie acquiesced. 'But would it be all right for me and Anton to visit one afternoon?'

'You're always welcome,' Frank said, with such emphasis that Marie knew he was lying. 'Anyway, I'd best be off.'

The next time Julie visited, Marie asked her what was going on.

'Marie, you really are hopeless,' Julie said. 'Why can't you just concentrate on getting better for the cutest boy in the world and the most wonderful husband and father on the planet? Mum isn't doing too well at the moment, but she'll be all right. Your illness has opened old wounds ... She's thinking a lot about Mads, these days, and you know what she's like when—'

'No,' Marie said, 'I don't know what she's like.'

'I don't want you to worry about Mum, promise me? It's scientifically proven that cancer patients who worry about all sorts of things don't recover as quickly as cancer patients who "only" have their cancer to worry about. There's no point in making things worse. I'm sure everything will be better in a couple of weeks, and then we can get together. Until then, all you have to do is rest – and, besides, Jesper's helping me, so you don't have to worry.'

'What does Jesper help you with?' Marie looked at her sister in surprise.

'He renewed Mum's prescriptions. He's done it before, but always argued that she really ought to see her own doctor for a check-up, but last week he could see how poorly Mum was. I don't know how I would have got her out of the house and taken her to the doctor's, but fortunately Jesper understood. And, anyway, she's been taking those pills for years so, frankly, I can't see—'

'When did Dad become a heavy drinker, Julie?' Marie interrupted her. 'He came round the other day and he stank like a brewery.'

'Marie, sometimes I find it hard to believe that you have benefited from higher education. Mum isn't the only one who finds it hard to cope with your illness. It's no picnic for Dad, either. You know perfectly well you were always his favourite.' Julie held up a hand when Marie was about to object. 'No, it's all right. It is what it is. I don't blame him. I happen to be closer to Emma than Camilla because Emma and I are so alike. It happens in families. And Dad is really worried about you, so, yes, perhaps he drinks a bit more than he normally would, but he's entitled to. Don't you worry about it now. You just concentrate on getting better, all right? Stop fretting.'

That evening Marie could no longer control herself and asked Jesper outright if he was having an affair. He went as white as a sheet and wanted to know how she could think something like that of him. Marie apologised, but it did not seem to appease him. He just spun around furiously and stared out of the window at the twilit garden.

Eventually Marie went to bed. Having left the door to the guest bedroom ajar, she read for a long time in the hope that Jesper had stopped being annoyed and would come in to talk to her. Around ten o'clock she finally heard his footsteps on the stairs, the door to the study open, then typing on the keyboard for a long time. Eventually the tap was turned on in the bathroom and finally she heard the door to the master bedroom close.

Most evenings Anton would tiptoe to Marie's room. Jesper had always been against children in adult beds and Marie had made a point of walking Anton back to his own bed until she became ill. These days she let him slip under her duvet. If the end was near, if Marie was dying, she wanted to have as much time with her son as possible.

That night Anton didn't come and Marie couldn't sleep. She opened her laptop and started composing a letter to Anton. She managed to write four sentences, but when she was about to save it, the tears started rolling down her cheeks. *To Antonsen from Mum.* It sounded so innocent, but the truth was, it was the saddest document in the world.

Little Anton, he would see on the screen. *When you read this, I will have been dead for far too many years. I wonder if you can remember me.*

Marie slammed the laptop shut.

When she finally fell asleep, she dreamed a new and disturbing dream about Storm. He was standing in Lecture Hall A at the Department of Immunology, banging his pointer against the board to emphasise the words he had written on it. He was angry that his audience did not understand what he meant and whacked the board harder and harder. Marie could not see what it said on the board either, until large flakes of slate started loosening under Storm's blows and fell to the floor. Then, suddenly, she saw it. It said, *Look under every stone.*

'You're slacking, all of you,' Storm thundered, looking straight at Marie. 'Especially you, Marie. You're asking the wrong questions, and you accept far too many easy answers.'

'I have more important things to think about,' Marie protested.

'More important than my research? I don't think so,' Storm said, and turned his back on her. At this point Marie was woken up by Anton, who had decided he did want to sleep under Marie's duvet after all. He fell asleep immediately and Marie snuggled up to him.

The dream echoed in Marie's head in the days that followed and she glanced furtively at Storm's parcels of reading material of which the last three remained unopened. Storm's research *was* important and she wished she wasn't suffering from such a lack of interest. Jesper was away on a course on South Sjælland and Julie called five times to ask if she was all right. Marie assured her that she was looking forward to a weekend alone with Anton and would manage fine on her own. Even so, Julie turned up with a casserole on Friday afternoon. She put the pot in the fridge and left some bread in the bread bin. 'And there's no need for you to wash the pot. I can do that.'

'Julie, I'm capable of washing up.'

'Do you and Anton have any plans?' Julie wanted to know. 'You really ought to get a second car. How are you going to get around now that Jesper has the car?'

'Julie, relax,' Marie said. 'We're not going anywhere, and if we decide to do something, we'll take the bus. Or we'll cycle.'

Julie looked horrified. 'Cycle? You can't be serious! You've just finished chemo. You can't go cycling around. It's far too cold.'

'It was a joke, Julie,' Marie said, and put her arms around her sister. 'Thank you for all your help. We might go and see Mum and Dad,' she added. 'I haven't seen them for weeks.'

'That's not a good idea,' Julie said firmly. 'Mum is in bed with the flu and your immune system is compromised. I don't want you to catch it. Promise you'll stay at home. I've put a lot of ginger in the casserole to make you feel better. I hope it's not too hot for Anton.'

'Julie, you fuss like a mother hen,' Marie said.

'That's what being a big sister is all about,' Julie said lightly.

On Sunday, 21 February, Marie almost felt well. She and Anton had pottered about all weekend, slept in, drawn mandalas, played Monopoly and made eight different smoothies to find out which tasted the best. It turned out to be blueberry and honey. The weather was cool but bright and clear, and Anton jumped for joy when Marie asked if he fancied making a surprise visit to Granny and Grandad's. If Joan was still poorly, Marie thought, she would keep her distance. It would be fine.

Frank looked surprised when Marie and Anton rang the doorbell. The day was starting to darken and he squinted as if he had trouble seeing them. He looked very tired and again Marie detected a smell about him: this time it was something fermented mixed with the odour of something unwashed.

'Oh. It's you, is it?' He pulled away with a jolt before Marie had a chance to hug him.

'Yes, we wanted to surprise you,' Marie said.

'Oh,' Frank said, but continued to block the doorway.

'Are you going to let us in?'

'Of course,' he said apologetically, and stepped aside. 'Are you hungry? I think we've got something in the freezer.'

Anton ran ahead into the living room and Marie heard Joan exclaim with delight: 'Well, hello, little one.'

'How are you, Mum?' Marie asked, when she joined them. Joan sat in her armchair with a rug over her legs. The living room was stuffy and dark, and Marie could hear the ticking of the grandfather clock. 'Were you asleep?'

'I must have dozed off,' Joan replied.

'How is the flu?'

Joan blinked. 'The flu?'

'Julie said you had the flu.'

'Oh . . .' Joan shifted slightly and a pill organiser, which had been hidden in the folds of the rug, slid onto the floor.

Marie picked it up. 'So it's safe for me to give you a kiss, then,' she said, and kissed her mother's cheek.

'But how are you, my love?' Joan asked, and her chin quivered. 'Any . . . news?'

Marie shook her head. 'I've had my last chemo and I'll start my post-chemo treatment soon. I'm tired, but I'm fine.'

The tears started rolling down Joan's cheeks and she squeezed Marie's hand hard and drew it up to her face. 'It's hard for me,' she whispered. 'I don't know what to think. Julie says— Where are my pills?' Joan interrupted herself and looked about the rug.

Marie handed her the pill organiser. 'Here,' she said.

At that moment Anton slunk into the living room with a bowl of Twist chocolates. He looked guiltily at his mother. Marie stroked her mother's hair and told Anton he could have three chocolates before dinner.

'Oh, go on, let him,' Frank said from the doorway.

'Three chocolates,' Marie said, giving Anton a stern look. She went out into the kitchen to Frank, who had his head in the freezer.

'Dad, we can just ring for a pizza, can't we?'

'No, no, we'll find something.' Frank was standing a little too close to the freezer and Marie soon concluded that he was not entirely sober. 'What do we have here? . . . Curried meatballs . . . Goulash . . . Hearts in a cream sauce. Oh, there was no need for her to make that.'

Marie looked into the freezer over Frank's shoulder and recognised Julie's neat handwriting on the many freezer bags.

On the bottom shelf there were meat dishes and at the top there were bags of bread rolls and parboiled rice. 'Did Julie make all this?'

'Yes. At first it pissed me off. You know how I hate being beholden to anyone, least of all Michael. I know it's only a matter of time before he wants to borrow my Orvis fishing rod and he thinks he's got a right to it because Julie's cooked all this food. But now that your mum isn't feeling too good, it's quite handy that I can just grab something from the freezer. Julie even bought me a microwave oven. Though I did give her five hundred kroner for that. That's what they cost, isn't it?'

'Sounds about right.'

Frank had got hold of a bag with a casserole of some kind and fumbled with the knot for ages before he started looking for a pair of scissors with irritated movements. He found them under a pile of cutlery, but when he tried to cut the knot, he dropped the freezer bag and it skidded across the floor, like a curling stone. He swore. Marie watched him. All her life Frank had been hard and outspoken in his opinions, in his rhetoric, in his verdicts. For better or worse. Now he was old and confused. With considerable effort he managed to pick up the bag from the floor.

'Please would you set the table?' he asked Marie. 'I'm just going outside to lock the shed. The neighbours had a break-in and I don't want the lawnmower . . .' He flapped his hand as if to say it was too complicated to explain.

Marie saw him walk past the kitchen window and went into the dining room to set the table. On the TV in the living room Poul Reichhardt was crooning in a barn doorway. Joan was sound asleep and a trickle of saliva stretched towards her jumper.

'I'm just going upstairs, Anton,' Marie said. 'Grandad has gone outside to lock the shed, but he'll be back soon and then we'll eat.'

The first floor of the house had not been decorated for twenty years at least and was in dire need of a makeover. Julie's old room still had the same wallpaper, with the tiny floral pattern, and sloping windows whose varnished frames were brown. Joan's sewing machine was still there, but it was covered with dust. Marie had always admired Julie's room. She'd kept it immaculate – even the desk drawers were organised, erasers lined up, paperclips and drawing pins in their respective boxes.

Lea and Marie's old room was now Frank's home office. At first they had shared the room, but later Frank had put up a partition wall and Marie remembered her relief when Lea picked the side with the loft hatch. They had been told never to climb up into the loft and Marie had always been scared of the hatch. Lea didn't care. Even as a little girl she had had the ability to bounce back like a rubber ball and it took more than a dark loft to scare her. Now the partition wall had gone and Frank had created a makeshift office for himself with an untidy desk and two cheap metal bookcases so laden with ring binders, books and trays stacked high with papers that he had had to screw them to the wall to stop them falling over.

Where had all the mess come from? As far as Marie knew, Frank was still working as a handyman, but the state of his office did not suggest that business was booming.

At the back of the room, Marie spotted the loft ladder. She climbed it and opened the hatch. She had never been up in the loft before and she quickly turned on the light. The space was crammed with junk. Lamps, chairs, boxes and black bin liners stuffed with old clothes and duvets. Tools, horseshoes, a pot. She spotted the old camp bed, which the girls had taken turns to use and which had been crudely repaired with big stitches. Leaning against the wall were several framed photographs of men and women whom Marie did not recognise. They must be distant relatives. They had had an uncle, Joan's brother, whom Marie vaguely remembered, but otherwise they had never had much contact with Joan's or Frank's family. Their maternal grandparents had died even before Julie was born and had left the house on Snerlevej to Joan and Frank. Frank's parents had also passed away long ago and his two brothers, who lived in Jutland, 'aren't worth knowing', he had always said.

At the far end of the loft Marie found four large photographs mounted on cardboard. One of Julie, one of Lea and, how funny, two of me, Marie had time to think before she realised that one of the portraits was of her twin brother. She picked it up and studied it under the loft light. Marie and Mads had resembled each other like two drops of water, though Mads was slightly darker and looked like a boy. Suddenly Marie could see the close resemblance between Mads and Anton. She had always wondered why Anton was darker than Jesper and herself, but now she knew where it had come from. What a little sweetheart, Marie thought, and looked at Mads's happy, chubby cheeks.

Marie noticed yet another, a framed black-and-white

picture of a young Frank and a man whom Marie did not recognise. Marie and Mads were standing between them; they must have been a couple of years old then, dark-haired and grinning. In the background, Joan was wearing a patterned dress with a fabric tie and a large, full skirt. Marie barely recognised her mother: she looked so carefree. Going out of the picture were two teenage boys, one with a football under his arm. Frank was beaming, and he and the unknown man had their arms around each other's shoulders. As if Frank had had a good friend and had put his arm around him. As if it was summer, the steaks were sizzling and the corn on the cob crackling. As if they were planning on dancing the whole night through.

Julie had often told her how much Frank and Joan had loved parties back in the old days. Joan especially would dance until dawn with Frank or with some of the other men from their street when they held garden parties. Julie loved one story in particular and she had told it over and over. Joan had danced with a police officer, who also lived on Snerlevej, someone high up in the ranks, apparently, and he had been tripping the light fantastic with her when the police turned up to tell them to turn down the music. 'Sorry for interrupting your evening, boss,' the embarrassed officer had said, when he recognised his superior. Julie remembered it very clearly, she had told Marie, because she always slept in a tent in the garden when the adults had their parties. When the patrol car had driven off and the music had been turned down, the adults had at first looked guiltily at each other before breaking into howls of laughter.

Marie spotted a woven tapestry wall-hanging sticking out

of a large box and dragged the box over to the light where she managed with considerable effort to unroll it. It was very dusty and a spider darted to safety. The subject was dramatic. A severed woman's head with a crazy, suffering expression and snakes in her hair. Other than the rug Joan had made for Anton, Marie had never seen evidence of her mother's craftsmanship or at least not her major works, which Julie had told her about. The subject was frightening, but Marie was fascinated. This was art, not just needlework, and although it was sinister, it was a shame that it was kept in a box in the loft.

Marie hauled the box with the wall-hanging, the portrait of Mads and the picture of her festive parents to the hatch and managed to lower everything to the floor in Frank's study. She intended to ask Jesper if she could put up the wall-hanging. She wanted to show Anton the portrait of Mads and suddenly began to wonder if she had ever told her son about him. She hung up the photograph of Frank and Joan and their friends on a vacant nail above Frank's desk. She wanted Frank to see it. She wanted to say, 'Look, Dad, once you had a friend and life was good. Once you made Mum happy.'

Something made Marie jump. 'You startled me, sweetheart!'

Anton was standing in the shadows of the passage outside Frank's office, opposite the stairs. 'I've been calling you lots and lots,' he said, and started to cry. 'Why didn't you come?'

'But, sweetheart,' Marie hugged him, 'I was only in the loft. Why didn't you just call Grandad?'

'I did.' Anton sniffed. 'But he didn't come. And Granny's asleep and the movie has finished and I didn't know where you were.'

'Never mind,' Marie said, and decided to distract him with the portrait of Mads. 'Hey, Anton, guess who this is?'

Anton turned to the photograph. 'It's me,' he said, and sniffed again.

Marie smiled and told him it was not. It was his uncle Mads. Marie knelt down and told Anton about her twin brother, who got so ill when he was three years old that the doctors could not save him. Anton listened with rapt attention.

'Doesn't he look nice?' Marie asked, and Anton nodded. The portrait of Mads was so light that she decided to carry it home. She could take the wall-hanging the next time, when Jesper was with her and they had the car.

'Come on, let's go down and have some dinner,' Marie said, and went down the stairs with the photograph. When she was three steps down, she noticed that Anton had not moved.

'If Uncle Mads and I look so much like each other,' Anton said, gazing down at his mother, 'will I get ill and die too?'

Marie thought about it. 'You might get ill one day,' she said, 'not because you look like Uncle Mads but because people sometimes get ill for no particular reason. But because you also look like me, you have a very special ability to get well again, just like I will. And do you know something?' Anton shook his dark hair. 'Anyone who cheats death once will live to be a hundred.'

'Is that true?'

Marie nodded. 'A hundred and four, in fact. Come on, sweetheart, let's go downstairs. I bet you're starving.' Anton nodded and followed his mother.

Marie put the portrait of Mads on the chest of drawers in the hall so that they could take it with them when they left.

In the kitchen the casserole was still in the microwave. It had been defrosted, but it was merely tepid so Marie turned on the microwave again. 'Please would you put some of these beetroots into a bowl?' she asked Anton, and put them out with a bowl for him. Marie found some glasses and filled the water jug. Then she went into the living room. Anton scurried after her, insisting on holding her hand. Joan was fast asleep. Marie called out to her softly, but she did not react. Her pill organiser had got lost in the folds of her rug again so Marie picked it up and put it on the coffee table next to her mother. Then she covered her carefully with the rug.

'Hmm, I think Granny's very tired,' she said to Anton.

'Dad?' Marie called down the passage to her parents' bedroom. She wondered if he had gone to the loo or was getting changed. There was no reply. Then she noticed that the garden door was open. 'Please would you find the Tiddlywinks? Then we can have a game after dinner,' she said casually, but Anton said no and refused to let go of her hand. Together they went out into the garden.

'You could always have a go on the swing?' Marie suggested. Anton shook his head.

It was eerily silent and dark in the twilight, except the shed, from which a rectangle of light fell on the ground through the open door.

'Right, sweetheart, I want you to stay over there,' Marie said, pointing firmly to one of the garden chairs. Anton sat down reluctantly.

Marie walked towards the shed. Had Frank had a fall?

No, Frank hadn't had a fall.

But it was only a matter of time.

He was blind drunk. Half a dozen miniature bottles lay scattered across the floor inside the shed and he was in the process of knocking back yet another while he leaned heavily against the shelving unit, which was crammed perilously full of heavy tools and tins of paint.

'Hiiiii, Marizzen,' he slurred, when he noticed her. His eyes rolled. 'I'm . . . I'm just coming. Is it time for din-dins?'

'Have you drunk all of those?' Marie asked in disbelief. There was Jack Daniel's and several small bottles of schnapps.

'No, no.' Frank wobbled dangerously and Marie grabbed his arm, guided him out of the shed and supported him to the terrace where Anton was waiting.

'What's wrong with Grandad?' Anton said. He sounded scared.

'Nothing,' Frank assured him, as he slumped across the garden table. Marie had to let go so that she wasn't dragged down with him.

'Grandad has got drunk,' she said calmly. 'It's not dangerous, but it is very stupid.' She spoke the last word in a loud voice as she turned to Frank, who was trying in vain to get to his feet. Marie managed to steer him back inside the house with considerable effort.

'Anton,' Marie groaned, under the weight of her father, 'please would you wait in the living room while I put Grandad to bed?'

Anton started to cry. 'I don't want to sit with Granny,' he said. 'I don't like it when she sleeps in her chair like that.'

Marie thought about it. 'OK, then. I want you to walk ahead of me to Granny and Grandad's bedroom, and pull back the duvet on Grandad's side.' Anton raced down the passage.

'I can't lift you, Dad,' Marie said to Frank. 'I'm still weak and I'm worried about the scar from my surgery. You need to walk on your own or at least try to.'

Anton had already pulled back the duvet when Marie and Frank finally reached the bedroom, and Marie let her father collapse on the bed. She took off his shoes and rolled him onto his side as best as she could. Then she covered him with the duvet and fetched a bucket, which she put on the floor within his reach.

They returned to the living room. Joan was still fast asleep in her armchair, but had turned her head to the other side. For a moment Marie had no idea what to do.

'We'll buy something for dinner on our way home,' she said, switched off the television and tucked the rug around Joan again. They put on their coats, took the portrait of Mads and walked down the street. On the bus, Anton insisted on sitting on Marie's lap the whole way, and she let him, even though he was rather too heavy. She could have done without Anton seeing his grandparents in that state. Why hadn't Julie just told her the plain truth? That Frank and Joan were in crisis and that it was best for Anton not to visit for a while. Why had she lied that their mother had flu?

On 12 March, less than a fortnight after Marie's last chemo, she was asked to attend a meeting with Mr Guldborg to review her future treatment options. Guldborg spoke as rapidly as if he was packing inflight meals on a conveyor belt. He said

Marie should have her ovaries removed, which would bring on the menopause so she could be treated with Aromasin. Marie's cancer was oestrogen sensitive, Guldborg explained, and by removing her ovaries and thus stopping her oestrogen production, he could treat her with Aromasin, an oestrogen inhibitor, and her oestrogen level would then be so low that her cancer would have poor growth conditions. It sounded like the right thing to do.

'Speak to Jesper about it,' Guldborg added.

Why did I get cancer? Marie wanted to ask. Why do some people get cancer while others don't? Why?

When you died, she thought, you didn't just leave the room for a pee or go abroad on a sabbatical. When you died, you ceased to *exist*. She tasted the word. There in her lap lay her hand. Across the desk, Guldborg's fleshy lips opened and closed, like the stoma on a leaf. In a little while, in a matter of weeks or months or possibly not for as many years as she had promised Anton, she would be gone.

Marie did not manage to ask Guldborg any questions. When she left the hospital, she sat down on a bench. She caught herself looking for Storm and watched the swallows that had just returned from their winter quarters in Africa. They soared vertically into the sky, turned sharply and dived with such speed that their screams chased after them, like serpentines of delayed sound.

Anton liked asking her, 'If you were an animal, Mum, which one would you be?' before he quickly added, 'I want to be a dog,' so that Marie couldn't be a dog as well. Marie had never known which animal to pick. Sometimes she would say a rabbit, other times a seahorse. Anton's rules meant that she was allowed only one animal. At that moment, Marie knew that she would say a swallow the next time Anton asked her. Swallows could fly all the way to South Africa and back again. They were tough. If Marie were ever to have a tattoo, and that was a big if, it would be a swallow.

On Thursday morning, 18 March, Marie received two packages. One was from Storm. With a pang of conscience she added it, unopened, to the pile of other unopened parcels of magazines and sugared almonds, reminding herself she should have told him that, sadly, he should not expect to hear from her for a while.

The other item was an eye-wateringly expensive wig she had ordered from Sweden. When she opened the bag, she had to laugh. She had specified a shoulder length, nut-brown bob, but the supplier had made a mistake. The wig she had been sent was every man's textbook fantasy. Long blonde hooker hair. Marie put on the wig in front of a mirror and laughed even louder. Then she found an eyeliner pencil and made up her eyes. She could not remember the last time she had worn makeup. When she applied lipstick, she smeared it on purpose. Then she took off all her clothes and studied herself in the mirror. Christ, she was skinny now. She looked like a one-breasted heroin addict. While she ran herself a bath, she examined first her one firm breast, and then the thick, pink scar that looked like the closed eye of a newborn baby. Guldborg had said that he would put her forward for breast reconstruction as soon as her treatment had finished and her test results were clear. Marie was sure that Jesper would start to fancy her again once she was put right.

She took off the wig and let herself sink into the bath water. The telephone rang and she let it ring: the water was wonderful. She closed her eyes and amused herself by imagining what type of woman Jesper was attracted to. The emaciated-junkie look was definitely not to his taste. But when they had watched season one of *Mad Men*, Marie had noticed that he really liked the character Joan Holloway. She was submissive, had a brilliant mind and she was sensual, and although her curvaceous figure and Marie's boyish shape had absolutely nothing in common, Marie had not minded. In the distance the landline started ringing again.

At the ward where Jesper worked, the nurses were bound to fancy him, she thought, and felt a sudden tingling of unease. Was that why Jesper had lost interest in her? Because there was a woman at work, a younger, undamaged woman? She added more hot water to the bath and was about to scrub her face when she heard the front door open, then a set of keys land in the bowl on the side table in the hallway. Jesper was home.

'Marie,' he called. 'Hello? Where are you?' Marie nearly slipped as she stood up in the bath. She had not expected him back for another five hours and she was terrified that something had happened to Anton.

When Jesper entered the bathroom, a dripping wet Marie had one arm in her dressing gown and her face was smeared with makeup. He flung his arms around her.

'Marie,' he said, and his thick voice made Marie gasp for air. 'Something terrible has happened. Your mother is dead, Marie. Joan is dead.'

'No!' Marie started to cry. 'What happened?'

Jesper handed her a towel.

'Julie called me at work. She was beside herself and I could barely understand a word she said. She'd tried calling you as well. When will you learn to answer your mobile? Julie couldn't get hold of your mother this morning so at ten o'clock she went over there because she was worried.' Jesper glanced at his watch. 'She found Joan dead in her bed. Marie, I'm really sorry to have to tell you, but Julie says your mother took an overdose.'

'She committed suicide?'

'I don't know. The police won't say anything until your mother has been examined. They haven't found a note, which makes it hard to know whether she did it on purpose or whether she accidentally took more pills than her body could cope with. Julie is distraught because it appears she counts out your mother's pills every Monday, but this Monday she couldn't come over because Camilla was doing something at school. Julie found Joan's pill organiser and it was empty. There were also some half-empty jars of pills on the bedside table, but we don't know how many she took. We have to wait until the police have had her examined.'

'Where is Dad?' Marie asked, and could immediately tell from Jesper's expression that there was more bad news to come.

'We can't get hold of him. His mobile is switched off. Julie says that the police are very keen to talk to him. He wasn't at home when Julie came over. His van is gone and Julie discovered an almost empty bottle of whisky next to his armchair before she went to the bedroom and found Joan. She rang one one two. Then she tried calling Frank, then you and finally me, because neither of you was picking up.'

'Do you think that Dad had anything to do with—'

'No, of course not, but the police . . . They really do want to talk to him. I've tried ringing Frank several times in the last hour, but my calls go straight to voicemail. What is it about you and mobiles in your family?'

'We have to go to Snerlevej,' was all Marie said.

When Marie and Jesper arrived, a police car was still parked outside. They entered the house and found a deathly pale Julie sitting at the dining table with two police officers. When Julie spotted Marie, she leaped up and threw her arms around her.

'They've just taken Mum away,' Julie cried. 'Oh, I can't bear it.'

While the police talked to Jesper, Julie and Marie sat on the sofa in the living room and hugged each other.

'Suicide is the coward's way out,' Julie wept.

'But we don't know yet that she did commit suicide,' Marie pointed out.

'Oh, don't be so naïve, Marie!' Julie said. 'Nobody takes so many pills that it kills them unless that's what they want. What do we tell the children?' she added, horrified. 'Do you think we should just tell them she's died? They won't understand what suicide is!'

'We certainly shouldn't say anything to the children about it being suicide before we know whether it was or not,' Marie said. 'We have to wait until we know the facts. Did Mum take five pills too many and accidentally overload her system or did she deliberately take a hundred and twenty pills to end her life? Whichever it is, lying to the children is a bad idea.'

'But it's not lying,' Julie said, shocked. 'It's protecting them. They'll never be able to understand how Granny could be such a coward.' Julie blew her nose.

'Please can we ring your mother and ask her if she can pick up Anton?' Marie asked Jesper, when he entered the living room. 'And could Michael's mother pick up your girls, Julie? Perhaps it's better that somebody else looks after the children until we know more about what's happened.'

Julie and Jesper agreed.

'And how about Lea? Has anyone called Lea?'

'Michael went to see Lea,' Julie said.

Marie frowned. 'Are you sure that was a good idea?'

'What choice did I have?' Julie asked. 'He called earlier and . . .' Julie glanced furtively at the door to the dining room, which was ajar. Officers were still milling about in there and they could hear the crackle of a distant police radio. Julie leaned towards Marie.

'Dad's there,' she whispered.

'With Lea?'

'Sssh,' Julie said. 'He turned up late last night. He was drunk and passed out on her bed. Michael has told Lea about Mum, but they don't yet know if Dad knows anything . . . Perhaps he found her during the night and started drinking. But don't you think he would have called if he knew she was dead?' Her eyes widened. 'We won't know until he wakes up.'

'Are you whispering because you haven't told the police?' Marie could not believe her own ears.

'Marie, darling, please could we find out what's happened

before we say anything to them? Please?' Julie looked beseechingly at Marie.

'Christ, Julie.'

Marie looked to Jesper for support, but he simply shrugged his shoulders and said, 'If Julie prefers finding out what happened first, where's the harm in that? All we need is to have a word with Frank.'

At that moment Superintendent Henrik Tejsner came into the living room. 'We've just had a call from the traffic police. It looks like Frank Skov crashed his VW Transporter into a sign outside a corner shop on Vesterbro some time last night. He appears to have abandoned the van, which was towed away by Falck this morning.'

Tejsner looked briefly at Julie, then at Marie. 'The key was still in the ignition and I'm sorry to have to tell you that we found quite a lot of blood on the steering wheel. CCTV recordings from the shop suggest he was bleeding heavily from his nose. Now, it may not be serious, but we'll issue a description in case he's out there somewhere and needs medical attention. Like I said, we very much want to talk to him so we expect to hear from you as soon as he comes home or calls.'

Jesper and Julie nodded quickly.

'Otherwise that's it for today,' Tejsner continued. 'If you require trauma counselling, please contact your doctor. I'll be in touch again when your mother's body can be released for burial, but you should prepare yourselves that it might be at least a week. And here is my card. I work in the Violent Crimes Unit, but please believe me when I say that there is currently nothing suspicious about your mother's death. We just need to get a couple of tests back from the Institute of Forensic Medicine, then have a chat to your father. But that's standard procedure. I'm sorry for your loss.'

Shortly afterwards the front door closed behind him.

Marie, Jesper and Julie drove to Vesterbro in Julie's car. Julie sat in the passenger seat next to Jesper, who was driving, and cried all the way into the city. Marie sat in the back and stared emptily out of the window. She had a strange feeling that Joan was better now. Much better. Julie kept asking questions and Jesper did his best to answer them.

'Should I have locked away her pills? I counted them out every Monday for the whole week when I brought them their meals and it never even crossed my mind that . . .'

'Julie,' Jesper said firmly. 'You can't stop someone killing themselves, if that's what they want. Joan would have got hold of the pills some other way. You can't control everything.'

'Why was she taking so many in the first place?' Marie asked, but no one was listening to her.

'I just don't understand why she would rather die than ask for help. All Mum had to do was call. I would have dropped everything and gone there immediately. You know I would.'

'Joan was a very private person,' Jesper said, and cleared his throat. 'I've known you all for quite a few years now and I've never got very close to Joan. Who knows how she was really feeling?'

'But she wasn't well,' Julie cried. 'Especially not since Marie got ill. The same goes for all of us. Obviously! The worst thing that can happen is losing someone you love and knowing there is nothing you can do about it, *nothing*!' Her voice was shrill. 'And, remember, we've been through it all before, Jesper, when I was ten years old. The night Mads died. I remember waiting in the hospital corridor and the look in the doctor's eyes when he came to tell Mum and Dad. Mum screamed. I couldn't bear to listen! She screamed and screamed. Eventually they had to give her a sedative and put her to bed. She's had to relive it because Marie is going to— is so ill. I do understand, but I still think it's cowardly towards the children. And to me. I could have done something!'

Marie sat in the back, speechless. This was absurd. It was as if she didn't exist.

'I'm not going to die,' she said out loud.

'No, of course not, my darling!' Julie exclaimed, as she reached out a hand to Marie. 'How can you say a thing like that? Of course you're not going to die. Is she, Jesper?'

'Of course not,' Jesper said.

'But you almost said I was going to die,' Marie said, but no one was listening.

Jesper parked outside the entrance to Lea's flat and they made their way up to the fourth floor. A tearful Lea opened the door. She wore no makeup and her hair was a mess – it was usually styled with great care. Marie threw her arms around her and they hugged for a long time. Michael was sitting in an armchair in Lea's living room, next to a desk with piles of books and a pad with densely written notes.

'It's a mess, that's what it is,' Michael mumbled, and patted Julie's leg awkwardly without getting up. 'A right bloody mess.'

'We haven't spoken to Frank yet,' Lea said in a low voice.

'But I don't think he knows anything . . . He staggered to the loo just now and he said—'

'Yeah, that was freaky,' Michael interrupted. 'He said, "Not a word to Mum. Or she'll kill me."'

'Shut up, Michael,' Lea hissed.

'Hey, relax,' Michael said.

'Yes, really, Lea,' Julie said, and started crying again.

Lea exploded. 'This is *my* home so I'll say whatever the fuck I like. What the hell do you think you're doing?' She glared furiously at Marie. 'I would never have thought this of you, Marie. The others, definitely. But you, never!'

'What?' Marie said.

'How could you even think of sending that dickhead to tell me my mother is dead? Eh? Of all people, you send him?' Lea pointed angrily at Michael and tears spouted from her eyes.

'Lea,' Marie said calmly, 'Michael had already gone to see you when Jesper and I arrived at Snerlevej. And you're right, it wasn't a very good idea.'

'That's it. I've had enough,' Michael said, getting up and grabbing his jacket. 'Here I was, thinking I was doing Julie a favour. What the hell have I done wrong this time?' He stormed out into the small hallway.

'Just go, will you?' Lea said.

The front door slammed and Julie wept. 'Honestly, Lea. Is this really the time and place?'

'Explain to me again what Dad said,' Marie said calmly.

'Something along these lines. Something about him wanting me not to tell Mum because she would be angry with him. He's still drunk.' Lea sounded deflated now.

'I'll talk to him,' Marie said. 'Julie, you go and make some coffee. A lot of coffee, strong coffee. And call the police, Jesper. Tell them they can come over in an hour and pick Dad up.'

'But—' Julie began.

'No buts; that's what's going to happen,' Marie said rather loudly.

Everyone looked at her in a stunned silence.

Marie sat on the edge of Lea's bed, where Frank lay like a beached whale across the duvet. She could smell vomit. Her father had dried blood down his clothes and his nose looked broken.

'Dad?' Marie whispered. 'Dad? Are you awake?'

'Mmm,' Frank grunted. 'Eh?'

'Dad,' Marie said, louder now. 'You have to wake up. Now. It's important.'

With infinite slowness Frank opened his eyes and gingerly touched his nose. Then he looked at Marie with swimming eyes before a smile spread across his face. 'Marizzen,' he slurred. 'Wouldn't you know it? It's my Marizzen.' He tried to sit up and succeeded after a few attempts.

'Dad,' Marie said. 'Why did you get so drunk? The police are looking for you.'

'Argh, bloody hell,' Frank mumbled. 'I didn't think I'd had that much until I tried to park. Bollocks. That's going to cost me a few points. Your mum will kill me when she finds out.'

'Dad,' Marie said. 'Mum is dead.'

For one moment Frank's eyes became completely lucid, then something crumbled around his mouth and a deep, unhappy sound escaped from it. 'No,' he wailed. 'No.'

Marie held out a hand to him. 'Yes,' she said. The tears rolled down her cheeks and she kept stroking Frank's hand. 'Julie thinks she killed herself. What happened yesterday? Where were you? The police are looking for you.'

But Frank just cried.

The police took Frank to Bellahøj Police Station; Julie and Michael followed. They would drive him back afterwards, and Julie promised to stay at Snerlevej that night. Marie and Jesper were free to drive home. Marie worried about Lea, but Julie said that Lea had called a friend who would stay over with her. Marie talked non-stop all the way home, while Jesper said nothing. When they were halfway to Hellerup, Julie called to say that the forensic examiner had established that Joan had not been dead for very long when Julie had found her, and as Lea had now confirmed that Frank had arrived at her flat at two o'clock in the morning and not left at any point, Frank was not under suspicion. The police would still like to have a proper chat to him about the earlier events that evening and he would inevitably be charged with driving under the influence.

'What do you get for drink-driving?' Marie asked, when she had finished talking to Julie. 'Months? Or are we talking years? How could it get this bad, Jesper? How can we live like this? I can't live like this!' she cried. Jesper sat stony-faced and still said nothing.

The house was freezing because Marie had not shut the windows before they had rushed off to Snerlevej. Jesper closed them and turned up the heating. Marie sat on the sofa wrapped in a blanket while he pottered about in the kitchen, where he opened a bottle of wine. Marie had not drunk alcohol for several months, but now a glass of wine was exactly what she needed. In fact, she wanted to knock back the whole bottle, summon up the courage to kiss Jesper passionately, suck his dick so hard that he almost came, then straddle and ride him until he did. She wanted to be close to him again and live as if each day was their first.

'Jesper,' she said, taking his hand. 'Why don't we try to . . .? I really want to . . . I miss you.'

'Marie, please let me say something first,' he said.

She looked at him and he glanced away.

'It's dreadful, but I have to say this. I can't wait any longer, because . . . there never will be a right time – and I can't do this any more.'

Marie gave him a puzzled look.

'I want a divorce,' he said.

The next morning the doorbell rang and Marie stared numbly at Merethe Hermansen, chief secretary at the Department of Immunology, who seemed subdued. It was raining and water was dripping from the edge of her hood.

'Marie,' she said, 'I'm afraid I have some terrible news. Storm is dead. He hanged himself. I didn't want to call because I know how much—'

Marie closed the door.

CHAPTER 5

On Sunday evening Søren was lying comfortably on the living-room floor at home in Humlebæk playing picture bingo with Lily while he enjoyed an unobstructed view of her mother's well-shaped rear through the kitchen door. The telephone rang and it was 'only me, Henrik'. Søren briefly considered ignoring it, but ended up answering. He regretted it almost immediately.

'So, what's up? Am I disturbing your Sunday downtime?' Søren was about to answer that, yes, Henrik was.

'Then again,' Henrik chuckled, 'Sunday, Thursday, same thing for the unemployed, innit?'

'What do you want?' Søren said.

'Now, now, don't go all helpful on me,' Henrik said. 'I want to talk to Anna, as it happens. Is she there?' He snorted.

'Anna, Henrik wants to talk to you,' Søren called, in the direction of the kitchen. His blood was boiling. The extractor hood was on so Anna just turned towards his voice and signalled she would be there in two seconds. 'She's coming,' Søren said. 'What do you want to talk to her about?'

'It's confidential,' Henrik said. 'Police business.'

Søren put the phone on the sofa and turned over a card.

'A watering can!' he said.

'Mine!' Lily said.

Søren turned over another card. He could hear Henrik say: 'Hello? Hello?'

'Triplets!'

'Mine!' Lily said.

'Hello?' Henrik shouted.

'Who is that little voice shouting?' Lily asked.

'Only Uncle Henrik,' Søren said loudly, and turned over another card. It was a trumpet and also Lily's. He threw a rug over the telephone.

Anna entered the living room, wiping her hands on her trousers and looking puzzled. Søren fished out the telephone and handed it to her. On realising that it was Henrik, she mouthed, 'WTF,' to Søren. 'Anna Bella here,' she said. They exchanged a few pleasantries, but then Anna suddenly disappeared down the passage to her study.

'Yes, sure,' Søren heard her say. 'All right, I might be able to . . . Fine. But probably not until after Easter – I've got an application deadline coming up . . . Oh, I see, that's a bit difficult to say no to . . . OK, deal.'

Søren could no longer hear what she was saying and Lily shouted, 'Bingo!'

'The police have hired me for a project,' Anna said, when she returned ten minutes later. 'As a kind of researcher.'

'They've what?'

'Yes – I'm to write a profile of Kristian Storm so that Henrik can understand his research and why it was controversial.'

'But why? I thought he killed himself.'

'Hmm,' Anna said. 'Henrik wasn't quite so sure. He's talked to Trine Rønn, who found the body, and her distress and her flat refusal to accept that Storm took his own life seem to have made an impression on him. Besides, he also wants to dig deeper into the contradictions. On the one hand Storm was a hero to all his students, while on the other he was one of the most vilified men in modern research. He said he was going to let everything simmer for a little while.'

'You're kidding?'

'No, I was rather impressed with Henrik,' Anna said. 'You can never tell, can you? I like the fact that he's prepared to keep an open mind while he gathers more information. That's not like him, is it? It's probably the prospect of the new baby that has mellowed him. By the way, when is Jeanette due? We haven't seen them for ages . . . Socially, I mean.' Anna stretched to give Søren a kiss, but he was as rigid as a statue.

'Hey, what's wrong?' Anna demanded, and sent him a teasing look. 'Henrik clearly isn't the only police officer who needs Anna Bella Nor's help to solve the case.'

'How much is he paying you?' he asked.

'More than enough for me to say yes,' Anna said, with a wide grin.

Monday morning was Søren's second unemployed weekday. He and Lily waved Anna off when she cycled to the station to catch the train to the university. By now Lily's rash was all over her body and face, and Søren let her watch television while he cleared up after breakfast, did the laundry and took some meat out of the freezer for dinner. Anna had been brimming with enthusiasm all morning, talking about her profile of Kristian Storm, and when Søren had asked about her incredibly urgent grant application, she had brushed it aside. They were bound to get it done sooner or later, she said, and, besides, she was waiting for Anders T. to finish his part of the project description.

Søren felt jealousy creep through him again as he cleared up. When he thought about it, Anna could always come up with a good reason for having to go to the university. There was always something that demanded her attention and dragged her out of the house into the Institute of Biology. Until now he had accepted it as the dedication of the scientist. After all, he knew what it was like. When he'd had an unresolved case on his desk, back in the days when he had a job, he could think of nothing else, and was only half present in any other activity until the killer had been caught. Even though scientific research was different, he was starting to understand. It was a permanent state that could last a lifetime, rather than a race against a killer who might strike again. He began to wonder if Anna was simply using the university as an excuse to get away from him and Lily, dried porridge and snotty noses. Anders T. was laidback, undemanding and bound to make Anna laugh. Søren loved it when she threw back her head and roared with laughter. In the beginning, in the heyday of their relationship, he had been the one to set her off.

He sat down with his coffee next to the computer in the living room and looked up the Institute of Biology and the Department of Immunology. Under *Staff* he found photographs of all employees and students, and a brief presentation of their area of research. He started by studying the photograph of Kristian Storm, a ruddy, pleasant-looking man, with nice eyes and a full head of hair. Next in line was Thor Albert Larsen whom, to Søren's surprise, the camera appeared to love. Søren continued clicking and paid special attention to the students' faces. Trine Rønn was an attractive blonde, whom Søren had never met so her friendship with Anna could not be close. Marie Skov Just, however, was surprisingly familiar, though Søren could not place her. She had bright blue eyes, nut-brown hair in a practical style and a clear, soft presence, like a watercolour painting. She was someone who definitely did not lose her temper when she got angry, Søren thought. If she ever did get angry.

Anna and he had lived together for more than eighteen months and Søren was still just as taken aback when Anna flew into a rage. She had been known to call him an idiot. One day the words 'monumental prat' had escaped her lips.

Monumental prat?

No one could accuse Anna of suffering from nice-girl syndrome.

She always apologised afterwards. She hadn't meant it. But, she explained, when she got angry she couldn't control what came out of her mouth. She said it was just like when she was little and got car sick and had to throw up straight away. There was no holding back. Søren had suffered dreadfully from travel sickness when he was a boy so he could empathise. But why did she have to take it out on him?

Søren studied the photograph of Marie Skov Just. Where on earth had he seen her before? It had to have been in connection with the campus murders. She was a lovely-looking woman so he must have noticed her subconsciously.

He went through the rest of the department and drafted a

group email to the students, signed it with his official police signature and hit *send* before he had time to change his mind. In his email he asked them to get back to him if, in connection with their work with Kristian Storm, they had noticed anything unusual. Even the smallest thing was of interest, he had stressed.

Lily called to him from the sofa: she was hungry again. Søren made her two slices of rye bread with liver pâté and fished out pickled beetroot slices from a jar, which he put on top. She told him she was thirsty, too; he gave her a glass of milk and she spilled a little on the sofa. He mopped it up and gave her another glass. Then he went for a shower, and just as he had massaged shampoo into his hair, Lily appeared in the doorway with her duvet.

'I spilled milk all over my duvet. It was an accident.'

Søren sighed, got out of the shower and resolutely shoved the duvet, still in its cover, into the washing machine.

Lily said, 'Søren, you can't wash a whole duvet,' but he assured her he could.

Then he felt her forehead and found she was not particularly hot. 'Come on,' he said. 'Put some clothes on and we'll go for a ride.'

'But I'm ill,' Lily objected.

'Don't be silly,' Søren said firmly. 'Measles need fresh air. Especially German ones. Otherwise they get cabin fever and start chewing the sofa.'

Twenty minutes later, Lily sat warmly wrapped up in her child seat on the bar of Søren's bicycle while they rode the two kilometres to Kystbanen. They took his bike on the train, got off at Nørreport station and cycled onwards to Nørrebro.

They stopped in Elmegade to buy takeaway bagels and three monstrously large slices of chocolate cake.

'What are we doing now?'

'Bringing your mum a surprise lunch,' Søren said. 'But first we'll make a quick stop to see if her friend Trine happens to be at work today. Do you know her?'

'No,' Lily said, and continued in a hopeful voice, 'Then are we going to the museum?'

'Not today, sweetheart,' Søren said. 'But perhaps tomorrow.'

'Oh, we're back here again, are we?' Lily said loudly, when she and Søren entered the Department of Immunology. Søren said a silent prayer that they would not bump into Thor Albert Larsen, who might well start to wonder if police officers made a habit of bringing their children to work every day. Fortunately the door to Thor's office was closed. However, the door to Trine Rønn's office was ajar and Søren knocked on it. Lily had lagged behind because she was busy admiring the sea of flowers in front of Storm's door, which had not reduced since last Friday. Søren heard her say, 'They're pretty.'

'Come in,' said a lovely voice from the office, and when Søren pushed open the door, a blonde woman gave him a quizzical look.

'Trine Rønn?' Søren said stupidly, and the woman laughed.

'I'm flattered, but I'm about twenty-five years older than Trine. Who wants to know?'

'Søren Marhauge from the Violent Crimes Unit,' Søren said, hoping that Lily would stay in the corridor so he could preserve his authority.

The woman held out her hand. 'Merethe Hermansen. I'm

the chief secretary here in the department. You're quite right. It is Trine's office, or Trine and Rasmus's office, to be precise. Rasmus is abroad and Trine isn't here either. She was the one who found Storm in . . .' Merethe's gaze slipped from Søren's face to hip height where Lily's head had appeared.

'Hello,' Lily said.

'Hello, you,' Merethe replied.

'Please may I play with that?' Lily asked, pointing to a Spanish flamenco dancer on the desk.

Merethe replied that, sadly, she could not. 'I'm just here to pick up some papers that Trine wants me to send to her. She's not feeling very well and decided to work from home today, so she called me to . . . ' Merethe came to a halt as if she had realised that her explanation was unnecessary. 'I'm sorry to ask,' she then said to Søren, 'but do you have any ID?'

'I promise I'll be careful,' Lily said and put on her cutest face, which Søren could never resist.

Merethe looked despairingly from Søren to Lily, and Søren was quick to exploit the situation. 'I must come clean and tell you I don't have my warrant card with me today because I'm not officially on duty. My daughter and I were just on our way to have lunch with my girlfriend, who is also Lily's mother, Anna Bella Nor, from the Department of Cell Biology and Comparative Zoology; do you know her?'

'Søren washed his warrant card,' Lily interjected. 'And it went all small.'

Søren flashed his most endearing grin and it worked.

'Of course I know Anna. Here,' she continued, as she handed the flamenco dancer to Lily. 'But promise me you'll be careful. It's not mine.'

Lily nodded so hard her head nearly fell off.

'Now that I've got you,' Søren said quickly, 'do you mind if I ask you a few questions, even though I'm not officially at work? An investigator is never really off duty . . .'

'An investigator?' Merethe said suspiciously. 'What are you investigating? We were told it was suicide. That he hanged himself.'

'That's correct,' Søren said, mentally kicking himself. 'But we like to explore all avenues before we close a case.' Merethe continued to look sceptical, but said that Søren should go ahead and ask.

'What was the mood like here in the department?' Søren began.

'Storm has created a really good working environment,' Merethe said, without hesitation, 'and the academic staff members are not embroiled in internal conflicts, as I know they are in some other departments. These days, scientists have become each other's rivals and they fight tooth and nail for funds and prestige. But not ours. Once your PhD thesis has been approved by either Storm or Thor, your career as a scientist is reasonably secure. No one walks around coveting what the others have, if they themselves have enough, do they? Now, I'm not a scientist myself but I've worked in this department for more than a decade.'

Søren nodded. 'So overall the mood is good?'

Merethe nodded, but then she wavered. 'The only thing I would say . . .' Suddenly she seemed embarrassed. 'Well, I don't suppose it's a very scientific point to make . . . almost the contrary. And it's not because I'm a superstitious person . . . But we have been struck by a run of bad luck, or rather Storm has, I suppose I should say, ever since he got involved in that project in Africa.'

'What do you mean?'

Merethe thought about it. 'I just think it's . . . remarkable, to put it mildly, that Storm has faced so many obstacles ever since he started the Belem project.'

'What kind of obstacles?'

'Well,' she said, 'to begin with it all looked very promising. Storm came back from Guinea-Bissau and was over the moon because he and his Swedish colleague, Olof Bengtsson, had made this ground-breaking observation in their dataset. He summoned us all for a briefing, and I had never heard him so . . . triumphant. What they had seen was quite simply huge and we should prepare ourselves for considerable attention, he said. We all got really excited about it and the corridor was practically buzzing. But things started going wrong almost immediately. First Olof Bengtsson jumped ship from the Guinea-Bissau project. Storm was completely down in the dumps that morning, and when I asked him what on earth had happened, he told me that Bengtsson had fobbed him off with some lame excuse about a new job. Storm soldiered on, but shortly afterwards, Silas drowned.'

'Silas?'

'Storm's PhD student and right-hand man. A dreadful accident in Africa. As you would expect, everyone was terribly upset, especially Storm and the whole Belem team who had known him well. Tim, Storm's other PhD student in Guinea-Bissau, grieved for months, and a statistician from Aarhus, Berit Dahl Mogensen, who was otherwise deeply committed to the project, flew back from Bissau as fast as she could and cut all links to Belem soon afterwards. As a result the work ground to a halt for several months. Then, on top of that, let's not forget the professional opposition Storm has had to battle. It would be enough to send anyone on sick leave with stress. One moment the future looked bright with the promise of publications and workshops all over the globe, but every time events were either cancelled at the eleventh hour or turned out to be irrelevant. Storm also had major problems securing the funding, even though he's a highly respected and experienced scientist. He ended up selling his own house to keep Belem going during a period when there was absolutely no funding available. Eventually the project was allocated an annual grant from the Serum Institute, and soon afterwards Marie Skov's PhD application was approved. Once again, the future looked bright but – wouldn't you know it? – just as Marie and Storm published their new results from animal tests carried out last autumn, and she had got her master's, she was diagnosed with breast cancer at the age of twenty-eight, and the DCSD accused her of scientific dishonesty, so everything came to a halt again. And now Storm is dead. Can't you see that the whole thing is remarkably ill fated?'

She shuddered and added, 'Storm always told me not to worry about it. That obstacles occur randomly. If you throw a die enough times, he would say, sooner or later you'll get ten sixes in a row, even though it sounds absolutely impossible. I was not to attach any importance to it. But I'm probably not quite as level-headed.'

'Were you surprised to hear that Storm had killed himself?'

'When I came to work last Thursday and the police were here, Thor told me what had happened. I was both shocked and surprised. Storm was like a cork – he would always bob up to the surface. But when I thought about it more deeply, I wasn't that surprised. Remember, I didn't see him socially, but I've worked with him for the best part of ten years. He was totally wedded to his work, and after he sold his house on Frederiksberg and moved to Baldersgade in outer Nørrebro, it became even more obvious. He had grown up in that house and he used to invite everyone in the department for Christmas drinks. The place was drowning in books and periodicals, as you would expect of a scientist, but it had a nice atmosphere. As if things other than just research were going on there. When he moved to his flat in Baldersgade, he started hosting the Christmas drinks party in the department's refectory rather than at his home. He said that the flat wasn't big enough, and I'm sure that was true, but one of the students told me the real reason was that Storm's home was no longer in a fit state to receive guests. The student had stopped by to pick up a book and could see Storm had yet to unpack his removal crates. There was still plastic packaging around the cooker, she told me. Storm was working the whole time and would often sleep here in the department. It's fair to say the last few years have been an uphill struggle for him and, though he held his head high and gave us all the impression that he was going to fight until the end, I'm sure it must have taken its toll on him. I think that the allegation of scientific dishonesty and Marie's illness were the last straw.' Merethe looked upset.

'It was truly awful to have to tell Marie,' she went on. 'She was at home because, like I said, she's ill, so I went to tell her in person, rather than call. She slammed the door in my face. She couldn't take it in at all. Poor girl.'

'Tell me a bit about Marie Skov,' Søren asked, showing his curiosity.

Merethe sighed. 'Storm worshipped her. Even while she was still an undergraduate, he let her co-write several of his publications and she's still not even thirty. There were jealous murmurings in the corners, but if you ask me, Storm's favouritism was wholly justified. Marie worked hard and she was not at all pretentious or calculating, which some of the others can be, whether they're prepared to admit to it or not. When Marie defended her master's dissertation in September, the audience rose to its feet and applauded her for almost five minutes when she had finished. She was completely bowled over, as if she didn't have the slightest idea of just how exceptional her presentation had been.' Merethe interrupted herself and Søren followed her gaze. Trine's flamenco dancer was pirouetting vertically off the door frame, as if she was on some kind of mood-enhancing substance. Søren firmly took the figure from Lily.

'Boring,' Lily said.

Søren put the dancer on the desk. 'Anyway, that brings us to the end of my questions,' he said, addressing Merethe. 'Thank you so much for your help.'

'You're welcome,' Merethe said. 'I'm afraid I can't go to Storm's funeral on Friday. My grandmother turns a hundred and I promised her months ago to help with the party. So I'll be travelling to Fyn tomorrow.'

'On Friday?' Søren merely said, but Merethe did not detect the hidden question.

'Yes. In St Stefan's Church on Nørrebro. Just what Storm would have wanted.'

Søren thanked Merethe warmly and marched off with Lily in tow.

For once it did not take Søren and Lily long to find Stairwell One where Anna had her office on the second floor. Lily had been to the Department of Cell Biology and Comparative Zoology lots of times and ran ahead up the steps. When Søren entered the office, she was already sitting on the lap of a happy-looking Anna.

'What a lovely surprise,' she said, and sent Søren a quizzical glance. Fortunately Anders T. was nowhere to be seen.

'German measles is nothing, is it, Lily?'

'No,' Lily said. 'They just need some fresh air. Or they'll bite.' Anna giggled, and they ate the bagels and chocolate cake. Between mouthfuls, Anna talked about her profile of Kristian Storm, which she had been working on all morning.

'So Henrik didn't call today?' Søren said casually. He had hoped that Henrik would have changed his mind and cancelled Anna. Henrik was not just wasting Anna's time, he was also doing his best to taunt Søren. Besides, Søren was convinced that Jørgensen would disapprove strongly of Henrik's decision to waste money on a profile. The police commissioned profiles only when they were hunting a killer who was still at large.

'Oh, yes, he rang a moment ago,' Anna replied, 'wanting to know when I expect to have finished. I believe he would like me to come to Bellahøj to present it. He's on loan to Station City this week because of those inner-city rapes, so he wanted to know exactly when I'll be there so he can be sure to make it. I'm working hard and promised him I'll have it ready by tomorrow, Wednesday at the latest. Is this common practice for the police? Hiring external researchers like this?'

'No,' Søren said.

'Well, it's the easiest money I've ever made in my career,' Anna said, with a smile. 'It's been super exciting. I'd had no idea that Kristian Storm was that famous and that ground-breaking, yet so vilified. I've read up on scientific dishonesty and the process that is set in motion when a scientist is reported to the DCSD. I used to think that the DCSD was a brilliant and typically Danish organisation, created to ensure that justice is done. But now I'm not so sure. I agree, of course, that scientists mustn't get away with cheating. We're talking about a lot of grant money here and it should go to honest scientists. But I don't like the fact that you can remain anonymous when you accuse someone – and it's unreason-able that the investigation process takes so long. Imagine waiting months or years for a conclusion and never knowing the identity of your accuser. I would start to suspect everyone! It must be an extremely stressful situation, especially once the media catch a whiff of it. Remember the Penkowa case? It was all she-said-he-said, and then Penkowa's invitation to the Palace was withdrawn because the Queen obviously couldn't attend a state dinner and sit next to a scientist under investigation and blah-blah. It's pure soap opera and it inevitably ends up on the front pages. Anyway,' Anna looked at her watch, 'I'd better get back to work. Please would you give me Henrik's number? Whenever he calls me, it shows up as *number withheld*, and I forgot to ask when I last spoke to him.'

'I don't mind calling him for you,' Søren said.

Anna raised an eyebrow. 'Don't tell me you're jealous of Henrik? Seriously, Søren, get a grip.'

'No, of course not,' Søren said quickly, and copied down Henrik's mobile number from his own phone. 'But I decide what you wear when you go to Bellahøj to present your profile,' he added. 'And it'll be something very baggy. Possibly a burka.'

Anna threw back her head and laughed. 'That's quite all right,' she said, and gave him a big kiss.

Henrik called as Søren was pushing his bicycle across the university car park in the direction of Jagtvej and Lily was jumping up and down next to him. Even though he told himself he was not going to, he took the call.

'What do you think you're doing?' he barked at Henrik. 'Have you officially closed the Kristian Storm case, but still not cancelled Anna's profile? How is that possible? And since when did we hire external researchers with no police background to prepare personal profiles of people who are already dead? This is ridiculous. Does Jørgensen know that you're spending the unit's budget on hiring Anna? He didn't order us to make savings on everything from printer paper to post-mortems only for you to blow the budget on hot air, did he?'

'Hey, easy does it. You told me yourself I should get a profile done,' Henrik reminded him.

'Yes, but I didn't mean you to hire an external consultant. You should form your own opinion. You're meant to do the thinking. You're superintendent now, Henrik. You're meant to think about what kind of person Kristian Storm was and consider if it has any relevance to his death. And you're stringing Anna along. She's working her socks off writing that profile and you won't be using it for anything.'

'You don't know that,' Henrik said, clearly unperturbed.

'But you've already closed the case?'

'Not officially. I'm still waiting for Bøje, that slowcoach. He hasn't filed his report yet.'

Søren thought he must have misheard. 'So why did you call Thor Albert Larsen to tell him the case is officially closed?'

'Because I've been talking to Bøje and he says he's a hundred per cent sure that Storm died as a result of hanging and that the injuries match those of the other thirty-seven suicides by hanging he has previous experience of. He told me so this morning. Only he hasn't had time to sign off his report yet, partly because . . . Yes, because he, too, is feeling the heat from above on account of the inner-city rapes – as would you be if you could be bothered to turn up for work where you would see that we're all running around like blue-arsed flies because of you and your lack of work ethic. Now get yourself back here, mate. We really need you. I haven't slept since last Thursday and I'm running on a bad mix of coffee and Red Bull.'

'Bloody hell, Henrik!' Søren bellowed. 'You can't officially close a case when you haven't got the final report. Have you completely lost the plot?'

'Thor Albert Larsen hasn't stopped calling me since last Thursday and is nearly driving me insane. Paranoid little toerag. He wants to know if, as he puts it, it's safe for him to go to work because, if there's even the slightest risk that Kristian Storm was murdered, then he could in principle be the killer's next victim. Dah, dah *daaaaah!*' he drumrolled. 'I know it's tough, Søren, but you just have to accept that you're currently in second place on my list of drama queens. Thor couldn't give a toss whether Kristian Storm was murdered or killed himself. What he really wants to know is how soon he can move into Storm's office without being accused of poor taste. He called again this morning, just after I'd spoken to Bøje and got his word that Storm committed suicide, so I told Thor he could safely start packing his removal crates and get ready to move up the ladder. He hasn't phoned me since . . . Funny, that. As for Tiger Pussy, she's over the moon about that profile so let her have her fun. She'll be done tomorrow, Wednesday at the latest, and we can find a few thousand kroner in the budget, don't you think, Søren? Even Jørgensen thought it was a good idea.'

'Jørgensen said you had two days to wrap up this case. Two days. And now it's suddenly OK to hire external experts to carry out research? Have you both lost your minds?' Søren was shocked, but then it struck him that Jørgensen was trying to tempt him back to work by involving Anna. But even if they hired Sherlock Holmes himself to solve the case, right under Søren's nose, there was no way he was going back.

'Talking about insanity,' Henrik added amicably, 'I'm actually calling you for a reason. You see, Kristian Storm's death wasn't the only suicide – pardon me, Mr Pedant, *presumed* suicide – we picked up last Thursday. A housewife from Vangede with mental-health problems emptied her medicine cabinet and never woke up again. Right from the start I was sure we were looking at suicide and it was only because the dead woman's husband had vanished without a trace that I chose to follow a good friend and ex-police officer's excellent advice and let everything simmer for a while. I spent the time looking into the dead woman's background and a number of things cropped up, which I think you'll find interesting. The first thing I came across was an assault charge – retracted in the summer of 1987 – when the woman's husband, Frank Skov, appears to have attacked his neighbour, a woman called Tove Madsen, as she was about to let herself into her house. According to the report, Frank Skov had accused Tove Madsen, who was his daughter's childminder, of shaking the kid. Guess who reported it?'

'Elvis Presley?'

'Elvis is dead, you numpty. No, your grandfather. Knud Marhauge.'

'Oh.' Søren was taken aback.

'So I made a note of the address of the Skov family. Number nineteen Snerlevej, in Vangede. If I'm not mistaken that's the street you grew up in.'

'Yes, number twenty-six.'

'I knew it!' Henrik said triumphantly. 'But hold your horses. Turns out that Tove Madsen was married to a police officer called Herman Madsen. I didn't know him personally, but when I mentioned him to Jørgensen, he knew exactly who he was. Herman Madsen's nickname was Cluedo because he followed a process of deduction and, despite his hopeless method, he had an incredibly high clear-up rate. Jørgensen also told me that Cluedo transferred to Aalborg Police District at some point . . .'

'Herman Madsen?' Søren wondered aloud. 'I knew him really well. I was friends with his son, Jacob, when I was little.

It's thanks to Herman Madsen that I applied to the Police Academy.'

'And, in truth, that was a day of joy,' Henrik said, 'but shut up for a second, will you, because there's more. Frank Skov was never charged because your grandfather retracted his accusation. Since then, Frank Skov has had contact with the police on only two occasions, once in February of this year and most recently last Wednesday, when we discovered his van near Enghave Plads with blood everywhere and found Skov in his youngest daughter's flat in Saxogade the following day, where he was sleeping off one hell of a night out.'

Søren and Lily had stopped at a bus stop just before the Tagensvej junction, and Lily was busy climbing onto and jumping down from the bench in the bus shelter, perilously close to a woman who was giving her evil looks.

'This is all very exciting, but I'm afraid I'm going to have to hang up,' Søren said.

'Hold on! I haven't got to the good part yet,' Henrik said. 'We picked Frankie-boy up and took him for a trip to Bella where we quizzed him for a bit, but soon decided it was a waste of time. We got a video recording from some dive on Kultorvet and later CCTV footage from a camera in Magasin's multi-storey car park, where Frank snoozed in his car for about an hour, and after that a recording from a kiosk in Istedgade where he's covered in blood and crashing into a shelf of crisps before being thrown out. Frank had been knocking it back all day and couldn't possibly have been involved in wifey's death. Didn't I tell you it was suicide? I have a nose for these things.' Henrik sniffed.

'Congratulations.'

'I personally drove Frank Skov home to nineteen Snerlevej, where I had the honour of meeting the eldest daughter in the family, Julie Claessen. While Frank Skov took a slash, I asked his daughter about the attack in 1987. The girl shut down completely. She couldn't remember any attack, she said, and even if she could, she didn't think it was important. Her mother had been very beautiful and her father very clever, so when their young son got acute meningitis and died, the neighbours couldn't stop twitching their curtains. Now that she thought about it, she did actually remember an unpleasant elderly couple across the road who had been quick to turn up their noses at them when her mother had had a breakdown. It wouldn't surprise her, she said, if they'd gone to the police simply to harass them.'

'Now that's bullshit,' Søren interrupted him, outraged. 'Knud and Elvira would never have dreamed of harassing anyone.'

'Hey, will you shut up? I still haven't finished. I asked if I could have a look around and—'

'Why on earth did you do that?' Søren demanded.

'I dunno. I find myself doing the strangest things, these days.' Henrik laughed. 'Anyway, we wander around the house for a bit and at one point we reach the first floor. Funny old house, by the way, untouched since the seventies, with big floral wallpaper and curry-yellow skirting boards, as if the last thirty years hadn't happened, which in itself might not be that unusual, but Frank Skov is meant to be some sort of builder or handyman and they're usually a bit house-proud, aren't they? The house was totally neglected. Anyway, there we were, upstairs, and when we went inside Frank's study, guess what the first thing I saw was?'

'I've no idea,' Søren said wearily.

'You!'

'Me?'

'Yes, in a photo in Frank Skov's study. The only photo on his otherwise bare walls. No page-three girl, mate – more evidence that he can't possibly be a builder, ha-ha – but, anyway, you're in that photo. True, you're in the background, but I still recognised you.'

'Are you sure? Why on earth would I be in a photo belonging to people I don't even know?'

'Of course I'm sure. There are two men in the foreground and Julie confirmed that one of them is Frank, but she didn't know who the other was. In fact, she'd never seen the picture before, she said. Between Frank and this unknown man, however, there were two younger children, whom Julie called the twins, and in the background to the right, there was one hot chick – you wouldn't believe how hot she was. Julie said that was her mother, the now late Joan Skov. In the background to the left, next to another boy, there you are with a football under your arm. Julie said she didn't know who either of you were, but I'm certain that one of them is you. You look like I don't know what. Christ Almighty, what an eighties outfit. Julie said that her family has owned the house for more than fifty years and that her grandparents lived there before Frank and Joan inherited it. Frank and Joan must have been there while Knud and Elvira lived in the same street. Perhaps Knud and Elvira were friends with them and you happened to drop by. There's no doubt it's you.'

'That's so weird,' Søren conceded. 'Hey, Lily, that's enough jumping for now, do you hear?'

'Yes, but I get bored when you're on the phone,' Lily protested.

'All right, I've finished now . . . Uncle Henrik just wanted to tell me something exciting.'

'. . . Marie Skov . . .' Søren suddenly heard Henrik say.

'What?' Søren pricked up his ears and held up his hand so that Lily would be quiet.

'I'm saying I was having a good laugh at your failed eighties haircut, when Julie Claessen suddenly mentioned that her younger sister had been through a tough time. Here she pointed to the little girl in the photo. First, Marie lost her twin, Julie said, waving at the little boy, and then she'd got breast cancer and now she's just lost her supervisor *and* her mother on the same day. "Supervisor?" I asked, thinking she was about to reel off some tedious Scientology sob story, but do you know which supervisor she was referring to? Kristian Storm.'

For one moment Søren's mind was a reverberating vacuum.

'That Marie Skov?' he then said. 'Kristian Storm's PhD student, who is currently on sick leave?'

'Bingo. What a small and very cute world we live in, eh? Made me laugh that the two of you seem to have known each other as kids. Isn't there something about everyone in the world knowing everybody else through six degrees of separation?'

'They can't have been friends of Knud and Elvira,' Søren said. 'I have no recollection of ever visiting them so it must be pure chance that I'm in the photo. I wonder if it was taken in Herman Madsen's garden. That would make more sense. I was there all the time – it was my home from home.'

'Well, I wouldn't know about that. A garden is just a garden and I'm glad I haven't got one.'

'Jacob and I hung out all the time and we played a lot of football. Perhaps he's the boy standing next to me. But whatever it is, what a coincidence— Maybe that was why Marie Skov seemed so familiar,' Søren exclaimed.

'Her mother, now she was a looker,' Henrik said dreamily. 'Though I would be lying if I said she'd passed her looks on to her eldest daughter. She's the size of a shed! The mother, you can't have forgotten her? Every teenager's wet dream of an older woman, even though she can't have been much over twenty-eight in that photo. Jesus, to begin with I couldn't believe that the woman in the picture was the one we found on Thursday morning after Julie's call to the emergency services. But Julie kept saying, "My beautiful mother," and touching the photograph. It's not often we get a good-looking corpse, but it happens.'

A silence followed, then Henrik said, 'Why am I telling you all this? I keep forgetting you're no longer a police officer. Your new hobby seems to be showing up and wrecking my investigation. I can't get over how naff you looked in that picture – I can't stop laughing when I think about it. OK, so the eighties was the decade style forgot, but even so . . . Jesus Christ, Søren, you looked like a plonker!'

'Says the man who still has a trucker moustache,' Søren muttered, under his breath.

'Anyway, this concludes today's anecdote from the real world,' Henrik went on. 'And I'm here now so I'd better hang up.'

'Where?'

'I've lent myself to Station City,' Henrik announced proudly. 'No more typing for Henrik Tejsner. I'm off to solve a couple of high-profile rapes and make the front page of *Ekstra Bladet*. I'll call you when I'm famous.'

'No need,' Søren said, but Henrik had already hung up.

Søren scooped Lily up, strapped her into her child seat and cycled to Nørreport station. She had grown unusually quiet and Søren concluded all that jumping must have worn her out, but on the train back to Humlebæk, he noticed that her eyes were shining and she seemed dopey. He put her on his lap and she fell asleep soon afterwards.

Was it really true that he was no longer a policeman?

After dinner that evening Anna disappeared into her study. Søren had hoped they would have some time to talk. They had put Lily to bed over an hour ago and they rarely had any time, let alone a whole evening, that did not revolve around practical tasks. He had even found a bottle of wine in the cupboard and already poured two glasses.

'Not for me, thanks. I have work to do,' Anna had said. 'I need to finish Kristian Storm's profile, and I've just had a text message from Anders T., telling me he has finally written his part of our application and I must read it before he calls me about it, so . . .' She glanced briefly at the wine bottle and the two glasses, gave Søren a quick peck on the corner of his mouth and disappeared down the passage.

Søren tipped the contents of one glass into the other and sat down to watch television. Five minutes later he was bored and got up to fetch his laptop to check his emails. He had received one reply to the group email he had sent to Storm's and Thor's students. It was from a Niels Sonne, whom Søren remembered from his visit to the Department of Immunology's website. He was one of the department's most recent postgraduate students, but didn't look a day over eighteen: his face was completely unlined and beardless.

Hi Søren Marhauge,

I'm a master's student at the Department of Immunology, but I've been away in Sweden on a Scout camping trip for the past five days. I only heard about the death of Kristian Storm this morning when I returned to the university. Thor Albert Larsen told me that you think Kristian Storm probably died between seven fifteen and eight fifteen Wednesday evening. However, I turned up at the department that Wednesday evening at seven fifteen where I said hello to Storm, who always worked with his door open. I believe I spent forty-five minutes in my office, and when I left, the door to Storm's office had been closed, but I could hear him shredding something in the printer room. It means the earliest Storm could have died would be eight thirty. Now, I don't know how literally you treat the time of death, but I thought I should contact you anyway. In fact, I called Bellahøj Police today and left a message for Henrik Tejsner to call me back, but he hasn't, and as I'm spending the next three days at Syddansk University, working on my master's, I thought I had better email you instead. I hope I haven't wasted your time, but you did say that everything was of interest.
Best wishes, Niels Sonne

Søren drummed his fingers on the table.

Suddenly he heard Anna laugh and he walked in his socks down the passage, checking first on Lily before stopping outside the half-open door to Anna's study.

'Anders, for Christ's sake, you muppet,' he heard Anna say, but she didn't sound cross at all. 'Then call me back when you *are* ready.' Søren accidentally brushed a picture on the wall and the sound made Anna turn on her office chair and give him a questioning look through the crack in the door.

'Would you like some tea?' he mimed. She nodded before turning her attention back to her computer and carrying on with the conversation. Søren went to the kitchen and put on the kettle. Anna's computer screen had shown that she was logged onto Facebook. Søren hadn't known she had a Facebook profile. While the water heated, Søren went on Facebook and searched for Anna Bella Nor. When her page came up, he clicked on it, but got a message informing him he had to be friends with her before he could access her profile. Søren created his own profile and sent Anna a friend request. A moment later he heard her giggle down the passage and two seconds later his friend request had been accepted. Flustered at how quickly she had replied, he started clicking around her profile. He found several photographs, including one of himself and Anna together, taken at the start of their relationship, the first party where they had officially been an item. Søren could remember the evening vividly. He had been delirious with happiness and Anna had teased him because he could not hide how besotted he was with her.

My gorgeous man, Anna had written on Facebook. *Now it's official.*

Congratulations, you look so sweet together, someone had commented.

Cute couple, someone else had said.

Although the comments were embarrassing, Søren couldn't help smiling. That was until he reached Anders T.'s comment.

Doesn't matter that the brother inherited the farm, he had written, *because the forces of law and order got the princess.* Now irritated by this stupid reference to the typicality of second sons becoming police officers, Søren clicked on Anders T.'s profile. It seemed more open than Anna's had been until she had accepted him as a friend. Søren was able to view several of Anders T.'s photo albums and was not surprised to discover that his profile picture was a carefully chosen shot of a surfboard and a tanned six-pack against an azure sky, but there were plenty of others as well. Anders T. had more than seven hundred friends and was chatting to some on his wall in a variety of languages. Søren returned to Anna's profile and started scribbling down her various posts.

Hi, read a message from someone called Sarah. *Nice bumping into you in the refectory yesterday! Let's do lunch soon.*

Anna had replied and Søren could see that she had posted a picture on Sarah's profile, a photograph of two very young biology students with backpacks, insect nets and their arms around each other. *Terrestrial ecology sucks*, she had written below.

Søren went through all of Anna's posts methodically and came across a few from Anders T. *Now go to bed, you night owl*, he had typed four weeks earlier. *I can see that you're still online.* Other messages told Anna that she had received a virtual cow, seven chickens, a goat and four rabbits from Anders T. Plus a pitchfork and eight fruit trees. What the hell was that all about?

Søren went through the rest of Anna's photographs. They were mainly pictures where other people had tagged her, mostly during field trips, it would appear, and a few parties at the faculty, including one where she was standing next to her former supervisor, the late Professor Lars Helland. One photograph nearly gave Søren a heart attack. It had been taken at last year's Christmas party at the Department of Cell Biology and Comparative Zoology and Anna and Anders T. were wearing matching Santa hats and sitting close together at a table with a red cloth. Anna looked as if she was having a whale of a time and Anders T. gazed at her as if she had just said the funniest thing he had ever heard. But it was his hand on Anna that really bothered Søren. It didn't rest on her shoulders, where a male friend would put his arm around a woman, but crept sneakily across the middle of her back and subsequently peeked out under the soft spot below Anna's arm, exactly where her breast began. With a stretch of the imagination.

Then he heard Anna come down the passage and quickly clicked back to his own profile.

'Did you make some tea? Only I think I would rather have some wine now. Anders T. is driving me up the wall. He's incredibly talented, but ever since he became single, he's seriously hard work. By the way, I didn't know you were on Facebook,' Anna said. She poured a little wine into a glass and asked if he wanted a top-up.

Søren shook his head. His mouth felt completely dry. 'I didn't know you were on Facebook either,' he said. 'And I only created my profile because there's something I want to check. The name of someone I used to know when I was little cropped up in conversation and I decided to see if I could track him down.'

Søren typed Jacob Madsen in the search field and several profiles appeared on his screen.

'Facebook is huge at the university,' Anna said behind him.

'Everyone's on it. It's not really my thing. But when I'm working and my brain cells curl up from lack of oxygen, it often helps to take a Facebook break. Everything there is lovely, superficial and a good counterbalance to my work.' She yawned.

'Oh, by the way,' she continued, 'Thomas called today. He's got a job at Rigshospitalet and is moving back to Copenhagen. He's coming over this weekend to do some house-hunting and would like to see Lily.'

'But Lily's ill.' Søren was flustered. 'She can't just be taken out and about.'

'Søren, even though you hate the thought, Thomas is Lily's dad and he also happens to be a doctor, so they'll be fine. And, anyway, it's not for another five days.'

'Yes, but what if Thomas wants visiting rights?' Søren asked, now terrified. 'What if he wants joint custody of Lily?'

Anna raised her eyebrows. 'Well, seeing that he *is* her dad, there's not a whole lot I can do about it. But let's not get ahead of ourselves. Thomas talks a good game, but when it comes to the heavy lifting, he usually favours a solution that's essentially to his own advantage. He would never ask to have Lily half the time, but possibly three to eight.'

'What does that mean?'

'Eight days with us and three days with him and Gunvor.'

'*Three days?*' Søren stared at her in disbelief. At that moment her mobile rang and she answered it.

'Hey, I'm talking to you,' Søren snapped.

Anna glared at him before she composed her voice, said, 'Just a moment,' into her phone and let it slide down her thigh. 'What's wrong with you today, Søren?' she said quietly. 'I've been waiting for Anders T.'s comments on our application for four days because he's been busy with all sorts of other things, but when he called me just now to get my feedback, he hadn't even turned on his computer. So I have to take this call now, OK? Do you think you could calm down?' And she went back to her office.

Søren sat on the sofa and scowled. When he thought back to his own childhood, Knud and Elvira seemed to have been there for him all the time. There was always someone at home when he came back from school, always someone who would make him a cup of tea and butter him a bread roll, always someone he could ask for help with his homework or talk to about his day. He knew that his memories might be a little rose-tinted: Knud and Elvira had been schoolteachers, but they had also been politically active so they could not possibly have been around for him the whole time. But it had felt like that and that was what mattered. Knowing he came first. It was important for children to know that, he thought. Lily wasn't even six yet: what did she know about adult priorities and how important research was to her mother? Nothing. Even so, Lily still sensed how her mother discreetly and deftly managed to occupy her with some activity so that she herself could turn on her computer or look something up in a book. Søren came third, he was well aware of it, and that was just how it was. But surely Anna would not give up Lily for three days after every eight without a fight. It was out of the question, he thought, and shuddered at the prospect.

When Søren's daughter, who had died as a baby, had been born, her mother, Katrine, and her partner, Bo, had wanted Søren to play a minor role in Maja's life, at least while she was little. But he had rights and he had pointed this out to them. Søren wanted to be in Maja's life even if it meant going through the courts. It had felt good to insist. But when it came to Lily, he realised to his horror that he had no rights. Any minute now Anna could announce that she was moving in with Anders T., or Thomas might waltz in and demand to have Lily for several days, weeks even, at a time, and there was nothing Søren could do about it.

Søren grabbed his computer and stared at the screen. Thirty-seven Jacob Madsen profiles had appeared. He clicked on the first three, but it was a hopeless task. The quality of the first profile picture was so poor that he could not be sure if he was looking at the right Jacob Madsen and he was about to give up when he spotted the last profile before the list disappeared off the screen. It was him! Some twenty-plus years older and with less hair, but quite definitely the Jacob Madsen he had known as a boy. Søren clicked on his profile, but could access only the profile picture and practically no information. On the picture, Jacob Madsen was sitting at a garden table with a small Asian boy aged four or five on his lap and an Asian girl of school age standing next to them. A smiling woman in running kit, with lots of curly, blonde hair, stood behind them. They all looked happy and in glowing health. Søren sent Jacob Madsen a friend request.

Just at that moment a friend request from Anders T. popped up on the screen. Søren could not believe his eyes. The nerve of the man. He could hear that Anna was still on the phone at the other end of the house, so Anders T. must be busy on Facebook while giving Anna his so-important-it-couldn't-possibly-wait feedback on their grant application. Søren slammed shut his laptop and went to bed. Facebook was definitely not for him. Free access to the green-eyed monster of jealousy.

On Tuesday morning the clouds hung like heavy bunting across the trees. Lily was still unwell, so when Anna had left for the university, Søren dropped all plans of going by bicycle and put Lily, wrapped in her duvet, into the child seat in the car. They drove to Copenhagen and Lily sang a snotty-nosed version of 'The Wheels on the Bus' as suburbs turned into city. Søren parked his car on Danasvej and rang Trine Rønn's doorbell.

'I'm Søren Marhauge from Copenhagen Police,' he said, into the intercom, when Trine replied. After a brief hesitation he and Lily were let into the stairwell. Walking up the stairs took them forever.

'You slowcoach,' Søren said, and swung Lily onto his shoulders. She was heavy and he was wheezing like a pair of punctured bellows when they finally reached the fourth floor. Trine had put the security chain on the door and was peering out at them. Søren explained that he was Anna Bella's boyfriend and that the child was Lily, Anna's daughter; she was with him because she was ill. Trine looked sceptically at them through the gap in the door.

'We have German measles,' Lily announced in a loud voice. 'And I get to play on Søren's mobile if I promise to be quiet as a mouse and not bother him, not one single time, and go to the loo on my own if I need a pee.' On hearing this Trine opened the door and invited them in. She looked upset. Her skin was pale, as if she had been awake for a long time, and she was still in her dressing gown. Søren made Lily comfortable on the sofa and handed her his mobile. Then he followed Trine into the kitchen.

'I'm alone at the moment,' she said. 'My sister is usually here, but she has just left to take my daughter to nursery and do a bit of shopping. My boyfriend is Spanish; he's in Barcelona visiting his mother, so I'm grateful for her help. I haven't been able to sleep properly since Thursday. I keep seeing . . . I keep seeing Storm. Would you like a cup of tea?'

Søren nodded and sat down.

They started talking. Trine wondered if someone like Søren was used to the sight of dead bodies and Søren said he was, but that it always made an impression.

'I just started shaking all over,' Trine said. 'His face was very frightening.'

'It must have been a distressing sight,' Søren said.

A strange silence arose, then Trine said, 'Why do you want to question me again? I spoke to the superintendent, Henrik Tejsner, on the phone yesterday and got the impression the police had already made up their minds that Storm killed himself. Tejsner kept saying that the pathologist had just called to confirm that Storm's death was suicide. I think he said it three times.'

Søren cleared his throat. 'I'm sorry if you feel you have to repeat yourself, but we often work in parallel when we investigate a case. That way we get a more nuanced set of observations than if I simply read my colleague's report.' When Trine nodded, Søren quickly continued, 'It's my impression that Storm didn't have any kind of private life. That he was married to his work. Is that correct?'

Trine confirmed it. To her knowledge, Storm had never been married and had no biological children, but he had been very paternal towards all of his students. 'Most postgraduates whinge about their supervisors, but you had no grounds for that if you were being supervised by Storm. He loved us. He called us "the pillars of the future", and he always involved us in his research. Evil tongues might say that he exploited us, but I fail to see how. Storm wanted Denmark to be part of the research elite and it was his mission to teach us to carry out proper research. He let us be co-authors on his scientific papers, even if we only contributed with a single graph or a minor statistical analysis, and there was absolutely no requirement for him to do that. But Storm knew that publishing is the only way to get a slice of the pie, both in terms of making a name for ourselves and when it comes to grants and funding. Take Marie Skov, for example. I think her name went on more than twenty papers and she was lead author on several, yet she hasn't even started her PhD! It would never have happened in another department, with another supervisor, and that was why people were jealous.'

Søren made a mental note that Marie Skov's name had cropped up yet again and wondered if Trine Rønn was among the jealous ones. She didn't seem the type.

'Seems you liked him.'

'Yes,' Trine said, and nodded. 'He belonged to a dying breed of scientists, you could say. He valued curiosity, the importance of making mistakes. He would read Karen Blixen stories aloud during his lectures and say that natural scientists could learn a lot from the baroness. Storm was obsessed with the Danish language.'

'The Danish language?'

'Yes.' Trine explained: 'He wanted us to be able to express ourselves in perfect Danish. Most immunology books are written in English or German, so you quickly end up speaking a kind of hodgepodge Danish with English and German terms thrown in, but Storm insisted that we knew our scientific terminology in Danish as well as in English. He even coined two neologisms and got them recognised by the Danish Language Council. He was genuinely worried about the future of Danish research. "At best we'll be overtaken," he would say. "At worst, simply steamrolled."'

Søren nodded. 'As you know, we're working on the theory that Storm killed himself,' he then said.

'I thought you were *totally convinced* that Storm killed himself,' Trine said sharply. 'That's what your colleague said yesterday.'

'And you don't agree?'

'No,' was all Trine said.

'Would you care to elaborate? Just a little bit?'

Trine smiled wryly. 'Sorry. I became very monosyllabic when your colleague rang me yesterday. But I can tell that you're genuinely interested in my opinion.' She took a deep breath. 'Storm taught me properly,' she began. 'My GP can no longer give me a prescription for penicillin without my asking hundreds of in-depth questions. I drive every expert crazy because I always want to understand what lies behind their statements. It's an occupational hazard. Storm's occupational hazard. Ha. If you knew how many of his students have argued with their families when writing their master's! Storm and his teaching style were notorious for this. He told his students to look through a range of lenses. He taught us to ask the right questions, then gave us the academic tools and the guts to discover the truth. Both professionally and personally. The bottom line is that I *know* something about Storm's so-called suicide just doesn't add up. I was on maternity leave all of last year and I've only been back in the department since Christmas. As you're aware, Storm had been abroad since the middle of February. But I'll still claim that I knew him well and he would never— And do you know something?' she burst out. 'Just think it through to its conclusion. It's completely illogical. Why would a man – who was so passionate about his research that he sold his childhood home to finance the Belem project – take his own life just as he was on the verge of a breakthrough? The Serum Institute believed him. The Danish National Research Foundation believed him. Even the editor of *Science* believed him! I was in Storm's office three days before he died, and he was ecstatic. Why on earth would he kill himself? It makes no sense.'

Søren nodded again. 'Tell me about the missing box,' he said.

Trine looked at him closely. 'So you believe me?' she asked.

'I believe that you believe what you're saying, and I take that very seriously,' Søren said.

'OK,' Trine said. 'Storm had had major problems surveying an area in southern Guinea-Bissau. For more than two years the figures that came back were unbelievably good and, frankly, they distorted Storm's other data, prevented him processing his statistics and thus drawing the conclusions that would enable him to write the paper which would finally convince the rest of the world that some of the WHO's recommended vaccines cause the child mortality rate in developing countries to shoot up. After Marie had defended her master's dissertation and presented her laboratory figures, which very much supported Storm's theory about the non-specific effects of the vaccines, Storm went to Guinea-Bissau to survey the whole of the problematic area one last time. He came back in February and spent almost three weeks analysing his data before he announced joyously to everyone in the department that he had finally cracked it. And, in the middle of this euphoria, he kills himself and his box of precious medical records just happens to go missing?' Trine gazed sceptically at Søren.

'I lost my temper with your colleague yesterday,' she continued. 'He kept going on and on about Storm's state of mind. Did he seem depressed at having been accused of scientific dishonesty? Was he prone to depression? Had something upset him recently? No, no, and again no. I kept bringing up the box and drawing parallels with the Belem project, I kept mentioning the professional heavy fire Storm was under. Only that Tejsner guy wouldn't listen. I'm telling you, not in your capacity as a police officer but as Anna's boyfriend, someone silenced Storm. His death had nothing to do with feeling low or ashamed at being accused of dishonesty. It's *much* bigger.' Trine closed her eyes briefly, then opened them. 'I just know it.' She put a hand on her heart. 'Now that's not very scientific, but Storm always said that a hunch was enough.'

'Now about that box . . .' Søren said. 'What was it made from?'

'Cheap, rough cardboard. It was quite battered and someone had scribbled on it with a ballpoint pen. It was about this big.'

Trine demonstrated with her hands. 'Do you know those IKEA archive boxes you assemble yourself? Roughly that size and the same kind of cardboard. And it was full of medical records.'

'What exactly did the medical records look like?'

'They're yellow notebooks,' she replied. 'About the size of a comic and the same format. The data is entered in pencil.'

Søren remembered Niels Sonne's email. Suddenly he had a very good idea of the location of the box and its contents.

Lily peeped into the kitchen where they were sitting. 'What are you doing?' she asked.

Søren got up and thanked Trine. They exchanged mobile numbers and Søren told her she was welcome to call at any time.

'Thank you for listening,' she said.

When Lily and Søren walked down the stairs, he heard Trine put the security chain back on.

Søren and Lily had lunch at a café in H.C. Ørsteds Vej, where Anna and Søren had had several dates two years earlier. Søren's mind was distracted while he removed first the onions, then the cucumber and finally the tomato from Lily's burger.

'I don't like the lettuce, either,' Lily said.

'So what you're saying is you just want the bun and the burger?'

'And the chips.'

'Hmm,' Søren grunted. The thoughts were buzzing around his head. It troubled him that— 'What was that, sweetheart?' Lily had said something, but Søren had been miles away.

'Uncle Henrik called and said that if you don't get back to him he'll come round and box your ears.'

Søren blinked. 'He said that?'

'Yes,' Lily said, and made loud gurgling noises with her straw.

'Lily, it's probably best if you don't answer my phone if it happens to ring while you're playing a game on it, OK?'

'OK,' Lily said. 'Where are we going now?'

'We're going to say hi to Linda,' Søren said.

When Søren and Lily arrived at the Violent Crimes Unit, Søren's secretary, Linda, leaped up from behind her desk and hugged Søren long and hard, as if he had been away on a sabbatical.

'Hi, Linda,' he said, hugging her back. 'Did you really miss me that much?'

'You're not serious about quitting, are you?' she said.

Søren shrugged. 'A desk job is not for me. Besides, my timing appears to be spot on. Anna is busy and Lily is a bit under the weather so I'm looking after her. We'll just have to wait and see.' He shrugged again.

'I really hope you decide to come back. Jørgensen seems really stressed and Henrik is fast losing the plot. His briefing this morning was one of the worst I've ever seen. By the way, is it true that we've hired Anna as a researcher?'

'Yes, she's writing a profile of . . . Kristian Storm.'

'The professor who hanged himself?'

Søren nodded and sneaked a glance at Linda's computer. 'Never mind about that, how are you?'

Linda replied that she was well and started to tell him about her elder daughter, who was finally pregnant after several IVF attempts. 'I'm going to be a granny.' She beamed.

'Congratulations,' Søren said, trying discreetly to work out if Linda was logged onto the intranet, but it was difficult to tell from where he was standing. The telephone rang and she answered it. Søren bent down and whispered to Lily, 'When Linda's finished talking on the phone, ask her if you can have a fizzy drink.'

'Can I?'

'You have to ask Linda,' he whispered, and winked at her, 'but I bet she'll let you.'

When Linda hung up, Lily said, 'Søren told me to ask you if I can have a fizzy drink.' Søren muttered curses under his breath, but all Linda said was, 'Oh, did he? I'm sure that's allowed.' She ushered Lily down the corridor towards the vending machine in the meeting room.

Søren sat down in front of Linda's computer and went on to the intranet where he quickly logged onto Polsas, the police case file system, and found a folder named *Kristian Storm*. It contained numerous documents so Søren selected the whole lot and hit *print*. He had just logged out of Polsas and stood up when he heard Lily's chatter as she and Linda returned.

When Lily had finished her drink, they went to Jørgensen's office to say hello and on the way Søren nipped into the printer room. The preliminary report and other documents on Kristian Storm lay warm and fresh in the printer tray; Søren rolled them up and stuck them in his inside pocket. Jørgensen turned out not to be in his office and somehow Søren was relieved. Jørgensen's secretary told him he was in a meeting and added, 'Have you really resigned? Aren't you going to come back?'

'Maybe,' Søren said. 'Say hi to Jørgensen and tell him I'm open to offers. Very attractive offers.'

'Where are we going now?' Lily said, when they were back in the car outside the police station. 'Please can we go home soon? I want to watch a movie.'

Søren looked guiltily at her. 'We have just one more person to visit and he can be bit difficult, so it's best if you wait in the car. But you can play a game on my mobile as long as you promise me you won't answer if it rings. Afterwards, we'll go home and watch a movie, OK?'

'Okaaaaay,' Lily said reluctantly.

Bøje Knudsen, the medical examiner, was eating his packed lunch when Søren arrived at the Institute of Forensic Medicine, which was located right next to Rigshospitalet. He sat with his feet on his desk as he munched what looked like a cheese sandwich. His uncombed hair stood out on all sides and he had day-old stubble – Søren had never seen him so unkempt. He had left Lily in the car with his mobile and, even though he had impressed on her that she must stay put, he was keen to get his visit over and done with before she made trouble.

The door to the dissection room was closed, but the stench of formaldehyde permeated everything, including the smell of cheese.

'Bon appétit,' Søren said, and felt his lunchtime burger somersault.

'If you're here to stress me out, you can piss off,' Bøje said, and carried on eating, unperturbed. 'This is the first time I've sat down today. I turned up for work at five o'clock this morning and my feet haven't touched the ground for the last four days due to the Kødbyen rapes. Bernt from Station City is heading the investigation and he's already called me three times today to moan – I'm sure he would have called me a fourth and fifth time if I hadn't told him exactly where he could stick his phone. It takes as long as it takes and that has to be fast enough. Even for the justice secretary.'

'I'm not here to stress you out,' Søren said. He wondered if Bøje knew that he had quit his job. Not long after Søren had been promoted to deputy chief superintendent, Bøje had called him to complain about Henrik.

'He has no manners,' Bøje had said at the time. 'He threw up in a dustbin twice the last time he was here. Stomach like a girl's. I preferred you.'

'I'm here because of that professor from the Institute of Biology,' Søren said. 'Are you carrying out an autopsy on him? Are you anywhere near finalising your report? And what's the state of the case?'

Bøje folded his arms across his chest and glared at Søren. 'You're right. I haven't finalised the case or written my report, but try asking me why I haven't done it, apart from the simple reason that I'm rushed off my feet with the double murders in Kødbyen.'

'Double murders?'

'Yes, another rape victim in intensive care died from her injuries last night, but don't try changing the subject. Ask me why I haven't closed the case.'

'Why haven't you closed the case?' Søren said obediently.

'Because the noose is missing.'

'The noose?'

'Yes – would you believe it? The body arrived at the morgue on Thursday morning and just after lunch I was pretty much set to close the case when I discovered that the noose, which the dead man supposedly used to kill himself, was missing. I called Bellahøj straight away, of course, and finally tracked down that moron of a new CSO, Lars Hviid, who confirmed that he had removed the noose from the neck of the deceased and put it in the evidence box along with other items bagged at the scene. Why would he even think of doing something so utterly stupid? And what exactly happened to the evidence box afterwards? He didn't know because he had been dispatched to a case on Østerbro. After I had bitten off Lars Hviid's head at the fifth vertebra, I called Tejsner to do the same to him, and do you know what he said? That anyone could see the guy had killed himself. Just take a moment to digest that one. I told Tejsner to get me that noose at once, even if it meant him crocheting a new one and hanging himself in it and – wouldn't you know it? – he sends over Mehmet, that mummy's boy, who turned up an hour ago to deliver it. One hour ago. He was very sorry, but the noose had been temporarily misplaced in the evidence room, he said. Just take a further moment to reflect on that.' Bøje gestured with the last bite of his cheese sandwich towards an evidence bag on the table with a woven red object. Then he turned to Søren. 'So you have that bunch of total amateurs you call your colleagues to thank for any delay in this case. And do you know what else I've heard? Rumour has it that Tejsner stomped all over the crime scene without protective clothing. But that's just too far-fetched even for me to believe it. Danish police simply haven't stooped that low yet.'

Søren cleared his throat. 'At the risk of losing my own head, when do you think you'll sign off this case?' he ventured.

'I thought you said you hadn't come here to stress me out. I'll get to it as soon as I can, depending on how busy that psycho in Kødbyen plans on being. Everybody has the right to opt out of life, but no one deserves to be attacked, raped and have their groin molested by a madman with a blunt knife, so, if you don't mind, I'll take the liberty of prioritising.'

'Yes, of course,' Søren said amicably.

'But apart from that, I happen to agree with Tejsner, to my intense irritation.' Bøje grunted. 'It really does look like suicide. And when something looks like a duck and quacks like a duck, it's usually a duck, isn't it, young Søren?'

'But you're still not a hundred per cent sure?' Søren persisted.

'No, and I never will be, not even if I do an autopsy. Only an idiot is ever a hundred per cent sure.'

'So, strictly speaking,' Søren persevered, 'we're still talking about a possible suicide, but not a confirmed one? I'm being pedantic purely because suicide was very far from the deceased's mind. And several of his close colleagues deny suicide is even an option. I'm just telling you.'

'If you insist on being pedantic, then, yes, it would be correct to call it a possible suicide. It's certainly not confirmed yet.'

'Do you have any idea how Superintendent Tejsner reached that conclusion, that it was suicide, and officially closed the investigation?'

'You bet I do,' Bøje fumed. 'It's because Tejsner is a bloody anarchist with only one agenda, and that's his own. You're his superior, Søren. You must cut him down to size. I haven't said anything to Jørgensen on this occasion, but the next time

Tejsner steps out of line like this, I'll report him. Anyway, I'd better not take it out on you. And, as for your observation that Storm's colleagues refuse to accept it was suicide, it's my experience that it's often very hard for people to come to terms with such things. The realisation that someone so close to you felt that bad and you didn't know it is never easy.'

'Thank you,' Søren said. 'And please would you do me a favour and call me when you have your conclusion?'

'I can email you the report. I'm too busy to natter on the phone. I'll deal with everything on email after midnight,' Bøje said.

'Fine. I'll probably be working from home for the rest of the week because my daughter is ill.' Søren scribbled down his private email address on a piece of paper and gave it to Bøje.

'Your daughter? I didn't know you had children.'

'No,' Søren said pensively. 'I can't tell you exactly when I became a dad, but I have a strong feeling that it's already happened.'

Once he was outside the Institute of Forensic Medicine, Søren called Anna and she picked up immediately. 'Do you have twenty minutes?'

'Twenty?'

'Yes.'

'Eh, yes.'

'Good, then I'll stop by with Lily in two minutes and pick her up again in twenty-two. I have an errand in your building.'

'An errand?'

'I need to ask the caretaker a question.'

'About what?'

'Anna, I promise to tell you tonight, OK? But Lily is tired and I want to get her home, only I just have to do this one last thing, so if you could tear yourself away for twenty minutes . . .'

'Of course,' she said, and Søren had almost hung up when she added, 'I love it when you knit backwards. Because that's what you're doing, isn't it?'

'Might be,' Søren replied.

Anna was already waiting in the car park by the entrance to Stairwell One when Søren and Lily arrived.

'Mum!' Lily cried, as soon as she spotted Anna, and jumped into her arms the moment Søren had unlocked her seatbelt.

'Let's go and browse in the museum shop,' Anna said. She seemed happy.

'OK, I'll meet you there.' He kissed her.

'Another,' she said, pulling him close.

Søren kissed her again.

Luckily the caretaker was in his office, which was to the right of the main entrance to the Institute of Biology. He had the radio on and was tinkering with something under a bright light. He was around sixty and looked old fashioned in his dungarees and flat cap. 'Now what was wrong with the old wooden pointers?' he wondered out loud, as Søren stuck his head round the door. 'This electronic rubbish keeps breaking and you can't whack the students with a laser.' The caretaker chuckled. Søren shook his hand.

'My name is Søren Marhauge and I'm with the police.'

'And you're Anna Bella's young chap,' the caretaker stated.

'How do you know that?' he asked, surprised.

The caretaker grinned again and pointed to two shelving units stacked to the rafters with odds and ends; in the gap between them Søren noticed a peephole-sized window where the caretaker had just witnessed them kissing.

'Aha,' Søren said.

'How can I help you?'

'I'm investigating a few details in connection with Kristian Storm's suicide – I'm sure you'll have heard about it.'

'Yes, of course. It's tragic. Storm was a nice man. I spoke to him almost every morning when he turned up for work. Many of the older professors around here can be a bit stand-offish, you know. They never say hello or anything like that. But Storm would always stop, and he even came in here for a cup of coffee once or twice . . . I was very sad when I learned what had happened. So what exactly are you investigating?' The caretaker peered at Søren.

'A hunch or two,' Søren replied.

'Proper police answer.' He chortled. 'But I'll do my best to help you.'

'Upstairs in the Department of Immunology they have a printer room with a shredder. What happens to all the shredded paper?' Søren asked.

'It ends up in a sack, which the cleaners remove every day.'

'Isn't it recycled? It's only paper.'

'Oh, yes, of course. The sacks end up in a recycling container in the basement. We have separate containers for test tubes and petri dishes and one for metals. They're emptied once a fortnight.'

'When was the last collection?'

The caretaker leaned to one side and checked a wall calendar. 'The eleventh of March.'

'Do you think I might be allowed to take a look at that container?'

The caretaker picked up a bunch of keys.

There were three medium-sized recycling containers lined up in the basement under Building One. In addition to the door through which the caretaker and Søren entered, a broad ramp with a sliding gate led from the basement up to the car park in front of the Institute of Biology.

'The recycling lorry reverses down it,' the caretaker said, pointing to the ramp. 'But there's also a small side entrance, used by several staff members who park their bicycles down here.' The caretaker opened the swing lid to the paper container. It was half full, mostly with strips of paper, but also newspaper and cardboard.

'Right. I'll take a look around. I'll be back when I've finished.'

'I'd be happy to help,' the caretaker offered, and looked very keen, but Søren declined. A moment later he was alone in the basement.

Søren checked the paper strips by grabbing an armful and dropping them on the floor in front of him. The first twenty times he did it were fruitless. White photocopier paper with typed letters, the remains of formulas, exam papers. But when he was a third of his way through the pile, he found what he was looking for: a section of yellow paper strips, which seemed more woolly to the touch than standard white photocopier paper, and shortly afterwards a mass of rough strips. He took a generous handful of both the yellow and the coarse strips, smoothed them out on the floor under a fluorescent light and photographed the result with his mobile. He sent the two best pictures to Trine Rønn, with a message, asking, *Is this the paper from Storm's medical records/box?* and found a plastic bag on a shelving unit, which he stuffed to the brim with strips. Before he had finished, Trine had already replied: *Yes, definitely. I recognise both the material and Storm's handwriting.* Søren switched off the basement light, returned to the caretaker and asked him to look after the bag with the strips. Then he thanked him for his help and headed for the Museum of Natural History. While he walked, he rang Henrik's mobile, but got no reply, and then Bellahøj, where he got hold of Linda, who promised to dispatch an officer to the Institute of Biology to collect the plastic bag and add it to Kristian Storm's case file.

When Søren reached the Museum of Natural History, he spotted Anna and Lily immediately. Anna was in the process of paying for a toy python and Lily looked enormously pleased with herself. When Anna saw him, she gave a guilty shrug and placed two hundred kroner on the counter.

Shortly afterwards, Lily and Søren drove home to Humlebæk. Every time Søren made a right turn, he found himself staring right into the face of the squishy python, which Lily had draped over the passenger seat. 'Otherwise it can't see out of the window,' she insisted.

CHAPTER 6

Marie grieved more for Storm than she did for her mother, and for the first few days, that made her feel deeply ashamed. But then she realised what she was really mourning. Two completely different movements had come to a standstill. Joan's confused, morose, downward spiral towards the darkness, her fading voice and her diffuse gaze versus Storm's unstoppable leaps towards discovery and his animated hands, which drew the horizon upwards, like a swarm of butterflies.

Anton had wept when Marie told him that Granny had died, and Marie comforted him as best she could.

'So is Granny better now?' he sobbed and, touched, Marie nodded.

Even Anton could see it. Joan had not been well and she was better now.

Storm was another story. He had had no reason to want to leave this world.

Marie called Merethe Hermansen at the Department of Immunology to apologise for slamming the door in her face, but she was not at her desk. Instead, she got Thor Albert Larsen and they spoke briefly. Thor said he could understand why Marie refused to accept that Storm had killed himself. Storm didn't seem like someone who would want to take his own life, but the accusations were a great blow to a scientist, especially if there could be some truth in them. Marie asked him what he was insinuating.

'The results from your animal studies were remarkably good and came at a very convenient time, Marie,' Thor said.

'It's called statistical significance,' she said. 'Besides, they were *my* results, not Storm's.'

'All I'm saying is that those numbers were very good,' he repeated. 'Never mind, the case is now officially closed, Marie, and the police concluded it was suicide.'

'Is that so?' Marie said. 'Only I received an email from a deputy chief superintendent at Bellahøj today who asked me to let him know if I'd noticed anything unusual.'

'If you're talking about Deputy Chief Superintendent Søren Marhauge, then I wouldn't worry about him. He stopped by to see me yesterday and emphasised that the police regard the matter as closed.'

Marie was about to protest, but Thor cut her off. 'I, too, am very shocked, Marie. We all are. And I wish that Storm had asked for help rather than checking out early like this, but don't forget that I've been in this business for a few more years than you have, and I know how science works. It's hard enough for a scientist to admit that he was wrong, even though that's completely legitimate in any scientific endeavour. It must be even harder to acknowledge that you accidentally manipulated—'

Marie hung up.

She lay down on the sofa and stared up at the ceiling.

Why had she ever veered from her first impression?
Thor Albert Larsen really was a prat.

Julie turned up at Ingeborgvej with books on how to handle
suicide. *It Affects the Whole Family* was the title of one; another
was called *How to Cope When a Grandparent Chooses Death*.
She perched on the edge of the sofa and carefully stroked
Marie's arm.

'I've heard,' she said. 'I can't believe it.'

Marie knew that Julie must be referring to Storm's death
because Jesper had pleaded with her not to tell anyone yet
that they were getting a divorce and Marie had agreed.

'Not until after Joan's been buried,' Jesper had said. 'Not
until we know if Frank gets a suspended sentence or whether
he'll have to serve time. We'll just hold off for a few weeks.
Also for Anton's sake, so that not everything comes tumbling
down at once. Our marriage has been on the rocks for a long
time. I'm sorry that I'm no better than the statistics, but
there's a reason why eighty per cent of all couples break up
when one gets cancer. It's tough and people change. We've
both changed. But now we have to think about Anton,' he had
babbled. Marie was sorely tempted to tell Julie everything,
but instead she turned, exhausted, to the wall, away from her
sister's affection.

'We need to concentrate on our family now,' Julie whispered. 'On the children. On Dad . . . and making you better,
right? Get some peace and quiet.' Julie was now stroking
Marie's neck and shoulder, and Marie was eventually forced
to stand up to get away from her touch.

'I went into Dad's office before Mum died.' Marie made

quotation marks in the air. 'His so-called office. No one had sat at that desk for months. Brown envelopes were piling up. What did they live on? Was he even working? I know he drinks more than he should, Julie. More than a few glasses a day, a lot more. You can deny it as much as you like. And Mum, how did she end up in that awful state? So awful that she took her own life. What have we been sleepwalking into?'

Julie's eyes welled up. 'What are you accusing me of?'

'I'm not accusing you of anything. I'm asking why we've been in denial all these years. Losing Mads was terrible for Mum and Dad, and for you, of course. I look at Anton and try to imagine how you can ever get over the loss of a child. But it's twenty-four years ago, and I have the impression that Mum never got back on her feet. And now she's dead. There's nothing more we can do. It's over.'

Julie burst into tears. 'We all knew that Mum had been in a bad way for a long time,' she sobbed. 'She had a delicate mind, just like her own mother. And we all fitted around it. But no one could possibly have foreseen that your illness would hit her quite so hard. That it would reopen so many old wounds. I tried to help as much as I could . . . but I have a family of my own, Marie, and . . . Camilla has just started her periods. She's only twelve! I couldn't possibly look after Mum all the time. I had to look after you as well.'

Marie pressed the palms of her hands into her eye sockets. She would never understand Julie. Their mother had overdosed on her medication, accidentally or on purpose, the result was the same, and their father would appear to have a serious alcohol problem and was now facing a possible prison sentence for drink-driving. Jesper was definitely having an affair and she herself had only one breast. And what did Julie do? She gritted her teeth, made packed lunches for everyone and labelled them with the days of the week.

'I wish we'd talked about it sooner,' Marie said. 'Perhaps I could have done something for Mum. Or Lea. Perhaps we could have done something together. I'm aware that Mum was feeling rotten, but she did have her good days, and she enjoyed her grandchildren and her art books, old Danish movies . . . and she had Dad. They were going to get a new dog! I don't understand how it could have got so far.' Now Marie's eyes welled up as well.

'It's my fault.' Julie continued to weep. 'I shouldn't have gone to that thing at Camilla's school. I should have counted out Mum's pills as I always do every Monday.'

'Stop it, Julie!' Marie hadn't intended to shout.

Julie stared at her, horrified. Then her face froze and she retreated into herself. Marie had seen that expression plenty of times when Frank criticised her or Michael bossed her about, but Marie had never triggered it. She sat down next to Julie and put an arm around her.

'I know you've put yourself out to support us all,' she said, to appease her. 'I'm all over the place. I have cancer. Mum is dead. Storm is dead and my career is in ruins.' And I'm also getting a divorce, she thought, and continued aloud, 'I knew that Mum wasn't always feeling too good, I just didn't know she'd deteriorated so rapidly since I fell ill. And as for Dad . . . He's always so quick to judge others. Keep your nose clean and work hard. And then he goes out and pulls a stunt like that—'

'Marie, why don't we visit Dad this Sunday?' Julie interrupted her. 'I've already spoken to Jesper about it. Cook lunch and perhaps play a game of Bezzerwizzer with the children, like we used to. Show them that life goes on. Show Dad that we're there for him, even though he's done something stupid. Besides, Dad would like us to go through Mum's clothing and things. I think he'd like us to clear it out as quickly as we can. I don't think he can bear to look at it. All those years in that house. Perhaps he should sell it.'

'I've been trying to get them to sell that house for years,' Marie said wearily.

'You have?' Julie sounded surprised.

'But Sunday's fine. Let's get it over and done with.'

'I don't want Lea there,' Julie added firmly. 'I can't cope with any more problems right now.'

'OK,' Marie said, and gave her sister a hug.

When Marie, Anton and Jesper arrived at Snerlevej 19 that Sunday evening, Julie, wearing an apron and followed by the scent of meat browning in butter, opened the door to them.

'I've been here since two o'clock,' she said, and blew up into her damp fringe. Michael and Frank were in the living room, and Marie could hear Emma and Camilla in the garden. The house had been vacuumed, the furniture rearranged, candles lit, and Joan's armchair was gone. Frank was wearing a clean shirt and was freshly shaven. He had a strong beer in his hand. The other adults also had beer. Marie asked him how he was and he shrugged.

Then Julie brought in some snacks. 'Dad's lawyer says he'll try for a suspended sentence and that, no matter what happens, Dad will get no more than three months,' she said, as she circulated the plate. 'He'll argue that Dad was mentally unbalanced at the time and that our family is going through a tough time because you're terminally ill with cancer – that's just something we're saying, obviously,' she added.

Jesper asked Frank about some legal details and was of the opinion that it would work out. 'Do you think so?' Frank said, sounding relieved. He intended to put the house on the market, he said, and make a fresh start.

'Dad, how long did you know that Mum was feeling so low she might take her own life?' Marie asked. 'Why on earth didn't you say something to me or Jesper? We might have been able to help.'

Frank slumped on the sofa. 'Marie, you know she's been in a bad way for years,' he said. 'I've just learned to live with it.' He looked tentatively at Jesper. 'And Jesper has helped. With pills and everything.'

'I thought Julie was in charge of Mum's pills.'

'I was,' Julie said. 'Every Monday. We put the pills in her pill organiser so all she had to do was empty one compartment every day. What Dad meant was that Jesper has helped with her prescriptions a couple of times.'

'How was I to know,' Frank said quietly, 'that she would even think of . . .? We had gone out to choose a new dog. A Jack Russell puppy. I'd even paid for it!' He buried his face in his hands.

'It's not your fault, Dad,' Marie said.

'Yes, it is,' Frank mumbled.

Julie disappeared into the kitchen and Marie got up and followed her.

Her sister was standing by the kitchen window. A wonderful

aroma was coming from the oven, of roast meat and sweet potatoes, thyme and love.

'Julie, sweetheart,' Marie said, and hugged her sister from behind.

'You don't have to comfort me . . .' she began, but then she burst into tears and leaned miserably against Marie.

'I can help out even though I'm ill,' Marie said, rocking her gently. 'Julie, I've been thinking about something recently. We never speak of it, but it must have been very hard for you when Mads died.'

'Yes, but it was also hard for . . .' Julie sobbed violently. 'I was only ten.'

'Weren't you offered any help?'

Julie shook her head. 'Not really. Tove, the woman who looked after you until you started school, she was nice. When I came to pick you up, she would sit me down on a chair in her kitchen and give me milk and biscuits, and when you wanted to have some, she would say, "Hands off! They're for Julie, they're just for Julie!"' She smiled at the memory. 'Though I really wanted to share them. I wanted to do everything for my family, especially you, Marie. You kept asking me where Mads was. You looked for him for months and pretended to play with him every day. While I ate Tove's biscuits, she would chat to me about all sorts of things. Who was my Eurovision Song Contest favourite? Could I solve a Rubik's Cube without cheating? She treated me as the child I still was.'

'But what about here at home?'

'Oh, you couldn't rely on Mum. One minute she was fine, the next she couldn't stand up. She was also terrified that something would happen to you or Lea or Dad, so at first she wouldn't allow anyone to look after you. What if a saucepan fell on top of you? What if you ran out into the road and got hit by a car? But eventually she agreed that Tove could be your childminder and that really helped.'

'But what about you?'

'I did the shopping, the cooking, made the packed lunches. Organised PE kits, did the laundry and so on. Somebody had to do it. Dad often came home late. Mum was always in the house, but you never knew what state she'd be in. Was she having a good day or a bad one?' Julie blew her nose.

'Julie, I don't know what I would have done without you. I only know that everything would have been much worse if Lea and I hadn't had you. But you also have to take care of yourself. Michael—'

'You've always needed me,' Julie said. 'You would jump for joy when I let you sleep in my bed, but Lea was completely different. Marie, I did a terrible thing.' Julie started to cry again. 'Lea grew much too fond of Tove. She used to cling to Tove and refuse to come home with me. And when we did get home, she wouldn't say hi to Mum. She started calling Mum and Dad, Joan and Frank, even though she was only three. Mum would cry and say that she had lost Lea too. So even though I really liked Tove, I told Dad I thought she had hit Lea and that she shouldn't look after her any more. I had shaken Lea the day before because she had knocked over a bowl of fruit compôte I'd just made. I showed Dad the bruises. Dad freaked out. He marched straight to Tove's house, screaming and shouting. So Lea started going to nursery instead and Dad told Lea not to visit Tove any more. Lea used to make a huge scene every time we passed Tove's house. That's why Lea hates me. I'm sure of it. She can't remember, but deep down she knows that I took Tove from her. You were always easier.'

'Julie, Lea doesn't hate you. Besides, you were just a child!'

Julie stared at her with wide eyes. 'Yes, but I did it on purpose. I wanted us to be normal, like we used to be. With a mum and a dad. Two lovely twins, a cute baby and their big girl of whom they were so proud. But then it all fell apart. And now everything is in pieces again. You only have one breast, Mum is dead, Dad is a criminal and I've grown so fat that people stare at me. I've become someone other people stare at! Can't you see it? I just want us to be a normal family.'

'Well, you shouldn't have married Michael,' Marie said drily. Julie looked startled. Then they both burst out laughing.

'How could you even think of sending Michael to Lea's?' Marie grinned.

'God knows! Perhaps I was scared that Lea would freak out and that I wouldn't be able to console her. Lea didn't want Mum when she was little, but in recent years she and Mum were close ... But you already know that. Or maybe not close, only as close as it was possible to get to Mum. Still they shared ... something. I do realise sending Michael was a mistake. I must apologise to Lea. Michael isn't very tactful. But he is my husband ... And I love him.'

'Why?' Marie asked.

'Oh, Marie. It is what it is. I'm fat. I should be grateful that anyone wants me.'

'Number one, you're not fat – besides, you could do something about that. Number two, Michael isn't exactly skinny.'

'He's the children's father, Marie,' Julie said. 'And not all women are as lucky as you when it comes to men.'

'Oh, I wouldn't say that,' Marie burst out.

'What's that supposed to mean?'

Marie was about to tell Julie that Jesper wanted a divorce when the children came running in from the garden. Anton's cheeks were fiery red as he asked for a glass of water. Then the timer pinged and the roast was ready.

There was a strange atmosphere while they ate. Joan had never said very much, yet her absence was remarkably noisy. After dinner Emma asked if they could play Bezzerwizzer and a sigh of relief rippled through the room. Joan had never joined in their games: she had preferred to lie on the sofa. Frank had drunk most of a bottle of red wine over dinner and warned the children, 'I'm going to thrash you lot, I am!'

While Marie and Julie cleared the table, Marie remembered the wall-hanging she had found upstairs. 'By the way,' she said to Julie, while they were loading the dishwasher, 'a few weeks ago I found one of Mum's wall-hangings in the loft. It's gloomy, but I like it. I want to take it home, if that's OK with you and Lea, and Dad, of course. I don't want any of Mum's things, just that wall-hanging.'

Julie looked quizzically at her sister. 'A wall-hanging? I wouldn't know anything about that. I'm fairly sure that the few major works Mum did manage to make were sold years ago. After that she only wove those pieces for the children. Do you still have Anton's?'

'Yes, of course,' Marie said. 'Don't you have Camilla's and Emma's?'

Julie shook her head. 'They didn't really match our style. It was nice of Mum to make them, but it's not our thing at all.'

'The wall-hanging I found was incredible. It's huge: two metres square and a really impressive piece of craftsmanship. It depicts a screaming woman. She has snakes in her hair.'

'That doesn't sound very attractive.'

'No, it isn't, but it is fascinating. Mostly because it says something about Mum that I . . . didn't know. That she was once a real artist.'

'What were you even doing in the loft?' Julie wanted to know. 'You know very well we're not allowed up there.'

Marie had to laugh. 'Julie, we're adults now. You don't think that Dad's rules apply after all these years, do you? Besides, there's some seriously cool stuff up there. Furniture and lamps. I was going to ask Dad if I can have some of it now that I'm going to be living on my own.'

'Live on your own? What are you talking about?' Julie sounded horrified.

'Jesper wants a divorce,' Marie said. 'He thinks my illness has wrecked our relationship.'

Julie dropped a serving dish on top of the plates she had already stacked in the dishwasher.

'The strange thing is that I'm not even particularly upset. Do you think I'm in shock?'

'But you can't live on your own,' Julie whispered.

'It looks like I might have to, Julie.'

Julie leaned over the kitchen table. 'Everything is falling apart,' was all she said.

When Marie had finished in the kitchen, she went into the living room where Frank and the children had laid out the board game. A big bowl of colourful sweets stood on the table.

'Ten pieces only, Anton,' Marie said, and fetched a small plate from the sideboard on which Anton carefully placed ten sweets.

'I want to be on Dad's team,' Camilla called.

'Good, then you're with your mum, Emma, and Marie and Anton can be together, and then . . . Where did Julie and Jesper go?' Frank looked at Marie.

'I think Julie popped to the loo and I don't know where Jesper is. But I guess they'll be back soon,' she said. 'Hey, Dad. Did you notice that I left one of Mum's old wall-hangings on the floor in your office? I found it in the loft a few weeks ago and I think it had been there for years. Would you mind if I take it home with me today, seeing as we've got the car?'

Frank looked blankly at her. 'A wall-hanging? No, I didn't see it. But take whatever you like. There's nothing but junk in the loft.' Frank refilled his glass to the brim. 'Right, kids, how about a trial game?' he said to the children. 'While we wait for those slowcoaches, also known as your parents.'

The children would like that.

Marie went up to the first floor and into Frank's office. The box with the wall-hanging was nowhere to be seen and the loft ladder was also missing. When Marie stood underneath the hatch, she could see that the padlock was back in place. She wondered if Frank's memory was going. Who else could have moved that wall-hanging? Suddenly she spotted Jesper and Julie through the window overlooking the street and quickly she retreated to the side. They were some distance down the road, outside the carport, and Marie could see that Julie was both upset and freezing cold. Marie carefully opened the window so that she could hear what they were saying.

'Yes, but you promised to wait, Jesper,' Julie said in a thick voice. 'You promised. For Anton's sake.'

'So you keep reminding me.' Jesper sounded irritated.

'And that was before this business with Mum and Dad! How could you even think of telling her *now*?'

'How many times do I have to say that waiting doesn't make it any easier, Julie? And has it crossed your mind that Marie might not die?' she heard Jesper reply. 'Have you thought about that? This has been going on since last autumn. I can't wait for ever. I need to think about Emily as well.'

'Do you know something?' Julie hissed. 'If there's one thing you can't expect me to do, it's worry about how your mistress is feeling. I couldn't give a damn if that bitch falls under a bus. This is about protecting Marie and Anton. And that was part of our deal. I keep my mouth shut and let Dad think you're the perfect son-in-law, and you don't move in with your whore until Marie is dead.'

Marie was in shock. She had never heard her sister use language like that before.

Jesper said something Marie couldn't hear and Julie blew her nose.

'Let's go back inside,' Julie said. 'We promised the children we'd play a board game with them.' Marie heard their footsteps come closer and then the front door was opened. Her heart was pounding.

When Marie came down to the living room, Jesper was already sitting at the table and flashed her a smile. Shortly afterwards, Julie emerged from the bathroom and Marie could see that she had tidied herself up.

'Can I start, Grandad?' Camilla asked.

'Anton starts. He's the youngest.'

Anton picked up the dice.

Jesper had another woman and Julie had known for a long time. And yet she had chided Marie for even thinking such a thing.

Julie had also known that they were getting a divorce.

For how long?

And why had she kept quiet?

Did she think she was protecting Anton? Julie could not be serious. Marie had sought advice from cancer charities and they recommended openness and honesty. Of course Anton was affected by his mother's illness. But, all things considered, he was doing fine.

Then the penny dropped: neither Julie nor Jesper had expected Marie to survive. Jesper might be telling himself that Marie was getting better so that he could justify his divorce rather than wait until she kicked the bucket. But Julie clearly believed that Marie was going to die. Marie felt like she had been punched in the stomach. Julie had always been her loyal helper: she had picked her up and carried her across burning hot sand when they were children and Marie was trapped on her beach towel wanting to go into the water; she had covered for her when Marie had overslept on the first day of a paper round, which Frank had told her she was too young to take on – she had only pulled it off because Julie had done half her deliveries. Julie had always believed in Marie. Until now. Marie could barely breathe, and when it was her turn to throw the dice, one fell on the carpet.

'Did you find that wall-hanging?' Frank asked and, for a moment, everyone's eyes were on Marie.

'No,' she said, and tightened her headscarf. 'It wasn't there.'

When they got home later that night, Jesper sought out Marie in the kitchen after he had carried Anton up to bed. He asked her if she would like a bottle of elderflower cordial and took one for himself from the fridge when she declined.

'Thank you for not saying anything today, Marie. I know it might sound feeble, but your family are important to me and I think it's better this way. Also for Anton's sake. Waiting, I mean.' Marie turned her back on him and replied through gritted teeth.

'I'm sorry, what did you say?' Jesper asked.

'I said I wish you wouldn't use Anton as an excuse to promote your own agenda. You're a grown man. Make your choices and stand by them. I heard you and Julie talking in the street earlier tonight. Several weeks ago, I told her that I thought you'd met someone. Your late-night phone calls, your sudden brotherly understanding for why we don't have sex. And do you know something? Julie managed to convince me that I must be mistaken. Imagine how guilty I felt for even suspecting you, the best husband and father in the world, of cheating on me. Who is she?' Marie turned to face him.

'Someone from work,' he said, flustered. 'Her name is Emily.'

'A nurse? Oh, no, I forgot – you prefer well-educated women.

Women without breast cancer so they're not too weak and feeble to wash your socks.'

Jesper flinched. 'Emily is an anaesthetist, and I don't think you're being fair,' he said. 'You have to admit that you've changed a lot recently. This past year. Since you started your master's. Believe me, I have tried. Only it didn't make any difference. And then I met Emily, and you can't control feelings like that and—'

'And then you tell Julie that you *have* met someone, but you give *me* some cock-and-bull story about how my cancer's worn us both down and blah blah blah.'

'Julie came to speak to me some time ago. She pretended she'd seen me with another woman. So I admitted everything. That Emily and I are in love and want a life together.' Marie looked blankly at him. 'And Julie made me promise I wouldn't say anything until you—'

'Until I was dead? You agreed not to say anything until I was dead. To protect Anton? To protect me?'

'Yes,' Jesper said.

'Are you both out of your minds?' she said.

'Marie, we all thought you were going to die.' Jesper was suddenly gazing tenderly at her. 'Frank, your mother, Julie, all of us. We prepared for it. We thought about what would be best for Anton.'

'You all thought about what was best for you,' Marie said in a deadpan voice.

'That's not true,' Jesper said angrily.

'Did you also consider what was best for Anton the first time you went to bed with Emily?'

'We fell in love, Marie. We didn't mean to – it just happened.'

Marie nodded. 'I'm starting to understand why Anton has nightmares,' she said, mostly to herself.

'And why is that?' Jesper said.

'Because it's more than enough for a six-year-old to deal with his mother being seriously ill. Your hypocrisy turned out to be the final straw.'

'I don't think you're being fair,' Jesper said.

'I no longer care what you think,' Marie said in a low voice.

The next morning Jesper and Anton were already at the kitchen table when Marie got up.

'Good morning,' she said, in a loud, clear voice, as she moved the sugar bowl out of Anton's reach.

'Will Granny get sad if people are happy, even though she's dead?' Anton wanted to know.

'No,' Marie said firmly. 'Granny will be happy if we're happy. I'm sure of it. Besides, you can be happy and sad at the same time. I'm sad because Granny has died and I might be a bit sad about it for the rest of my life. But I'm also happy to be here because I'm not dead at all,' she threw a glance at Jesper, 'and here's my beautiful son eating sugar with cornflakes on top.' Marie kissed Anton's hair and started making a pot of tea.

Jesper glanced furtively at her and flicked through yesterday's paper.

'Have you made your packed lunches?' Marie asked, and when Jesper said no, she started looking for rye bread and cold cuts. Suddenly she became aware that Jesper was watching her and she turned to look at him. The newspaper was open on the table, but he wasn't reading it. Marie smiled briefly at him. Then he turned the page and Marie buttered some bread, but when she turned again to ask Anton where his lunchbox was, Jesper was still watching her.

'What?'

'You've put on weight,' Jesper said.

'Since yesterday?' Marie asked.

'No, Mum, that's not possible.' Anton grinned.

'I think it depends on how many sweets you eat when you visit Granny and Grandad's,' Marie said, and winked at him.

'I miss Granny,' Anton said, and started crying.

'So do I,' Marie said.

'Are they not going to get a new dog now?' Anton asked.

'I don't know, sweetheart.'

Jesper didn't say anything. Marie grabbed the property section and settled down at the table with her tea. Twenty minutes later, when Anton and Jesper were ready to go, Marie had circled several rental flats in red. Jesper looked at the paper and then at Marie, but she ignored him.

Three days later, Marie and Anton moved into a flat at Randersgade 76 in Østerbro. The owner had got a job in Greenland and was thrilled when Marie rang to say she would like to rent the flat immediately. There was only one bedroom: for Anton to have a room of his own, Marie would have to sleep in the living room, and they had to remember to rescue the lavatory paper before they took a shower because the bathroom was the size of a broom cupboard. Anton chose lime-coloured wallpaper with a car pattern for his room and

Marie bought a new bed, but apart from that . . . 'We have to get really good at saving money,' she explained to Anton.

'Won't I be living with Dad any more?' Anton asked, and Marie reassured him that of course he would. Sometimes.

'But Dad is no longer my boyfriend,' she added. 'Dad has a new girlfriend called Emily. Grown-ups can stop being boyfriend and girlfriend or get new girlfriends, but you can never stop being someone's mum or dad, so Dad and I will continue to be your parents.'

Anton mulled it over for a little while. 'Aren't you angry that Dad has another girlfriend?'

'Yes,' Marie said. 'But I don't want to be his girlfriend if he doesn't like me best of all.'

'But he has to like you best of all!' Anton said anxiously.

Marie thought about it for a moment and then she lifted Anton onto her lap. 'Dad says that I've changed because I've been ill. He liked the old me better. But do you know something?' Anton shook his head. 'I like the new me much better.'

'I like you better always,' Anton said, and gave his mother a hug.

Jesper had protested when Marie announced that she and Anton were moving out, but Marie could tell from his face that he was also relieved. Now he was a free man. Free to work, to explore his relationship with Emily and to see Anton whenever he could fit him in. He could even use Marie's illness as a valid reason as to why a marriage that everyone had thought was perfect had foundered after all.

'Voilà,' Marie said drily.

'I'm sorry, what?' Jesper said.

'Nothing,' Marie replied.

In addition to Anton's things, she took a bookcase, her desk, her books and her clothes, then called Frank and asked him to move their stuff to Østerbro.

'To Østerbro?' he said.

'Jesper has met someone,' Marie said, 'and Anton and I have rented a flat in Randersgade.'

'Why didn't you say anything last Sunday?' Frank asked.

'Because I didn't know at the time,' Marie said.

When Frank arrived in his van, he stormed inside the house looking for Jesper. 'Where is he? I'm going to bloody kill him.'

Marie set about making coffee while Frank searched every room in the big house. 'He's at work. Anton is at nursery. And there's no need for you to kill him, Dad. It's all right. He's the very least of our problems right now.'

Frank flopped into an armchair. 'Got any beer?' he asked.

The funerals of Joan and Storm were each the culmination of a very different life. Joan's service was held in Vangede Church, exactly one week after her death, and only close family attended. The vicar spoke about Joan, her love of dogs, her creativity and the trials God sent to test us. Mads was mentioned, and Marie thought the vicar was referring to her when he said that God's trials took many shapes. All Marie could think about while he spoke was that Joan was almost as invisible in death as she had been in life. Marie mourned that. When the service had ended and the hearse had left, Marie squeezed Anton's hand. When it was her time to die, she thought, be it in four months or fifty-four years, she hoped that Anton would feel, just for a brief moment, that something huge had been taken from him.

Frank stood with his hands stuffed into his pockets and Marie saw Lea put her arm around his shoulders. Julie clung to Michael's arm and cried her heart out. They ate sandwiches at Snerlevej 19. Frank drank heavily and refused to speak to Jesper, who looked relieved when he got a call at just after three o'clock and announced that he had to go to the hospital as he was on duty. When Jesper had left, Michael and Frank retreated to the garden shed with a couple of beers. Once Lea had gone, Marie and Julie stayed in the living room to talk. Julie had had a few glasses of wine and was becoming maudlin.

'Have you really forgiven me for not telling you about Jesper?' she asked, and hugged Marie tightly.

'Of course,' Marie said, and meant it, but pulled back a little because Julie's breath smelt strongly of alcohol.

Marie had rung her sister to confront her the day after she had overheard Jesper and Julie talk outside the house on Snerlevej. Julie had broken down completely and claimed that she was just looking after Marie. Trying to make it a bit easier for everyone and protect Anton. Not exposing Marie to stress, if she was going to . . . pass on soon. Marie had said that Julie should start taking care of herself instead. That she would manage and might not be dying in the immediate future anyway.

It had only made Julie sob even louder.

'But how will you manage for money?' Julie wanted to know. 'How will you survive? In a one-bedroom flat?'

'When my post-chemo treatment is finished, I'll return to the university, Julie. I have a PhD grant waiting for me at the Department of Immunology and it pays me an excellent salary. Enough for Anton and me to manage. Jesper will also help me financially. He promised me that when I threatened to write a letter to every single one of his colleagues at Rigshospitalet and tell them he had been unfaithful to his cancer-stricken wife and had now abandoned her in favour of a woman with two breasts.'

Julie stared at Marie in disbelief. 'Did you actually say that to him?'

'No, of course not!'

'Oh, I thought you might have,' Julie mumbled. 'It's like you've become . . . I don't know. I miss the old Marie . . . I miss Mum. I miss the days when everything was . . . normal.'

Yeah, right, Marie thought.

Storm was cremated on Friday, 26 March, the day after Joan's funeral, with a service at St Stefan's Church on Nørrebro, and more than a hundred mourners attended. Marie recognised the *pano* in earth colours that covered the coffin. Storm had had two *pano*s on his office wall and Marie knew that the finely woven rugs were a part of birth, wedding and funeral ceremonies in most of West Africa. She looked for the second *pano*, a scarlet one she had often admired in his office, but it was not there. Seven people spoke, one played the saxophone and suddenly the church doors were opened and a group of West African men came dancing all the way up to Storm's coffin while they played their *mbiras*.

When Thor Albert Larsen announced that there was a reception in Lecture Hall A at the Department of Immunology, Marie wondered whether she should go. She had a feeling that people were staring at her. She had considered wearing her wig, but feared that people who knew her might not recognise her if she did. She decided she would rather look ill; it wasn't as if people didn't already know. In the end she had tied the yellow scarf around her head.

Marie had a lump in her throat when she entered Lecture Hall A. It had been Storm's favourite auditorium and candles had been lit on every desk. People had been asked to send in their favourite photographs of Storm, and while the mourners chatted, grinned and shared anecdotes, photographs from Storm's life were projected on the wall behind the lectern. Thor tapped his glass and gave a brilliant eulogy about the proud, indefatigable scientist. At no point did he bring up the allegation of scientific dishonesty. Marie appreciated that and afterwards she complimented him on his speech, then congratulated him: she had heard that he had been made acting head of the department and she was convinced it was only a formality before the appointment became permanent. Halfway through their small talk, Thor suddenly said, 'Marie, I'm aware you still find it hard to accept Storm's exit, but don't you think that somehow we owe it to the old chap to respect his choice?'

'Yes, but . . .' Marie said.

'I honestly believe that he was totally ground down, Marie,' Thor ploughed on. 'He couldn't cope with any more challenges to his integrity. He wanted peace at last.'

'Peace?' Marie looked sceptically at Thor.

Thor nodded.

During Thor's speech about the proud scientist who had dedicated his life to his subject and never given up, Marie had started to have doubts. Perhaps she hadn't known Storm as well as she'd thought. Perhaps he had succumbed to the temptation to extrapolate his empirical data to fit his theory. Perhaps he had ultimately ended up carrying out strategic – far too strategic – research, despite his stated contempt for it. When she heard Thor's words, she regretted her doubts.

'But Storm loved challenges,' she said. 'The greater the scientific controversy, the happier he was. Had you forgotten?'

'Sometimes it's hard to believe that you're real scientists,' Thor snapped back.

'You?'

'You and Tim. I know that you both cared about Storm and that's all well and good. I was incredibly fond of him myself. But I'm starting to lose patience. You have a master's and a PhD respectively, and you ought to back the conclusion that is best supported by the evidence.'

'Tim who? Tim Salomon?'

'Yes. He came to Denmark last Thursday. He keeps pestering me because he thinks Storm's suicide makes no sense. And, as far as I could gather from the police, he also visited Bellahøj to express his doubts. I understand that you're upset, Marie; we all are. But stop being so naïve. It doesn't suit either of you. Tim, by the way, is sitting just over there.'

Thor pointed to the far end of the bottom row of the raked seating and Marie spotted a hunched figure in a suit, with a head of short, curly hair. Tim Salomon was sitting alone and staring at the pictures that continued to flash up on the wall above the lectern.

Marie went to join him, but it was some time before he turned to her, as if he had been completely lost in his own thoughts. He was tall, Marie could see, although he was sitting down, and his upper lip had a sharp edge that was also fragile.

It culminated in an easy smile at the corners of his mouth. Only his eyes were black.

'Hello,' Marie said in English. 'My name is Marie. I've heard a lot about you.'

Tim looked at her with delight and kissed her on both cheeks. '*Tudo bém*, Marie! I have heard a lot about you too. How are you?' Tim looked at her closely, first at her face, then at her scarf. 'Storm said that you were seriously ill. He was very sad about it.' Tears started trickling down Tim's cheeks and he made no attempt to hide them.

They talked for a long time. Anton was with Jesper and Marie had no plans so they ended up having dinner together. They walked the short distance to a Thai restaurant on Tagensvej that Marie knew. They were silent, but it wasn't an awkward silence. Tim was emotional all through dinner and Marie was fascinated by and in awe of his openness. He asked if she would like a glass of wine, but she declined and added that he was welcome to have one himself, of course.

'No,' he said. 'I don't drink alcohol.'

So they drank sparkling mineral water with lemon and continued to talk.

Tim had grown up in the capital, Bissau, the third of four children. Their father was a Kenyan missionary who had come to Bissau to convert the Guineans. A strict man who beat his eldest son, he would undoubtedly have gone on to beat Tim, had he not died unexpectedly. It was hard for Tim's mother to make ends meet after the death of her husband and one by one the children had to leave school to work in the cashew plantations. When it was Tim's turn, his teacher came to their house. 'Tim is too clever for the cashew plantations,' the teacher said to his mother.

'All my children are clever,' she replied, 'but we still have to eat.'

Shortly afterwards, Tim was awarded a full scholarship to Kingston University in London. The scholarship had been set up several years before and the teacher had recommended Tim, who was the first Guinean ever to receive it.

'Ébano, my big brother, was angry that our teacher had submitted my school papers rather than his,' Tim said, with a wry smile. 'Normally, you know, it's the duty of the eldest son to provide for the family and there's certainly nothing wrong with Ébano's head. Only he was never academically gifted. When we went to school, Ébano couldn't sit still for two minutes before he had to go out and chase the chickens.'

Five years later Tim returned to Guinea-Bissau with a master's in biology and fell into a void. 'An education is like a sack of grain that never runs out,' his teacher had said, but now his teacher was dead and Tim could not find a job.

Ébano, however, had taken it all in his stride. '"*Ka bali mom di branco.* Useless white hands. You're home! That's what matters. Now you're nothing but a proud black man in Bissau who has to work in the cashew plantations alongside his brothers,"' he said. But I couldn't share Ébano's joy. Of course I was glad to see my family again, but the thought of a life in the cashew plantations sent me into a deep depression.'

When Tim had hit rock bottom, he had met Storm. He was on his way to the plantation one morning when a girl he barely knew came running to him: she needed help with a royal python. It had moved into the wall in a house she was cleaning and she had been told that the house must be ready today because a Danish scientist was arriving. Tim agreed to help her and that afternoon he had just cemented up the hole in the wall when Storm dumped his suitcase on the floor behind him and said hello. Storm asked if Tim wanted a bottle of Maaza juice because Storm fancied one himself and wasn't it hot today? Tim and Storm started talking and Storm noticed his impeccable English.

'What a stroke of luck,' Storm had exclaimed joyfully, when Tim told him about his degree. 'I need an interpreter for the next eight weeks and it's a bonus that you also know scientific terminology. I will pay you twenty thousand CFA francs per week because you're an educated man. What do you say?'

'I said yes, of course,' Tim said, and his eyes welled again. 'When the eight weeks were up, Storm asked me if I would consider writing a PhD thesis. He was setting up the Belem Health Project and he needed local people. He helped me with my grant application and the day the funding came through was the most important of my life. At that point, Silas had come to Bissau to assist Storm, who wanted the rural areas between the Dulombi-Boe parks surveyed again, and Silas, Storm and I celebrated my grant in a restaurant by the seafront.' The tears rolled down Tim's cheeks and Marie put her hand on top of his. She jumped when he immediately grabbed her wrist and held it tight.

'My brain still refuses to accept that he took his own life,' he said quietly. 'It makes no sense.'

'No, it makes no sense,' Marie echoed.

'I came to Copenhagen last Thursday,' Tim continued, 'and I went straight to the police. They were courteous and professional, but they insisted it was suicide. Afterwards, I visited Thor Albert Larsen at the Department of Immunology. I have met him before and I usually like him, but not that day. He kept saying that Storm's behaviour in the days leading up to his death was unstable and paranoid. I asked him what else he had expected. Storm had just discovered an error in his dataset, which had prevented him saving thousands of children's lives in Guinea-Bissau for two years. Storm was also trying to figure out who could be so callous as to put a spanner in the works by sabotaging his data. Of course he was unstable! He was standing before a major scientific breakthrough and he was all nerves. I'd never seen him in such a state. One moment he was overcome by grief at Silas's death and was raging at the mangrove and the useless fisherman who had sailed the boat, and the next he was going out of his mind with fresh worry about you. He read the email where you told him about your illness fifteen times, turning over every word and wanting my opinion. Were you really OK or were you just pretending? The day he learned of the allegation of scientific dishonesty made against your master's was the final straw. I had been out on an errand and when I returned to the research station Inés, who helps out, was cowering in a corner while Storm paced up and down his office without realising he was stomping on books and papers that he, according to Inés, had knocked off the shelves in his rage. He didn't give a damn about the flimsy, trumped-up accusations the DCSD was prepared to waste its time on, he thundered, as he marched up and down, but he was outraged at how easy it was to cast aspersions on a promising young scientist. Didn't they know the harm it did? I helped him tidy up the books and he began to calm down. But from what I heard it only got worse when I went to America in January. According to Nuno, one of our regular drivers, Storm was bordering on paranoia when he drove him to the airport to fly to Denmark after the last survey. Storm refused to let go of the box with the medical records and had a heated argument with the cabin crew before he was finally allowed to take it with him inside the plane. Storm, who is usually so calm. There's no doubt that he wasn't himself. But from there to suicide? He was so full of . . . life. I told all of this to Thor, but he refused to budge. The next day Thor called me at my hotel. I apologised for getting angry and explained that I was distraught at Storm's death. He told me that the police had found Storm's medical records from Guinea-Bissau. At first I didn't believe him, but he told me to phone—'

'They have?' Marie was perplexed. 'So where were they?'

Tim looked nervously at her. 'Storm shredded them, Marie. I thought you knew.'

Marie clasped her hand over her mouth. 'No,' she whispered.

'Yes,' Tim said. 'And he also wiped the hard disk on both his computers.'

'No,' Marie repeated in despair.

'I don't know what to believe any more. Common sense tells me that Storm must have killed himself. But my heart tells me that something is wrong.'

'And a hunch is enough,' Marie whispered.

Tim nodded. As if to put the matter out of his mind for a while, Tim ordered Thai coconut pancakes with lime and honey, and Marie watched him eat. 'So now what?' she asked.

'Yes, now what?' Tim pushed his plate aside.

'You have honey on your lip,' Marie said, and he licked it without success.

'I'm going to Bissau tomorrow. I need to sort out the Belem Health Project. Storm put so much work into it, and whether or not his criticism of the DTP vaccine was an aberration, he created the foundation for a fantastic demographic moni-toring system. It's a unique structure for the country and, besides, it provides jobs for a hundred and fifty local people. I'll do whatever it takes to continue the project. I need to gain an overview of our finances, of any articles we need to finish writing, and decide who will take charge after Storm. It was Storm's ambition to train locals and strengthen Guinea-Bissau from the inside. If I can help realise that dream in any way, I will.'

'What about the figures from Dulombi-Boe?'

Tim suddenly looked desperate. 'Why did he shred the med-ical records, Marie, if they were an accurate and complete set of data? Why?'

'What if Storm didn't shred them?' Marie said. 'Someone else could have done it. Someone who wanted to destroy Storm.'

'That was my first thought too,' Tim said, 'and I asked Thor if the police were sure that Storm did it himself. But they have a witness who heard Storm shred a lot of material the same evening he died. One of Thor's master's students called Niels Sonne.'

'Heard?'

'Yes, the door to the printer room was closed, but Niels Sonne had just said hello to Storm and there was no one else in the department. The next morning, before Trine Rønn found Storm, the cleaners took the waste paper down to the basement under the institute. That was where the police found it. Reduced to spaghetti.' Tim threw up his hands in despair.

'I always knew I would end up with Thor as my supervisor.' Marie heaved a sigh.

'I wouldn't be so sure,' Tim said. 'Thor has yet to defend his PhD and, following Storm's untimely departure, he could easily be overtaken on the inside by stronger candidates. Stig Heller from the Karolinska Institute, for example. He has a list of publications as long as your arm and he defended his PhD last year.'

'Stig Heller?' Marie exclaimed. 'When Storm called to tell me that we had been accused of dishonesty, he mentioned Stig Heller's name. He said he wouldn't be surprised if he had reported us to the DCSD. He called him a sourpuss.'

Tim smiled. 'I've heard him refer to Heller like that. But I think he was more upset that the two of them had fallen out. He was very fond of him. And Heller is a good man. He does research into vitamins and public health, and is just as committed to helping developing countries as Storm was, but in his own, more conservative, fashion. By the way, do you know what Storm called you?' Tim added. Marie smiled and shook her head. '*Andurinha*. It means "little swallow" in Creole.'

'Is that true?'

'He said you looked like a ruffled baby bird the first time you stepped inside his office. Still wet from the yolk sac, helpless and confused. But he knew that you would turn into an indefatigable swallow and one day fly very far away without a murmur, just like the swallows that migrate to Africa.'

Marie wanted to cry. 'Did he really say that?' she whispered.

Tim nodded. 'That reminds me, I have something for you,' Tim said, and rummaged in his pockets. 'Here.'

Tim placed a small, flat package on the table in front of her. Marie unwrapped it. 'Oh, it's beautiful.'

It was a swallow, carved from ebony. The bird had spread its wings and held its head proudly.

'Storm bought it in a market last autumn when you wrote to him that you were ill. But he forgot it on his desk in Bissau and emailed to ask if I could look after it until he came back. So that's what I did.'

Marie's eyes welled up and she closed her hands around the swallow.

Tim smiled. 'Incidentally, he called me Kinder Egg,' Tim continued. 'Brown, white, sweet and full of surprises.' They burst out laughing.

'What a flattering nickname.' Marie grinned.

'At first I didn't have a clue what he meant. You see, we don't have Kinder Eggs in Guinea-Bissau. But now I can see that it's vaguely amusing. But only vaguely. My brother always teases me by saying that I travelled to London as black as ink and came home as white as snow. Ébano doesn't think that a black man can be well educated without becoming white in the process.' He asked Marie what she was going to do now.

'I don't really know,' she said quietly. 'I'm still recovering and I start my post-chemo treatment in a couple of weeks. Perhaps I'll die,' she said. 'Perhaps I won't. I try not to think too much about it because lots of people are in the same boat as me. I've become so grateful for all sorts of things I never used to appreciate.' Marie gulped. 'My son and I have left his father. My mother died recently. So, to begin with, I guess I want to learn to stand on my own two feet. When I stop being so tired, I want to return to the university. I can't imagine what else I would do. Research is the one thing I'm good at.' Marie shook her head. 'But right now I don't even know if my master's is valid, given that I've been accused of scientific dishonesty.'

'I'm very sorry to hear that your mother has died,' Tim said. 'You must be very upset.'

Marie took a deep breath. 'I don't really know what I am,' she said softly. 'In one way, it's a relief that she's dead. I'm ashamed to admit it and I haven't been able to say it out loud until now. She had been very unhappy for many years and I think she didn't want to go on living.'

'My mother died recently too,' Tim said. 'I bought her a house in Bissau with the money I earned working for Storm and she loved it. But she was worn out.'

They sat for a while looking at each other. Suddenly Tim said, 'We should write that article together, Marie.'

'Storm's article?'

'Yes. Terrence Wilson from *Science* promised Storm he would print his article in the May issue, and if I go straight to Xitole and Dulombi-Boe to survey the area again and you write the introduction, describe our method and present the conclusion, based on the numbers we already have, we might just make it. I'll come back to Denmark as soon as I have the new figures and then we'll finish the article.'

'But—'

'I promise you I'll work night and day. I'll take my brother

Ébano with me and three other assistants who know the drill. And if we really pull our socks up, then, with a favourable wind, I think we can do it in three weeks, maybe only two. I'll come back as soon as I can. Please, Marie.' Tim reached across the table and took her hand again.

'OK,' Marie said. 'Let's do it.'

A smile spread across Tim's face. 'Storm always said I could count on you,' he said.

'That's funny – he said the same thing about you,' Marie replied. 'And . . .' She hesitated, and Tim looked at her expectantly. 'I have a favour to ask you,' she said.

On Saturday, 27 March, Marie rose with the sun. She stood by the window and looked across Copenhagen. Tim's room was on the top floor at First Hotel on Vesterbrogade and the rooftops glistened after the overnight rain. She was wearing only knickers and stood for a moment savouring the morning light on her smooth, warm skin. Tim was still asleep on his stomach with one arm dangling over the edge of the bed and the pillow over his head. His ticket to Bissau lay on the bedside table and his blue rucksack was on the floor. Marie tiptoed to the bathroom and splashed water on her face. At first she was afraid to look at herself in the mirror, but when she did, she was surprised. The right breast was perfectly round and the nipple stood proud. The perfect breast. But the scar on the left side suddenly looked raw, she thought. She was still horribly skinny, but at the centre of her stomach where once Anton's bottom had stretched her skin, she spotted a tiny bulge of wonderful belly. She ran her hand across her stomach, up to her healthy breast, onwards across the scar, which Tim had kissed with his honey mouth, and to the top of her head where a dark shadow revealed that new hair was growing. She had been terrified that she might be unable to have sex with him. That she would be dry. Fearful. Shy. But it had been fine. For a moment she allowed herself to be filled by a magical feeling that she was no longer ill. Then she got dressed and carefully slipped out of the door without waking Tim.

On her way down in the lift, she fished out her mobile and looked at the display. Eight unanswered calls from Jesper. Shit! Her heart was pounding when she called him.

'Marie, Goddammit, why didn't you pick up? What's the point of having a mobile when you never answer it? You don't even have voicemail!' Marie could hear from his uncensored irritation that nothing too serious had happened.

'We had a break-in last night while Anton and I were asleep,' Jesper continued. 'The side windows of the Range Rover were smashed and someone tried to start a fire in the garage. It's really most unpleasant. The police have just left. I've been calling you a million times because Anton is refusing to go on his playdate today and has been screaming and crying all morning, but I'm due at work at eight so you have to take him. I can drop him off on the way. Thirty minutes?'

'No,' Marie said, shocked. 'Are you all right?'

'Oh, we're fine, but it's obviously not very pleasant, is it? And the burglar appears to have made himself at home because a lot of the food in the fridge has been eaten. I'm just glad I finally managed to get hold of you. We'll be there shortly.'

'I have to get home first,' Marie said. 'I'll catch the next bus and I don't think there will be a problem, but— Did they take anything? What did the police say?'

'They dusted for fingerprints and took a look around, but because nothing was stolen, they're of the opinion that it was simple vandalism. They asked me if I had any enemies and I said, "Why don't we all just calm down?" The only thing I don't understand is that I didn't hear anything, not even when the car windows were smashed in. So I've no idea when it happened . . . Where are you, then?'

'On Vesterbrogade on my way to Rådhuspladsen,' Marie said. 'But what did the police say? Will they take any precautions? What if the vandals return?'

'What are you doing on Rådhuspladsen?'

'Jesper, I didn't sleep at home last night. I'm happy to give you the details, but I think you'd prefer it if I didn't. I asked you what the police are going to do.'

There was a deathly silence at the other end.

'Nothing really,' he said eventually. 'They've been driving around the neighbourhood and they gave me a number . . . So who do you know on Vesterbrogade?'

'Oh, look, there's my bus! I'll get on it now and I'll be home in twenty minutes. You can drop Anton off any time after that.' Marie hit the *off* button and couldn't help smiling. Jesper was stunned, she knew.

They had originally agreed that Jesper would collect Anton again that evening, but he called to ask Marie if Anton could stay with her until Tuesday. Jesper wanted to tidy up the house after the break-in, and had also been given extra shifts at work.

Anton and Marie spent Saturday and Sunday chilling out.

They lazed around.
They sucked sour sweets.
Anton lost a tooth.
They put it on his bedside table.
They played Stratego.
And they cheated.

They also spent a lot of time talking about Granny. Anton asked many questions and Marie answered them to the best of her ability. He wanted to know if maybe they could take on the dog Grandad had bought for Granny. After all, Grandad had paid for it. Marie said that they couldn't have a dog in their small flat, but perhaps they should consider getting a dragon. Anton thought that was a good idea and they discussed at length whether to buy a fire-breathing one or a more common type. Then Anton wanted to know if he could have a Nutella sandwich. No. How about liver pâté? All right, then. Are you going to die, Mum? Marie keeled over theatrically with her tongue lolling and Anton couldn't help laughing.

'I told you I'll live to a hundred and four,' she said.

'OK,' Anton said happily, and watched a bit of a movie, played with his *Star Wars* figures, drew a picture and asked when his sandwich would be ready. Marie watched him, and when he was immersed in playing or his film, she sneaked out her laptop and dealt with her mental to-do list.

She had an appointment with Mr Guldborg at Rigshospitalet on Monday morning and she had to prepare for it. Her recovery period would be over in two weeks and Mr Guldborg would then want to perform the surgery to remove her ovaries so she could start her post-chemo treatment with Aromasin.

However, Marie's doubts about losing her ovaries were

growing. She had found several articles about Aromasin on PubMed and she carefully reread the more relevant ones while her throat tightened. She had to concede that there was some medical evidence to suggest that Aromasin was more effective than other post-chemo treatments, but the difference was vanishingly small. And she thought that the loss of her ovaries was a high price to pay.

She found herself gazing at Anton. He was far away in his fictitious universe and his lips were moving. She had only to cough and he would look up and ask what was happening to his sandwich, but if Marie stayed quiet, another hour could easily pass before he remembered it. She would like to have more children.

'We can freeze your eggs,' Guldborg had said, when she had raised this objection. 'And you can have hormone treatment, if the urge to have more children should occur.' Guldborg sounded as if he was talking about a verruca rather than her ovaries. Was she ready for that? Losing her ovaries before she was even thirty?

When she had finished on PubMed, she used her access key to log on to Biosis, the scientific article database, and did a general search of articles on the non-specific effects of vaccines, only to have it confirmed that, apart from Storm's, there was hardly any research within that field. At one point she came across a reference to the Nobel Committee and, out of sheer curiosity, she clicked on www.nobelprize.org and read a press release about Stig Heller's recent admission to the committee. The chairman of the Nobel Committee, Göran Sandö, was quoted as saying what a joy it was to welcome such young and promising new blood to the committee. In the photograph, Heller was grinning from ear to ear and didn't look in the least like a sourpuss.

On Sunday morning Marie and Anton made popcorn in a saucepan without a lid and played Monopoly on the floor below the bay window. Marie thought about Tim when she bought Grønningen with the last of her money. He must be back in Bissau now and might already have travelled on to Dulombi-Boe where Internet coverage was limited. Her groin tingled when she thought about him.

'Why are you laughing, Mum?' Anton said.

Marie placed a finger on her lips. 'Sssh.'

Anton and Marie climbed inside the broom cupboard in the hall and closed the door, so it was completely dark. There was a smell of old coats even though the cupboard was almost empty. Marie chortled like a troll, ho-ho-ho, so deeply that her throat tickled. Anton pretended to be a small miser, hih-hih-hih. This made Marie laugh because she had no idea how Anton would know how a miser might laugh, but he said he had read it in a Donald Duck comic. And when would his sandwich be ready?

In the afternoon they caught a bus to Østerbrogade and went for a walk on Kastellet. Marie was soon out of breath so they slowed down. There was a wonderful scent in the air of the strange overlap between two seasons, the birds swooped on the tips of their wings and the city traffic sounded like grains of sand pouring into a bottle far away. Afterwards they lugged home several shopping bags filled with their favourite food. They had bought spring rolls, feta cheese, tuna, blood orange juice and a giant box of fondant chocolate turtles on special offer.

When Marie had unpacked their shopping, she checked her mobile and saw five unanswered calls from Julie. She called her sister and could hear immediately that something was wrong. Julie spoke three words and burst into tears.

Frank's lawyer had called to let them know that the trial had been set for 2 July and added that they should prepare themselves for a custodial sentence, a fine and the loss of Frank's licence for a minimum of three years. It turned out that he already had a suspended custodial sentence for drink-driving.

'A suspended sentence?' Marie said. 'Since when?'

'That was my reaction,' Julie wept. 'I called Dad afterwards and he couldn't even be bothered to lie. It was in February, he said. He was stopped on Lyngbyvejen on his way home and his blood-alcohol level was ninety milligrams per hundred mills, so he got a suspended sentence and a fine.' Julie was now sobbing uncontrollably and Marie struggled to understand what she was saying.

'Everything is in ruins,' Julie stuttered at length. 'Everything we stood for, it's all ruined. You can't help it . . . And Mum couldn't help it . . . But Dad, what was he thinking? I'm so ashamed of him! Dad is always the first to pick on Michael. And do you know something?' she exclaimed. 'Lea has known all along! Dad admitted that he called her and asked her to pick him up from the police station. Lea? Since when did Dad ever ask her for help? And why didn't she say anything? Maybe we could have helped him. You must call her. I want her to tell us right now why she kept quiet. She owes us an explanation.'

Marie tried as best she could to console her while her brain continued to spin. Eventually she brought the conversation to an end because Julie kept repeating herself. Marie ran a hand across her sprouting hair. What was going on? She had never heard Julie lose her temper before and now she had witnessed it twice in less than a month. She had been planning to ask Julie to come with her to her hospital appointment the following day, but that didn't seem such a good idea now. She wondered if she could ask Lea instead. For years Lea had been distant and closed off to Marie, but her carapace had started to crack in the last few weeks. Lea had spontaneously put her arms around her at Joan's funeral and Marie couldn't remember the last time that had happened, and when it became official that Marie and Jesper were divorcing, she had caught Lea watching her with interest. She found Lea's number in her phone, but when she rang it the call went straight to voice-mail. She left a message.

On Monday morning Anton was in a terrible mood despite their lovely weekend.

'I don't want to go to nursery,' he sobbed. 'I want to be with you all the time.' He clung to her and refused to let go.

Marie did not need much persuading and Anton dried his eyes. 'But it's on one condition,' she said. 'You have to wait in the corridor while I'm with the doctor. And you must be as quiet as a mouse. Afterwards we'll go into town and get an ice cream.'

He promised.

Anton and Marie walked to Rigshospitalet via Trianglen and Blegdamsvej. Anton had brought along his scooter and would slip in front of her or lag behind as he liked. They had plenty of time.

For once Marie answered her mobile when it rang.

'Marie?'

'Yes.'

'Success at last! It's Merethe from the Department of Immunology. Am I disturbing you?'

'Hi!' Marie said. 'No, it's fine. I've been trying to get hold of you too. I wanted to apologise for the way I behaved when you came to tell me that Storm had died.'

Merethe said that was all right. Then they spoke a little about Storm's funeral and Merethe said that she was sorry to have missed it because of her grandmother's hundredth birthday. 'But Thor told me it was a very fine service.'

'It was,' Marie said. 'Thor gave a beautiful eulogy and there was a good turnout.'

'The real reason I'm calling is because I have various messages for you,' Merethe said. 'I've just got them from Ane Berg, the secretary from Population Ecology, who was temping for me last week.'

'Messages for me? Who from?' Marie wondered. She had been on sick leave since shortly after Christmas and there were messages for her?

'There are four from Göran Sandö,' Merethe said. 'He asks you to call him back on a Swedish phone number. Do you have a pen?'

'Four messages from Göran Sandö?' Marie exclaimed, astonished. 'Please could you email me his number? I don't have a pen.'

'Will do,' Merethe said and added, 'You can say a lot about Sandö, but he's one persistent gentleman.'

'What do you mean?'

'I mean,' Merethe said, 'that it's only a few weeks ago since he was calling Storm morning, noon and night, but Storm refused to speak to such a "self-promoting, self-glorifying arse-hole who thought that research was all about polishing your own trophies". Or words to that effect. Sandö would appear to have taken an interest in Storm's Guinea-Bissau research recently, but Storm was convinced that Sandö had somehow found out that Terrence Wilson from *Science* had promised him an article in the May issue, and wanted to see if he was in time to put himself down for a little of the glory.'

'I'll call him,' Marie said. 'And the other messages?'

'I believe there are several from Stig Heller in Stockholm. Probably wants to express his condolences.'

'Is that right?' Marie said drily. 'But if he calls again, tell him I'm on sick leave. I have nothing to say to him.'

'What has he done?'

'Storm and he fell out some years ago, and Storm suspected Heller of reporting my figures as dishonest.'

'OK,' Merethe said, and went on, 'The last message is from Tim Salomon. He came here last Wednesday to ask after you. Ane Berg told him you were on sick leave and he asked for your address because he wanted to send you something. I hope it was all right that she gave him your home address and mobile number.'

'Yes, of course. I met him at the funeral reception,' Marie said. 'He gave me a present from Storm. A wooden swallow. But . . .' Marie hesitated. 'Are you sure he didn't call in last Thursday?'

'Ane Berg wrote Wednesday on the note. Why?'

'Because he didn't arrive in Denmark until Thursday.'

'Oh, well, Ane probably just made a mistake. I think she was quite flustered over just how hot he was.'

Marie smiled. 'Yes,' she said, 'and she's right.'

As Marie and Anton walked through the hospital swing doors, Marie's thoughts jumped around like fleas. She couldn't imagine what such an important man as Sandö wanted with her. As far as Stig Heller was concerned, he could jump off a cliff. It was just too late to start playing nicely.

They took the lift up to Oncology on the seventh floor where Marie settled Anton in the corridor outside Guldborg's office and went in for her appointment. The consultant shook her hand and at that moment an angry shower of rain started pelting the window. Distracted, Marie turned her head in the direction of the sound. Tim had been closer than sound.

Guldborg said, 'It looks good, Marie.' He glanced up from her medical record. 'You look good. Your figures are fine and the scanning shows no solid tumours.'

'So I'm well?'

'You're currently not ill,' Guldborg corrected her. 'Just be happy that you're currently not ill.' Guldborg started going through the procedure for her oophorectomy. He spoke the word without stumbling. Marie tried saying it to herself a couple of times, but it proved difficult. The surgery itself would take one to two hours, Guldborg explained, but Marie should expect to be in hospital for three to five days. He would perform a Caesarean section. Following surgery she would experience vaginal bleeding for up to four weeks. Marie watched him without moving. He was telling her something about his experience with suture versus metal clamps.

'Do you know what I spent most of my weekend doing?' she interrupted him.

'Eh, no,' Guldborg said.

'Looking for statistical evidence which proves that removing my ovaries and treating me with Aromasin afterwards will increase my chances of survival, compared to other treatments where I get to keep my ovaries.'

'Please may I continue and we can take your questions at the end?' Guldborg said.

'On Friday, I formulated my H^0-hypothesis while Anton watched Disney cartoons,' Marie lied. 'I choose a simple H^0-hypothesis: "The survival rate among female breast cancer patients treated with Aromasin is significantly higher."'

'Marie, this is all well and good, but please may I—'

'On Saturday I collected raw data from twenty-four primary articles about post-chemo treatment with Aromasin from PubMed, ran them through an X^2-test and ended up rejecting my H^0-hypothesis. On Sunday I made up my mind to keep my ovaries for a little longer.'

Guldborg watched her for a while. 'That's a very bad idea, Marie.'

'When I look purely at the figures, I can see that there is a slight difference in survival rates among women who choose to have their ovaries removed so they can be treated with Aromasin and those who are treated with, for example, Tamoxifen, but the difference isn't statistically significant.' Guldborg screwed up his face, and Marie quickly continued, 'I would like you to note down the following in my record. "The patient has considered the question of whether her ovaries should be removed and there is no need to discuss this

further with her. She will keep her ovaries for a little longer."'
Marie looked straight at Guldborg and she was sweating under
her jumper.

At length Guldborg nodded. 'I'm bound to accept your
decision,' he said. 'But you're taking a chance.'

'Yes,' was all Marie said.

Silence ensued. Marie looked cordially at Guldborg until he
cleared his throat. Then they started planning her Tamoxifen
treatment.

'That's great,' Marie said, when they had finished.

She took the paperwork he handed her and had bent down
to pick up her bag when Guldborg said, 'I think you should
reconsider the ovaries one more time and I really would like—'

Marie straightened up. 'I don't believe you've read my medical record recently, Mr Guldborg,' she said.

Guldborg looked momentarily at a loss.

'At this point, it should say,' she continued, 'that "The
patient has considered the question of whether her ovaries
should be removed, and there is no need to discuss this further
with her. She will keep her ovaries for a little longer."'

The silence was now deafening. Marie got up and held out
her hand to Guldborg.

'I'll see you in a fortnight when I'm ready for the next stage
of my treatment,' she said.

Then she took her bag and left.

At first Marie could not find Anton, but when she finally
tracked him down, she had to laugh. He had discovered a
water cooler and had managed to fill about thirty-five cups
with water and had lined them up in a long row.

'People here are really busy, you know,' he said contentedly, 'so I make sure they get a glass of water on their way.' Marie gave her son a big hug.

'What a thoughtful boy you are,' she said. 'Come on, let's go into town and visit Aunt Lea. Maybe she'll fancy having ice cream with us.'

'Yippee,' Anton said, and as they skipped hand in hand down the hospital corridor, an ampoule of happiness exploded behind Marie's forehead and spread like a chemical throughout her entire organism. She was well. The most undervalued word in the world by everyone in good health. She didn't care that Guldborg was too much of a pessimist to use the word. She was going to.

They drifted lazily through Magasin du Nord and spent at least half an hour in the toy department where they paid special attention to remote-control cars and Slinkys that could walk downstairs. Then Anton needed a pee, and when that had been taken care of, they took the lift to the Du Nord Spa on the fifth floor where Lea worked as a nail technician. The entrance was glazed with frosted glass and a young woman smiled obligingly when Marie and Anton stepped out of the lift.

'May I help you?' she asked. It said *Adèle* on a badge on her chest. Marie explained that she was Lea Skov's sister, Marie, and that she had come on the spur of the moment, but wondered if she could possibly disturb Lea briefly.

Adèle looked blankly at Marie. 'Lea? We have a Majken and a Malene, but no Lea,' she said.

Marie frowned.

At that moment the telephone rang and Adèle asked if there was anything else she could help Marie with. Marie was just about to leave when another woman appeared from inside the spa.

'Hi,' she said, looking at Marie with curiosity. 'My name is Sandra. I'm the manager of Du Nord Spa and Lea is a friend of mine. You're Lea's sister, aren't you? She's told me about you. Lea no longer works here, but she did once. Adèle is new – that's why she hasn't heard of her.' Sandra smiled.

'Oh,' Marie said. 'I'm confused. She told me just before Christmas that she had a job here.'

'There must be some mistake,' Sandra said. 'I'm sorry I can't help you. I don't know where she works now. She has been very busy recently and, eh . . . We haven't seen much of each other. But if you see her, tell her Sandra says hi, won't you?'

'I will,' Marie said slowly. 'I'll say hi to Lea when I see her. From Sandra, her friend. Who doesn't know where she works now. Thanks for your help.'

'You're welcome,' Sandra said, still smiling.

Marie and Anton walked back to the lift and Anton pressed the button. Just as they stepped inside, Marie glanced over her shoulder. Adèle had the telephone wedged under her chin and was making a note in a big diary; Sandra was standing next to her, busy writing a text message. Her thumbs flew across the screen. When she looked up, Marie fixed her with her gaze.

Marie's brain was working overdrive as they travelled down in the lift.

Sandra was lying. But why?

*

On Tuesday morning Anton was willing to go to nursery, and when Marie had dropped him off, she lingered on the pavement, not knowing what to do with herself. Jesper would pick Anton up from nursery and Marie would not see him again until after the weekend. For a moment the emptiness was echoing, but then she made up her mind and walked briskly towards Hellerup station. She took the S-train to Vesterport and headed down Istedgade. At a bakery she bought fresh cinnamon whirls with sticky cinnamon filling oozing over the tall sides and two extra-large takeaway lattes. The front door to Lea's stairwell in Saxogade 88 was open, so she went straight in and slowly made her way up the stairs. She was out of breath by the time she reached the fourth floor and had to ring the doorbell with her knee because her hands were full of pastries and cups. Marie could hear someone in the flat, yet no one came to the door. She rang the bell again and ended up putting the coffee on the floor before she rang the bell a third time. Still no reply, even though it was now obvious that Lea was at home. Marie could hear her cough and a radio playing at low volume. She called through the letterbox.

Shortly afterwards the door was opened.

'Oh, it's you,' Lea said. 'Why didn't you let me know you were coming? I'm not at home to anyone.'

'Hello, Lea,' Marie said. 'I'm sorry for turning up unannounced, but I did try to call you. Why aren't you at home to anyone?'

Lea wandered back inside the flat and Marie took that as a sign that she was welcome to follow. She put the coffee cups and the pastry bag on the table in the small kitchen-diner. They sat down and, without a word, Lea grabbed one of the coffees, flicked off the lid and added three teaspoons of sugar from a bowl on the table. She tore open the paper bag with the pastries and devoured one in large bites. The silver tongue bar clicked against her teeth as she chewed. 'How are you doing in your new flat without Jesper, the boy wonder?' she asked, as she picked up her coffee and rocked back in her chair. As always, Lea looked beautiful, but Marie detected a hint of black circles under her eyes and her hair was casually piled on top of her head.

'All things considered, I'm doing fine,' she replied slowly, ignoring Lea's provocation. 'Every minute is a whirlpool of emotion, but you probably know what that's like. Anton has spent the last couple of days with me and that was wonderful. He likes his new room.'

Lea rolled her eyes.

Marie studied her briefly. 'Or maybe you think it's silly to be six years old and like your new room,' she said. 'Otherwise, why are you rolling your eyes at me? I didn't come here to argue with you, Lea. I'm here because you don't answer your phone when I call. Mum is dead and Dad is on the verge of a breakdown. We have to stick together.'

'I'm not sticking together with you lot,' Lea said calmly. 'I can manage on my own. I have done since I lost my first tooth. Yuk, this coffee's cold,' she said, and got up without warning. First she spat in the sink, then she put her coffee into the microwave to reheat it.

Marie had yet to touch hers.

'You don't work in the spa in Magasin, like you told me at Mum's birthday party,' Marie continued, aware that she was close to tears. 'I went there yesterday and one of the girls who work there had never heard of you and the other, Sandra, acted strange, but asked me to say hi. You're lying.'

Lea gave Marie an icy stare. 'I'm lying?' she said. 'Perhaps. And you are and always will be Julie's sister.'

'I'm not like Julie,' Marie said, offended. 'Julie gave up on you long ago because being with you is always such incredibly hard work. But I haven't given up on you.' Marie was tempted to add *yet*, but swallowed it. Lea looked at her diffidently, then drained her coffee in two large gulps and ran her pierced tongue around the rim to suck up the foam. When she had finished, she helped herself to Marie's pastry from the open bag and gobbled it with the same appetite with which she had wolfed down the first.

Julie would have said something very shrill.

And Lea would have laughed, and either given her the finger or stuck her tongue out at her, displaying both the masticated food and the bar.

Whereupon Julie would have burst into tears and Marie would have comforted her and said, 'Honestly, Lea.'

And they would have gone round in circles as they always did. And it would have foundered as it always did.

Marie took a deep breath. Then she removed the lid from her coffee cup, added three teaspoons of sugar, got up and heated it for thirty seconds in the microwave, put the coffee in front of Lea and kissed her cheek. Then she sat down again on her own chair.

Lea had averted her gaze. She didn't touch the coffee; she didn't say one word.

Just under a minute passed. Lea was still staring at the table top.

Then the tears rolled down her cheeks.

'Do you know how much I loved you when we were children?' she said quietly. 'I loved you so, so much. Every night I prayed to God to be allowed to keep you. All the years I was growing up, you were the only one I trusted. You never bullied me, you never hated me, you never belittled me.'

'Lea, no one hates you . . .'

'Believe me, they hate me,' Lea said angrily, wiping away her tears. 'But they don't hate you. And that's why you can't see it. But trust me. One hundred and fifty hours of therapy later, I know I was always the scapegoat in the Skov family. My whole fucking life I've borne the burden of Julie's frustration, Frank's megalomania and Joan's wasted artistic talent. Frank and Joan should obviously never have had me. You don't need to study psychology to see that. Two immature idiots with four young kids. Julie and the twins would have been more than enough. Julie, Marie and the dead twin far exceeded their capabilities. Little Lea was the last straw. Mum and Dad were each other's tragic destiny. They married far too young, far too blinded by the last thing in this world on which you should base a marriage. Joan was Frank's talented, pretty trophy girl, whose tiny waist he could span with his manly hands: his ticket to a higher social sphere. Frank, for his part, was Joan's tower of strength, her guardian, her symbol of greatness and might. But then Mads died and the fantasy couldn't be sustained any longer. Joan was no longer beautiful – she was ugly and grieving and whimpering and demanding – and it became obvious to everyone that Frank was and always would be a loser who turned into a bully so that no one would ever know that he was a fraud. Julie was ten years old when she started pouring oil on troubled waters. She looked after all of us. Our mentally ill mother, our disappointed father, their immature agendas, you and me – I was only a baby. I should have been given up for adoption, Marie. It would have been better for me. Mum and Dad weren't able to take proper care of me and Julie broke her neck trying. Of course she did. She was only a child herself.'

Marie was knocked for six. 'But I loved you,' she objected.

'Yes,' Lea said, 'you did, and I never doubted you – not then. You were also cool, in your own unremarkable way. As if everything that happened just bounced off you. You were with us, yet you lived in a world of your own: in your books, in your homework, in the ridiculous brain-teaser puzzles you spent all your pocket money on. You didn't pander to Frank or suck up to him, like Julie did; you never told tales, you formed no alliances. You just got on with your life. You were very well behaved, but not because you were trying to get something from Frank, rather because you sought to avoid something, I think, and I loved you for that. You were the real deal.' Lea's voice started to quiver.

'But then you met Jesper. Being introduced to him was my worst nightmare. A polished, well-educated mini Frank. An updated version of Michael, with a university degree. Everyone in the family gazed at him in admiration, but I threw up, literally, in the bog, while you sat beaming like the sun in the dining room, happy that you'd finally honoured Frank's twisted fantasies. I brought up peas and gravy, three times the amount I'd actually eaten of Frank and Joan's crappy food. Suddenly bullying was legitimised. Because Jesper had such a way with words. He ignored anything Julie said, more so even than Michael. He told you what to say – he was even better at it than Dad. And you never told your husband to shut his fucking mouth. Not once did you speak up for yourself. You sold out totally and nothing has ever hurt me more than to witness that. I gave up on *you*, Marie.'

Marie was shocked.

'You've no idea how much it suits you to be rid of Jesper,' Lea added. 'Fuck, even having cancer suits you. Finally there's some fight in your eyes. And you look cool with that chemo haircut.'

'Thanks,' Marie said. 'By the way, I still love you.'

'Oh, just shut up,' Lea said, as she wiped away a treacherous tear with the back of her sleeve.

'But it's hard to show it,' Marie continued cautiously. 'Because you're permanently angry. All three of us grew up at nineteen Snerlevej, but we deal with it in three different ways. Being Frank's favourite wasn't always easy.'

They sat for a while until they suddenly looked tenderly at each other. Then Lea said, 'In case you're interested, I'm study-ing psychology at the University of Copenhagen. I submitted my final-year project in January, but I have to do a resit due to illness before I get my degree. My viva is at nine o'clock on Wednesday. Saying I was going to be a beauty therapist was just a joke. To wind Frank up. But, Jesus Christ, you all fell for it. Even you, which, by the way, I regard as the ultimate proof that Jesper brainwashed you. Did you seriously think I was going to spend the rest of my life massaging people's faces? Thanks for the vote of confidence.'

Marie was speechless.

'Sandra in Magasin is a friend of mine,' Lea continued. 'She's

super-cool. I met her at a tattoo fair at the Bella Center some
years ago. In the beginning, pulling the wool over your eyes
was fun. Here was I, getting to grips with late post-modernist
family relationships and clinical psychology, and you thought
I was dyeing eyelashes and eyebrows. Ha-ha, it was hilarious.
It wasn't until I started my own therapy, which, incidentally,
is something you have to do, that I realised it wasn't hilarious
at all. In fact, it was tragic.' Lea gave a light shrug.

'Does Dad know?' Marie asked.

Lea nodded.

'He found out the night Mum died. He turned up here out
of the blue and I was on study leave so all my books and papers
were lying around. That's another reason I don't open the
door to anyone or answer the phone. Frank was furious. Typical Frank. He managed to spin it, of course. How could I do
this to *him*, lying to *him* like that? He was ranting and raving.
Finally he passed out on my bed. When he woke up the next
morning, he was still drunk, but now he was as meek as a
lamb. "I'm so proud of you, Loopy-Lou. My clever little
Loopy-Lou,"' Lea mimicked. 'He hasn't called me Loopy-Lou
since I was five. I told him that he was the most pathetic,
worst-educated, academic-arse-licking snob I had ever met. He
got seriously pissed off, of course, and tried to stand up to
leave because there was no way in hell he was going to visit
an ungrateful bitch like me. "Ungrateful, yes, but to everyone's
surprise a super-well-educated bitch, if you please," I said to
him. He never got further than the edge of the bed. He slumped
backwards and fell asleep again. In the middle of it all, Michael
rocked up to tell me that Joan had died, about as casually as
when he told me he'd quit smoking. And, to add insult to

injury, he put on his chirpy hospital-porter voice. "Oh, yes, I can see you've just had your leg torn off at the hip, but I'll roll you down to Ward Fourteen." Very compassionate face, very understanding eyes, firm hands, which he kept resting heavily on my shoulders. Christ on a bike. Well, that's another story. I'm trying hard to forgive you for making him the messenger.'

'I didn't send him, Lea.'

'Ah, well, Julie did. Same difference.'

'No,' Marie said firmly. 'It isn't.'

'Convince me,' Lea said.

'Let me in,' Marie said.

'First show me your breast,' Lea said.

Without hesitation Marie pulled her T-shirt over her head and Lea studied her upper body for a long time before she exclaimed in awe, 'Fucking wow.'

They talked all afternoon. When they got to Frank's drink-driving, Marie asked if Lea had known about Frank's suspended sentence from February all along. Julie was angry about it, she said.

'Oh, I tremble,' Lea said laconically. 'Is Julie angry with me? She's one to talk. No one trumps her when it comes to keeping things hidden. Besides, Frank asked me not to say anything.'

'Only drink-driving is what . . . losers do,' Marie mumbled.

'Marie, our dad is the very essence of a loser! All his moral bullshit about right and wrong. Based on what? Cirrhosis of the liver and an impressive lack of education? He's lived rent-free in his wife's house for thirty years and falls out with his children the moment they fail to agree with every word he says or don't stand to attention when he tells them to. He's not even particularly intelligent, if you ask me – he just talks about himself long enough to make people believe he's a shining light. Trust me, if Mads hadn't died and bound Frank and Joan together in their shared destiny, they would have got divorced long ago. Frank would have been nursing a can of strong lager somewhere, boasting about his achievements, and Joan would have been an artist permanently in receipt of state support.'

'But Frank despises drink-drivers . . .' Marie said, but even she could hear how stupid that sounded.

'It was a few months after you'd dropped your breast-cancer bombshell. Frank and Joan were both heading up Shit Creek, to put it mildly. A total Freudian regression. It was so obvious that your illness ripped open all their old wounds. Frank started drinking during the day, and I know this because I saw him several times around Nørre Farimagsgade when he clearly wasn't sober. One day we literally bumped into each other when he came stumbling out of Funchs Vinstue and I was on my way to uni to meet my supervisor. It was the most awkward moment of my life. Fuck, my own dad shook my hand, he was that out of it. He was so flustered that he asked me if I wanted a beer. I had half an hour, so we went back inside Funchs Vinstue where we had a beer – or, rather, Frank had three. For the first time ever we had something that resembled a conversation. Frank told me that Joan was going out of her mind because of your illness. That she had stopped sleeping and barely ate. That she got up at night, howling like a sick animal, and that when he hushed her and tried to get her back to bed, she would lash out at him. Frank asked me for help. Julie came a couple of times a week to organise Joan's pills, but Frank thought the medication only made things worse. At any rate, Joan had practically stopped eating and hardly ever left the house.

'I went to Snerlevej a few days later. When I arrived, Joan was watching television in the living room, still in her dressing gown, obviously sedated and rather unwashed. I made some coffee and managed to rouse her a bit. She even ate something. I started by explaining to her that a breast-cancer diagnosis doesn't equate to a death sentence. That more than eighty per cent of people diagnosed with breast cancer were still alive five years later. That they had lost Mads in the most brutal manner, unexpected and sudden, but it was by no means certain that they would lose you as well. Then I gently suggested that she should seek professional help to process Mads' death so that she could start to feel better and relate realistically to your disease rather than bury you prematurely. "The sick person here is really you, Mum," I said to her. She fell silent. "But I feel the way I always feel," she said then. I offered to make an appointment with her GP, if she wanted me to. Her GP could refer her to a psychiatrist who could help. At this point she gave me a horrified look. She couldn't tell Dr Henrik something like that. She'd die of shame, she said. Because then everyone would know. Everyone in the waiting room, everyone in Vangede and on Snerlevej. "Why are you sticking your nose into my business?" she cried. "You're wicked; it's all your fault." The next moment she collapsed in my arms and pleaded with me to help her and I stroked her spine for a long time. Marie, she was skeletal. I reiterated that I would very much like to help, but that I didn't think pills were the answer and certainly not on their own. I said I would get the address of the nearest psychiatric emergency clinic where she could seek help without worrying about Dr Henrik.

'"Frank can drive you there as early as tonight. Or as soon as you want," I said, and Joan nodded. Yes, she'd like that.

'That evening Julie called me and blew her top, and I mean completely blew her top. It's not the first time she's lectured me – Christ, I'm practically immune to it now, but she went berserk. She asked me who the hell I thought I was, thinking I knew anything about what was good for Mum. I tried telling her that pills are nothing but a short-term treatment of symptoms and that Joan was addicted to medication and needed acute help. Julie was totally out of control. I've never heard so many foul words come out of such a prim mouth. At last I said, "OK, Julie, I'll hand over the responsibility to you, but I'm telling you, if it carries on like this, Mum will be dead before the year is out." At this point she screamed for me to stay away from Mum and Dad, that I'd caused more than enough pain for *everyone*. I was blown from here into the fucking living room, let me tell you.'

Marie gulped.

'Even so, I found the number of a psychiatric emergency clinic, familiarised myself with the admission procedure and left a leaflet at Snerlevej. Frank even rang to thank me, but said that Joan was feeling much better now. She had started new medication, which she tolerated better, and Julie had managed to persuade her to join an occupational-therapy group twice a week to do some sewing. The time was coming up when I needed to revise for my orals and, to be honest, I was relieved that there was nothing more I could do. I needed to knuckle down.

'About two weeks later, just before three o'clock in the morning, Frank called me from Bellahøj Police Station. He had run the car off the road, he said, and was prepared to admit that he hadn't been entirely sober. He wanted me to come and get him.'

'But surely you don't have a driving licence?' Marie said stupidly.

'Of course I have a driving licence. I've had one since I was nineteen. Paid for with my own money because I was a bad girl who'd started smoking so Frank refused to pay for it. Even though he smoked like a chimney himself, in those days. But anyway. I took a taxi to Bellahøj at some shitty hour so I could drive Frank home. His blood alcohol level was ninety milligrams, so he wasn't binge-drinking drunk, just mild midweek intoxicated. He had had a few drinks in town, he said, and had been on his way home when he came off the road. When the police arrived, they produced a breathalyser and the trap shut. When we turned into Snerlevej, Frank asked if I could pull over further down the road, and when I had stopped the car, he gave me five hundred kroner for a taxi home. He clearly didn't want me to come inside the house in case Joan was asleep in front of the television and woke up. She wouldn't have been able to understand what I was doing there in the middle of the night. Dad asked me not to say anything to anyone.

'He had never asked me to keep schtum about anything before and it felt good to be his ally. That's why I didn't tell anyone. And what would Julie have done differently, had she known? Frank is a grown man and he chose to drive while drunk. In February it was a minor offence and now it's a lot more serious. Frank knows how the Danish legal system works, so if he'd wanted to avoid a custodial sentence and losing his licence, he should have stayed at home that night. That's a fact even Julie can't change.'

'What do you think happened on the day Mum died?' Marie whispered. 'Did they have an argument? Did Dad say something to her that made her kill herself? Why did he even get drunk in the first place? I lie awake at night and I can't help thinking about it.'

'Worrying is futile,' Lea said, 'because it won't change a thing. I'm not convinced that Joan killed herself. She hadn't eaten properly for weeks and she took far, far too many pills. I think her system gave up that Wednesday evening rather than the week before or the week after when it might just as easily have happened. I know that Julie is outraged that Joan would do something so selfish but, quite honestly, I don't believe for one moment that she made a conscious decision to end her life. She was incapable of making decisions. She felt like shit and that evening she took some extra pills – who was counting? – and Frank drank whisky rather than red wine and got it into his head to drive into town for a pub crawl rather than sit at home next to his dried-up twig of a wife. Seven fateful hours later he had crashed into a sign on Vesterbro and Joan had slipped into a chemical coma from which she never woke up. I'm sorry if I sound cynical, but that's my view of what happened.'

'How did you become like this?' Marie asked. 'So insightful and composed, so sure of yourself and your way of seeing our family?'

'How do we become the people we are?' Lea shrugged her

shoulders. 'Genes, the environment, obstacles, who knows? I'm intelligent – it's my strongest life skill. And yours, incidentally. It also helps that I'm not exactly ugly and that my entire life I've had a firm conviction that what was going on at home was plain wrong. Frank and Joan made me what I am, for better or worse. They hurt me badly because they couldn't cope with me, but at the same time they did me a favour because without all their baggage I would never have turned into the person I am now. I'm rather proud of myself, Marie.'

'Do you think it made a difference that Tove Madsen looked after you?'

Lea was temporarily baffled. 'Tove Madsen? Who's she?'

'Tove looked after you when we were little. She looked after me too, but when I started school, she carried on looking after just you. Do you remember her?'

Lea did not.

'She lived on Snerlevej too,' Marie said. 'Further down the road. I can vaguely remember her. She had a husband and older children and a beautiful doll's house, which I was jealous that you got to play with. Julie says that you once asked Frank if you could go and live with Tove and her husband. He didn't like that at all.'

Lea's gaze was completely blank. 'It doesn't ring any bells. It might be that Tove made a difference. They do say that a kind neighbour or a caring teacher can have a huge impact on a neglected child.'

Marie fell quiet. 'Is that really what we were?' she said eventually. 'Neglected children?'

'It depends who you ask,' Lea replied. 'Julie can't even

handle it if I say that we had the same meal over and over again, but we did sometimes. All right, perhaps I exaggerate occasionally and focus too much on the negatives, but only to balance out Julie's massive denial. I need to call a spade a spade and a difficult upbringing a difficult upbringing. Otherwise I can't deal with it. It's the same with my tattoos. They're pictures of the reality I have to face or my fear will grow stronger.'

'I admire your integrity,' Marie said.

Lea roared with laughter. 'You had plenty of integrity while you were growing up. I don't know exactly what happened when you married Jesper but look at you now! You've dumped him, thank God. You have a wonderful son, a master's in biology and a PhD grant waiting for you. At the age of twenty-eight you've earned the admiration of one of the wisest and most highly respected scientists in the world; you have one breast and almost no hair, but in my eyes you're more beautiful than ever.'

'Do you know who Kristian Storm is?' Marie asked, surprised, pleased to be able to ask a question while she recovered from her embarrassment.

'Yes, of course. Science theory is a mandatory subject on the psychology course and Kristian Storm had some much debated and interesting attitudes to both paradigm shift and the acknowledgement of subjectivity in science. I've read several of his articles on science theory.'

Lea and Marie talked at length about Marie's master's, her research, Storm's discovery in Guinea-Bissau, other scientists' rejection of Storm's ideas about non-specific side-effects of vaccines, the police theory about his suicide, the break-in on

Ingeborgvej, Marie's nagging doubts, and the article Tim wanted to write with her. Lea listened attentively.

'Storm always said that a hunch is enough,' Marie said. 'And my intuition tells me that something is wrong.'

'Hmm,' Lea said. 'That does depend on whether your intuitive radar is properly calibrated. Do you think Julie can trust her intuition? I think it misleads her, big time. I think Julie's intuition tells her that if she lets anything bad happen to anyone, she'll die, and that's why she tries desperately to make sure that everything in the garden is rosy.'

Marie thought about it. 'I don't indulge in make-believe any more, Lea,' she said quietly. 'I'm much too disillusioned for that.'

Lea placed her hands on the table and made to get up. 'Start writing your article, Marie. My experience is that the missing pieces turn up when you work on the empty spaces.

'And now I'm afraid I'm going to have to throw you out, sis,' she said. 'I need to revise. Or I won't pull it off on Wednesday.'

'I'm glad we had a talk,' Marie said.

'So am I,' Lea said. 'Incredibly glad.'

When Lily had fallen asleep on Tuesday evening, Anna disappeared into her study and Søren sat down at the dining table with his laptop. He had not got round to closing the curtains in the dining room and an eerie darkness crept in from the forest behind the house. It occurred to him that maybe he should sell both of his properties and buy a flat on Nørrebro instead. Ha, that really would irritate the hell out of Thomas, especially as he was intending to buy a house in Espergærde to be close to Lily. Then Anna could live at the university, but cycle home in ten minutes whenever she needed a change of clothes, and Søren could get a paper round by Søerne. Overall the idea had a lot going for it. But then Søren remembered Lily loved the forest. Soon the mewling fox cubs would emerge from their earth and there was soft moss on the stones, which Lily always greeted reverently with the equally soft tip of her nose. There was nothing like that in the city.

Søren took out the preliminary report on Kristian Storm, which he had printed from Linda's computer, and read it in detail. The first thing that leaped out at him was the phrase AWAITING CONFIRMATION, which was stamped in red across the front.

'The inspection of the body at the scene was supervised by Benny Dam, medical examiner,' Søren read. 'Time of death is estimated to be between 19.15 and 20.15, Wednesday, 17 March 2010. Blood effusion observed in the conjunctiva and the sclera of the eye and also in the mouth and along the ligature mark. The ligature mark is pale. Evidence of slackness in the neck, along with presumed damage to the os hyoideum and thyroid cartilage, but a full autopsy must be performed in order to provide evidence of a fracture. Teeth are intact.' At the bottom of the preliminary report, Bøje had scribbled, 'Where the bloody, bollocking hell is my noose, you useless amateurs?'

Søren looked at the report with a growing sense of unease. It really was very unfortunate that Henrik had officially closed the case by concluding that Storm had killed himself *before* he was in receipt of the final medical report. Søren reviewed various witness statements and noted that practically everyone interviewed had initially expressed surprise that Storm would take his own life, but rowed back the moment the conversation moved towards the scientific-dishonesty allegation. Only Trine Rønn continued to insist that suicide was out of the question, regardless of the dishonesty allegation.

At the very back of the file Søren found a copy of Kristian Storm's suicide note. When he had read it, he pushed back his chair and went out into the kitchen to make himself a cup of coffee.

It was an odd suicide note, clumsily phrased and littered with Anglicisms. That was particularly strange because Trine Rønn had stated that Storm had made a point of using correct Danish. Henrik would have picked this up, Søren thought irritably, if only he had bothered questioning Trine Rønn properly.

He flicked through the report to find a witness statement from Marie Skov, but there was nothing. Søren could not understand why she had not yet been interviewed. In the few days since he had taken an interest in the case, her name had cropped up all the time. Nor had Henrik spoken to Berit Dahl Mogensen, the statistician from Odense, whom Merethe Hermansen, the department's chief secretary, had mentioned. Berit Dahl Mogensen was the woman who had left Guinea-Bissau in such haste. Why would Henrik hire Anna to write a totally superfluous profile on Kristian Storm, but fail to talk to the very people who had known Storm and the Belem Health Project? Søren was convinced that Henrik had asked for Anna's help purely to make him jealous, and it was this side of Henrik that bothered him. Quite simply, Søren did not know what game his so-called friend was playing. Deep down Søren trusted very few people, possibly only three: Vibe, his ex-girlfriend, with whom he still had sporadic contact; Linda, his secretary, who had followed him loyally ever since his appointment; and then, of course, Anna. At least until now.

But he didn't trust Henrik.

It only made matters worse that Søren had started having nightmare visions of Anna making passionate love to other men, and that these men were almost invariably Anders T. or Henrik. In Søren's imagination, Anders T. was always irritatingly cocky, as only a young guy with no life scars other than those sustained when he'd scraped his knee on the Great Barrier Reef could be, and Søren was able to rise above it. The scenario of Henrik and Anna together, however, almost drove him insane. In his nightmare, Henrik was taking Anna from behind, hard, the way Anna liked it, but he was rougher and more ruthless than Søren would ever think of being. Søren was convinced that in reality Anna would not enjoy it at all, but in his nightmare she moaned with pleasure. Every time the image appeared, Søren attempted to block it out, which had almost the opposite effect.

Søren knew that Anna would have no truck with his jealousy. He could imagine her roaring with laughter. She had announced long ago that she was a realist and, for his information, did not waste her time on intrigues, gossip and paranoid fantasies. She did not discuss men with her girlfriends, or at least not in the way men imagined. For instance, she would never dream of talking about him behind his back; nor would it ever cross her mind to be unfaithful to him, she had said. If she desired another man, it was because she no longer wanted him and she would tell him so to his face before she did anything with anyone. This reassured him, of course, but just occasionally he wished that Anna could be less direct when it came to irrational feelings. Slam dunk. There was such a thing as too much honesty.

So Søren suffered in silence with his dreadful vision of Henrik taking Anna from behind; a couple of times he had resorted to putting on his trainers and going for a run in the forest to shake off the horror of the image.

Søren logged onto Facebook and visited Anna's profile. He could see that she had just received a virtual fruit basket, a beech sapling and four pineapple palms from Anders T. It was part of an idiotic game called Farmville, Søren saw, and before he knew it he had added the application and selected a small avatar that stood on a barren field, looking totally ridiculous with its oversized head and a pitchfork. Weirdly, a friendship request from Anders T. popped up on his screen almost immediately and when Søren clicked frantically on the invitation to make it go away, he accidentally accepted it, and suddenly an equally ridiculous figure appeared next to his, saying, *H* in a speech bubble. Søren checked the game page to find out how to reply, but before he had discovered that, another speech bubble popped up: *Unemployed public sector worker gets new job. Time to get the harvest in!* At the same time Søren got a message telling him he had received a plum tree and a garden chair as a present from Anders T. Søren clicked *chat*, wrote *Piss off*, hit *enter* and logged out of Facebook.

Then he heard a ping and checked his inbox. *Lovely surprise*, it said in the subject field, and when Søren opened the email, he saw that it was from his childhood friend Jacob Madsen. The tone was hearty. When they were children, Søren had often wondered whether Jacob was jealous of him. Herman Madsen, Jacob's father, had taken a special interest in Søren and his investigative abilities and never sought to hide it, and in the latter part of their friendship, before the Madsen family had moved, Søren had had the distinct feeling that Jacob could not wait to see the back of him. But any past tension had clearly been forgotten.

Dear Søren, How nice to hear from you! I often think about you. And I see that your name appears in the paper every now and then. The old man is obviously as proud as a peacock and claims at least half the credit for your success. As you may remember, we moved to Aalborg and here we have stayed. I teach PE and Danish at Aalborg

Free School. My wife, Birgitte, teaches at another school and we have two children, Max and Jasmin, whom we adopted from China. We are all very well. The only sad news is that my mother died just over a year ago. Jasmin, our daughter, was seven years old at the time and we had just come back from China where we had collected Max. Max was nearly four years old when we adopted him, so it was something of an upheaval for both him and for us, and in the middle of it all my mother was diagnosed with cancer, a very aggressive form, unfortunately. It really got us down, especially the old man, who has had to learn to manage on his own. Dad has moved to a small terraced house because, although he is still as bright as a button, his legs are starting to fail and he fell down the stairs a couple of times in their old house. His mood isn't what it used to be, either. He has grown quite gloomy since Mum died and often struggles to get out of bed in the morning. As it happens, I am going over to see him tonight, and he will be so pleased to hear that I am in contact with you! I think he is slightly disappointed that you became Denmark's most famous detective, rather than me. If you ever come to Aalborg, you must visit him. It would make him so happy. But how are you? Do you have time for a family alongside your career? Are your grandparents still alive? Please post some pictures on your profile so I can keep up! By the way, I made friends on Facebook with Vibe a few months ago, though it was her who found me. I understand that Vibe is married with children of her own now. And I was sure that you and she would stay the distance. Even though we were all so young, there was something very settled about the two of you. Anyway, good to hear from you. Let's keep in touch. Best wishes, Jacob

Søren clicked on Jacob Madsen's friends list and quickly found Vibe's profile. He sent her a friend request and spent a moment looking at her profile picture. It was several months since they had last seen each other, possibly as many as six. Vibe had not lost weight after having two children, but she looked happy. Simple and uncomplicated. And that was precisely what you couldn't stand, Søren reminded himself. Not enough of a challenge. Yet now he found himself almost missing their predictable life together. The certainty of their quiet love, which they didn't have to choose every day. Neither did it have to be reviewed and tested. Søren could not recall Vibe ever being irritated by him. Or provoked by him, was probably more accurate. She was nothing like Anna. Søren had a mental image of Anna constantly watching him, wondering when it was time to pull the pins out of a couple of hand grenades so that anything that looked remotely like the budding shoots of harmony could be levelled to the ground. Vibe was a fundamentally more contented person with normal, everyday expectations, which had been easy for Søren to meet. That they had ultimately split up because Vibe wanted children and Søren didn't was another and, as it had turned out, more complicated story.

Suddenly Søren noticed that Anna and Vibe were also friends on Facebook. That really pissed him off.

Consequently, when Anna came into the living room shortly afterwards and turned on the television to watch an episode of a series she was following, he was perfectly aware how out of order he sounded. Anna glared at him.

'Did you seriously just ask me why I'm friends with Vibe on Facebook, as if that's not allowed because she's your friend, or what?'

'But—'

'On Facebook, you can be friends with the world and his wife, Søren. That's the whole point. Besides, Vibe and I really like each other. I thought you'd be pleased that we get on.'

'I don't like Facebook,' Søren grunted.

'Fine, so you shouldn't have created a profile,' Anna said breezily. 'Are you going to watch *Six Feet Under* with me? It's a repeat, but I didn't see the first episodes when it was last on.'

'No,' Søren said.

'Please yourself,' Anna said, and started watching television.

Søren relocated to the kitchen with his laptop and made a point of closing the door firmly and turning on the radio with the volume a little too loud.

Dear Jacob, Yes, thank you, I'm all right. I live with an unbelievably demanding and self-centred woman who drives me crazy on a daily basis. She is one of those modern 'wimmin' who has ultimately no need for a man because she is more self-sufficient than an ecosystem on steroids, but she deigns to let me live on the margins of her life so she can have regular sex without the risk of catching a nasty venereal disease and to make sure there's someone to look after her daughter when she catches German measles and gets in the way of Mummy's career plans.

Søren had dashed it off as a single thought and now he drew breath. Then he deleted everything and started again.

Dear Jacob, Please give your father my very best wishes. I often think of him with great affection because if it hadn't been for him I would never have applied to the police. I am sorry to hear that he is starting to age. I can't imagine Cluedo being anything other than sharp as a knife. I was also sorry to hear about your mother. Cancer is a merciless disease which sadly claimed the lives of both Knud and Elvira some years ago.

Søren read what he had written before he continued.

I live with Anna who is a dinosaur scientist and works at the Department of Cell Biology and Comparative Zoology; I guess you can say that she is the female equivalent of Ross from *Friends*. She has a daughter, Lily, from a previous relationship, and I have grown to love Lily as if she were my own. We live in Humlebæk, on Skovvej, in a house bordering the forest, but I still own Knud and Elvira's old place on Snerlevej. I'm currently wondering whether to sell it, but then again, the market isn't exactly buoyant.

Hey, by the way, do you remember a family who lived across from us at number nineteen? Their surname was Skov. They had three daughters who were younger than us. I don't remember them myself, but they have popped up in as many as two cases at work and I have grown curious, not least because one of my colleagues has found an old photograph of the family in which I also feature. I haven't seen the picture, but I have been told that I have a football under my arm and am standing next to another teenager wearing eighties clothing, and surely that can only be you. I was just wondering if you can remember them. Curiosity will be the death of me, just ask your father! And, yes, I'll definitely visit Aalborg soon because I would also really like to see him. Let's keep in touch. It's nice to know you're doing so well. Cute kids!

Best wishes, Søren

When Søren had made himself a sandwich and drunk a glass of milk standing at the kitchen table, he walked through the living room, where Anna was still watching television, and down the passage to their bedroom.

'Good night, Big Sulk,' Anna called out cheerfully after him.

When Søren had checked on Lily, he cleaned his teeth and made sure to squeeze the toothpaste in the middle, then leave a couple of fat blobs in the washbasin. He doubted that Anna would notice, but it still felt good.

On Wednesday morning Lily was more ebullient than usual when Søren came out of the shower. She was in the kitchen wearing only knickers and sticking her tummy out while Anna inspected the remains of the German measles.

'The rash has almost gone,' Anna said. 'And she doesn't have a temperature. I think she's well enough to go to nursery.'

'Oh,' Søren said.

'You sound almost disappointed.' Anna laughed and flung her arms around him.

'Give her a kiss,' Lily shouted, and started jumping up and down. Anna offered Søren an exaggerated pout and he bent down to kiss her.

'Right, if you're going to nursery, Lily, we need to get a move on,' Søren said. 'Go and get dressed.' Anna and Lily disappeared down the passage, chatting, and soon afterwards he heard a Kaj and Andrea song playing. He began making Lily's packed lunch.

A moment later Anna popped her head into the kitchen. She was in her underwear, with mascara on one eye. 'Two things. Turns out I'm not going to Bellahøj after all to present my profile of Kristian Storm and—'

'Why not?'

'I've just checked my email and Henrik writes that the case is officially closed, but he doesn't say why. Only that he's sorry for the inconvenience and that I should send him an invoice. Never mind. I had fun doing it. The other thing is that I've just realised the nursery is closed next week as it's Easter. And I was wondering . . . I mean, if you have stuff to do where you can't take Lily, please do you think you could get it done this week? It's just that . . . well, Thomas is coming over this weekend and would like to have Lily on the Saturday, but on the Sunday Anders T. has asked me if I would go with him to his parents' summer house on Sjællands Odde. He can't concentrate on that application – it's hopeless – but he insists that if we drive up there, we can write it in no time. Would that be all right? I'll be back on Wednesday, a week today. And on Maundy Thursday Cecilie and Jens have invited us to Easter lunch and Lily can stay there for a sleepover, and then I thought the two of us could do something together . . . Stay in a hotel or something. Just like all the other boring couples who need to have sex.' Anna grinned.

During all the time Anna had been talking, Søren had been buttering rye bread and had made rather too many sandwiches for a five-year-old.

'Are all those for Lily?' Anna asked, astonished.

'Some are for me,' he said quickly.

'Where are you going?'

'I thought I'd pop over to Snerlevej and tear down the old shed in Knud and Elvira's garden,' he said. 'Finn, my tenant, called to say that the roof is hanging on by a thread after the last storm.'

'Oh, all right. That's a shame – I would have liked to come with you. I'd love to see that house one day. Remind me again why we don't live there.'

'Bad memories,' was all Søren said.

'Bad memories from your childhood? I thought you were happy in that house.'

'Anna.' Søren spun around. 'I can't step inside it without smelling cancer. I know perfectly well it's all in my mind because I aired it for two months after Knud died, but I can still smell it.'

'Then why don't you sell it?'

'Because ... I'm not ready,' Søren replied, and turned his attention back to the packed lunches.

'OK,' Anna said thoughtfully. 'We need to talk about that. But what about the stuff I just said?'

'That's fine with me, Anna Bella.' Søren was busy fitting cherry tomatoes and snack boxes of raisins into the lunch box next to the stacks of sandwiches.

Anna hugged him from behind. 'Hey, are you really OK with that?'

'Yes,' Søren said. 'And you don't have to book some pathetic hotel break to ease your guilty conscience.'

'I don't understand,' Anna said, and let go of him. 'What am I supposed to feel guilty about? And why is it pathetic that I'd like some alone time with you?'

At that moment the doorbell rang.

'Now who could that be? It's only eight thirty,' Anna said. 'Do you mind answering it while I get dressed?'

*

Henrik was at Søren's throat the moment he opened the door.

'What the hell—' Søren defended himself by pushing Henrik so forcefully that Henrik ended up on his backside on the hall floor.

'What do you think you're doing?' a startled Søren roared.

'What am I doing?' Henrik shouted back. 'What do you think you're doing? You handed in your warrant card a week ago. You quit. That means what you're doing is fucking illegal.'

Henrik's gaze was manic.

'Right,' Søren said, 'and what exactly am I supposed to have done?' Henrik had got to his feet again and raised his hand to jab Søren in the chest. Søren shoved him outside and closed the front door behind them. Henrik pointed a finger angrily at him.

'You had no business talking to Bøje without your warrant card,' he said. 'And, what's more, you fucking asked Bøje to email you a copy of his report, forgetting to mention the small detail that you don't have the authority any more. That's classified information for police eyes only, man. And you've been sniffing around the Institute of Biology, chatting to people and, oh, yes, discovered some, in your opinion, vitally important confetti in the basement, which meant I was hauled in front of Jørgensen when I came back from Station City yesterday. Why hadn't I had the brilliant idea to look for those papers in the basement under the Institute of Biology? Why hadn't I spoken to the caretaker? That was what Jørgensen wanted to know. But what fucking difference does it make to the case, eh? None. On the contrary. No normal person shreds their life's work unless it's an admission that the whole thing was a con. But what does common sense matter when you spy an opportunity to humiliate Henrik Tejsner, eh?'

'I don't see why you feel humiliated, Henrik,' Søren said calmly, and folded his arms across his chest. 'Besides, I tried calling you first. Twice. But I reckon you were too busy showing off at Station City to do your job properly.'

'You take that back, you bastard!' Henrik yelled, and took a step towards Søren while he jabbed the air, this time in the direction of Søren's face. 'I'm not putting up with this crap. Take it back.'

'No,' Søren said.

'I think you're jealous,' Henrik spluttered.

'Of what?'

'Jealous that I took over your old job and appear to be so good at it that Station City wants me to work for them. All you're doing is sitting around here breastfeeding. Jealous that I hired Tiger Pussy and that she purrs whenever she sees— What the hell are you doing?'

Søren had taken a step forwards and shoved Henrik further onto the lawn where he stumbled. Henrik regained his footing and looked furiously at Søren. 'Don't you fucking push me!'

'Hey, Henrik, you're—' Søren exclaimed, raising his hand to his own nose.

'You're out of order this time. Either come back and do your job or keep your detective nose to yourself. If you don't, I'll—'

'Henrik—'

'You've made me look a right prat, man, and—'

'Henrik, you're bleeding!'

Now Henrik realised that blood was dripping from his nose and over his mouth. 'You hit me!' he howled.

'No,' Søren said.

'You bloody hit me, man!'

'I only pushed you and you know it.' Søren opened the door, grabbed a woolly hat from the coat stand in the hallway and chucked it at Henrik, who pressed it against his nose.

'I'll bloody report you,' Henrik said. 'If I catch you sniffing around my turf one more time, if you stick your big nose into my business, I'll report you.' Henrik had walked further down the garden path now, still pressing the hat to his nose. His skin was deathly pale and Søren noticed that his free hand was shaking.

'Hey, are you sure you don't need some help with that?' Søren asked.

'Just shut the fuck up,' Henrik shouted, and hurled the hat to the ground.

Then he disappeared. A moment later Søren heard him drive away.

Startled, Søren walked back to the house. There was blood on the garden path and all the way into the hall, so he fetched a cloth and a bucket of water and cleaned it up. He put the woolly hat in the laundry room. It belonged to Lily so he should probably try to wash it even though it was soaked with blood and he was sorely tempted to bin it. Back in the kitchen he washed his hands and poured himself a cup of strong black coffee. Now his hands were shaking too.

Lily came bouncing down the passage, with Anna behind her.

'Who was that?' Anna asked. Søren looked closely at her, but there were no signs that Anna or Lily was aware of what had just happened.

'Licensing people,' Søren said.

'You haven't paid our TV licence?' Anna was surprised.

'Have you?'

'I don't watch TV, do I?'

'You watched TV yesterday,' Søren said.

'Yes, for the first time in two months.'

'Kiss him now,' Lily said, stamping her foot.

Anna kissed the corner of Søren's mouth and grabbed Lily's lunch box.

'Will you be picking me up today, Søren?' Lily asked.

'Absolutely,' Søren replied.

When Anna and Lily had left, he knocked back the last of his coffee, even though it tasted foul.

Then he took a moment to reflect.

Having made up his mind, he went straight to the laundry room, retrieved the blood-soaked woolly hat from the laundry basket and placed it on top of a freezer bag on the kitchen table. In Lily's room he found a petri dish from the Institute of Biology, which Anna had brought home to Lily. He carefully wrung out the hat and a couple of viscous drops landed at the bottom of the petri dish. Then he covered the dish with cling-film and put it in the fridge.

Something was wrong with Henrik.

Søren had cabin fever and needed to get out of the house. He called his tenant on Snerlevej and left a message. Twenty minutes later Finn texted back that Søren was welcome to take a look at the garden shed, even though he and his wife were at work. The key was under an artificial stone to the left of the front door, so he could just let himself in. He would find tools in the basement. Søren put his excess production of sandwiches and a bottle of water into a plastic bag and grabbed his own toolbox. When he was ready to leave, he took the petri dish with Henrik's blood and put it into a small cool box, which Anna used for Lily's sandwiches in the summer. Soon he was on his way to Copenhagen.

Søren scanned the car park outside the Institute of Forensic Medicine, but fortunately he could see neither Henrik's car nor any others from Bellahøj Police. When he walked down the ramp to the basement under the institute, he spotted Bøje at the centre of a semicircle of rapt students in white coats. Bøje was facing Søren and he looked worse than he had yesterday, pale and exhausted, which his recent shave only served to highlight. His eyebrows shot up when he saw Søren, who gestured that he would wait in Bøje's office.

'I've worked with you for . . . how many years is it now?' Bøje asked him brusquely when he stepped inside his office five minutes later and closed the door behind him.

'Nine or ten,' Søren said. 'Thereabouts.'

'Whatever. At any rate, this is the first time you've seriously disappointed me.'

'I'm sorry,' Søren said. 'I just didn't want to put you in a moral dilemma.'

'Oh, I've worked that out and that's why I'm disappointed,' Bøje continued. 'When you waltz in with a question for me, I assume you have a bloody good reason for asking it and it would never cross my mind to question your motives. Maybe ten years ago when you were an irritating rookie, but certainly not now when we've worked together for so long and we respect each other. So I'm a bit pissed off that you didn't tell me yesterday that you and Bellahøj are taking a break. Had I known that, I would obviously never have mentioned your visit to Henrik Tejsner. He totally flipped out. You could have spared me the sight of the most embarrassing loss of composure I've witnessed so far in a grown man. Why on earth did you quit?'

'I'm not suited to a desk job. Not like that,' Søren replied. 'And I'm sorry I didn't trust—'

'That is the biggest load of tosh I've ever heard,' Bøje snapped. 'You are your job, just like I am. It's a calling, a passion, and it's not something you just quit. Take a leaf out of my book and make a highly undervalued move down the ladder. It's more refreshing than green tea.'

'Yes, because you seem so incredibly laid-back, these days,' Søren remarked drily. 'But you're right. I appear to have painted myself well and truly into a corner.'

'Nonsense,' Bøje said. 'Sometimes you have to make a really big mistake to learn your lesson. And if Jørgensen doesn't realise soon that he made a massive howler and give you your old job back, there's bound to be another bright commissioner in one of Denmark's eleven other police districts who would be happy to benefit from your expertise.'

'You may be right,' Søren said, 'but it's also . . .' Suddenly Bøje looked as if he was about to faint. Søren grabbed his arm, pulled out a chair and sat him down. 'Are you all right?' he asked, alarmed.

'Yes, yes,' Bøje snapped. 'I'm just terribly behind with my work and I didn't sleep very much last night. I worked late to finish a case so the undertaker could pick up the body this morning.'

'You need to get some sleep,' Søren said anxiously. Bøje had gone as white as a sheet and Søren thought he was having trouble breathing.

'Yeah, yeah. You can sleep when you're old.'

'You *are* old,' Søren said gently.

'Rub it in, why don't you? Besides, this time I have only myself to blame. I downgraded the case because at first glance it didn't look suspicious in the least. Depressed, heavily medicated fifty-seven-year-old woman in early retirement took too many pills one night last week and snuffed it somewhere in Vangede. At first I thought I could whizz through it in a couple of hours, but I was wrong. First I needed to determine how many drugs she was on, and while her medication chart listed nine, eleven different types were found at her address, some of which were out of date, some no longer being produced and some were medication given only to hospital patients. However, according to her medical records, the deceased had not been hospitalised since 1995. I began to get a bad feeling about it, especially when I found three dark hairs wrapped around the deceased's thumb, index and middle finger. Too dark to belong to the deceased herself, if you get my drift. I've probably grown paranoid from lack of sleep, but I ended up performing a full autopsy and sent blood, tissue, urine, nail scrapings and the three hairs as an urgent case to the Department of Forensic Genetics. Even if it proves to be a storm in a teacup, it'll still feel good to have squandered some of your miserly boss's budget. Anyway, I didn't finish until three o'clock this morning and by that time it was too late to go home, wouldn't you say? My new shift of students arrived at eight.'

Søren looked attentively at Bøje. 'I happen to know about

the Vangede case,' he then said. 'I believe the dead woman's name is Joan Skov.'

Bøje Knudsen shrugged. 'You could be right. I know her better as OK133-2010.'

'She's the mother of a girl who grew up in the same street as me, and that girl, Marie Skov, is the professor's closest assistant. Or she was.'

For a moment Bøje seemed baffled. 'The professor?'

'The other body on your table. The man from the Institute of Biology.'

'Really? Is there a link I ought to know about?'

'No, I don't think so. I'm just saying it's a small world.'

At this Bøje gave Søren a sly look. 'Now I get why you're sniffing around without permission, you nosy parker.'

Søren gave a light shrug. 'Anna, my girlfriend, works in the building next to the Department of Immunology, and she knows the woman who found Kristian Storm and then ... Well, it just seemed a bit odd that everything led back to the street where I grew up, so, yes, it did make me a bit nosy. But I'm also annoyed at how Henrik is handling this case. He talks nonsense and draws easy conclusions ... And he flirts with Anna,' Søren blurted out.

Bøje stared at Søren in disbelief. 'You lot are nothing but a bunch of bitchy little divas. One minute one of Denmark's leading police officers is stamping his foot like a toddler having a tantrum, and the next his superior, possibly Denmark's most famous police officer, comes to cry on my shoulder because somebody's been flirting with his girl. Jesus Christ, Marhauge, if you can't rise above that inflated hothead, your relationship with your girlfriend is in big trouble. Now, I have better things to do than sit here offering you free therapy.' Bøje stood up, swaying perilously, but stayed on his feet.

'You really should go home and get some rest,' Søren said.

'Do you still want a copy of my report on Kristian Storm when I get round to finishing it?' Bøje said, ignoring him.

'Yes, please,' Søren replied. Bøje was right. He should easily be able to rise above Henrik. 'And if you accidentally attach your post-mortem report on the woman from Vangede, with her blood tests and the forensics results, I wouldn't mind.' Søren fluttered his eyelashes in an exaggerated manner.

'Got something in your eye, have you?' Bøje grunted.

'Hey, wait, there's another thing!' Søren said.

Bøje had got as far as the door and placed his hand on the handle. He gave Søren a weary look.

'Please would you take a look at this blood sample?'

'What blood sample?' Bøje said.

'It's from . . . a friend. Someone I'm worried about. So I guess you could say it's a personal favour.'

Bøje narrowed his eyes. 'You're pushing it, Marhauge. But put it in the fridge on the right.' He pointed first at one of the two steel doors and then at Søren. 'And then get out of here. Dry your eyes and man up, OK?'

'Thanks!' Søren called after him, but the door had already slammed.

Shortly afterwards, as Søren walked towards the lift, he heard Bøje's voice: 'Right, people, the first person who throws up buys a round. This isn't a profession for the faint hearted.'

After visiting Bøje, Søren drove to Snerlevej and concluded almost immediately that trying to repair the old shed in

Knud and Elvira's garden was pointless. It was crumbling and dilapidated, even potentially hazardous. He sent a text message to Finn that he would be back the following day to knock it down. He walked around the house, which brought back memories of Knud and Elvira. They had been good, loving people, who had brought up Søren to be committed and realistic at all times, which made their decision that he couldn't handle the truth about his parents' death even more mysterious. He would never understand it; perhaps that was why he felt so low whenever he visited the house. It was not the smell of cancer or the memory of first Elvira and soon after Knud, wasting away in front of his eyes; it was a feeling of having been deceived. He was not angry, not in the least, just sad.

It was at that moment he made up his mind to sell the house.

He knew he would never live there again.

As Søren unlocked his car, he glanced down the road to number nineteen, the home of the Skov family. He could not remember noticing the house before, and now that he had, he instinctively took against it. Most houses on Snerlevej were attractive and well maintained, but number nineteen looked decidedly run-down. No flowers. No kitsch wreath on the door or a bird bath in the flowerbed to suggest that someone, regardless of taste, had at least made an effort. Just then the front door opened and a man and a woman appeared. The man was an undertaker, that was plain, and he offered the woman a sympathetic handshake. The woman must be the eldest daughter, Julie Claessen, whom Henrik had described as 'the size of a shed'. It was not entirely fair. Curvaceous would have been a more generous word. But what jumped out at Søren more than anything was how old-fashioned she looked. Her skirt was long, reaching right down to her calves and she wore an awful blouse with a loose, floppy bow. The style was completely wrong for a woman who was at most in her mid-thirties. At that moment, Julie raised her eyes and looked directly at him, only for a second, and Søren quickly got into his car. As he drove off, he saw in his rear-view mirror how Julie waved to the undertaker, then lingered wistfully on the garden path in front of the house before she went back inside and closed the door behind her.

Søren made a quick U-turn. When he passed number nineteen, he turned his head to study the house and was rumbled when he spotted Julie in the window. She followed his car with her eyes, then made a point of closing the curtains. Søren drove on past Herman Madsen's old house. It lay less than a hundred metres from the Skov family home.

Lily was drawing at a table in her nursery when Søren arrived to collect her.

'She's been a bit quiet today,' the nursery teacher said, 'and she liked sitting on my lap for a cuddle, didn't you, Lily?' Lily nodded and ran to the pegs in the hallway to fetch her snowsuit.

'Forgive me for asking,' the nursery teacher said quietly, 'but is everything all right at home? I don't wish to intrude, but Lily said a couple of things today that made me think you might be having problems.'

'Oh,' Søren said. 'I'm surprised to hear that.'

'Before our fruit break she said you had a fight with your brother this morning.'

'My brother?'

'Yes,' the nursery teacher said. 'She said, "Søren said it was the TV-licence people, but I knew it was Uncle Henrik."'

Søren was momentarily at a loss. 'Aha,' he said. 'I'll talk to her.'

Once they were in the car, Lily sang 'The Wheels on the Bus', but made up most of the lyrics, which alternated between being involuntarily poetic and deliberately provocative. Søren couldn't get a word in edgeways until they reached home and he had parked the car.

'Lily, I want to ask you a question. When you looked out of the window this morning, did you see something that frightened you?' he said.

'I might have,' Lily replied.

'Did you see me push Uncle Henrik?'

'Yes,' Lily said. 'Mum was drying her hair so she didn't hear anything, but I sat on the windowsill counting my birds' eggshells, and that's when I saw you push Uncle Henrik and I also saw a lot of blood. Why were you angry with Uncle Henrik and why did you say he had come about the TV licence? It's naughty to lie.' Lily looked sternly at Søren.

Søren thought hard. 'I said it was about the TV licence because your mum heard someone ring the doorbell and wanted to know who it was, but I didn't think you had heard or seen anything, and Uncle Henrik was really very sad, and I thought if you found out you would be sad too, and there was no reason for you to be. So I said it was the TV-licensing people. I didn't see you in the window.'

'Don't be cross with Uncle Henrik.' Lily looked upset.

'We'll make it up,' Søren assured her. 'It's just like when you fall out with Hannah or Martha at nursery and—'

'I didn't like Uncle Henrik's eyes,' Lily said. 'I waved to him and he looked right up at me and his eyes were huge and swirly.' Lily made spiral movements in front of her eyes. 'Just like Uncle Anders' when he stayed over.'

'Uncle Anders? From the children's TV programme?'

'No,' Lily said. 'Anders who works with Mum.'

Søren's stomach lurched. 'When was that?' he said casually.

'I don't know. Oh, yes, I do – it was when you came home with that mermaid Barbie for me, which Mum didn't like one bit but you said that she was a marine biologist and had written a doctoral something or other.' Lily unclicked her seatbelt and jumped out onto the pavement. 'And I want my Hello Kitty hat back,' she insisted. 'Please may I play Oline on the computer now?' Søren nodded and stayed in the car when Lily had slammed the door and raced up the garden path.

He was in shock.

He had bought that Barbie for Lily in Vordingborg where he had spent two days attending a strategic leadership course last October. Anna had mentioned that Anders T. and another PhD student from the department had come round for dinner because they were writing a song for their head of department whose anniversary was imminent. Søren had thought nothing of it. It had been wonderful to come home because Anna and Lily had thrown their arms around his neck and been extraordinarily pleased to see him. On Anna's part, almost suspiciously pleased, he could see that now.

Lily was busy stacking cushions on a chair in order to reach the laptop when Søren entered the house; shortly afterwards he could hear low, animated voices and Lily replying. For a long time he stood leaning against the kitchen table, unable even to pick up the phone when Anna called just before five.

Besides, he knew why she was calling: to say that she was running late because of something work-related. He'd bet on it.

Søren was lying on the sofa, watching the news, when Anna got home. Lily had had a bath and was in bed, but she was still awake and looking at some picture books. Anna brought the scent of early spring with her into the living room and her eyes shone after her walk back from the station.

'Oh, isn't it wonderful that it's getting lighter? I do so love spring,' she said, and kissed Søren. 'I'm sorry I'm so late. Did you get my message?'

'Yes,' Søren said, and tried to watch television around Anna, who was squatting on her haunches by the sofa.

'Am I in your way?' She grinned.

'Lily's still awake. Do you think you could go and say good night? She's been waiting for you.'

Anna went down the passage and Søren heard her read aloud three books at least. During all that time, he lay seething on the sofa. Part of him wanted to march into Lily's room and demand to know why Anna had never mentioned that Anders T. had stayed over, while another part ordered him not to. Anna had told him so very little about her relationship with Thomas, Lily's biological father, but she had said one thing that was scorched into Søren's memory.

'When we met each other,' she had said, 'Thomas wanted

everything and preferably by yesterday. He pressured me into living with him, he said "I love you" almost straight away, and he took me to meet all his friends and family in Jutland even though we had only dated for a few weeks. But once he got to know me properly, he didn't like me at all. He didn't like my personality, he didn't like my body, he didn't like my passion. If I hadn't already been pregnant at that point, we would have split up. It was all wrong. He thought I was the woman of his dreams, but I was someone completely different. It was the worst experience of my life, and I swore that if I were ever to have another boyfriend, he would have to love me for who I was.'

Søren knew that Anna would be furious if he so much as hinted that she had cheated on him. She had already told him she would never contemplate doing anything of the sort. She would break up with him before she started a relationship with another man, she had said. But she had not split up with him. And that business with Anders was six months ago, if it had even happened.

He would die if he lost her.

'What's wrong with you?' Anna asked, when she came back into the living room. Søren had curled up and was facing the back of the sofa. 'She's asleep now. Did you save some dinner for me?'

'No,' Søren said. 'We had porridge.'

'Porridge?'

'Yes, I couldn't be bothered to cook,' Søren said.

'Is something wrong?'

'No.'

'Then why are you being like this?'

'I'm just tired.'

Anna sat down on the sofa next to him and held him tight.

'Kiss me,' she said, in a low voice. Soon, his jeans were around his ankles and Anna was straddling him.

'Put your hand over my mouth,' she moaned, and when he did, she came loudly, murmuring into his palm.

'I needed that,' Anna said afterwards. She was lying with her neck on the edge of the sofa, her half-dressed body on the floor and her hand around Søren's ankle. He was still sitting on the sofa and was completely exhausted.

'Working with Anders T. is a bloody nightmare,' Anna said, after a lengthy silence. 'He's a great guy, charming and funny, but trying to organise anything with him is a joke. He can't concentrate at all. It beats me how he ever got his master's. Seriously, I suspect him of having bought his degree on the Khao San Road during a transit stop in Thailand, and I genuinely worry about his PhD. You have to work consistently for all three years, but Anders T. is acting as if he were still an undergraduate and he can just pull a few all-nighters before the exam. I won't apply for any more grants with him. He's uncontrollable, like a puppy, but very entertaining.' Anna shook her head, but couldn't stop herself smiling. Then she got up and went out into the bathroom. Soon after, she returned in her dressing gown and headed for the kitchen where Søren heard her tip cornflakes into a bowl.

'I'm going to bed,' she said, a moment later, when she reappeared in the living room. 'And, Søren?'

'Yes?'

'It was good to be close to you again. It's been a whole week since the last time. What's happening to us?' She gave a fleeting smile and disappeared out of the living room.

What was she really saying?

When Søren checked his inbox, Bøje had sent him two emails with attachments. One he had named *OK133 -2010* and the other *Your friend's blood sample*.

Dear Søren, I'm attaching Joan Skov's autopsy report, with the preliminary investigation report. You'll get the rest as soon as they're back from Forensic Genetics. Should anyone ask, you nicked everything and I know nothing about it. Unfortunately I didn't get round to Kristian Storm today because a girl was found dead in Hedehusene. Personally, I don't believe her death is related to the girls in Kødbyen, but of course I had to drop everything again. After orders from above, obviously! So, on that account, please be patient. I think it will be tomorrow at the latest because Storm's funeral is this Friday. Best wishes, Bøje. PS: I really hope the blood sample you gave me this morning isn't actually yours. As in 'Dear Agony Aunt, my friend has genital warts, what do you think my friend should do?' But we can have a chat about that another time. Remember, I'm always on your side.

Søren opened the file *Your friend's blood sample* with a sense of foreboding.

'Shit,' he exclaimed, when he had finished reading the document.

He took his mobile out of his pocket, found Henrik's number and then he stopped.

'Shit, shit, shit,' he swore again.

He called Jeanette instead.

Henrik and Jeanette had been married since Henrik was at the Police Academy. They had two teenage daughters, and a baby on the way. That baby must be due any time soon, Søren thought. He believed Henrik had mentioned April as the due date. His call went to Jeanette's voicemail and Søren asked her to call him as soon as possible.

Then he opened Joan Skov's report, but his mind was no longer on the job. He kept thinking about Henrik. Suddenly he heard a ping from his laptop, and when he checked, there was a long email from Jacob Madsen.

Dear Søren, I'm really sorry to hear that Knud and Elvira are both dead. I realised that they had reached old age, but they always seemed indomitable to me. Cancer is a dreadful thing. We have changed our lifestyle completely since my mother died. It's no guarantee, I know, but we have both started exercising, we try to eat healthily and be less stressed. Yes, I know it sounds a bit holier than thou, but when I saw my mother waste away in front of my eyes, I decided to do what I could to ensure my cause of death will be something else. What kind of cancer did Knud and Elvira die from?

Søren kept thinking about Henrik and he had just made up his mind to read Jacob's kind email another time when the next sentence caught his attention.

It's funny that you should ask about the family at number nineteen. Dad moved house about a month ago, and when we were sorting through his and Mum's stuff, the old man suddenly picked up a black-and-white photograph from a box, of my mother hugging a little girl, and said he would send it to the Skov family. I had no idea who he was talking about, but Dad explained that they were our former neighbours from Snerlevej and that Mum used to look after their youngest daughter, Lea. She was the girl in the photograph and Mum was very fond of her. Sadly the care arrangement ended dramatically when her father, Frank Skov, accused Mum of having bruised Lea's arms. He grabbed my mother's arm in the street and your grandfather saw it. My mother didn't want to report Frank Skov because she feared he would take it out on Lea, but your grandfather – who was a strong believer in the rule of law – reported him. However, when the police came to interview Mum, she folded her arms across her chest as only she knew how and said she had no idea what they were talking about. Anyway, Dad got it into his head that Lea Skov should have that photograph as a memory of Mum and when we looked up the Skov family on the net, we learned that the parents, Frank and Joan, still lived on Snerlevej. Dad was going to ring them and ask for their daughter's address, he said. A few weeks later I asked how he was getting on with the picture and Dad said that it hadn't gone very well. He had managed to get hold of Joan Skov, who had also agreed that Lea would be pleased to have the picture, but had asked him to please ring back in the evening when her husband was at home because she couldn't remember Lea's address. But before Dad had time to call back, he received a call from Julie, the eldest daughter in the Skov family, who very bluntly and somewhat aggressively said they didn't want the picture and it should be thrown away. But Dad didn't want to do that. He remembered how Julie had always been very controlling of her sisters so he called back in the evening and got Lea's address from Frank, who was perfectly polite. A few days passed, and before Dad got round to posting the photograph, Julie Skov called him, screaming and shouting that he had killed her mother. At first Dad did not understand one word, but then he realised that Joan Skov had committed suicide, and Julie thought it was because Dad had reminded her of the dreadful time when she couldn't look after her own children. Dad was distraught and got in touch with his old friend and colleague Benny Jørgensen, from Bellahøj Police. You know him, I gather. He's your chief superintendent, and you work at Bellahøj, don't you? But it was true: Joan Skov had killed herself on the night between Wednesday and Thursday, Jørgensen was able to tell him, but obviously it had had nothing to do with Dad's call or the photograph. Nevertheless Dad has been very upset by the incident ever since, glum and despondent, as if he has completely lost the touch that, back in the day, made him such a good police officer. I hope you won't think I'm putting pressure on you, but I was going to ask if you fancy actually visiting him in the near future. It would really cheer him up to talk about the old days and about police work. Anyway, I had better hit *send*. Apologies for such a lengthy palaver, but don't forget, I'm a Danish teacher ☺ Best wishes, Jacob

On Thursday morning Søren drove to Snerlevej after taking Lily to nursery. Finn had not yet left for work and offered Søren a cup of coffee and a crusty bread roll when he turned up with his toolbox and chainsaw.

They chatted for a while about this and that, and Søren was struck by how tired he was. Dead tired. He leaned back, happy to let Finn do the talking. Suddenly he realised that, although the kitchen had been modernised, he could see straight through the living room directly to the Skov house across the road. He adjusted his chair slightly to get a better view.

A man and two smartly dressed girls were standing on the pavement. The front door opened and Julie Claessen, dressed in black, emerged with a man whom Søren guessed must be the infamous Frank Skov. They debated something, after which Frank put his keys into his pocket. Together they walked in the direction of a parked car and Søren could see their faces clearly now. Frank looked like a petty criminal, he thought. A weasel. Not evil or repulsive, but someone who was always ducking and diving. He drank, that was plain to see. His hair had been combed, but it was greasy at the back with marks from the comb and he had the kind of dentures worn by someone who is ageing and trying to disguise it. As a police officer, Søren had seen his fair share of weasels and, though he knew perfectly well not to judge a book by its cover, he couldn't help it. The man who had been standing on the pavement with the two girls now helped Frank into the car's passenger seat and closed the door. They drove off, leaving a white VW Transporter in the carport.

'She's being buried today,' said Finn, who had followed Søren's gaze. 'The mother, Joan. You probably know them because I believe they've lived there for over thirty years.'

Søren shook his head. 'I don't know them, but . . .' He was about to tell Finn about the photograph Henrik had found and the link to Kristian Storm, but fell silent.

'Frankly, I can't say we were surprised when we heard that she had died. We hardly ever saw her, and on the few occasions that we did, she looked ill. Always in her dressing gown, and fragile, as if she could barely tolerate sunlight. But I've heard that she was artistic when she was younger and studied at Kunstakademiet before she had children. My wife is friends with the woman who took over Joan's job teaching art at Dyssegårdsskolen – that's how I know. I believe she killed herself. The police were here for two days in a row so it's probably not an ordinary death. Do you know anything?' Finn looked curiously at Søren.

'Even if I did, I couldn't tell you.' Søren smiled.

'They have a very beautiful daughter,' Finn said. 'Lea, their youngest. My son has just turned seventeen and has a huge crush on her. Their middle daughter is also pretty, but more ordinary-looking. The neighbour told my wife that she has breast cancer, so that family has been hit hard. Frank is a nice guy. I've borrowed tools from him a few times. His shed is really well equipped, but you should see their back garden. It's unbelievable. Enclosed by bushes on three sides so you can't see in from the other gardens, and it's not until you're inside it that you realise you're in a small version of Vigeland Park.'

'Vigeland Park?'

'That sculpture garden in Oslo – only Frank's garden is dotted with the most peculiar clay figures, partly ruined by the wind and the weather. When you look at those figures, it's hard to believe she ever showed promise.'

'I believe they lost a little son many years ago,' Søren blurted out.

'Gosh, is that right?'

'What else do you make of them?' Søren said.

'Hmm,' Finn said, draining his coffee cup. 'Their eldest daughter visits frequently, sometimes with her two daughters, but mostly alone. I believe she's a carer – well, she drives one of those cars with *Copenhagen Council Homecare* on it. She looks nothing like her sisters although they share the same colouring. All three have their father's dark brown hair and blue eyes. But the two younger girls are both petite – my son would probably describe them as fit, especially the youngest – while the eldest girl is very large. Not massively overweight, but … big. The youngest visited a lot at the start of the year, come to think of it. I haven't seen her for a few months, though, and the middle daughter comes from time to time on a Sunday. I believe she has a child and a husband … That's right; I'm sure about the husband because he's an orthopaedic surgeon at Rigshospitalet. Jesper Just is his name. My wife is an anaesthetics nurse and she recognised him one day when we were … curtain twitching.' Finn chuckled. 'Simple pleasures, eh? Anyway, I'd better get to work. Just lock up when you're done.'

'Can you remember the name of the other son-in-law?'

'I don't know it. However, every time I came to borrow something, Frank would make sure to mention Jesper. As if he was trying to impress visitors with his son-in-law the doctor. He never mentioned the other, not once. They're a strange family. Tanja and I have spent a lot of time discussing them in the last few years – yes, I'm sorry, but they're that kind of family. You just can't help talking about them. They stand out, somehow, if you know what I mean. Marie, the middle daughter, is a shining academic light while the youngest is a nail technician, and Frank might have been studying civil engineering once, at the dawn of time, but he doesn't seem that bright to me. He cracks bad jokes and is a bit of a racist. I think he makes his money doing odd jobs. That family just doesn't make much sense, is what I'm trying to say. Anyway, I'd better be off.'

Get a life, Søren thought, when Finn had left.

Two hours later it was Søren's turn to stand behind the curtain in Finn and Tanja's living room, spying on the Skov house. He had managed to tear down most of the wooden shed in the garden and reduce it to an unruly pile behind the house, but he still had several hours of work ahead of him. The Skov family was clearly not back from the funeral yet because Frank's Transporter was still sitting abandoned in the carport. Søren narrowed his eyes and tried to conjure up just one memory from his childhood that included the Skov family, but it proved impossible. Not even the supposedly gorgeous daughter rang any bells, but then again she would have been just a few years old in those days. Lily would definitely grow into a beauty, he then thought, because she took after her mother, luckily, not Thomas. Søren already knew that next Saturday, when Thomas had Lily, would be the longest day in the history of the world, and he wondered if he should go to Odense to visit a friend and former colleague, who kept asking him when he was coming over. Then it would be Anna's turn to wonder where *he* was. His thoughts turned to Henrik. He would have to confront Henrik with what he knew. However he looked at it, Henrik was his friend and Søren had to steel himself for a difficult conversation.

Eventually two cars drove down Snerlevej and pulled up outside number nineteen. Søren retreated behind the curtain. At first he watched Frank Skov get out, then the man who had waited on the pavement with the two girls and finally Julie and her daughters. Julie was sobbing openly and the girls pressed themselves anxiously against her. Three people got out of the second car: a man of around thirty-five, who fitted the description of the son-in-law with the medical degree, and two younger women, who had to be Marie and Lea. Søren studied them with interest. Lea really was striking. Even so, Søren was instantly more attracted to Marie. She was petite, wore no makeup and, compared to her sister's black-lace-meets-studs outfit, her clothes were decidedly dowdy, but she had intelligent eyes, whose sparkle Søren could see from across the street, and she wore a defiant yellow scarf around her head. He was fascinated by the dynamics of the Skov family. Julie continued to cry and everyone took it in turn to comfort her, somewhat awkwardly. Frank was silent, but Søren could see that he was upset. The other son-in-law, Julie's husband, clearly had no idea what to do with himself and kept checking something on his mobile, while the surgeon shifted his weight from one foot to the other and exuded authority. Marie and Lea were both distressed; that was obvious. However, Søren realised, to his surprise, they were also very guarded.

He jumped when his mobile rang.

It was Jeanette.

For a moment he struggled to remember why he had asked her to call him back. He knew he was a bad friend for not going straight to Henrik with his discovery and deep down he did not want to be that kind of person, but the result of Henrik's blood sample had temporarily knocked all common sense out of him.

'Hi, Jeanette!' he said. 'How are you? Have you had your baby yet?'

'What do you want, Søren?' Jeanette said icily.

'Are you OK?' Søren asked, mystified.

'How many times have you been to my house in all the years we've known each other? Eaten my dinners and drunk my wine in my kitchen while we put the world to rights? Lots. The girls and I cheered you on when you ran the Eremitage Race. I'm aware that you're mostly Henrik's friend, but I thought you and I were friends too. Good friends, even.'

'Yes. Aren't we?' Søren was stumped.

'No, we're not. Because if we were, you would have called to ask me how I was. How the girls were. Asked if you could bring me some dinner or help me put together the changing unit or spend just one evening listening to me. It's been really tough and I've never been so miserable in all my life. I'm pregnant and I've got pelvic-girdle pain and I'm overdue and I'm being induced tomorrow – and do you know something? I always thought you were better than that because—'

'Jeanette, what are you talking about?'

'I've always really liked you, Søren. But I was wrong about you.'

'Jeanette,' Søren said, 'I've no idea what the hell you're talking about. Please take a deep breath and slow down. Where is Henrik?'

'How the hell would I know? I haven't seen him for six months.' She was crying her eyes out now. 'Six months! Ever since he came home and announced out of the blue that he was off, see you later. Don't tell me you didn't know, you bastard. The least you could have done was call to ask how the girls and I were coping. And, since you ask, I feel like shit. We're going to have a baby, a little boy, and I'm convinced Henrik is screwing someone on the right side of forty, the right side of thirty, even, who doesn't have floppy tits from breastfeeding his kids and—'

'But I thought you had, eh . . . new breasts?' Søren asked

and wanted to kick himself, but he had blurted it out before he'd had time to think.

'What the hell are you on about?' Jeanette was now sobbing and raging at the same time. 'What possessed you to ask me such a stupid question? Is that what she's got, Henrik's bitch? You must tell me if you know something.'

'Jeanette,' Søren said, 'I haven't got a clue what you're talking about. As far as I know, you and Henrik are happy after that crisis a few years ago and you're expecting a baby. I know nothing about him not living at home for six months, or that he's supposed to have a girlfriend, and I can't imagine that he does! He's thrilled that you're pregnant—'

'Then why did you make that comment about me getting new breasts?' Jeanette bawled.

'Because some time ago Henrik mentioned that you were considering having breast implants. I don't know why I said it. I'm just so shocked that . . . It appears he's been lying to both of us.'

There was silence at the other end.

'And you're telling me the truth?' Jeanette said at last.

'Jeanette,' Søren said, 'in the past year, Henrik and I haven't been getting on all that well. In fact, I'm really pissed off with him and . . . quite worried. I haven't heard anything about . . . anything.'

Jeanette was weeping quietly now. 'He just came home from work on a totally ordinary day and announced that he was moving out. He wouldn't give me an explanation, only that we were better off without him. Me, the girls and the baby. I begged him, but there was nothing I could do. "It's over," he said. I'd never seen him so cold. I thought I knew him and that I could reach him, but no. He just stood there with his sports bag and his bloody Xbox under his arm, as cold as ice. I didn't know what to tell the girls. They've hardly seen him since and they're really upset! Once they met in town, at a patisserie, and afterwards they said they'd barely recognised him. That he was all twitchy. After my twenty-two-week scan, I called Henrik. I'd just found out that we were going to have a boy and that all was well. I was sobbing when I called him and I could feel how he softened. "Jeanette ..." he said. He dropped his guard for a moment. "Love me," I said to him, "love us." It went completely quiet. And you know why? Because he'd hung up. I hate him, Søren. I hate him.' Jeanette started sobbing again.

'OK,' Søren said.

'OK?' Jeanette said.

'Jeanette,' Søren said, 'I didn't know about any of this, believe me. Not a thing. Perhaps because I'm as thick as two short planks and haven't paid attention to anything other than myself over the past year, or perhaps because Henrik has a damn good reason for doing what he's doing. Whatever it is, I'll have a word with him, I promise. Have you got someone who can be with you at the birth tomorrow?'

'Yes – my friend Solvej is coming with me.'

'Good,' Søren said. 'Try to forget Henrik for a few days and concentrate on your baby and your girls. And, Jeanette? I wish you'd called me earlier.'

When Søren had finished his conversation with Jeanette, he called Henrik three times in a row, the first two without leaving a message. The third time he said, 'Henrik, Søren here. I need to talk to you now. Please call me back when you get this message. Thanks.'

Two hours later he had finished demolishing the garden shed, and at about the same time, a lorry set down a skip outside the house. It took Søren an hour to carry the wood to the skip and every time he dumped an armful, he would throw a glance at number nineteen. Once he saw the three grandchildren open the front door, but they were quickly called back inside. Apart from that, it was quiet on Snerlevej. Just before three o'clock, he left to fetch Lily.

On Friday morning Søren dropped Lily at nursery and drove back home to change into a suit. At midday he entered St Stefan's Church and managed to find himself a seat on one of the rear pews in the densely packed church. Storm's coffin was covered with an earth-coloured, finely woven fabric and blue flowers. The ceremony was moving. There were several eulogies, there was music and dance, and liberating laughter echoed around the church when the vicar remarked that Storm would have been enormously pleased with his send-off. Eventually Søren spotted Marie. She was sitting near the front, on the opposite side of the central aisle, and once again Søren got the distinct impression that she was on her guard. Several times she turned her face to the stained-glass windows, away from the service, and when the vicar made everyone laugh again, Marie was practically the only one who kept a straight face. The tears did not start rolling down her cheeks until an elderly man stood up and, his voice shaking, said, 'With Storm a whole school of exemplary research has died.' When it was announced that there would be a reception in Storm's lecture hall at the Institute of Biology, Søren decided to attend.

He continued to keep his distance at the Institute of

Biology, but he rarely let Marie out of his sight. She knew most people, at least on nodding acquaintance terms, and mingled quietly from group to group. Many people were surprised and delighted to see her and Søren heard her say, 'Yes, but I'm still on sick leave,' and, 'Yes, but I'm feeling better and expect to start my PhD soon.' She spent a long time talking to Thor Albert Larsen, and Søren made sure to position himself so that Thor would not see him. It looked as if they had a disagreement. Suddenly Søren heard his mobile ring deep in his pocket and failed to get to it in time. When he looked up again, Thor was talking to a fresh group of mourners and Marie had disappeared. He wandered around the lecture hall until he saw her talking to a black man at the far end of the raked seating. Pictures from Storm's life were projected onto the wall above the lectern and a photograph of a smiling Storm with two young men appeared. One was a Danish-looking guy with dreadlocks and the other was the man Marie was talking to. Marie and the man peered up at the photograph, seeming deeply moved.

Søren was suddenly overcome with embarrassment and decided to look for the exit. What the hell was he doing there, spying on a private gathering? He wasn't investigating a case because there was nothing to investigate. And, besides, he had quit his job.

Out of nowhere Thor Albert Larsen was behind him. 'Excuse me,' he said, and when Søren turned, he continued, 'I thought I recognised you.' They shook hands.

'It's not that you're not welcome, of course,' Thor smiled, 'but is there any particular reason for your being here?'

'Just doing a bit of observation,' Søren said. 'Something

doesn't add up. I'm aware that you scientists don't have a lot of time for hunches, but in my job a hunch is often enough—'

'Are you taking the piss?' Thor interrupted him.

'No,' Søren said, and flashed him a smile.

'And what is your hunch telling you?' Thor wanted to know.

'It's telling me that you're a creep,' Søren said, and before Thor had time to pick his jaw up from the floor, Søren had turned on his heel and left.

In the car park outside the Institute of Biology, his mobile rang again and this time Søren managed to get to it in time.

'Hi, Søren,' a chirpy voice said.

'Who is it?' Søren said brusquely.

'It's Jacob! Jacob Madsen.'

'Hi,' Søren said, surprised.

'Did you get my email?'

'Yes! Thank you! I was going to reply today but—'

'Don't worry about it, it's not urgent. And I did bang on a bit.' Jacob laughed.

'No, that's quite all right.'

'I'm calling to ask a favour,' Jacob continued. 'I know you're too busy to come to Aalborg right now, but would you mind giving the old man a call? Have a chat to him, one police officer to another. It was my wife's idea. I told her I'd emailed you about what had happened and she thought talking to you might cheer him up. He's still very low because of Julie Skov's far-fetched accusation. Nothing we've tried seems to help so I thought perhaps you could . . . ring him. For old times' sake.'

Søren thought about it. 'I'd like to visit,' he then said.

'Great!' Jacob exclaimed. 'Then the two of us would have a chance to meet up as well. When?'

'How about tomorrow?'

'Tomorrow?'

'Yes, if I can get a plane ticket, I'd like to fly out tomorrow.'

'Right then – of course, but—'

'I'll see if I can get a ticket and I'll call you back in a sec.'

'Brilliant,' Jacob said.

It took Søren five minutes to learn that he could catch a plane to Aalborg at nine fifty-five the following morning and return to Copenhagen at six forty in the evening.

'I've already told Dad,' Jacob said, when Søren called back. 'You wouldn't believe how happy it made him. Thank you, Søren.'

Søren had parked in Hillerødgade and had made his way on foot to the university in the wake of the large crowd of mourners and now he had to go back to fetch his car. It was a twenty-five-minute walk, rain was spitting and it was cold, but he felt better for it. At Nørrebro Runddel, his mobile pinged to let him know he had a new text message and he fished out his phone. No wonder people were chronically stressed these days. Being constantly accessible, whether you were walking, on the loo or asleep, was a nightmare. He had only had a smart phone since his promotion and he suddenly missed his ancient Nokia 3210, which had been a useful servant, not something that controlled his life.

Dear all, Nature beat me to it. I went into labour at three o'clock this morning and at six ten I gave birth to a lovely boy weighing almost 4 kg. Mother and baby are doing well

and Solvej has been a great support. The girls already love
their baby brother, as do I. We have decided to call him
Storm because he arrived at gale force 10. The maternity
unit is Y2, and I'm in side ward 228, but we would also
welcome visitors when we get home in a couple of days. Lots
of love, Jeanette, Olivia, Sara and Storm

A picture of Olivia and Sara holding their newborn baby
brother was attached to the message. Søren stopped in his
tracks.

When he had recovered, he called Henrik again, but this
time his call did not even go to voicemail.

Then he called Linda at Bellahøj.

'You're calling to let me know you'll be coming back to
work after Easter,' she teased him. 'Oh, that's great news.
Jørgensen will be so thrilled!'

'Hold your horses,' Søren said. 'I'm not making promises
either way. I still haven't heard a word from Jørgensen so, as
far as I'm concerned, it's merely my secretary's humble desire
that I return for the simple reason that I'm a nicer boss than
Henrik.'

Linda laughed.

'Speaking of Henrik,' Søren went on, 'did you know he's
moved?'

'No,' Linda said. 'Has he?'

'I'm not sure—'

'Why don't you just call Jeanette and ask her where
they're living? By the way, isn't that baby of theirs due any
minute now?'

'Have you seen Henrik today?'

'Yes, when he gave the nine o'clock morning briefing. Or, that is, the nine-fifteen morning briefing, because he was late. I haven't seen him since, but he's spending a lot of time at Station City this week.'

'What's that about?'

'Don't tell me you haven't heard about the serial rapist?' Linda said.

'Of course I have.'

'For a moment I was worried you'd gone completely off the grid. Anyway, I believe Henrik has been helping Bernt, the head of investigation at Station City.'

'Helping him how, exactly?'

Suddenly there was silence. 'I'm really sorry, Søren, but we had a group email from Henrik today. He wrote that you've handed in your warrant card so you no longer have the authority to participate in any kind of investigation so I probably shouldn't . . .'

'Fair enough,' Søren said amicably. 'But would you do me a favour? I've bought a few bits and pieces for Henrik and Jeanette's baby, some clothes, a teddy and so on. From me and Anna. And I'm standing outside Henrik's stairwell at number seven, Jacob Erlandsens Gade, only they don't appear to live here any more. So please would you check if the National Register of Persons lists Henrik at a different address? I want to drop off their presents because, like you said, that baby's due any minute now.'

Linda agreed, and Søren heard her typing on her keyboard.

'No,' she said. 'His address is still listed as number seven, Jacob Erlandsens Gade . . . However, I can see that another private number has been added to his file, but that was way back in October, months ago. I thought the two of you were friends outside work as well?'

'Yes, and I'm ashamed I haven't visited them yet. I haven't even seen Jeanette pregnant. Is there a mobile number?'

'Yes,' Linda replied. 'Do you want me to look it up for you?'

'Yes, please,' Søren heard the clatter of the keyboard again.

'Oh,' Linda said. 'But surely that can't be right . . .'

'What?'

'The mobile number is registered to an address on Amager. Twenty-seven Amagerfælledvej. But that's the Urbanplanen Estate. Social housing with tiny flats. Henrik and Jeanette wouldn't move there with two teenagers and a baby on the way, would they?'

'Must be a mistake,' Søren said. 'What house number did you say it was?'

'Twenty-seven; fourth floor. But why do you want to know if it's a mistake?'

'Linda, my love, you work faster than an energy drink,' Søren said, and hung up.

Twenty-seven Amagerfælledvej.

Søren had reached his car by now and called Lily's nursery to let them know he was running late. It was already two thirty: he still had to get to Amager and it would be nearly five before he got to the nursery. The teacher simply thanked him for letting them know, but when Søren had ended the call, he felt guilty because Lily hated being picked up late, especially on a Friday when most children were collected early. *Please would you pick up Lily today?* he texted Anna. *I won't get home until 5 o'clock.* Before Søren had even turned the key in the ignition, she had already texted him back: *Not much notice, but OK. I'll pack up now.*

Søren flew into a rage and texted back: *Anna Bella, I have picked up Lily three days out of five this week, and besides, she is your child.*

The moment he had hit *send*, he regretted it. It sounded as if he didn't love picking Lily up from nursery and he did. There was no reply. Yet another reason to hate mobiles, he decided. If he had had to rummage around in his pockets for loose change, then track down a payphone, he would probably never have said anything quite so idiotic. He beat himself up all the way from Nørrebro to Amager.

Amagerfælledvej was a grim sight: a short appendix of a road with dull 1970s houses that looked as if they were made from chipboard that had been coated only with primer before the builders had thrown in the towel. Søren parked outside number twenty-seven. He got out and inspected the doorbells: an H. Tejsner was listed as living on the fourth floor. Søren rang the bell with a heavy heart, but there was no reply. He took a few steps back and tried the mobile number, still no reply and still no voicemail. Søren got back into his car to text Henrik, but after a couple of failed attempts, he tossed the mobile onto the passenger seat and drove to Amagerbrogade where he located a florist. He ordered a totally extravagant bouquet in blue spring colours and wrote a card:

Dear Henrik. Congratulations on your son who was born at 6.10 today, 26 March 2010. Your wife and son are doing well and they are at Rigshospitalet, maternity unit Y2, side ward 228. Call me. Cheers, Søren

When Søren was satisfied that the card would be dropped into the letterbox even if the recipient was not at home, he paid for the flowers and drove north.

Anna and Lily were already at home and playing Snap! at the dining table. Søren kissed them both and instantly picked up Anna's frostiness.

'Hey, I didn't mean it like that,' he said, when they had a moment to themselves because Lily had run off to the loo.

'That's what it sounded like. And, Søren, don't ever pat yourself on the back on account of how wonderful you are. You're lucky to know Lily – you're not earning any brownie points by picking her up which you can write down in your little book of good deeds. Lily is not an irritating duty.'

Anna was furious and accidentally jabbed Søren in the chest.

'Funny you should say that,' Søren said, 'because sometimes that's exactly what it seems like, that she *is* a burden – for you. When was the last time you collected her from nursery just because you wanted to, eh?'

'Don't!' Anna hissed. 'Don't even go there! We have a child *together*, and if you had been at a crucial point in your career and I was the one who was unemployed, we wouldn't be having this conversation, would we?' Anna's eyes flashed. Søren could not remember the last time he had seen her so incensed.

At that point, Lily came bouncing down the stairs wanting to play cards again with her mother.

When she had been put to bed, Anna disappeared into her study, and for the first time for as long as Søren could remember, he did not follow to ask if she wanted a cup of tea.

CHAPTER 8

It was just past six o'clock on Tuesday evening when Marie got home to Randersgade from Lea's home on Vesterbro. The flat was quiet, and for a moment she was gripped by unease and stood frozen in the hallway. Eventually she went into the kitchen and opened the window overlooking the courtyard – the washing-up she had not got round to dealing with was starting to smell; she put the kettle on to make tea and thought about Lea. They had finally managed to have a proper talk.

In the living room she checked her mobile, then tossed it onto her bed. No calls. Then she sat down at her desk and opened her laptop. She got butterflies in her stomach when she saw that Tim had written:

Dear Marie, I'm writing to you from Xitole about 150 impassable kilometres from Bissau where I have sweet-talked my way to Internet access from a German scientist whom I met at a restaurant this evening. I left early Sunday morning and am already two long days into surveying the area. So far so good. I expect to be gone four weeks, maybe five, and afterwards I will come straight to Denmark. If it's at all possible, I will email you again soon. Have you been in touch with

Terrence Wilson? As soon as you know the deadline for the *Science* article, please email me. Thank you for a lovely meeting in every possible sense. See you soon. Tim

She read it twice.

She skimmed the rest of her emails and opened one from Göran Sandö. She had yet to call him back and he was clearly not used to being ignored because he had written PLEASE CALL ME BACK in capitals in the subject box. She wondered briefly at his email address – which was a very unofficial sounding, sayhitogoran@gmail.com – and was suddenly intrigued. Why on earth would Göran Sandö write to her from his private email account?

Dear Marie Skov, I have tried to contact you in the past week without success. Please ring me. This is my private phone number and you're welcome to ring me any time that's convenient for you. It's important. Thank you.

When Marie had fetched herself another cup of tea, put on her slippers and turned up the heating, she sat down in her armchair in the bay window, which overlooked Randersgade, and called Sandö.

'Yes, Göran here,' a sing-song Swedish voice answered.

'Göran Sandö?' Marie cleared her throat. 'This is Marie Skov.'

'Marie!' Sandö exclaimed. 'Finally. I was about to resort to drastic measures to get your attention.'

'What's this about?' Marie asked suspiciously.

'You probably don't like me,' Sandö said. 'It wouldn't be the first time one of Storm's students has taken against me. Do you have ten minutes? Or, better still, half an hour?'

Marie said she had.

'Good,' Sandö said. 'To start with, I can't even begin to tell you what a tragedy it is that Storm is dead. I spoke to him only a few days before his death and he was brimming with the enthusiasm that, in spite of everything, earned him so much prestige in modern science . . . I simply can't grasp that he's gone.'

'No one can,' was all Marie said.

'I had known Storm for many years and we always respected each other, even when we disagreed,' Sandö continued. 'But when I hired Olof Bengtsson for Pons and Olof decided to stop working with Storm in Guinea-Bissau, that was the first time Storm fell out with me and rang me up to tear strips off me.' Sandö laughed briefly. 'Storm called me a coward, a weakling, a cynic driven by money – he laid it on thick. I tried to explain that Olof had pulled out of the Guinea-Bissau project because he wanted an office job and more time with his family. It had nothing to do with me. *Pons* means "bridge" in Latin and that's the whole point of our work! We build bridges between universities, between countries, between the public and private sector. I would happily have lent Olof to SIDA, had he wanted to go.' Sandö paused. 'But, saying that, I was relieved when Olof withdrew from the Belem project. Pons is a young research hybrid in its start-up phase and every year our funding is decided by a tough board comprised of representatives from the Swedish universities and the international pharmaceutical industry. I'm not ashamed to admit that I try to avoid negative publicity, although Storm despised me for it – do you know why? Because I believe in Pons. We're an important research hybrid, the first body ever to position itself successfully between industry and the universities, and I'm convinced that we're creating precedents. As I see it, we scientists have a choice between letting commercial interests dominate, which means that the pharmaceutical industry and politicians will soon dictate all modern research based purely on what is profitable, or we can enter into closer collaboration with them along the lines of if-you-can't-beat-them-join-them. Pons favours the latter. Storm thought it was all nonsense, of course. He didn't think industry should be allowed to interfere at all. He said it was like asking the wolf to guard the sheep, and on an ideological level I agree, but in the real world it's completely unrealistic to exclude commercial interests, and even an old hippie like him should have been able to see that, I told him. We actually ended up having a good discussion about the world of research and what we could do to promote it. At this point Storm admitted that he was mostly disappointed with Olof. He had enjoyed working with him and it was simply beyond him that personal priorities could matter more than their discovery in Guinea-Bissau. But, then again, he didn't have a family, he said, at least not a biological one, so perhaps he just couldn't empathise. I said I wasn't married and had no children either, and that scientists like us probably ended up identifying with our research, for better or worse. We had a little laugh at that. Our conversation ended on a good note and I wished him the very best with his exciting observation in Guinea-Bissau, which I, from a research point of view, obviously hoped he intended to pursue.'

'But then what happened?' Marie asked, slightly mollified.

'In the two years that followed, we had no direct contact, but I watched from the sidelines, both the scientific turbulence that hit Storm and his slow, but steady progress, which resulted in a couple of major workshops and more column inches for his subject in general. I was delighted. Groundbreaking research always takes a while to gain a foothold, and if anyone could stand the heat, it was Storm, I thought. About two years after Storm's bollocking, I sent Olof Bengtsson on a fact-finding mission. At this point Pons was six years old, and as our staffing levels grew, we needed to gain greater insight into how major organisations led and distributed their work. Olof travelled first to the US, then Canada, then Japan and ended up at the WHO in Geneva where he sat in on various meetings, including the WHO's Epidemiology Task Force, WET. When Olof came back, he was brimming with ideas as to how we could optimise Pons. However, he confided in me that something strange had happened during a taskforce meeting. The topic under discussion was how the WHO could streamline its processing of the many unsolicited letters it received. There was a consensus that there had to be certain requirements as to the seriousness of a request, some parameters which must be met, so that not every crazy housewife who found a dead bird in her back garden could trigger a pandemic scare, while at the same time, the filter must allow local epidemics to be registered and responded to. Olof had made detailed notes because we in Pons sometimes find it difficult to determine the priority of the research projects people want to see realised. At one point, Olof said, a representative from the expert group had presented an example of a request to the WHO, which had made it through three sorting rounds, even though it was so unauthorised and so unscientific that it should have been eliminated much earlier. It was a request from a Greek scientist who in 2004 had accidentally discovered that the accumulated mortality rate among children in Tanzania correlated with national immunisation. The scientist had got in touch because he was very concerned. Olof obviously couldn't help thinking of the close relationship between the observation of the Greek scientist in Tanzania and the observations he and Storm had made in Guinea-Bissau. He was inclined to think, he told me, that he had in fact heard a reference to Storm's letter and that the WHO had disguised it by changing the geography and the nationality of the scientist precisely so they could use it for educational purposes. I agreed with him that that was likely to be the case, but for some reason I couldn't get the incident out of my head. Eventually I contacted WET and spoke to Paul Smith, whom I know from our student days in Paris.'

'Paul Smith as in *the* Paul Smith, who has published several articles about the many excellent qualities of the DTP vaccine? Paul Smith who, every time Storm tried to make himself heard internationally, did everything he could to block Storm's articles and was quick to publish denials in WHO's own publication? *That* Paul Smith?'

'Marie,' Sandö said, 'I'm aware that Paul Smith and Storm disagreed strongly on a professional level, and that Paul Smith can be stubborn, but you must understand that he has spent most of his career researching the characteristics of the DTP vaccine. It will take a bit more than a few casual observations to convince him that he's wrong. That's just how it is. I know Paul Smith. He's a clever scientist and a very nice man and, as far as I know, he's been more open to Storm's thinking recently, but if you'll just let me finish . . . I asked Paul directly if the rejected request to the WHO, of which Olof had made a note, was really Kristian Storm's letter from Guinea-Bissau, but he denied it. A request really had been submitted by a Greek scientist back in 2004 and the WHO had sent him their standard reply that he was welcome to contact them again once his observation met the required standards of a scientific observation, but they never heard from him. I asked what the name of the Greek scientist was and Paul Smith promised to find out and get back to me. Which he did that same afternoon. The name of the scientist was Midas Manolis and he was a professor at the University of Athens but had lived in Tanzania, where he studied tropical diseases, up until his death in 2005. I thanked Paul Smith for his help and regarded the matter as closed. It wasn't until I happened to bump into Kristian Storm at a conference in Helsinki a couple of months later that I remembered the Greek's observation and told Storm about it. He didn't seem particularly surprised and said he already had figures from both Ghana and Haiti which proved exactly the same point and that he would make himself heard eventually. He said the latter to me with thinly veiled contempt and it was clear to me that he had yet to forgive me for that business with Olof. Eventually I decided to leave him alone. He was clearly not interested in making small talk with me—'

'You were his favourite aversion,' Marie exclaimed. 'He thought your self-promotion was refreshing and he loved teasing you.'

'Did he now?' Sandö said, sounding amused. 'I think I'll

take that as a compliment, coming from the old codger. Anyway, I returned home from the conference with Storm and his observation on my mind. That same spring I joined the Nobel Committee and I was appointed general secretary of the committee soon afterwards. In May, once the names of that year's Nobel Prize winners had been published, I went on a two-week safari in Tanzania. On this trip, deep in the Serengeti National Park, I got talking to one of the other tourists. I had kept mostly to myself, but when I heard her speak fluent Swahili with our guide, I got curious and asked her how she knew the local language. She told me that she had lived in Tanzania for twenty-five years because she and her husband had both worked there as scientists. However, following the death of her husband, she had moved back to Greece to their children and grandchildren, but she visited Tanzania every year. I told her that I, too, was a scientist and we soon started namedropping and entertaining ourselves with how small the world of science and research is. At one point we shook hands and introduced ourselves. Her name was Bibiana Manolis. It was possibly because I was on holiday that the penny didn't drop until later that evening. When I asked her, she confirmed it immediately. She and Midas Manolis had been married for forty years, they had three children and eleven grandchildren, and it was a great shock when she lost him so unexpectedly in 2005. Bibiana and I kept in touch after the safari and last autumn she called me. She was in Stockholm and wanted to know if we could have dinner together. I said yes, of course, and we had a really nice evening. We spoke about her husband and she told me more about his death. He had drowned in Tanzania. He had gone out with some local fishermen but never came back. He had fallen overboard and got trapped in some nets. Before the men on the boat could rescue him, he had drowned.'

The hairs on the back of Marie's neck stood up. 'No,' she whispered.

'Wait,' Sandö said. 'Please let me go on. I was shocked, obviously, even more so when Bibiana told me that her husband was about to make a major scientific breakthrough. He had made some observations in Tanzania, she told me, and had been in the process of writing an article that, in Midas's own words, would "lance a global boil". I told her that I was aware of Midas's WHO request. "Yes, they just dismissed it," Bibiana said sadly, and Midas had been knocked back for several months. I asked Bibiana if she had ever heard of Kristian Storm's research. I told her that Storm had made the same observation in Guinea-Bissau.'

'Yes, and that's where Silas drowned,' Marie said. 'In the same way as—'

'Yes, I know,' Sandö interrupted. 'But there's more. As you probably know, Stig Heller recently joined the Nobel Committee. We enjoyed working together from day one, and I quickly decided to attach him to a couple of Pons's projects to strengthen our links to the Karolinska Institute, where he works. Three weeks ago I met Heller to review some proposed collaborations. I can't remember how exactly, but we ended up talking about your and Kristian Storm's research. Heller said that Storm had been like a father to him during his master's and PhD, but their relationship had been increasingly strained, particularly once it became clear that Storm didn't like criticism, especially not from Heller, whom Storm had expected to follow in his footsteps. Heller mentioned you. The first time he heard of you, he thought you had arrived at the perfect moment. A timid, reticent and brilliantly gifted puppet, was his impression. When you and Storm published your master's results, Stig Heller didn't think for one moment that you had reached them honestly. Their fit to Storm's theory was simply too neat. Much too neat. But when I got to know him better, he confided in me that he had tested your experiment down to the last detail . . .'

'My experiment?' Marie was taken aback. 'But how would he have got hold of the protocol?'

'I've absolutely no idea,' Sandö said honestly. 'From someone at the Department of Immunology, I guess.'

Marie fell silent. 'I know exactly what you're about to say,' she said after a time. 'You're about to tell me that Heller reached the same results I did.'

'Yes,' Sandö said. 'He was in shock and needed to talk about it. So that was what we spent the rest of our evening doing. I called Olof Bengtsson to ask if he still had the raw data from the three original surveys in Guinea-Bissau that he had taken part in, and he had. It took some persuading to convince him to email me the figures, but after I had promised him on my life that I would never compromise Storm, I got them. He had also attached the figures that Storm had been sent by his colleagues in Ghana and Haiti, and which Storm had emailed to Olof to convince him to carry on working with him. It then struck me that I could ask Bibiana if she would supply us with her husband's figures from Tanzania. If we could gather data from four different locations, process them statistically and get the same statistically significant results from them all, well, it would appear that we owed Storm an apology and the restoration of his reputation. Stig Heller asked why I didn't just contact Midas Manolis directly, so I explained to him that Midas had unfortunately died in an accident in 2005. I told him that the Greek scientist had fallen overboard from a fishing boat, got caught up in some nets and had drowned before the crew could rescue him. Heller went white as a sheet.

'I had heard, of course, that Storm had lost a PhD student in Guinea-Bissau in 2007. That kind of information spreads like wildfire, but because it coincided with the Department of Marine Biology at the University of Stockholm losing a female diver at Kullen, I hadn't paid attention to the specific circumstances of the death in Guinea-Bissau. A visibly upset Heller told me that Storm's PhD student in Guinea-Bissau had died in exactly the same circumstances as Manolis. We agreed that I would contact Storm immediately.

'As early as Monday, the eighth of March, I tried to get hold of Storm. I left at least ten messages with the departmental secretary, but he never called back. I also tried emailing him, but I soon suspected that he must have blocked my email address because, except for my very first email, in which I'd written that I had something important to discuss with him, all my emails bounced back.

'On Tuesday morning, a whole week after my first attempt, I was well and truly annoyed. I can take flak and I accept that Storm fundamentally thought me a research whore. But it would have reflected well on him to take a request from a colleague seriously and, for the first time, I could see why

Storm had a reputation for being exceptionally stubborn. I decided that if he hadn't got back to me by Wednesday I would travel to Copenhagen. On Thursday morning I got my secretary to book me a plane ticket for that afternoon. I was in the refectory when I learned of Storm's death. One of our PhD students had heard it from another student at one of the other departments at the Institute of Biology. The pressure following the allegation of scientific dishonesty had apparently become too much for him, was the explanation. Distraught, I tried contacting Heller, but didn't succeed until Saturday. He hadn't heard that Storm was dead and was deeply shocked when I told him. Ever since then we have both been trying to track you down. We have to go to the police, Marie. Something is terribly wrong.'

Sandö fell silent and Marie wanted to say something, but she couldn't get a word out.

'Are you still there?' Sandö asked.

Marie gulped. 'I am,' she said. 'But I'll have to call you back tomorrow. I have to . . .'

When Marie had ended the call, she couldn't breathe. Frightened, she got up from her armchair in the bay window, but had to sit down again. She clutched the armrests with shaking hands. Five minutes passed, then ten, before she gingerly got up and went to lie down on her bed. She concentrated only on taking deep breaths. After half an hour she had almost calmed down, but was overwhelmed by a boundless feeling of grief.

Everything was going to be taken away from her.

She had left her mobile by the armchair and it took nearly all her strength to get up and fetch it. She found Lea's number and called her younger sister. The moment she heard Lea's voice, she burst into tears.

'I can't breathe,' she sobbed. 'I'm scared. I'm so scared.'

'I'm on my way,' Lea instantly responded.

When they had hung up, Marie called Jesper. 'Jesper, I want you to drive Anton to Julie's right now,' she said, when Jesper picked up.

'What? I've just put him to bed.'

'I want you to drive Anton to Julie's right now,' Marie screamed.

There was total silence at the other end.

'Has something happened?' Jesper asked.

'I don't know what's going on,' she said in a low voice. 'I think Storm was murdered and I'm scared that the two of you aren't safe in that house. I'm scared that the break-in and the arson last week might have had something to do with Storm's article. That the intruders were looking for something. I know it sounds completely far-fetched but they might come back. They might burn down the house. They might kidnap Anton. Three people are dead – three people. So I want you to drive Anton to Julie's right now.'

'But—'

'You can take Anton to your girlfriend's and stay there, if that's easier,' Marie said. 'I don't mind, Jesper. Just promise me that you won't stay in the house tonight. I'll call the police as soon as I've worked out a plan. I'll let you know what's happening. Now do as I say.'

And for the first time since they had met, all Jesper said was, 'OK, Marie. OK.'

Marie curled up in her bed and waited for Lea. Twenty minutes later the intercom buzzed and, having looked out of the window, she let her sister in.

'Calm down, you're having a panic attack. It's horrible, but you're not going to die, even though that's how it feels. And I'm staying here tonight,' Lea said firmly, and threw a holdall onto Marie's bed, 'but I need to leave early tomorrow morning. My exam starts at nine o'clock.'

'But are you prepared? I don't want to—'

'This is more important,' was all Lea said.

During the next half-hour Marie told her everything. When she had finished, Lea looked pensive. Then she said, 'Come here. Sit on the floor and I'll massage your shoulders.'

Grateful, Marie sat between Lea's legs and rested her forehead on her knees. For the next ten minutes they hardly spoke and Marie gradually began to calm down. Lea got up to make tea and Marie went to lie on her bed, covered herself with a blanket and concentrated on her breathing.

Lea pottered about in the kitchen and Marie heard her speak quietly on the phone.

Suddenly Marie had a flash of inspiration. She flung the blanket aside and sat on the edge of her bed. When Lea returned with tea and biscuits on a tray, Marie was rummaging in her removal crates.

'What are you looking for?'

'I'm looking for—' Marie interrupted herself. 'Oh, here they are.'

'What?'

'Storm's bundles of reading material.' Marie took out a pile of unopened packages from a box. There were ten, six yet to be opened. 'All through spring, Storm sent me reading material,' Marie said. 'But you can have too much of a good thing. I was in bed, vomiting up my insides, as bald as an egg, and all Storm could think of was sending me science literature and sugared almonds. At the same time it was incredibly sweet of him. But I've just had an idea . . .' Marie flicked through the packages, checking the postmarked stamps one after the other.

The postmark on the last package read 16 March, fourteen days ago, in another life. With a pounding heart, she opened the envelope and found herself with a copy of Storm's Guinean medical records in her hands. A folded letter lay on the top.

'Are you all right?' Lea said, with a frown. 'You look as if you've seen a ghost.'

Marie unfolded the letter. 'It's from Storm,' she said, and read aloud:

Dear Marie,

In the last few days I have had a growing feeling that someone is watching me. I have noticed that a blue car with tinted windows is always parked outside the Institute of Biology, also late at night when all other cars are gone. On at least three occasions I have observed how the driver starts the engine and drives off the moment I go home. I'm probably just a paranoid old git, but I feel better for knowing that you have a physical copy of the medical records from Dulombi-Boe. On another matter, I have finally finished the statistical processing of all the data and, as I warned you on the phone, there is a strong correlation between the DTP vaccine and the number of dead children. It's beautiful. In all its horror, of course. Is there any way we can meet next week? We simply have to write that article now!

Much love, Storm
PS: The registration plate of the blue car is JF 40 173. Just in case I'm found in a nearby river with my hands tied behind my back . . .

Marie lowered the letter. Her ears were blocked and, for a moment, she could hear only the roar of her own blood. She had the Guinean medical records. She sat on her bed and handed the letter to Lea.

'This is definitely not a letter written by a man who kills himself a few days later,' Lea asserted. 'You have to call the police.'

Marie nodded. 'I'll do it tomorrow,' she whispered.

Lea made more tea and Marie texted Jesper. He replied almost immediately that he and Anton were with Emily and could easily stay there for a few days.

'Aren't you jealous?' Lea asked, when she returned to the living room with more tea and Marie told her where Anton and Jesper were.

'No,' Marie said, 'and I don't really understand why not. I was very upset when I found out that he had been seeing someone all the time I'd been ill, for longer, probably, and I lost all respect for him when he tried to blame it on my illness. It was pathetic. But now I'm almost relieved and I know how strange that must sound. Divorcing Jesper would never even have crossed my mind, but now that he's made the decision for me, life without him suddenly makes total sense. Life is . . . well, it's just too short to waste on Jesper.'

Lea couldn't help laughing.

'I'm not being mean,' Marie said. 'I'm sure that Jesper's life is too short for me as well, even though he doesn't have cancer. Simply because life *is* short. We never brought out the best in each other.'

Lea looked at Marie for a long time. 'Actually, I believe you brought out the best in him. And that was what I hated. He grew bigger and bigger while you almost disappeared completely. I've seen that happen once already with Mum and Dad. So I'm thrilled that you've realised you can live without him. Now all we've got to do is get Julie to see sense.'

'Don't you dare to compare Jesper with Michael.' Marie was outraged.

'No, out of two evils, I, too, would have picked Jesper,' Lea said, with a smile, 'but there are limits. I haven't had a lot of steady relationships in my life because Frank and Joan cured me well and truly. So I have very high standards.'

They went to bed close to midnight, and when they had said good night and turned off the light, Marie had another panic attack. It felt as if the void was filling with earth and soon she would be buried underneath it. She tried telling herself that she was safe, that no one knew where she lived and that Lea was lying next to her, breathing calmly, but suddenly she was no longer certain of anything. First her legs started to shake, then her arms.

'Lea,' she whispered.

'Are you all right?'

'No,' Marie whispered. 'Not really.' Lea put her arms around Marie from behind and held her tightly. Marie continued to tremble, but Lea did not let go. Eventually she began to calm.

'Why don't I turn on the light?' Lea said.

'I'm sorry for keeping you awake,' Marie said. 'Your exam and all that . . .'

'It's OK. I'm glad I can do something for you.'

Marie turned to face her sister and they lay talking in the light from the reading lamp, close and intimate, just like they used to do a long time ago in their bunk beds. Marie studied her sister's tattooed arms, shoulders and chest. 'What do your tattoos mean?' she asked.

Lea looked momentarily self-conscious. 'Do you really want to know?'

'Yes.'

'The demon child, that's me,' she said, stroking a black tattoo of a strange, diabolic child with sad eyes. 'The sun rising above the sea is my longing for new experiences,' she continued, pointing to the orange sun on her left shoulder, which had just broken through the horizon. 'And the snake is the unpredictable element in every human life.' She moved her finger to a green snake whose body crept dramatically over her shoulder and disappeared along her spine. 'Breast cancer, break-ups, lies, death. It could be anything. Everything you can't control.'

'But why—'

'Every day when I wake up and see my tattoos in the mirror, I'm reminded of my reality and how I can't or never should try to escape it. The truth is that I grew up in a family that runs away from grief, represses pain and extinguishes joy.'

Marie listened. 'What does that one mean?' she asked, pointing to a Chinese symbol on Lea's left forearm.

'Freedom,' Lea replied. 'That's my most important tattoo. It was a present to myself when I let go of an impossible task: changing the past.'

'They're all incredibly beautiful.'

'Are you serious?'

'I've always thought they were beautiful,' Marie said, surprised.

'I didn't think so. You were always silent when Frank and Julie expressed their unreserved opinion about my ink. I thought that meant you agreed.'

'I've always wanted one myself,' Marie said.

'What image?' Lea asked.

'A swallow. Not one of those kitsch cartoon ones holding a banner saying Live well or something, but a real swallow, shooting vertically up into the sky, flying thousands of kilometres to Africa, because it can. And when it dies, it simply drops out of the sky. Doesn't make a fuss. Storm used to call me "Little Swallow".' Marie's eyes welled and Lea stroked her hand.

'My best friend is a tattoo artist. His name is Mattis and he's very good. He designed this one himself,' she added, pointing to the demon child with the sad eyes. 'I can give you his number.'

Marie giggled.

'What?' Lea said.

'Dad would have a heart attack if I showed up with a tattoo.'

It was said in jest, but Lea was stony-faced. 'Frank lives his life,' she said at length, 'and I live mine.'

When Marie fell asleep, she dreamed that Anton was having a mandatory vaccination on his seventh birthday, but somehow she knew it was lethal. She sat in the surgery trying to argue against the vaccine while the doctor unwrapped the syringe and drew the fluid into the chamber. He listened to her attentively, but showed no signs of stopping the procedure, and before Marie could say anything else, he had plunged the needle into Anton's arm. While he pressed the plunger, yellow handwritten pieces of paper suddenly appeared out of nowhere and started whirling up towards the sky, which, in Marie's nightmare, spanned even wider than the horizon. 'It's not at all certain that he will die,' the doctor shouted through the rustling pieces of paper. 'The child mortality rate in Denmark is very low, you know. Nothing to worry about!' Suddenly the doctor turned into her father. Marie could barely see him for whirling paper, but it looked as if he was slumped drunkenly across his desk and had fallen asleep.

The next morning Marie sat up wide awake in bed with a jolt. It was six thirty and day was slowly dawning. Lea was still sleeping and for a moment Marie studied her beautiful sister's silhouette before she tiptoed out into the kitchen. While the tea was brewing, her brain worked overtime. She could not believe that she had a copy of the medical records. That she had had them all along. But why had Storm destroyed the originals? It made no sense that for weeks he had slept, eaten and gone to the lavatory with the medical records only to end up shredding them. And why had he wiped his hard disk? People only ever did that if they had something to hide. It suddenly occurred to her that Storm might have been acting under duress. What if he had only made her a copy for safekeeping, not knowing that soon it would be the only material in existence?

Marie took the envelope that had contained the Guinean medical records and checked the postmark again. It said 16 March, so it would have left the faculty on the Tuesday and Storm had died on Wednesday evening. When she rang the police, she would ask if they had a theory that might explain why Storm had deleted his hard drive and shredded the medical records. And what evidence was there that he had committed suicide? Why were they so sure of themselves? Marie had seen a few programmes about crime investigation on TV, and whenever police investigated a murder, it was almost unbelievable what they could deduce based on dust and bits of fibre. Did it mean that absolutely no suspicious pieces of evidence had been found? Not even one? Marie could not believe that Storm had climbed up on his desk of his own free will and looped the noose around his neck without a fight. Had the police really found no defensive wounds, no sign of a struggle, no unidentified DNA evidence, no sedatives in Storm's body – nothing? Her mind was racing.

She found the email she had received from Deputy Chief Superintendent Søren Marhauge last week, copied down his mobile number on a Post-it note and stuck it to the armrest of the chair she was sitting in.

Then she wrote an email to Tim:

Dear Tim,

It was lovely to meet you too. I have good news and bad. The good first: I have found a copy of the medical records! All the records are there, including the most recent ones from Dulombi-Boe. They were in a parcel Storm sent me just before he died. Drop everything you're doing right now and hurry back to Denmark so we can write the world's most earth-shattering paper. I will call the editor of *Science* today and get a deadline. And now the bad news: I had a call from Göran Sandö yesterday and he told me . . .

Marie stopped. It could be days or weeks before Tim got Internet access again, but she had to stop him wasting a month in the middle of nowhere collecting data they already had. The article was their top priority now and she needed his help. She quickly finished her email, and when she had sent it, she went onto the homepage of the Belem Health Project and found a telephone number for the research station. One of their drivers must go out to look for Tim.

Marie had to make three attempts before she finally got through.

'*Bom dia*, Belem Health Project,' a sleepy voice said.

Marie introduced herself and said she was looking for Tim Salomon.

'Ah, Marie. This is Malam Batista, Storm's assistant.' Malam explained that he was alone at the research station. Tim had asked him to guard it when he travelled to Xitole last Sunday. He had left with three assistants and a driver and said that he would be back in three weeks at the earliest.

'Are there any other drivers around?'

'I believe a team is returning from Bissora today. Hang on, let me check the board.' Marie could hear Malam's footsteps across the floor. 'Yes,' he then said. 'They're expected back today. Nuno is the driver. Do you want me to dispatch him to Xitole?'

'Yes,' Marie said, even though she did not have the authority to do so. 'Ask them to find Tim as quickly as possible and tell him to check his emails. It's urgent.'

When she had ended the call, she wrote an email to Sandö. She apologised for breaking off their conversation yesterday, but she had come up with a plan now. She would contact the police later today and keep him updated, obviously. She also wanted him to know that she and Tim Salomon would finish Storm's article; to that end she needed the figures from Tanzania and Stig Heller's laboratory figures immediately. Marie felt embarrassed at being so demanding, but she had little choice. The article would be more persuasive if she included those figures and, besides, it was the ultimate test of Sandö's and Heller's loyalties. If they gave her the figures without protesting, she would consider trusting them. At the end of her email she added that Sandö was welcome to give her mobile number to Heller.

When she had sent the email, she looked up the European editorial office for *Science*, which had its headquarters in Cambridge. She made a note of the number of their editor-in-chief, Terrence Wilson, who had promised Storm an article in their May issue provided he could produce a complete set of data. It had just gone seven when Marie gently roused Lea.

'Did you manage to get some sleep?' Lea said, as she stretched.

'More than I expected,' Marie said, 'but not much.'

'No one knows where you are,' Lea reminded her again. 'Jesper and Anton got out of the house. You have the evidence to write that paper.'

Marie nodded. 'I need to ring several people today,' she pointed to a number of Post-it notes, 'and when that's done, I'm barricading myself in here to write. I'm meant to have Anton this weekend, but if I don't finish in time, perhaps he could go to Julie's. It's a long time since he last played with Emma and Camilla.'

'I don't mind having him,' Lea said. 'I need to start looking for work, but there's no hurry. And I'm happy to stay over, if you need me to. Just call me. By the way, have you spoken to Julie recently? I tried getting hold of her most of yesterday, but she doesn't pick up and she doesn't return my calls.'

'I haven't seen much of her since Mum's funeral. We've spoken on the phone a few times and talked about meeting up, but nothing came of it,' Marie said. 'Then again, I think Camilla's been ill and Michael has been working nights this week. We last spoke on Sunday when she was very upset about Frank and his drink-driving in February. Is that why she won't pick up the phone? Because she's still angry with you about that? She'll calm down eventually, but . . .'

Lea shrugged her shoulders and arched her back. Her dark hair fell to one side and Marie caught a full view of the green snake.

'I'm never going to apologise to Julie, Marie,' Lea burst out. 'Never. She's heaped guilt and shame on my shoulders ever since I was a little girl. *You shouldn't have eaten the chocolate in the fridge, Lea. Now Dad will be very cross with you. You shouldn't have had a tattoo.* I'm a grown woman and I'm entitled to my privacy, as is our dad, especially since he didn't want his screw-up to be common knowledge. Otherwise why call me?

He could just as easily have rung Julie. She has a car and she could have picked him up. But he called me.'

'Lea, you don't have to justify yourself to me,' Marie said. 'I'm just suggesting that Julie might be punishing you with her deafening silence because she's angry with you over this business with Dad.'

'I think she's angry about something else,' Lea said.

'What?'

'Me wanting to know about Tove. That's what I said in my message.'

'Tove?' Marie's mind had gone blank.

'The woman you said looked after me when I was little. I don't remember anything from when I was a child, Marie. Nothing. I don't remember Mum ever being well. I don't remember Mads. I don't remember anything, and I can't trigger any memories with photographs because we have almost none from the early years as Mum cut them up when Mads died. I know Julie has told us lots, but I don't trust what she says. She censors reality and presents it the way she wishes it had been: that Mum was beautiful and kind and artistic, that Frank was such a good and patient father, but then Mads died and big, evil clouds gathered over our paradise. But I refuse to believe it was quite as rosy as that before Mads died and I'm curious to hear what this woman, Tove, made of us. What she made of Frank and Joan. What she made of me. Julie can't handle my dragging up the past and I think that's why she's giving me the silent treatment. But I could be wrong.' Lea shrugged again. 'I do understand how upset she is. Julie has always taken on much too much responsibility, so of course she believes it's her fault that Mum died because she didn't turn up to count her pills that Monday. But I want to know if she remembers anything about Tove. The number of the house she lived in, her surname, anything. I can take it from there myself.'

Marie tried to think back. 'I remember that Tove's house was on the same side of the street as ours because I ran down the pavement with the buggy to pick you up. And I'm fairly certain she had adult children. At any rate, she let you play with a doll's house she had on display with real curtains and tiny lamps, and I remember being so jealous . . . And I have a feeling that her husband was a police officer,' Marie added suddenly.

'Why do you think that?' Lea asked.

For a moment Marie stared blankly into the air. 'I've just remembered that a police officer lived on Snerlevej and he helped Dad hose down the road when Bertha was run over. His nickname was the same as that board game, we had . . . Professor Plum, was it? And as far as I remember, he was married to Tove, but I could be wrong.'

Lea laughed. 'Professor Plum? With a dagger in the library? I remember that game. Cluedo.'

'That was his nickname!' Marie exclaimed in amazement. 'Cluedo!'

'But you don't remember his real name?'

Marie shook her head. 'Why don't you ask Frank?' she suggested.

'I have asked Frank,' Lea said. 'Or I've asked his answering machine. But he doesn't return my calls, either.'

Once Lea had left for her exam, Marie called Detective Chief Superintendent Søren Marhauge.

'Hello?' The clear voice belonged to a small girl.

'Eh, my name is Marie Skov,' Marie said. 'Have I called Detective Chief Inspector Søren Marhauge's phone?'

'He's having a great big poo,' the child said. 'I know this because he takes the newspaper to the bathroom and stays there a really long time. Would you like to speak to my aunt Karen instead?'

'Er . . .' Marie stuttered. At that moment she heard a male voice in the background.

'Lily, for goodness' sake, I told you not to touch my mobile when it rings. Who is it?'

'Someone called Marianne Skov. She doesn't say very much.'

'No, I don't suppose she could get a word in edgeways. Give me the mobile. Hello, Søren Marhauge here.'

'My name is actually Marie Skov,' Marie said, 'and you sent me an email a couple of weeks ago.'

'Oh, hi.' Søren Marhauge sounded pleasantly surprised, as if he had waited years for her call.

'Yes, sorry for calling you so early, and I didn't know it was your private number. But in your email you asked me to get in touch if I had noticed anything unusual about Kristian Storm. I . . . It's true I hadn't worked with him since last autumn, but I was his— I need to talk to the police urgently. There are various matters . . . Can we meet? It's complicated.'

'Of course,' Søren said. 'Where do you suggest?'

Marie thought about it. 'The Laundromat Café at the corner of Randersgade and Århusgade? Five o'clock?'

'Deal,' Søren Marhauge said.

After the call, Marie Googled Søren Marhauge and found a photo from a press briefing after the notorious campus murders two years ago when the zoologist Lars Helland had been found dead in his office. Marhauge was an earnest-looking man in his early forties with chestnut hair and eyes so brown it was hard not to describe him as having a dark look. Marie stared at the photograph with a feeling that she knew him from somewhere, probably from the investigation two years ago when the Institute of Biology had been teeming with police officers and crime-scene technicians for days. She printed out the picture, folded it up and put it into her handbag.

When she checked her emails again, she saw that Göran Sandö had forwarded the email with the Tanzania figures attached, as she had asked. Heller would send his laboratory figures separately, he wrote, and Marie's heart sank. Intuition told her that she could trust Sandö. That he was a good guy. But she had her doubts about Stig Heller. It bothered her that he had managed to wrangle her detailed experiment protocol out of someone from the Department of Immunology and that Storm had believed it was Heller who had reported her master's results to the DCSD. It was hard to trust a man you suspected of so much. At that moment her computer pinged and Marie found a brief email from Stig Heller in her inbox.

Hi, Marie Skov

Please find attached my rerunning of your experiment. I'll be in Copenhagen on Friday and would very much like to meet you. Is that possible? My number is + 46 8 524 800 00.
Best wishes, Stig Heller

Marie opened the file and quickly skimmed Heller's results. Both the set-up and the figures were identical to her own, even down to the methodology, which she had kept in a folder on the steel table in Storm's laboratory and later included as part of her master's dissertation. Marie sent a return email to Heller:

Dear Stig Heller,
Thank you for your laboratory figures. I really appreciate your co-operation, but I need to know how you got hold of my experiment protocol, and if you are the person who reported my master's results to the DCSD in February. I expect you to answer both my questions on Friday. We can meet at eleven o'clock at O'Leary's Sports Bar at Copenhagen Central Railway Station.
Best wishes, Marie

Marie held her breath until the email had gone and then she smiled. Being assertive felt great.

She called Terrence Wilson, editor-in-chief of *Science* in England – in Cambridge he was known as the 'Eye of the Needle' because every scientific article had to pass through him before you could even begin to hope for a career in science. He was in a meeting, she was told, but would be back at one o'clock.

For the next couple of hours Marie immersed herself in her work, interrupted only by sporadic cups of tea and a snack. When she had finished processing the figures from Guinea-Bissau and printed out the graphic presentation, she pushed her removal crates to one side and stuck the sheets of paper on the bare wall. For a long time she sat on a chair studying the graphs, making notes on a pad or getting up and writing something directly on the papers. Then she ran the statistics on the remaining figures from Haiti and Tanzania, and put the graphs on the wall alongside the others.

When Marie took a step back and examined her work, the positive correlation became so obvious that it sent a chill down her spine. Storm's observations were not local in the least. The WHO's DTP vaccine killed children across the globe.

At one o'clock precisely she called *Science* in Cambridge again and this time she was put through.

'Terrence Wilson,' a deep voice said.

Marie introduced herself and explained the reason for her call.

Terrence Wilson heaved a sigh. 'Miss Skov,' he said. 'I had a huge amount of respect for Kristian Storm. He was a brilliant scientist and undoubtedly a very decent human being. I spoke to him fairly frequently. It's true that before Christmas I promised him an article in the May issue, if he had a complete set of data, but I have heard nothing from him since and the space went to someone else long ago. And now Storm is dead, I can't see—'

'Mr Wilson,' Marie interrupted, 'Storm returned to Guinea-Bissau after speaking to you and I have the complete set of data in front of me. I've analysed the figures and the results show significant correlations. Just do the maths! The DTP vaccine kills children in Guinea-Bissau, thousands of them!'

'Aha.' Wilson sounded sceptical. 'Isn't there something you've forgotten to mention?'

'What?'

'The dishonesty allegation regarding your laboratory figures. Surely you realise I can't print results based on figures that are currently under investigation, at least not until the DCSD has cleared you. Even if I did agree to accept the new figures, we would still have to wait.'

'A scientist from the Karolinska Institute repeated my clinical experiment,' Marie quickly interjected, 'and he arrived at exactly the same result. Stig Heller.'

'Stig Heller?' Wilson sounded incredulous. 'Who distanced himself completely from Storm's research?'

'Not any more,' Marie said.

Terrence Wilson cleared his throat. 'OK, let me see if I've got this right. Storm returned to Guinea-Bissau where he surveyed the problematic area again and you have the new figures?'

'Yes.'

'Who carried out the statistical work?' Wilson asked.

'Storm, before he died.'

'And now you want to write Storm's article and back it up with lab results currently under investigation, but which you hope that I'll approve because Stig Heller, star scientist and a member of the Nobel Committee, has suddenly seen the light and now supports Storm's theory? Please don't take this the wrong way, Miss Skov, but even you must admit that it sounds a little—'

'Have you heard of Midas Manolis, Mr Wilson?' Marie interrupted him.

'The name rings a bell but—'

'He was professor of immunology at the University of Athens, but spent time in Tanzania. He was the first person in the world to monitor population mortality in a developing country in the hope of lowering the child mortality rate.'

'I thought Kristian Storm was the first,' Wilson objected.

'Yes,' Marie said. 'So did we because Midas Manolis never managed to publish his survey and the observations he had made. In 2004, shortly after he had contacted the WHO's Epidemiology Task Force with an observation that had, in his own words, "shaken him to the core", he died. He fell overboard during a sailing trip, got caught in some fishing nets and drowned. But I have his figures.'

There was total silence at the other end.

Marie quickly continued. 'Do you know of Silas Henckel, Storm's former PhD student?'

'I know his name from several of Storm's articles, of course, yes.'

'Silas died in Guinea-Bissau in 2007 when he fell overboard from a fishing boat, got caught in some nets and drowned. He was twenty-seven.' Marie let it sink in before she went on. 'At that point Silas had tried to contact Storm for three days and we're convinced it was to tell Storm why the figures in south-eastern Guinea-Bissau kept playing up. Silas had discovered that someone had sabotaged them, you see. But he never got hold of Storm. Because it was Christmas, because Storm was away on holiday and because Silas then died. After my master's exam last year, after he had spoken to you, Storm went to Guinea-Bissau to finish Silas's survey in the problematic Dulombi-Boe region, and that was when he realised the full extent of what Silas had discovered. In the data, sixty-five children were listed as being alive, even though they had died long ago. Somewhere between Xitole and Bissau someone had altered the medical records, so the figures became far too optimistic and kept distorting the statistical calculations. This time Storm never let the records out of his sight during his journey back to Copenhagen, where statistical tests showed that the DTP vaccine is linked to a significant increase in the mortality rate among children under five years old. And now Storm is dead. Don't you think that's a remarkable coincidence or is that just me?'

'But . . . we were told that Storm killed himself,' Wilson said.

'Do you know something? In a way I wish he had . . .'

'I don't follow.'

'I'm scared, Mr Wilson. Three people have died because of some research results that are currently burning a hole in the desk in front of me. The house I've just moved out of has been burgled – someone ransacked the place as if they were looking for something before they tried setting fire to it. My six-year-old son lives in that house, Mr Wilson. So, yes, it would have made everything so much easier if Storm had taken his own life because he was ashamed of the dishonesty allegation, but I do not believe that for one second. So I'm asking you, Mr Wilson, please give that article a chance.'

There was another silence.

'OK,' Terrence Wilson said at length. 'I'll take a look at your article. I'm not making any promises, but I will read it. However, it won't be in the May issue. That issue has already been laid out— Unless . . .' he suddenly said. 'There might be one article which I should be able to . . . How many words do you need?'

'Four thousand,' Marie said.

Terrence Wilson laughed. 'No way,' he said. 'That's a feature and you don't get one of those. You can have an intro column space, if I approve your article in the first place. If I like it, I'll consider giving you a bit more space in our online version. But get a move on, young lady! You have until Monday morning at nine o'clock, and we're talking Central European Time.'

'Thank you,' Marie said. She closed her eyes.

'And, Miss Skov?' Terrence Wilson said.

'Yes?'

'Watch your back.'

When Marie had hung up, she expelled all the air from her lungs and wrote another email to Tim:

Hope you're reading this. Our deadline is Monday at 0900 hours CET. Yes, you read correctly!

CHAPTER 9

It was not until Søren was on the plane to Aalborg that he finally had time to read the police report into the death of Joan Skov properly. The call had come in on 18 March 2010 at ten twelve in the morning and an ambulance and a patrol car had been despatched and reached Snerlevej 19 exactly fourteen minutes later. Joan Skov's body temperature had been twenty-five degrees when the crew arrived and Bøje had estimated the time of death to be between seven and nine the previous evening, Wednesday, 17 March. There were no external or internal signs of violence. The deceased had badly maintained teeth, a possible needle mark in the crook of her left elbow and an untreated bunion on her left foot. Bøje had listed the following symptoms to indicate ill health: clinical depression, severely underweight, moderate calcification of the artery in the neck, slight enlargement of the heart, a healed fracture on the thighbone and surgery following a fall in 1995, and scarring to both lungs as a result of pneumonia. In her stomach Bøje had identified the remains of a few tablets and partially dissolved medication capsules and had consequently concluded that the probable cause of death was poisoning with prescription drugs. Blood and tissue samples, with three dark human hairs, had been sent to Forensic Genetics for testing.

Søren drummed his fingers briefly on the tray table in front of him before turning to Bøje's review of the police report.

On 18 March 2010 at 10.08 a.m., the deceased was found in her bed at her home address, Snerlevej 19. The deceased was discovered by her eldest daughter, Julie Claessen, who called the emergency services. The ambulance and the police arrived at the address at 10.26 a.m. Julie Claessen stated that she had spoken to her mother on the telephone the previous night around seven o'clock and that her mother had seemed 'completely normal'. It was not until the following morning after several failed attempts to contact her mother that she went to the address and discovered her mother dead. For details regarding the scene, see separate report. Joan Skov's prescription history, as supplied by her GP, stated that the deceased had been prescribed Cipramil, mirtazapine and diazepam for depression and anxiety attacks, as well as Matrifen against strong pain in her left hip. In addition, the following medicines were found at the address of the deceased:

Søren ran his finger down the list where the only drug he recognised was flunitrazepam, a sleeping tablet.

The flight attendant announced over the speakers that the plane was preparing for landing at Aalborg airport and Søren folded away the tray table. As they landed, he skimmed the report on the discovery of the body at the scene, but nothing stood out. In fact, the only remarkable thing about the death of Joan Skov was that Bøje had found 'a *few* tablets and partially dissolved medication capsules'. Was that really all it took to kill someone? It sounded unlikely. Joan Skov had been addicted to prescription drugs for years and was severely underweight and weak. Søren had mixed feelings about medication. On the one hand he disapproved of the amount of drugs pumped into society, and when he looked at the vast profits made by the pharmaceutical industry, he was inclined to think that the medical profession was only too keen to issue prescriptions. He felt reluctant even taking a headache pill, and on two occasions Anna and he had scrunched up a penicillin prescription for Lily because they had used their common sense and concluded that she was not ill enough to need it.

However, he had been forced to resort to medication a couple of times in his adult life and he had been grateful for the pain relief the doctors had offered to Knud and Elvira when they were terminally ill. Knud had had a small morphine pump, which enabled him to administer his own dosage, and short squeezes had bought Søren valuable moments with his grandfather in the days leading up to his death.

If you could medicate against jealousy, Søren would have swallowed that pill without hesitation.

Jacob had insisted on picking Søren up from the airport although Søren would have preferred to rent a car and be in control of his afternoon. Søren spotted him immediately. A cheerful, waving man, whose receding hairline reminded Søren that he himself was no longer in the first flush of youth. Somehow Søren had imagined that the adult Jacob would look different. Herman Madsen had been eagle-eyed, observant and direct, but Jacob did not appear to take after his father very much. He yakked on and on, and when they parked outside Herman Madsen's small terraced house, in a development of sheltered accommodation, Søren knew practically all there was to know about Jacob's life.

Herman Madsen, however, looked like himself, only a much older version.

'Yes, there's no denying I've grown old,' he said, when he caught Søren sizing him up. 'Positively ancient.'

'Oh, I'm sure it's not that bad,' Søren said.

Søren greeted Max and Jasmin, and Birgitte emerged from the kitchen and held out her hand. 'I've heard a lot about you,' she said warmly. 'Ever since I first met Jacob. The great detective, hatched by our very own Grandpa.' Birgitte patted Herman Madsen gently on the back.

'I'm sure he would have hatched just fine without my help,' Herman Madsen grumbled. They sat down for lunch and Birgitte put the remaining dishes on the table. There were hard-boiled eggs with prawns and mayonnaise, pork meatballs and Easter herring.

'No, the credit is yours,' Søren insisted. 'If it hadn't been for you, I would never have thought of joining the police.'

Herman Madsen did not say anything, but Søren could see that he was proud.

While they ate their herring, Herman Madsen told anecdotes from his years with Aalborg Police and Søren smiled, nodded and asked questions. The old man was in his element and Søren saw Birgitte squeeze Jacob's hand.

'Jørgensen!' Herman exclaimed, when the conversation

moved on to police officers they both knew. 'He was just a pup in those days! I would never have believed that he would make it to chief superintendent. Back when I was his boss, he was a bit of a fool, but a nice one.'

'He's a good boss,' Søren said. 'Under pressure from the new police reforms, of course, and forced to make cuts, so he's not always popular, but that's part of the job.'

'Reforming the police districts was a huge mistake,' Herman Madsen grunted. 'It sounded good on paper, I suppose, getting officers away from their desks and out on the beat. But so far the benefits remain to be seen.'

'Are you and Jørgensen still in contact?' Søren asked.

Herman Madsen shook his head. 'Not really, though I did call him the other day. I believe Jacob told you.'

Søren nodded. 'I agree with Jørgensen. It's highly unlikely that anyone could trigger a suicide like that, so please stop blaming yourself. Besides, I'm starting to wonder if it really was suicide. I know the case.'

'It wasn't suicide?' Herman Madsen exclaimed. 'But Julie Skov said so. In fact, she screamed it at me before calling me a bastard and hanging up.'

'I read Joan Skov's autopsy report on the plane coming here,' Søren said, 'and she hadn't taken very much medication – in fact, very few people would have died from that amount. But Joan Skov had been addicted to prescription drugs for many years and weighed only forty-five kilos. My view is that her body gave up, Herman. Pure and simple. It's possible that your call stirred up old feelings in her, but I don't believe for one second that you caused anything. I'm seeing our forensic examiner tomorrow to discuss a few things with him, and I'm fairly sure that his conclusion will be that Joan Skov's system just packed up.'

Herman Madsen looked relieved. 'Joan Skov was already ill back when we lived at Snerlevej,' he said. 'Or ill probably isn't the right word . . . But she was unstable and moody even before their son died, if you ask me. We saw them from time to time at the start of the 1980s, but I believe Jacob has already told you that. Local get-togethers with neighbours – indeed, your grandparents came to some of them, I recall. It could all be a bit strained, but quite fun on occasion. The children enjoyed it, especially since many of them knew each other from school and clubs. Whenever it was Frank and Joan's turn to host, we would all hold our breath until we knew how Joan was feeling. When she was in a good mood, she'd be walking on air and was a brilliant hostess, serving elaborate salads and making everyone kick off their shoes and dance in the garden. Other times she shut down completely. Tove and I used to wonder why they didn't simply cancel the party. Joan would go to bed before the evening had even begun, if she felt like it. Frank, however, would just smile and carry on as if nothing had happened. But he was always a bit of a tough guy and it became more pronounced when their son died.'

'How?'

'Frank grew harder while Joan became even more fragile. They were always a mismatched couple and the death of their son widened the cracks. It was a very rocky marriage. I remember how once, during one of Joan's better periods, she wanted to learn to drive their car again. I happened to pass one evening when Frank was teaching her how to get the car into the carport and I overheard him screaming and shouting at her because she was doing it wrong. Frank had tied a string to a tennis ball and suspended it from the roof in the carport. The moment the tennis ball touched the windscreen, Joan was meant to apply the brakes, but she kept driving too far. Frank lost his temper and I waited, sheltered by the hedge, while I tried to work out how angry he was. But it blew over as quickly as it had started. "You'll get the hang of it eventually, darling," he said to her, now all smiles. "Let's go inside and have ourselves a drink." It was the same with that dog of theirs – Bertha, I think it was called. They got it shortly after their boy had died and I saw Frank take it for a walk down Snerlevej where he yelled at it and humiliated it until it crept along the pavement. But you should have seen him the day Bertha was run over. It was before all that business with Lea, and he came over and rang our doorbell, crying like a baby. Bertha lay dead in the street and what was he going to say to the girls? I helped him put the dog into a box and told him he had to go inside and tell them the truth. He cried all the way up the garden path, so it wasn't as if he didn't care about the dog.'

'How did the boy die?' Birgitte asked.

'Meningitis,' Søren said.

'Oh, that disease terrifies me,' Birgitte exclaimed. 'We go totally overboard checking the kids' necks whenever they get a temperature, don't we, Jacob?'

Jacob nodded.

Herman Madsen cleared his throat. 'But it wasn't true,' he said quietly.

Søren looked at him with a frown. 'What do you mean?'

'He died in an accident in the family's garden. But Frank and Joan Skov told everyone that he died from meningitis.'

'Dad, you've never said that before,' Jacob said.

Herman Madsen looked at his son and tilted his head. 'No, Jacob. I'm a police officer and I have a duty of confidentiality. Besides, I didn't discover it until two years later when Frank assaulted Mum . . . I believe Jacob has told you about that?' Søren nodded. 'When Tove refused to report him, I had to accept it, but without telling her, I decided to have him checked out. I called a colleague who worked in the police archives and had him look up Frank Skov for me. But there was nothing. No undeclared income, no fraud, not even so much as a small tax problem or a missed payment. Except for the alleged assault, which we had already decided not to proceed with, Frank had only been in contact with the police on one other occasion, my colleague told me, and that was two years earlier when his son had been killed in an accident in the family's garden.'

'How awful,' Birgitte said.

'I was shocked,' Herman Madsen said. 'Before he attacked Mum, we had been . . . if not friends, then at least quite good neighbours. We had sat in their garden on many occasions, eating and drinking. Now, you can never know how you would have reacted yourself, but I don't think I could have continued to live in a house where my son had been killed.'

'You don't know what kind of accident we're talking about?' Søren said.

'No. My colleague asked if he should request the case files for me from the basement archive, but I didn't want to know the details. Suddenly everything made a lot more sense: the children, who were always on edge and Joan, who was falling apart; Frank, who was paranoid to the extent that he could even suspect Tove, who would never hurt a fly, of having shaken Lea. Besides, we moved soon afterwards. In many ways it was a relief to get away from Snerlevej.'

It grew silent around the table. All they could hear was the cartoons from the television in the adjoining living room.

'Then again, Frank Skov's back garden never was very child-friendly,' Herman Madsen said at length.

'Why not?' Søren asked, and remembered what his tenant Finn had said about it.

'Because it was full of rubbish. Frank was a hoarder who collected all sorts of junk and piled it up at the bottom of the garden. He had read engineering at some point, or so he said, and he was always in the process of building something or other. It became a standing joke among the neighbours on Snerlevej. Frank was forever bragging about his specialist tools we absolutely had to borrow – a bevel box or pliers for constant-velocity joints, which no one had heard of – and he was always keen to offer you expert tips, as he called them. But he forgot to apply his good advice to himself. The front garden was nice enough and you would often see Frank outside the house fixing something, cleaning the windows or weeding between the flagstones, while the house itself was in desperate need of a lick of paint and the rubbish mounted up at the back. Their old garden shed had burned down because of an electrical fault and Frank had started building a new, completely over-the-top one. The garden looked like a building site while the burned-out remains of the old shed were left lying around. It would have taken no time to replace the scorched grass with fresh turf. I know it bothered some of the mothers on Snerlevej so much that they didn't turn up for the get-togethers whenever it was Frank and Joan's turn to host. Anyone with young children didn't get a moment's peace because they were constantly running after their kids to make sure they didn't scratch themselves on rusty nails or drink caustic soda.' Herman smiled at the memory. 'Not that it was funny, it was just typical Frank Skov. He really was one of a kind. When the boy died, I do remember Frank making some progress with the chaos, but it didn't last. New junk simply took the place of the old stuff.'

'But surely it's against the law to live in a place that's dangerous for children.' Birgitte was outraged.

'No, my love,' Herman Madsen replied. 'A gun must be locked in a gun cabinet, and if it's fired accidentally, the owner can be sent to prison for not keeping it safe. But there are no rules about living in a messy house and that's just as well. It's the parents' own responsibility to look after their children. And how do you keep a nosy three-year-old safe from harm? Just take Max.' Herman Madsen cast his gaze into the living room where Jasmin was still watching cartoons, like a good girl. Max, however, had quietly pushed his chair over to his grandfather's bookcase, placed a pouffe on top of the chair, scaled the shelves and was in the process of removing his grandmother's Royal Copenhagen china figurines from the top. Jacob and Birgitte shot up from their chairs.

'We need to fix those bookcases to the wall before the children start having sleepovers at your house, Grandpa.' Birgitte sighed when she returned after having shouted at Max and rescued the china figurines.

'Life is a risk,' Herman Madsen just said.

Søren and Jacob washed up and Jacob talked nineteen to the dozen.

'Dad's had a really good day today because you came. Thank you so much, Søren. I would hate him to continue beating himself up over this and I have a feeling that what you said did some good.'

'Don't mention it,' Søren said.

When they returned to the living room, Herman Madsen was listening to the news on the radio. 'Please would you take this photograph to Copenhagen?' he said to Søren, as he turned down the volume. The unsent photograph of Tove and Lea lay on the coffee table.

Søren promised he would.

They had coffee and cake. When Max learned that Søren was a police officer, he begged him to tell him a riddle. 'I've guessed all Grandad's,' he explained. 'I've heard them over a million times.'

'Now, now,' Herman Madsen said, and smiled.

Søren said that of course he would and set the little boy a brain teaser.

Max thought until his head hurt, but it was his sister who came up with the right answer.

'Bingo, Jasmin,' Søren said, and winked at her.

When it was time to say goodbye, Søren had a moment alone with Herman Madsen while Jacob and Birgitte got the children into their coats. Søren said he had been delighted to see him again. Really pleased.

'Likewise,' the old man said. 'I'm proud of you, Søren. And I'm sure you have strong reasons for resigning, but you need to reconsider. Having a talent puts you under an obligation.'

Søren looked at the old man in astonishment.

'Jørgensen let the cat out of the bag,' Herman explained.

'It's more complicated than that,' Søren said. 'I got greedy and now I'm paying the price.'

'Nonsense. It's not greed. You made a mistake. It's what real people do.'

Søren held out his hand to Herman. 'See you soon,' he said.

When Søren landed at Copenhagen Airport at seven o'clock on Saturday evening, he had two missed calls from Bøje Knudsen's number at the Institute of Forensic Medicine and a frantic message on his voicemail: 'Fucketty fuck. Why the hell haven't you been in touch, you layabout? I've sent you three emails now. Bloody well get on and read them, will you?'

Three emails? Søren checked his inbox immediately, but there was nothing from Bøje. 'Hey, you old whinger,' he emailed back, 'I think you forgot to send me those oh-so-urgent emails. Please try again. I'm waiting with bated breath.'

Søren put the photograph of Tove Madsen and Lea Skov in the glove compartment and had just started his car when he received a text message from Anna. She wanted to know if he intended to come home at some point and was wondering where he was.

He felt only slightly sheepish when, rather than drive straight home, he twisted the knife by going to Palads Teatret to watch *Avatar*. If Anna could spend three whole days in a seaside cottage with David Hasselhoff, surely he could do his own thing for one lousy day. It was almost midnight by the time he arrived home and found her asleep on the sofa with a book on her chest. He sat beside her and gently roused her. Anna stretched, confused, and Søren thought how much he loved her when she let her guard down. For one moment she looked openly at him, as if sleeping had dissolved their disagreements, but then she retreated.

'Where have you been?'

'Has Lily come home?' Søren asked.

'Yes, she's asleep.'

'Has she had a good day?'

'I think so. She seemed happy. Turns out Thomas and Gunvor won't be moving to Copenhagen after all. Thomas has been offered a job at Bærum Hospital in Oslo so they'll be moving to Norway instead. I told you so!'

'What?'

'Yes. Didn't I advocate caution? I said there was no need for you to worry about joint custody and all that. I knew it! Thomas has never put his child first. Lily has to fit into his life.'

Søren could not resist gloating inside.

'That makes you happy, doesn't it?' Anna smiled and yawned.

'Yes, to be honest, it does. I can't imagine Lily living somewhere else for several days at a time.'

'Me neither,' Anna said.

'I thought you said it was a good idea?'

'Listen, I might still be angry with Thomas for failing to take his share of the responsibility and perhaps I'm ultra-keen to strike while the iron is hot to further my career, so maybe that's how it came across. But once I'd had time to think it through, I didn't think it would work at all. It's far too confusing for Lily. So I'm delighted that we don't have to deal with it. Sometimes I forget I'm not alone any more. Being a single parent and writing my master's – and then there was all the business with my parents – was really tough. Oh, and don't forget the tiny detail that my supervisor was murdered. So I guess I was a little bitter when you met me.'

A little? Søren controlled himself because it was so rare for Anna to admit to anything.

'But now I've got you, and that's fantastic,' she said, and kissed his cheek. 'Nature in her wisdom requires two people to make a baby and I'm not just talking about conception, just so you know. It's mindboggling how much easier it is to be two.'

'Does that mean you want another?' Søren said, before he could stop himself.

Anna had sat up on the sofa and looked at him inscrutably. 'Not right now, Søren. I think that things need to be . . . running a bit more smoothly before we make that decision. Everyone says having two children is more than twice the work of one.' Then she got up and disappeared down the passage.

Søren stayed in the living room. One day he would clock Thomas for all the hurt he had caused.

Before he went to bed, he quickly checked his emails, but there was still nothing from Bøje. Ah, well, he thought, it couldn't have been that important.

On Sunday morning Søren slept late for the first time in years. He did not wake until just after ten and heard the tap running in the bathroom. There was a cup of instant coffee with milk on his bedside table, but it was almost cold, so it must have been some time since Anna had put it there. Was she waving a white flag or did she feel guilty because she already knew what would happen in the seaside cottage on Sjællands Odde? Søren leaned back in bed and closed his eyes. Every now and again he wished he could switch off his brain. Just for an hour. Soon afterwards Anna came into the bedroom. She was naked, except for a towel around her hair.

'Good morning,' she said, and disappeared into the wardrobe where she struggled to pull down the weekend bag from the shelf above the garment rail. He ate her up with his eyes and all he could think about was her climbing, damp and fragrant, under his duvet and staying with him for a long time, stripped of ambition and to-do lists, paying attention only to him.

'By the way, Jørgensen called yesterday,' Anna suddenly remembered. 'Sorry, I forgot to tell you. He thanked me for the profile on Kristian Storm. I think he felt bad that the case had been closed before I'd had time to present it, but I told him not to worry about it. These things happen. They couldn't have known that last week. Besides, it would never cross my mind to complain about wasted work that's so well paid.'

'Didn't he want to talk to me?'

'Sure, but you weren't here yesterday. Where were you, incidentally? You never told me last night.'

'In Aalborg.'

'Aalborg?'

Søren looked at the weekend bag, which Anna had managed to get down and was busy packing. 'How long will you be gone, did you say?' he asked.

'What were you doing in Aalborg?' Anna wanted to know.

'Investigating something in connection with the case.'

'What case?'

'Actually, that's a bit difficult to explain,' Søren said, and swung his legs over the edge of the bed.

Anna froze mid-movement and Søren was terribly distracted by her brown nipples.

'Søren,' she said, 'would you ever cheat on me?'

The question stunned him. Why did she ask him that now? Was it the kind of question that revealed the thought had crossed her mind and she was now, in some weird, complicated psychological way, trying to turn it against him?

'No,' he said. 'Why?'

'I just want to know,' she said. 'Anders T.'s partner cheated on him last year and he found out. That's why he's been in such a state. He said something the other day that I haven't been able to get out of my mind: that it wasn't the first time it had happened. Anders T. says that, in his experience, if people can cheat once, they'll do it again and that he was an idiot for giving the relationship a second chance. And then I remembered that you had cheated on Vibe ... and ... well, that was why I asked.'

Søren had no idea what to say. It was true that he had cheated on Vibe and that it had had huge consequences because the woman involved, Katrine, had got pregnant, but he did not see himself as a serial cheat who fitted into some convenient category invented by Anders T. It was just something Anders T. had said to undermine Søren and Anna's relationship and thus pave the way for himself.

'How long will you be gone?' he asked again.

'I'll be back on Wednesday at the latest.' At this stage Anna had got around to putting on socks, but nothing more and Søren had to avert his eyes. He hated being so attracted to her. 'Hello? Is that all right?' Anna asked again and Søren shrugged.

'I guess so,' he said. 'It's not like I've got a job to go to.'

'Talking about jobs, I had the distinct feeling that Jørgensen really wants you back.' She zipped up the weekend bag and finally finished getting dressed. Søren was desperate for the loo, but after watching Anna walk around in just her socks, it would be a while before he'd be able to pee.

'Why?'

'He pumped me for information.'

'What about?'

'About whether I thought you'd be willing to return to work if you could have your old job back.'

'Are you serious?'

'Of course.'

'But that job has gone to Henrik. Jørgensen will fall foul of every member of the Police Union if he moves Henrik to reappoint me, especially now when Henrik has . . . when he's . . .' Søren ground to a halt. 'Besides, I wouldn't want to return to Bellahøj as the guy who elbowed a colleague out of the way. I made a mistake when I agreed to that promotion and I'm delighted to hear that Jørgensen thinks he made a mistake by offering it to me in the first place, but it's too late now. It's like infidelity. You can't turn back time, can you? Some actions have huge consequences.' Søren looked straight at Anna. 'But I'll start job-hunting after Easter. I'll begin in Copenhagen and work my way outwards. It wouldn't be too bad if I ended up in Hillerød, but there's always a risk that I'd have to go to

Odense or all the way to Jutland, where the soil is black and the echo on the telephone line is hollow but—'

Anna laughed. 'You could always have a go at being a street poet on Strøget.'

'Will you come with me if I get a job in Jutland?' Søren asked her seriously.

'Søren,' she answered, just as seriously, 'please can we deal with that one if and when it actually happens? I love Copenhagen and I'm seriously banking on a full-time contract at the institute once I finish my PhD, so right now it would be something of an upset. Please can I think about it once you've been offered a job in Tarm or anywhere else that the soil is dark enough? Besides, Jørgensen sounded as if he had no idea where Henrik was. Please would you talk to him before you move us all to the far-flung corners of Denmark?'

'He couldn't find Henrik?'

'No. He asked if we'd seen him and I said we hadn't. Funny thing was Lily disagreed. Thomas had just brought her back when Jørgensen called and she got involved in the conversation. She said that Uncle Henrik was probably hiding because you had given him a bloody nose. Did you give Henrik a bloody nose?'

'No, of course not,' Søren said.

'Well, in that case, I've no idea what she was talking about. But I do think you ought to ring Jørgensen. He sounded really quite desperate and stressed and willing to offer you almost anything. Gosh, I've got to get a move on.' Anna looked at her watch. 'Anders T.'s picking me up in twenty minutes.'

'But I thought you'd already packed?' Søren said. 'Or are you taking the furniture as well?'

'No, but I still have to dry my hair and put on mascara.'

'Why?'

'Why what?'

'Why do you need to wear mascara when you're going to a seaside cottage to be nerds?'

'Because I don't want to look like crap,' Anna retorted sharply. 'Lily is watching children's television, but only until eleven, then that's enough for today. I don't want her watching TV all the time.' Then she grabbed her weekend bag and disappeared down the passage. Moments later Søren heard the hum of the hairdryer.

'Pretty please, Lily, my love,' Søren said, once Anna had left.

Lily looked at him and narrowed her eyes. 'Only if I get an ice cream with three scoops and a marshmallow on top.'

'There's no way you can eat three scoops *and* a marshmallow,' Søren objected.

'Yes, I can.'

'All right, then, it's a deal.'

When Søren parked in front of the Institute of Forensic Medicine, Lily piped up in anticipation: 'Can I stay in the car and play games on your mobile?'

'No, not today, sweet pea. I'm expecting a call and you need to spend a little more time at secretarial college before I'm ready to hire you full-time.'

'What's secretarial college?'

'A place where you learn to answer the phone without scaring people off. Just like Linda can.'

'I've decided I'm not going to be a biologist when I grow up. I want to be a doctor,' Lily declared. 'Just like my dad.'

That stung.

'Did you have a nice time with him yesterday?'

'It was all right,' Lily said. 'We walked right past BR Toys and he wouldn't even let me go inside to have a look. You would definitely have bought me something, and that's what I told my dad. Not a big toy, just a treat.'

'I would definitely have bought you a giant toy,' Søren said, with a smug grin. 'A Barbie castle or a whole grocery shop in plastic.'

Lily took Søren's hand. 'No, you wouldn't,' she said, and laughed.

'What are we doing here?' Lily asked, when she and Søren reached the Institute of Forensic Medicine by Rigshospitalet.

'Just saying hello to my friend Bøje.'

'You really can't be called that, can you?' Lily said.

Søren knocked on the door to Bøje's office, but there was no reply and the door was locked.

He took out his mobile and called Bøje's number, only to hear the telephone ring behind the locked door.

'He doesn't seem to be at home,' Søren said.

'Does he live *here*?' Lily sounded shocked.

'No, no,' Søren said. 'Hey, sit down for a moment, will you? I need to knock on some other doors and it's best if you stay put.'

'Why?'

'It just is.'

'Boring. Please can I play on your phone?'

'Nope,' Søren said. 'I'll only be a sec.'

At that moment a young pathologist arrived whom Søren

had met a few times before he was promoted to deputy chief superintendent and had stopped visiting the morgue quite so frequently. He was tall, with fiery red hair, and his name was Morten La Cour.

The two men shook hands and Søren said that he was looking for Bøje Knudsen.

Morten La Cour paled. 'Oh, I'm terribly sorry, but Bøje had a heart attack last night and was admitted to the ICU. It's not looking good.'

'What?' Søren exclaimed. 'No!'

Lily came racing over and took Søren's hand.

'When did it happen?'

'Last night in his office when he was writing post-mortem reports. I wasn't there myself, but four junior doctors were next door performing an autopsy. They heard a loud noise coming from Bøje's office and found him lying on the floor with severe chest pains. He was taken to A and E where he was stabilised and now he's in the ICU. He's still unconscious and it's too soon to say if he'll be OK. I'm really sorry to be the one to tell you.'

'But he called me last night,' Søren said. 'Between six and seven. Four times.'

'It happened just before nine o'clock,' Morten La Cour said.

'What is it, Søren?' Lily asked.

'My friend Bøje is ill,' Søren said, picking Lily up. 'He's had something called a heart attack and that's very serious.'

'They're already saying it will have consequences for management,' Morten La Cour added. 'I know it's only just happened, but I believe there'll be an investigation.'

'Why?'

'Because Bøje had worked seven days in a row. He stayed here every night and I don't think he got all that much sleep, a few hours max. He didn't even take the time to eat properly and his wastepaper basket is full of junk-food wrappers and Coke cans. There's supposed to be some kind of safety net in the public sector so people don't work themselves to death. I've barely been able to recognise him in the last few days. We've worked together for six months now and I've never seen him so stressed or with such a short fuse. His patience had run out, even with the junior doctors, and Bøje always stands up for the novices. He was totally exhausted yesterday, his skin grey. It's a terrible thing to say, but it didn't come as a great surprise.'

'Bloody hell,' was all Søren could say.

La Cour indicated that he had to go and Søren quickly asked about Kristian Storm's autopsy report.

'I'm trying to get an idea of what's on Bøje's computer. We need to finalise his reports. I promise to call you as soon as I've located it, OK?'

'Thank you. It's rather urgent.'

'Everything is, these days,' La Cour said, sounding as if he had turned sixty overnight.

Lily held Søren's hand all the way to St Hans Torv and kept giving him anxious looks.

'Are you very sad about your friend?' she asked.

'Yes,' Søren said.

'Then it might be a good idea for you to have an ice cream as well,' Lily said, and Søren smiled. He couldn't remember the last time he'd had ice cream. They spent a long time admiring the colourful selection in the ice-cream parlour before Søren chose a modest tub and Lily picked her three scoops with a coconut marshmallow on top. They crossed the road and sat outside Café Pussy Galore where Søren ordered himself a double espresso. Five minutes later Lily dumped her half-finished ice cream on Søren's saucer and went off to play.

'Try not to get too wet,' Søren called out.

'I won't,' Lily said, as she made a beeline for Jørgen Haugen Sørensen's fountain in the middle of the square.

Søren found Jørgensen's private telephone number on his mobile and rang it, even though Jørgensen had warned him not to call that number on a Sunday unless the Queen had been kidnapped.

'Hello, Søren,' Jørgensen grunted, when Søren had introduced himself.

'Have you heard about Bøje Knudsen?' Søren said. 'I've only just found out.'

'I have. It's not good.'

'And what's that about you not being able to find Henrik?'

'I had to suspend him last Friday, I'm sorry to say. Ever since then we haven't been able to track him down.'

'Why on earth did you have to suspend him?'

Søren heard Jørgensen hesitate. 'It's supposed to be a confidential human-resources issue between the management of Bellahøj and Superintendent Henrik Tejsner but ... I was about to call you to beg you to come back to work and hopefully you're about to say, "Sure, when do you want me to start?" so you'll need to know anyway. And, mark my words, I really am prepared to beg.'

'Big words coming from such a stubborn man,' Søren said. 'But let's start with Henrik.'

'OK. As you probably know, Tejsner was on loan to Station City for most of last week. They're rushed off their feet with the student rapes, as they have been christened by the ever-tasteless media, and the commissioner has asked all stations in Copenhagen to contribute manpower. Tejsner has handled the assignment very well, with credit, in fact. I know that you and Tejsner don't always get on, but he's a good police officer, Søren.'

'Henrik is a good police officer,' Søren agreed. 'A really good man in the field. And I've never claimed otherwise. He's just a horrendously bad manager, but that probably reflects more on those who appointed him.'

'And blah-blah-blah,' Jørgensen said irritably. 'But right now I'm not interested in your opinion of my managerial skills, Søren. Last Thursday, they finally got a breakthrough in the serial rapist case. They found some CCTV footage of the rapist's most recent victim, Emilie Storgaard, talking to a man. They couldn't identify the man from the footage, but something important happens in it. One of our confidential informants, a black guy called Solo, suddenly wanders into the frame and proceeds to greet the man Emilie Storgaard is talking to like a long-lost friend. Solo comes from some godforsaken place on the Ivory Coast, but has been granted permission to stay in Denmark in return for reliable intel from the drugs scene on Vesterbro. He speaks fluent Danish and is fairly observant, and even though we know he deals cocaine, we look the other way because he's helped us on several occasions. We brought him in, of course, and he spent all of

Thursday refusing to talk. Rathje and Hansen, the investigators tasked with interviewing him, tried everything, but he said not a word. Even threatening to deport him had no effect. "Let me tell you something. If I give you the name of the man in that film, I'll be dead before sunrise," he said. "I'd rather be sent home. At least there I've got a chance to see the week out."

'At one point Tejsner went to the loo and on his return he went straight for Solo and managed to break his nose and knock out both his front teeth before Rathje and Hansen got him under control. Afterwards Tejsner refused to explain what had triggered the attack and Station City had no choice but to report him to his superiors. Rathje drove Tejsner back to Bellahøj where he was sent to my office to explain himself. I confiscated his warrant card and sent him to HR to hand in his service weapon, but he never turned up. Since then I've called him dozens of times, but his mobile is switched off. The irony of it all is that I have good news for him. When Rathje and Hansen resumed questioning Solo – now with a brace on his nose and no front teeth – he immediately gave us the name of the guy on the CCTV footage. He's Martin Brink Schelde, some hotshot lawyer from a highly regarded law firm in the city, whom we arrested last Friday afternoon and he's been sweating in Station City ever since. He's denying everything, of course, but we got a tongue scraping, so it's only a matter of time before we get a DNA match. We all think he did it, so the powers that be have decided to overlook Tejsner's stunt. This is Denmark, don't forget, so we're not allowed to play good-cop-bad-cop, but for once a broken nose and two missing teeth were a godsend. The justice secretary has publicly praised us for our arrest, the public's rating of us has risen by six per cent in two days and Brink Schelde hasn't even confessed yet.'

'Listen to yourself,' Søren said. 'Anyone would think you worked in advertising. But let's get back to Henrik. I think I know what's going on. I'll find him and have a word with him.'

'Good,' Jørgensen grunted. 'And what about you? Can I persuade you to give me a helping hand? It's bad enough that I've had to manage without a DCS, but now that Tejsner is down, it won't do and—'

'Fine. I'll return to work,' Søren interrupted.

'That was easier than I expected!'

'Yes, but I have some conditions.'

Jørgensen heaved a deep sigh. 'Let me have them,' he said.

'I want my old job as superintendent back, but only until Henrik returns from paternity leave.'

'Paternity leave?'

'Yes, his wife had a baby last Friday.'

'Jesus Christ, that explains why he's hiding. And what happens when Tejsner's paternity leave is over?'

'We'll have another brainstorming session.'

'But am I right in thinking you don't want to be deputy chief superintendent any more?'

'One hundred per cent correct.'

'Even if it means a lower salary and a smaller pension?'

'Yep.'

'I don't get you, Marhauge,' Jørgensen said. 'Everybody else is busy fighting their way up the greasy pole. Anything else?'

'Yes, I want total freedom to reopen Henrik's cases. The

deaths of Professor Kristian Storm at the Institute of Biology and of Joan Skov at Snerlevej in Vangede, which happened the same evening.'

'But both cases have officially been closed.'

'Do you know how to spell "giant cock-up"? Bøje Knudsen hasn't even submitted the official autopsy report yet.'

'Autopsy reports for suicides?'

'*Alleged* suicides, not confirmed,' Søren said. 'Small word, big difference.'

Jørgensen considered it. 'But surely Tejsner wouldn't have closed two cases without first getting the green light from the Institute of Forensic Medicine?'

'If you ask me, Henrik's suffering from stress and I believe one of the symptoms is a diminished sense of reality and a tendency to rush decisions.'

'Stress?' Jørgensen thundered. 'Who the hell doesn't suffer from stress these days? It's a national disease, Marhauge! You think I'm not stressed? That doesn't mean I can't do my job.'

'So you didn't sign off his reports?' Søren asked sweetly. 'Funny . . . It looked like your signature.'

'You bastard,' was all Jørgensen said.

'Then we have a deal,' Søren said.

When Søren had hung up, he went to rescue Lily. She was soaking wet and her teeth were chattering, so he threw her over his shoulder and jogged back to his car outside the hospital.

'I told you not to get wet,' Søren scolded her. 'You've just been ill.'

'I didn't do it on purpose,' Lily wailed.

'No, of course you didn't and Dumbo has small ears.'

'No, he hasn't.' Lily carried on howling.

When they got to the car, Søren made her take off all her clothes and climb onto her car seat wearing only her pants. She complained pitifully. Then he took off his jacket and sweater and turned the car heating to maximum. By the time they reached Vibenshus Runddel, Lily had stopped whingeing.

'Tomorrow and the day after, Granny will be looking after you,' Søren said, as they drove down the Lyngby motorway.

'Yippee!' Lily cried.

On Monday, 29 March, Søren walked down the corridor to the briefing room at the Violent Crimes Unit at Bellahøj Police Station as if nothing had happened. It was five past nine in the morning and he was five minutes late because the detour to Nørrebro to drop Lily off at Cecilie's had proved a big mistake in the rush-hour traffic. The police officers were waiting for the morning briefing to start; a few were reading newspapers and the rest were batting small talk back and forth across the table. Søren knew them all well, except a new sergeant from Aarhus, Inge Kai, to whom he had been introduced but hadn't worked with. Søren hung his jacket over a chair and cleared his throat. 'Good morning,' he said. 'I'm your supply teacher this week because your usual teacher is ill.'

Most people laughed and there was even scattered applause.

'You can call me Acting Superintendent Søren Marhauge. Shall we get started?'

'So what you're saying,' Mehmet taunted him, 'is that not only have you been demoted, you're also on probation?'

Most people laughed again.

'Something along those lines.'

'So where is Superintendent Tejsner then?' Sergeant Sara Holbæk wanted to know.

'He's just had a baby,' Søren replied.

The gathering fell about laughing.

When Søren had said hi to Linda, assured her that she was not hallucinating and that he had indeed returned to work, he went to search Henrik's office. The room was dark and smelt sour, so Søren opened the window and adjusted the blinds. Henrik's desk was a frightful mess of loose-leaf paper, case files, crushed Red Bull cans, screwed-up paper and more case files. In the middle of it all, the Penal Code lay open: without any obvious logic, Henrik had marked at least two hundred of the three hundred paragraphs with yellow Post-it notes. Søren opened the desk drawers. The top left one was locked. Søren briefly considered forcing it, but dropped the idea. He already had an inkling of what it contained.

Instead, he put on his jacket and went down to his car.

Fifteen minutes later, he parked outside Henrik's stairwell on Amagerfælledvej 27 at the Urbanplanen Estate. There was no reply when he rang the doorbell. When a young guy came thundering down the stairs, Søren slipped inside the stairwell before the door slammed. First he checked Henrik's postbox and, as far as he could see, it had been emptied. On the fourth floor he rang Henrik's doorbell hard before he peered through the letterbox. In addition to an unmade-up mattress on the floor and Henrik's biker boots, which he had refused to part with even though he had sold the bike long ago, Søren spotted half a dozen empty or nearly empty bottles of spirits. There were no curtains in front of the window and even through the letterbox he could detect the stale smell of alcohol. Søren tried the door, but of course it was locked.

Back in the street he found a corner shop where he bought a copy of *Politiken* and *Euroman*, a cup of coffee and a chocolate bar. Then he made himself comfortable in his car and waited for Henrik. It had just gone twelve, so he braced himself for a very long afternoon.

He had received a text message from Anna, telling him she had arrived safely at Sjællands Odde, but apart from that, Søren had heard nothing from her. Their days of frequent, frantic text messages were over. Søren had not had time to give their relationship much thought today, but as he sat in the silence, it crept up on him. He downloaded the Facebook app to his smart phone and logged on. The photograph of Anna was like a punch to his stomach. Her cheeks were flushed and she was wearing her running top against a picturesque background of bark steaming with frost and the sense of spring. Anders T. had tagged her and the caption simply read: *Bella*.

Suddenly Søren sensed a shadow in the side window and turned his head.

Henrik was standing outside. He had lost weight and his gaze was manic. Søren made to get out of the car and tried to open the door, but every time he did, Henrik would push it shut. Finally Søren rolled down the window.

'Please can I get out?' he asked calmly.

'Leave me alone,' Henrik said. 'Don't ever talk to me again.' Then he turned on his heel and walked back to his stairwell.

Søren closed the window, got out of the car and locked it with a click.

'Wait,' he called after Henrik, but Henrik had already disappeared up the stairs and the door had slammed. Irritated, Søren systematically rang every single bell and got all the way down to the ground floor before he had any luck. 'Police,' he said brusquely, and was admitted after a brief hesitation. An elderly woman looked at him sceptically from the gap in her door and he quickly flashed his warrant card at her and said, 'Hello, madam,' before he took the stairs two steps at a time.

Søren banged on Henrik's door. 'Did you get my card?' he shouted through the letterbox. 'Come on, let me in. I want to talk to you.'

There was no sound from the flat and when Søren looked through the letterbox, he saw only the scene from earlier.

'Henrik,' he called. 'Let me in. I know you and Jeanette have split up. Why the hell didn't you say anything? Henrik, God damn you, open the door so I don't have to stand out here shouting at you.'

There was still no sound from the flat so Søren sat on the steps, trying to work out his next move.

He could call a locksmith. He could drive back to Bellahøj and fetch 'the big key', as it was known at the station: an iron pipe with handles the police would sometimes use during raids. Or he could kick down the door.

So that was what he did. He pushed down the handle and aimed his kick at the lock; at his third well-placed attempt the door flew open.

From the hallway he could see directly into the room with

the mattress, the bottles and the biker boots. To his left, over-looking Amagerfælledvej, there was another room, unfurnished except for a dilapidated sofa and a low coffee table. On the table lay a mirror and a razor blade. Henrik was nowhere to be seen.

'As you'll be aware, I have the right to shoot you in self-defence.' Søren spun around. 'Section thirteen of the Penal Code. Self-defence when a person or their property is attacked.'

Henrik was sitting up against the wall behind the door. His pupils had contracted to pinpoints and he rested his hand on one knee as he pointed his service pistol at Søren. He took a swig from an almost-full bottle of whisky on the floor.

'Lower your weapon,' Søren said.

'Lower your weapon,' Henrik mimicked, with a snarl, but showed no sign of doing so.

'You have a son.' Søren found his mobile and held it in his outstretched arm so that he could search for the picture of Olivia and Sara cradling their newborn baby brother while maintaining eye contact with Henrik. 'A bouncing baby boy weighing four kilos. His name is Storm.'

'I don't want to see him,' Henrik roared. 'Put that phone away or I'll fucking off you. Trust me, I've nothing to lose.'

Søren changed tactic. 'I know you're doing cocaine, Henrik.'

Henrik looked deadpan at him, but Søren sensed a hint of surprise behind the flat expression.

'You thought you could hide it, did you? That makes you just as stupid as every other drug addict on the planet. Besides, I took a blood sample from Lily's hat, which you used as a compress last Wednesday. Your nosebleed gave you away and I got Bøje to confirm it. I'm guessing you've got a habit. I'm guessing that the top left drawer of your desk at Bellahøj is locked because you can no longer get through a day's work without a line or two. And I'm guessing that you're snorting confiscated cocaine, which you stole from the evidence room.'

'No shit, Sherlock. Did you ever think of joining the police?' Henrik quipped sarcastically, then took another gulp from the bottle.

For a while, the two men said nothing while they stared each other down. Søren had rarely felt so ridiculous.

'I panicked when Jeanette told me she was pregnant,' Henrik suddenly said. 'I didn't want another bloody baby. Sara and Olivia had finally grown old enough to enjoy a lie-in and they can make their own breakfast, then Jeanette decides she wants to go back to square one. Nappies and bottles and puke? I'm just not good with babies. I go mental when they wake up screaming at night.' He jabbed himself in the temple with his free hand. 'At long last, our sex life was starting to pick up again. And then she tells me she's bloody pregnant. She claims she told me she'd stopped taking the pill and asked me to take precautions, but that's a big fat lie!'

'I thought the two of you were good,' Søren said. 'That you were all right after . . . your affair. Because that's what you said. You were over the moon when you told me you were having another baby.'

'What choice did I have? Jeanette might be telling everyone she's forgiven me for the affair with Line, but the truth is she's been punishing me non-stop ever since. Whenever I screw up, she makes it all about her and how I betrayed her two years ago. Even the girls are on my back. "Where are you going,

Dad? Isn't it a bit late to be going to the corner shop, Dad? Dad, you've made Mum cry again."' Henrik spat out the words. 'Besides, I've had it up to here with your and Anna's jammy little lives. Makes me want to vomit the way you go on about her. You and I haven't had one night out since you started living with her. We haven't gone for a beer on Friday after work once. You don't want to play squash any more. It's not normal, man. Before you met Anna, you'd hang out with your mates every now and again. But now you're too busy to waste your time on us losers. Jeanette agrees with me that you've become stuck-up. We haven't had dinner once since you and Anna moved in together. Because we're not good enough for your intellectual girlfriend? It's not like you went to university, either, you prick. And do you remember me telling you that Jeanette wanted fake tits? You swallowed it whole. As if that would ever even cross Jeanette's mind. You know her. She's a nursery-school teacher and gets organic vegetables delivered every week, for Christ's sake. But I saw the look on your face. You've become such a bloody snob since you moved in with that bitch.'

He took another swig from the bottle.

Søren was astonished. There was no point in him saying he hadn't known how to react when Henrik had mentioned Jeanette's new breasts. What did he know about women's midlife crises? was all he had thought at the time.

So he just said, 'You're wrong, Henrik.'

'Jeanette and I had a massive row about that baby,' Henrik continued. 'I told her to get an abortion and she went mental. Eventually I walked out, and if you hadn't been such a crap friend, I might have called you and asked if we could go for

a beer. Instead, I got drunk on my own somewhere on Vesterbro and did coke with a random guy who offered me some;
quite a lot, as it turned out. At one point that night I got the
urge to screw a hooker, so that's what I did. I would have killed
for just half an hour of being the boss of my own life. And do
you know something? I felt totally free. I was king of the
world, right until the condom burst and I found myself on top
of some twenty-year-old black girl who couldn't even look me
in the eye.' He laughed a hollow laugh. 'I went to the doctor
immediately and the first test was negative. The doctor gave
me a post-exposure prophylactic injection and told me only
to have safe sex until I got the final test. But I couldn't start
wearing rubbers when I was with Jeanette, could I? The first
few weeks were all right because Jeanette had morning sickness, but when that passed, she couldn't understand why I
wasn't in the mood. She would whine and accuse me of not
loving her any more, of having another affair – who was she
and where did she live? She irritated the hell out of me. In
the middle of it all I got promoted. And thank God for that. I
started working twenty-four/seven and didn't have to go home.
I even rented a room on Nørrebro where I could sleep, and
whenever Jeanette complained, I said I had a camp bed in my
office, that this promotion was a once-in-a-lifetime chance and
that she shouldn't expect me to give up my big break to
change nappies.'

'I wish you'd told me about you and Jeanette,' Søren said.

'Why? So you could play at being my therapist and fuck
with my head? I don't think so. But what a boost to my career,
eh? I've always hated taking orders from people, especially
you, but now finally I was in charge. I had my own digs where

I spent more and more time, I was on a roll, and the best thing was that no one knew a thing. When Jeanette's best friend called to ask what the hell I thought I was doing, I blurted out that I had met someone and told her to mind her own business. That shut her up. Then I found this flat where no one ever tells me to take off my shoes when I get home, no one changes the channel without asking me first, no one makes me eat broccoli and no one leaves their disgusting jamrags with the red side upwards in the bathroom. Finally Henrik Tejsner was living it up with a little help from his friend.' To illustrate, Henrik pressed a finger against one nostril and sniffed.

'But then that girl was raped in north-west Copenhagen,' Søren said.

Henrik drank some more whisky. 'I couldn't handle it,' he said after a while. 'Fourteen years old. Same age as Olivia. I met the girl's father, a gentle Syrian guy who just sat there while the tears rolled down his cheeks, and there was nothing I could do. If it had been my daughter, I would have killed myself. But he just sat there, saying he knew we were doing everything we could. But what could I tell him? The rapist was still at large. I spent half the night at Bella trawling through old microfilms. I searched high and low on the Net. I interviewed the family again, hoping we had missed something. I spent far too much time on that case and I fell badly behind with everything else. Besides, I was running out of money . . . So you're right, I nicked the bag from the evidence room. I never thought anyone would find out.'

Henrik got up and went over to the sofa. He lifted a sofa cushion and fished out the confiscated bag of cocaine. Søren saw the numbered police evidence tag dangling from it. Henrik looked at Søren with disdain, then lined up a fat stripe, which he distributed between his nostrils, taking care to keep his service pistol and the whisky bottle within reach.

'What happened at Station City?'

'I was the boss.' Henrik cheered and clapped his hands hard. 'I was Bernt's new golden boy. I aced that case. I was one hundred per cent better than you and your stupid backwards knitting.'

'What happened to Solo?'

'I could tell from his face that he knew something. Rathje and Hansen were far too easy on him. We didn't owe him shit. There are plenty of potential CIs out there who want to work for us. But Rathje and Hansen treated him like bloody royalty. Little coke-pushing creep contaminating Denmark from the inside . . .'

'So you went to the Gents and snorted a line to build up some Dutch courage, and when you returned, you knocked out Solo's teeth and broke his nose.'

Again Henrik looked deadpan at Søren before he suddenly moved the pistol to his own temple. 'I'm not going back to Jeanette,' he said. 'It stopped being fun long ago. And I've lost the girls. Jeanette has turned them against me with all that guilt crap. I haven't got a snowball's chance in hell of winning them back. And the boy? Jeanette will turn him against me too. Just you wait and see.'

'Give me your gun,' Søren said quietly.

'And now I've got the sack.'

'Give me your gun,' Søren said.

Henrik looked at him blankly.

'Give me your gun now,' he said again.

'I'm a man,' Henrik said, pressing it harder against his temple.

'Solo gave us the name of the man on the footage,' Søren said, 'and we've arrested a young lawyer who works in the city. Martin Brink Schelde. Jørgensen asked me to tell you that your suspension has been lifted. You can go back to work again.'

'You fucking liar.' Henrik looked emptily at Søren for a moment and then he pulled the trigger.

Søren squeezed his eyes shut.

Then Henrik laughed. 'You're such a prick. Did you really think I was going to shoot myself? The chamber's empty, you idiot. You should have seen your face. Oh, I can just imagine you telling that bitch of yours how you almost saved me.'

For a moment Søren stared at him in shock, then anger took over. 'I've told Jørgensen that you're on paternity leave for a month.'

Henrik scoffed.

'That means you have a month to sort yourself out. Get your shit together. I'm giving you one chance. If you don't take it, I'll report you for the theft of eighty grams of cocaine from the evidence room. You'll get a two-year custodial sentence minimum and your police career will be over.'

Henrik was still looking at him with contempt.

'And Anna isn't a bitch,' Søren added quietly.

'Anna isn't a bitch,' Henrik mocked, and took another swig from the bottle.

'And I'm nothing like what you said,' Søren continued.

'Get out. You're not my friend. You never were.'

'Do you know something?' Søren said. 'You were never my friend either.'

Then he left.

On his way into town Søren was shaking so much that he had to stop at a service station to compose himself. When he had calmed down, he called Lea Skov, but his call went straight to voicemail. It was only five thirty so he decided to stop at her flat and try the doorbell. He checked that the photograph of young Lea and Tove Madsen was still in his glove compartment and it was. But Lea Skov was not at home, or she was not answering her door. Søren did not want to leave the photograph in Lea's letterbox: it required an explanation. Instead he drove out to Lily and Cecilie on Nørrebro.

CHAPTER 10

At four thirty on Wednesday, 31 March, Marie switched off her computer and went out into the kitchen to grab some food before her meeting with the police. While she ate, she wondered who could check the finished article for her. She had written several academic papers in English and Storm had praised her for picking up the language so quickly. Nevertheless, she would prefer an expert to read the text before she emailed it to Terrence Wilson. Ideally that person would be Tim because he was her co-writer and because his English was perfect, but what if he didn't get her message in time? She had to come up with a plan B, then cross her fingers that Tim would respond during the weekend so they could still meet the Monday-morning deadline. Why not ask Trine Rønn? It would also give them a chance to catch up. Marie put her plate in the sink and picked up her handbag. Just as she was about to leave, Lea called.

'Hi, sis! I'm now officially a psychologist!'

'Congratulations!' Marie was delighted. 'Sorry, I was going to call you. How did it go?'

'Great, I think. I won't know for sure for another couple of weeks, but I have a good feeling about it. I'm convinced that

I passed. And you'll never guess what my oral exam was about. Advanced defence mechanisms.'

'What are they?' Marie said and sat down on her bed.

'Repression, denial, displacement and regression. That kind of stuff. But I knew my terminology inside out. Oh, I wonder why,' Lea said drily. 'Talk of the devil, Frank called me a moment ago to tell me to stop "harassing" Julie. That was the word he used. I could hear that he'd been drinking.'

'Where was he?'

'I don't know. He just called to say that Julie is really upset about "what she's done" and needs to be left alone, so did I think I could stop harassing her.'

'I must talk to her,' Marie said, exasperated. 'It makes no sense for her to think she killed Mum because she failed to sort out her pills.'

'And I'm not harassing her,' Lea added. 'Christ, I only asked if she could remember Tove, her surname or a house number, anything. Why is she so scared of what Tove might tell me? That our family fell apart when Mads died because it was already teetering on the edge of the precipice with a highly strung mother and an immature fantasist of a father who should never have got married? I realised that years ago. Mum and Dad piled far too much responsibility onto the shoulders of a ten-year-old girl and sometimes she had no choice but to give her little sisters tinned spaghetti three days in a row because Frank had forgotten to come home and Mum was spaced out on the sofa. Anyway, it doesn't matter now because it turns out that Tove is dead.'

'Dead? How do you know that?'

'I Googled "Tove, police officer, Cluedo and Vangede", and

found a possible connection: Herman Madsen. He was an investigator with Copenhagen Police, but moved with his wife, Tove, and their three children from Vangede to Aalborg in 1998. Their elder daughter, Helle Madsen, founded Aalborg's first choir for children who are hard of hearing, and by comparing a picture from a local paper I found on the web, where she's standing between her parents, with several Facebook profiles of women also called Helle Madsen, I ended up being so sure that I messaged her on Facebook. I've just read her reply on my mobile. She writes that her family used to live on Snerlevej, at number twenty-five. She also writes that she remembers me well because her mother had a photograph of me. I got very emotional when I read that. I have no memory of Tove, but I meant so much to her that she kept my picture all these years. Sadly, she died of cancer last year, Helle Madsen wrote. I only wish we'd talked about her sooner. I would have loved to meet her. It's definitely to her credit that I didn't end up as fucked up as the rest of you.' Lea chuckled. 'Sorry, sis.'

'What else did her email say?' Marie was intrigued.

'That was all,' Lea said. 'Only that Tove had died and then this business about the photograph. I'm going to write back to Helle tonight and ask if I can have it. It would be all right to ask, wouldn't it?' Lea sounded anxious.

'It's a funny thing with you,' Marie said pensively. 'Most of the time you're so assertive, then suddenly you get insecure about the oddest things. Of course you can ask her if you can have that picture! All she can do is say no.'

'It's called having low self-esteem, but lots of confidence. Just ask a psychologist. Anyway, it's nice to know that I meant something to Tove. Hey, by the way,' Lea continued, 'I spoke to Mattis and you're welcome to give him a call if you're serious about your swallow tattoo. He has a waiting list of two months, but because you're my sister, he'll see you without an appointment. Tonight, for example, he said.' Lea laughed.

'I really don't think I can—'

'Of course you can! You can do anything you want to, Marie. Anything. And you can take my word for it. I'm now officially a psychologist!' Lea said triumphantly.

'You're a tough cookie.' Marie smiled to herself.

'So are you.'

They hung up and Marie rushed out of the door. She was running late and she was due to meet Søren Marhauge at the café in two minutes. She stopped on the pavement, found her mobile and began composing a text message to him. And that was when she saw it.

A dark blue Ford with tinted windows.

It was parked diagonally across from Marie's stairwell.

Marie started to walk quickly down Randersgade and crossed Strandboulevarden. Had someone been watching her? Was she being followed now? Then again it might be nothing. It could be a different car from the one Storm had seen. Maybe she was just paranoid. But three people were dead. When she crossed Vordingborggade, her chest began to tighten and she had to give up walking and texting at the same time. Never mind, she was almost there. She recognised Søren from a distance. He was tall and he was locking his car. When he had dropped the keys into his pocket, he turned and looked straight at her.

'Walk with me,' she said, and as she passed him, she grabbed his arm. For a split second he reacted with surprise, then they continued down the street like just another couple.

It was not until they reached Bopa Plads that Søren said, 'Are you being followed?'

'Wait. I . . . can't . . . breathe,' she panted.

She dragged Søren across the square and into a typical Copenhagen courtyard with a picnic table, a battered playground, small patches of grass and some sheds. She carried on walking, now with Søren in her wake, and it was not until they were behind a leafless beech tree in the centre that she set down her bag, unzipped her jacket, crouched with her hands on her knees and gasped for breath.

'Are you all right?' Søren asked, and put his hands on her shoulders.

'No,' Marie wheezed. 'I . . . I can't breathe . . . I need to sit down . . .' Søren managed to get her to the picnic table.

'Take deep breaths,' Søren said calmly. 'All the way down to your stomach. Easy now. You're hyperventilating, but it's not dangerous. There you go, easy does it.'

Eventually Marie regained some control over her breathing, and a few minutes later, she was back to normal.

'I saw a blue car,' she said. 'A Ford with tinted windows. Right outside my front door. But I've only lived in that flat for a week and I haven't officially changed my address yet. No one knows I live there.'

'Slow down,' Søren said. 'Take it from the start.'

It took Marie half an hour to tell Søren everything.

When she had finished, Søren drummed his fingers on the table for a long time without saying anything.

'I know that you have officially closed the case and classified it as suicide,' Marie said despairingly, 'but surely you can see that something doesn't add up.'

'Marie,' Søren said, 'I can't tell you very much right now, only that we're investigating the case again. It has been reopened. I don't believe that Kristian Storm killed himself, either.'

'You don't?' Marie said, and tears rolled down her cheeks. 'Oh, thank you, thank you for believing me.'

Søren resumed drumming his fingers. 'I would like your opinion on Storm's so-called suicide note.' Søren made quotation marks in the air. 'I'll email it to you later.'

'Sure,' Marie said.

'In return I want you to give me the registration number he copied from the car he saw parked outside the August Krogh Institute. I'll try to track it down.' Marie nodded.

'Did you make a note of the number of the car you saw just now?'

'No,' she said sheepishly. 'I just ran.'

They sat for a little while. Marie concentrated on her breathing. She was cold, but there was something reassuring about the chilly air mixed with the smell of wax from the police officer's jacket.

'Incidentally, I have a totally unrelated question for you,' Søren said at length. 'Please could you give me your younger sister's email address?'

Marie looked at him in surprise. 'Why?'

Søren cleared his throat. 'It has nothing to do with the case,' he said. 'It's a private matter. But you and I grew up in the same street. Now, I'm somewhat older than you, so we never had much to do with each other. It was my colleague, Superintendent Henrik Tejsner, who drew my attention to it the other day. Can I start by saying that I was really sorry to hear about your mother?'

'Thank you,' Marie said. Eagerly, she added, 'You must have known my parents. Or did yours know mine? Only Lea wants to talk to someone who knew us when we were little. If your parents remember something, perhaps Lea could talk to them?'

'My parents died when I was five,' Søren said, 'and I was brought up by my maternal grandparents, who lived across the road from your family. They're no longer alive and I think they only knew your parents superficially. From local get-togethers in the early eighties. How old are you?'

'Twenty-eight,' Marie said.

'Then you would have been only five when I left home and ... Normally I wouldn't have said anything because I prefer to keep things separate, but ...' Søren cleared his throat '... I've tried and failed to get in touch with your sister in the last couple of days.'

'Really, why?'

'I have something for her. A photograph. Your sister had a childminder when she was little and—'

'Yes,' Marie said. 'Tove. But she's dead.'

'Yes,' Søren said. 'But she left a photograph that her husband, Herman, really wants Lea to have. Tove was very fond of your younger sister and she had kept the photograph all these years. Herman has tried getting in touch with Lea, but that ... didn't work out. So when I visited him last Saturday, he asked me to take the photograph with me to Copenhagen and give it to her. The connection with you and Kristian Storm is purely coincidental and I wouldn't have brought it up, only I haven't been able to get hold of Lea myself. I tried phoning her and calling at her flat. All to no avail. If I had her email, I could ask her to contact me – that is, if she wants the photo-graph.'

'Lea has been revising for an important exam so she has ignored everyone. But I can email you her email address as well as the car number, and I promise to mention it to her when I next speak to her, probably later today. I know she'll be delighted to have that picture. When my twin brother died, Mum was so distraught that she cut up almost all our family photographs . . . And I think the rest were destroyed when our shed burned down because our family photographs were kept inside it.' Marie seemed momentarily confused. 'What-ever the reason, there are hardly any pictures from when we were young. It's never really bothered me because our elder sister has told me lots about the past. But I'm sure Lea would be thrilled to have that photograph,' Marie said again.

'How did your brother die?' Søren asked.

'He got meningitis,' Marie said. 'Though I don't remember anything about it myself,' she added.

'I know what it's like to lose a child,' Søren said. 'I'm sorry. I don't know why I said that. That was exactly why I didn't want to bring up my connection to Snerlevej. I like keeping things separate.'

'It's fine,' Marie reassured him. 'That must have been awful. I would never get over it myself. Cancer, possibly; my mother's death, Storm's. But my son Anton's – never. I think I need to go now. I must finish Storm's article.' For a moment she looked awkwardly at Søren. 'Please would you walk me home?'

'Of course,' Søren said. 'We'll check out the blue Ford at the same time. There's no need for you to worry if it turns out it's not the same car.'

'I'm really embarrassed about my earlier behaviour,' Marie said.

'Don't be,' Søren said. 'Being careful never killed anyone.'

When they stopped outside Marie's stairwell in Randersgade, the dark blue Ford had gone.

'It's not here,' Marie said.

'Who knows you live here?' Søren asked.

'No one. Except my family: my ex-husband, my dad and my sisters.'

'Does Tim Salomon know where you live?'

Marie shook her head. 'I think I mentioned I'd moved to Østerbro. But that wouldn't mean anything to someone who doesn't know Copenhagen. Why do you want to know? I trust him completely.'

'I'm a police officer,' Søren said. 'I ask random questions to clarify points. Is your new address listed in the university's database?'

Marie blinked. 'They have my mobile number and my old address in Hellerup. But I have yet to register my change of address with the National Register of Persons. I moved out at very short notice.' She was staring at him anxiously.

'Try not to worry, Marie. You have my phone number. If anything happens, you call me straight away. I can dispatch a car from Bellahøj in less than five minutes. Be on your guard, but try to stay calm.'

'OK,' Marie said, subdued. She glanced up and down the street, but everything was normal. 'Thank you for walking me home.'

'Don't mention it,' Søren replied. 'I'll wait here until you're upstairs in your flat. You can let me know over the intercom.'

'Thank you,' Marie said, but she stayed where she was. 'Funny business about Snerlevej,' she began. 'I Googled you earlier today so that I would know what you looked like and I thought you seemed familiar. But surely I wouldn't be able to recognise you from twenty years ago. I know I have a photographic memory, but there are limits.'

Søren smiled.

When Marie had let herself into her flat, she quickly put on the security chain and assured Søren over the intercom that he was safe to leave now.

'Talk to you soon,' his voice crackled, and shortly afterwards she watched him head down Randersgade towards his car. Even from the third floor he looked tall.

When Marie had emailed the blue Ford's registration number and Lea's email address to Søren, she sat down at her desk to work. Her thoughts were flapping about like headless chickens and she found it hard to concentrate on her article. Storm, the blue Ford, Tim, who was risking his life in the wilderness of Guinea-Bissau, and her shock at learning from Sandö how Midas Manolis had died.

Dear Tim, Emailing you feels strange because I don't know if you get my messages. I hope that you got my last email, and/or that Malam Batista has got hold of you by now. Are you on your way to Denmark yet? I'm working on the article, but I would feel so much better if you were writing it with me and especially if you could proofread it. Warm wishes, Marie

PS: I gather that you visited the institute last week to get my address and telephone number from the faculty secretary. The telephone number is correct, but I have moved and am now living at number 76 in Randersgade on Østerbro. I hope that you will email me or call me soon, so that I know we have made contact. More than anything, I hope you'll be back in Denmark soon!

When she had sent the email, she worked without a break for almost two hours until Julie called her out of the blue.

She was in her usual fussing mode. 'How are you? Are you eating?' she wanted to know. 'And how was your appointment at the hospital last Monday, Marie? I suddenly remembered it yesterday. Why didn't you remind me? I thought I was coming with you.'

Marie replied that she'd thought Julie had enough on her plate, but it had gone fine. Her numbers were good and she had decided to keep her ovaries.

'Are you sure that's wise?' Julie sounded worried. 'The doctors usually know what they're doing and I—'

'I'm not sure of anything,' Marie interrupted her. 'But it's my choice. I've looked into the scientific arguments for and against and I know what feels right for me, so I said no.'

'But, Marie—'

'Anyway, how are you doing?' Marie asked.

'Oh, I'm all right,' Julie said in a small voice.

'Why do you mind so much that Lea wants to know about that woman who looked after her when we were little?' Marie said. 'She says you no longer return her calls.'

'Lea shouldn't be stirring things up,' Julie said.

'Julie,' Marie said, 'you can't control other people. Do you hear me? I love you and I know you mean well, but you can't control everything.' She heard a sharp intake of breath.

'You're been talking to Lea behind my back,' she said. 'I would never have believed that of you, Marie. After everything I've done for you.' She practically hissed the last words.

'I love both my sisters,' Marie said miserably, 'and I wish we could all get on together. Sometimes I can see where Lea is coming from. You and Dad are always so angry with her.'

'What are you trying to tell me, Marie?' Julie's voice had turned icy.

'Nothing, Julie. You're not to blame for Mum's death. It was kind of you to organise her pills for all those years, kind of you to cook meals for Mum and Dad's freezer when they couldn't manage it themselves, and all the other things you've done for them, but Mum didn't die because you failed to turn up that Monday to sort out her pills and went instead to your children's school to see them in a play. It's not your fault, Julie. You have to stop it.'

'I would never have believed that of you,' Julie repeated quietly.

'Believed what?'

'That you would turn on me. After everything I've done for you for all these years.'

'Listen, this is ridiculous, Julie . . . Hello?' But Julie had already hung up.

Marie sat dumbstruck at her desk. Julie had never hung up on her before.

When she had composed herself, she tried to turn her attention back to her writing.

Overall, routine vaccinations have beneficial effects on child survival rates in high mortality countries. However, routine vaccinations may have non-specific effects (NSE) on child survival rates – that is, effects not explained by prevention of the vaccine-targeted infections.

Her thoughts kept returning to Julie. Her elder sister had never been angry with her before, either, not like this. But why did Marie feel so guilty about it? All she wanted was to have a reasonable relationship with both sisters, even if the other two didn't get on very well. It should be possible. Marie called Julie back, but no one picked up the phone. After two more attempts, she left a message. 'Julie, I think we were cut off,' she said. 'Please call me back. Lea isn't trying to harass you. She just wants to know more about her childhood and I don't see what's wrong with that. Why does this matter so much to you? You don't have to relive the past if you don't want to. We all know that it's extra hard for you just now, but you haven't done anything wrong. I love you and I love Lea and I wish that the three of us could find a way of getting on. Please call me.'

When she had hung up, she sat down to do some more work, but after half an hour, she gave up and opened the windows for some fresh air. She stood behind the curtains, scanning the cars in the street, but in the evening twilight they all looked dark blue. Suddenly she was filled with in-articulate rage and rummaged in a removal crate until she found the blonde wig and put it on. She pulled a woolly cap over her hair, put on her coat and boots and walked down the stairs. Halfway down she met the man who lived in the flat below and who had welcomed her to the building the day before, but he showed no sign of recognising her. This made it seem highly unlikely that the driver of the blue car would realise who she was. Marie walked down Randersgade, then briskly down Østerbrogade without making eye contact with anyone. A sudden impulse made her reach for her mobile in her pocket. Before she knew it, she had called Mattis, Lea's tattoo artist. She heard loud rock music in the background when the call was answered and Mattis shouting, 'Hang on a sec.' The volume was turned down.

'Who did you say you were?' he asked. His Danish was slightly accented and Marie surmised that he must be German.

'Marie Skov, Lea Skov's sister. She gave me your number because I was thinking of . . .' Marie ground to a halt.

'Ah, Marie!' he exclaimed cheerfully. 'Yes, I hear you want a swallow . . . Ha-ha, Lea Skov, that sounds really weird.'

'Why?' Marie asked.

'Among us, she's known only as Lea Sky.'

'Lea Sky?'

'Yes. I knew she had another surname but I'd forgotten it was Skov. Skov, Jensen, Hansen, a common surname like that doesn't really suit Lea, does it? Right, so when are you coming over? We have a waiting list of two to three months, but not for Lea Sky's secret sister.'

'Is now a good time?'

'Great,' Mattis said. 'Do you have a picture of a particular swallow?'

'No,' Marie said, 'but I know exactly what I want.'

'Then just come over,' Mattis said. 'Nansensgade seventy-three, basement. See you shortly.'

Marie caught the bus to Nørreport station and quickly located the tattoo parlour in the basement in Nansensgade.

The sign on the door, which had security bars, said *Closed*, but it was wedged open and Marie could hear Queens of the Stone Age. She walked down the few steps and peeped inside. A young guy with a black punk hairstyle was busy sweeping the floor while he sang very loudly and very out of tune. His arms were covered with tattoos and a cigarette was dangling from the corner of his mouth, which he managed to drop twice while Marie was watching him. Suddenly he looked up and waved her inside the shop.

'There you are,' he said. 'Yes, I can see that you're sisters, even though you're not . . .'

'Nearly as good-looking?' Marie said, with a smile. She didn't mind. Lea had always been the beautiful one.

Mattis sized her up. 'Nearly as hard core, I was going to say. And at least as good-looking. It's lovely to meet you at last. Lea has told me loads about you, but I was starting to think you didn't exist.' Mattis kept on scrutinising her. He had small, clear blue eyes, a dimple in his left cheek, a piercing in his right ear and an incredible amount of hair, which had been cut short at the back and sides and was standing straight up on his head in a Mohican.

They chatted while Marie removed first her woolly hat, then her wig.

Mattis told her he was twenty-six, had moved from Berlin to Copenhagen and had met Lea in Pumpehuset at a Fear Factory concert in 2006.

'Anyway, tell me what kind of tattoo you want.'

Marie produced Storm's wooden swallow from her pocket and handed it to him. 'This,' she said.

Mattis turned over the swallow in his hand.

'It's a barn swallow,' Marie explained. 'They fly fifteen thousand kilometres to South Africa every autumn and back again every spring. No, this way round.' Marie rearranged Mattis's hands. 'I want its wings spread out as it soars vertically up into the sky.'

'OK,' Mattis said. While he started sketching the swallow on a piece of transfer paper, Marie took off her top and sat on a couch in a cubicle with curtains on three sides.

'Why a swallow?' he asked, while he drew. Marie was in her jeans, naked from the waist up and wondering if she had discarded too much clothing. Perhaps Lea hadn't told him that she had had a breast removed and he would be shocked.

'Because it's tough,' Marie said, and made herself comfortable on the couch with her back to him. She straightened when Mattis entered the cubicle and jumped when he applied disinfectant to her shoulder.

'I'll start by transferring the image, yes? Then we can double-check if that's what you had in mind.'

Mattis's palm brushed Marie's back and he had just placed the transfer paper with the swallow on her skin when Marie called, 'Stop!'

'What's wrong?' Mattis said, and removed the transfer paper.

'Please would you tattoo me here?' she asked, turning to Mattis. She watched his face, searching for any sign of revulsion in his eyes.

'There, above my heart, well away from my scar. Please can you tattoo me there?'

'Of course,' he said, not missing a beat. 'I can tattoo you anywhere. Are you sure?'

'Yes,' Marie said.

'Turn towards me a little more.' Marie did so and Mattis gently pressed the image against her heart.

'Go over to the mirror. If it's where you want it, we'll get started.'

Marie stood in front of the mirror and inspected herself. The downy shadow of new hair on her head had become a little more obvious and the swallow imprint, the size of her childhood glitter stickers, sat exactly where she wanted it.

'I don't want it filled in,' she said. 'I want it exactly as it is now. An outline.'

'Sure,' Mattis said, sizing her up again. 'But then I think we should turn it, just a little bit so it flies diagonally. Just in case you decide to have your breast reconstructed one day because then there will be more of a curve here.' He tilted his head and pointed. 'But even if you decide not to, it'll still look super-cool.'

They exchanged only a few words while Mattis tattooed her. His hands brushed her while he worked and she felt his breathing like a feather against her upper body as he inspected his work. It took almost an hour. She could smell ink and blood. Her mobile rang a couple of times and the CD had fallen silent. When Mattis had finished, Marie got up and returned to the mirror while he cleaned his equipment. She studied the swallow. Her skin was red and swollen and she was lost for words.

Suddenly Mattis was right behind her, looking with her into the mirror over her shoulder.

'Bloody hell, that's fantastic,' was all he said.

Mattis drove her home in his mother's green Morris Minor even though he lived in the opposite direction. They hardly spoke during the journey and Marie wondered what he made of her, Lea's colourless sister, whom he had been kind enough to compliment. When they pulled up outside her flat, Marie asked shyly if Mattis would please wait until she had turned on the light and waved to him from her window, and he said he would be happy to, without asking prying questions about why she was afraid. She was grateful for that when she stood in her window behind the curtain and watched his small car rattle down Randersgade.

It was not until she had been to the lavatory and cleaned her teeth that she remembered her mobile had rung a few times while she was getting her tattoo. She saw that the number had been withheld, but Søren Marhauge had left a message. He had emailed her Storm's suicide note and would like to speak to her urgently.

It was past midnight.

Marie checked her emails and saw that Søren had written *Call me as soon as you can* in the subject box. There was also an email from Stig Heller, which she skimmed. He wrote that he would be at O'Leary's Sports Bar at Copenhagen Central Station this Friday morning at eleven o'clock. With a heavy heart she opened the document with Storm's final note.

When she had finished reading it, you could have knocked her down with a feather. She had not seen such badly written, pompous Danish riddled with Anglicisms for a long time. She was convinced that Storm had not written it.

She quickly sent a text message to Søren Marhauge:

Sorry for not getting back to you earlier. I guess it's too late now, but I really want to talk to you ASAP. Best wishes, Marie

Her mobile rang three minutes later.

'That note is absurd,' Marie said, without introduction. 'Storm never wrote it. I'm sure of it.'

'Hmm,' Søren said. 'I had a hunch.'

'Why didn't you show it to me before? Or to someone from the department? Anyone who knew Storm could have told you that he would never have written such nonsense. His Danish was flawless and he detested Anglicisms. His killer must have written it. Isn't there a fingerprint on it or something? There must be something you can do.'

'There are no fingerprints on the paper, not even Storm's. Our technician actually made a note about it in his report. Does Tim Salomon speak Danish?'

Marie gulped. 'Not as far as I know,' she said. 'I spoke English to him. He's Guinean and lives in Bissau, and all scientific communication outside Denmark is done in English. Why would he speak Danish?'

'Can you think of anyone who could have written this note in bad Danish?'

Marie could not. 'But why do you keep asking about Tim? He flew to Guinea-Bissau last Saturday. He loved Storm like his own father. He would never—'

'It was Tim Salomon who rented the blue Ford, Marie.'

'I don't believe you,' Marie said.

'According to Hertz, Tim Salomon rented the car from their Gammel Kongevej branch on the thirteenth of March. The booking was paid for with a Visa card and Hertz took a copy of the international driving licence Tim produced before they gave him the keys. I have copies of both and I would like you to confirm that the picture on the driver's licence really is of Tim. Besides, Hertz has reported Tim to the police because the car was never returned. Marie, are you there?'

'There must be some mistake,' Marie whispered.

'I'm afraid that looks unlikely,' Søren said.

'But what can it mean?' She was in tears. 'That Tim is the man who was watching Storm and now he's watching me? That Tim killed Storm? But why? The Belem Health Project was Tim and Storm's joint venture. Their pride and joy.'

'Right now I don't know what it means,' Søren said frankly. 'But we need to look into it and I would like to—'

'Tim didn't arrive in Copenhagen until the twenty-fifth of March and he flew back to Guinea-Bissau on the twenty-seventh,' Marie interrupted triumphantly. 'And only this morning I spoke to Malam Batista in Bissau, and he said that Tim went to Xitole and Dulombi-Boe last Sunday.'

'But it's still a fact that Tim Salomon hired the car that Storm observed outside the August Krogh Institute. I've sent copies of both the driving licence and the credit card to our document technician so he can check if they're fake. And tomorrow I'll look into Tim's travel activity in and out of Denmark. Did he say anything to you about when he was leaving?'

'I only know that he left on Saturday afternoon,' Marie said. 'But I know from Storm that all flights to Guinea-Bissau go via Lisbon. The only airline in Europe to fly there is TAP. Then again, Guinea-Bissau is an old Portuguese colony. And I saw his ticket!' she cried out. 'It was lying on the bedside table!'

'I'll call you again tomorrow,' Søren then said. 'Keep your phone to hand and switched on.'

'Google Translate!' Marie exclaimed.

'What?'

'The letter. Storm's suicide note. It was definitely put through Google Translate!'

There was silence for a moment, then Søren said, 'Christ, I think you might be right.'

The night before Thursday, 1 April, Marie's sleep was more broken than a dropped Ming vase. At three a.m. she gave up hope of getting any rest and turned on her computer.

Dear Tim, What if Storm was wrong? What if a hunch isn't enough? That certainly wasn't the impression I had about you. Please explain to me why you rented a blue Ford in Copenhagen. Best wishes, Marie

When she had pressed *send* she had second thoughts. Should she have run it past Søren Marhauge first? She climbed into bed and finally fell into a deep sleep.

Jesper's call woke her at just after nine o'clock.

'Are you trying to make me jealous?' he screamed, the second a bleary-eyed Marie answered her phone.

'What?' Marie swung her legs over the edge of the bed and caught sight of herself in the mirror, which was propped against the wall. Bloody hell, that's fantastic, Mattis had said. Her skin was fiery red along the outline, but she was inclined to agree with him. She saw only the swallow, not the missing breast.

'You were seen at First Hotel,' Jesper ranted. 'Last Friday. By

THE ARC OF THE SWALLOW | 414

a good colleague of mine who happened to be enjoying a drink in the bar after a conference. You've just been ill, you're still ill, and then you go and screw some big African guy.'

Marie was speechless for a moment. Then she said, 'May I remind you that you were the one who wanted a divorce because you'd met someone else?'

'But, Christ Almighty, I don't go around rubbing your face in it. You could at least be a little discreet.' It was rare for Jesper to be angry.

'Who saw me?' she asked, and regretted the question immediately. She did not have to justify herself to anyone.

'It doesn't matter. A colleague. Someone who happens to have covered a lot of shifts for me so I could be with you whenever you had chemo. How do you think it makes me look when three seconds later you're holding hands with someone in a hotel?'

'Jesper,' Marie said, 'you had an affair while I had chemo. You wanted the divorce, not me. I'm entitled to hold hands with whomever I want to, be they Chinese, Eskimo or African, though I fail to see what that has to do with anything.'

'So you admit it?' Jesper snarled.

'Yes,' Marie said, and then the devil got into her. 'I do. I might be dying, Jesper, and I don't want to die curious.'

Marie could hear Jesper gasping for breath before he spluttered, 'So you decided you wanted to know what it's like to have sex with a black man with a big dick?'

'No, Jesper. I decided I wanted to know what it feels like to make love to a man who is actually interested in making me feel good. Just for once in my life.'

There was a brief silence.

'Do you know what the difference between the two of us is?' Jesper said. 'I respected you enough to keep my affair secret. Emily and I have been together for five months now and not once have we been out for dinner, not once have we gone to the cinema. We've never even been out for a walk because I didn't want to risk bumping into someone who might know you. I've been very discreet.'

'Five months? That's interesting,' Marie said.

'And, if you really must know, your lover boy came to Ingeborgvej to ask after you.'

'My lover boy?' Marie said, and felt a shiver down her spine.

'Yes, I didn't see him myself because we've been forced to leave the house, in case you'd forgotten. But yesterday was Wednesday and Natascha came to clean. When she was almost done, a black man rang the doorbell and pushed his way into the hall. He said he was your friend and asked if you were in. Natascha said no and quickly rang me. Is that a little Freudian slip that you just happened to give him the wrong address?'

'I haven't told anyone where I live,' Marie said quietly.

'I want Anton this weekend,' Jesper insisted angrily. 'My brother's rented a holiday cottage in West Jutland and Anton hasn't seen his cousins for a very long time. But Anton says he's only prepared to go if he's allowed to come back to yours today. So I'll bring him round in two hours and pick him up again early tomorrow morning, OK? And let me tell you something, Marie, if that guy is with you, you have exactly one hour and fifty-nine minutes to get him out of the flat. I don't want Anton spending even one minute with your new boyfriend.'

Before Marie had time to object, Jesper had ended the call.

Marie rose and stood for a moment in the living room, not knowing what to do.

Then she called Søren Marhauge, who didn't answer his phone. She went to the lavatory, and when she came back, there was a missed call from an unknown number. She was about to ring him back when she got a text message:

Is everything OK? Søren wrote. *I'm on the other line.*

Everything is OK, Marie wrote. *Call me as soon as you can.*

Marie toasted two slices of rye bread and boiled an egg. She slathered butter on the bread and finished off her meal with half an avocado and twenty-two almonds. She wanted to put on some weight. Then she took a quick shower, and when she had got dressed, she discovered she had missed yet another call and rang Søren back. This time his number was engaged and she left a text: *Sorry, I was in the shower, but I'm around now.*

She sat down at her desk, determined to crack a seriously tricky section of the article. Storm would undoubtedly have spun in his grave, but Marie wanted to include the most valid objections from their opponents, such as Paul Smith. He was still in charge of the WHO's Epidemiology Task Force in Geneva and had gone from diametrical opposition to Storm to being less dismissive. The January issue of a Canadian periodical even quoted Smith as saying that Kristian Storm's research could no longer be ignored and made it necessary to form a working group that would concern itself exclusively with the non-specific effects of vaccines.

Big words from a former opponent.

However, Marie had her doubts about Peter Bennett, the

highly respected American immunologist and professor at Stanford University. Bennett was the scientist who, in the last five years, had expended the most energy on rejecting Storm's ideas about the non-specific effects of the vaccines, so there was plenty of material from which to choose. Worse, in October 2008 Bennett had stood up and trashed Storm's research in front of every international immunologist at the workshop in London. Storm would indeed spin in his grave if he knew that Marie was considering giving Bennett more column inches.

Bennett had a list of publications to his name as long as the Great Wall of China, Marie discovered, and there could be little doubt that he was a leading expert. Even so, she had a strong feeling that his almost hysterical attacks, especially in scientific periodicals, were about something more than Bennett merely demonstrating his own superiority. Storm had often mentioned how scientific periodicals had been just as badly hit by the financial crisis as the rest of the publishing industry, and it followed that editors in part gave column inches to Bennett because he was famous.

Hang on a minute . . . Now that was interesting. Despite his fame, Bennett had himself been accused of professional misconduct, not for scientific dishonesty, but he had been suspected of corruption in connection with the WHO's pandemic warning about the swine flu virus H1N1 in 2009. Storm had never mentioned that and Marie was mystified until she discovered that Bennett had been cleared, which had only heightened his popularity. In 2010 alone he had been the main speaker at every international immunology symposium and the lead author of thirteen articles.

By now Marie had got the bit between her teeth and she followed a link to a summary of the pandemic scandal.

In June 2009 Elizabeth Chung, general secretary of the WHO, had issued an international pandemic warning when several mysterious deaths in the US and Mexico had turned out to be the result of a rare flu strain called H1N1. The decision to issue the warning was based on an assessment by the WHO's Emergency Committee and instantly triggered the production of millions of doses of vaccines. For a brief moment the world held its breath. Given the WHO's reaction, people began to think that humanity might be on the verge of extinction.

The first criticism of the pandemic warning appeared in a liberal German newspaper when a journalist questioned why members of the Emergency Committee were anonymous. All other WHO committee members were known to the public, the journalist pointed out, and he wondered why the same principle did not apply to a committee that had the power to make decisions affecting the whole world. His criticism was soon echoed by both *El País* and *The Times*, and in July the same year, the WHO issued a press release, which stated that the reason for the committee members' anonymity was to avoid any attempt at manipulation by the pharmaceutical industry. Furthermore, the WHO promised, once the pandemic was over and the risk of manipulation of individual members had passed, the names of the committee members would, of course, be released.

However, there must have been a leak because a few weeks later a French journalist published the name of every single member of the Emergency Committee in a major feature in

Le Monde. No one knew how he had got hold of the list, but there was a huge scandal when it turned out that practically all members of the committee were shown to have close links to the pharmaceutical industry. No less than seven members sat on the boards of various pharmaceutical companies, and four of those companies turned out to produce constituents that went into the H1N1 vaccine. Things went from bad to worse when a pharmaceutical-company contract for one of the committee members was published. It stated in black and white that the bonus paid to each board member was linked directly to the profit of the company. A hefty sum, the journalist concluded archly, because the WHO's pandemic warning had resulted in a massive rise in the production of influenza vaccines and there had been in total an increase of seventy-five orders with a value of two billion euros for Tamiflu alone.

The WHO cares more about the pharmaceutical industry than public health!

The WHO is in the pocket of Big Pharma!

The world's media went crazy.

The WHO was forced to dismiss several members of the Emergency Committee as more and more came under the spotlight, including Bennett. It turned out that he was an adviser to and director of several vaccine-constituent producers, including the rapidly growing Japanese pharmaceutical company Sixan Pharmaceuticals, which manufactured an aluminium-based constituent for the influenza vaccine.

Two factors saved Bennett from professional beheading. First, he could prove that he had resigned from the board of Sixan Pharmaceuticals *before* he had joined the WHO's Emergency Committee. Second, it turned out that he was the only one of the twelve committee members to have voted *against* the pandemic warning. He had stayed silent while the scandal unfolded, but the moment he was cleared, he uploaded a press release on his homepage in which he wrote:

I can only agree that a close relationship between an organisation like the WHO and the pharmaceutical industry is completely inappropriate, but it doesn't justify a witch-hunt of individuals.

And it might be said that he had a point.

Marie got up from her computer to stretch her legs and stopped in front of the window to look down on the street. There was no blue Ford today. She thought about Tim. Last Friday night she had melted like butter in his arms and shyly inhaled his overpowering scent of unknown continents, caressed the soft skin of his palms and tickled his foot with hers. 'You're exploring me.' Tim had laughed in the darkness. Yes, and for a moment, she had let her guard down. But if Tim really did want to hurt her, why hadn't he just killed her there and then? One blow and she would have been dead.

One explanation could be that the Guinean medical records had still been missing at that stage. And now, when Tim had got her email telling him she had found them, she would become the next target to be destroyed. But what about Malam Batista, who had sounded utterly convincing when he told her that Tim was travelling in the province? Had that been a lie? It hadn't sounded like one. But Marie knew from Storm that in Guinea-Bissau everything was for sale. An alibi, a ministerial post or a container full of cocaine. It was always about the money. Had Tim paid Malam to lie if anyone from Denmark should call to ask for him?

Marie's thoughts were interrupted when Søren rang her.

'Did you get some sleep last night?' he asked.

'Not much,' Marie said, and quickly told him what Jesper had said.

'And I don't know any African men except Tim,' Marie said miserably. 'I don't know what to believe any more.'

'I'm investigating Tim's travel activity,' Søren said. 'As soon as I've got something, I'll call you. But we should consider moving you to a safer place.'

'All right,' Marie said feebly.

'Perhaps you could stay with Lea? I've just spoken to her.'

'You finally got hold of her?'

'Once she got my email, I had a breakthrough – I think you could call it that,' Søren said. 'She rang me the second she'd read it. I'm going over there later today to give her the photograph.'

When Marie had ended the call, she got a message telling her she had four missed calls. An unknown number had tried once and Lea three times. Marie was about to call her younger sister when Lea's name flashed up on the display.

'I've just spoken to a policeman called Søren Marhauge,' Lea said, without introduction. 'He would appear to have grown up on Snerlevej and has just come back from Aalborg. Well, he did try to explain the whole convoluted business to me, but how it all connected was beyond me. Bottom line is that he has the photograph Tove kept. I'll get it tonight.'

'I gave him your email address. I thought you'd be pleased,' Marie said.

'You? How long have you known him?'

'Since yesterday when I called the police about Storm. We met and I told him everything. At one point, he mentioned that he knew who I was and that he, too, had grown up on Snerlevej.'

'I don't remember him at all,' Lea said.

'No, but you must have been very young when he moved out.'

'Yes, but— Hey, by the way, Mattis called! He says your ink is super-cool! I can't wait to see it. If you didn't have such an ancient mobile, you could have sent me a picture. Incidentally, he's crazy about you,' Lea went on.

'No, he's crazy about *you*,' Marie said.

'Mattis? No way. We're just friends. Besides, he knows I'm into women.'

For a moment Marie thought she'd misheard. 'You're what?'

'Into women. One hundred per cent. It took me four turbulent teenage years and way too many bad experiences to realise I don't like men. Or, at least, not in that way. But Mattis is cool. Go for it.'

Marie was speechless.

'Are you shocked, sis?' Lea asked. 'You've gone awfully quiet.'

'No,' Marie said. 'But sometimes it amazes me how blinkered we can be when it comes to our own family.'

'It's called a survival mechanism, sweetie,' Lea said. At that moment, the doorbell rang.

'I have to go. That'll be Anton,' Marie said. 'But I'll call you later. Would it be all right if we slept at yours tonight?'

'What do you think?' Lea laughed. 'I'll rush out and buy a bunk bed.'

'I'm so glad that we've finally grown up,' Marie said.

She ended the call, looked out of the window at the roof of Jesper's 4x4 and saw Jesper standing on the pavement. He was getting thin on top.

'You can run upstairs on your own,' she heard Jesper say to Anton.

Marie pressed the button to let Anton into the stairwell, put a cardigan over her nightie and went down to meet him.

'What have you got there?' Anton asked, pointing to Marie's tattoo, which peeped out at the neckline of her nightie.

'A tattoo,' Marie replied.

'Just like Aunt Lea?'

'Yep.'

'Won't it ever come off?'

'Nope.'

'Wow! Dad will be so mad.'

'But do *you* like it?'

'Yes,' Anton said. 'Can I have a tattoo of a dog?'

'Yes,' Marie said. 'But not until you're a grown-up. When you're a grown-up, you can do anything you like.'

Together they walked up the stairs.

Anton and Marie made space aliens out of salt dough, which they painted once they had baked them until they were hard. Marie peered furtively at her computer and had to keep a tight rein on herself not to let the approaching deadline panic her. Three times she went to the window, but there was no blue Ford. When push came to shove, it probably was not *that* Ford she had seen. When Anton went to his room to play, Marie sat down at her desk. Now, where was she? Bennett's homepage. She had to smile when she saw it. Dressed in cashmere, Bennett was leaning casually against his bright red sports car, suitably rugged and suitably professorial. Marie thought he looked a little like Sandö, but Sandö had turned out to be OK, and Marie reminded herself never to judge a book by its cover. She clicked around Bennett's homepage for a while and discovered that he had spent several years in West Africa, sent out by the now defunct American aid organisation Trust to build health centres. There was also a picture of Bennett with his beautiful daughter, Louise, aged twenty-three, who, according to the caption, was studying medicine at Stanford University and 'made her old dad proud'.

Marie was starting to understand why Storm had disliked the man. Bennett's homepage stated that he had decided to study medicine because 'as a young man he had often found it difficult to sleep due to his strong desire to save Africa'. Later he had specialised in vaccine constituents, focusing on improving the reaction of the immune system to the vaccine, and in 1988 he had been awarded the Nobel Prize for his research.

All of which was very heroic.

Marie explored the website further and came across a statement written by the WHO's legal officer confirming that every rule had been followed to the letter in connection with Bennett's resignation from the board of Sixan Pharmaceuticals and his joining the WHO's Emergency Committee in 2009. Legally everything was above board, the lawyer stated. Marie followed a link to the website of Sixan Pharmaceuticals where she skimmed the names of current board members, conspicuous for Bennett's absence. She also found a list of Sixan

Pharmaceuticals' 'friendship universities', but the University of Copenhagen was not among them. However, the University of Stockholm was. The Swedish academics appeared keen to become blood brothers with the world of commerce. The University of Oslo was not mentioned either, but Sixan Pharmaceuticals was friends with several prestigious institutions, such as Stanford and the University of California in Berkeley. And – who could have guessed it? – Universidad Colinas de Boé in Bissau of all places! It was a bit of a mixed bag.

Marie decided to condense Paul Smith's views to give Bennett more space. It was common knowledge that Storm and Bennett disagreed, and Marie was convinced that her article would have a stronger impact if she let Bennett appear in all his impressive academic expertise before she, just as expertly, of course, took him apart.

Søren rang back. 'I've got some fresh information,' he said. 'I've been in contact with the border control officers at Copenhagen airport and a passenger by the name of Tim Salomon did indeed board an SAS flight to Lisbon on the twenty-seventh of March at fourteen fifty-five. From there he caught a TAP flight to Bissau at twenty-one fifteen. Portuguese border officials have confirmed that he boarded the plane in Lisbon and that it took off on time.'

'Oh, I'm so relieved,' Marie exclaimed. 'I told you it couldn't be true.'

'Marie,' Søren said, 'Tim returned to Denmark this morning.'

'What?' Marie whispered.

'He hasn't tried to contact you, has he?' Søren asked.

'No,' Marie said, but then she remembered the call from

the unknown number. 'Have you called me from mobiles other than your own?' she asked Søren. 'An unknown number rang a few times, but I just presumed it was you calling me. From the police station, perhaps.'

'I've only called you from my mobile,' Søren said. 'Can you tell me exactly when the calls came in?'

'Around nine thirty and again around eleven.'

A pause followed.

'Tim's plane landed at eight fifty-five a.m. at Copenhagen airport,' Søren said. 'Listen, Marie, you should go to a safe place. I know that you trust him, and I'm sure you have good reason to, but even so, I want you to pack a bag. I'll be around later and take you to your sister's. I'm going to see her anyway with the photograph. I'll be a couple of hours because I . . . I'm having Easter lunch with my mother-in-law, but I'll be with you as soon as I can get away.'

'OK,' Marie said.

Anton was sitting on the floor playing with his *Star Wars* figures when Marie peeked into his room. His lips were moving in an inner monologue and he did not look up. Marie found a sports bag and packed some clothes and a few books. Then she texted Lea to say they would be there in a couple of hours and returned to her desk. Suddenly Anton touched her arm and she jumped.

'You startled me!' she cried, and pulled him onto her lap.

'I forgot to give you the envelope from Dad,' he said. 'It's in my rucksack.'

'What envelope from Dad?' Marie said.

Anton darted out into the hall to fetch his rucksack. He

pulled out a big yellow hospital envelope and gave it to Marie. On the front Jesper had written: *Marie Skov, Randersgade 76, 2100 Copenhagen Ø*, and it was franked with eighteen kroner, ready to be posted. Marie noticed that he had left out 'Just' from her name and shook out a pile of letters.

'They're for you. Natascha forgot to post the envelope,' Anton said, 'and Dad says I can have the stamps and that they're worth eighteen kroner because they haven't been post-marked.'

'Of course,' Marie said. 'We can steam them off in a moment.'

There were about ten letters in the large envelope, a magazine she subscribed to and a small soft package, poorly wrapped in brown paper. Marie flicked through the letters. Bills, a reminder of a dental appointment and a patient-satis-faction survey of her treatment at Rigshospitalet.

'Aren't you going to open your parcel?' Anton asked.

Marie turned it over and looked at the address:

Marie Skov
Ingeborgvej 24, 2900
Hellup

'Yes,' Marie said, but then she stalled. The address was wrongly spelled.

'Please may I watch a movie?' Anton asked.

'Yes, but in your own room or on my bed wearing head-phones. I need to work a little longer. Later we'll go and see Aunt Lea.'

'On your bed with headphones,' Anton said, when he had considered the offer. Marie made him comfortable and returned to her desk. When Anton was engrossed in his movie, she took the parcel to the kitchen.

It contained a long, narrow piece of cloth whose ends were tied together. Marie was in no doubt: the fabric had been torn off Storm's bright red *pano*, which she had looked for in vain at the funeral. Mystified, she held up the rag, then threw it down as if it had burned her hand.

Someone had sent her a noose.

Marie called Søren Marhauge, but got no reply. Then she sent him a text message asking him to call her immediately. She locked herself into the bathroom and sat on the toilet seat with her head between her legs. Fortunately Anton was wearing headphones and could not hear how long she struggled to get her breathing under control. When the panic attack started to subside, she flushed the toilet and glanced into the living room. Anton was exactly where she had left him, totally absorbed in his movie.

Marie returned to the kitchen where the woven noose was still lying on the floor. She found a freezer bag, picked up the noose with her hand inside the bag and turned the bag inside out. She carefully studied the envelope. The postmark said: *Nørrebro Post Office, 24 March.*

Marie gulped.

Merethe Hermansen's temp had said that Tim had dropped by the Institute of Biology on Wednesday, 24 March, asking for her address because he wanted to send her something. Marie had presumed this to be the wooden swallow, which he had given her in person.

At that moment Søren rang. 'I'm sorry I didn't take your call,' he said. 'I'm on my way to your flat now. Be ready to leave as soon as I arrive. Marie, I've just had a call from the Institute of Forensic Medicine and it's now clear that Kristian Storm was murdered. He was suffocated with a plastic bag and afterwards his body was suspended from a noose in the ceiling to make it look like suicide.'

'Someone has sent me a noose,' Marie whispered, terrified that Anton might be able to hear her even though he was still watching his movie.

'I'm on my way,' Søren said.

CHAPTER 11

On Tuesday, 30 March, Lily had got out on the wrong side of bed. First she couldn't open her eyelids, then she didn't like the yoghurt, then her tights were itchy and she definitely did not want to visit Granny, but insisted on being looked after by Anna, who was away in Sjællands Odde. When she was finally strapped into her car seat, still wearing pyjamas, dressing gown and wellies, because Søren had given up trying to get her dressed, she declared she was starving, but it was now too late, Søren said: he had offered her breakfast and she had said no, so she would have to eat when she got to Granny's. As a result, Lily felt dreadfully car-sick all the way to Nørrebro.

'When did you say Anna is back?' Cecilie asked, when Søren dropped Lily off. 'It's just that Jens and I have been invited to Fyn for an Easter get-together with some old friends, so we need to leave no later than eleven o'clock tomorrow morning. Is that OK with you?'

Søren promised to find a solution and kissed his mother-in-law on the cheek. 'But now I really have to run or I'll be late.'

'I knew you'd go back to work,' Cecilie said. 'Jens and I had a bet on how long you would last. Jens said two months.

"Given how pig-headed he can be," he said. But I said two weeks max, so I win!'

Søren sped down Hillerødgade to make the nine o'clock morning briefing and everything went according to plan until he reached Borups Allé where a lorry had turned over. The police had just started cordoning off the street and Søren had to get out of his car and wave his warrant card before he was finally let through. He was sweating profusely when he parked in front of Bellahøj at ten minutes past nine. He was slow-clapped as he entered the briefing room.

'You're worse than Tejsner,' Mehmet quipped. Søren was about to reprimand the young police officer, but thought better of it.

'It's called life,' he said amicably, 'and every now and then it gets in your way.'

When the morning briefing was over, Søren dealt with a few things at his desk, feeling somewhat put out that no one at the station had believed he had ever been serious about quitting. Everything in his office had been left untouched. Even an old coffee cup with dried-on stains. He tried calling Lea Skov again and wondered why she was so difficult to get hold of. Then, for the third time, he listened to Bøje's incandescent message from three days ago.

'Bollocking bollocks' meant that Bøje had discovered something. That much Søren understood. But what? Søren replayed the message again. An outburst of rhetorical thunder disguising feelings of agitation, but no actual information. Søren played the message for a third time, trying to ignore the words and concentrating purely on the emotion. Could it be shame?

It was probably the last feeling Søren would associate with Bøje Knudsen, but once the thought had crossed his mind, that was exactly how it sounded. Søren slammed his fist hard on the desk. He needed the emails Bøje had never got round to sending him. And he needed them now.

Suddenly one name sprang to mind. Berit Dahl Mogensen, the statistician from Odense who had left the Belem Health Project in a hurry. It proved to be difficult, but eventually Søren managed to track her down at the Faculty of Business and Social Sciences at Syddansk University where she worked. He wrote her a brief email asking her to call, but received an instant auto reply. Berit Dahl Mogensen was currently on maternity leave until 1 February 2011, and all requests should be directed to her temporary replacement. Bother. He tried the online telephone directory, but there would not appear to be a single Berit Dahl Mogensen in the whole of Denmark. He called Linda.

'Ah,' she said. 'How lovely to hear your voice again.'

'It's nice to be back,' Søren said, and asked her for information on Berit Dahl Mogensen. 'And I'll need her private email address as well because she has just gone on maternity leave. If they can't help you at Syddansk University, then try the Institute of Biology at the University of Copenhagen. Berit Dahl Mogensen used to work on the Belem Health Project, but there has to be someone at the Department of Immunology who can come up with a private email address or telephone number. You could try Merethe Hermansen, the chief secretary. She seems reasonably well informed. Otherwise, try the National Register of Persons.'

'I'm on it,' Linda said.

Søren called the Department of Forensic Genetics to find out when the results of Joan Skov's tissue and blood samples would be ready and, more importantly, the analysis of the nail scrapings and the three hairs Bøje had found wrapped around her fingers. He spoke to Klaus Mønster, a technician he knew.

'Do you have a case number?' Klaus Mønster said, when they had exchanged pleasantries.

'Hang on,' he said, when Søren had given him the number of Joan Skov's autopsy report.

Søren drummed his fingers on the desk while he waited.

'Oh, it's that case,' Klaus Mønster said, sounding weary when he came back on the phone. 'I could have told you that without having to look it up. The results aren't in yet.'

'Really? I gathered from Bøje Knudsen that this was an urgent matter,' Søren said.

'All of his cases always are, aren't they?' Mønster said drily. 'However, DNA sequencing of hair takes as long as it takes. Besides, he called Friday morning and overrode his own orders.'

'Overrode himself?'

'Yes with a new, incredibly urgent case. Four pieces of plastic and five close-up pictures of secondary ligature marks, which appeared to have become visible on the neck of a body and which Bøje Knudsen demanded to have analysed as quickly as possible. "Preferably yesterday, you lazy sods," as he so elegantly put it. As a rule we try to accommodate the phenomenon that is Bøje Knudsen with good grace, but at times it's a struggle. This department isn't Bøje Knudsen's private fiefdom, is it? We've been rushed off our feet with the student rapes, and last Friday everything was total chaos because the police had remanded a potential rapist in custody.

I certainly intended to take a closer look at Bøje Knudsen's bits of plastic as soon as I could, but I didn't get round to it last Friday.'

'So you still haven't checked them?'

At this Mønster chuckled. 'Yes, because do you know what Bøje did? He turned up at my home Friday evening while my wife and I had guests. I still haven't worked out how he got my home address, but there he was in a grubby white coat and his hair standing up on all sides. He had already sent me four reminders by email, he said, and demanded that I come with him immediately and analyse the plastic pieces and the ligature marks. Of course I refused point-blank, but I couldn't get rid of him until I had promised to take a look at them first thing the following morning. So that was what I did and I sent the results to him around noon. The plastic fragments had been torn off a yellow Netto shopping bag, and the secondary ligature marks, which had appeared, were from a regular strangulation and not the ligature marks of a hanging, which was what Bøje had initially presumed.'

'Which case do the secondary ligature marks and the four plastic fragments relate to?' Søren asked, holding his breath.

'No idea,' Mønster said. 'I was never given an autopsy report, a police report or a crime-scene report. Just an evidence bag with four plastic fragments and five close-up photographs of ligature marks.'

Søren swore in frustration.

'Never got as much as a thank-you from him, and though I know perfectly well why not, it's still bad form.'

'What did you know perfectly well?'

'That he's embarrassed. No matter how much Bøje screams

and shouts, ultimately it's on his head that he didn't take a proper look at the case until now, regardless of how busy he was. As far as I know, the deceased has already been cremated and the case is officially closed, so it's always a total nightmare to have to reopen it, but you would know more about that than me. Bøje doesn't exactly come out of this smelling of roses, does he? Still, let's not make a mountain out of a molehill. We do have a full autopsy, so all we need is for the old man to swallow his pride and admit that he made a mistake. It would suit him. Anyway, give him my best and tell him it's the last time I do him a favour without a thank-you. Especially on a Friday evening.'

'Bøje had a heart attack on Saturday,' Søren said. 'He's in a coma.'

There was silence at the other end.

'Good grief, I'm really sorry to hear that,' Mønster said, and promised to email his report on both the plastic fragments and the ligature marks immediately and also to call as soon as there was news from the samples in the Joan Skov case.

Søren walked past Linda, who was still trying to find Berit Dahl Mogensen's address, and told her he would be away from his desk for a couple of hours. Then he went to Rigshospitalet.

'I would like to visit Bøje Knudsen,' Søren said, when he had shown his warrant card at the entrance to the intensive care unit. 'I'm aware that he's in a coma, but Bøje is . . . a sort of friend. If people in our line of work have friends, that is.'

The duty doctor shook his hand. 'No one knows how much coma patients take in,' he said, 'so I'm glad you've come. You're his first visitor. He's in side ward eight.'

The room was cool and quiet and the only sound was that of the ventilator. Bøje had practically disappeared under the white sheets.

'So, now it's your turn,' Søren said, and thought about how many hundreds, if not thousands, of times Bøje had stood bent over a lifeless body. 'I went back to work yesterday,' he went on. 'As acting superintendent, would you believe it? I think you've started a trend, old friend. Before we know it everyone will want to move down the ladder.' Then he patted Bøje's hand. 'And that's all. I'm going now. I'm not very good at talking to people in a coma. But I promise to drop by one of these days. Bye-bye.'

Søren walked down the corridor and slammed his hand against his forehead at his own idiocy. Who the hell said *bye-bye* to a man in a coma?

At the Institute of Forensic Medicine, Morten La Cour, the young pathologist, would appear to have taken over Bøje's stress in a one-to-one ratio.

'Don't I know it,' La Cour said wearily, when Søren told him he was in urgent need of the missing autopsy report. 'I've looked for it, believe me. But total chaos reigns on Bøje's computer or perhaps he had a system known only to him. I really couldn't say. It's an impossible task for an outsider to make sense of his logic, or lack of it, not least because he had several versions of the same half-finished autopsy report open at the same time, and used filenames such as "the long wrinkly one" and "Snow White's eighth and hitherto unknown little friend". I ended up sending his computer to our internal computer analyst to unravel the mess. We're talking about twenty-seven unfinished autopsy reports.'

'That's just not good enough,' Søren snapped at him. 'When do you think your guy will be done?'

'In a few days. He gave me his word. So tomorrow, Thursday at the latest. Trust me, you're not the only one chasing this. I've also got Chief Superintendent Bernt from Station City breathing down my neck, but not quite as politely as you, in case you're interested,' La Cour said.

'But Thursday is a public holiday,' Søren objected.

'Not this year, it isn't. Before Easter is over, another fifteen bodies will have piled up, which makes it very much in my own interest to clear up after Bøje so we don't drown in unfinished cases. I'll call you as soon as I hear from him. But this was suicide, wasn't it? I thought that case had been closed.'

'No, it wasn't. We're investigating a murder,' Søren said grumpily. 'Only I can't prove it yet.'

When Søren got back to Bellahøj, he sat for a while drumming his fingers on his desk. Then he called Lea Skov for the umpteenth time and for the umpteenth time his call went straight to voicemail. He had to change tactic and get her email address. Perhaps Marie Skov could give it to him and then he could question her at the same time.

However, he decided to call Julie Claessen, the Skov family's eldest daughter, instead, but got no reply on her mobile or landline and didn't want to leave a message. He went on to look up Frank Skov's telephone number and had pressed all the digits before he changed his mind and hung up. In the open-plan office, Mehmet and Inge Kai were reviewing interviews in connection with a suspected arson case in Gladsaxe. Mehmet was clearly bored out of his skull while Inge Kai was wearing her reading glasses and looking industrious.

Five minutes later Søren and Inge Kai were on their way to Frank Skov's house. They were in plain clothes and Inge Kai was driving. Mehmet had been put out when Søren had picked her, but it couldn't be helped.

Søren leaned back in the passenger seat and felt exhausted. He could not believe how blind he had been. With the benefit of hindsight it was obvious that Henrik's arsy behaviour in recent months was all about how terrible he felt. Were Anna and Søren really so fixated on each other that they had lost sight of the rest of the world? If that was true, it was only half true. Søren was prepared to concede that he might be fixated on Anna, but Anna was not nearly as obsessed with him as he would like. The truth was he was permanently terrified that she would pull the plug on their relationship without any warning. He would die, he thought, and, at the same moment, wanted to kick himself for being such a girl. *Die*. His baby daughter had died from drowning. Knud and Elvira had been eaten up by cancer. The worst that could happen to him was that his heart would hurt very, very much for a very long time. It was not the same as dying. It would just feel like it. Besides, he had no reason not to trust Anna. Only he just didn't. He was constantly on his guard. She was like a suitcase with a false compartment: there was something about her he didn't know. Houses, streets and people passed by in a steady flow outside his window; Inge Kai was a good driver. Or did he have a hidden compartment? he suddenly thought. And had the lid sprung open because he had never loved as deeply as he loved Anna and Lily? His biological daughter's short life had fertilised the soil and now the tree of that love had borne its first bittersweet fruit. The sweet touch of Anna's body nestling against his back at night and the joy of Lily's hand in his when they walked through the snow mixed with the bitter taste of fear.

Shit. Henrik had been right. Søren always managed to make everything that happened about Anna, and he had just done it again. He was a crap friend. He was self-obsessed. Imagine him not even suspecting that Henrik and Jeanette had split up. It was beyond awful.

They had reached Vangede, and Inge Kai parked the car outside the Skov family's home. She had not spoken one word the whole way and Søren was grateful for that.

Søren threw a glance at Knud and Elvira's house. 'That's my house,' he said.

'You live here?' Inge said, surprised. 'I thought you lived in Humlebæk.'

'I do,' he replied. 'But I still own that house. It's where I grew up.'

'It's a lovely place,' was all she said.

The Skovs' place was not lovely. The front garden was well kept, but only in the way that a freshly shorn sheep could be described as neatly trimmed. It was mostly lawn with a few flowers and bushes and a straight flagstone path that led to the front door. The house gave the same impression. At first sight it was in good condition, but on closer inspection it was badly in need of some TLC. Søren noticed that someone had reattached a section of the gutter to the roof with cable ties. An effective solution, but not one for the long term.

Søren rang the doorbell and they did not hear footsteps from inside the house until his third ring. Shortly afterwards the door was opened.

Frank must have been asleep because he had the imprint of a cushion on his cheek, but when Søren showed him his warrant card, he livened up and tried to smooth his hair. He reeked of stale booze and Søren had a flashback to Herman Madsen's description of him as a 'tough guy'. That must have been a long time ago.

'Come in, come in,' Frank said obligingly. 'What can I do for you?'

Søren said that he had a couple of questions and Frank ushered them into the dining room.

'Anything for the police,' he fawned. 'I've got to give it to you, you've been real sports. I know I screwed up big-time, but I'm sober now,' he lied, holding up two fingers like a Boy Scout. 'Thanks to you.'

'Actually, I'm from the Violent Crimes Unit.' Søren watched Frank closely for a reaction. There was none. 'So your offence on Vesterbro isn't my department.'

Søren and Inge Kai sat down at a large, extendable Brazilian rosewood table in the dining room; Frank disappeared into the kitchen and returned shortly with coffee cups and a plate of biscuits. He talked a lot. About Julie's many good qualities – imagine, her mother had just died and she was already back working as a carer, helping people in need – about Marie's brilliant career as a scientist and about Lea, who would soon graduate as a psychologist and what-have-you. And about the house, which might be old, but sound, no trace of mould, about the Børge Mogensen sideboard, which they hadn't even known was designed by Børge Mogensen until their son-in-law, who was a consultant at Rigshospitalet, had seen the exact same one on Lauritz.com, would you believe it, about the weather and about a dog they had once had, which had been run over in the street and whoever had done it had never reported it to the police, but Frank had his suspicions.

During all the time Frank was talking, Søren wondered what was really going on in the man's mind, and when he paused, purely to draw breath, Søren concluded that this was about distraction.

'More coffee?' Frank enquired.

'No, thank you,' Søren said.

For a while everything was quiet. Søren made a point of not saying anything and merely smiled at Frank.

Frank was being slow-roasted over a fire.

'May I ask the reason for your visit?' he then said, as if it had not occurred to him until now that it might be a little odd. 'My wife has just passed away and I'm due in court for my little screw-up on the second of July. It's all arranged. There's nothing more for you here. So, if you don't mind, I'd like some time to myself.'

'We're wondering why your wife had so many different types of medication for the same conditions,' Søren said. 'Much of it was out of date so I suppose you just hadn't got around to throwing it out, but we also found drugs that she would not appear to have been prescribed in the first place. Do you know where they came from?'

'Oh, no,' Frank said. 'I wouldn't know anything about that. Julie was in charge of my wife's medication. She came here to count her pills every Monday and put them in one of those pill organisers so that her mum was set up for the whole week. I know nothing about pills. Never been anything wrong with me.' Frank thumped his chest, then started to cough.

'What was wrong with your wife?' Søren asked.

'Wrong? I wouldn't say there was anything specifically wrong with her as such. My wife had been on all sorts of tablets ever since the boy's accident and it's a long time since I had any knowledge of what she was taking and why.'

Søren raised his eyebrows. 'So she never told you anything when she had been to see her doctor? About being prescribed new drugs or that her dosage had been increased or reduced?'

Frank looked at Søren in surprise. 'My wife never went to the doctor's,' he said. 'I mean, she used to go, but she hadn't been anywhere for years. She didn't like going out. Luckily our son-in-law is a doctor so he could easily renew her prescriptions and ring them through to the chemist where Julie would go to pick them up.'

'How did your little boy die?'

'He got meningitis. He was gone just like that.' Frank snapped his fingers. 'He got a fever late one afternoon and it soon got so high that we called an ambulance. Mads died at Rigshospitalet.'

'I'm so sorry,' Søren said sincerely.

'Yes,' Frank said. 'It was awful.'

For the first time Søren thought he had caught an uncensored glimpse of the man. Frank's eyes grew moist and he quickly looked down at the Brazilian rosewood table.

'Is it all right if I ask you a question?' Inge Kai said, when they were almost back at Bellahøj station. 'I'm sure you've got a lot on your mind, but I want to become a better investigator and I don't know when I'll get another chance to have a one-to-one with you.'

Søren straightened up in his seat. 'That's quite all right; I'm sorry I've been so monosyllabic today.'

Inge Kai cleared her throat. 'When Frank said that Joan Skov had taken pills ever since "the boy's accident", I made a mental note to ask you what kind of accident, but shortly afterwards you asked specifically what he died from, and when Frank Skov then answered "meningitis", I began to wonder.'

'That's good because you were supposed to.'

'Yes, I was, wasn't I?' Inge Kai said eagerly. 'Because no matter how acute someone's illness is, no one would ever describe death from an illness as *an accident.*'

Søren nodded. 'He slipped up. The truth is Mads Skov died in an accident in the Skov family's garden, but they tell everyone that he died from meningitis.'

'Aha,' Inge Kai said instantly. 'So they're ashamed. No one is to blame for meningitis, but if a child dies in an accident, people might think that someone failed to look after it properly.'

Søren was impressed. 'Yes, that would be my guess too,' he then said, 'and I know exactly where they're coming from. My daughter drowned in Thailand some years ago. During the tsunami. She was with her mother and I wasn't even there. Nevertheless, I felt horribly guilty that I had allowed it to happen.' He had no idea why he was blurting all this out. 'But how would I feel if she had died in my house while I was in the garden or watching television? I would be racked with guilt.'

Inge Kai nodded. 'What do we do now?' she asked at length.

'We need to do a bit of digging into the circumstances surrounding the death of Mads Skov,' Søren said.

Inge Kai nodded again.

'Did you notice anything else?' Søren asked her.

'That dentures by definition appear more suspicious than one's own teeth,' Inge Kai said. 'In an old-school way. Big teeth, false beard, spectacles and a hat.'

Søren smiled. 'Yes, it was conspicuous how he kept grinning at us with those teeth. As if he was trying to divert us.'

'That's another source of his shame,' Inge Kai said pensively.

'His teeth?'

'No, his alcoholism,' Inge Kai said. 'My father was an alcoholic and he died from drink, but right up until the very end he denied he had a problem. He felt he was above it. He was a successful bookkeeper from a provincial town in Jutland, known and respected by all. He despised addicts. He looked down on them. It never occurred to him that he was one. After all, *he* wasn't a loser. A good business, two delightful children and a lovely wife. I picked up the same vibe today. Frank Skov doesn't want to face reality. Maybe he can't because it's associated with too much pain, but the outcome is the same. He lives in a fog and drinks to cope, which makes the fog even denser so he drinks more. How old is Frank Skov? Late fifties? My father would have been sixty this year. My sister calls them "the double-standards generation". They have strong views about how other people should live their lives, but no one has the right to tell them how to live theirs.'

Søren nodded slowly. He had totally revised his opinion of the young police sergeant from Aarhus.

Back at the station Søren pulled up another chair and asked Inge Kai to take a seat in his office. 'We'll start by looking up the case in Polsas,' he said. He logged onto the police case handling system. 'Let's see what it says,' he said, as he ran his gaze down the screen. '"Mads Benjamin Skov, born on the twentieth of December 1982, died in an accident in his home on the twenty-seventh of June 1986. Categorised as 'other investigations'. Autopsy requested. Investigators present: Amundsen and Sandholt."

'What do you make of that?' he asked Inge. 'There are no wrong answers. I just want your reaction.'

'"Other investigations" means that the death is not regarded as suspicious,' Inge Kai said. 'Even so, an autopsy was requested, but that's standard practice in situations where an otherwise healthy child dies unexpectedly. But . . .'

'But?'

'Is that really all it says? Surely they must have interviewed the family about the accident.'

'Yes, I'm absolutely sure they did,' Søren said. 'But the case is closed now. Besides, there were no suspicious circumstances so Polsas only gives us a brief summary. If we want the complete case file with appendices and autopsy photographs, we have to go to the National Police Archives. We'll do that tomorrow.'

Later that evening Søren drove to Nørrebro to have dinner with his mother-in-law and to pick up Lily. As he drove, he called Anna at the holiday cottage. She sounded happy when she answered her phone and Søren asked when she would be coming home.

'Tomorrow evening,' she replied.

'As late as that?'

'Yes – don't you remember me telling you?'

'You said Wednesday, but you never mentioned it would be the evening.'

'Is that a problem? We'd like to be able to work the whole day.'

'Do you know something?' Søren snapped. 'So would I. And Cecilie and Jens are going to Fyn tomorrow morning. So please could you get back a little earlier? That way I can do my job too.'

'You having a job is a somewhat recent development,' Anna said drily, but even though Søren was well aware that she was only teasing him, he refused to play ball. 'Anyway, got to run,' Anna continued. 'If you absolutely have to work, then call Karen. She's just texted me to say she's off work this week and wants to see Lily. I'm sure she'd love to babysit. I'll text you her number. Bye.'

A moment later he received a text message with Karen's telephone number; Anna hadn't signed off with love or a kiss. Søren rang Karen, a childhood friend of Anna's, and they agreed that she would come over and look after Lily the next day. She would arrive for coffee at ten o'clock, she said, and offered to cook dinner for them when Anna got home so Søren could work late if he needed to. Later, perhaps, the three of them could have a glass of wine, Karen suggested, just like they used to do when Anna and Søren had first started seeing each other.

It was nine thirty that evening before Søren and Lily got home after dinner with Cecilie. Lily had long since fallen asleep in her car seat. When Søren had carried her to bed, he sat down on the sofa with his laptop. There was an email from Linda.

Hi Søren

After much searching, I managed to track down Berit Dahl Mogensen, but she wasn't terribly co-operative. She kept stressing that she has no links to the Department of Immunology, Kristian Storm or the Belem Health Project and that, as far as she's concerned, it's all in the past. Besides, how could she be sure that I really was calling from the police, she kept asking, and refused to give me further contact details. However, she did suggest that we could set up a meeting with Fyn Police and she was willing to go to the police station in Hans Mules Gade. She sounded a bit paranoid, but I gather that her baby daughter is only a few weeks old, so I guess she has a valid excuse. I then called Sergeant Uffe Nielsen from Fyn Police. He has booked a meeting room for you tomorrow morning at one o'clock and Berit Dahl Mogensen has promised to be there.

Best wishes, Linda

Søren put aside his laptop and picked up a book, but he couldn't concentrate and kept glancing furtively at his mobile. He had not heard a word from Anna since the afternoon, when she had seemed in a hurry to get rid of him. He missed her and he had to give himself a severe talking-to to prevent himself stalking her and Anders T. on Facebook and working himself into a frenzy. He set the alarm on his mobile for ten twenty, so he had time to make coffee and go to the loo before

Deadline started on DR2, and settled down for a nap on the sofa. This turned out to be a futile exercise. Anna writhed on his retinas, naked and glistening on the actual skin of a tiger that Anders T. had shot – because he would have, wouldn't he? – in front of a fire in a seaside cottage on Sjællands Odde while Anders T. slowly pushed his enormous dick into her and pulled it out again just as slowly.

Søren sat up on the sofa and rang Inge Kai. 'Am I disturbing you?' he asked.

'No.' She sounded surprised. 'I'm trying to stay awake so I can watch *Deadline* at ten thirty. How about you?'

Søren grinned. 'You don't want to know,' he said, and felt his mood rise by at least twelve degrees. He explained to her that he had to go to Fyn the following day and that she would have to pick up Mads Skov's file from the National Police Archives without him.

'Of course,' Inge Kai said.

The next morning, when Karen arrived to look after Lily, Søren gave her a big hug. Her unruly curls were even frizzier than usual and Søren had forgotten how infectious her laughter was.

'So, where have you been hiding?' Karen said, with a smile, when Lily finally let go of her and ran off to her room. Søren and she were seated with coffee and fresh rolls. 'I thought the infatuation stage was meant to last ten months, not ten years.'

'Oh, I think it's work rather than Cupid,' Søren said. 'And the winter.'

'Yes, phew,' Karen said. 'But when it finally gets warmer, the two of you need to climb down from your ivory tower.

Throw a barbecue or something. Otherwise having a garden by a lake is a total waste.' She laughed.

They talked about the exhibition Karen was preparing. She was taking her finals from Kunstakademiet in two months. Søren also asked about Karen's boyfriend, Jeppe, and Karen told him that he had a job at Syddansk University and was now commuting.

'Turned out to be a blessing in disguise,' Karen said. 'It makes seeing each other extra special.' Karen always looked on the bright side.

Lily emerged from her room and asked Karen and Søren if they could watch *Bamse and Kylling* while they made bead necklaces.

Karen was up for it, but Søren needed the lavatory. When he came out again, his mobile had rung and Karen was bent double laughing at something Lily had said to the caller. Søren told Lily off and snatched back his mobile.

The caller was Marie Skov and they agreed to meet at the Laundromat Café on Nørrebro at five o'clock that afternoon. Ten minutes later Søren was in his car and heading for Fyn.

When Søren reached Odense Police Station, he was met by Sergeant Uffe Nielsen in reception and shown to the interview room they had made available for him. Twenty minutes later Berit Dahl Mogensen arrived, a woman of around thirty-five with discreet, round glasses and short hennaed hair. She held out her hand to Søren. 'Anyone would think I had been accused of something,' she said, with a wry smile, as she glanced around the interview room. 'I only have an hour. My baby is just three weeks old so I can't leave her for very long.'

'Of course,' Søren said, and asked her to take a seat. 'Let's get started. As you know, Professor Kristian Storm killed himself on the seventeenth of March.' Berit nodded. 'However, we're no longer sure that it was suicide and we have reopened the case.'

Berit clapped a hand over her mouth. 'I knew it,' she said.

'You knew what?'

'That it couldn't be true. Storm wasn't the type who would even think of killing himself. He didn't care one jot what people thought of him, be it good or bad. He was a decent man, very skilled at motivating his students. But he was also brutally single-minded. He had his own agenda and there was *them* and then there was *us*, and in order to belong to *us*, you had to commit just as wholeheartedly to his area of research as he had. But when your colleague . . . Hans Tejsner, is that his name?'

'*Henrik* Tejsner.'

'Yes, that's it, when Henrik Tejsner called to say that the police were sure of their suicide theory, I started to doubt myself. Tejsner said there was plenty of evidence, including a suicide note, so eventually I was forced to accept that I might not have known Storm as well as I thought I did. A part of me was relieved, I guess.'

'Why?'

Berit's eyes flitted. 'Something happened in Guinea-Bissau while I was there. It made me feel very unsafe and I started having panic attacks, which I have only just learned to deal with. So when your colleague said it was definitely suicide, I told myself that it had nothing to do with the events in Bissau.' Suddenly she looked at Søren with wide eyes. 'Was it really murder?' she whispered. 'I'm starting to feel quite ill.'

'I'm afraid it looks like it,' Søren said. 'That's why it's import-ant that you tell me exactly what happened in Guinea-Bissau. Everything could be important.'

Berit sighed. 'I'd made up my mind to put Bissau behind me, but if Storm was murdered, I realise I have to . . .'. Søren nodded.

'I arrived at the start of January 2008, a few days after Silas had drowned. The whole research station was deeply affected by the tragedy, and although Storm had flown back to Copen-hagen at that point, you could feel it all the way to Africa that he had lost his grip on the project. Everything was a mess. There were twelve locals on the project's payroll, but not one tenth of the work was carried out because Storm hadn't left any instructions and Tim was in shock. It was deeply frus-trating for me because I was new. Of course I was affected by the accident, but I also wanted to get on with my work. In order not to go crazy with frustration, I decided to instigate some daily routines and I persuaded Tim that the two of us should just crack on. In the weeks that followed, we worked our socks off to gain insight into our data, ordered whatever materials we needed and made sure the laboratory was prop-erly equipped. Once the basics were in place, I was finally ready to start the statistical data analysis. It would be months before the data was complete, but we agreed that I might as well start analysing what we had collected, so that was what I did.

'I loved my work, but I never felt comfortable at the research station. We were constantly the victim of petty thefts and vandalism, which initially I attributed to Storm's decision to locate the research station right in the middle of Belem, an impoverished part of the city, rather than in the gated white community where the other expats lived. I spent most evenings alone because Tim didn't live on the premises and I started to feel increasingly unsafe. We did have a security guard, George, but he was deaf, blind and old, and not so much a guard as Storm's private aid project. One evening a man managed to walk straight past George and into the house. I was in the lavatory when I suddenly heard things being smashed and knocked over in the room that doubled as our office and living room, and I screamed so loudly out of the window that someone from the neighbouring barracks came to my rescue. When the police arrived . . .' Berit looked knowingly at Søren '. . . when the completely hopeless and corrupt Guinean police arrived, the burglar was obviously long gone. The office had been trashed. Books and pictures all over the floor. Papers had been ripped up and the computer monitor had been smashed, but fortunately the computer itself was bolted to the floor because Storm had had a break-in once before, years back, so it was still there. I was deeply shaken. What if I'd been in the living room? I persuaded Tim to move into the research station, but even though he was now living there, I still felt uneasy. Finally, I rang Storm to ask him to hire a guard who was actually up to the job, in case we had another break-in. Storm wasn't keen on the idea, but when I threatened to return to Denmark, he hired Tim's older brother, Ébano, a broad-shouldered guy straight from the cashew plantations. Ébano was a very different type from the toothless George and I started to enjoy my work again. But my respite was short-lived. One evening, about four weeks later, when Tim and I came home late after visiting the state laboratory, the research station was on fire. The blaze had already got a solid hold of the two guesthouses and most of the station's atrium had burned to the ground. Ébano was distraught. He had been to the market to do our shopping and on his return found everything in flames. Again, the police were unhelpful and slow, and none of the neighbours had seen anything. That night I wondered for the first time if the vandalism might have been an attempt to sabotage Belem's scientific work.

'If it hadn't been for Tim, I would have left at that point. But when I voiced my concerns, he held a rousing speech about civic courage and the importance of the work Storm was carrying out in Guinea-Bissau. He persuaded me to finish the statistics on the positive effect of the measles vaccine on the child mortality rate, but he didn't try to conceal the fact that he hoped I would stay and process the problematic DTP data. I couldn't promise the latter, I said, but I stayed on. Tim had a word with his brother, who started acting as my body-guard. He didn't stick to me twenty-four/seven because that would have driven me crazy, but if I was doing anything in the evening or felt unsafe if I had an errand in town, I could always ask Ébano to come with me. That worked really well until one evening when I was doing the washing-up in the small kitchen at the research station. Suddenly someone came up behind me and, before I had time to react, put a sack over my head and tightened it. I tried to scream because I knew that Ébano was sitting just outside the gate, playing dice with some men, but my attacker put his arm across my throat, so I couldn't make a sound. Then he dragged me backwards down the passage to the office, where he ordered me, in English with an African accent, to delete the contents of the computer.

I said I couldn't see anything and he cut two holes in the sack covering my head with his knife and repeated, while he held my neck in an iron grip so I couldn't turn my head, that I had to delete the hard disk or he would kill me. When I had deleted everything, I clicked desperately on the screen so that my attacker could see that everything was gone. Then he turned the sack around so that I was blinded again, tied my hands behind my back with a cable tie and threw me onto the sofa.

'Two days later I was on the first available TAP flight out of Bissau to Lisbon, and when the plane took off from Bissau, I knew that that was the end of my involvement. Storm lived for his research, but I don't. Not in that way. Statistics is my work, but I've no intention of dying for it. Storm called me several times to express his concern, but it was always in the air that he wanted me to return. He even offered me a pay rise. When he realised that I had made up my mind, he called me one more time and asked me to be discreet about what had happened. He didn't want to scare off other young scientists, he said, and thus damage the research, and that was what I was referring to earlier. Storm was a fascinating man and his work in Guinea-Bissau was outstanding and, in my opinion, the only form of aid work that really makes a difference. But the moment I left the magic circle, he lost interest in me.'

'Have you kept in touch with Tim?'

'Yes, but only sporadically. He emailed me a few times to ask how I was. I know that his mother died recently and that he and Ébano took it very hard.'

'What do you make of Tim's brother?' Søren asked.

'He's different from Tim, even though they look alike. Ébano isn't stupid, not at all, but he's not academically gifted like Tim. More muscle and stamina.'

Søren had an idea. 'Does Tim know where you live?'

Berit look nonplussed. Then she went deathly pale. 'You're not suspecting Tim, are you? That's not what you're saying? That you suspect him of killing Storm? He knows where I live. He got my address last year because we joked that we wanted to see how long it would take a Christmas card from Bissau to reach me. But . . .' Berit's hands were shaking so much when she found her mobile that she dropped it twice on the table.

'Easy now,' Søren said. 'Don't panic. I don't think you're in danger. You have officially withdrawn from the project and are working on something completely different. Are you worried because your daughter and her babysitter are at your home address?'

Berit nodded and the tears rolled down her cheeks.

'Is there somewhere you can go for a few days? Somewhere you feel safe. That's the most important thing. As I said, I don't think you're in danger.'

Berit nodded. 'I don't know why I'm reacting like this. The fear has never really gone away. I don't believe for a moment that Tim did it. He's a good man. You don't meet many like him. He's a bit like how people used to describe Storm. He has no hidden agenda. I refuse to believe that he did it.'

The tears continued to trickle down Berit's cheeks as she pressed the number. 'Are you all right?' she said, into her mobile. 'OK, good . . . No, nothing's wrong. I'm coming home now.' She hung up.

'I can stay with a friend for a few days,' she said.

'That sounds good,' Søren said.

'I should never have agreed to meet you,' she added. 'I'm sorry, it's nothing personal. Only I thought I had finally beaten my anxiety attacks.' She put on her jacket and slung her bag over her shoulder.

'If Tim didn't do it, then who did?' Søren asked.

'Someone who doesn't value human life,' Berit said promptly, 'especially not African lives. Someone from the pharmaceutical industry.'

'But if the WHO is refusing to review the vaccination programme, then surely they're the guilty ones?'

'The WHO is an old conservative institution that doesn't want to lose face or prestige. But it's only a matter of time before they have to accept the new truths. Along with other scientists across the globe, who are starting to back Storm's theories about the non-specific effects of vaccines, the WHO will have to change its attitude. But it takes time, and although it's frustrating, ultimately it's right that it should be so. The WHO is the cornerstone in the world's understanding of health and they cannot, nor should they, jump on every new research trend. No, if someone murdered Storm to shut him up, then it's someone who is making money out of his death. Money is the only thing that can drive people to such extremes.' Berit's eyes blazed again. 'I knew it was more than common vandalism. I knew it! Storm thought I read too much into it. Perhaps he didn't even understand the extent of what he was meddling with. In that way he was naïve. Idealists often are. But I really need to go now.'

Søren nodded. 'I'll keep you informed, and if there's anything, just call. Here is my private number.' Søren handed Berit his card.

'Thank you,' she said.

She had taken two steps when she stopped and looked anxiously at Søren. 'Give Marie Skov my best wishes and tell her to watch her back,' she said.

Søren drove from Odense straight to Østerbro and parked in front of the Laundromat Café just before five o'clock. He took the photograph of Lea Skov from the glove compartment and studied it again. It might be important for children to have their parents around, he thought, but the most important thing was for them to have someone who took notice of them. If someone did that, they would be all right. He had called Lea Skov at least fifteen times and got nowhere. The easiest thing – for him – would be to give the photograph to Marie Skov and ask her to pass it on. But something stopped him. Herman Madsen wanted Lea to have it. Not Julie, not Frank and possibly not Marie, either. He had to get Lea Skov's email address. Then Lea could reply to him if she wanted the photograph or ignore him if she did not. Søren put the photograph back in the glove compartment, got out of the car and locked it. He saw a woman walking towards him and recognised Marie Skov from the university homepage, but something about her expression was wrong.

After his meeting with Marie, Søren drove home and for once he valued the half-hour drive so he could put his thoughts in order. The blue Ford, the identical drowning accidents of Silas Henckel and Midas Manolis, the arson on Ingeborgvej and then Marie, who was clearly frightened. Rain lashed the wind-screen and Søren turned on the wipers. He called Inge Kai, but when there was no reply he left a message on her voice-mail asking how she had got on with Mads Skov's report. He added that he also needed information about two fatal drown-ings in Africa, one in Gambia on 27 December 2007 and the other on a – to him – unknown date in Tanzania two years earlier. He also needed the report on the attempted arson on Ingeborgvej the previous Saturday night. 'It's not urgent. Tomorrow morning is fine,' he finished, hoping that Inge Kai had a sense of humour.

A driver sounded his horn because Søren had taken his foot off the accelerator and the car was slowing down.

Søren had asked Marie how her brother had died. He had watched her face closely when she said, 'Meningitis.' It was clear that she knew nothing about the accident.

Søren got home at seven thirty that evening. When he opened the front door, he knew instinctively that Anna was back. He could not see her jacket or her bag and the door to the hallway was closed so he could not hear her either. Even so, he knew that she was there. And he was proved right. Karen and Anna were busy cooking supper. Anna stood by the chopping board preparing salad and Karen was stirring something in a saucepan. They both had a glass of wine, there was music coming from the radio and condensation ran cheerfully down the inside of the kitchen window.

Anna beamed at him as he entered the kitchen. 'Hi,' she said, and kissed him. 'How are you?'

'Fine,' Søren said, and kissed her back, but not as deeply as he normally did because Karen was watching them – or so he told himself.

Or perhaps because he was too busy sniffing her? Did she smell different? Was she acting differently? Her cheeks were certainly flushed and her hair was exactly like Søren loved it, unstyled with plenty of natural waves. Anna poured him a glass of wine, but he'd have preferred a beer.

Lily came running to show Søren an egg shell with blue spots, which Anna had brought back from Sonnerup Forest, and a fossil she had found on the beach.

His mobile beeped. Marie Skov had sent him the registration number of the blue Ford and Lea Skov's email address.

Søren left the kitchen and called a colleague at the police station at Copenhagen airport, who promised to check the registration number against the airport's eight different car-rental firms and get back to him as soon as possible.

Inge Kai called back. She was still at Bellahøj and the report into the attempted arson on Ingeborgvej 24 on the night of 27 March was now on his desk. However, the fatal drownings required her to contact Interpol, which she could not do until the following day.

'Fine,' Søren said. 'And Mads Skov?'

Inge Kai sighed. 'I have a copy of the full police report in front of me. To summarise, Mads Skov died when a metal shelving unit fell on top of him in a garden shed. There would appear to have been a toolbox on the top shelf and, when the shelving unit keeled over, the toolbox hit the boy on the head and killed him instantly. The police requested the autopsy to be absolutely sure that he hadn't been the victim of abuse and there are quite a few autopsy photographs, which we can look at tomorrow. But there's nothing suspicious about the death itself, even though it was traumatic. I read in the report that the Falck emergency crew struggled to take the dead child from the mother. Afterwards, the whole family was offered counselling, but only the eldest daughter, Julie, accepted the offer. However, she only attended a few sessions.'

'Let's deal with it tomorrow,' Søren said.

Dinner was ready. Karen and Anna talked and laughed while they ate, and Søren entertained them with his demotion. 'What does that mean?' Karen asked, and Anna explained that Søren had realised it was much more fun to be in the field than gathering dust behind a desk.

'I'm thrilled about it. A small step back for Søren, but a quantum leap for the mood in this house,' she said, and winked at him.

He smiled back, but on the inside he was fuming. Anna herself hadn't been a bundle of laughs recently. They drank coffee with warm milk, and Anna and Karen started discussing research and grants, which would appear to be in short supply at Syddansk University, too, where Karen's boyfriend worked. They had just been through a round of cuts, Karen explained, but fortunately Jeppe had survived.

At some point Søren managed to interject that it was time for him to hit the hay, and he hoped that Anna would get the hint. Karen certainly did and promptly said it was time for her to go home, but Anna would not hear a word of it. It was pitch black outside, she said, so why didn't Karen just stay the night? 'I insist,' she added.

When Søren went to bed, Anna and Karen were busy making

up Karen's bed in the living room. Søren could hear them giggling and chatting and finally he could no longer keep his eyes open.

At almost half past midnight he was woken by a text message from Marie Skov. When he'd had a pee, he called her. They spoke for a long time, first about Storm's note and then about the discovery that Tim Salomon had hired the blue Ford. Anna had yet to come to bed, so they could speak undisturbed. When he had ended the call, he tiptoed downstairs to the living room and found Anna and Karen fast asleep on separate sofas. Anna had even gone to fetch her duvet. She no longer loved him. They had had something together and it had been invincible. Now it was gone.

On Thursday, 1 April, Søren arrived at work to find the station in uproar.

'Result!' Mehmet exclaimed, when he saw Søren. 'Martin Brink Schelde has confessed to five rapes and two murders!'

Søren went straight to Jørgensen's office and learned that the results of Martin Brink Schelde's DNA profile had come back. 'A hundred per cent match,' Jørgensen said contentedly. 'And he admits everything.'

'And then some, I understand.'

'Seven open cases, would you believe it? Including the rape of the Syrian girl in north-west Copenhagen. It's scant comfort, but I can't wait to tell the girl's father. Do you remember him? Poor man. I've just sent the file to Station City. Tejsner did an excellent job on that case. Would you like to tell him that we got the bastard? As far as I remember, that case hit him hard.' Jørgensen looked warily at Søren. 'I would like to stress that last week was a disaster. But let's move on. There's no reason to sacrifice a good police officer on the scaffold for a single mistake, is there?'

'Or a chief superintendent for that matter,' Søren said sweetly, and left.

At the morning briefing, Søren listed and allocated the day's assignments and sent ten of his twelve officers out of the building. The two who remained were Inge Kai and Peter Bjørn, and he took them into the big meeting room to bring them up to speed. It now looked likely that Professor Kristian Storm had been suffocated with a plastic bag, but unfortunately Bøje's autopsy report was still missing. The very nanosecond it appeared, Søren stressed, he wanted a thorough investigation of the murder. All students and employees at the Department of Immunology must be brought in for questioning. Students and colleagues at the other departments of the faculty must be interviewed as well. Possible motives must be identified both in Denmark and abroad, and they needed to apply for a court order so they could establish the identity of whoever had reported Kristian Storm and Marie Skov to the Danish Committees on Scientific Dishonesty. In the meantime they should concentrate on any task that did not depend on the autopsy report, such as investigating Tim Salomon's travel activities and familiarising themselves thoroughly with the profile that Superintendent Tejsner had asked an external researcher to prepare on Kristian Storm.

Inge Kai and Peter Bjørn nodded, and Søren returned to his office.

Just five minutes later Inge Kai knocked on his door. 'Per

Andersen from the National Investigation Centre says he'll call you regarding Tim Salomon's travel activity as soon as he hears from Scandinavian Airlines. They're usually pretty efficient.'

'Great,' Søren said, and returned to the papers he was working on.

'Why don't we round off our investigation of Mads Skov right now?' Inge Kai asked.

Søren nodded, and they sat at a meeting table. Inge Kai opened the file. 'It's tragic, but not suspicious,' she said, 'and the Skov family is entitled to keep the accident a secret, so . . . The only thing I question is why the eldest daughter, Julie, was allowed to give up counselling so quickly. She was barely eleven when it happened and, according to the report, she witnessed the accident.' Inge Kai flicked through the report. 'Julie was looking after her three siblings in the garden behind the house. At one point, the telephone rang and Julie ran inside to answer it. It was a friend from her school and they spoke for a few minutes until Marie came into the house to fetch her. The children were banned from the garden shed, but Mads had gone inside. Julie went to the garden shed, where the accident happened in front of her. It must have been very traumatic and that's why I'm surprised that the counselling afterwards was allowed to peter out. According to police records, Julie attended three times, then stopped going. The police psychologist handed her over to the family's own GP, with whom I've been in contact . . . Her name is Pia Tongaard at the Vangede Bygade medical practice. According to her records, she made offers of counselling to the whole family, but nobody took it up. Approximately six months after the accident, the school psychologist at Dyssegårdsskolen visited the family. Julie's teacher was concerned because Julie seemed tired and distracted and had cancelled a school trip she had otherwise been looking forward to because, as she put it, she "couldn't leave her sisters at home alone". However, the school psychologist found no fault with the Skov family . . .' Inge Kai took out a sheet of paper and read aloud: '"Joan Skov is on sick leave and at home with the children, but seems to be coping well. The same applies to the family's three children; the home is clean and tidy." But it's not about putting on a front for forty-five minutes when the school psychologist visits, is it? A tragedy like that is life-changing.'

'Did the police psychologist manage to form an impression of Julie Skov before she stopped her sessions?'

'Yes,' Inge Kai said, and produced the police psychologist's report. 'The psychologist noted various minor issues . . . Hang on.' Inge Kai trailed her finger down the report. 'Julie Skov displays extreme maturity and performs far above average at school . . . She is extremely protective and attentive to her younger siblings and her behaviour shows some evidence of too much responsibility for a child of her age . . . Very articulate for an eleven-year-old girl . . .' Inge Kai looked at Søren. 'Among other things, the psychologist quotes Julie as having said: "My mother is an artist and you know what artists are like. Flighty and unreliable and wrapped up in themselves. But my father and I support my mother in her creativity. My father comes from a deprived background where no one ever made anything of themselves. He has other wishes for his wife and his children."' Inge Kai looked at Søren. 'Isn't it rather absurd for an eleven-year-old to speak like that?'

'Hm,' Søren said. 'She sounds old beyond her years. It's almost as if someone coached her to say those words.'

'If you ask me, the police trauma counselling team should have kept a close eye on the Skov family, especially Julie. After all, she witnessed her little brother's death. And probably felt responsible.'

'I agree totally,' Søren said. 'The only problem is that you can't force people to accept help. Denmark is full of families who stagger along, managing as best they can. But something is bothering me . . .' He drummed his fingers on the table.

'What?'

'Yesterday when I asked Marie Skov how her brother died, she said meningitis straight away. I'm convinced that she doesn't know. I would imagine that the third sister, Lea, doesn't know either, because she was even younger. How old were they exactly when the accident happened?'

Inge Kai checked. 'Marie was three and a half and Lea was two and a half.'

'Do you remember anything from when you were three years old?'

'Nothing,' Inge Kai said.

'No, and that's another thing that's bothering me.' Søren cleared his throat. 'When I was five, my parents were killed in a car crash. They drove straight out in front of a lorry. My grandparents have always told me that I was on holiday with them when it happened. But two years ago I discovered that I was in the car with my parents and trapped for more than an hour before the emergency services freed me. I don't know why my grandparents chose to hide the truth, but I'm sure they meant well. And I can see why they did it. Has discovering the truth made me a happier person? I don't know.'

'And now you wonder whether you should tell Marie Skov that her brother died in an accident in the home, rather than from meningitis,' Inge Kai said.

'Yes,' Søren said. 'I'm guessing the family kept it secret to protect the two younger children. Times were different. I'm not convinced that our current obsession with honesty and letting it all out is necessarily a good thing. Marie told me yesterday that Lea is curious about the past, but that their mother destroyed most of the family photos when Mads died, so Lea is struggling to learn anything. And that's when I started having doubts as to whether or not I can allow myself to take that responsibility.'

'Responsibility for what exactly?'

'Knowing but not telling her something that might be the missing piece she's looking for.'

They sat for a moment in silence. Then Inge Kai slammed shut Mads Skov's file. 'Think it over and I'll do the same. Meanwhile, let's concentrate on Kristian Storm,' she said, and got up.

Inge Kai had barely left Søren's office before his telephone rang. It was Per Andersen from the National Investigation Centre. Tim Salomon had indeed left not only Denmark, but also Europe on 27 March. However, he had returned this morning.

'Are you sure?'

'Totally. Tim Salomon landed at eight fifty-five a.m. with SAS from Lisbon.'

Søren called Marie Skov and told her to pack a bag. It was probably both paranoid and unnecessary, but he would sleep better if she and Anton stayed the night in a different location rather than the most obvious one. Just until he had tracked down Tim Salomon and discovered why he had returned to Denmark and where he had been on 17 March when Storm was murdered.

Suddenly Søren noticed that it was twelve forty-five and, unless he got a move on, he would be late for his mother-in-law's Easter lunch.

Cecilie and Jens were on sparkling form. Jens, especially, could not stop praising the delicacies on the Easter table, his grand-daughter's countless talents or bringing up the news that he had been offered a regular column in the Sunday edition of *Berlingske Tidende*. 'Just the other day I was complaining that older journalists have been frozen out of the business, and then I land a deal like this,' he said. 'How are you doing, Søren? I hear that you enjoyed a brief period of unemployment before you ate some humble pie.'

'Yes, you could say that,' Søren said. 'I've got my old job back, but only for a month.'

'Oh, what happens in a month?'

'I'm temping for Henrik Tejsner,' Søren said. 'His paternity leave ends in four weeks and I reckon he'd like to have a job to come back to.'

'Henrik's on paternity leave?' Anna said. She was cutting rye bread and Søren had been unaware that she was following the conversation. 'Isn't taking paternity leave somewhat out of character for Denmark's last male chauvinist?'

'Erm,' Søren said, 'I guess you could say that. But Henrik has decided to take a month off.'

Anna sent Søren an icy stare, then turned back to the kitchen table and stuck the knife into the bread.

Søren didn't know what he had done to upset her, but she refused to look him in the eye during the meal. Jens and Cecilie, with a couple of their friends who had also been invited, were having a great time and kept raising their glasses, but it was clear that Anna was just pretending. Every time Søren tried to talk to her or put his arm around her, he was met with permafrost. Frustrated, he helped himself to a beer before he remembered that he was on duty and put it back on the table.

Lily asked him to help her put on her fancy dress and, when he had zipped her up at the back, his mobile rang. He went to Cecilie's bedroom to take the call.

It was La Cour from the Institute of Forensic Medicine.

'You've found the autopsy report and you're calling to tell me it's in my inbox,' Søren said.

'I'm afraid not,' La Cour said.

'Bollocks! Then why bother calling me? This is a murder case, unless you've forgotten. I need that autopsy report found right now.'

'Oh, I'm aware of that,' La Cour said, unperturbed. 'You may have mentioned it once or twice. And now you've shouted it as well. But it's not me whose hard drive was in a fearful mess, nor was I told to fix it, so it's a bit unfair to take it out on me, don't you think?'

'Sorry,' Søren mumbled.

'I'm calling to tell you to check your spam folder.'

'My spam folder?'

'Yesterday our IT guy mentioned that the spam filter used by the police force was upgraded last Friday, and just now Bernt from Station City rang to offer me the closest that man can get to an apology for having bitten off my head the other day. He had happened to check his spam folder and found the email with the autopsy report he had been looking for. Bøje had sent it to him last Thursday and the subject field said: *Here's hoping this will make you shut your arse*. The spam filter disapproves of such language, as indeed does Bernt. I think Bøje should consider himself lucky that he's already in a coma.'

Søren ended the call and returned to the open-plan kitchen where the happy Easter mood was now subdued.

'Is everything all right?' Cecilie asked.

'Yes, I'm sorry for shouting, but . . . Please may I use your computer?'

'Of course. It's in the living room. It's already on.'

Søren logged onto his email account, found the spam folder, scrolled past various penis-extension offers and eligible Russian girlfriends and reached his emails from 26 and 27 March. Here he found three emails from Bøje Knudsen.

Bøje had chosen to call the first email, sent 26 March, *Fucking call me, you massive bell end*. The second was entitled, *This is a major fuck up. Ring me, you bastard*, and the third, sent just after five thirty p.m. on Saturday, 27 March, was headed, *Are you taking the piss, you wanker?*

Søren dragged all three emails to his inbox and was asked to confirm that they were not spam. Then his mobile rang.

His hands were shaking when he opened the first email:

Søren, this is a cock-up. I'm not apologising for anything, it's just a massive cock-up. I'm attaching the final autopsy report along with the analysis from the Department of Forensic Genetics and I expect that you'll be turning up as soon as you have read it. It's probably the biggest howler of my career. Perhaps it's time I retired. I've grown old. Best wishes from your friend, Bøje

Søren's eyes welled. 'It's OK, Bøje,' he said quietly. 'Real people make mistakes.'

Then he clicked on the attachment, which was named OK139-2010, and quickly read the autopsy report:

Clear secondary horizontal ligature marks visible along with dotted bleeding under the primary ligature marks. I decided to perform a full autopsy and I don't give a toss that it will cost the Police Force 30,000 kroner. Autopsy commenced 25 March 2010 at 23.45, and concluded at 02.45. Four plastic fragments detected. One under the tongue, which measures 3 x 4 millimetres, a larger piece in the throat, measuring 7 x 8 millimetres. I examined the noose and found two further pieces of plastic, one on the noose itself and one in the evidence bag (used by Lars Hviid, a massive bell end because he – contrary to his instructions – not only cut and removed the noose from the body and secured it in an evidence bag at the scene, but also sent it to Bellahøj station where, up until 23 March, it had vanished without trace between a highly suspicious office stapler and two equally suspicious ring binders). I sent all four plastic fragments and the noose, with photographs of the secondary ligature marks, to the

KTC Forensic Laboratory as a priority case immediately. The body was collected on 26 March 2010 by a (fraught) undertaker at 9.30 (idiot). Call came in from KTC the same day at 16.30. The secondary ligature marks are 98 per cent identical to prototype photographs from KTC's archive of injuries caused by suffocation with a plastic bag, and the four plastic pieces are a 100 per cent match to a Netto carrier-bag. Now follows the unqualified opinion of the forensic examiner, Bøje Knudsen (me), if I can be left alone to do my job properly: the victim was suffocated with a yellow Netto bag and subsequently hanged from a noose. Sherlock Hviid has secured 121 different fingerprints from the victim's office, but failed to take a single one from the victim or the noose, either because he forgot (which wouldn't surprise me) or because the killer wore gloves. A note regarding the noose: by comparing the scarlet, finely woven cloth also found among the secured and bagged evidence at Bellahøj station, KTC concludes that the noose was torn from this cloth. However, another strip from the same cloth appears to be missing and it was nowhere to be found at Bellahøj station. Perhaps Lars Hviid used it to wipe his arse.

While Søren had read the autopsy report, a text message from Marie had arrived. He rang her with a heavy heart to tell her there was no longer any doubt that Storm had been suffocated, but he could hear that something was very wrong. Someone had sent her a noose in the post.

'I'm on my way,' he said.

'I'm afraid I have to go,' Søren said to the other guests. 'I'm sorry, but I have an urgent case and there has just been a development I need to respond to.'

'Oh, what a shame,' Cecilie said, 'but of course.'

Søren quickly shook hands with everyone and kissed Anna. He aimed for her mouth, but she offered him her cheek.

While he was putting on his shoes and coat in the hallway, she suddenly appeared in the doorway. 'I just want to tell you,' she said, 'that I know you're lying.'

'Lying?'

'Yes. I met Jeanette at Copenhagen Central Station yesterday. She and Henrik have split up and no way is he on paternity leave. I don't know what the two of you are up to, but how could you think that I would be dumb enough to—'

'Please can we talk about it later, Anna? I really must go.'

'Screw you,' Anna said.

Søren picked up Marie and Anton and drove them to Saxogade where he walked them all the way up to the fourth floor.

'I see you've got yourself a bodyguard,' Lea remarked, when she opened the door. She looked Søren up and down. 'Who are you?'

'Søren Marhauge. We spoke earlier regarding a photograph from your childminder.' He handed it to her.

She took it carefully, as if it was a piece of fragile ancient parchment, and studied it for a long time. Marie looked with her. 'I do remember that you were seriously cute,' she said.

'Please can I have a look?' Anton said, and Lea tilted the photograph. 'You look like me,' he said.

At first Lea said nothing. Then a tear rolled down her cheek.

'Why are you crying, Lea?' Marie said, alarmed.

Lea pointed to Tove. 'I'm happy. Look at her face. She loves me.'

Søren said goodbye and went downstairs. He got into his car but did not turn on the engine. He was kicking himself. He had missed an opportunity to bring up their brother's accident.

He called Anna, but she did not answer her phone. *We need to talk*, he texted. *I'm driving home now. Do you want me to pick you up? I just don't have the energy to walk all the way up to Cecilie's flat.*

No reply. Søren drove to Cecilie's and rang the bell.

'Hi, won't you come up?'

'I'm sorry, Cecilie, but I've had a long day. I need to get home. I just wanted to know if Anna and Lily want a lift or if they'd prefer to catch the train later. I tried calling, but Anna didn't pick up.'

'Oh, they've already gone,' Cecilie said. 'They left soon after you did.'

Less than forty minutes later, Søren was at home. The house lay in darkness; the only light was the magic cat glowing in Lily's window. When Søren let himself in, he knew that they were not back yet. Even so, he searched the whole house for them before he flopped down on the sofa where he was overcome by debilitating exhaustion. He decided to put on fifteen kilos and find himself an ugly girlfriend who was always thrilled when he came home. He would screw her with all the enthusiasm of a fat panda.

He took out his mobile. *Darling Anna,* he texted. *Darling, darling Anna.*

Then he hurled his mobile against the wall with all his might.

On Friday, 2 April, Søren delivered his most incoherent morning briefing to date. The twelve police officers gawped at him in silence. When the assignments had been allocated and everyone had been updated on the Kristian Storm case, he hurried to his office, slammed the door behind him, closed the blinds and sat in darkness.

Soon afterwards his mobile rang, his old orange Nokia 3210, which he had found in his desk drawer and into which he had inserted his Sim card.

He considered ignoring it. He couldn't take any more right now.

'Søren Marhauge,' he said gruffly, when he answered it.

'Søren, it's Klaus Mønster from the Department of Forensic Genetics. I've got some preliminary results regarding Bøje Knudsen's original priority case . . . By the way, how is Bøje doing? I didn't mean what I said; you know that, don't you?'

'Bøje is the same,' Søren said curtly, and turned on his computer. 'What have you got for me?'

'The results of the blood sample from OK 133-2010, the woman from Vangede. Do you have a moment? I want to add a few comments.'

Søren said he had.

'Our chemists have identified five different drugs,' Mønster went on. 'Four anxiety suppressants and some sleeping tablets. We're talking about diazepam, nordiazepam, Cipramil, mirtazapine and zopiclone. At first glance it's a crazy number of drugs for the same condition, and it would have set alarm bells ringing, if it hadn't been—'

'Yes, and not only that,' Søren interrupted him. He had opened the police report on Joan Skov and quickly trailed his finger down the screen. 'We found more types of medication than the deceased had been prescribed by her GP.'

'Yes, I'm sure you did,' Mønster said. 'But the point I want to make is this: as I was about to say, I, too, would have wanted to investigate this further except that the concentration is so low that it couldn't possibly have been fatal. Besides, nordiazepam is a breakdown product of diazepam, which can be traced in the body up to ten days after ingestion and, judging from the concentration found in the blood sample, the deceased must have taken this drug on several days up to the time of her death.'

'Oh, really?' Søren said, baffled.

'Yes, what killed her was 2.6 diisopropylphenol, commonly known as propofol.'

'Propofol?'

'Yes, and that is suspicious. You see, propofol is administered intravenously and is used exclusively on patients in an intensive-care unit or who are about to undergo surgery with a general anaesthetic. You need specialist training to administer this drug, so something here doesn't add up, but that's your department. Where should I send the results of the blood test? The DNA sequence of the three hairs will follow shortly.'

Søren gave Mønster his email address. When they had said goodbye, Søren opened his browser and carried out an extended web search on propofol. Then he got up and opened the blinds. The needle mark.

Søren scrolled through Bøje's autopsy report on the screen and quickly found what he was looking for. On the first page Bøje had written, . . . *possible needle mark in the crook of the left elbow* . . .

Someone had injected Joan Skov with propofol so expertly that Bøje had been in doubt as to whether there was a needle mark.

Getting confirmation of a murder was always an ambivalent feeling.

Euphoria and shock.

When he had digested the news, he went to the open-plan office where the police officers were working and found Inge Kai.

'Come on, we're off to Rødovre,' he said.

This time Søren was behind the wheel and he was speeding. Ten minutes later, when they pulled up outside Julie Claessen's terraced house on Hvidsværmervej, he had brought Inge Kai up to date with the recent developments in the case.

'I'll do the talking,' Søren said. 'You keep your eyes and ears peeled.'

As they walked up the flagstone path leading to the house, they spotted Julie Claessen busy with something on the kitchen counter or in the sink. She did not look up until Søren and Inge Kai were only a few steps from the front door. She jumped, then made a movement that suggested she was drying her hands on her apron.

'I know your face,' Julie said, when she opened the front door. 'But I can't place it. Do you want Michael? He's not back yet.'

Søren and Inge Kai took turns shaking hands with her and Søren explained that they were from the Violent Crimes Unit.

'Violent Crimes Unit?' Julie sounded alarmed.

'I also grew up on Snerlevej,' Søren continued, 'which probably explains why you recognised me. I lived with my grandparents diagonally opposite you. We didn't know you all that well, but then again I'm a few years older than you.'

Julie tightened her lips. 'I remember your grandparents very well,' she said coolly. 'What do you want? My children are here. And we're expecting guests for lunch tomorrow so I'm busy cooking.' Julie folded her arms across her chest and showed no signs of wanting to invite Søren and Inge Kai inside.

'Please may we come in?' he asked.

Julie Claessen stepped aside reluctantly.

The ground floor of the small terraced house was a modern open-plan kitchen-diner and living room. At the far end there was a big corner sofa upholstered in bright white wool; on it two chubby girls were watching television with a bowl of sweets between them.

'Please may we speak in private?' Søren enquired politely, nodding towards the girls.

'They can't hear us,' Julie said, and Søren had to concede that the volume from the television was loud.

They sat down at the dining table where mixing bowls and cake tins had been put out. Julie pushed them aside.

'First of all, may I say that I'm sorry for your loss,' he began. 'I—'

'What do you want?' Julie said sharply. 'My mother is dead and buried and that's all there is to say about that. If this is about my father, I'm ashamed of him. Deeply ashamed.'

When Søren explained that they had found traces of propofol in Joan Skov's blood and that the police were investigating, he saw the colour drain from Julie's face.

'You can't do this to us,' she said. 'Don't you realise that the whole family is falling apart? My mother has just died. My younger sister is dying from cancer and about to get divorced. My father is a drunk-driver and due in court on the second of July. And now you come here telling me that you intend to stir everything up? To what end? It's not going to bring my mother back, is it?' Tears welled in her eyes. 'You just can't do this to us.'

'Unfortunately we have a duty to follow up any evidence that arises as part of an investigation,' Søren said.

'Oh, and what kind of evidence would that be?' Julie snarled. Her cheeks were flushed and Søren had an inkling that while the two girls might still be looking at the screen they were paying careful attention to their mother's behaviour.

'Well, as I've just told you, we found traces of a pharmaceutical product in your mother's blood and we don't understand where it could have come from. The drug is called propofol and is used mainly on intensive-care unit patients.'

Julie stared vacantly into the distance. 'But my mother hasn't been in hospital since 1995 when she broke her leg,' she said.

At that moment the front door opened and a man whom Søren concluded must be Michael, Julie's husband, entered. 'What the hell are you doing with a man in the house?' he exclaimed.

'This is Søren Marhauge from the police,' Julie said, 'and . . . What did you say your name was?'

Inge Kai said her name again.

'Bloody hell,' Michael said. 'What's my father-in-law got up to this time?'

'It's not funny, Michael,' Julie said.

'Oh, just chill, will you?' Michael said, and looked at Søren. 'What's the problem?'

'They found something in Mum's blood called propofol,' Julie said anxiously.

'Right,' Michael said. 'Then they'd better talk to Jesper. Jesper is the family pill pusher.' The latter was addressed to Søren before Michael walked through to the living room to say hi to his daughters. Afterwards he headed upstairs to have a shower. 'I've been pushing nearly dead meat around all day,' he said, sniffing his armpits.

What a charmer, Søren thought.

'I understand,' Søren said, when Michael had disappeared, 'that you were in charge of your mother's medication. Is that right?' Julie was still looking at him in a hostile manner and Søren burst out, 'Could you try to be a bit more co-operative, please? I've come to tell you that we found traces of a suspicious substance in your mother's blood, for which there might be a perfectly innocent explanation, but in theory it could mean that someone killed her. And let me tell you something. I didn't give your mother propofol, so do you think you could set your antagonism aside for a moment?'

A single tear rolled down Julie's cheek. 'I'm sorry,' she said. 'I just can't take any more. I will help you. Killed her?' she said, and looked frightened. 'What do you mean, killed her?' Suddenly she grinned from ear to ear and flapped her hands excitedly. For a moment an astonished Søren thought that the woman had completely lost her marbles until he realised she was waving to the two girls on the sofa. They had long since stopped watching the television and were staring anxiously in their mother's direction.

'Everything is fine, girls. Mummy will be with you in a minute,' Julie said, in a loud voice, and the girls turned back to the television.

'My mother has been ill for many, many years. Ever since I was a little girl. I've always known it, of course, and helped out as best I could, but I didn't realise just how ill she was until the last few years. I really did everything I could to help her. I got her onto an excellent occupational-therapy programme some years ago where she did gymnastics and sewed patchwork along with other patients who had mental health issues and, yes, I was actually starting to think that her life was becoming bearable, as far as that's possible when you have a dark mind. Unfortunately, my younger sister fell ill last autumn.' Julie glanced furtively at her daughters and whispered, 'Breast cancer. It was very hard on all of us, especially my parents. They lost Marie's twin, Mads, when he was three years old, and . . . I'm sure your grandparents must remember that? The flags were at half-mast on all of Snerlevej – people were very kind. But it's not something you can survive twice, is it? So when Marie got ill, my mother had a breakdown. I've read in a book that it's common. I believe it's a form of regression. If something happens in the present that you can't cope with, it's like you're catapulted back in time. My mother had been very poorly ever since Marie's diagnosis, but I must admit I never thought for one moment that she would kill herself.'

Another tear trickled down Julie's cheek.

'But you handled her medication?'

Julie nodded. 'Yes, except for the week when she died,' she said quietly. 'I worked in a different district from my usual one, far away from Vangede, and that evening there was a performance at Camilla's school, so I simply couldn't fit it in. The next day Emma was ill, which meant I had to take time off work, both Tuesday and Wednesday. But I rang my father, obviously, and asked him to sort out the pills, which he did because he called me twice with questions. I can't imagine why Michael made that comment about Jesper being our pill pusher. Typical Michael. Always trying to be the class clown. My mother got her medication on prescription from her GP, but it's true that Jesper renewed her prescriptions a few times. Given that he's a doctor, all he needs to do is ring them through to the chemist. I was incredibly grateful to him because getting my mother to the doctor's was such a palaver, especially in recent years.'

'What pills did your mother take?'

Julie reeled off the various drugs. 'Sadly, that's something you know by heart when you've been counting them out for so many years,' she added, with a small smile.

'Have you ever given her an injection?'

'No, of course not,' Julie said.

Had she said it too quickly? Søren wasn't sure.

'Could anyone else have given her an injection? Your brother-in-law? Your father? Or one of your sisters?'

'Definitely not my father. He can't stand the sight of blood. And I doubt that Jesper would do it. He doesn't mind renewing my mother's prescriptions, but he always told us to go to our own GP with anything else. And my sisters? Lea, possibly? But definitely not Marie. Like I said, she's been very ill herself these last six months.' Julie whispered the last bit and turned in her chair to look at her daughters.

'And your daughters don't know anything about that?' Søren asked, in an equally low voice.

'No, of course not,' Julie said. 'There's no reason they should know anything. They're only ten and eleven.'

'Didn't they wonder why Marie had lost her hair? It's only just starting to grow back now.'

'Children don't notice things like that. Besides, I brought them up not to pry. I hate it when people pry.' Julie looked beseechingly at Søren. 'Neither do they know anything about what their Grandad has done and nor should they. As far as they're concerned, he's still just their Grandad.'

Michael returned to the kitchen and took a beer from the fridge. 'When is dinner?' he wanted to know.

'Oh, I was hoping you and the girls could have a pizza. I have so much cooking to do for tomorrow,' Julie said.

'Pizza again? I thought your dad was hosting this Easter lunch, not us,' Michael said in a surly voice. 'Switch on the oven, will you? Have we got any crisps?' Julie got up, found a bag of crisps in a cupboard and filled a bowl to the brim. Søren's blood was boiling.

Michael sat on the sofa. He and the girls started watching a programme on cable TV, which made them break out into hysterical fits of laughter.

'You said "Lea, possibly"?'

It was a moment before Julie was back on track. 'I don't trust my sister,' she then said. 'We've never got on and I've no idea what she's capable of. Anything would be my guess.

She's covered in tattoos and revolting piercings. I don't understand her. I never have. When she was little, she was naughty all the time. This spring she started interfering in the management of my mother's illness, wanting her to travel all the way to West Jutland for therapy at a rehabilitation facility for addicts. Lea is fanatically opposed to any kind of medication. But my mother couldn't handle Lea's so-called good intentions at all. Whenever Lea had preached to her, it took days before she calmed down again. Lea didn't understand that Mum was seriously ill – she was adamant that all Mum needed was to talk about Mads. Let it all out. She almost convinced my father to jump on her bandwagon. Lea has always been selfish. Just because it helps her to let it all out, she automatically assumes the same goes for everybody else. But losing a child is the most terrible thing that can happen, and life after a tragedy like that is survival, pure and simple. There is no need to rip open old wounds after all these years.'

'How old were you when your brother died?'

'Ten. I turned eleven soon afterwards.'

'That must have been terribly difficult.'

'I've never complained,' Julie said abruptly. 'What's the use of that? Nothing. That's what Lea doesn't understand. I have no time for such fads. I read a lot of books. Self-help ones, that kind of thing. And I've been known to give someone a copy of a book I thought was good and which you could learn something from, but I never lecture anyone. And, quite frankly, Lea is a nail technician, but she acts as if she has a degree in psychology . . . That really gets my goat. Marie had just been told she had . . .' Julie pointed discreetly to her own swelling breast and glanced towards the sofa '. . . and that was more than enough for my parents to take on board. And Lea wants Mum to start seeing a psychologist on top? Honestly.'

'I remember you now,' Søren lied, and smiled at her.

'You do?'

'Yes, from Snerlevej. You used to visit Tove Madsen often, I believe. She was married to Herman Madsen, who was a police officer – he's retired now. He was my role model and I spent a lot of time at their house, as did you, didn't you? Or am I mistaken?'

'I didn't go there very often,' Julie corrected him. 'But Tove looked after Lea until we got her a place at nursery. The arrangement came to a rather sudden end because Tove shook Lea.'

'Shook her?' Søren exclaimed, as if he had never heard the story before.

'Yes, she had bruises on her arm one day and how else could she have got them? Lea never set foot in Tove's house after that.'

'How did Lea react when Tove wasn't allowed to look after her any more?'

'God have mercy on us all,' Julie burst out. 'She went crazy and smashed lots of things, including a very fine earthenware jug my mother had inherited from her mother. In the end I had to lock her in the cupboard under the stairs.' Julie looked embarrassed. 'My mother sat there with her broken heirloom and looked so sad because Lea could only think of herself.'

'Did this happen before or after the accident?' Søren asked lightly.

'Accident?' Julie said. 'What accident?'

'Your brother's.'

'My brother died from a very aggressive strand of meningitis,' Julie stated. 'It happens to only one in a hundred thousand children, but of course it would have to happen to us.'

Søren looked closely at her. 'But that's not true,' he said softly.

Julie blinked. 'I'm sorry, what did you say?'

'What does your husband do for a living?' Søren asked, and smiled.

'He's worked as a porter at Bispebjerg Hospital since 1998,' Julie said. 'Why?'

'Curiosity.' Søren smiled. 'An occupational hazard.'

'I want you to leave now,' Julie said, and her lips quivered.

'When will dinner be ready?' Michael called out from the sofa.

'I've already said I'll heat up a pizza for you,' Julie said, in a shrill voice.

'Oh, calm down, will you?' Michael called back. 'Bring me another beer and some pop for the girls.'

Julie got up, as did Søren and Inge Kai.

'Right. I think that's everything for now.'

Julie walked them to the front door and offered them a limp handshake.

They went down the flagstone path, and as Søren got into his car, he glanced up at the house. Julie was back behind the kitchen window. She looked terrified.

Søren and Inge Kai drove in silence for five minutes, then Inge Kai said, 'Christ on a bike.'

'Give me your honest opinion,' Søren said.

'A swollen finger couldn't be more infected,' Inge Kai said. 'And Michael might have looked as if he was watching television with his children and relaxing, but his ears were glued to our conversation. When you asked Julie about his job, he nearly fell off the sofa.'

'And Julie?'

'Where do you want me to start?' Inge Kai said. 'She's . . . she's . . . I don't know how to put it . . . sick?'

'A house of cards crashing down,' Søren said.

Fifteen minutes later they parked outside Rigshospitalet.

'And now?' Inge Kai asked.

'The intensive-care unit,' Søren said.

'This is Sergeant Inge Kai,' Søren introduced her when he had shaken hands with the duty doctor at the ICU. Fortunately it was the same doctor as last time.

'Hello,' the doctor said. 'You already know where Bøje is, so just go through.'

'Thank you,' Søren said, 'but before I do, I have a question for you. Do you know a drug called propofol?'

'Of course I do,' the doctor said, with a smile.

'Can you give me a quick guide?'

'Eh, yes,' the doctor said. 'Propofol is an anaesthetic that we use in this unit every day. Doctors like it because it disperses swiftly to all tissue, including the brain, while at the same time it has a short half-life, which means you can quickly get your patient conscious again. The drug has only two side effects, but they're serious. Number one, propofol can cause you to stop breathing. Number two, it heightens the impact of all other medication in the patient's system. Consequently, we only administer it to patients who are being monitored twenty-four/seven, and/or who are on assisted breathing. That was the trouble with Michael.'

'Michael?'

'Yes, Michael Jackson. MJ. You know, the King of Pop. When pathologists carried out his autopsy, they found propofol in his blood and today that's the core argument in the case against his doctor, Conrad Murray. As a doctor, Murray should have known the side effects of propofol, so to give his patient a shot to calm him down when he was at home, then leave him to his own devices was obviously completely irresponsible. As far as I'm aware, MJ had taken a fair amount of anti-anxiety medication, but not necessarily more than he usually did. It was only because he was given propofol that the effect of the pills he normally took was heightened and caused his heart to stop. You see, there is an upper limit to how relaxed your muscles can be before you snuff it. Trust me, Murray will be found guilty of manslaughter, and when he is, it'll be the right verdict. It's a very serious error for a doctor to administer propofol to a patient whose history they know well. It should never be given to anyone outside the ICU. And that's what the law says – or it does in Denmark.'

'So you would be surprised,' Søren said, 'if you came across a patient with propofol in their blood unless they had been in intensive care?'

'Yes, absolutely.'

'How does a layperson get hold of propofol?' Søren asked.

'Well, it's not something you just pick up from the chemist,' the doctor said, with a smile, 'so you need to either work in the health service or be a thief. Or possibly both.'

Søren pondered this. 'Who is in charge of the purchasing and distribution of medication at this hospital?'

'That would be the head of pharmacology, Nadia A. Jensen,' the doctor said. 'Her office is on the floor above the hospital pharmacy. She doesn't work alone, of course. I think about twenty pharmacologists are employed here to purchase and issue medication.'

'Thank you,' Søren said.

'Wait, you forgot to visit the patient,' the doctor called, as Søren and Inge Kai left.

The head of pharmacology was called Nadia Abdul al-Haq Jensen and Søren nearly swooned at her beauty. She had sparkling dark eyes, wore a bright blue hijab and a white gown, and did not look a day over twenty-four, but when he pressed her hand, he distinctly felt the gravitas of an adult woman. Even Inge Kai was gawping at her.

'Police?' Nadia said, when Søren had explained the reason for their visit. 'Looking for stolen propofol. That sounds exciting. How much are we talking about?'

'Enough to kill someone,' Inge Kai said.

'So a hundred or two hundred mills or an ampoule the size of this eraser.' Nadia picked up an eraser from her desk and, before Søren and Inge Kai had time to say anything, the eraser had vanished and Nadia held up two empty palms to them. 'I don't think that would be difficult to steal,' she said, with a smile, and Søren blushed. 'Drugs are left out during the day on the anaesthetist's trolley in the operating theatre, for example. Now, an operating theatre is obviously a restricted area, but all you'd need to do is to open the door, go in and leave without being seen. We know there is a certain loss every year, but it isn't something we register systematically because we can't possibly know if the loss is due to theft or simple wastage.'

'Where are we going now?' Inge Kai wanted to know, when they had said thank you and goodbye to the head of pharmacology and Søren was marching purposefully towards the lift at Entrance Two.

'Paying a visit to the orthopaedic ward,' Søren said.

'To do what, if I may ask?'

'The way I see it,' Søren said, when the lift doors had closed, 'we have several potential propofol thieves in this case. Joan Skov's eldest daughter, Julie Claessen, who dropped out of her nursing training, now works as a carer and would therefore definitely know how to administer an injection. Her husband, who works as a porter at Bispebjerg Hospital. The middle daughter, Marie Skov, has been in and out of hospital since last autumn, and has had plenty of opportunity to steal the drug and learn a few tricks, and last, but not least, Marie's ex-husband, Jesper Just, who is an orthopaedic surgeon at this hospital. So I thought we would pay him a visit since we're here anyway.'

'Nice to know,' Inge Kai said drily.

'I've just finished my shift and I'm about to leave,' Jesper Just said, when Søren had shaken his hand.

Jesper Just had the steady gaze that signalled authority. He was a handsome man who was starting to go bald. Søren had taken an instant dislike to him. His self-assurance was like a tight second skin; he was all hard edges, no softness. Søren could not see Marie Skov and Jesper Just together in his wildest imagination. 'I only need ten minutes,' Søren promised him, and smiled.

'Very well, then,' Jesper Just looked most put out. 'But not a minute more. I need to pick up my son from Vesterbro and drive all the way to West Jutland in time for dinner.'

Søren smiled again.

'Let's step inside this meeting room,' Jesper said. 'Do go ahead. I need to text my sister-in-law to let her know that I'm running ten minutes late.' He stressed the ten minutes.

Søren and Inge Kai were studying the photographic posters of prosthetic body parts when Jesper entered the meeting room. He turned on the ceiling light and, after a series of crackling flashes, the room was bathed in a harsh, white glare.

'That's bordering on excessive,' Jesper said, looking irritably at the light fitting. 'How can I help you?'

'Are you're familiar with a drug called propofol?'

'Of course I am,' Jesper said. 'I'm an orthopaedic surgeon. We use propofol during practically every operation in addition to the general anaesthetic.'

'So you have access to the drug on a daily basis?'

'Yes, why?'

'We found traces of propofol in your mother-in-law's blood. "Traces" might be the wrong word because the concentration was fairly high. In fact, ten times higher than the concentration of the other drugs we found in her blood.'

Søren watched Jesper Just closely and paid special attention to his reaction.

'I've no idea how that could have happened,' Jesper said.

'Propofol? But how? To my knowledge, she hadn't been in hospital recently. No, I'm sure of it – I would have known.'

'So it's nothing to do with you?'

For a moment Jesper stared at Søren in disbelief. 'What the hell are you insinuating?' he exploded. 'I took a medical oath! You have no right to accuse me of anything of the sort. This is outrageous.'

'Does the medical oath say anything about it being all right to be "the family pill pusher"?' Søren asked.

'Pill pusher?' Jesper frowned.

'Earlier today I learned that it was standard practice for you to renew your mother-in-law's prescriptions, to save her a trip to her GP. Is that right?'

'Who told you that?' Jesper asked vehemently. 'I'm entitled to know who it was.'

'I'm afraid I can't tell you who used the term "pill pusher". I can only say that the expression was used. Isn't that right?' Søren looked at Inge Kai, who nodded.

'I'm a doctor,' Jesper said, 'and in my capacity as a doctor I have the right to issue prescriptions and you know it.'

'But you're an orthopaedic surgeon,' Søren responded, 'and as far as I can gather, the pills your mother-in-law was taking were mainly sedatives and anxiety suppressants. But perhaps orthopaedic surgeons know a great deal about psychiatry.'

'I didn't prescribe them. I merely renewed existing prescriptions so my mother-in-law wouldn't have to go to her GP, which she disliked doing. Besides, the pills she took were completely harmless,' Jesper said. 'Half the population of Denmark takes them. But it goes without saying that you must take them responsibly. And that's not the case, if you intend to commit suicide. Do you know how many tablets crossed the chemist's counter in 2009 alone? I read the figures only yesterday in *Dagens Medicin*.'

'No, I don't know,' Søren said, like an obedient schoolboy.

'Almost seventy million benzodiazepines and benzodiazepine-type drugs for the treatment of severe anxiety, and a hundred and sixty-six million antidepressants of which a hundred and twelve million are so-called happy pills. Every Dane has access to enough drugs to kill themselves and their neighbour. But that doesn't mean they do it, does it?'

'But don't they say that antidepressants without talking therapy are like a pacemaker without a battery?' Søren asked innocently. 'And shouldn't you – precisely because of your medical oath and your clear conscience in general – have made sure that your mother-in-law's mental health issues were addressed?'

'My mother-in-law suffered from a chronic condition,' Jesper spluttered, 'and you didn't need to spend more than five minutes in her company to know that she was a hopeless case. I helped her to the best of my ability, partly because leaving the house gave her panic attacks. I renewed her prescriptions whenever my sister-in-law asked me to and, besides, it's my understanding that Julie had been in touch with my mother-in-law's GP several times in the last few years, but you would have to talk to her about that. The pills were, as I have already told you, completely harmless if taken as prescribed, but they would do vast harm if you decided to wash them all down at once, and that's what my mother-in-law did. I'd like a copy of that blood-test result – how do I know that you didn't make a mistake when you analysed it? It's not like you're a doctor, is it?'

'The analysis was carried out by the Department of Forensic Genetics, but I'll make sure they send you a copy.' Søren smiled and handed the doctor his card. 'Thank you for your help. If you want to talk to me, you're welcome to give me a call any time.'

'I can't imagine that happening,' Jesper said. He hurled Søren's card into the wastepaper basket and stormed down the corridor.

When they were back in the car, Søren said, 'I only hope that Lea Skov is either a lesbian or has better taste in men than her sisters.'

'Yes, neither is more charming than the other,' Inge Kai said.

'But this one was telling the truth,' Søren said. 'He knew absolutely nothing about the propofol business.'

They both scratched their heads.

'Where are we going now?' Inge Kai wanted to know.

Søren smiled. 'You sound just like Lily,' he said. 'She's five.'

'No woman, no matter how old she is, can read a man's mind,' Inge Kai said. 'And you're one of the less informative ones, just so you know. I'm sure you drive your girlfriend crazy.'

'My girlfriend . . .' Søren gulped.

At that moment his mobile rang.

'Marie,' Søren said. 'Is everything all right?'

He listened.

'How did it go?' He listened again. 'OK . . . No, it's fine, I can do that. We're outside Rigshospitalet. Where are you? . . . No, I'd feel better if we did. It's not a problem. We'll pick you up.' He ended the call. 'We need to take Marie Skov to her flat in

Randersgade so she can pick up a notebook that got left behind in the rush yesterday. She's been working at the Royal Library today, but she can't make progress without her notes. So that's what we're going to do. We'll pick her up at Nørreport. See? I can communicate with a woman, can't I?'

'Oh, absolutely.' Inge Kai grinned.

CHAPTER 12

Once Søren had driven Marie and Anton to Lea's flat, Marie was able to relax properly for the first time in days. Finally she got a good night's sleep and woke up just after nine o'clock. She could hear Lea and Anton chatting in the kitchen and went to join them. Anton had emptied his rucksack onto the table and was explaining to his aunt the various features of his *Star Wars* Lego, while Lea listened attentively.

'Good morning,' Marie said.

Anton jumped up and gave his mother a hug, and Lea poured her a mug of tea. 'Hey,' she said. 'Do you know what I remembered after you fell asleep last night? Your new tat. I still haven't seen it! Come on, show me the goods!'

Bashfully, Marie pulled up the T-shirt in which she had slept to reveal the swallow. Lea was mesmerised. 'Wow, how clever of Mattis not to colour it in. It's a simple outline. It's . . . elegant. Not like the vulgar sailor's tats I run around with,' she said, with a grin.

'I'm really pleased with it,' Marie said.

'I want a dog tattoo when I grow up,' Anton said.

'A V-19 Torrent would be cool, too,' Lea said, grabbing Anton's arm. 'Here, maybe? Or here?' She tickled him.

'What's a V-19 Torrent?' Marie asked.

'One of these,' Anton said, and flew around with a spaceship that resembled a giant bug.

'Yes,' Lea said, 'and Anakin Skywalker flew it at the Battle of Geonosis.'

She and Anton made it sound very important.

'Does Anton really have to go to that cottage in West Jutland with Jesper?' Lea whispered, when he was busy building something on the floor.

'Yes,' Marie said. 'Jesper's brother's rented it for the whole family. We can't change it now. Jesper is pissed off enough as it is. He'll be here around half past three to fetch Anton. Thanks for looking after him.' Marie gave her sister a kiss.

'No problem,' Lea said. 'I've just discovered I'm a really cool aunt who's crazy about *Star Wars* Lego. So what's young Jesper's problem?'

'Oh,' Marie said, glancing furtively at Anton, 'I haven't got the energy to talk about it. It's just Jesper and his ... principles.'

'While we're on the subject of principles,' Lea said, 'is it all right if I give Anton his completely over-the-top and massively unhealthy chocolate Easter egg for breakfast? I meant to give it to him tomorrow.'

'Tomorrow?'

'Yes, when we meet up for Easter lunch.'

'You're joining us for Easter lunch?' Marie's jaw dropped.

'Sure. Dad invited me and I said yes.'

'Seriously?' Marie said.

'Yep,' Lea said. 'Do you want some toast?'

'Yes, please,' Marie said. 'But, Lea ...'

'But what? Will I promise to behave?' Lea laughed. 'I'll do my best. I don't know why, but my mood has shot up a thousand degrees since I got that photo of me and Tove yesterday. It was the last thing I looked at before I fell asleep and the first thing I looked at this morning. I tell myself I'm even starting to remember Tove. Not clearly, it's more a feeling. The feeling of sitting on her lap and snuggling up to her, the feeling of tripping over and scraping my knee and someone comforting me. Perhaps it's all in my mind, but who cares? For the first time ever it'll be relatively easy for me to attend a family get-together because, if I feel like I'm about to explode and that everyone hates me, I'll just think of Tove.'

'No one hates you, Lea,' Marie said.

'Call it whatever you like,' she said. 'I'm off to have a shower.'

After Marie, too, had showered, she had a long debate with herself about whether to wear her wig for her eleven o'clock meeting with Storm's former student, Stig Heller, or whether to tie the yellow scarf around her head. Finally, she decided on the wig. Lea and Anton had started building the ice planet Hoth out of salt dough and eating Easter eggs, and Anton barely had time to say goodbye to her.

'Super-cool aunt,' Lea mouthed behind his back, pointing two thumbs at herself.

Marie walked down Istedgade in the direction of Copenhagen Central Railway Station, wondering why Stig Heller wanted to meet with her. She was twenty minutes early, so she ordered a Ramlösa mineral water and had time to read through her article on her laptop before he appeared at her table.

'Marie Skov?' he said.

Marie held out her hand to him.

'Sorry, I wasn't sure that it was you. I've seen a couple of photos, but I thought you had brown hair. But I've also heard that—'

'People change,' Marie interrupted him. 'You ought to know that better than anyone.'

Stig Heller sat down and ordered a coffee. 'Marie, please can we bury the hatchet? I haven't got the energy and, besides, you're not being entirely fair. Storm and I fought like two men who both wanted to win, giving no quarter. Storm dying before we had made peace wasn't part of the plan. But he did, and now I have to find a way to live with that.'

'Fine,' Marie said. 'If you say so.'

'That didn't sound terribly convincing,' Heller said.

They fell silent while the waiter served his cappuccino and Marie ordered more mineral water.

'No, but perhaps I still need convincing,' Marie said, when the waiter had left. 'I understand from Sandö that you've altered your view of Storm's research. And so what? It doesn't change the fact that you've been on his back for years, and it most certainly doesn't change the fact that you repeated my experiment purely to prove that Storm and I had fiddled the figures. You could have come to us directly and taken an interest in what we were doing, in Storm's unique project in Guinea-Bissau, the adaptive immune system and the non-specific effects of vaccines, rather than discredit him. So I'm sorry if it's a little difficult for me to take your sudden urge to reconcile seriously. Storm was very disappointed in you.'

Marie had said her piece and looked expectantly at Heller.

'Daddy isn't upset, Daddy is merely disappointed with you,' Heller said archly. 'But the fact is I turned into exactly the scientist Storm trained me to be. Hard, precise and stubborn.'

'Yes, and he would probably have valued those qualities much more if you hadn't used them to fight him.'

Heller shrugged. 'Do you know why Storm was such a brilliant scientist?'

'Because he was driven purely by curiosity,' Marie said.

'Wrong. Because he attracted disciples, Marie. He could spot the weak from miles away, those in need of a mentor, those who struggled to stand on their own two feet. He would train them and make sure they ended up thinking the way he did.'

'That's not true,' Marie said. To her irritation she felt the tears well in her eyes.

'What's so terrible about that?' Heller asked. 'Storm was an outstanding scientist and a very warm human being who happened to be manipulative. I had to rebel against that.'

'Why?' Marie asked.

Heller looked down for a moment. 'Storm cherry-picked me when I was eighteen. I was a first-year biology undergraduate, and after a lecture I asked him a question he thought was intelligent. Later he told me he knew at that very moment that I possessed the skills to become his successor. Always such grandiose words. Always the best for Storm's disciples. To begin with, being Storm's protégé was like winning the lottery. Bachelor assignments but, of course, a fascinating master's with built-in exotic travel destinations, a PhD following in its wake, no problem. Until one day I'd had enough. I was twenty-six and had almost completed my PhD and I was fed up with always being in Storm's shadow. So I started dismantling his arguments. The science magazines loved it, of course. Nothing sells like a good feud. When ours was at its peak, I applied to be a lecturer at the Department of Immunology, but that job went to Thor Albert Larsen, even though everyone knew I was the better candidate. Storm was on the appointment panel and I was convinced that he had voted against my appointment because deep down he couldn't handle being contradicted—'

'But Storm voted for you,' Marie interrupted. 'It was the rest of the panel who thought that your and Storm's profiles were too similar and that was why they appointed Thor Albert Larsen instead.'

'Yes, I heard that later,' Heller said, with a pale smile.

'But what was the point of testing my lab experiment? And how did you even get hold of my protocol in the first place?'

'The Danish Committees on Scientific Dishonesty asked me to test your experiment and they sent me the protocol. To my surprise, I discovered no irregularities. Nothing.'

Marie was silent for a moment. 'So you didn't get the protocol from someone at the Department of Immunology?'

'No, of course not. That would have been underhand.' Stig Heller looked at his watch. 'I understand from Sandö that you're finishing Storm's article and I've also spoken to Terrence Wilson from *Science*. He called to ask me to confirm that I had obtained the same results as you had. Which I did, of course. He told me that your deadline is Monday.'

'Yes,' Marie said, and glanced at her watch, too.

'Right. Listen to me. I have a slot at the International Immunology Congress in Amsterdam at the end of August. I was going to give a paper on malnutrition and infant mortality,

but I'm going to give you my slot. The world's leading immunologists will be there and they must hear what you have
discovered.'

Marie was astonished. 'Is that even allowed?'

'No, of course not,' Stig Heller said. 'But then again killing
someone to shut them up isn't allowed either.'

'So you already know that Storm was murdered?'

'Two identical drowning accidents are plenty of evidence
for me,' Heller replied. 'Besides, I've been summoned for an
interview at Bellahøj Police Station on Monday. I had a call
from an officer this morning saying they have fresh evidence
in the case. I need to be at the station at nine o'clock.'

'So who did it?' Marie whispered.

'Someone from the pharmaceutical industry,' Stig Heller
said, without hesitation. 'No one else benefits that much by
silencing Storm.'

'So it wasn't Tim Salomon?'

Heller laughed out loud. 'Tim? Have you met him?'

'Once, very briefly.'

'What you see is what you get. Tim would never hurt
anyone, least of all Storm. He owes Storm everything.' Heller
checked his watch again and quickly rose to his feet. 'Got to
run – I have a train to Jutland to catch.'

'One last question,' Marie said. 'Do you happen to . . .?'

Heller smiled. 'I'm afraid not,' he pre-empted her. 'I can't
tell you who reported you to the DCSD because I don't know.
However ridiculous it sounds, Danish scientists are free to
stab each other in the back whenever they feel like it. Whoever reports something is covered by the DCSD's anonymity
policy and no one knows their identity, not even the experts

the DCSD hire to investigate the accusation. Sorry.' He held out his hand to Marie. 'It was nice to meet you finally.'

Marie pressed it firmly. 'Likewise, Stig.'

When Stig Heller had left, Marie sat for a moment longer, then walked across central Copenhagen to the University Library in Fiolstræde. She worked undisturbed for almost three hours, but by four o'clock, she was starving and in need of her notebook, which she had left behind at her flat. She ate a sandwich at a café, then called Søren Marhauge. She was sorry to be a nuisance, but she needed her notes. She didn't mind picking them up herself, but did he think it would be safe? Twenty minutes later Søren met her at Nørreport and Marie shook hands with Inge Kai across the seats.

Søren parked outside Marie's building and they got out of the car. 'I'm happy to come with you,' he volunteered.

At that moment his mobile rang and he stepped aside to answer it. 'But where *did* you sleep last night?' Søren said, in a low voice. Inge Kai had stayed in the car and was busy with her mobile.

'I'll just pop upstairs,' Marie signalled to Søren. 'Five minutes.'

Søren looked sceptical, but he nodded.

Marie let herself into the flat and went straight to the kitchen to open the window because it was starting to smell of unwashed dishes again. She wondered if there might be a problem with the drain. She took off her wig, drank a glass of tap water and put four apples into the fridge to stop them going off.

Then she screamed.

Tim was standing in her hallway. 'Marie?' he said and took off his cap.

The door to the stairwell behind him was still open and Marie could see his rucksack on the steps leading up to the next floor. He must have been waiting for her.

'Marie?' he said again.

'Gosh, you scared me,' Marie said. Tim filled the whole of her small hallway and was blocking the front door.

'I've tried calling you,' he said, sounded resigned, 'but there aren't many payphones left in Copenhagen.'

'I did get some missed calls yesterday. From an unknown number,' Marie said.

Tim came out into the kitchen where Marie was and her heart started pounding. He looked dreadful, and when he made to embrace her, she could smell his stress. She retreated with a jolt.

'The police are just downstairs,' she said quickly.

Tim stopped and let his hands flop. 'Why do you say that?' The light changed in his eyes. 'Ah, you think . . . Please tell me you don't think that I . . .' He looked completely lost.

'I no longer know what to think,' Marie said.

Tim sat down on a folding chair, rested his head against the wall and closed his eyes.

'You go and get the police,' he said. 'I'll wait here.'

CHAPTER 13

On 17 July 2007, Tim's brother, Ébano, was alone at the research station, busy putting up a sign saying *Belem Health Project* above the entrance to the garden, when a *branco* walked past the barracks and continued in his direction. Two days previously, Tim and Storm had travelled to a conference in Conakry and they had asked Ébano to keep an eye on the place in their absence, but they had forgotten to tell him they were expecting a VIP. For a moment Ébano watched the man coming towards him with confusion before he climbed down, wiped his hands on his trousers and held it out to the stranger. The man asked for Kristian Storm and Ébano told him that Tim and Storm were away. 'Oh, what a shame. I'm only here for three days and I'd hoped to meet Storm. We're old colleagues,' the man explained. 'My name is Pedro, and you are?' Before Ébano had time to say anything, Pedro had walked through the gate and continued across the research station's small courtyard garden. Ébano hurried after him. Pedro wanted to know all sorts of things. Where did they store the blood samples and which chest freezers were protected against power cuts? Which stat- istical analysis programs did Storm use and how did he store the empirical data? Ébano could remember most of what

Tim had told him and answered the questions to the best of his ability.

'So you're not a member of the academic staff?' Pedro asked. He sounded surprised.

'No,' Ébano said. 'But my brother went to university in London and works for Kristian Storm. Tim Salomon. Do you know him?'

'Tim Salomon? Yes, of course. He's a bright guy,' Pedro said, and continued, 'But you seem like a bright guy, too. Why didn't you go to university?'

'Tim was the best in our school,' Ébano said, 'so he got a scholarship.'

'Aha,' Pedro said, and invited Ébano to the A Pérola restaurant. Ébano could pick whatever he liked from the menu, and when he had eaten his way through several courses and drunk a fair amount of imported beer, the *branco* asked, 'What do *you* dream about? If you could have anything you wanted?'

'Dream about?' Ébano said, and mulled it over. 'My own cashew plantation. A big one with lots of workers. I'm good at cultivating the soil. But it'll be a long time before I'll be able to afford it.'

'Why don't you ask your brother for help? I imagine he makes good money at the research station. Or does he just rake it in and leave you to struggle?'

'Oh, no,' Ébano said, and burst out laughing at the *branco's* misconception. 'Tim is a good man. He helps me whenever he can. Like now, with the sign I was putting up today. He gave me seven hundred CFA francs for the carpenter, but said I could keep the rest if I could find it cheaper. Tim has never let me down.'

Pedro asked if Ébano fancied making some extra money. Ébano said that he did.

'I'll pay you a hundred and fifty thousand CFA francs every month,' Pedro said.

A hundred and fifty thousand CFA francs every month! It was an unimaginable sum for a plantation worker.

But once Ébano heard what Pedro wanted him to do, he turned the offer down. He didn't like Kristian Storm all that much, but even so . . . No. Besides, Storm did a lot of good for the Guinean community.

'Oh, like what?' Pedro was clearly surprised. Ébano explained how Storm had discovered that one of the vaccines recommended by the WHO was harmful, and that he was now doing everything in his power to save the lives of Guinean children.

'That's a whole lot of nonsense,' Pedro said amicably. 'I've been following Storm's work for years and I know that he's barking up the wrong tree. The WHO saves millions of lives, and only a blind fanatic like Storm would claim otherwise. Incidentally, not that many people take Storm seriously, these days, you know. That was actually what I came here to talk to him about, one friend to another. Storm needs to start watching his otherwise excellent professional reputation.' Pedro suddenly looked worried. 'Is your brother a bit naïve? Yes, forgive me for asking, but I think it would be a real shame for him to waste his considerable talent. But you must do what you think is right, of course. I imagine there are others in Bissau who would like to earn a hundred and fifty thousand CFA francs a month.' Pedro winked at Ébano and handed him his card. 'Anyway, why don't you think it over?'

Pedro ordered another couple of beers and asked for the bill. Ébano's head was spinning.

Six months later, in January 2008, Ébano was asked if he would like to work full-time as security man, bodyguard and caretaker at the Belem Health Project. Storm had hired a new statistician, Berit Dahl Mogensen, and she had threatened to fly straight back to Denmark if Storm did not improve security immediately. Ébano took the job and Storm had a small porter's lodge built for him near the main entrance to the station. Silas had drowned before Christmas and Tim was devastated. That was the price you paid for making friends with the *brancos*.

Being Berit's bodyguard was hard work. Every day Ébano followed at her heels and every night he had to make sure that the place was safe and locked up. At the same time he had to learn lots of other tasks: cleaning, shredding paper, putting new documents in binders and making sure that the cisterns of the toilets at the research station were full and that all storerooms were well stocked. For doing all that he was paid 125,000 CFA francs per month.

Ébano complained to Tim, but Tim got angry and said that Storm paid his people well and, more importantly, on time *every* month, in contrast to the Guinea-Bissau government. As far as Tim was aware, the local doctors had not been paid for over two months now and they made only 75,000 CFA francs a month. But Ébano was welcome to look for another job, Tim had said, sounding annoyed on Storm's behalf.

Ébano got angry. He hated being patronised by his younger brother, who had been lucky enough to have a full scholarship to London fall into his lap. How dare he side with the *brancos* against his own brother who had worked his arse off, first in the plantations and now as Storm's errand boy? Besides, Tim made much more money than Ébano, so it was easy for him to be blasé. However, in contrast to Ébano, Tim never spent any of his money because he didn't drink and he never went out. All he cared about was his research and trying to impress Storm. Ébano, on the other hand, was desperate for cash. He wanted to buy his own plantation and build something up, something that would support him rather than him having to toil for others.

That night Ébano rummaged around his belongings and found the white man's business card. Their collaboration began soon afterwards. Easy little jobs, almost innocent.

One week Ébano was told to disconnect the chest freezers for four hours; the next week he started a fire in the garage when the cars were out. One day he got a luxury assignment: he had to pretend to be a professor at Universidade Colinas de Boé and join the board of a Japanese pharmaceutical company. Ébano was sorely tempted to show Tim his smart leather briefcase with the letter confirming his appointment, with the name *Sixan Pharmaceuticals* embossed on the first page. Why study for years if it was this easy to become a professor and join the board of a pharmaceutical company?

An ugly, pockmarked Senegalese man, who refused to give his name, communicated Pedro's various jobs to Ébano, but it took Ébano only half an hour to discover that this man's name was Ibrahima N'Doye and that he was the hired muscle for the American Representative Office in Bairro de Penha. Underestimating Ébano had been a mistake.

Ébano had been working for Pedro just a few months when he had enough money to buy a small plot of land. He showed it to Tim with a wide grin. Tim wanted to know how he had got the money and Ébano said he had saved up. Tim flung his arms around his big brother and told him he was proud of him. Ha, Ébano thought. It was the easiest money he had ever made. He didn't even have moral scruples when he let Ibrahima N'Doye into the research station to attack Berit in the living room. Ébano sat outside the house playing dice with the neighbouring security guards while the attack happened; besides, Ibrahima N'Doye had promise not to hurt Berit.

When Berit flew back to Denmark, Storm asked Ébano to travel with him to the province to help him collect data and Ébano was too scared to say no. First, Tim had said that Storm was very pleased with him and planned to give him bigger and more interesting jobs if he handled this one well, and second, Ibrahima N'Doye had given him orders from Pedro to go with Storm without 'fucking anything up'. N'Doye emphasised his words by pressing a knife against Ébano's throat. It would appear that Ébano's predecessor had 'fucked up'. The incompetent fool had been so indiscreet that first Silas and later Berit had become suspicious.

'And that's why neither Silas nor that other fool is alive any more. Do you understand, *buro*? And Berit should thank her lucky stars that she left of her own accord.'

N'Doye's revelations shocked Ébano. He had never really liked Silas, but Silas had been a good friend of Tim, and Ébano started to wonder if he should come clean with his brother.

But the days passed and he said nothing, partly because he was reluctant to give up his well-paid work for Pedro but also because it was impossible to get through to Tim once they had left to carry out the survey. Tim and Storm spent all their time engrossed in discussion about why the child mortality rate in the Dulombi-Boe area was so low, lower even than in Denmark. They simply could not understand it. Ébano could understand it perfectly well because every night, when the others were asleep, he changed the entries in the medical records. It took him only five minutes.

In the autumn of 2009, when Ébano had worked at the Belem Health Project for eighteen months, Storm returned to Bissau to carry out what he called the 'the absolutely final survey trip'. Once more, Ibrahima N'Doye ordered Ébano to accompany his boss to the Dulombi-Boe area, and Ébano did so, but again unwillingly. The rainy season was nearly over and Ébano needed to plant his land. Instead he was faced with the prospect of several months in the back of beyond with Storm and Tim, and matters did not improve when Tim had to leave the survey prematurely when he was offered a place on a PhD course at Yale University. Suddenly Ébano found himself alone with Storm. Storm, who went to bed early, Storm who never touched a drop of alcohol, Storm who had nothing on his mind other than his medical records, yet was still so dumb that he failed to spot the sabotage Ébano had managed to carry out with something as simple as an eraser. The days passed at a snail's pace and for once Ébano had to agree with Storm: it would absolutely have to be the last survey.

When the team finally returned to Bissau in the middle of February, Ébano was both exhausted and desperate. None of his schemes had got him anywhere near the medical records for even ten seconds. Storm had slept with them, taken them to the lavatory and kept them constantly within his reach. When Ibrahima N'Doye came to pay Ébano and wanted to know how things had gone, Ébano lied and said that everything had gone according to plan and that the medical records had been destroyed. There was nothing for Pedro to worry about.

One week later, Storm flew back to Copenhagen, and three weeks later, all hell broke loose.

Ébano was reading in his porter's lodge when Ibrahima N'Doye opened the door and brandished a knife at him. Ébano was taller and stronger than Ibrahima N'Doye, but Ibrahima still inflicted a deep cut across Ébano's stomach.

Pedro had heard rumours that Kristian Storm had made it to Copenhagen with a complete data set and had been given the green light for a publication that could ruin everything. 'Do you understand, *tarpasêro*? Ruin *everything*.'

Soon afterwards, Pedro ordered Ébano to Denmark. Ibrahima N'Doye organised his passport, ticket and visa; the latter was granted on the basis of an invitation from Stanford University, which requested the presence of Professor Ébano at a conference on human trafficking in Copenhagen on 16 March.

'Tell me, how long can I expect to be away?' Ébano asked.

'That depends on how quickly you do your job,' Ibrahima said.

'Yes, but it says here I'm not flying back until June.'

'That's because Pedro doesn't trust you, Ébano. But as soon as Pedro is happy, you can go home.'

Ébano thought about his fields. If he did not start planting soon, the trees would not grow sufficiently robust before the next rainy season started. 'I won't stay there for three months,' he insisted. 'I'm telling you.'

'You don't have a choice, *tarpasêro*.' Ibrahima took out his flick knife and started playing with it, but without opening it.

'What am I meant to do in Copenhagen?' Ébano said.

'We'll tell you later. It's easy,' Ibrahima said.

'How much will you pay me?' Ébano asked.

Ibrahima grinned. 'Since when do you get paid for clearing up your own mess? But you know Pedro. If he's happy, he'll pay you well.'

'And if I refuse to go?' Ébano said.

'Then I will stick my knife a little deeper into you,' Ibrahima said, and plunged the closed weapon into Ébano's stomach before he left.

In the transfer hall at Lisbon airport, a stranger came up to Ébano and handed him an envelope with instructions for the job Pedro wanted him to do. Ébano almost panicked when he realised that the job was killing Storm and making it look like suicide. There was a note in Danish in the envelope, which Ébano was meant to leave by the body. In addition, both the original medical records and Storm's computers with potential copies must be destroyed. The envelope also contained three thousand Danish kroner in cash and a reversed-charges telephone number, which he could ring in an emergency. When the job was done, Ébano would be sent an electronic ticket so he could get back to Guinea-Bissau.

It was freezing cold when Ébano arrived in Denmark and he had to spend five hundred kroner on a thick jacket. How would he make Pedro's cash last? On the first night he tried sleeping on a bench to save money, but it was no good. He would be ill unless he slept indoors. He found the Guinean community club in Copenhagen, three smoky rooms in Mysundegade. The Guineans welcomed him warmly, especially when Ébano explained that he was a professor from the university in Bissau and had come to Denmark to work with the world-famous immunologist Kristian Storm – did they know him? They did not, but they were very impressed. Most educated Guineans had to start again when they came to Denmark, the oldest Guinean told him, taking jobs in abattoirs, even though they were bookkeepers, or clean public toilets, although they were bakers.

'You do us great honour, *nha ermon*,' they said, and Ébano glowed with pride.

Ébano found a hotel near the Guinean club that he could afford. It was called Hotel Nebo. After giving the receptionist his passport to put in the hotel safe, he was about to pay with Pedro's cash, but instead he handed her a credit card he had found in Tim's desk drawer in Bissau, just to see if it worked. It did, and suddenly he had plenty of cash. That same evening, he dined out for over five hundred kroner on his younger brother's credit card and the next day he hired a car. He showed them Tim's international driving licence, which he had found with the credit card. Again everything went smoothly. The car was brilliant and Ébano enjoyed driving it around Copenhagen. It was warm and comfortable and it even had tinted windows so he could sit inside it undisturbed and watch life in Denmark. Ébano turned up the radio and thought about his future. Maybe he would even be able to build a house on his land with the money Pedro would pay him.

Ébano began by observing Storm's daily routines. Every morning at nine o'clock Storm would park his bicycle outside the Institute of Biology and, after a chat with a caretaker, he would disappear inside the building. Then the world's dullest day would start for Ébano, who had a full view of the institute from a parking bay diagonally opposite. Except for fetching his lunch from the refectory around noon, Storm would appear to spend all his time in his office, which overlooked the University Park, and he did not leave until the lights in the other windows had long been switched off.

Ébano spent the endless hours in the car wondering if Tim was even aware that he had left Bissau. They had not had much contact while Tim had been doing his PhD course at Yale, so Ébano did not think so. This was how it had become whenever Tim was abroad. He would forget all about Ébano. Come to think of it, Tim had emailed him only twice, once to apologise for his untimely departure from the Dulombi-Boe survey and to hear if it had been completed without any problems, and again to let him know that a parcel containing spare parts was on its way from Denmark and that Ébano was to give it to the engineer who was coming to look at a defective cooling system. That was all. When Tim was home, it was another story. Then he would constantly give Ébano jobs to do.

The problem wasn't that Ébano minded helping Tim, because he always had done. He had made sure Tim didn't get beaten up at school and talked him into coming with him on dangerous adventures so he didn't completely lose the respect of the other boys. When Tim returned from London with his fancy education, Ébano had even introduced him to his friends and got his brother a job at a cashew plantation. Ébano wanted to help Tim. But he no longer wanted to help Storm: the more he thought of it, the more he was convinced that Storm exploited both of them.

What was the likelihood that Ébano would ever get interesting work that matched his intelligence? It was just something Storm had made Tim believe in order to make Ébano work even harder. And what was the likelihood that Tim would ever get a senior position as a scientist? Tim would always be second-in-command, if not to Storm, then to the next white scientist who showed up backed by money from a rich country. Pedro had called Tim naïve, but Ébano was not like his brother.

Finally, the light was turned off in Storm's office and shortly afterwards Ébano saw Storm fumble with his bicycle lights. It was dark and deserted outside the faculty and Ébano was angry. He could easily have killed Storm there and then, but he had been ordered to make it look like suicide. At that moment, Storm leaped onto his bicycle and disappeared across the large car park.

When an exhausted, furious and frustrated Ébano returned to Hotel Nebo, the receptionist wanted a word with him. His credit card had been declined, the receptionist said, so they needed another card or cash as security.

'No problem,' Ébano said. 'I have another card upstairs in my room. I'll just go and get it.'

Back in his room he quickly packed his few belongings. Denmark was insanely expensive and he had just two hundred kroner left of the three thousand Pedro had given him. He did not know what to do without Tim's credit card. He opened the window. His room was on the first floor, so it was a long way down to the dark, narrow courtyard. Fortunately, there was a shed in the adjacent courtyard, and when Ébano had sat on the windowsill for a while to steel his nerves, he pushed off. He landed hard on the edge of the shed. He scrambled across the roof and leaped down into the neighbouring courtyard. Someone shouted, but he did not turn; a few seconds later he had scaled an iron gate and was heading down a side street, away from Hotel Nebo. He had got away – but his passport was still in the hotel safe. How would he now get back to Bissau?

He walked to the Guinean club in Mysundegade where he was instantly invited inside by the men who were still hanging out there. 'Tell us about your research,' one of the men said, when Ébano had been given a cup of coffee. Ébano told them and they listened with awe. It turned out that in fact one remembered Kristian Storm because a relative of his had taken part in one of the very first surveys back in 2004, and Ébano smiled and said he had better be going because his first lecture was at eight o'clock the following morning. 'Tell me, where are you staying?' the oldest man wanted to know and Ébano replied that he was at Hotel Nebo, but that the university was looking for more permanent accommodation for him because it looked likely that he would be staying in Denmark for a while. The old man said that he was always welcome to stay with him, and Ébano nearly accepted, but checked himself. The men must never know that he had lied.

He slept in the back of his car that night. The next morning he woke up, achy and miserable. He had to get Pedro to send him a new passport because he wanted to go home to Guinea-Bissau *now*.

He drove from Vesterbro to the university, parked the car across from the Institute of Biology and began his wait. He nodded off several times, but so what? Storm wasn't doing anything but sit in his office; it was enough to drive anyone crazy. As evening approached, the faculty gradually became deserted and Ébano saw the lights in the wing facing the park go out one by one.

All the time, he kept thinking that Storm was a conman who exploited Guinea-Bissau. He hadn't fully understood what Pedro had told him about the vaccines, but Storm got his money from Denmark and any idiot knew that Danish money was worth far more than the Guinean currency. Even so, Storm had always paid both him and Tim according to Guinean standards. Storm must have pocketed the difference himself – it was obvious now. And what was his lousy excuse? That he saved thousands of children from dying from vaccines. But that was a lie. Ébano and Tim's mother had been one of thirteen children and seven of them never made it past their fifth birthday because the vaccines had only just been introduced to their country. Their mother had told them this and that was the reason she had always made sure that Ébano and his brothers and sisters were vaccinated at the health centre. What Storm was doing was a crime and, thanks to the ignorant governments of absurdly wealthy countries, he was becoming filthy rich in the process.

With that thought in his mind, Ébano put on a pair of rubber gloves and grabbed the plastic bag with the rope he had bought. Then he found the entrance to the Department of Immunology. It was almost eight o'clock and the Institute of Biology lay in silent darkness. First he would get that business with Storm out of the way and then he would destroy the records, both the Guinean medical records in the box and the information on Storm's computer. He was shaking now.

When Ébano suddenly appeared in the doorway to his office, Storm looked shocked. For a moment, he had no idea what was going on.

'Ébano! What on earth ...? Has something happened? What's wrong?' Ébano closed the door behind him, and Storm took fright. Everything happened very quickly. Storm reached for the telephone, but Ébano made it to his desk in two quick strides. He twisted Storm's arm hard behind his back and grabbed the plastic bag with the rope.

'Whoever is paying you,' Storm cried out in desperation, 'I'll pay you three times as much.'

Storm's words made Ébano see red. Why did white men always think they could buy Guineans? He tipped the rope out onto the floor and put the plastic bag over Storm's head. It took three minutes and it felt like three hours.

Afterwards he felt completely empty and needed time to recover. He looked at the pictures on Storm's wall, and when he discovered the photograph of Storm between Silas and Tim, rage welled in him again. Tim had been too trusting and Storm had tricked him well and good. Ébano snatched the photograph and flung it onto the floor.

Ébano spotted a Guinean *pano* on the wall and took it down. This would be much better than the rope. It was a symbol that would make people think that Storm had committed suicide by hanging himself in a traditional cloth from the country he had exploited. Storm was tall but lean, and Ébano managed to string him up, in a noose he made from the *pano*, without much effort. Then he left the note on the desk. He panicked when he couldn't see the medical records, but then he spotted them: the familiar box was on the floor under Storm's desk. He followed the instruction from Lisbon to the letter and deleted first all the data on Storm's PC tower and then on his laptop. When that was done, he opened the door and listened out, but the department was quiet. His orders were to destroy the medical records, but how? At that moment he noticed a shredder, like the one Storm had in Bissau. It was in a room across the corridor with two photocopiers and shelves of office stationery. Ébano entered the printer room and closed the door behind him. The shredder was terribly loud, but it took him less than two minutes to destroy the medical records. The paper strips disappeared into a bag and out of Ébano's life.

By now he was desperate to leave and it was not until he was outside in the dark area in front of the institute that he was finally able to breathe properly. He chucked the rest of the *pano* and the unused rope into a nearby bin, but had second thoughts and fished them out again. No evidence, Ibrahima had said.

In the days that followed, Ébano called the reversed-charges number he had been given several times, but every time a recorded message informed him that the call had been declined. Over the weekend, Ébano's desperation grew. He needed a new passport and a new plane ticket so that he could fly home.

On Sunday afternoon he went to the Guinean club in Mysundegade where a cleaner told him that no one ever visited on a Sunday. Ébano was tempted to ask if he could please come in anyway, but was too scared. Everything was going down the toilet. By now he should have returned the hire car, but he couldn't do that since the credit card had been declined and he ended up parking the car in a deserted street far from the city centre. He used it only for sleeping in because it was just a matter of time before the police started looking for it. He had practically no money left and it was not until Monday when people started frequenting the Guinean club again that he had a proper meal because one of the men invited him home for supper.

On Wednesday morning Ébano finally got hold of Pedro.

'Why the hell do you keep calling me?' Pedro rebuked him. 'Don't you know it's important to lie low for at least a week? Until everything calms down. Stay put, you idiot. And you really are an idiot. I told you to destroy the medical records, not leave them to be found in the university basement six days later. I know that the Guinean police are useless, but Danish police officers aren't imbeciles, so there's a real risk that the medical records are now lying in neat strips at a police station.'

'How do you know?' Ébano exclaimed.

'Because I called the Department of Immunology to express my condolences at the death of Kristian Storm,' Pedro said, 'and I learned that the medical records had been found in a recycling container in the basement. I also learned that Marie Skov, Kristian Storm's fellow author, has been on sick leave all year and hasn't been seen at the faculty since she defended her master's last September. So how the hell do you know that Storm didn't send her a copy of his data? I want you to find Marie Skov's computer.'

'But how do I do that?'

But Pedro had already hung up and Ébano had not even had time to say that he needed a new passport.

Ébano was reluctant to return to the Faculty of Natural History, but fortunately the secretary at the Department of Immunology was away, so Ébano was directed to a secretariat in a completely different building, far away from Storm's office. Here he introduced himself as Tim Salomon and got Marie Skov's address and telephone number without any problems.

Afterwards he sat on a bench and suddenly missed Tim terribly. It had been great when Tim had returned from his studies in London, proud and optimistic, but nothing had worked out the way Ébano had imagined. And now here he was. All alone.

He had to track down Marie Skov, but how would he find out if she had Storm's data? And how would he get his hands on it? This was risky. He had never met her in Bissau, and he knew nothing about her. What if she lived with a towering Viking husband and four giant dogs on Ingeborgvej? Ébano was terrified of dogs.

Then it occurred to him to send her a section of Storm's *pano* in the shape of a noose. Marie Skov would almost certainly put the two *pano* fragments together, get the message and keep her mouth shut. Ébano took the *pano* and tore off another strip. He found a post office and posted the *pano* noose. He called Pedro the same day to tell him what he had done, but Pedro didn't answer his call on the Thursday or the Friday.

On Friday evening Ébano was hanging around a *shawarma* bar near Copenhagen Central Railway Station where he ate scraps of food that people had abandoned on the tables outside. Eventually the owner noticed him and Ébano slunk away. Suddenly he spotted Tim in a crowd on the pavement. It really was him! He walked past Ébano and he was holding hands with a girl who must be Guinean, as far as Ébano could make out from the bright yellow scarf peeking out behind Tim. Ébano's heart skipped a beat. Tim must have wondered what had happened to his brother. Tim had decided to look for him. Bring him home. Everything would be all right now. But Tim didn't see him. He had eyes only for the girl – he was completely mesmerised by her. And she wasn't Guinean at all, Ébano could see that now, but white, and she had no eyebrows. Ébano felt dazed as he watched them disappear down the street.

That same night, he made his way to Marie Skov's home and forced his way into the house through a window in the basement. He was starving and in the kitchen he ate meatballs and sausages from the fridge before he searched high and low for copies of the medical records, but found nothing. Neither did he find Marie Skov's laptop. Finally, out of sheer desperation, he tried setting fire to the house by lighting some cardboard boxes in the garage, but he could not make them burn properly. Before he drove away, he smashed two windows of the 4x4 vehicle parked outside.

Five days in hell followed. Pedro didn't answer his phone and Ébano wandered from phone booth to phone booth. He had run out of money and was forced to beg in the street and steal food wherever he could. The only place he was met with kindness was the Guinean club in Mysundegade where he stopped by every night to say hello. His clothes needed washing, as did he, but the men there did not seem to notice. They were always welcoming and one of them even asked Ébano if he would like to meet a grandchild, who wanted to be a nuclear physicist and study in London. Wasn't that where Ébano had studied? Ébano said that he would love that.

Tuesday afternoon Pedro finally picked up the phone and was suddenly very obliging. Of course he would get Ébano a new passport. Things had calmed down, he said, and the case had been filed as suicide. As soon as Ébano had got hold of Marie Skov's copies of the medical records, he could fly home. Ébano argued that he had searched her house, but that the medical records were not there. 'Oh,' Pedro said, 'but you did find her laptop, didn't you?' Ébano did not dare do other than tell him the truth. Suddenly Pedro no longer sounded quite so friendly. He said that Marie Skov had been in contact with Terrence Wilson, the editor of *Science*, and convinced him that she had a copy of the medical records and that, as a result, Wilson would have to give her some column inches for his next issue.

'So go back to her house and search it properly. Steal her handbag, find her laptop, whatever it takes. And when you have done that,' he added, 'you can come home. Your money is already waiting for you in Bissau. Ten million CFA francs in an envelope, which will be handed to you the moment you land.'

'Ten million?' Ébano could not believe his ears.

'Yes, because you've done a really great job, Ébano,' Pedro said warmly.

Ébano returned to Ingeborgvej for a second time and parked a short distance from Marie Skov's house. At first glance it looked empty and Ébano could not see the expensive car anywhere. Then he spotted a woman inside the house. A cleaner, he realised, as he came closer and saw that she was dusting. Ébano rang the doorbell and forced his way into the hall when she opened the door. He introduced himself using Tim's name and title and said he was meeting Marie.

'I don't see how that can be,' the cleaner said, 'because Marie has moved out.'

Ébano was about to force his way further inside the house when someone appeared on the steps behind him. It was the postman and the cleaner said something to him in Danish in a shrill voice. The postman told Ébano kindly, but firmly, to leave. Ébano had no reason to stay, anyway, because he had had time to see the address on a large envelope lying on a chest of drawers in the hallway. *Marie Skov*, it said. *Randersgade 76, 2100 Copenhagen Ø*.

Ébano drove straight to Randersgade and parked opposite Marie Skov's stairwell. Suddenly he was overcome by exhaustion and sorely tempted to give up. He had imagined this trip to be a nice easy earner, but now he had spent more than two weeks in Denmark. And he was freezing cold.

He had to rest, just one or two hours in the car, so he could think straight and make plans.

He had just settled down on the back seat when he spotted the girl Tim had been engrossed in outside the railway station last Friday. It was definitely her. Same petite build, same bright yellow scarf. She emerged from Marie Skov's stairwell and stopped momentarily to press buttons on her phone. Then she slipped the mobile into her pocket and, if it hadn't been for the car's tinted windows, he would have been discovered because she looked straight at him. Then she disappeared down the street with rapid footsteps.

The girl with the yellow scarf was Marie Skov. Tim's girlfriend.

It knocked him for six.

Ébano drove down Randersgade and parked further down the street. Then he slumped over the wheel. If he killed Tim's girlfriend, he and Tim could no longer be brothers. He would have to spy on Marie, just like he had spied on Storm, and snatch the medical records one day when she was not at home.

Ébano watched Marie's block all Thursday. He could not find anywhere to park and ended up sitting on the bottom step of number 93, from where he had a clear view of Marie Skov's front door. It was not until a young guy demanded to know what Ébano was doing there that he had to abandon his observation post. At that moment a parking space became available on the corner of Randersgade and Ébano fetched and parked the car so he could watch the entrance from the back seat without being seen. Absolutely nothing happened. A couple of times he saw Marie look out of the window, but she never left her flat. Late in the afternoon, Ébano suddenly spotted the 4x4 whose windows he had smashed less than a week ago. The glass had been replaced, but he was still convinced that it was the same car. Ébano craned his neck and saw a small boy jump out of the 4x4 and disappear into Marie Skov's stairwell.

One hour later Ébano had to stretch his legs and get something to eat. He was lucky and found a supermarket nearby with fruit and vegetables displayed outside; he stole some apples and oranges. When he was back in the car, he saw Marie in the window again, glancing anxiously up and down the street. When it started to grow dark, he gave up. He would have to come back the next day and hope that she was going out. He didn't want to hurt her, but he was losing patience. All he could think of was getting home to Bissau.

He drove back to Vesterbro and parked close to the Guinean club, his mood now much improved at the prospect of a bite to eat and a good chat with his own people.

'Professor Ébano,' the old man said, stretching out his arms. 'Welcome.' A pot had just been put on the table and Ébano ate hungrily from the plate, which was put in front of him. The old man cleared his throat. 'Professor Ébano, your brother has been here several times today asking after you. We told him that you were staying at Hotel Nebo and he went there to look for you. Since then he has been back twice, most recently an hour ago. He left you this note.' The old man gave Ébano a piece of paper. 'I hope it was all right that we told your brother where to find you.'

Ébano shook his head and got up.

'Won't you stay for a little while?' the old man asked. Everyone was looking at him.

'No, I have to go,' Ébano said, and retreated backwards out of the club.

He ran back to the car as he read the note from Tim.

My brother, my friend, I have paid your bill at Hotel Nebo and I have your passport. I'm staying at First Hotel on Vesterbrogade 23. I'll wait for you there. Love from your brother, Tim

Ébano clutched the note. *My brother, my friend.* Had Tim written this to entrap him? Suddenly Ébano had doubts. What if the police were waiting for him at the hotel? Had Tim taken sides and chosen Storm's? Or did Ébano still have time to explain to Tim that he had been wrong? That Storm suffered from white man's megalomania and was skimming off money that really belonged to Guinea-Bissau? Ébano wavered. He loved his brother, but he also loved his acquisitions. The plantation and the money to cultivate it. Then he caught sight of his own reflection in the tinted car windows. What had he really gained? A scrawny body and the beggar's loss of dignity. He looked briefly into his own eyes. Then he walked to Vesterbrogade.

Ébano had barely knocked on the door to Tim's hotel room before Tim tore it open. The two brothers stared at each other until Ébano averted his eyes. Then Tim dragged him into the room and slammed the door shut. 'What the hell have you done?' Tim screamed, and pushed Ébano into a chair.

'Storm is using you,' Ébano said. 'He makes a fortune saying vaccines kill children, but it's a big fat lie. Vaccines save lives and . . .'

Tim glared at Ébano in disbelief. 'Yes, of course vaccines

save lives,' he shouted. 'And Storm never ever claimed otherwise. Any idiot knows that vaccines are the most amazing thing to happen to global health. But we need the WHO to evaluate the DTP vaccine, yes, all vaccines. They have to admit that it's possible that vaccines have non-specific effects, which we have to deal with.'

'Storm is using you,' Ébano tried again. 'He—'

'Don't say another word,' Tim interrupted, and flopped down on the edge of the hotel bed. Ébano had never seen him so furious and disappointed.

'I know what you have done,' Tim continued. 'I got suspicious the moment I returned to Bissau and you weren't there. But I refused to believe it. I kept telling myself that my brother wasn't that heartless or that stupid. But when I kicked down the door to your house and found the contract between you and Sixan Pharmaceuticals in Tokyo and your visa papers for Denmark, my worst fears were confirmed. I pressed Nuno until he admitted that he had driven you to the airport. On the plane on my way to Denmark everything fell into place. *You* sabotaged our figures, *you* killed Silas, *you* took Storm from me—'

'I didn't kill Silas,' Ébano objected, 'that was the man who came before me.'

Tim ignored him. 'You made quite an impression on our brothers in Mysundegade, eh? Ébano the brilliant professor, the clever boy from Bissau, their pride. You're nothing but a killer, Ébano.'

Tim heaved a deep sigh.

Once again Ébano tried to explain to Tim what Storm had done to Guinea-Bissau, how he had defrauded Tim and lined his own pockets in the process. The words stumbled over each other, then petered out. Finally, there was silence in the cool hotel room.

Tim sat looking down at his hands and his face was tortured. 'You deserve the greatest possible punishment,' he said at length, and then he got up.

CHAPTER 14

'Ébano confessed to everything,' Tim said to Søren and Marie, 'and then he asked me if I could forgive him.'

'And could you?' Søren asked.

Tim smiled a pale smile.

'"If your brother sins, rebuke him; and if he repents, forgive him,"' he said wearily. 'The Gospel according to Luke. Our mother was a deeply religious woman. When Ébano had obtained my forgiveness, he grabbed his passport and did a runner. I haven't seen him since.'

'Who is Pedro?' Søren asked.

'I'm convinced it's Peter Bennett, a Nobel Prize winner and scientist who researches into vaccine constituents. Pedro is Peter in Creole,' Marie said. 'He left the board of Sixan Pharmaceuticals in February 2009, a few months before he joined the WHO's Emergency Committee, which was forced to sack two thirds of its members soon afterwards when it emerged that their relationship with the pharmaceutical industry was very far from disinterested. At the time Bennett did actually appear to be a good guy as he was one of the few scientists not to profit from the pandemic warning. But the truth was he was just twice as devious. By ensuring that Ébano officially took over his seat on Sixan's board, he could keep his position on the WHO's Emergency Committee without being suspected of corruption.'

Søren cleared his throat. 'Pardon me for asking, but what does that have to do with Kristian Storm?' he said.

'Sixan Pharmaceuticals is one of the world's biggest producers of aluminium hydroxide,' Marie explained. 'It's a constituent added to vaccines to heighten their antibody response. Whether it actually does or not is another matter. Nevertheless, that's Bennett's area of research.'

'But . . .' Søren said.

'Two thirds of the international pharmaceutical industry's aluminium hydroxide production goes to vaccines, including the DTP vaccine,' Tim said. 'And the DTP vaccine is given to more than a hundred million children a year. We're talking about a business worth billions.'

The police officer suddenly looked as if the penny had dropped. 'So Peter Bennett made a fortune out of the DTP vaccine,' he said.

'No,' Marie corrected him. 'Bennett and Sixan Pharmaceuticals made a fortune out of producing aluminium hydroxide, but given that vaccines are the biggest users of aluminium hydroxide in the world, it's in both Bennett's and Sixan's interest to preserve the status of all vaccines as the cash cow of medicine. Any negative re-evaluation would mean losses running into millions. That was why Bennett joined the WHO's Pandemic Emergency Committee. He needed to get close to the very people who ultimately held the purse strings. And he needed to silence Storm, who persisted in blowing the whistle.'

'And he succeeded,' Tim said in agony.

There was deep silence in the kitchen.

'It's so callous that I struggle to believe it,' Marie said.

When Tim had repeated his explanation at Bellahøj Police Station, and Marie had contributed any information she could, she and Tim said goodbye to Søren Marhauge and walked down Frederikssundsvej holding hands. It was close to midnight and they were shivering. Even so, Marie unbuttoned her jacket and let in the cold air. They did not say a word to each other until they reached the corner of Tagensvej and Jagtvej and the university came into view.

Tim stopped and cupped Marie's face with his hands. 'I'll never forget you,' he said. 'You will always be my friend.'

'Likewise,' Marie said.

Tim took a deep breath. 'I let Ébano go,' he confessed.

'That's what I thought,' Marie said.

A group of cyclists passed them and wolf-whistled.

'I loved Storm,' Tim whispered, 'but I couldn't sacrifice my brother. I bought him a ticket home and I put him on the plane. They can close every border, they can look for him all over Europe, but they won't find him. He's already in Bissau. I'm not asking you to understand, Marie, but I couldn't let him down.'

'OK,' was all Marie said.

'I'll be leaving tomorrow morning,' Tim continued.

'Tomorrow morning? But what about the article? And, besides, Søren Marhauge said that—'

'Søren Marhauge will be fine without me,' Tim said. 'And so will you. Send me the article on Sunday and I'll give you my comments, though I doubt I'll have any. Storm always said you're a perfectionist.'

'But . . .' Marie fell silent.

'The most important thing right now is the Belem Health Project. Storm had started investigating the different effects of vaccines on each sex and found evidence that the negative effect was gender dependent. More girls than boys die from side effects. I need to start writing a paper about that as soon as possible.'

'But what about *our* article?' Marie said. 'And Storm's?'

'No, Marie. It's your article. When you turn eighty and are awarded a Nobel Prize, think of me. That's all I ask.'

The tears started rolling down Marie's cheeks. 'It sounds almost as if you're saying goodbye.'

'I'm saying see you later, *Andurinha*,' he said, and kissed her. 'Visit me in Bissau and we'll go dancing.'

'I don't think I could—'

'You'll never see Ébano, Marie. I promise.'

When Marie let herself into her flat, she stood for a moment in the darkness and listened. The water pipe groaned, but apart from that it was quiet. She took a shower and made herself a cup of herbal tea. Then she climbed into bed. Suddenly she was sobbing. She could breathe without any difficulty so she knew she wasn't having a panic attack. She lay under her duvet, alone in her flat, crying until she had no more tears left. She had almost fallen asleep when her mobile rang. It was Jesper.

'Jesper?' Marie was alarmed. It was almost one thirty a.m.

'Hello, Marie,' he said.

Marie told herself she could hear the sea in the background. 'Is everything all right?'

'Yes, yes. Anton has eaten his own bodyweight in Easter eggs and all the kids fell asleep five minutes into the movie they'd been pestering us to be allowed to watch. Only I couldn't sleep.'

'What's up?'

'The police came to see me today. At the hospital. Superintendent Søren Marhauge. He wanted to talk to me about your mother's blood analysis.'

'Mum's blood analysis?'

'That's what forensic examiners call a blood sample they send to the Department of Forensic Genetics if they suspect something is amiss.'

'Right. So what does that mean?'

'They have found a substance in their analysis and they don't understand where it could have come from. An anaesthetic called propofol. I use it every day in surgery. What they don't understand is how it could have ended up in your mother's blood, and neither do I. It's used only in patients who have been admitted to hospital. But your mother hadn't been in hospital recently, had she?'

'No, I don't think so.'

'I get the impression that the police are investigating it.'

'But don't you think there's bound to be some perfectly logical explanation?' Marie said.

'I struggle to see what it could be,' Jesper said. 'I think now would be a very good time for Frank to tell us if Joan had been in hospital. A private clinic perhaps? And why? He's already in a very delicate situation and I think the police are trying to dig up as much dirt as possible, so if there is anything . . . anything at all they're ashamed of . . . Well, perhaps you should try talking to your dad about it. But . . . there was something else I wanted to tell you.'

'What is it?'

'Emily and I didn't work out. We had a row. Anton and I have been staying with Frans, a colleague from the ward, until it's safe for us to return to Ingeborgvej. Emily didn't come with us to West Jutland, either. It's over.'

'OK,' Marie said quietly.

'Is that all you have to say?' Jesper said. 'Are you in love with that other guy, is that it?'

'I'm very fond of Tim,' Marie said. 'I'm not in love with him.'

Jesper sighed. 'Please would you give me another chance? I know it's insane, but I haven't been able to sleep properly since I found out about you and . . . Tim. That has to count for something, doesn't it? I spoke to my brother about it and he agrees with me.'

'Agrees with you about what?'

'Lars says I've been a fool and that I should have been able to handle you being so ill.'

'Jesper,' Marie said gently, 'I have to get some sleep now. It's been a long day and . . . to tell you the truth, I don't want to give you another chance.'

'So you are in love!' Jesper burst out.

'It has nothing to do with anyone else, Jesper. It's about us. I like being who I am. A one-breasted biology nerd. Who is at least as ambitious as a man. And I don't think you know how to love someone like that.'

'But I love well-educated, ambitious women,' Jesper said, sounding astonished. 'You already know that.'

'In theory, yes. But in real life?'

'I don't understand you, Marie,' Jesper said.

'Precisely,' Marie said, with a smile. 'Good night, Jesper.'

On Saturday morning Marie stayed in bed when she woke up. She touched first her healthy breast and then her flat chest where the sick breast had been. The scarring was still a little swollen. Jesper would definitely have wanted her to have breast-reconstruction surgery immediately. But if she chose to do that, it would be because *she* wanted it and not because Jesper couldn't bear to look at her.

It was hard not to feel a tiny bit flattered at Jesper's pathetic attempt to give their relationship another shot. But it was also hilarious. Jesper in his rigid mind-set had come to the conclusion that their relationship could be made to work. Once upon a time she had been attracted to his dominance. That was a long while ago.

Marie got up, made tea and ate some muesli. Then she took her laptop and returned to bed. Tim's plane had taken off several hours ago and would soon land in Bissau and, if she knew him right, he would start planning work for the future first thing the following morning. Storm could not have wished for a better successor.

She was about to email him when she noticed an email from Søren Marhauge. It appeared to have been sent at three thirty a.m. She opened it and read it three times.

Søren wrote that her brother, Mads, had not died from

meningitis when he was three years old. He had died in an accident in their garden at Snerlevej.

A shocked Marie rang Lea immediately.

Julie and Michael were already at Snerlevej when Marie arrived. Julie opened the door, wearing an apron and sporting a new hairstyle that seemed to have involved curlers at some point. Marie gave her a hug. Emma and Camilla were watching television in the living room.

'Where are Dad and Michael?' Marie asked, and Julie pointed to the garden.

'They're fixing a hole in the roof,' she said, 'so hopefully the first floor won't be flooded before Easter is over.'

The table had already been laid, but was one setting short.

'I've taken care of everything,' Julie said happily. 'I made the bacon quiche and fried the meatballs yesterday, so they only need serving. And I've bought Easter eggs for everyone. What a shame that Jesper and Anton aren't with you. Couldn't they have gone to that cottage some other time? It seems all wrong that they're not here, don't you think?'

'Julie, Jesper and I are no longer together, so why did you invite him?'

Julie gave Marie a knowing look. 'Oh, so he hasn't said anything yet? Well, I'd better not say anything but, Marissen, you'll be ever so happy!'

'If you're hinting that he wants to give our marriage another chance, then he's already told me.'

Julie beamed with joy. 'Isn't it wonderful?' she said. 'I was so thrilled when he called yesterday to tell me he realised what a big mistake he'd made.'

'He called me last night, Julie,' Marie said. 'But I said no.'

'You said no?'

'I'm in love with someone else,' Marie said, 'and, besides, Jesper and I were never happy together.'

'But that's not true.' Julie was outraged. 'You've always been the perfect couple. The two of you . . . Who are you in love with?'

The doorbell rang.

Julie went to answer it. Seconds later she stalked through the living room and slammed the kitchen door shut behind her.

Lea entered the living room with red eyes. She wore tight leather trousers, high-heeled platform boots and a fairly transparent top. Her eyes were heavily made up, as usual, but she had removed the piercings.

Marie gave her a hug. 'Are you OK?'

'Not really,' she said, and the tears welled in her eyes again. 'I can't stop crying. But what's wrong with Julie? Didn't she know I was coming?'

At that moment, Michael appeared in the door to the garden. 'What's she doing here?' he said. 'Where's Julie?'

'Hello, Michael, you handsome beast.' Lea put on a brave face. 'And hello, Dad.'

Frank had appeared behind Michael, and Marie could see that he was already drunk. He balanced on the threshold and stumbled back out into the garden. It was not until Michael had gone to join Julie in the kitchen that Frank recovered his footing and came into the living room. Marie had never heard Lea call Frank 'Dad' before.

'Hello, Marizzen; hello, Loopy-Lou, sweetie,' he said, and

kissed them both on the cheek. 'What would the ladies like to drink? I have a fine Barolo.'

'Why didn't you tell Julie you'd invited me?' Lea asked.

'Ah,' Frank said, handing them each a glass of wine. 'Didn't I? It must have slipped my mind.'

Julie and Michael came into the living room.

'I'm sorry, Dad, but we're leaving,' Julie announced.

'Eh?' Frank said. He was busy pouring red wine into his own glass.

'Yes, it's her or us,' Julie said. 'You have to choose.'

'Well, then, happy Easter, everyone,' Lea said. 'Cheers.'

'Dad?' Julie said.

'But how can I—' Frank knocked over his glass, which broke, spilling wine across the sideboard.

Julie looked irritated, then summoned Emma and Camilla. They were watching one of Joan's old movies and didn't want to put on their coats.

'Come on,' Julie hissed. The girls got up reluctantly and went to the hallway.

'Wait,' Lea said. 'I'll leave.' Lea placed her glass on the dining table and looked at Marie. 'I should never have come.'

Frank was now drinking directly from the bottle. 'Oh, come on, girls,' he said. 'How about some Easter peace?'

And then Marie let out a roar. A strange, guttural sound, which made the whole gathering stare at her in shock. She roared on her entire exhalation. Total silence ensued. Marie filled her lungs with air again.

'Dad,' she said. 'I've received an email from the police stating that Mads didn't die from meningitis but in an accident in the garden. In the shed. The police say he died instantly and that Julie witnessed it. Is that right?'

Julie gasped and Marie's legs threatened to buckle under her.

'Bullshit—' Michael began.

'Be quiet, Michael,' Marie said, looking only at her father. 'Is that right, Dad?'

Frank put the bottle to his lips and emptied it in three large gulps. 'The police are lying,' he said, glancing at Julie.

'The police are lying?' Marie said. 'The original police report from the twenty-seventh of June 1986 is a lie?'

Frank glanced at Julie again and Marie looked at her elder sister. All the blood had drained from Julie's face and her mouth was a grey line. Then she exploded and threw Lea hard against the wall. 'You spoiled brat,' she screamed. 'This is all your fault. Why do you think I've kept it secret all these years? To protect you. So that no one would know you're a killer. I had to look after all of you the whole time. I was only gone for five minutes but, oh, no, you couldn't behave for just five minutes and Dad, well, he was asleep as usual. You killed our brother.' She pointed at Lea.

Julie marched to the hall and nearly knocked Michael over in the doorway. She turned to Frank. 'I'll never forgive you for this, Dad,' she then said.

Michael quickly followed Julie.

'Aren't we going to say goodbye to Grandad and Aunt Marie?' they heard Camilla ask.

'Not today, darling,' Julie said. The front door slammed.

Lea was leaning up against the wall. Marie walked up to her and flung her arms around her.

'Is that true?' Lea said. 'Oh, God, please tell me it's not true.'

'We can't possibly know, Lea,' Marie said, to comfort her. 'You know what Julie's like when she's angry. But, Lea, love, you're shaking all over.'

They heard the sound of a cork being pulled out of a bottle and Frank drinking straight from it. 'Julie's telling the truth,' he said. 'Only I wasn't asleep. My engineering studies were going down the drain, while your mum was more productive than ever. She wove one gloomy tapestry after another. But we needed her to make pretty things I could sell. We had a huge row about it. Your mum called me a loser who didn't know anything about art. Afterwards, I drank a beer to calm myself and then another. Finally, I went to lie down on a sun lounger in the garden. My plan was to revise for my exams. But I wasn't asleep. I heard Lea say that she wanted her dolly, which Julie had put on the shelving unit in the shed. I heard Julie say that Lea had to say sorry first. I heard the telephone ring inside the house. I heard Mads say, "Don't go in the shed, Lea. Please come out," and I heard Marie say, "I'm going to get Julie now." I'd told you kids a hundred times not to go into that shed! Suddenly there was a huge crash and I jumped up. Marie had fetched Julie and she was standing in the doorway to the shed. Then she screamed.' Frank clutched his head. 'Lea had managed to open the door to the shed and climb up on the workbench. How she did it, I've no idea. Julie had put her doll on the top shelf because Lea had been naughty. But there was no stopping Lea. She stood on the workbench clutching her doll and the shelving unit had toppled and was wedged against the opposite wall ... The toolbox had slipped down and hit Mads. It was too late.' Frank broke down.

The tears trickled down Marie's cheeks and Lea was now shaking so violently that Marie struggled to hold her. 'Why didn't you ever say something, Dad?' Marie sobbed. 'This is insane.'

For a moment, Frank stared vacantly into the air. 'We had to move on, Marie. Three small children and a mother who was already mentally unstable. I burned that shed to the ground. I removed everything that could remind your mum of Mads. She destroyed all the photos herself. We all started to feel better when we decided to forget about the accident . . . Julie was fantastic. She took care of everything. Even in those days, she organised your mum's pills and—'

'You let your eleven-year-old daughter organise Mum's pills?'

Frank looked down. 'Julie was better at it than I was.'

'Yes,' Marie said. 'She was forced to be, wasn't she? But, Christ, Dad, she was a child.'

'Julie loved looking after her mum. She was good at calming her down,' Frank slurred.

'What happened the day Mum died?' Marie asked.

'The tapestry wall-hanging . . . The one you couldn't find . . . Your mum found it in my office and went crazy. I must have told her that I sold it to Helsingør Town Hall for four thousand kroner. I don't remember anything about that, but it's probably true. So as to not upset her, you see . . . Of course no one ever bloody bought it!' Frank was now so drunk that he struggled to speak. 'I didn't want to listen to her any more, so I went into town. The next day she was dead.' He collapsed on a chair and slumped over the table.

For a long time no one said a word.

'I can understand if you hate me,' Lea said to Marie at last.

'I don't hate you,' she whispered. 'That shed should have been locked. Julie should not have been in charge of three young children. Dad should have roused himself from his drunken stupor. It's not your fault.'

They sat on the floor, listening to Frank snore. Then Marie got up. 'I'm really worried about Julie,' she said.

'I've always believed that Julie hated me and was punishing me for something,' Lea said into space. 'But she was protecting me all along.'

CHAPTER 15

It was almost midnight that Friday evening before Søren left Bellahøj Police Station. He offered to drive Tim Salomon and Marie Skov home, but they wanted some fresh air and he saw them disappear up Frederikssundsvej holding hands. It had taken Søren and Inge Kai almost three hours to get the whole story in place because, although Marie and Tim had supplemented each other very neatly, several pieces were still missing before the picture could be completed. Which made it all the more annoying that Ébano Salomon had dropped off the face of the earth. They had issued his description to every police station, border crossing and airport in Denmark, and Søren gave Ébano three days max. Then he caught himself hoping that, for once, he was wrong. Tim had wept over his brother and Marie had said, 'We mustn't forget that the real criminals are Sixan Pharmaceuticals and Peter Bennett. Storm would have said the same.' And she was right. Bennett had exploited a rejected brother's yearning for a better life.

Søren drove home. He had called Anna and left several messages, but her only response had been a text message in the late afternoon: *Leave me alone, Søren.*

It was over.

When he got home, Søren was starving but he had no appetite. He ended up reheating the leftovers from Anna and Karen's dinner the other night and washed them down with a cold beer. He sat in the kitchen for a long time without moving.

'I'm going to sprinkle some happiness on your house,' Anna had said, when she moved in.

'Our house,' Søren had corrected her.

'*Mi casa es tu casa.*' Anna had grinned and hung up a chain of colourful fairy lights over the kitchen window, bought shocking pink scatter cushions for the living room and chucked out a dead mind-your-own-business, in return for a promise always to buy fresh flowers. And she had done. Until recently.

'That's just how it is,' she had responded, when Søren had asked about the fresh flowers. 'At the start of a relationship, you make a huge effort. Then it becomes routine.'

'Oh.' Søren had been hurt. 'So I could have kept my plant, after all?'

'But why?' Anna had replied. 'It was dead.'

He decided that he had to be the problem. He was hard to love. He couldn't even keep a pot plant alive. Perhaps Anna had never loved him. Was that why he had had to reel her in like a stubborn perch? But if she really loved him, she shouldn't have needed convincing.

Søren, for example, had not needed convincing at all. He had just rolled over with all four paws in the air. He loved Anna just as much today as he always had. Even when she called him a monumental prat.

Søren took another beer from the fridge and walked down

the passage. He closed the door to Lily's room. Anna would have to come for her things one day when he was out. He leaned his forehead against the closed door and couldn't even cry. The pain was numbing. Suddenly he heard a noise and spun around.

The door to the bedroom opened and a sleepy-eyed Anna appeared in the doorway. She was wearing jeans and a T-shirt, and she scratched her head.

'Anna,' Søren exclaimed, stunned. 'I didn't think you were home.'

'Karen said I was chicken,' Anna said. 'She said it was beneath my dignity not to grab the bull by the horns. So I came home. Lily stayed with her.'

'Well, then, let me hear it,' Søren said bullishly. 'Get it over with.' Suddenly the devil got into him. 'Come on, I'll help you pack,' he said. 'I think we've got some boxes here.' He opened one of the built-in cupboards in the passage and found a box that had previously contained their new Hoover. 'Let's start in Lily's room. Afterwards you can rip out my heart. Will she be taking all her teddies?' Søren had turned on the ceiling light in Lily's bedroom and started throwing books, teddies and various objects into the cardboard box. 'Or do I get to keep one, so she has a teddy whenever she visits me – *if* she's allowed to visit me, that is?' Søren held the box under one of Lily's shelves and swept everything into it.

'What the hell do you think you're doing?' Anna screamed. 'Are you out of your mind?'

'Are you out of *your* mind?' Søren roared. 'We live together. We have Lily together. I love Lily! You promised this would never happen.'

Søren got ready to empty the next shelf into the box and braced himself for Anna's reaction. Napalm. But she did not say one word. She just stood there staring at him.

'What did I promise would never happen?' she said.

'You promised you would never stop loving me,' Søren said.

'I never, ever promised that,' Anna said.

'You promised you would not take Lily from me,' he added.

Søren had turned to the window where the curtains had yet to be closed. The front garden was dark, and hundreds of monsters and demons were waiting on the other side of the glass.

'But I still love you,' she said. 'I thought that you—'

'But please can we be friends?' Søren snarled. 'Spare me, Anna. I know that you screwed Anders T. I know he slept here. How can you stoop so low? A totally ridiculous poser who highlights his hair.'

Anna looked at him in shock. Then she started to laugh. 'Don't tell me you're jealous of Anders T.,' she said.

'And what if I am?' Søren yelled. 'I'm not done with you. I love you, Anna.'

Anna crossed Lily's room and went straight to Søren. 'Number one, you have no cause for jealousy,' she said, putting her arms around him. 'Because I love only you. And number two, Anders T. is gay.'

They made love on the floor in Lily's bedroom. Afterwards a small plastic ocelot was stuck in Anna's hair, but Søren decided not to say anything. They sat down in the living room and spoke without a break for two hours. Anna couldn't believe that Søren hadn't realised that Anders T. preferred men.

'He's about as gay as they come,' she said. 'Anyone could tell from miles away. He has a diamond stud in his right ear! I'm sure I told you!'

Last year Anders T. had discovered quite by accident that his boyfriend had cheated on him with a guy they both knew. Even so he had decided to give their relationship another try. Soon afterwards he learned that it was not the first infidelity and that his boyfriend was a notorious slut, who had screwed half of 'Cosy Bar', as Anders T. had put it.

'Anders T. then ended the relationship for good, but he was totally cut up about it. I didn't know him very well at the time, but that evening when we wrote the song for the head of the department's party, we drank some wine and he told me the whole story. At one point he produced a bag of cocaine and sniffed some. I had a bit, but I didn't like it. Partly because Anders T. kept lining up more, but also because of you. Imagine if someone had found out there had been drug-taking in your house. And, besides, Lily was at home at the time. "Don't be so such a prude," Anders said, before he finally accepted that I didn't want any. Since then he's denied that he's still doing cocaine, but I know that he gets off his face every weekend. That's why he feels like crap for the first three days of every week. Recently I had to inform our supervisor, and we agreed that I would make it clear to Anders T. that if he doesn't get his act together, he'll forfeit his PhD. The first twenty-four hours we were at his parents' cottage were OK, but then he got fidgety and kept wandering outside, and I'm not an idiot, am I? I gave him an ultimatum. Either he pulled himself together or it was the end of him and me working together. He went straight to our supervisor last Wednesday and I believe he's going into rehab somewhere on Fyn. He'll have to take leave, but at least there's a small chance that he might finish his PhD later. Meanwhile, I hope I can find a study partner who takes their work a bit more seriously.'

When Anna had finished, Søren told her about Henrik. About the missing bag of cocaine from the evidence room, about Jeanette's call and about the blood test from Lily's Hello Kitty woolly hat, which had confirmed Søren's worst fears.

'But that's massively illegal,' Anna said, and looked closely at Søren. 'Isn't there a risk you'll get into trouble as well? Now that you know he stole it?'

'Yes,' Søren said. 'But only if Henrik lets the cat out of the bag, and he won't. Besides, I can always deny it. No one knows I visited him in his new flat. I want to give him one last chance, Anna. Everyone deserves that.'

'I feel simply awful that I haven't called Jeanette,' Anna said. 'Trust me, I kept meaning to. But I thought she was busy nest-building, enjoying Henrik and her bump. Why on earth didn't she call us? I know we don't see them very much, but we're still friends.'

'I'm starting to believe they didn't see it that way,' Søren said.

'I'm going to call her,' Anna declared.

They sat for a while in silence.

'We need to talk about us,' Anna said at length.

'Yes,' Søren said.

They fell silent again.

'You go first,' Anna then said.

Søren cleared his throat. 'I think you've started to pull back,' he said. 'You keep finding excuses for going to the university or burying yourself in work when you're at home and Lily's in bed. It's hard not to see it as a sign that you're avoiding me. And surely you had a child so that you could be with her, and even though we've fallen into a routine, ultimately we're a couple because we want to be together, aren't we?'

Anna got up abruptly and closed the curtains.

'Please don't get angry,' Søren said. 'Not now.'

'But I *am* angry,' Anna said. 'Because I had Lily with the wrong man. I should have waited for you but . . . then Lily wouldn't have been Lily, would she? Fortunately you love her as if she were your own.'

'Yes, I do,' Søren said.

'Well, then, why isn't it OK for me to pull back a little? I'd been a single parent for years when I met you. Neglected my studies, put my career on the back-burner and gone to bed early every single Saturday night – yes, some might say, "Tough, that's what life's like when you choose to have a kid." But I never planned on being a single parent, did I? Thomas abandoned us without warning and moved to another country. Since then he hasn't taken on anything that looks remotely like serious responsibility, but now I have you and you love Lily unconditionally, she loves you and I love you both. That's wonderful. So I'm taking the opportunity to work hard. I can see that Lily is thriving and I thought that you adored being with her. I really want a career now. And I can do it, Søren. I'm good. That's all this is about. I want to be with you and I want this.' She pointed to her head. 'And I think that's OK. I give you my child, the most precious thing in my life, and the price you pay is that you take on half the work, and you do, more sometimes, so I don't really see what the problem is.'

'I think I've just been missing you,' Søren said. 'And I adore being with Lily.'

'But I've missed you too,' Anna said, and sat down next to him on the sofa.

'If that's how we feel, then why do we argue all the time?' Søren said.

Anna looked surprised. 'You think we do?'

'Yes,' Søren said. 'We argue far too much.'

'I rather like that we know how to argue,' Anna replied. 'Thomas was completely uptight. Every time I raised my voice, or felt anything that wasn't a hundred per cent positive, he'd shut down and practically give me a sedative. As if my temper was a disease. I love . . .' Anna thought about it '. . . I love that you're a real man who can still get a hard-on for me even though I'm angry about something.'

'That's one way of looking at it,' Søren said, with a grin. 'But even so, I don't want Lily to grow up with a mum and a dad who argue.'

'But why not?' Anna persisted. 'We always make up. And she sees that as well.'

They sat for a little while.

'Now it's your turn,' Søren said.

'I've been wondering if you're suffering from depression,' Anna said frankly.

'Depression?'

'Yes. Sometimes you sit there,' she pointed to the furthest dining chair by the window, 'staring out into the darkness, into nothing. And I don't think you're even aware of it. But you give off some seriously . . . bad karma. I've tried guessing what could be wrong and, of course, I thought I had something to do with it. We haven't had as much sex recently and usually that . . . Well, what I'm trying to say is, in the past whenever I've wondered if you were bored with me, I'd remind myself that you still fancied me. In the months before Thomas's sudden departure, we had no sex, and he seemed as if . . . he no longer fancied me. So I've been telling myself that no matter how stressed you seemed or how irritable you were, you were always interested in sex. But in the last few months you seemed to have lost interest. In fact, I was convinced that *you* had met someone. Especially after I met up with Jeanette last Wednesday. It sounds stupid, but I suddenly imagined that you and Henrik had set up some kind of bachelor pad where you partied all the time.'

Anna smiled at her own embarrassment.

'Being unfaithful to you would never even cross my mind, Anna,' Søren said. 'That time with Vibe was . . . different. I'm not the unfaithful type and I think even Vibe would agree with me on that. But I needed to end that relationship and . . .' Søren shrugged his shoulders. 'I'm not proud of what happened and it will never happen again. You mean far too much to me.'

'Then why aren't you happy?' Anna asked cautiously.

'But I am happy,' Søren said. 'I love living here with the two of you. I love that we're a family, but . . . You're right that something's nagging at me. Only I don't know what it is. A feeling that . . . I'm out of step with myself.'

Søren lay down on his back and folded his hands under his neck. Anna snuggled up to him.

'I have a confession to make,' she said, when they had been lying like that for a while.

'Now what?' Søren said, with bated breath.

'It's my fault that Lily got German measles. I forgot her booster vaccination when she turned four. I feel incredibly bad about it. How much of a crap mother are you allowed to be? Thomas will hit the roof if he finds out. He's very particular about such matters.'

Søren laughed.

'What's so funny?'

'Because for a moment I thought . . . Never mind.' Søren grew serious. 'You're not a crap mother, Anna Bella, and who gives a toss what Thomas thinks? He's not part of our life. Besides, German measles doesn't kill you. Or it doesn't at our latitudes,' he added.

They lay for a while in silence.

'What happened back then?' Søren asked at last. 'When Thomas walked out on you.'

'I don't know,' Anna said.

'You don't know?'

'No, and that's why it's so hard to talk about it.'

'Try,' Søren said.

Anna mulled it over for a while. Then she said, 'It was Christmas and Thomas's parents were visiting us from Jutland. We had a discussion about something and we disagreed strongly. I got worked up, but not half as much as I had done at least a thousand times before, when, for example, I'd been discussing politics with my dad, but enough for Thomas's parents to leave the next morning. In fact, I haven't seen them since and I don't think Lily has either. A few weeks later, Thomas got a job in Sweden and announced that we were no longer a couple. He said he couldn't live with my emotional meltdowns and I ought to seek professional help. I knew that he had grown up in a home where people were terrified of showing their feelings, but even so I was in shock. I begged him to change his mind. I lost eight kilos. I nearly died, or that was how it felt. But it was no good. I had broken some unwritten rule and made a fool of myself.' Anna half got up and cupped Søren's face in her hands. 'Love me for who I am, Søren,' she pleaded with him softly. 'I'm sorry I fly off the handle every now and again but, believe me, I really am trying to control my temper. I had no idea that it got on your nerves. Shortly after we'd started seeing each other, you said that your and Vibe's relationship had been far too restrained. You said you welcomed a relationship with more passion.'

'Did I really say that?'

'Yes,' Anna said.

'That was probably just a ruse to snare you,' Søren said, with a smile.

'Well, it worked,' Anna said, and settled down with Søren's arm around her once more.

Shortly afterwards, Søren got up and lit the fire in the wood-burner, and Anna fetched two glasses of wine from the kitchen.

'I'm working on this case,' Søren said, when she came back and they had made themselves comfortable on the sofa. 'At first we thought it was suicide, but it turned out to be murder. As part of the investigation, I've stumbled across a secret. This family lost a son in 1986. He died in a tragic accident in the family's back garden, in the shed, when a metal toolbox fell from a shelf and killed him instantly. However, his two younger sisters were told that he died from meningitis. They were only two and three years old when it happened and don't remember anything. Now, that has nothing to do with the case, at least not directly. The problem is that now I don't know whether to tell the two sisters the truth. I have a feeling that the whole family is constructed around that secret, and I'm frightened that I might do more harm than good by telling them what I've discovered. It's a nightmare.'

Anna sipped her wine. 'I'm probably the wrong person to ask,' she said, 'but perhaps that's why you're asking me.'

'What do you mean?'

'Because you already know my answer.'

They went to bed and snuggled up to each other. When Anna was asleep, Søren got up and sat down with his laptop.

Dear Marie,

Do you remember me telling you that I prefer to keep things separate? It is almost four o'clock in the morning and there is something I need to tell you. Not as a police officer, but as . . . your friend?

Your brother, Mads Skov, didn't die of meningitis. He died on 27 June 1986 in an accident in your parents' garden. In your father's shed. I have read the police report and I know that a shelving unit keeled over. A toolbox hit Mads on the head and killed him instantly. The police report states that Julie witnessed the accident. I have been wondering a great deal about whether you and Lea were there, but the report doesn't say. It was an accident, an utterly tragic and horrible accident.

Best wishes, Søren

Søren noticed that he had received an email from Klaus Mønster from the Department of Forensic Genetics. It had been sent just before six the previous evening.

Hi, Søren,

We have completed the DNA sequencing of the three hairs. I can't send you the final report, which includes the official forensic genetics statement, until Monday when everything has been double-checked, but I thought you would like to know the results now. The hairs stem from a woman who is related to Joan Skov, but they are not Joan Skov's own. So there you are. Good luck finding the owner.

Best wishes, Klaus

Søren opened the attachment while he drummed his fingers on the table. He had been hoping to take a day off tomorrow, but it looked like he could forget about that.

Just after noon the following day, Søren was sitting at his desk at Bellahøj Police Station, his heart four planets and a tank lighter than the day before. He printed out the report from the Department of Forensic Genetics and entered the DNA sequence into the police's DNA database. No match. When he had come to terms with his disappointment, he looked up Julie Claessen in the criminal records register, but there was no entry for her; neither was her DNA on file.

Next he looked up Lea Skov and here he was in luck. The entry related to a shoplifting incident in 1997. Lea and her friend had been out walking her friend's dog on Strandvejen and had come across an already broken shop window; the girls had nicked shoes and jeans and got fifty metres down the street before the police arrived. The girls had been taken to the station where a report had been made, their finger-prints taken along with pictures and a DNA sample, which was standard police procedure for minor as well as major offences, but even so Søren got the distinct impression that the duty officer had done this mainly to give the girls a warning fright. However, it meant that Lea Skov's DNA was registered in the police database.

Søren drummed his fingers on the table. The hairs originated from a woman who was related to Joan Skov, but he could eliminate Lea because she was in the register – they would have immediately matched her records when they ran the DNA from the strands. And it could not be Marie Skov because she was bald. At that moment his mobile rang. It was Jesper Just.

'Oh, hello,' Søren said, as he remembered the business card that Jesper Just had tossed into the bin. 'What can I do for you?'

'I couldn't sleep last night,' Jesper said, 'for several reasons, but partly because your people found propofol in my mother-in-law's blood. I've remembered something my brother-in-law asked me two months ago. It was about injections. He said he had noticed that doctors in TV series and in films always push a little fluid out of the syringes prior to injecting and he wanted to know why. My brother-in-law works in a hospital, but he's not the sharpest knife in the box, so ... Anyway, I explained to him that this practice is to prevent blood clots caused by air bubbles, and afterwards we spoke no more about it.'

'And now you're wondering why he wanted to know?'

'Yes,' Jesper said. 'In the light of ... Well, I don't know. It's dreadful even to suggest that my own brother-in-law ...'

'Thanks for your call,' Søren said.

When he had ended the call, he saw a text message from Marie: *Thank you* was all it said.

Søren sat for a moment, then called Inge Kai, but she did not answer. Forty-five seconds later she popped her head around his door. 'Peekaboo,' she said.

'I thought today was your day off,' Søren said.

'Funny, I thought the same thing about you,' Inge Kai said. 'And you would be right. But I couldn't sleep last night so I came to work early this morning to look into Peter Bennett. He's rich, powerful and doesn't give a damn about anyone. I'll die a slow, agonising death if he escapes justice.'

'We'll get him. We have Ébano's electronic ticket from Bissau to Copenhagen, the reversed-charges calls, the instructions from Ibrahima N'Doye. One day we'll be able to prove that Bennett hired Ébano to do his dirty work.'

Inge Kai shook her head. 'I've checked everything, lock, stock and barrel. The ticket was paid for in cash at a travel agency in Paris, but on the same day Peter Bennett gave a lecture at a university in the US, so unless Bennett can time travel . . . Even the visa invitation, which made it possible for Ébano to enter Denmark, can't be traced. I've just spoken to the head of the Centre against Human Trafficking and he was able to confirm that, on 1 March 2010, the centre did indeed receive a request from Stanford University to invite Ébano Salomon, professor in African-European human trafficking at the Universidade Colinas de Boé, to their conference, so they did. But that's just standard practice and no one knows who at Stanford made the request.'

'Right,' he said. 'Then we'll have to rely on Ébano's evidence when we catch him. How far can he have got? As far as Poland? The moment he tries to get into Germany, the trap will shut.'

'He's back in Bissau,' Inge Kai said.

'What?'

'His plane took off yesterday at twelve fifty-five, he changed in Lisbon and caught an evening flight to Bissau at twenty-two fifteen. It's all been confirmed.'

'But I thought he had no money,' Søren said.

Inge Kai looked at him under a raised eyebrow. 'Baby brother bought and paid for his ticket online from the computer in the airport two and a half hours before the plane took off.'

Søren was speechless. 'Tim Salomon sent his brother back to Bissau?'

'Yes.'

'Do you think Marie knows?'

'I'm sure she does.'

'They let him go?' Søren was livid. 'Ébano killed Storm. He tried setting fire to the house where Marie's ex-husband and son were asleep. Jesus Christ, he *stalked* Marie. He sent her a noose! And they let him go?'

Inge Kai said nothing.

'And you think that's all right?' Søren said indignantly.

'I think it's about catching and punishing the guilty,' she replied after a pause. 'That's why I joined the police force. Ébano is poor. Exploited. Disenfranchised. He did the deed. But is he guilty? I really don't know.'

'Well, we need to get Tim back to the station,' Søren said, slamming both palms on his desk.

'That's going to be a bit tricky,' Inge Kai said.

'Why?'

'He flew to Lisbon at six fifteen a.m. The flight connects directly to a TAP departure to Bissau at eleven forty a.m., which is now thirty-five minutes ago. He'll be landing in Guinea-Bissau in three and a half hours.'

'Bollocks, that's—'

'But I have an idea,' Inge Kai said.

'Oh, good,' Søren said. 'And what is it?'

'We follow the money,' Inge Kai said.

Just before three o'clock that afternoon, two civilian police cars pulled up outside the Claessen family's terraced house on Hvidsværmervej in Rødovre. Søren and Inge Kai walked up the garden path while officers Bundgaard and Larsen stayed in the second car. To Søren's relief it looked as if the Easter lunch had been called off. Through the kitchen window he could see the two girls watching television, but the table was not set and no candles were lit. Søren rang the doorbell.

'Yes?' Camilla had opened the door.

'Hello, my name is Søren Marhauge and I work for Bellahøj Police,' Søren said. 'This is my colleague, Inge Kai.'

For a moment the girl stared blankly at them, then turned to the stairs leading to the first floor and screamed, 'Daaaaaaaaaaaad, it's that police officer from yesterday,' after which she asked politely if Søren and Inge Kai would like to come inside and if she could take their coats.

Shortly afterwards Michael came thundering down the stairs. 'Oh, it's you again. Now what?'

'Actually, we wanted a word with your wife. Is she in?'

'Yes, but she's locked herself in the bathroom.'

'Has your Easter lunch been cancelled?' Søren asked.

'Yes – I think it's safe to say so.'

'Why, if I may ask?' Søren had noticed two sweaty patches under the armpits of Michael's shirt.

'Well, it was meant to be held at my father-in-law's, wasn't it? In Vangede. But it turned out he had also invited Lea, the wife's youngest sister, and the two of them don't get on. So we left.'

'What was the row about?'

Michael ran a hand over his short hair. 'I've got to be honest with you, I'm really shocked. Turns out my wife's little brother ... I guess I can tell you, can't I? I mean, you *are* a police officer?'

'Yes, absolutely. The police have a duty of confidentiality,' Søren said.

'Right. I did know that the wife's little brother had died, yeah? She never stops talking about him. How sweet he was, how cute. But I always thought he died from meningitis. It was only today we found out that he died from something completely different.' Michael leaned forwards and closed the door to the living room so that, for a moment, they stood in darkness.

'Oh, where the hell is the switch? Here. Turns out Lea bloody went and killed him,' Michael whispered. 'Can you believe it?'

'No,' Søren said, surprised. 'How did she kill him?'

'She had been naughty and broken something. But she wouldn't say sorry.'

'But she was only two and a half!'

'Yes, but good manners are very important to Julie so Lea knew the word "sorry", only she refused to say it. So Julie put her doll on the top shelf in my father-in-law's shed. The kid climbs up to get it and knocks the whole shelving unit down and the wife's baby brother gets a toolbox on his head and dies on the spot. I'm really shaken,' Michael said again. 'No wonder the whole family is gaga. Normally the wife won't shut up, but when we drove home from my father-in-law's, I couldn't get a word out of her. But she did say that it's one of those, you know, family secrets. Shit, man, a two-and-a-half-year-old killer, I ask you.'

'Do you know why it was kept secret?'

'My mother-in-law couldn't bear to be reminded of it. I was told she went out into the garden just after it had happened and refused to let go of the dead kid. It took two Falck emergency crew members to make her release him. It wasn't much fun for the other kids either, and that's why my father-in-law and Julie decided to keep it a secret. It must never come out. Julie has no idea how her sisters discovered it.'

'Where's the bathroom?'

'On the top floor,' Michael said.

Søren walked up the stairs and heard Inge Kai say, 'Michael Claessen, the time is fifteen twelve. I'm arresting you and charging you with being an accessory to the murder of your mother-in-law, Joan Skov, on the seventeenth of March 2010. As you are now under arrest and have been charged, you do not have to speak to the police and you have the right to a solicitor.'

'Eh?' Michael said. 'Are you taking the piss?'

'No,' Inge Kai said. 'Come on, we'll walk out to the car, nice and easy now, and get into it. No point in upsetting your daughters, is there? Is there someone we can call who can come over and pick them up?'

'Well, there's my mum,' Søren heard Michael say.

The terraced house was on three floors and, on the first, Søren discovered two girls' bedrooms with everything pink and sparkly. Through the window to the front garden he saw Inge Kai march Michael Claessen down the garden path; Bundgaard and Larsen got out of their car. Søren walked up to the top floor and stepped inside a typical IKEA bedroom with a double bed, a white bedspread and a wardrobe with sliding doors. The door to the en-suite bathroom was locked.

'Julie Claessen,' Søren said, as he knocked on the door, 'I'm Søren Marhauge from Bellahøj Police.'

No response. Søren tried looking through the keyhole to catch a glimpse of Julie, but all he could see was a basket of white towels on the windowsill.

'I want to talk to you,' Søren said. 'Please would you open the door?'

No reply.

A sudden impulse made him place a well-aimed kick above the lock, practically taking the door of its hinges. Julie was sitting on the closed toilet seat; her head flopped against the wall. Her breathing was shallow. Colourful pills were scattered across the floor and on the edge of the sink was a small perforated injection vial. Julie had tied a fitness band tightly around her arm and a syringe just touched the skin in the crook of her elbow; one swift movement and the needle would go in.

Søren perched carefully on the windowsill next to the towels. 'How are you?' he asked.

Julie snorted with derision. 'Everything started going wrong when Marie got breast cancer,' she said drowsily. 'Mum got even worse. She'd cry and scream for no reason, as if she was

THE ARC OF THE SWALLOW | 564

possessed. I gave her a few more pills, but it didn't work. And then Lea decided to stick her nose in, with all her useless suggestions about rehab and closure and all that claptrap. Mum couldn't take it on board, and every time I had to pick up the pieces. Mum would sit in her armchair staring at the telly, which wasn't even on. "Lea says I'm the one who is sick," she would say. "Is that right, Julie?"

'In the middle of it all, that idiot Herman Madsen called from Aalborg, wanting to give Lea some photograph. Mum had just spoken to him when I called in to organise her pills. She wanted to know why we had no photographs from when we were kids. We had been over this a thousand times before. Mum herself cut them up, but previously we had always told her that the photo albums had been in the shed when it burned down. So that she wouldn't feel bad, see. She got it into her head than someone might have stolen the photographs. She started wandering around the house, tearing her hair out until I managed to calm her down and—'

'Calm her down with what?'

'One red, one blue and one purple.' Julie had closed her eyes, but Søren was convinced she was still watching him. 'Just after Mads had died, I would give her the prettiest pills, but only until she stopped screaming. If I gave her all of them, she would go all groggy and I didn't like that.'

'Go on,' Søren said gently.

'The last week before Mum died, she started losing her mind and I had to go to Snerlevej constantly. But I also had my own family to take care of. Michael likes dinner on the table at six thirty and the girls always need taking somewhere. I couldn't supervise Mum all the time, could I? Michael complained about the number of ready meals we were eating and I also have a full-time job. The day after that business with the photograph, Michael told me about a drug they use a lot at Bispebjerg Hospital. He couldn't remember what it was called, but he'd heard a consultant say it was a brilliant sedative because it didn't make you too groggy. Michael had thought straight away that it might be something for Mum. Shortly afterwards he came home with a couple of vials. I walked around with the vials and the syringe in my handbag for weeks, and I kept meaning to look up the dosage. Only I never had the time. Camilla fell ill and then . . .'

'You don't have to justify yourself to me,' Søren said evenly.

'That Wednesday afternoon, Mum rang and screamed at me down the phone. At first I tried to calm her down as best I could, and when that didn't work, I tried getting hold of Dad, but his mobile was turned off. Eventually I jumped into the car and went to Snerlevej where I found her on the living-room carpet. She was rocking herself back and forth saying, "Your dad's a liar. Liar, liar, liar," in a deep, throaty voice. I don't know how I managed to get her to her bedroom, but I did. When she was in bed, she refused to swallow her pills and lashed out at me. "Lea says you're poisoning me," she yelled. "That you've always been poisoning me." Every time I managed to get a pill into her mouth, she spat it out. In the end I had to force her to swallow them. She tore out some of my hair. Finally the pills started working and she settled down a little. She said she just wanted to sleep, and it was then that I remembered Michael's medicine. "This will make you really relax," I promised her, "and you won't be groggy at all."'

Julie's eyes filled with tears.

'When I found Mum dead the next day, I knew it was my fault. But then again, I never did become a proper nurse. I'm no good at anything.'

'Does Michael know?'

Julie looked straight at Søren. 'He hasn't mentioned the drug since he gave it to me,' she said. 'But a couple of days after Mum's death, he said, "Nice to have a bit of peace and quiet at last, innit?"'

Julie stared vacantly into space.

'Give me the syringe,' Søren said.

Suddenly Julie straightened up, still keeping the syringe pressed against her skin. Her eyes flashed. 'You sit there, all holy. But I know exactly what you did, and at least I only killed my mum, not *both* my parents.'

'I have no idea what you're talking about,' Søren said.

'Oh yes you do. Your grandmother told Mum and a couple of the other women from the street the whole story at a garden party, and I heard *everything* because I was lying in a tent in the garden. They were all pally, as if they suddenly wanted to be friends with Mum, but it was to trick Mum into sharing her secrets. The women in that street were all gossips and your grandmother was the worst.'

'You must be mistaken,' Søren said calmly. 'My grandmother was a decent woman.'

'Ha! You didn't even know you killed your parents, did you?' Julie said.

'Of course I didn't kill them,' Søren said. He began to ache all over.

'Oh yes you did. You and your parents had spent a week in a cottage and your father had driven around with you on the country lanes without making you wear your seatbelt. When it was time to go back to Copenhagen, you had to wear your seatbelt again. You refused and your father told you off. You then climbed onto the passenger seat where your mother was sitting. But your mother was heavily pregnant so there was no room for you. Your father got even angrier and ordered you to get back to your own seat and put on your seatbelt and – *bang*. He had overlooked a give-way sign near the main road and been torpedoed by a lorry. You were trapped in the car for over an hour before the emergency crew cut you free. Your father survived long enough to tell them what had happened. Then he died.

'Your granny was wringing her hands, saying they should have told you the truth, but now it was too late. And that was when Mum told your granny all about how Mads really died. Ha! I can tell from the look on your face that you didn't know a thing. I almost feel like gloating!' Julie grinned.

Suddenly Søren spotted Marie standing in the doorway, outside Julie's field of vision.

'What do you get for murder?' Julie wanted to know. 'Twelve years? After all, I'm not a child who can get away with it. Not everyone is as lucky as you and Lea.' Julie pressed the needle harder so it was no longer resting on the skin, but had perforated the vein.

Søren slowly got up.

'Mads's death was a tragedy,' he said. 'The system should have taken care of you. It wasn't fair to let a little girl try to fix the broken pieces. You'll be acquitted.'

'You're lying, double murderer,' Julie said furiously.

Søren took a step towards Julie.

'One more step and you'll be a triple killer,' Julie hissed, clutching the syringe.

'There's nowhere near enough propofol in that syringe to kill you. Your mother was severely underweight and heavily medicated. At most, you'll pass out.'

Søren took another small step. 'What was going through your mind when you injected your mother? You wanted to calm her down? In Denmark, you'll be punished according to your intent, and you didn't intend to kill her, did you?'

'Yeah, right,' Julie said. 'I've spent the last twenty-seven years of my life protecting my mother, only to kill her in the end. What do you think?'

'I think it was an accident and that's why you won't be punished.' He took another step towards Julie. He could tell from her gaze that she was listening.

'You will be charged with manslaughter, according to Section 241 of the Penal Code. But you'll be acquitted. I promise you.'

Julie wavered and Søren seized his opportunity.

He grabbed Julie's wrists. She tried kicking out at him, but he pinned her down.

'Marie,' he called.

Marie was in the bathroom and at her sister's side in three strides.

'Hello, Marie,' Julie said, and suddenly sounded completely normal.

Very carefully Marie removed the syringe from Julie's arm and pressed her finger against the needle mark. It was not until then that Søren let go of Julie, picked up the syringe and left the room.

'Oh, Julie,' he heard Marie say. 'Darling, darling Julie.'

'Why do you say it like that?' Julie said. 'You sound so worried. You don't have to worry about me, you know that.'

Søren found Inge Kai outside the house and handed her the syringe. 'For analysis,' he said.

'Are you OK, Søren?' she asked. 'You've gone all white.'

'I just need to . . .' His legs gave way.

Inge Kai caught him as he fell and supported him to the threshold where he sat down.

'Are you ill?' she asked, frightened.

'No,' Søren said. 'I just need . . . some air.'

CHAPTER 16

On 23 August, Marie and Søren flew to Amsterdam to attend the 2010 International Immunology Congress. They had gone through their plan of action countless times and barely spoke on the trip. Stig Heller and Paul Smith, the British head of the WHO's Epidemiology Task Force, sat further down the plane; both had been updated and briefed to the hilt. Everyone was ready for their joint mission.

Tim was meant to have been with them, but had cancelled at the eleventh hour. The reorganisation of the Belem Health Project was taking up all his time, he had explained to Marie on the phone. The head of Statens Serum Institute had visited him in July, and since the WHO had announced their arrival in September, Tim and his team were busy getting everything ready. Tentatively, Marie had asked if Tim could possibly delegate some of the work. Belem now had two Danish and three Guinean PhD students and they were all dedicated and highly skilled – he had told her so himself.

'I can't come,' Tim had burst out. 'It's too painful.'

When they landed in Amsterdam, they were met by Søren's Dutch colleagues, who escorted the small group to the congress venue outside Amsterdam. Marie and Søren were admitted through a side entrance, while Stig Heller checked out the venue itself.

'Peter Bennett has arrived,' Heller said, when Marie and he met backstage, five minutes before his allocated slot at the podium. 'He's in the middle of a packed group in the foyer and they all have seats in the centre of the auditorium, row nine.'

Marie nodded. She was starting to get nervous.

'Ready, Mr Heller?' the co-ordinator said, and attached a clip-on microphone to his lapel. They could hear applause from the hall as the previous speaker left the stage and exited through the wings.

'Ready, Miss Skov?' Heller whispered, and winked at Marie. 'We're on.'

Stig Heller strode onto the stage and Marie positioned herself so that she had a full view of the audience through a gap in the curtain. Peter Bennett was sitting in the middle, dressed in black, his hair neatly swept back. Her knees were shaking.

'Honoured colleagues from across the globe,' Heller began, when he had arranged Marie's papers on the lectern and connected her laptop to the video cable.

'My name is Stig Heller, and I research nutrition at the Karolinska Institute in Stockholm. Before I commence my presentation, I would like to take the opportunity – now that I have your attention – to remember a good colleague and friend, Kristian Storm, professor of immunology at the University of Copenhagen, whom we lost in March. It is said that an anonymous allegation to the Danish Committees on Scientific Dishonesty triggered his suicide.' A controlled hush rippled through the gathering and was followed by a reverent silence.

'Allow me to introduce Kristian Storm's closest colleague, biologist and PhD student Marie Skov, who has come here today to say a few words about her mentor. Miss Skov?'

Marie stepped onto the stage. She had Storm's wooden swallow in her pocket. Stig Heller attached the microphone to her blouse and took a step back.

Marie began her PowerPoint presentation. The first slide was a picture of Kristian Storm and Olof Bengtsson in front of a health centre in Bissau in 2004. The hall was deathly quiet.

'It began with a single unplanned observation,' Marie said.

She managed another ten sentences before the first protest rang out from the audience.

'Excuse me, but I'm here to listen to Stig Heller talk about the link between nutrition and infant mortality,' someone shouted out. 'And are you even allowed to present results currently being investigated by the Danish Committees on Scientific Dishonesty?'

'We've been cleared,' Marie said, and clicked on the acquittal letter from the DCSD. 'Two weeks ago.'

A woman was making a noisy and dissatisfied shuffle down the row of seats to the exit and Marie quickly clicked on her article.

'Not only were we cleared,' she said, 'but Kristian Storm's and my article on the non-specific effects of vaccines and the adaptive ability of the immune system will be published in the journal *Science* this Monday.'

At this the hall fell silent and Marie hastened to continue: 'Vaccines are an amazing discovery and save millions of lives every day. However, that doesn't change the fact that there are problems with the DTP vaccine.' Marie slowly clicked through four graphs showing the correlation between the vaccine and mortality rates so that no one could any longer be in doubt.

'Since 2006, Kristian Storm has repeatedly drawn the WHO's attention to his observations, but he was never taken seriously. Why? Because the WHO's vaccination programme has become global politics, and how can you criticise something that has been in place for years? But Kristian Storm's research results didn't care about politics or practice, and his figures tell us everything we need to know. The DTP vaccine, which is given to more than a hundred million children across the world every year, is linked to severe health issues and death. Professor Kristian Storm's figures must be taken seriously. Now.'

Marie let the information sink in before she went on. 'The WHO is used to having a monopoly on the truth and they are obviously scared to lose face. The WHO is a conservative institution resting on the dogmatic assumption that one must never criticise global immunisation. After all, it's the greatest success of medical science to date. The saviour of mankind. A paradigm shift is a difficult process and that's exactly as it should be. That's why I'm even more excited that the WHO is finally ready to broaden its view of immunisation. I'm delighted to hand over to the head of the WHO's Epidemiology Task Force, Paul Smith.'

Paul Smith stood up in the middle of the hall. 'Thank you, Marie,' he said, in a clear voice so that the whole assembly could hear him. 'The WHO has set up a working group, which we have named Storm, whose sole purpose from the first of

September 2010 will be global research into the non-specific effect of vaccines. I would like to take this opportunity to announce that the Bill Gates and Melinda Gates Foundation has just granted us fifty million dollars to extend the study of vaccine effects in developing countries. We are many who have come to realise that we can no longer afford to ignore the research of Kristian Storm and Marie Skov. Thank you.'

Paul Smith nodded to Marie and sat down again.

You could have heard a pin drop.

'Scepticism towards a paradigm shift is reasonable and, ultimately, it benefits us all. However, killing innocent children through individual greed is not.' Marie was now looking directly at Peter Bennett as she clicked on the next slide. It showed two photographs, one of Midas Manolis and one of Silas Henckel.

'Someone in this room murdered these two men,' Marie said. 'Midas Manolis and Silas Henckel: two scientists who were separately researching the negative effects of the DTP vaccine. Both were on the brink of a scientific breakthrough when they died. Furthermore, Silas Henckel was Professor Kristian Storm's PhD student.'

'So what are you really saying?' someone cried out from the back of the hall, but he was immediately hushed.

Marie clicked on a slide of Ébano Salomon and watched Bennett's reaction, but there was none. 'This man,' Marie said, 'is called Ébano Salomon and he worked as a security guard and odd-job man for Kristian Storm at the Belem Health Project. Danish police can prove that Ébano Salomon was paid on several occasions in 2008 and 2009 to sabotage Kristian Storm's research, and they can also prove that, on the seventeenth of March this year, Ébano Salomon murdered Professor Kristian Storm in his office in Copenhagen and made it look like suicide.'

Still no reaction from Bennett.

'In February 2009,' Marie continued, now changing tactic, 'an American scientist and Nobel Prize winner known to all of us stepped down from the board of a Japanese pharmaceutical company.' Marie clicked onto the letter of resignation stating that Peter Bennett was resigning from the board of Sixan Pharmaceuticals. Marie had Tippexed out Bennett's name but Sixan Pharmaceuticals' was left untouched; a murmur of surprise spread through the audience.

'This person had resigned from the board of Sixan Pharmaceuticals; the whole world could see that. However, no one noticed that someone else joined Sixan's board at the same time. This man –' Again Marie clicked and the photograph of Ébano Salomon appeared – 'the odd-job man from Kristian Storm's research station in Bissau. According to Ébano Salomon's contract of appointment to the board, he would receive an annual fee of twenty thousand dollars for attending Sixan Pharmaceuticals' board meetings *plus* an annual bonus linked to the company's turnover.' Marie clicked on the section of the contract that related to remuneration. 'Not a bad deal, is it? Sixan Pharmaceuticals is the eighth biggest pharmaceutical company in the world. It specialises in vaccine constituents and has shown healthy profits every year since 1991. So why did Ébano Salomon never receive one cent? Because the money was transferred to a trust-fund account with the American National Bank where, once a year, it was used for paying tuition fees to Stanford University.' Marie clicked again and another slide appeared. 'Here's the lucky recipient. A promising young medical student by the name Louise Bennett.'

At this, Bennett shot up and started edging his way violently past his colleagues in row nine. Three hundred people stared at him, and at the end of the row, Søren Marhauge and two Dutch police officers were waiting for him.

'The time is eleven forty-eight,' Søren said in English. 'I am arresting you and charging you with commissioning three murders and the fraudulent use of board funds.'

'Get your hands off me,' Bennett sneered.

But Søren put him in handcuffs.

CHAPTER 17

Dear Søren,

Henrik came back for a visit this weekend and he is doing really well in Jutland. He has been clean for almost two months now and says that the staff at the rehab centre are brilliant. And they must be doing something right, I think. For the first time for as long as I can remember, Henrik was truly present with us and was able to spend time with Olivia and Sara. He even asked to hold Storm (photo attached).

We don't yet know what will happen to him and me, but time will tell. As you probably know, he has taken leave from work for the rest of the year, but he is already talking about how much he is looking forward to returning after Christmas. I know that the two of you haven't spoken yet, but I'm sure that is only a matter of time. I just want you to know that we are very grateful. You are a good friend.

Love, Jeanette

Søren clicked on the photograph and spent a long time looking at Henrik cradling his little son. It was impossible not to get emotional. Storm gazed up at his father as only babies know how. Then Søren braced himself and went into the living room to Anna, who was busy proofreading an article for a vertebrates magazine.

'I really want us to have another baby,' he said.

Anna looked up. 'Right now?' she enquired.

'Soon,' Søren said.

'Will you be taking paternity leave?'

'Of course,' Søren said.

'OK,' Anna said, and carried on reading.

'OK?'

'Yes, just let me finish this,' Anna said, without looking up.

'No, I'm not going to just let you finish that,' Søren said, and snatched her papers. 'You're going to go to our bedroom, where you will take off your clothes.'

Anna was about to protest, but then she smiled at him.

'As you wish,' she said, and got up.

CHAPTER 18

The last weekend of August was unseasonably mild and warm, and Marie and Anton paid a visit to Julie and her daughters on Hvidsværmervej. Camilla and Emma were reading teenage magazines under a parasol in the back garden, while Julie and her mother-in-law were busy planting colourful flowers in terracotta pots. At the start of July, Julie had been acquitted of manslaughter at Lyngby Court. She had not been present when the verdict was read out because she was a patient in the psychiatric unit at Frederiksberg Hospital, where she had been diagnosed with post-traumatic stress disorder. She had started seeing a therapist and since the middle of July she had lived at home on Hvidsværmervej with Camilla and Emma, who had been looked after by Michael's mother. Michael was serving a three-month custodial sentence for the theft and illegal handling of prescription drugs.

Marie embraced her sister when she and Anton came out into the garden. Julie had gained weight from the medication she was taking, but despite that she seemed unusually relaxed, with a trowel in her hand and her hair in a mess. She started fussing about Marie the moment they sat down under the parasol with elderflower cordial and sandwiches, but then she stopped herself. Instead, she presented Marie with some pearl-encrusted slides for her new hair.

'Isn't it a little too short for these?' Marie laughed.

'It'll grow,' Julie said.

'So how are you doing, sis?' Marie said, when the children had said thank you for their meal and disappeared inside the house.

'I'm doing well,' Julie said. 'Being in therapy is hard, but I have a feeling that . . . the fog is lifting.'

Marie nodded.

'Michael and I are getting a divorce,' Julie added.

'OK,' Marie said, glancing furtively at Michael's mother, who was still pottering around at the bottom of the garden.

'There's no need for you to whisper,' Julie said. 'My mother-in-law already knows. The most important thing for her is that the children are all right. Michael will probably move here when he comes out of prison. The girls can visit him. It'll be fine. My mother-in-law loves waiting on him and, well, you know Michael.'

Marie smiled. 'How are you and Lea getting on?' she then asked.

'It'll happen, Marie,' Julie said. 'When I'm ready. I promise you. We've spoken on the phone and we'll meet soon. Soon. Tell me, how are you doing?'

'Really well,' Marie said, and found it hard to conceal her smile.

'And when do we get to meet your chap?' Julie asked, and winked.

'It won't be long,' Marie said.

'I'm very excited,' Julie said. 'Dad said that he was nice, even though . . .'

'. . . he has a lot of tattoos?' Marie asked, with a grin.

'Yes,' Julie said. 'Really nice, even though he has a lot of tattoos. Sorry, Marie. I just don't like them. I don't understand it . . . what it's about. It's so . . .' She fell silent.

'It's OK,' Marie said. 'You don't have to like Mattis's tattoos to like him, and I'm sure you'll like him.'

'And how about your PhD?' Julie asked.

'When I've had my next appointment with Mr Guldborg on the twenty-eighth of September, I'll officially enrol as a PhD student at the Department of Immunology.'

'Have you found out who'll be your supervisor?'

Marie shook her head. 'Thor Albert Larsen has resigned,' she said, 'so both Storm's and Thor's jobs are vacant. The deadline for applications is the first of September.'

'You never liked Thor Albert Larsen, did you?'

'No, and I had good reason not to. It turned out it was he who reported Storm and me to the DCSD. We found that out when the police got a court order that overrode the DCSD anonymity guarantee. He resigned soon afterwards. I almost feel sorry for him because the whole institute gave him the cold shoulder. Then again, you have to be a complete idiot to accuse your closest colleagues of scientific dishonesty, especially if you do it anonymously.

'I visited Dad yesterday,' Marie added.

'Did he show you the apple tree?' Julie asked. 'He planted it right where Mads died. Ingrid Marie apples.'

Marie nodded. 'It's nice,' she said. 'He also gave me Mum's tapestry wall-hanging. The Medusa one.'

'Oh, Marie,' Julie exclaimed. 'You're not going to put that up? After everything that's happened?'

'No,' Marie said. 'I won't. Not yet, anyway. But I wanted to have it. Mum was a brilliant artist, Julie. The tapestry is fantastic.'

They sat for a while, admiring the flowers in their pots.

'Dad still drinks far too much,' Marie said at length. 'But I didn't say anything. And even though he pretends it doesn't matter, I think he's very nervous about going to prison. I had to promise him yesterday that we'd look after the dog. It's really not terribly convenient now that we live in a flat, but I said yes all the same. We can probably manage it for those two months.'

'What dog?' Julie frowned.

'Didn't you know? He bought a Labrador puppy. Anton is over the moon about it. Dad's picking it up on Monday.'

'Well, we can only pray that it doesn't turn out to be a Great Dane,' Julie said, and they burst out laughing.

ACKNOWLEDGEMENTS

I would like to thank the following for their help with specialist and scientific questions: Christian Kaarup Baron, Birgitte Brock, Pernille Dickow, Peter Gravlund, Malene Jensen, Laura Li, Vitor Santos Lindegaard, Anders Lund, Trine Møller Madsen, Eva-Marie Helsted Ravn and Kristian Valbak. Last, but not least, a huge thank you to Nikolaj Friis Hansen, forensic examiner from the Institute of Forensic Genetics at the University of Copenhagen, and Uffe Jensen, investigator with the Violent Crimes Unit at Aarhus Police.

Very special thanks to Lene Wissing, Christine Stabell Benn and Peter Aaby (all three of you have been unique in your own inimitable way), my bonus sisters Down Under, Donna Lee Carlson and Kim Reid, my wonderful parents, Janne Hejgaard and Paul Gazan, and of course my children Lola and Willow Reid Gazan and their wonderful daddy and my husband, Mark Reid Gazan. You make me so happy.

Check out www.bandim.org.

For more than thirty years the Danish-founded research group, the Bandim Health Project, BHP, has operated in one of the world's poorest developing countries: Guinea-Bissau in West Africa. BHP has build up a database on more than 200,000 women and children to investigate the real-life effects of health interventions.

In the late 1980s BHP showed that the new high-dose measles vaccine which was introduced in low-income countries was associated with a two-fold increase in mortality among girls. After similar reports from other countries, the vaccine was – surprisingly quietly – withdrawn by the World Health Organisation, WHO. Based on BHP's figures, had it not been withdrawn, it could have cost at least half a million additional female deaths per year in Africa alone.

The vaccine protected fully against measles, so the observation indicated that vaccines could have other, 'non-specific' sex-differential effects; and this led the researchers at BHP to study other vaccines for their potential non-specific effects. Subsequent studies have indicated that *all* vaccines may have non-specific effects; most of them are, fortunately, very beneficial, so the vaccines actually increase survival more than could be expected.

These findings are very controversial, and many researchers, and the WHO, have refused to believe them. To this day the group continues to struggle to get their pioneering observations accepted; not least because if the vaccines have non-specific effects along with the specific disease-protective effects, the potential to improve child survival is very high.

It was only recently that BHP's struggle finally paid off in some way. In April 2014 the WHO decided that more research into non-specific effects of vaccines was warranted. It's BHP's hope that this is the first step towards a more general acceptance of the existence of non-specific effects.

It has been such a great honour for me to be invited to follow the BHP research group for a period of two years. I feel I have witnessed the genesis of a revolutionary scientific breakthrough. I have no doubt that BHP's research will one day soon change our view on the current vaccination programme forever. With this novel I hope I have contributed just a little to this awareness.

Read more at www.bandim.org

Sissel-Jo
Berlin, 28 August 2014

NATUREGUIDE
ROCKS
AND MINERALS

DK NATUREGUIDE
ROCKS
AND MINERALS
Ronald Louis Bonewitz

**LONDON, NEW YORK, MELBOURNE,
MUNICH, AND DELHI**

DORLING KINDERSLEY

Senior Editor Peter Frances	**Senior Art Editor** Spencer Holbrook
Jacket Editor Manisha Majithia	**Jacket Designer** Laura Brim
DK Picture Library Rose Horridge	**Picture Researchers** Jo Walton, Julia Harris-Voss
Production Editor Rebekah Parsons-King	**Production Controller** Erika Pepe
Managing Editor Camilla Hallinan	**Managing Art Editor** Michelle Baxter
Associate Publishing Director Liz Wheeler	**Publisher** Sarah Larter
Publishing Director Jonathan Metcalf	**Art Director** Philip Ormerod

DK INDIA

Managing Editor Rohan Sinha	**Deputy Managing Art Editor** Mitun Banerjee
Deputy Managing Editor Alka Thakur Hazarika	**Senior Designer** Ivy Roy
Senior Editor Soma B. Chowdhury	**Designers** Arijit Ganguly, Mahua Mandal, Tanveer Zaidi
Editors Pragati Nagpal, Neha Pande, Priyaneet Singh	**Assistant Designer** Sanjay Chauhan
DTP Designers Sourabh Challariya, Arvind Kumar, Arjinder Singh, Jagtar Singh, Rajesh Singh, Bimlesh Tiwary, Tanveer Zaidi	**Consultant Art Director** Shefali Upadhyay
	Picture Researcher Sakshi Saluja
Production Manager Pankaj Sharma	**DTP Manager** Balwant Singh

CONSULTANT

Dr. Jeffrey E. Post, Geologist, Curator-in-Charge, National Gem and Mineral Collection, National Museum of Natural History, Smithsonian Institution

First published in Great Britain in 2012
by Dorling Kindersley Limited
80 Strand, London WC2R 0RL
Penguin Group (UK)

2 4 6 8 10 9 7 8 5 3
006 – 181829 – Jul/2012

A CIP catalogue record for this book is available from the British Library

ISBN 978 1 4053 7586 3

Reproduced by Bright Arts, China, and MDP, UK
Printed and bound in China by Leo Paper Products

Discover more at
www.dk.com

CONTENTS

HOW THE ROCK AND MINERAL PROFILES WORK

profile information (including illustration of crystal system in mineral entries)

name of mineral or rock group

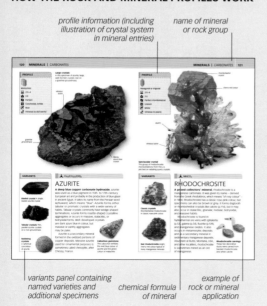

variants panel containing named varieties and additional specimens

chemical formula of mineral

example of rock or mineral application

KEY

- ⏚ Hardness
- ⬦ Specific gravity
- ▨ Cleavage
- ◪ Fracture
- ◩ Streak
- ⬦ Lustre
- ▲ Type
- ⊕ Origin
- ⬤ Temperature of formation
- ⬒ Pressure of formation
- ⊞ Structure
- ◉ Grain size
- ◼ Major minerals
- ◻ Minor minerals
- ✳ Colour
- ◀◀ Precursor rock
- ⊛ Fossils

INTRODUCTION

WHAT IS A MINERAL?

A mineral is a naturally occurring solid with a specific chemical composition and a distinctive internal crystal structure. Most minerals are formed inorganically but some, such as those found in bone are formed organically (by living organisms).

WHAT MINERALS ARE MADE OF

Most minerals are chemical compounds composed of two or more chemical elements. However, copper, sulphur, gold, silver, and a few others occur as single "native" elements. A mineral is defined by its chemical formula and by the arrangement of atoms within its crystals. For example, iron sulphide has the chemical formula FeS_2 (where Fe is iron and S is sulphur). Iron sulphide can crystallize in two different ways. When it crystallizes in the cubic system (pp.22–23), it is called pyrite;

Same composition but different structure
Though pyrite and marcasite have the same chemical composition and are both iron sulphide, their differing crystal structures make them different minerals.

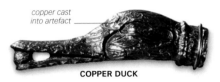

copper cast into artefact

COPPER DUCK

Native elements
Native copper was probably the first metal used by humans. This duck's head was made in North Africa about 1,900 years ago.

brassy yellow colour

cubic habit

PYRITE

rosette-shaped aggregate

metallic lustre

MARCASITE CRYSTALS

when it crystallizes in the orthorhombic system, it becomes the mineral marcasite. Minerals are classified by their chemical content: for example, those containing oxygen ions are called oxides and those having carbon and oxygen ions are called carbonates.

Native sulphur
Sulphur is mined at Kawah Ijen, Java. Volcanic gases escaping from small openings in the ground (fumaroles) carry sulphur vapours to the surface, where it is deposited as a yellow crust.

Volcanic rhyolite
The Rhyolite Hills in Iceland are formed of rhyolite, a silica-rich rock produced as a result of volcanic activity. Rhyolite is made up of crystals of high-silica minerals.

ELECTRICAL CHARGE AND COMPOUNDS

A mineral compound is based on an electrical balance between a positively charged metal and a negatively charged part. In many minerals, negative charge is carried by a "radical": a combination of atoms acting as a single unit. For example, carbon and oxygen combine in a 1:3 ratio to give the CO_3 radical, which acts as a single, negatively charged unit.

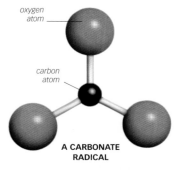

oxygen atom

carbon atom

A CARBONATE RADICAL

Simple and complex compounds
In carbonates, a simple carbon and oxygen group known as a radical combines with one or more metals.

COMMON MINERALS

There are more than 500 known minerals, but only about 100 of these are common. Silicon and oxygen make up about three-quarters of the crust by weight, and silicate minerals such as quartz, feldspar, and olivine are by far the most common minerals in rocks, making up about 90 per cent of the rocks at Earth's surface. The carbonates calcite and dolomite form sedimentary rocks, such as limestone.

Silicates
Silica tetrahedra link to form quartz. They can act as a radical to combine with one or more metals or semimetals to form other silicate minerals.

crystal face

QUARTZ CRYSTAL

each silicon atom is bonded to four oxygen atoms that form a tetrahedral shape

silica tetrahedra join at the corners to form a helix

STRUCTURE OF QUARTZ

MINERAL GROUPS AND ASSOCIATIONS

Some minerals belong to chemical groups or series called solid solutions. In some circumstances, minerals are found together in groupings known as associations or assemblages. These patterns of occurrence can provide clues as to the minerals' origin.

SOLID SOLUTIONS

Some minerals do not have specific chemical compositions. Instead, they are homogenous mixtures of two minerals. These homogenous mixtures are known as solid solutions. For example, the olivine group of silicates includes forsterite and fayalite. Forsterite is a magnesium silicate, while fayalite is an iron silicate. Most olivine specimens are homogenous mixtures of the two, with the relative content of magnesium and iron varying in specimens. These minerals are described as part of a solid-solution series, in which forsterite and fayalite are the end members.

tabular crystal

FAYALITE

light colour from magnesium

FORSTERITE

Fayalite and forsterite
The olivine minerals fayalite and forsterite form a solid-solution series, with magnesium-rich forsterite as one end member and iron-rich fayalite as the other.

PRIMARY AND SECONDARY MINERALS

Primary minerals crystallize directly from magma and remain unaltered. They include essential minerals used to assign a classification name to a rock and accessory minerals that are present in lesser abundance and do not affect the classification of a rock. Secondary minerals are produced by the alteration of a primary mineral after its formation. For example, when copper-bearing primary minerals come into contact with carbonated water, they alter into secondary azurite or malachite.

crystalline copper

massive copper

Primary copper mineral
Primary minerals, such as native copper, form directly in igneous rocks and remain unaltered. Their eventual alteration products are secondary minerals.

chrysocolla

botryoidal malachite

rock groundmass

Secondary copper mineral
Chrysocolla and malachite are secondary minerals derived from the chemical weathering of primary copper minerals, such as native copper and bornite.

MINERAL ASSOCIATIONS

Some minerals are consistently found together over large areas because they are found in the same rock type. Other associations occur in encrustations, veins, cavities, or thin layers. The fact that certain minerals are likely to be found together can help in the discovery and identification of minerals. Lead and zinc ore minerals are often associated with calcite and baryte, while gold is frequently found in association with quartz.

Associated minerals that form almost simultaneously and are usually present in a specific rock type make up an assemblage. Orthoclase, albite, biotite, and quartz form an assemblage for granite, and plagioclase, augite, magnetite, and olivine for gabbro. Assemblages are key indicators of the environments in which minerals form.

garnet

mica gives silvery sheen

Metamorphic mix
The assemblage of garnet, quartz, and mica in this specimen indicates that this rock formed at moderate pressure and low temperatures (up to 200°C/400°F).

apophyllite

stilbite

Mineral association
Minerals belonging to the zeolite group of silicates, such as these crystals of apophyllite and stilbite, are often found in association with one another.

Layered rocks in the San Juan River
Erosion at this canyon in Utah, USA, has exposed layers of shale. Differences in the assemblage of minerals in various shale layers can reveal much about the geological history of the region.

CLASSIFYING MINERALS

Classification of minerals is an ongoing study among mineralogists – geologists who specifically study minerals. The ability to delve deep into the structure and chemistry of minerals has increased dramatically with advances in instruments and techniques.

MINERAL OR NOT?

The term "mineral" is commonly applied to certain organic substances, such as coal, oil, and natural gas, when referring to a nation's wealth in resources. However, these materials are more accurately referred to as hydrocarbons. Gases and liquids are not, in the strict sense, minerals. Although ice – the solid state of water – is a mineral, liquid water is not; nor is liquid mercury, which can be found in mercury ore deposits. Synthetic equivalents of minerals, for example emeralds and diamonds produced in the laboratory, are not minerals as they do not occur naturally. The "minerals" referred to in foods are also not strictly minerals, as they refer to

elements, such as iron, calcium, or zinc.

Synthetic ruby boule
Rubies and other gems grown synthetically are not classified as minerals. Some gems, such as yttrium-aluminium garnet, do not even occur in nature.

CHEMICAL FORMULAE

A chemical formula identifies the atoms present in a mineral and their proportions. In some minerals, the atoms and their proportions are fixed. Pyrite, for example, is always FeS_2, denoting iron (Fe) and sulphur (S) in a 1:2 ratio. In solid solutions, the components may be variable. For olivine, where complete substitution is possible between iron and magnesium (Mg), the formula is $(Fe,Mg)_2SiO_4$, indicating that iron and magnesium are found in varying amounts.

CHEMICAL ELEMENTS

Symbol	Name	Symbol	Name	Symbol	Name	Symbol	Name
Ac	Actinium	Er	Erbium	Mo	Molybdenum	Sb	Antimony
Ag	Silver	Es	Einsteinium	N	Nitrogen	Sc	Scandium
Al	Aluminium	F	Fluorine	Na	Sodium	Se	Selenium
Am	Americium	Fe	Iron	Nb	Niobium	Si	Silicon
Ar	Argon	Fm	Fermium	Nd	Neodymium	Sm	Samarium
As	Arsenic	Fr	Francium	Ne	Neon	Sn	Tin
At	Astatine	Ga	Gallium	Ni	Nickle	Sr	Strontium
Au	Gold	Gd	Gadolinium	No	Nobelium	Ta	Tantalum
B	Boron	Ge	Germanium	Np	Neptunium	Tb	Terbium
Ba	Barium	H	Hydrogen	O	Oxygen	Tc	Technetium
Be	Beryllium	He	Helium	Os	Osmium	Te	Tellurium
Bi	Bismuth	Hf	Hafnium	P	Phosphorus	Th	Thorium
Bk	Berkelium	Hg	Mercury	Pa	Protactinium	Ti	Titanium
Br	Bromine	Ho	Holmium	Pb	Lead	Tl	Thallium
C	Carbon	I	Iodine	Pd	Palladium	Tm	Thulium
Ca	Calcium	In	Indium	Pm	Promethium	U	Uranium
Cd	Cadmium	Ir	Iridium	Po	Polonium	V	Vanadium
Ce	Cerium	K	Potassium	Pt	Platinum	W	Tungsten
Cf	Californium	Kr	Krypton	Pr	Praseodymium	Xe	Xenon
Cl	Chlorine	La	Lanthanum	Pu	Plutonium	Y	Yttrium
Cm	Curium	Li	Lithium	Ra	Radium	Yb	Ytterbium
Co	Cobalt	Lu	Lutetium	Rb	Rubidium	Zn	Zinc
Cr	Chromium	Lw	Lawrencium	Re	Rhenium	Zr	Zirconium
Cs	Cesium	Md	Mendelevium	Rh	Rhodium		
Cu	Copper	Mg	Magnesium	Rn	Radon		
Dy	Dysprosium	Mn	Manganese	S	Sulphur		

CLASSIFYING MINERALS

Minerals are primarily classified according to their chemical composition. Shown below are the major chemical groups, with an example of each. Minerals are further classified into subgroups, with each subgroup taking its name from its most typical mineral. A radical is a group of atoms that acts as a single unit.

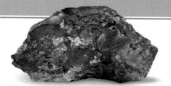

CHALCOCITE

Sulphides
The sulphides are formed when a metal or semimetal combines with sulphur. In chalcocite, the metallic element is copper.

Native elements
Minerals formed of a single chemical element – metals such as gold and copper and nonmetals such as sulphur and carbon – are called native elements.

GRAPHITE

RUBY

Oxides
When oxygen alone combines with a metal or semimetal, an oxide is formed. Corundum is aluminium oxide, with a red variety called ruby.

BRUCITE

Hydroxides
Hydroxide minerals contain a hydroxyl (hydrogen and oxygen) radical combined with a metallic element. In brucite, the metallic element is magnesium.

Halides
A halogen element (chlorine, bromine, iodine, or fluorine) combined with a metal or semimetal makes a halide. Sylvite is a compound of chlorine and potassium.

SYLVITE

coating of blue smithsonite

Carbonates
The carbonate radical, consisting of carbon and oxygen, combines with a metal or semimetal to form carbonate minerals. In smithsonite, the metal is zinc.

SMITHSONITE

APATITE

Arsenates, phosphates, and vanadates
In these minerals, a radical of oxygen and either arsenic, phosphorus, or vanadium combines with a semimetal or metal. Apatite is a phosphate.

COLEMANITE

Borates and nitrates
Borates contain radicals of boron and oxygen, and nitrates those of nitrogen and oxygen. In colemanite boron and oxygen combine with calcium and water.

Sulphates, chromates, tungstates, and molybdates
Sulphur, molybdenum, chromium, or tungsten form a radical with oxygen that combines with a metal or semimetal. Celestine is a sulphate.

CELESTINE

Silicates
In this group, silicon and oxygen form a silica radical that combines with metals or semimetals. Silica occurs alone as quartz, as in this amethyst specimen.

AMETHYST

AMBER

Organic minerals
This group includes some naturally occurring substances, such as shell and coral, that are generated by organic means. Amber is a fossil resin.

IDENTIFYING MINERALS

There are certain physical properties determined by the crystalline structure and chemical composition of a mineral. These can commonly help to identify minerals without the use of expensive equipment. Even a beginner can readily use these pointers.

COLOUR

Some minerals have characteristic colours – the bright blue of azurite, the yellow of sulphur, and the green of malachite allow for easy identification. This is not true of all minerals – fluorite occurs in virtually all colours, so it is best identified by other properties.

In minerals, colour is caused by the absorption or refraction of light of particular wavelengths. This can happen for several reasons. One is the presence of trace elements – "foreign" atoms that are not part of the basic chemical makeup of the mineral in the crystal structure. As few as three atoms per million can absorb enough of certain parts of the visible-light spectrum to give colour to some minerals.

Colour can also result from the absence of an atom or ionic radical from a place that it would normally occupy in a crystal. The structure of the mineral itself, without any defect or foreign element, may also cause colour: opal is composed of minute spheres of silica that diffract light; and the thin interlayering of two feldspars in moonstone gives it colour and sheen.

botryoidal habit

Azurite
Some minerals can be identified by their characteristic colour. The copper carbonate azurite is always azure blue.

GREEN FLUORITE

YELLOW FLUORITE

PURPLE FLUORITE

Colour range
These specimens show only a few of the many colours that can occur in fluorite. Different coloration depends on a number of factors.

Colour variation in opal
The play of colours or fire in opal is due to the arrangement of microscopic silica spheres. A microscope image shows opal's fractured surface.

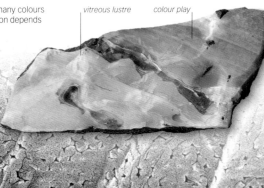

vitreous lustre   *colour play*

LUSTRE

A mineral's lustre is the appearance of its surface in reflected light. There are two broad types of lustre: metallic and nonmetallic. Metallic lustre is that of an untarnished metal surface, such as gold, silver, or copper. These minerals tend to be opaque. Minerals with nonmetallic lustre commonly show transparency or translucency. Vitreous describes the lustre of a piece of broken glass; adamantine, the brilliant lustre of diamond; resinous, the lustre of a piece of resin; and pearly, the lustre of mother-of-pearl or pearl. Greasy lustre refers to the appearance of being covered with a thin layer of oil, and silky, the appearance of the surface of silk or satin. Dull lustre implies little or no reflection, and earthy lustre the nonlustrous look of raw earth.

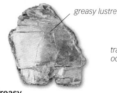

nonreflective lustre

Dull
A dull lustre is seen in this specimen of hematite. It is nonreflective but not as granular in appearance as earthy lustre.

glass-like lustre

Vitreous
Many silicate minerals, such as this quartz crystal, have a vitreous lustre. This lustre appears similar to the surface of glass.

satin-like sheen

Silky
The borate ulexite exhibits a silky lustre, with the surface sheen resembling a bolt of satin or silk.

translucent crystal

Resinous
Native sulphur crystals are transparent or translucent, with a resinous lustre that resembles the surface of tree resin.

bright sheen

Metallic
The sulphide galena has a metallic lustre and a distinctive cleavage. Metallic lustre looks like the reflection from new metal.

greasy lustre

Greasy
Orpiment can appear greasy – resembling an oily surface – or resinous. The difference between the two lustres is subjective.

transparent octahedron

Adamantine
Adamantine is the brightest of lustres, with an appearance similar to the surface of this diamond. It is brighter than vitreous lustre.

dry, soil-like look

Earthy
Minerals with an earthy lustre, such as this fine-grained calcite, have the look of freshly broken, dry soil.

STREAK

The colour of the powder produced when a specimen is drawn across a surface such as unglazed porcelain is known as streak. A mineral's streak is consistent and is a more useful diagnostic indicator than its colour, which can vary from one specimen to another. Streak can help distinguish between minerals that are easy to confuse. For example, the iron oxide hematite has a red streak, while magnetite, another iron oxide, gives a black streak.

CROCOITE

CHALCOPYRITE

Consistent streak
The streak of a mineral is consistent from specimen to specimen, as long as an unweathered surface is tested. It is the same as the colour of the powdered mineral.

CLEAVAGE

The ability of a mineral to break along flat, planar surfaces is called cleavage. It occurs in the crystal structure where the forces that bond atoms are the weakest. Cleavage surfaces are generally smooth and reflect light evenly. Cleavage is described by its direction relative to the orientation of the crystal and by the ease with which it is produced. If cleavage easily produces smooth, lustrous surfaces, it is called perfect. Distinct, imperfect, and difficult indicate less easy kinds of cleavage. Minerals may have different quality cleavages in different directions. Some have no cleavage at all.

cleavage plane

Perfect cleavage
This topaz crystal exhibits perfect cleavage. It breaks cleanly parallel to its base, and is thus said to have perfect basal cleavage.

cleavage planes cross each other

Clear breaks
The cleavage planes of this baryte crystal are clearly visible. Baryte has perfect cleavage in different directions, as seen in this specimen.

FRACTURE

Some minerals can break in directions other than along cleavage planes. These breaks, known as fractures, help to identify minerals. For example, hackly fractures (with jagged edges), are often found in metals, while shell-like conchoidal fractures are typical of quartz. Other terms for fractures include even (rough but more or less flat), uneven (rough and completely irregular), and splintery (with partially separated fibres).

conchoidal fracture

hackly fracture surface

glassy texture

irregular surface

Conchoidal
This obsidian nodule shows conchoidal fracture, with fractures shaped like a bivalve seashell. It is commonly seen in silicates.

Hackly
This gold nugget shows hackly fracture, with sharp edges and jagged points. It is characteristic of most metals.

Uneven
This specimen of chalcopyrite shows uneven fracture. Its broken surface is rough and irregular, with no pattern evident.

TENACITY

The term tenacity describes the physical properties of a mineral based on the cohesive force between atoms in the structure. Gold, silver, and copper are malleable and can be flattened without crumbling. Sectile minerals can be cut smoothly with a knife; flexible minerals bend easily and stay bent after pressure is removed; ductile minerals can be drawn into a wire; brittle minerals are prone to breakage; and elastic minerals return to the original form when bent.

Ductile copper
Like many other native metals, copper is ductile. This means that it can be drawn into a wire without breaking.

Malleable gold
The malleability of gold allows it to be wrought into elaborate shapes. It can also be hammered into sheets thinner than paper.

HARDNESS

The hardness of a mineral is the relative ease or difficulty with which it can be scratched. A harder mineral will scratch a softer one, but not vice versa. Minerals are assigned a number between 1 to 10 on the Mohs scale, which measures hardness relative to ten minerals of increasing hardness. Hardness differs from toughness or strength; very hard minerals can be quite brittle. Most hydrous minerals – those that contain water molecules – are soft, as are phosphates, carbonates, sulphates, halides, and most sulphides. Anhydrous oxides – those without water molecules – and silicates are relatively hard.

Fingernail test
The fingernail is about 2½ on the Mohs scale and can scratch talc and gypsum. The hardness of other common items is also noted on the scale.

THE MOHS SCALE OF HARDNESS

Hardness	Mineral	Other materials for hardness testing
1	Talc	Very easily scratched by a fingernail
2	Gypsum	Can be scratched by a fingernail
3	Calcite	Just scratched with a copper coin
4	Flourite	Very easily scratched with a knife but not as easily as calcite
5	Apatite	Scratched with a knife with difficulty
6	Orthoclase	Cannot be scratched with a knife but scratches glass with difficulty
7	Quartz	Scratches glass easily
8	Topaz	Scratches glass very easily
9	Corundum	Cuts glass
10	Diamond	Cuts glass

REFRACTIVE INDEX

Light changes velocity and direction as it passes through a transparent or translucent mineral. The extent of this change is measured by the refractive index: the ratio of light's velocity in air to its velocity in the crystal. A high index causes dispersion of light into its component colours. Refractive indices can be found using specialized liquids or inexpensive equipment.

Double refraction
A calcite rhomb is said to be double refractive. It refracts light at two different angles, thus creating a double image.

FLUORESCENCE

Some minerals exhibit fluorescence – that is, they emit visible light of various colours when subjected to ultraviolet radiation. Ultraviolet lights for testing fluorescence can be obtained from dealers selling collectors' equipment. Fluorescence is an imperfect indicator of a mineral's identity because not all specimens of a mineral show fluorescence, even if they look identical and come from the same location.

calcite cluster

fluorescence from manganese

Manganoan calcite
This yellowish specimen of manganese-rich calcite fluoresces rose pink when lit by ultraviolet light. Its fluorescence varies with manganese concentration.

CALCITE UNDER NATURAL LIGHT

CALCITE UNDER ULTRAVIOLET LIGHT

WHAT ARE CRYSTALS?

Virtually all minerals are crystalline – solids in which the component atoms are arranged in a particular, repeating, three-dimensional pattern. All crystals of a mineral are built with the same pattern. Some are several metres long; others can only be seen with a microscope.

ATOMIC STRUCTURE

A crystal is built up of individual, identical, structural units of atoms or molecules called unit cells. A crystal can consist of only a few unit cells or billions of them. The unit cell is repeated in three dimensions, forming the larger internal structure of the crystal. The shape of the unit cell and the symmetry of the structure determine the positions and shapes of the crystal's faces.

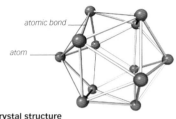

atomic bond

atom

Crystal structure
Stick-and-ball diagrams, such as this one, show how each atom in the structure of a crystal is bonded to others.

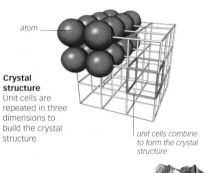

atom

Crystal structure
Unit cells are repeated in three dimensions to build the crystal structure.

unit cells combine to form the crystal structure

Crystals of many different minerals have unit cells that are similar in shape but are made of different chemical elements. The final development of the faces of a crystal is determined by the symmetry of the atomic structure and by the geological conditions at the time of its formation. Certain faces may be emphasized, while others disappear altogether. The final form taken by a crystal is known as its habit (pp.20–21).

MARCASITE CRYSTALS

metallic lustre

rosette-shaped aggregate

Structure of marcasite
Crystals of marcasite are created from repeating arrangements of atoms of iron and sulfur.

CRYSTAL SYMMETRY

All crystals exhibit symmetry because each crystal is built up of repeating geometric patterns. These patterns of crystal symmetry are divided into six main groups, or crystal systems (pp.22–23). The first of these symmetrical patterns is the cubic system in which all crystals exhibit cubic symmetry. The characteristics of cubic symmetry may be explained as follows: if opposite face centres of a cube-shaped cubic crystal, such as halite, are held between the thumb and forefinger and the crystal is rotated through 360 degrees, the pattern of faces will appear identical four times as the different faces and edges come into view.

All cubic crystals have three axes of fourfold symmetry. They have other axes of symmetry, but these differ among classes within the cubic system. For example, cube-shaped crystals of halite have three axes of fourfold symmetry, in addition to its four axes of threefold symmetry.

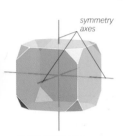

Cubic symmetry
All cubic crystals, such as those of halite (right), have three axes of fourfold symmetry.

symmetry axes

cubic crystal

rock groundmass

HALITE

chlorine atom

sodium atom

Halite atomic structure
This diagram shows the cubic arrangement of sodium and chlorine atoms in the halite structure.

TWIN CRYSTALS

When two or more crystals of the same species (a group of minerals that are chemically similar), such as gypsum or fluorite, form a symmetrical intergrowth, they are referred to as twinned crystals. Twins can be described as interpenetrating or contact. Penetration twinning may occur with individual crystals at an angle to one another – for example, forming a cross. It can also occur with individual crystals parallel to one another, as in Carlsbad twinning. If a twin involves three or more individual crystals, it is referred to as a multiple twin or a repeated twin. Albite often forms multiple twins. Many other minerals form twins, but they are particularly characteristic of some, such as the "fishtail" contact twins of gypsum or the penetration twins of fluorite.

parallel twins

area of intergrowth

CONTACT TWIN

CARLSBAD PENETRATION TWIN

Contact and penetration twins
Parallel twinning is a kind of contact twinning in which two or more crystals share a common face or faces. Penetration twinning results from crystals growing into each other.

centre of twinning

Cyclic twin
Cyclic twins occur when more than two crystals are twinned at a common centre. This specimen of cerussite shows the cyclic twinning of three crystals all at 60° angles to each other.

CRYSTAL HABITS

Habit refers to the external shape of a crystal or an assemblage of intergrown crystals. It includes names of crystal's faces, such as prismatic and pyramidal, names of forms, such as cubic and octahedral, and descriptive terms, such as bladed and dendritic.

CRYSTAL FACES

The three types of crystal face – prism, pyramid, and pinacoid – are determined by their relationship to a crystallographic axis (p.22). Prism faces are parallel to the axis; pyramid faces cut through the axis at an angle; and pinacoid faces are at right angles to the c axis. A crystal may have numerous sets of pyramid faces, each at a different angle to the c axis. Crystals may also have major and minor prism faces with edges parallel to each other. In most crystals, some faces are more developed than others.

pinacoid face
pyramid faces
prism face

c axis

Naming crystal faces
The names of crystal faces and their relationship to the c axis are shown here. The predominant crystal face gives the crystal its habit name.

pinacoid face
prism face
pyramid face

Prismatic topaz
Although this topaz crystal exhibits prismatic, pyramidal, and pinacoidal faces, the bulk of the crystal is defined by its prism faces and it is therefore called prismatic.

long prismatic habit

prism face

Prismatic
Prism faces clearly predominate in this long specimen of beryl. Its habit is therefore described as long prismatic.

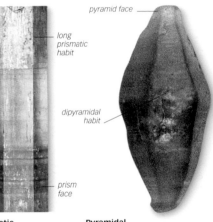

pyramid face

dipyramidal habit

Pyramidal
If pyramid faces dominate in one direction, the habit is pyramidal. If pyramid faces dominate in both directions, as in this specimen of sapphire, the habit is dipyramidal.

CRYSTAL FORMS

Habits can be named after crystal forms: "cubic" implies crystallizing in the form of cubes; "dodecahedral", in the form of dodecahedrons; and "rhombohedral", in the form of rhombohedrons. When crystals of one system crystallize in forms that appear to be the crystals of another system, the habit name is preceded by the word "pseudo". When terminations take different forms in the same crystal, the habit is known as hemimorphic.

Octahedral
This magnetite specimen has crystallized as an octahedron and is said to have an octahedral habit.

crystal forms as an octahedron, with eight plane faces

octahedral face

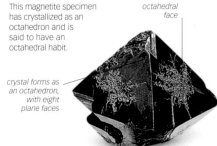

AGGREGATES

Aggregates are groups of intimately associated crystals. In general, aggregates are intergrowths of imperfectly developed crystals. In some aggregates, the crystals may be microscopic. The type of aggregation is often typical of a particular mineral species. Terms used to describe aggregates include granular, fibrous, radiating, botryoidal, stalactitic, geodic, and massive.

massive habit

fibrous strands

Massive
The massive habit occurs when there is a mass of crystals that cannot be seen individually, as in this specimen of dumortierite.

Fibrous
The fibrous habit is an aggregate, consisting of slender, parallel, or radiating fibres. This tremolite specimen is a good example.

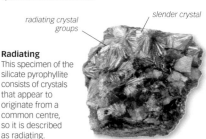
radiating crystal groups
slender crystal

Radiating
This specimen of the silicate pyrophyllite consists of crystals that appear to originate from a common centre, so it is described as radiating.

grape-like bunch

Botryoidal
This hematite specimen has formed in globular aggregates that resemble a bunch of grapes. This habit is described as botryoidal.

CRYSTAL APPEARANCE

Some habits are descriptions of the general appearance of a crystal. The term "tabular" describes a crystal with large, flat, parallel faces; "bladed" describes elongated crystals that are flattened like a knife blade; "stalactitic" describes crystal aggregates shaped like stalactites; and "blocky" or "equant" describes crystals with faces that are roughly the same size in all directions.

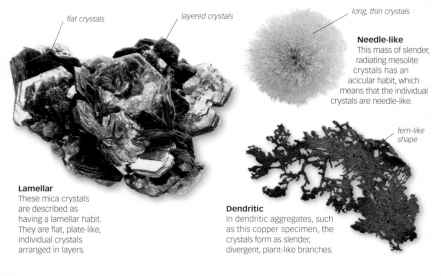
flat crystals

layered crystals

long, thin crystals

Needle-like
This mass of slender, radiating mesolite crystals has an acicular habit, which means that the individual crystals are needle-like.

fern-like shape

Lamellar
These mica crystals are described as having a lamellar habit. They are flat, plate-like, individual crystals arranged in layers.

Dendritic
In dendritic aggregates, such as this copper specimen, the crystals form as slender, divergent, plant-like branches.

CRYSTAL SYSTEMS

Crystals are classified into six different systems according to the maximum symmetry of their faces. Each crystal system is defined by the relative lengths and orientation of its three crystallographic axes – imaginary lines that pass through the centre of an ideal crystal.

CUBIC

Cubic crystals have three crystallographic axes (a_1, a_2, and a_3) at right angles and of equal length, and four threefold axes of symmetry. The main forms within this system are cube, octahedron, and rhombic dodecahedron. Halite, copper, gold, silver, platinum, iron, fluorite, and magnetite crystallize in the cubic system, which is also known as the isometric system.

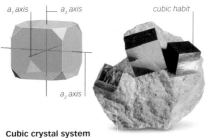

a_1 axis a_3 axis   cubic habit

a_2 axis

Cubic crystal system
Pyrite crystals commonly form as cubes, but they can also occur as pentagonal dodecahedra and octahedra, or combinations of all three forms.

TETRAGONAL

Tetragonal crystals have three crystallographic axes at right angles – two equal in length (a_1 and a_2), and the third (c) longer or shorter. These crystals have one principal, fourfold axis of symmetry. Crystals look like square or octahedral prisms in shape. Rutile, zircon, cassiterite, and calomel are minerals that crystallize in the tetragonal system.

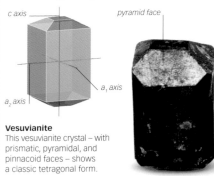

c axis   pyramid face

a_1 axis

a_2 axis

Vesuvianite
This vesuvianite crystal – with prismatic, pyramidal, and pinnacoid faces – shows a classic tetragonal form.

HEXAGONAL AND TRIGONAL

Some crystallographers consider hexagonal and trigonal crystals to comprise a single system, whereas others regard them as forming separate systems. Both crystalline forms have three crystallographic axes (a_1, a_2, and a_3) of equal length. These are at 120 degrees to one another and to a fourth axis (c), which is perpendicular to the plane of the other three axes. Trigonal crystals have only threefold symmetry, whereas hexagonal crystals have sixfold symmetry. Minerals that crystallize in the hexagonal system include beryl (emerald and aquamarine) and apatite. Some of the minerals that crystallize in the trigonal system are calcite, quartz, and tourmaline.

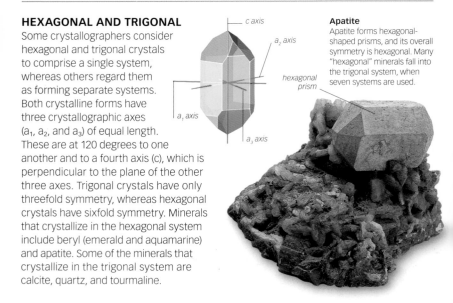

c axis

a_2 axis

hexagonal prism

a_1 axis

a_3 axis

Apatite
Apatite forms hexagonal-shaped prisms, and its overall symmetry is hexagonal. Many "hexagonal" minerals fall into the trigonal system, when seven systems are used.

MONOCLINIC

The term "monoclinic" means "one incline". Monoclinic crystals have three crystallographic axes of unequal length. One (c) is at right angles to the other two (a and b). These two axes are not perpendicular to each other, although they are in the same plane. The crystals have one twofold axis of symmetry. More minerals crystallize in the monoclinic system than in any other crystal system. Examples are gypsum, orthoclase, malachite, and jadeite.

c axis

Gypsum
The parallelogram shape of this crystal of gypsum demonstrates the two unequal crystallographic axes and the third axis at right angles of the monoclinic system. Orthoclase, which belongs to the same system, often forms twinned crystals.

a axis | b axis

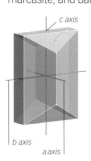

crystal with unequal sides

twinning

ORTHOCLASE

transparent, diamond-shaped crystal

GYPSUM

ORTHORHOMBIC

Orthorhombic means "perpendicular parallelogram". Crystals in this system have three crystallographic axes (a, b, and c) at right angles, all of which are unequal in length. They have three twofold axes of symmetry. Minerals that crystallize in this system include olivine, aragonite, topaz, marcasite, and baryte.

pyramidal face

c axis

b axis
a axis

Topaz
The mineral topaz often forms beautiful, orthorhombic prismatic crystals that are usually terminated by pyramids or other prisms. The mineral baryte also forms orthorhombic prisms.

TRICLINIC

Triclinic crystals have the least symmetrical shape, with three crystallographic axes of unequal length (a, b, and c) inclined at angles other than 90 degrees to each other. The orientation of a triclinic crystal is arbitrary. Minerals that crystallize in this system include albite, anorthite, kaolin, and kyanite.

c axis

a axis

b axis

triclinic axinite crystal

Axinite
The silicate axinite is a classic triclinic mineral. Several feldspars, including albite and microcline, are also triclinic.

GEMS

A gem is any mineral that is highly prized for its beauty, durability, and rarity. It is enhanced in some manner by altering its shape, usually by cutting and polishing. Most gems begin as crystals of minerals or as aggregates of crystals.

HISTORY OF GEMS

The use of gemstones in human history goes back to the Upper Paleolithic Period (25,000–12,000 BCE). People were initially drawn by the bright colours and beautiful patterns of gems. When the shaping of stones for adornment first began, opaque and soft specimens were used. As shaping techniques improved, harder stones began to be cut into gems. Beads of the quartz varieties hard carnelian and rock crystal were fashioned in Mesopotamia (now Iraq) in the 7th millennium BCE. Records of the time suggest that people thought that stones had a mystic value – a belief that persists to the present.

wings embedded with gems

Ancient masterpiece
This ancient Egyptian chest ornament is inlaid with gold, finely cut lapis lazuli, carnelian, and other gems. It is from the tomb of Tutankhamun (c.1361–1352 BCE).

lapis lazuli

Iraqi carnelian necklace
This necklace was made in Mesopotamia (modern day Iraq) from lapis lazuli, carnelian, and etched carnelian. It dates from about 2500 BCE.

etched carnelian

GEM MINING

Gemstone deposits form in different geological environments. Perhaps the best known are the "pipes" of kimberlite, from which most diamonds are recovered by the hard-rock methods of drilling and blasting. Other gems also recovered from the rock in which they form are quartz varieties, opal, tourmaline, topaz, emerald, aquamarine, some sapphires and rubies, turquoise, lapis lazuli, and chrysoberyl. Hard and dense gemstones that are impervious to chemical weathering are carried by water to placer deposits such as river beds, beaches, and the ocean floor. Placer mining techniques mimic the creation of the placer by separating denser minerals in running water. The simplest methods are panning and sieving, or passing gravel through a trough of flowing water with baffles at the bottom. The lighter material washes away but denser gemstones remain.

Gem panning
Many gemstone minerals, such as sapphire and ruby, are heavier than normal stream gravels. These can be recovered using the slow but thorough panning method.

Diamond mine in Siberia
Russia has become a major supplier of diamonds. In this mine, diamonds are being recovered from a diamond pipe.

FACETING

Gemstones can be shaped in several ways. Opaque or translucent semiprecious stones, such as agate and jasper, are tumble-polished, carved, engraved, or cut with a rounded upper surface and a flat underside. Grinding and polishing of flat faces on the stone is called faceting. Facets are placed in specific geometric positions at specific angles according to the bending of light within a particular stone. Transparent stones, such as amethyst, diamond, and sapphire, are faceted to maximize their brilliance and "fire" or enhance colour. Although much material is ground away while cutting, the final value is much enhanced.

Cutting a brilliant
While faceting gemstones, care must be taken to preserve the maximum material and produce the best brilliance and colour.

Rough choice
The faceter selects his rough based on colour, clarity, and shape, which determine the cut for the final gem.

Sawn in two
The rough is sawn to roughly the final shape of the gem. Accurate sawing saves time in the grinding process.

Faceting begins
The major facets are first ground onto the gem. The accuracy of these determines the final brilliance.

Further facets
Smaller facets are cut after the major facets. Based on the cut, there may be only a few or dozens of these.

Finished off
After the first side of the stone is cut, it is reversed and facets are placed on the second side in the same order.

GEM CUTS

There are three basic types of facet cut: step (with rectangular facets), brilliant (with triangular facets), and mixed (a combination of the two). The first faceting probably involved diamond cutting in Italy prior to the 15th century. First, only the natural faces of octahedral diamond crystals were polished. The rose cut was developed in the 17th century. By about 1700, the brilliant cut (today's favourite for diamonds and other colourless gems) was created. The emerald cut was soon developed to save valuable material, as its rectangular cut conforms to the shape of emerald crystals. Today there are hundreds of possible gem cuts.

Gemstone shapes
A principal criterion for the cutter in choosing a gemstone shape is the shape of the rough gemstone. This ensures that a minimum of valuable material is lost.

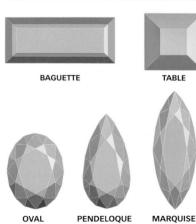

BAGUETTE

TABLE

SQUARE

SCISSOR

OCTAGONAL

CUSHION

OVAL

PENDELOQUE

MARQUISE

ROUND

MIXED

WHAT IS A ROCK?

A rock is a naturally occurring and coherent aggregate of one or more minerals. There are three major classes of rock – igneous, sedimentary, and metamorphic. Each of these three classes is further subdivided into groups and types.

TYPES OF ROCK

Igneous rocks form from melted rock called magma. When magmas solidify underground, intrusive rocks such as granite are created. Intrusive rocks are also known as plutonic rocks. If the magma flows onto the surface of the land or ocean bed, extrusive rocks such as basalt, are formed.

Sedimentary rocks are usually made of deposits laid down on Earth's surface by water, wind, or ice. They almost always occur in layers or strata. Stratification survives compaction and cementation and is a distinguishing feature of sedimentary rocks. Some sedimentary rocks are of chemical origin,

grey quartz crystals • black mica • pink feldspar

Pink granite
In this specimen of igneous pink granite, the three essential components of all granites can be seen: quartz, alkali feldspar, and mica.

having been deposited in solid form from a solution. Others are of biochemical origin and are composed predominantly of the compound calcium carbonate.

When existing rocks are subjected to extreme temperatures or pressures, or both, their composition, texture, and internal structure may be altered to form metamorphic rocks. The original rocks may be igneous, sedimentary, or metamorphic.

Pegmatite dyke
Light-coloured bands of igneous hydrothermal pegmatite, composed principally of quartz, can be seen here cutting across darker bands of metamorphic gneiss.

Volcanic growth
The eruption of extrusive magmas can create volumes of igneous rock measured in cubic kilometres on the surface of Earth.

Marble quarry
This dazzling white marble being quarried at Carrara, Italy, is metamorphosed from a very pure limestone.

Meteorites are not considered igneous, sedimentary, or metamorphic but are a group of their own. Many are remnants of asteroids, which are themselves remnants of the formation of the Solar System. Some meteorites are remains of the nickel-iron cores of asteroids; some contain nickel-iron and minerals such as olivine from the mantles of asteroids; and others are made up principally of silicate minerals.

Sedimentary layers
The Colorado River cuts through layers of sedimentary rock in the Grand Canyon, USA. The highest layers are the youngest, while the deepest are the oldest.

THE ROCK CYCLE

The series of processes by which rocks are created, broken down, and reconstituted as new rocks is known as the rock cycle. These processes depend on pressure, temperature, time, and changes in environmental conditions in Earth's crust and surface. At various stages in the rock cycle, old rocks are broken down, new minerals form, and new rocks originate from the components of the old. Thus a rock that began at the surface as an igneous rock may be reworked into a sedimentary rock or be converted into a metamorphic rock or new igneous rock to continue the cycle again.

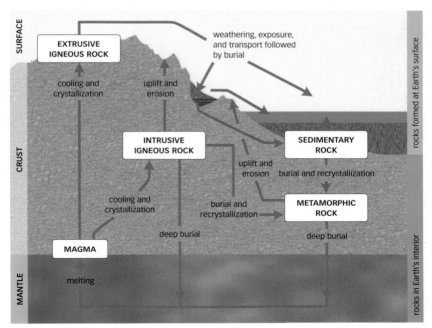

The rock cycle
This diagram summarizes the various elements of the rock cycle, from the creation of fresh igneous rock through erosion, deposition, and its reconstitution into new rock.

COLLECTING ROCKS AND MINERALS

The world of rocks, minerals, gems, and fossils offers endless possibilities for the hobbyist. Only a small amount of specialized knowledge is required to open a whole world of enjoyment of some of nature's finest creations.

WHERE TO LOOK

Most collectors begin by just accumulating rocks, minerals, and fossils. As their collection grows, they start being more selective, keeping only specimens with better colour and crystallization and more interesting crystal forms. A wide range of specimens can be purchased from dealers, but it is often more enjoyable to find your own. In many countries, there are guidebooks that give precise directions to collecting localities for rocks, minerals, and fossils.

Sample collection is not without its constraints: working mines and quarries have legal restrictions on people permitted on their premises; old mines are dangerous; old mine dumps have been gone over for decades by other collectors; and public access to land is often restricted. However, traditional collecting sites, such as road cuttings and eroded cliffs on shorelines, continue to provide excellent opportunities for collectors.

Field experience
Rock collecting can be a hobby for a lifetime, as the collector develops knowledge and skills to enhance the activity.

Road cutting
The bank of a road cut through this pegmatite rock reveals giant feldspar crystals. Many fine rock and mineral specimens are derived from road cuttings.

Looking for gold
The gold pan is an essential piece of kit for a collector. Many gemstones, such as garnet and sapphire, can be found by panning.

There is also an increasing number of collecting localities that are open to the public on the payment of a fee. Some clubs for collecting enthusiasts have their own collecting sites, and they also arrange trips to sites that are otherwise inaccessible to the public. Collectors should bear in mind that permission must always be sought to collect samples on private property.

Old working
While mine dumps are good sources of specimens, hidden workings and old machinery can pose a hazard to unwary collectors.

SAFETY AND THE COLLECTING CODE

Tempting tunnels
Old mine shafts can be tempting, but are often highly dangerous places. In most cases better specimens are usually found in the mine dumps outside.

While mineral collecting is generally a safe hobby, there are a few definite hazards that a collector needs to be aware of. The most dangerous collecting localities are around old mines and workings. Tunnels should never be entered – shoring timbers rot quickly, and cave-ins and rock falls are almost guaranteed to happen. Collectors must also pay attention to what is underfoot – old shafts are sometimes covered over. In any case, there is often remarkably poor collecting inside old mines, as most material of value has usually already been removed by miners. Mine dumps, by contrast, can be a good source of specimens. However, caution should be exercized as mine dumps are often loosely piled and can be unstable.

When collecting in beach cliffs, road cuttings, and rock falls, pay attention not only to loose material underfoot but also to anything that may fall or roll from above. It is best to avoid a collecting locality if you are not sure that is safe.

TAKING NOTES

When they start out, new collectors often ignore the need to write down information about their finds. But experience soon shows that investing in a notebook and devoting the minimal amount of time it takes to keep at least basic notes is essential. It is especially important to make notes about exactly where specimens were found. A considerable time may go by before you revisit the locality, and by then, in the absence of notes, you will probably be unable to find the spot again. It is useful to make a sketch of important landmarks or outcrops, because these can help relocate a specific spot.

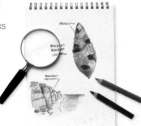

Drawing locations
It is useful to make drawings in notebooks of locations and the specimens they have yielded.

Map and compass
Tools such as a compass and a map or a GPS receiver are essential for identifying localities and relocating them at a later date.

Correcting fluid
Number each specimen with a note about their find-spot. A dab of correction fluid makes a good label and can be removed if necessary.

EQUIPMENT

Mineral collecting is a safe hobby, but some simple pieces of equipment increase the safety factor dramatically. Just a few basics, such as the right hammer and chisel, a hard hat, goggles, gloves, and things you already have, will get you started.

FIELD EQUIPMENT

In addition to the basic collecting tools described here, safety equipment should be considered essential. Access to some collecting localities requires safety clothing such as a hard hat and fluorescent vest. Carry a mobile phone with a fully charged battery with you even if you are only going a short distance from the car. A fall into a ravine

Head and hand protection

Flying rock splinters and falling rocks cause injuries to collectors each year. Hands, eyes, and heads are particularly vulnerable areas. Goggles are recommended when breaking or splitting stone.

HARD HAT

LEATHER GLOVES

SAFETY GOGGLES

straight head for splitting hard rock

lump hammer head

sharp end to break rock with precision

flat end

sharp point

rubber or leather grip

wooden handle

GEOLOGISTS' HAMMER

TRIMMING HAMMER

CLUB HAMMER

SAFETY CHISELS

Hammers

Every year rock collectors are injured – sometimes blinded – by using the wrong hammers. Geologists' hammers are made of special steels. Their striking ends are bevelled to prevent steel splinters from flying off.

Chisels

Like rock hammers, the chisels used by geologists are made from special steels that resist splintering. Not all are essential but having two or three of different sizes will make cutting rock safer.

trowel
brush for light cleaning
flat brush
sieve

Extra tools
The experienced collector has a range of equipment for all collecting possibilities, from sieves and pans to various brushes and trowels. Most of these can be bought a few at a time as new collecting localities are visited.

or another low spot may take you out of sight of potential help and add hours to the time it takes to find you. In desert country, an adequate supply of water is essential, and if you are in snake country take an appropriate snake-bite kit. Clothing suitable to the weather and terrain is, of course, vital. Leave your low-cut shoes and trainers at home. Leather boots

offer better protection from snake bites, cactus spines, sharp stones, jagged metal, and rolling stones, and ensure much better traction.

MAGNIFICATION
There is an entire area of mineral collecting devoted to tiny crystals known as micromounts. Small crystals often develop superb forms and groupings that are obscured as the process of crystallization progresses. Micromount collectors need effective microscopes, or at the least large magnifiers, to examine and enjoy these minute specimens. For collectors not wishing to incur the expense of a microscope, a simple hand lens will reveal much of the beauty of the tiny micromounts.

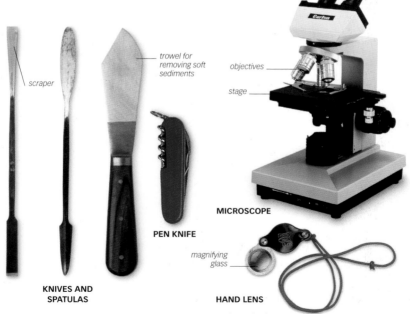

scraper

trowel for removing soft sediments

eyepiece

objectives

stage

MICROSCOPE

PEN KNIFE

magnifying glass

KNIVES AND SPATULAS

HAND LENS

Cleaning tools
There are two types of cleaning tool: those for field use and those for cleaning specimens at home. Tools for field use are more robust and are used for separating specimens from adhering rock.

A closer look
Most collectors of small crystals have a microscope to examine their specimens. The field equipment of every geologist and collector should include a hand lens with a magnification of about 10 times.

ORGANIZATION, STORAGE, AND CLEANING

Finding mineral specimens is only the first stage of collecting. The number of specimens damaged in the course of the journey home or while cleaning can be large. Care must therefore be taken from the moment a specimen is collected.

TRANSPORTING SPECIMENS

Wrapping of some sort is essential when transporting newly collected specimens, whether they are being carried in a rucksack or a car. Delicate specimens should be wrapped first in tissue and then in newspaper. If your wrapping material is used up, try leaves, grass, or pine needles as a natural alternative. Unwrap wet specimens and let them dry as soon as you get home. Cotton wool and cellulose wadding should be kept entirely away from specimens, as the fibres are almost impossible to remove.

In the bag
Rock samples can be carried in a cloth specimen bag. More sensitive specimens require elaborate wrapping so that they can be transported safely.

CLEANING SPECIMENS

As a general rule, clean specimens as little as possible, starting with the gentlest methods first. Begin by using a soft brush to remove loose soil and debris. Hard rock specimens, such as gneiss or granite, are unlikely to be damaged by vigorous cleaning. With delicate minerals, such as calcite crystals, it is essential to use a fine, soft brush. Never use hot water to wash a specimen, as the heat may

cause some minerals to crack or shatter. Toothbrushes that use a pulsing water jet are useful cleaning tools. Soaps should be avoided, but if you must use them, choose liquid dishwashing soaps rather than hand or toilet soaps that have additives that can penetrate specimens. The use of ultrasonic cleaners is not recommended, as they can shatter delicate specimens even at low intensities. Certain acids are

Muddy rocks
Many specimens will be muddy or dirty when collected. Most dirt is more easily removed when it is dry and can be lightly brushed off.

DISTILLED WATER **HYDROCHLORIC ACID**

Cleaning liquids
Distilled (or deionized) water is good as a final wash for minerals. Weak hydrochloric acid is good for cleaning silicates, but always be aware of the risks involved.

BRADAWL **FINE POINTED SCRAPER**

suitable for cleaning specific minerals. Silicates are not harmed by weak acids, but carbonates and phosphates can be damaged by them. If you do use acids, seek specific information on their use from specialized books or other collectors.

Cleaning up
Removing rock with fine specialist tools is often necessary when collecting fossils. The mineral collector, by contrast, is more likely to brush or wash off dirt from specimens.

STORAGE AND DISPLAY

Once specimens have been collected and cleaned, they need to be stored or, in the case of the most attractive pieces, displayed. Many collectors like to store specimens in card trays inside shallow drawers. Once collected, some minerals are liable to experience physical and chemical effects that may either change or sometimes destroy them. Fortunately, these problems are well known and preventative measures can be taken in advance.

Every specimen collected should be accompanied by a label with as much information about it as is feasible. For display, use a sturdy, preferably glass-fronted cabinet or shelf. Many guests will wish to handle specimens, but they may not be aware that handling can damage delicate examples.

Mineral preservation
Minerals such as orpiment and realgar are sensitive to light and need special storage methods. Other minerals may require either dry or humid conditions.

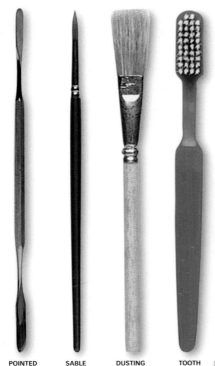

| POINTED SCRAPER | SABLE BRUSH | DUSTING BRUSH | TOOTH BRUSH |

Cleaning tools
A variety of tools is useful for cleaning specimens. Each specimen will present a different cleaning problem, so a selection of tools is necessary.

Informative display
People will admire your best specimens and also value information about them. Some collectors choose to provide museum-style information about specimens.

MINERALS

NATIVE ELEMENTS

There are 88 chemical elements known to occur in nature. Of these, less than two dozen are found uncombined with other elements. This group is called the native elements. Only eight of these native elements are found in significant quantities.

COMPOSITION

The native elements are classified into three groups: metals like copper and gold; semimetals like arsenic; and nonmetals like sulphur and carbon. The metals rarely form well-defined crystals; the semimetals typically occur as nodular masses; and the nonmetals form distinct crystals.

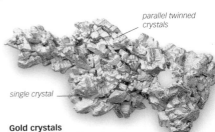

parallel twinned crystals

single crystal

Gold crystals
This crystallized gold specimen is a rarity, because native metals rarely form well-defined crystals. Most occur in wire-like and branching forms or as nuggets.

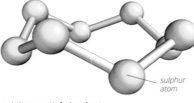

sulphur atom

Sulphur crystal structure
In the orthorhombic crystal structure of sulphur, strongly bonded rings of eight sulphur atoms are weakly bonded to neighbouring rings.

OCCURRENCE AND USES

Native elements are known to form under a wide range of geological conditions and in a variety of rock types. A native element can occur in several different environments. Some are found in sufficient concentrations to form economically important deposits.

Native gold and silver have been media of exchange for three millennia, and native copper and meteoric iron were among the first metals to be used by humans.

Industrial tools
This tool-maker is producing a diamond-edged industrial cutting tool. Although partly replaced by synthetic diamond, natural diamond continues to be used as an industrial abrasive.

Sulphur crust
Native sulphur builds up around fumaroles, where sulphur-rich gas is vented around volcanoes. These fumaroles often produce magnificently crystallized specimens.

Native copper
This specimen of native copper is accompanied by accessory quartz.

crystalline copper

massive copper

accessory quartz

VARIANT

Dendritic copper A specimen of crystalline copper in the branching form

Cu

COPPER

In its free-occurring metallic state, copper was probably the first metal to be used by humans. Neolithic people are believed to have used copper as a substitute for stone by 8000 BCE. Around 4000 BCE, Egyptians cast copper in moulds. By 3500 BCE, copper began to be alloyed with tin to produce bronze.

Copper is opaque, bright, and metallic salmon pink on freshly broken surfaces but soon turns dull brown. Copper crystals are uncommon, but when formed are either cubic or dodecahedral, often arranged in branching aggregates. Most copper is found as irregular, flattened, or branching masses. It is one of the few metals that occur in the "native" form without being bonded to other elements. Native copper seems to be a secondary mineral, a result of interaction between copper-bearing solutions and iron-bearing minerals.

Plumbing joint
Since it is easy to shape and roll the metal, copper is widely used to make household pipes.

PROFILE

Cubic

⚖ 4–4½

⚖ 14.0–19.0

▰ None

⤬ Hackly

▱ Whitish steel-grey

⤬ Metallic

Platinum nugget
Although most of the platinum mined from placer deposits occurs as small grains, sizeable nuggets are sometimes found.

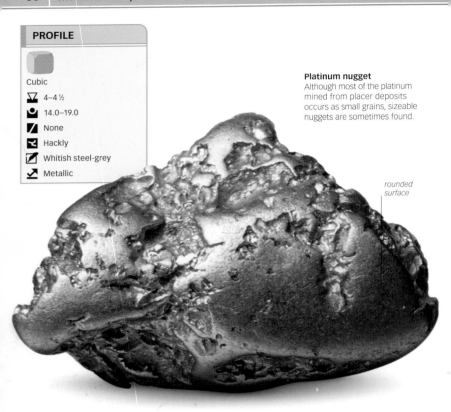

rounded surface

VARIANTS

Granular habit Most platinum is recovered as small grains

cube-shaped crystal

Platinum crystals Isolated cubic crystals of platinum

⚛ Pt

PLATINUM

The first documented discovery of platinum was by the Spaniards in the 1500s, in the alluvial gold mines of the Río Pinto, Colombia. They called it *platina del Pinto*, from *platina*, which means "little silver", thinking that it was an impure ore of silver. It was not recognized as a distinct metal until 1735. It is opaque, silvery grey, and markedly dense.

Platinum usually occurs as disseminated grains in iron- and magnesium-rich igneous rocks and in quartz veins associated with hematite (p.91), chlorite, and pyrolusite (p.80). When rocks weather, the heavy platinum accumulates as grains and nuggets in the resulting placer deposits. Crystals are rare, but when found they are cubic. Most platinum for commercial use is recovered from primary deposits. Native platinum typically contains iron and metals such as palladium, iridium, and rhodium.

Platinum ring
A 2.5-carat, brilliant-cut diamond has been set in a platinum mounting in this ring.

Iron meteorite
Most native iron is in Earth's core, but iron from meteorites, such as this one, was used from about 3000 BCE. Native iron is usually alloyed with nickel.

intermixture of kamacite and taenite crystals

metallic appearance

crust formed as surface melts and then solidifies on entry to Earth's atmosphere

PROFILE

Cubic

 4

7.3–7.9

Basal

Hackly

Steel-grey

Metallic

Fe,Ni

IRON

Five per cent of Earth's crust is made up of iron. Native iron is rare in the crust and is invariably alloyed with nickel. Low-nickel iron (up to 7.5 per cent nickel) is called kamacite, and high-nickel iron (up to 50 per cent nickel) is called taenite. Both crystallize in the cubic system. A third form of iron-nickel, mainly found in meteorites and crystallizing in the tetragonal system, is called tetrataenite. All three forms are generally found either as disseminated grains or as rounded masses.

Kamacite is the major component of most iron meteorites (p.335). It is found in most chondritic meteorites (p.337), and occurs as microscopic grains in some lunar rocks. Taenite and tetrataenite are mainly found in meteorites, often intergrown with kamacite. Iron is also plentiful in the Sun and other stars.

Viking axehead
This iron Viking axehead from Frykat, Denmark, has a shape commonly used in weapons.

Crystalline bismuth
This group of intergrown bismuth crystals shows typical metallic lustre and iridescence.

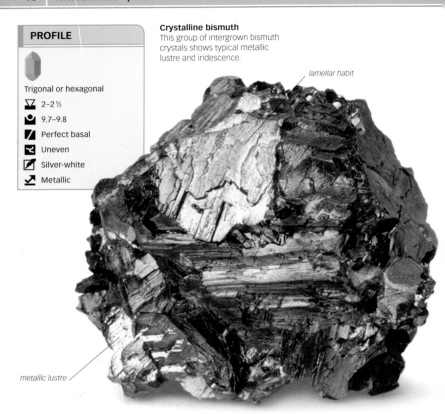

lamellar habit

metallic lustre

VARIANT

Native bismuth Partly crystalline bismuth on rock

♣ Bi

BISMUTH

As a native metal, bismuth has been known since the Middle Ages. A German monk named Basil Valentine first described it in 1450. Bismuth is often found uncombined with other elements, forming indistinct crystals, often in parallel groupings. It is hard, brittle, and lustrous. It is also found in grains and as foliated masses. Silver-white, it usually has a reddish tinge that distinguishes it. Specimens may have an iridescent tarnish.

Bismuth is found in hydrothermal veins and in pegmatites (p.260) and is often associated with ores of tin, lead, or copper (p.37), from which it is separated as a by-product. Bismuth expands slightly when it solidifies, making its alloys useful in the manufacture of metal castings with sharp detailing. Bismuth salts are often used as soothing agents for digestive disorders.

Hopper-shaped crystals
Laboratory-grown bismuth crystals with cavernous faces like these exhibit an array of colours.

PROFILE

Trigonal or hexagonal

	3–3½
	6.6–6.7
	Perfect basal
	Uneven
	Grey
	Metallic

Massive antimony
This specimen of massive antimony has a pale silvery grey colour and the occasional small crystal.

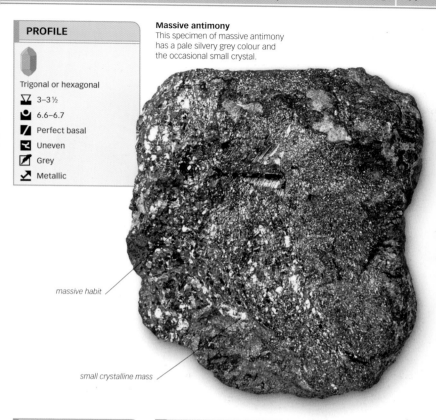

massive habit

small crystalline mass

VARIANT

metallic lustre

Antimony star A starry pattern of antimony formed when molten antimony is cooled

Sb

ANTIMONY

Although recognized as a metal since the 8th century or earlier, antimony was only identified as an element in 1748. Crystals are rare but when found are either psuedocubic or thick and tabular. Antimony usually occurs in massive, foliated, or granular form. It is lustrous, silvery, bluish white in colour, and has a flaky texture that makes it brittle. It almost always contains some arsenic and is found in veins with silver (p.43), arsenic (p.45), and other antimony minerals.

Antimony is extremely important in alloys. Even in minor quantities, it imparts strength and hardness to other metals, particularly lead, whose alloys are used in the plates of automobile storage batteries, in bullets, and in coverings for cables. Combined with tin and lead, antimony forms antifriction alloys called babbitt metals, which are used as components of machine bearings. Like bismuth (p.40), antimony expands slightly on solidifying, making it a useful alloying metal for detailed castings.

PROFILE

Cubic

- 2½–3
- 19.3
- None
- Hackly
- Golden yellow
- Metallic

scaly gold

Scales of gold
This specimen with thin plates of gold embedded in a quartz groundmass is from Baita, Transylvania, Romania.

mass of soft, pure gold

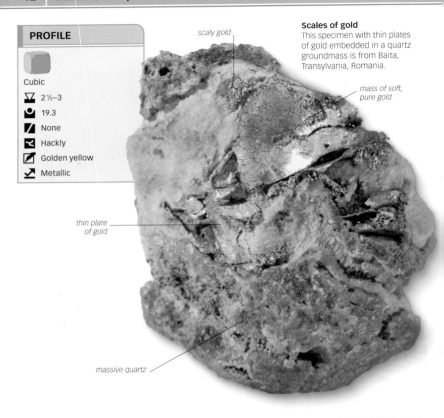

thin plate of gold

massive quartz

VARIANTS

Gold nugget An irregularly shaped gold nugget

quartz

Gold crystals Crystalline gold in a dull quartz matrix

Au

GOLD

Throughout human history, gold has been the most prized metal. It is opaque, has a highly attractive metallic golden yellow colour, is extremely malleable, and is usually found in a relatively pure form. It is remarkably inert, so it resists tarnish. These qualities have made it exceptionally valuable. Gold usually occurs as tree-like growths, grains, and scaly masses. It rarely occurs as well-formed crystals, but when found these are octahedral or dodecahedral.

Gold is mostly found in hydrothermal veins with quartz (p.168) and sulphides. Virtually all granitic igneous rocks – in which it occurs as invisible, disseminated grains – contain low concentrations of gold. Almost all of the gold recovered since antiquity has come from placer deposits – weathered gold particles concentrated in river and stream gravel.

Garnet in gold
This gold ring has an unusual demantoid (yellow-green) garnet set in it.

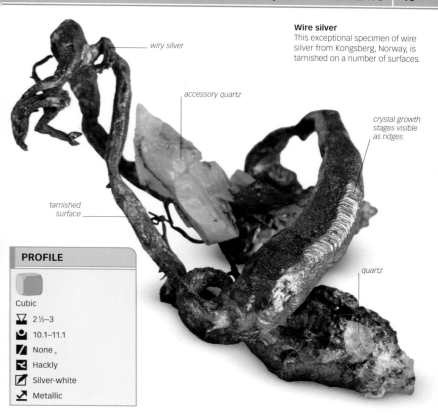

Wire silver
This exceptional specimen of wire silver from Kongsberg, Norway, is tarnished on a number of surfaces.

wiry silver

accessory quartz

crystal growth stages visible as ridges

tarnished surface

quartz

PROFILE

Cubic

2½–3

10.1–11.1

None

Hackly

Silver-white

Metallic

VARIANTS

Tarnished silver A tarnished specimen of wiry silver

tree-like crystal

metallic lustre

Dendritic silver Superbly crystalline, dendritic silver

Ag

SILVER

The earliest silver ornaments and decorations were found in tombs that date as far back as 4000 BCE. Silver coinage began to appear around 550 BCE. Opaque and bright silvery white with a slightly pink tint, silver readily tarnishes to either grey or black. Natural crystals of silver are uncommon, but when found they are cubic, octahedral, or dodecahedral. Silver is usually found in granular habit and as wiry, branching, lamellar, or scaly masses.

Widely distributed in nature, silver is a primary hydrothermal mineral. It also forms by alteration of other silver-bearing minerals. Much of the world's silver production is a by-product of refining lead, copper (p.37), and zinc. Silver is the second most malleable and ductile metal, and it is important in the photographic and electronic industries.

Silver inkwell
This Guild of Handicraft textured silver inkwell of square, tapering form has a blue enamel cabochon.

Orthorhombic

🔻 1½–2½

📦 2.1

▨ Indistinct

◩ Conchoidal to uneven, brittle

▨ White

↗ Resinous to greasy

Sulphur crystals
Yellow orthorhombic crystals of sulphur are set in a rock groundmass in this specimen from Conil, Andalucía, Spain.

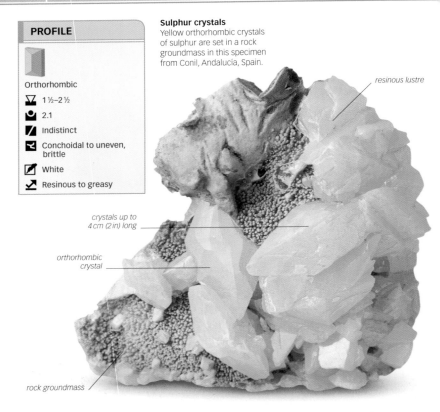

resinous lustre

crystals up to 4 cm (2 in) long

orthorhombic crystal

rock groundmass

VARIANTS

Fumarole crystals A crust of very small sulphur crystals from a fumarole in Java, Indonesia

needle-like crystal

Acicular sulphur Elongated sulphur crystals on rock

⚛ S

SULPHUR

The ninth most abundant element in the Universe, after oxygen and silicon, sulphur is the most abundant constituent of minerals. It occurs in the form of sulphides (pp.49–64), sulphates (pp.132–41), and elemental sulphur. The bright yellow or orangish colour of sulphur makes the mineral easy to identify. Sulphur forms pyramidal or tabular crystals, encrustations, powdery coatings, and granular or massive aggregates. Crystalline sulphur may exhibit as many as 56 different habits.

Most sulphur forms in volcanic fumaroles, but it can also result from the breakdown of sulphide ore deposits. Massive sulphur is found in thick beds in sedimentary rocks, particularly those associated with salt domes. Sulphur is a poor conductor of heat, which means that specimens are warm to the touch.

Powdered sulphur
Sulphur is used in a number of industrial and medicinal applications including in the production of sulphuric acid.

PROFILE

Hexagonal or trigonal

3½

5.7

Perfect, fair

Uneven, brittle

Grey

Metallic or dull earthy

Botryoidal arsenic
In this specimen, native arsenic has a metallic lustre and exhibits a typical botryoidal habit.

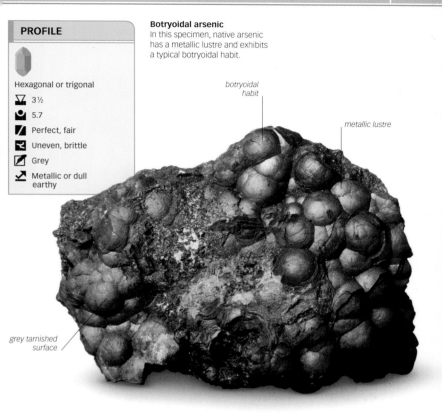

botryoidal habit

metallic lustre

grey tarnished surface

VARIANT

Massive arsenic A darkly tarnished, massive specimen of native arsenic

As

ARSENIC

Known since antiquity, arsenic is widely distributed in nature, although it is unusual in native form. It is classified as a semimetal, because it possesses some properties of metals and some of nonmetals. Crystals are rare, but when found they are rhombohedral. Arsenic usually occurs in massive, botryoidal to reniform, or stalactitic habits, often with concentric layers. On fresh surfaces, arsenic is tin-white, but it quickly tarnishes to dark grey.

Native arsenic is found in hydrothermal veins, often associated with antimony (p.41), silver (p.43), cobalt, and nickel-bearing minerals. It is highly poisonous, although it is used in some medicines to treat infections. Arsenic-based compounds can be used in alloys to increase high-temperature strength and as a herbicide and pesticide.

Arsenic paint
Ancient Egyptian artists used orange-red colours made from powdered arsenic sulphide.

Hexagonal

1–2

2.2

Perfect basal

Uneven

Black to steel-grey, shiny

Metallic or dull earthy

Massive graphite
As seen in this massive specimen, graphite has a soapy or greasy feeling when touched.

perfect cleavage

massive habit

metallic lustre

Black graphite A lump of compact, black graphite

Crystalline graphite A graphite crystal exhibiting metallic lustre

C

GRAPHITE

Like diamond, graphite is a form of native carbon. It takes its name from the Greek term *graphein*, which means "to write" – a reference to the black mark it leaves on paper. Graphite is opaque and dark grey to black. It occurs as hexagonal crystals, flexible sheets, scales, or large masses. It may be earthy, granular, or compact.

Graphite forms from the metamorphism of carbonaceous sediments and the reaction of carbon compounds with hydrothermal solutions. Graphite looks dramatically different from diamond and is at the other end of the hardness scale. Graphite's softness is due to the way carbon atoms are bonded to each other – rings of six carbon atoms are arranged in widely spaced horizontal sheets. The atoms are strongly bonded within the rings but very weakly bonded between the sheets.

Graphite pencil
The familiar pencil "lead" contains graphite. The first use of graphite pencils was described in 1575.

PROFILE

Cubic

10

3.4–3.5

Perfect octahedral

Conchoidal

Will scratch streak plate

Adamantine

Diamond in a matrix
An octahedral diamond crystal rests in the kimberlite matrix in which it was found.

yellowish octahedral crystal

rock groundmass

adamantine lustre

VARIANTS

Carbonado A form of black industrial diamond

Bort diamond A crystal of black bort diamond

Pink diamond A rare pink diamond crystal

C

DIAMOND

The hardest known mineral, diamond is pure carbon. Its crystals typically occur as octahedrons and cubes with rounded edges and slightly convex faces. Crystals may be transparent, translucent, or opaque. They range from colourless to black, with brown and yellow being the most common colours. Other forms include bort or boart (irregular or granular black diamond) and carbonado (microcrystalline masses). Colourless gemstones are most often used in jewellery.

Most diamonds come from two rare volcanic rocks – lamproite and kimberlite (p.269). The diamonds crystallize in Earth's mantle, generally more than 150 km (95 miles) deep, and are formed up to Earth's surface through volcanism. Diamonds are also found in sediment deposited by rivers or melting glaciers.

Hope Diamond
Blue in colour, the 45.5 carat Hope diamond is probably the world's most famous diamond.

SULPHIDES

Sulphides are minerals in which sulphur (a nonmetal) is combined either with a metal or a semimetal. Some sulphides are brilliantly coloured, and most of them have low hardness and high specific gravity. Sulphides are common and are found widely in nature.

Red River deposit
Sulphide deposits in the Rio Tinto area of southwestern Spain have been mined for silver, zinc, and copper since 800 BCE.

COMPOSITION

Most sulphides have simple atomic structures, in which sulphur atoms are stacked alternately with metal or semimetal atoms and arranged as cubes, octahedra, or tetrahedra. This yields highly symmetrical crystal forms. Except in a few sulphides, such as orpiment and realgar, the symmetrical form also gives rise to

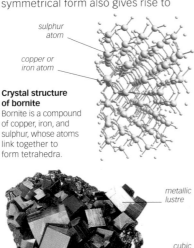

sulphur atom

copper or iron atom

Crystal structure of bornite
Bornite is a compound of copper, iron, and sulphur, whose atoms link together to form tetrahedra.

metallic lustre

cubic habit

Crystalline pyrite
The iron sulphide pyrite, also called fool's gold, is one of the most common sulphides. The cubic crystals of pyrite reflect its simple atomic structure.

many of the properties also found in metals, including metallic lustre and electrical conductivity.

OCCURRENCE AND USES

Sulphides tend to form primarily in hydrothermal veins, from fluids circulating within fractures in Earth's crust. Sulphides such as pyrite and marcasite can form in sedimentary environments; others may form in magmas. It is common to find several sulphide minerals together.

Sulphides are the major ore minerals of many metals, including lead, zinc, iron, antimony, bismuth, molybdenum, nickel, silver, and copper – all of which have industrial uses. Gold is commonly found in sulphide deposits.

Die production
Sphalerite – a zinc sulphide – is the principal ore of zinc, which is used for die-cast components to galvanize, or coat, iron and steel.

PROFILE

Monoclinic

2–2½

7.2–7.4

Indistinct

Subconchoidal, sectile

Black

Metallic

uneven fracture

metallic lustre

lustre less brilliant on exposed surfaces

darkened, weathered surface

Blocky, prismatic crystals
In this pseudomorph specimen, argentite has replaced acanthite, while retaining the outward form of acanthite's cubic symmetry.

VARIANT

Thorny acanthite Dark, spiky acanthite crystals

Ag₂S

ACANTHITE

A silver sulphide, acanthite is the most important ore of silver. It takes its name from the Greek *akantha*, which means "thorn" and refers to the spiky appearance of some of its crystals. It also occurs in massive form and has an opaque, greyish black colour. Above 177°C (350°F), silver sulphide crystallizes in the cubic system, and it used to be assumed that cubic silver sulphide – known as argentite – was a separate mineral from acanthite. It is now known that they are the same mineral, with acanthite crystallizing in the monoclinic system at temperatures below 177°C (350°F).

Acanthite forms in hydrothermal veins with other minerals, such as silver (p.43), galena (p.54), pyrargyrite (p.70), and proustite (p.72). It also forms as a secondary alteration product of primary silver sulphides. When heated, acanthite fuses readily and releases sulphurous fumes. The most famous locality of acanthite, the Comstock Lode in Nevada, USA, was so rich in silver that a branch of the US mint was established at nearby Carson City to coin its output.

PROFILE

Orthorhombic

⬇ 3

💧 5.1

▨ Poor

✂ Uneven to conchoidal, brittle

◪ Pale greyish black

⬈ Metallic

massive habit

uneven fracture

iridescent surface

purple oxidation

Massive bornite
This specimen of tarnished bornite shows the oxidation colours that give it the names "purple copper ore" and "peacock ore".

VARIANT

brownish red on fresh surface

Bornite crystals Well-developed bornite crystals with curved faces

♣ Cu$_5$FeS$_4$

BORNITE

One of nature's most colourful minerals, bornite is a copper iron sulphide named after the Austrian mineralogist Ignaz von Born (1742–91). A major ore of copper, its natural colour can be coppery red, coppery brown, or bronze. It can also show iridescent purple, blue, and red splashes of colour on broken, tarnished faces, which explains its common name, "peacock ore". Bornite is also known as "purple copper ore" and "variegated copper ore".

Bornite crystals are uncommon. Although they exhibit orthorhombic symmetry, crystals, when found, are cubic, octahedral, or dodecahedral, often with curved or rough faces. Bornite is frequently compact, granular, or massive and alters readily to chalcocite (p.51) and other copper minerals upon weathering. It forms mainly in hydrothermal copper ore deposits with minerals such as chalcopyrite (p.57), pyrite (p.62), marcasite (p.63), and quartz (p.168). It also forms in some silica-poor, intrusive igneous rocks and in pegmatite veins and contact metamorphic zones.

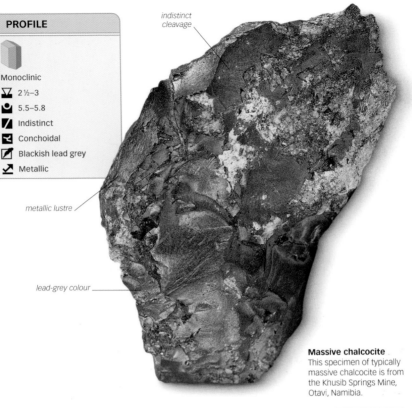

Monoclinic

⊻ 2½–3

🔨 5.5–5.8

▧ Indistinct

▨ Conchoidal

▧ Blackish lead grey

⬈ Metallic

metallic lustre

indistinct cleavage

lead-grey colour

Massive chalcocite
This specimen of typically massive chalcocite is from the Khusib Springs Mine, Otavi, Namibia.

VARIANT

Prismatic crystals Short prismatic chalcocite crystals on dolomite

Cu_2S

CHALCOCITE

The name chalcocite is derived from the Greek word for copper, *chalcos*. Chalcocite is one of the most important ores of copper. It is usually massive but, on rare occasions, occurs in short, striated prismatic or tabular crystals or as pseudohexagonal prisms formed by twinning. It is opaque, dark metallic grey, and becomes dull on exposure to light. Chalcocite was formerly known as chalcosine, copper glace, and redruthite, but these names are now obsolete.

Chalcocite forms at relatively low temperatures (up to 200C°/400°F), often as alteration products of other copper minerals such as bornite (p.50). It is found in hydrothermal veins and porphyry copper deposits with other minerals – bornite, covellite (p.52), sphalerite (p.53), galena (p.54), chalcopyrite (p.57), calcite (p.114), and quartz (p.168). Deposits in Cornwall, England, have been worked since the Bronze Age. Concentrated in secondary alteration zones, chalcocite can yield more copper than the element's primary deposits.

iridescence

foliated habit

metallic blue colour

oxidized material

Iridescent covellite
This spectacular, massive covellite specimen showing classic purple iridescence is from the Leonard Mine at Butte, Montana, USA.

VARIANT

tabular crystal

Tabular covellite Rare covellite crystals in their tabular habit

CuS

COVELLITE

Named in 1832 after the Italian minerologist Niccolo Covelli, who first described it, covellite is a copper sulphide. A minor ore of copper (p.37), covellite is opaque, with a bright metallic blue or indigo colour. It is easy to recognize because of its brassy yellow, deep red, or purple iridescence. Covellite is generally massive and foliated in habit, although sometimes spheroidal. In crystalline form, it occurs as thin, tabular, and hexagonal plates, which are flexible when thin enough. Plates formed from its perfect basal cleavage are likewise flexible. It fuses very easily when heated, emitting a blue flame.

Covellite is a primary mineral in some places, but it typically occurs as an alteration product of other copper sulphide minerals such as bornite (p.50), chalcocite (p.51), and chalcopyrite (p.57). It sometimes forms as a coating on other copper sulphides. It rarely occurs as a volcanic sublimate, as on Mt Vesuvius, where Niccolo Covelli first collected it. Covellite is abundant in the massive copper mines in Arizona, USA.

Cubic

3 ½–4

3.9–4.1

Perfect in six directions

Conchoidal

Brownish to light yellow

Resinous to adamantine, metallic

Sphalerite crystals
These superbly formed sphalerite crystals occur with well-crystallized pyrite and quartz. They are from Casapalca, Lima, Peru.

complex sphalerite crystal

quartz

pyrite

resinous lustre

VARIANTS

Massive sphalerite The most common habit of sphalerite

dark red crystal

Ruby blende Brilliant red crystals of ruby blende sphalerite

ZnS

SPHALERITE

Sphalerite is the principal ore of zinc. Pure sphalerite is colourless and rare. Normally, iron is present, causing the colour to vary from pale greenish yellow to brown and black with increasing iron content. Its complex crystals combine tetrahedral or dodecahedral forms with other faces. Sphalerite gets its name from the Greek *sphaleros*, meaning "deceitful", since its lustrous dark crystals can be mistaken for other minerals. It is often coarsely crystalline or massive, or forms banded, botryoidal, or stalactitic aggregates.

Sphalerite is found associated with galena (p.54) in lead-zinc deposits. It occurs in hydrothermal vein deposits, contact metamorphic zones, and replacement deposits formed at high temperature (575°C/1,065°F or above). It is also found in meteorites and lunar rocks.

Oval cut
This oval cut shows off the golden brown colour of sphalerite. Such stones are cut for collectors.

PROFILE

Cubic

2½

7.6

Perfect

Subconchoidal

Lead-grey

Metallic

Galena crystals
Galena is usually found in cube-shaped crystals, but the crystal shape can also incorporate the faces of octahedra, as here.

octahedral face cuts across cubic crystal

metallic lustre

accessory dolomite

VARIANT

Perfect cleavage Cubic galena crystals with perfect cleavage in three directions

PbS

GALENA

There are more than 60 known minerals that contain lead, but by far the most important lead ore is galena, or lead sulphide. It is possible that galena was the first ore to be smelted to release its metal – lead beads found in Turkey have been dated to around 6500 BCE. Galena is opaque and bright metallic grey when fresh, but it dulls on exposure to the atmosphere. Its crystals are cubic, octahedral, dodecahedral, or combinations of these forms. Irregular, coarse, or fine crystalline masses are common.

Galena is common in hydrothermal lead, zinc, and copper (p.37) ore deposits worldwide and is often associated with sphalerite (p.53), chalcopyrite (p.57), and pyrite (p.62). It is also found in contact metamorphic rocks. Galena weathers easily to form secondary lead minerals, such as cerussite (p.119), anglesite (p.132), and pyromorphite (p.151). Galena is both the principal ore of lead and the main source of silver (p.43) – it often contains a considerable amount of silver in the form of acanthite as an impurity. It can also be a source of other metals.

Massive pentlandite
This typical massive
specimen of pentlandite
also contains pyrrhotite.

granular habit

pyrrhotite

uneven fracture

PROFILE

Cubic

 3½–4

 4.6–5.0

None

Conchoidal

Bronze-brown

Metallic

 $(Fe,Ni)_9S_8$

PENTLANDITE

Named in 1856 after the Irish scientist Joseph Pentland, its discoverer, pentlandite is a nickel and iron sulphide. Nickel is usually a smaller component than iron, but both may be present in equal parts. Pentlandite mainly has a massive or granular habit, and its crystals cannot be seen by the naked eye. It is opaque, metallic yellow in colour, and has a bronze-like tarnish.

Pentlandite occurs in silica-poor, intrusive igneous rocks. It is almost always accompanied by pyrrhotite, with other sulphides such as chalcopyrite (p.57) and pyrite (p.62), and with some arsenides. The chief ore of nickel, pentlandite is relatively widespread, but commercial deposits are scarce. In Ontario, Canada, nickel from an ancient meteorite is thought to have enriched the ore. Pentlandite is also found as an accessory mineral in some meteorites. Silver (p.43) can be present in the pentlandite structure, yielding the mineral argentopentlandite; when cobalt replaces the iron and nickel, the mineral becomes cobaltpentlandite.

Crystalline cinnabar
This massive specimen from
Monte Amiata, Tuscany,
Italy, also contains
cinnabar crystals.

calcite

cystalline
cinnabar

rock
groundmass

VARIANT

adamantine
lustre

Massive cinnabar A specimen
of massive cinnabar with a
non-metallic, adamantine lustre

🔬 HgS

CINNABAR

A mercury sulphide, cinnabar takes its name from
the Persian *zinjirfrah* and Arabic *zinjafr*, which mean
"dragon's blood". It is bright scarlet to deep greyish red
in colour. It is the major source of mercury. Crystals are
uncommon but when found they are rhombohedral,
tabular, or prismatic. It usually occurs as massive or
granular aggregates, or sometimes powdery coatings.

Cinnabar is often found with other minerals – such as
stibnite (p.61), pyrite (p.62), and marcasite (p.63) – in veins
near recent volcanic rocks.
It is also found around hot
springs. Cinnabar is believed
to have been mined and
used in Egypt in the early
2nd millennium BCE. It has
also been mined for at least
2,000 years at Almadén,
Spain. This site still yields
excellent crystals.

Powdered cinnabar
Since ancient times, artists
have used bright red
powdered cinnabar for
the pigment vermillion.

PROFILE

Tetragonal

⊻ 3½–4

🪨 4.2

◪ Distinct

◪ Uneven, brittle

◪ Green-black

◪ Metallic

quartz crystal

twinned chalcopyrite crystals

metallic lustre

brassy yellow coloration

Chalcopyrite crystals
Crystallized specimens of chalcopyrite can sometimes contain both twinned crystals and quartz crystals.

VARIANTS

metallic lustre

Massive chalcopyrite A specimen with an iridescent tarnish to it

tetrahedral habit

Brassy yellow chalcopyrite
A specimen with an uneven fracture and tetrahedral habit

🔬 CuFeS$_2$

CHALCOPYRITE

One of the minerals worked at Rio Tinto, Spain, since Roman times, chalcopyrite is a copper and iron sulphide. It is opaque and brassy yellow when freshly mined, but it commonly develops an iridescent tarnish on exposure to the atmosphere. This tetragonal mineral forms tetrahedral crystals, which can be up to 10cm (4 in) long on a face. It commonly occurs as massive aggregates and less frequently as botryoidal masses or as scattered grains in igneous rocks.

Chalcopyrite forms under a variety of conditions. It is mostly found in hydrothermal sulphide veins as a primary mineral deposited at medium and high temperatures (200°C/400°F or above), and as replacements, often with large concentrations of pyrite (p.62). It is also found as grains in igneous rocks and is an important ore mineral in porphyry copper deposits. Rarely, it occurs in metamorphic rocks. Chalcopyrite is an important ore of copper owing to its widespread occurrence. In some cases, selenium can replace a portion of the sulphur.

Realgar crystals
These bright red, prismatic realgar crystals are in a rock groundmass and accompanied by grey quartz.

rare prismatic
realgar crystal

rock
groundmass

light grey
quartz

PROFILE

Monoclinic

▽ 1½–2

📏 3.6

🪨 Good

💥 Conchoidal

🎨 Scarlet to orange-yellow

↗ Resinous to greasy

 AsS

REALGAR

An important ore of arsenic, realgar is bright red or orange in colour. Crystals are not often found, but when they occur they are short, prismatic, and striated. Realgar mostly occurs as coarse to fine granular masses and as encrustations. Realgar disintegrates on prolonged exposure to light, forming an opaque yellow powder, which is principally pararealgar. Therefore, specimens are kept in darkened containers.

Realgar is typically found in hydrothermal deposits at low temperature (up to 200°C/400°F) often with orpiment (p.59) and other arsenic minerals. It also forms as a sublimate around volcanoes, hot springs, and geyser deposits and as a weathering product of other arsenic-bearing minerals. Realgar is often found with stibnite (p.61) and calcite (p.114).

Powdered realgar
Scarlet to orange-yellow in colour, powdered realgar was once used as a pigment and in fireworks.

uneven fracture

Foliated orpiment
Made up of thin layers, this specimen shows classic orpiment foliation. It has a resinous lustre and uneven fracture.

foliated appearance

resinous lustre

PROFILE

Monoclinic

 1½–2

 3.5

 Perfect

 Uneven, sectile

 Pale yellow

Resinous

VARIANT

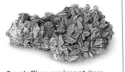

Crystalline orpiment Rare, stubby, prismatic crystals

As_2S_3

ORPIMENT

An arsenic sulphide, orpiment is a soft yellow or orange mineral. Widely distributed, it is typically powdery or massive, but it is also found as cleavable, columnar, or foliated masses. Distinct crystals are uncommon, but when found they are short prisms. Orpiment occurs in hydrothermal veins at low temperature (up to 200°C/400°F), hot spring deposits, and volcanic fumaroles and it may occur with stibnite (p.61) and realgar (p.58). It also results from the alteration of other arsenic-bearing minerals.

When heated, orpiment gives off the garlic odour typical of arsenic minerals. The lustre is resinous on freshly broken surfaces but pearly on cleavage surfaces. It was used as a pigment, mainly in ancient times in the Middle East. It was also used later in the West but soon replaced due to its toxicity.

Yellow pigment
Powdered orpiment was used as a yellow pigment, especially to make gold-coloured paint.

PROFILE

Hexagonal

3–3½

5.5

Perfect

Uneven, brittle

Greenish black

Metallic

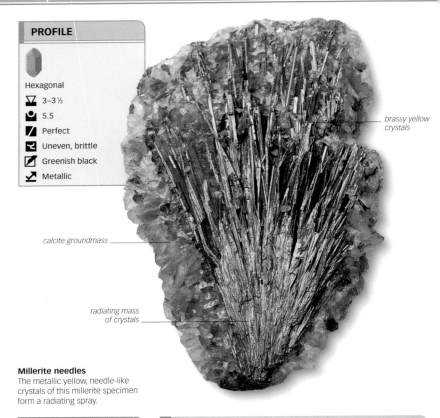

brassy yellow crystals

calcite groundmass

radiating mass of crystals

Millerite needles
The metallic yellow, needle-like crystals of this millerite specimen form a radiating spray.

VARIANT

hair-like crystal

geode

Millerite geode Thin, radiating crystals of millerite have formed in this hollow space

NiS

MILLERITE

A nickel sulphide, millerite commonly occurs as delicate, needle-like, opaque golden crystals. It can form free-standing, single crystals or occur as tufts, matted groups, or radiating sprays. It is also massive and frequently found with an iridescent tarnish. Nickel is more abundant in Earth's crust than copper (p.37), but it is generally more dispersed. Millerite is an ore of the element nickel, which is used in corrosion-resistant metal alloys, especially in the copper-nickel coinage that has replaced silver. It was named in 1845 after the English mineralogist W.H. Miller – the first person to study it.

Millerite normally forms at low temperatures (up to 200°C/400°F). It is often found in cavities in limestone (p.319) or dolomite (p.320), in carbonate veins and other associated rocks, within coal (p.253) deposits, and in serpentinite (p.298). It can occur as a later-formed mineral in nickel sulphide deposits and as an alteration product of other nickel minerals. Millerite is also found in meteorites and as a sublimate on Mount Vesuvius, Italy.

PROFILE

Orthorhombic

⚡ 2

🔨 4.6

▨ Perfect

◨ Subconchoidal

◩ Lead-grey to steel-grey

↗ Metallic

Stibnite crystals
This group of long, prismatic, striated stibnite crystals is on a quartz and baryte groundmass.

prismatic crystal

striations on prism face

quartz and baryte

VARIANTS

Stibnite sheets Thin layers of stibnite with sheet-like cleavage

Acicular stibnite A mass of radiating, needle-like crystals

🜍 Sb_2S_3

STIBNITE

The principal ore of antimony, stibnite is antimony sulphide. Its name comes from the Latin *stibium*. Lead-grey to silvery grey in colour, it often develops a black, iridescent tarnish on exposure to light. It normally occurs as elongated, prismatic crystals that may be bent or twisted. These crystals are often marked by striations parallel to the prism faces. Stibnite typically forms coarse, irregular masses or radiating sprays of needle-like crystals, but it can also be granular or massive.

A widespread mineral, stibnite occurs in hydrothermal veins, hot-spring deposits, and replacement deposits that form at low temperatures (up to 200°C/400°F). It is often associated with galena (p.54), cinnabar (p.56), realgar (p.58), orpiment (p.59), pyrite (p.62), and quartz (p.168). It is found in massive aggregates in granite (pp.258–59) and gneiss (p.288) rocks. Stibnite is used to manufacture matches, fireworks, and percussion caps for firearms. Powdered stibnite was used in the ancient world as a cosmetic for eyes to make them look larger.

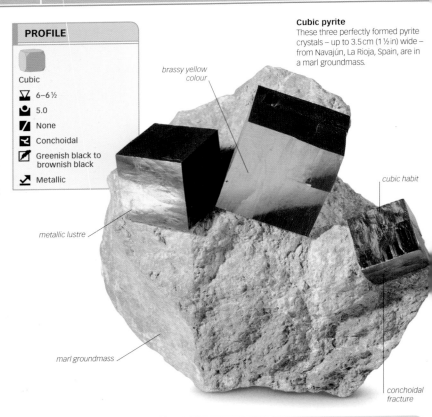

Cubic pyrite
These three perfectly formed pyrite crystals – up to 3.5 cm (1 ½ in) wide – from Navajún, La Rioja, Spain, are in a marl groundmass.

brassy yellow colour

cubic habit

metallic lustre

marl groundmass

conchoidal fracture

VARIANTS

Octahedral pyrite A group of octahedral crystals with quartz

brownish coating

Pyrite nodule A ball-shaped, nodular group of pyrite crystals

Pyritohedral pyrite A classic pyrite pyritohedral crystal

🝙 FeS_2

PYRITE

Known since antiquity, pyrite is commonly referred to as "fool's gold". Although much lighter than gold, its brassy colour and relatively high density misled many novice prospectors. Its name is derived from the Greek word *pyr*, meaning "fire", because it emits sparks when struck by iron. It is opaque and pale silvery yellow when fresh, turning darker and tarnishing with exposure to oxygen. Pyrite crystals may be cubic, octahedral, or twelve-sided "pyritohedra", and are often striated. Pyrite can also be massive or granular, or form either flattened discs or nodules of radiating, elongate crystals.

Pyrite occurs in hydrothermal veins, by segregation from magmas, in contact metamorphic rocks, and in sedimentary rocks, such as shale (p.313) and coal (p.253), where it can either fill or replace fossils.

Pyrite beads
With care, brittle pyrite can be ground into beads, such as those strung together in this necklace.

PROFILE

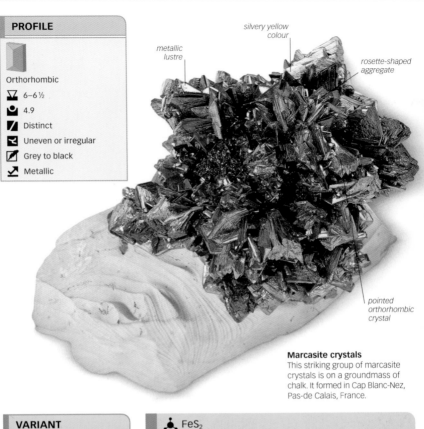

silvery yellow colour

metallic lustre

rosette-shaped aggregate

Orthorhombic

◭ 6–6½

● 4.9

◨ Distinct

◩ Uneven or irregular

◪ Grey to black

⭧ Metallic

pointed orthorhombic crystal

Marcasite crystals
This striking group of marcasite crystals is on a groundmass of chalk. It formed in Cap Blanc-Nez, Pas-de-Calais, France.

VARIANT

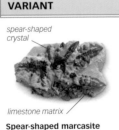

spear-shaped crystal

limestone matrix

Spear-shaped marcasite
Several groups of spear-shaped, twinned crystals

FeS_2

MARCASITE

An iron sulphide, marcasite is chemically identical to pyrite (p.62), but unlike pyrite it has an orthorhombic crystal structure. Marcasite is opaque and pale silvery yellow when fresh but darkens and tarnishes on exposure. It has a predominantly pyramidal or tabular crystal form. It is also found in characteristic twinned, curved, sheaf-like shapes that resemble a cockscomb. Nodules with radially arranged fibres are common. Marcasite can also be massive, stalactitic, or reniform.

Marcasite is found near Earth's surface. It forms from acidic solutions percolating downwards through beds of shale (p.313), clay, limestone (p.319), or chalk (p.321), where it often infills or replaces fossils. Marcasite also occurs as nodules in coal (p.253).

Art Deco jewellery
Marcasite was a popular choice for Victorian and Art Deco jewellery, although most of the material used was actually pyrite.

Layered masses
The crystallized molybdenite masses in this specimen show a typical layered structure.

granite groundmass

metallic lustre

hexagonal, foliated mass

PROFILE

Hexagonal or trigonal

1–1½

4.7

Perfect basal

Uneven

Greenish or bluish grey

Metallic

 MoS_2

MOLYBDENITE

A molybdenum sulphide, molybdenite is the most important source of molybdenum, which is an important element in high-strength steels. Molybdenite was originally thought to be lead, and its name is derived from the Greek word for lead, *molybdos*. It was recognized as a distinct mineral by the Swedish chemist Carl Scheele in 1778.

Molybdenite is soft, opaque, and bluish grey. It forms tabular hexagonal crystals, foliated masses, scales, and disseminated grains. It can also be massive or scaly. The platy, flexible, greasy-feeling hexagonal crystals of molybdenite can be confused with graphite (p.46), although molybdenite has a much higher specific gravity, a more metallic lustre, and a slightly bluer tinge. Molybdenite occurs in granite (pp.258–59), pegmatite (p.260), and hydrothermal veins at high temperature (575°C/1,065°F or above) with other minerals – fluorite (p.109), ferberite (p.145), scheelite (p.146), and topaz (p.234). It is also found in porphyry ores and in contact metamorphic deposits.

SULPHOSALTS

Sulphosalts are a group of mostly rare minerals that contain two or more metals in combination with sulphur (a nonmetal) and semimetals such as arsenic and antimony. Sulphosalt minerals have a high density, a metallic lustre, and are usually brittle.

COMPOSITION
Sulphosalts have complex crystal structures. The structures of many sulphosalts appear to be based on fragments of simpler sulphur compounds. Metals commonly found in sulphosalts are lead, silver, thallium, copper, tin, bismuth, and germanium.

OCCURRENCE
Sulphosalts occur in small amounts in hydrothermal veins formed at low temperatures (up to 200°C/400°F). They are generally associated with the more common sulphides. A single Swiss deposit is known to have yielded up to 30 different sulphosalt minerals.

USES
Sulphosalts are typically found in small amounts but in a few deposits are economically important. Sometimes, they can constitute minor ores of silver, mercury, and antimony.

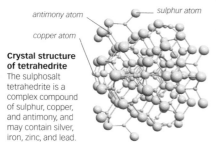

antimony atom — *sulphur atom*

copper atom

Crystal structure of tetrahedrite
The sulphosalt tetrahedrite is a complex compound of sulphur, copper, and antimony, and may contain silver, iron, zinc, and lead.

Silver coins
Pyragyrite, a sulphosalt mineral, yields the metal silver, which was used to produce the ancient coins seen here.

prismatic crystal

quartz groundmass

Bournonite
This specimen shows crystals typical of the sulphosalt bournonite. Twinned crystals growing parallel to each other give the mineral its informal name, cogwheel ore.

Sulphosalt deposit
Many sulphosalt minerals are found in Cornwall, England. These stone buildings once housed steam engines to pump water from mine shafts.

Crystalline tennantite
This mass of tetrahedral tennantite crystals is set in a rock groundmass and has an iridescent tarnish.

iridescence | tetrahedral crystal

VARIANT

steel-grey colouring

Massive tennantite A specimen of massive tennantite from Cornwall, England

 $(Cu,Fe)_{12}As_4S_3$

TENNANTITE

Named in 1819 after the English chemist Smithson Tennant, tennantite is a copper iron arsenic sulphide. Iron, zinc, mercury, bismuth, and silver may substitute for up to 15 per cent of the copper in tennantite. Tennantite is grey-black, steel-grey, iron-grey, or black in colour. It forms cubic and tetrahedral crystals. It may also occur in massive, granular, and compact forms. Tennantite is an end member of a solid-solution series with the similar mineral tetrahedrite (p.73). The two have very similar properties, making it difficult to distinguish between them. Their crystal habits are similar and both exhibit contact and penetration twinning.

Tennantite is found in hydrothermal and contact metamorphic deposits, often associated with sphalerite (p.53), galena (p.54), chalcopyrite (p.57), fluorite (p.109), baryte (p.134), and quartz (p.168). Deposits are found in Freiberg, Saxony, Germany; Lengenbach, Switzerland; and Butte, Montana, and Aspen and Central City, Colorado, USA.

uneven fracture

Enargite crystals
These superb enargite
crystals are striated and
show a prismatic habit.

metallic lustre

striation

PROFILE

Orthorhombic

 3

4.4–4.5

Perfect

Uneven, brittle

Black

Metallic

 Cu_3AsS_4

ENARGITE

A copper arsenic sulphide, enargite takes its name
from the Greek word *enarge*, which means "distinct" –
a reference to its perfect cleavage. An important ore of
copper, it has a bright metallic lustre, is opaque, and has
a grey-black to iron-black to violet-black colour when fresh.
It turns dull black on exposure to light and pollutants.
Enargite may occur in massive or granular habits. Crystals
are usually small, either tabular or prismatic, sometimes
pseudohexagonal or hemimorphic (with different
terminations at each end), and have striations along
the prism faces. Enargite crystals occasionally form
star-shaped multiple twins.

Enargite forms in hydrothermal vein deposits at low
to medium temperature (up to 575°C/1,065°F) and in
replacement deposits, where it is associated with
bornite (p.50), covellite (p.52), sphalerite (p.53), galena
(p.54), chalcopyrite (p.57), pyrite (p.62), and other copper
sulphides. It also occurs in the cap rocks of salt domes,
with minerals such as anhydrite (p.133).

Fibrous habit
This jamesonite specimen, set in a rock groundmass, has the fibrous habit typical of the mineral.

metallic lustre

rock groundmass

fibrous crystals

PROFILE

Monoclinic

2–3

5.5–6.0

Good

Uneven to conchoidal

Greyish black

Metallic

 $Pb_4FeSb_6S_{14}$

JAMESONITE

Named in 1825 after the Scottish mineralogist Robert Jameson, jamesonite is a lead iron antimony sulphide. It is opaque lead-grey, but can often develop an iridescent tarnish. Jamesonite is normally found as needle-like or fibrous crystals combined together into columnar, radiating, plumose (feather-like), or felt-like masses.

Jamesonite occurs in hydrothermal veins at low or medium temperature (up to 575°C/1,065°F), where hot, chemical-rich fluids have permeated joints and fault lines, depositing minerals during cooling. In hydrothermal veins, it often occurs with other lead and antimony sulphides and sulphosalt minerals. Jamesonite also occurs in quartz associated with carbonate minerals, such as calcite (p.114), dolomite (p.117), and rhodochrosite (p.121). Jamesonite is a minor ore of antimony, which is used as a strengthening agent in alloys. It is widespread in small amounts, with good specimens coming from Freiburg, Saxony, Germany; Yakutia, Russia; Trepca, Serbia; Dachang, China; Cornwall, England; and Oruro, Bolivia.

short, tabular crystal

pseudohexagonal outline

metallic lustre

twinned crystals

Pseudohexagonal crystals
Many short, prismatic crystals in this stephanite specimen show pseudohexagonal twinning.

PROFILE

Orthorhombic

 2–2½

 6.2–6.5

 Imperfect

 Subconchoidal to uneven, brittle

 Iron-black

 Metallic

Ag_5SbS_4

STEPHANITE

A silver antimony sulphide, stephanite was named in honour of Archduke Victor Stephan, the mining director of Austria, in 1845. It is sometimes called brittle or black silver ore. It is opaque, iron-black to black in colour, and has a metallic lustre on fresh faces. Stephanite crystals range from short prismatic to tabular and are repeatedly twinned to form pseudohexagonal groups. Stephanite may also occur in massive and granular habits.

Stephanite is generally found in small amounts in late-stage hydrothermal silver veins associated with native silver (p.43), sulphides, and other sulphosalts, such as acanthite (p.49) and tetrahedrite (p.73). It was found in sufficient quantity to be an ore of silver in Comstock Lode, Nevada, USA.

Historic silver processing
This 1550 woodcut from Georgius Agricola's treatise *De Re Metallica* shows silver ore being processed.

prismatic crystal

dark red colour
darkens further on
exposure to light

twinned crystals

adamantine lustre

Dark ruby silver
The dark red colour of pyrargyrite
can be seen in these superb
twinned, prismatic crystals.

 Ag_3SbS_3

PYRARGYRITE

An important ore of silver, pyrargyrite takes its name from the Greek words *pyros*, which means "fire", and *argent*, which means "silver" – an allusion to its silver content and its translucent, dark red colour. Also known as dark ruby silver, pyrargyrite turns opaque dull grey when exposed to light. Therefore, prized specimens are stored in the dark. Pyrargyrite is typically massive or granular. It can also occur as well-formed prismatic crystals with rhombohedral, scalenohedral, or flat terminations, different at each end and frequently twinned.

Pyrargyrite forms in hydrothermal veins at relatively low temperature (up to 200°C/400°F) with the minerals sphalerite (p.53), galena (p.54), tetrahedrite (p.73), proustite (p.72), and calcite (p.114). It also forms by the alteration of other minerals.

Roman silver
This Roman *denarius*
(silver coin) of the first
century BCE shows
gladiators fighting.

PROFILE

Orthorhombic

⚡ 2½–3

🔩 5.8

▨ Indistinct

◈ Subconchoidal to uneven

▨ Steel-grey

↗ Metallic

Cogwheel ore
This specimen of bournonite, accompanied by white baryte, shows the twinned habit that gives the mineral its informal name.

blades of baryte

twinned crystals forming cog-like shape

VARIANT

prismatic bournonite crystals

quartz groundmass

Prismatic bournonite A group of twinned prismatic crystals of bournonite

♣ PbCuSbS$_3$

BOURNONITE

A lead copper antimony sulphide, bournonite occurs as heavy, dark crystal aggregates and masses, as well as interpenetrating cruciform (cross-like) twins. When repeatedly twinned, bournonite has the appearance of a toothed wheel, giving rise to the informal name cogwheel ore. Untwinned crystals of this opaque mineral are tabular or short prismatic and usually have smooth and bright faces. Bournonite was first mentioned as a mineral in 1797 but was named only in 1805 after the French mineralogist Count J.L. de Bournon.

A widely distributed mineral, bournonite is found in hydrothermal veins at medium temperatures (200–575°C/400–1,065°F) and associated with sphalerite (p.53), galena (p.54), chalcopyrite (p.57), pyrite (p.62), tetrahedrite (p.73), and other sulphide minerals. Particularly prized specimens of bournonite come from the Harz Mountains of Germany, where a few crystals exceed 2.2 cm (¾ in) in diameter. This mineral has been used as a minor ore of antimony (p.41).

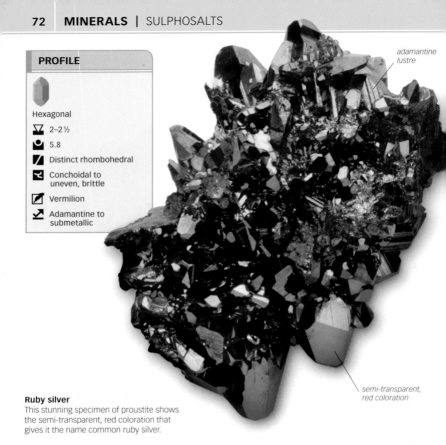

adamantine lustre

semi-transparent, red coloration

Ruby silver
This stunning specimen of proustite shows the semi-transparent, red coloration that gives it the name common ruby silver.

VARIANTS

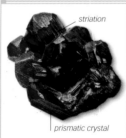

striation

prismatic crystal

Striated proustite A prismatic, semi-transparent crystal

Dull proustite A dull, opaque specimen after exposure to light

 Ag_3AsS_3

PROUSTITE

As its original name ruby silver ore suggests, proustite is translucent and red and is an important source of silver (p.43). It has also been called light red silver ore. The name proustite comes from the French chemist Joseph Proust, who distinguished it from the related mineral pyrargyrite (p.70) by chemical analysis in 1832. Its striated, often brilliant crystals are typically prismatic with rhombohedral or scalenohedral terminations, often resembling the dogtooth spar form of calcite (p.114) in habit. Proustite also occurs as massive or granular aggregates. The mineral turns from transparent scarlet to dull opaque grey in strong light, so specimens are stored in the dark.

Proustite forms in hydrothermal veins at low temperature (up to 200°C/400°F) with other silver minerals, such as acanthite (p.49), stephanite (p.69), and tetrahedrite (p.73), and with native arsenic (p.45), galena (p.54), and calcite (p.114). It also forms in the secondary zone of silver deposits. Large crystals come from Chañarcillo, Chile, and Freiburg, Saxony, Germany.

Tetrahedral crystals
This group of relatively rare tetrahedrite crystals shows twinning and coats a rock groundmass.

triangular crystal face

quartz crystal

twinned, tetrahedral crystals

$(Cu,Fe)_{12}Sb_4S_{13}$

TETRAHEDRITE

The name tetrahedrite comes from this mineral's characteristic tetrahedral crystals, although it also occurs as massive, compact, or granular aggregates. Tetrahedrite is opaque, metallic grey, or nearly black, and it sometimes coats or is coated with brassy yellow chalcopyrite (p.57). It forms a continuous solid-solution series with the similar mineral tennantite (p.66), in which arsenic replaces antimony in the crystal structure. Bismuth also substitutes for antimony and forms bismuthian tetrahedrite or annivite.

Tetrahedrite is an important ore of copper and sometimes silver. It forms in hydrothermal veins at low to medium temperature (up to 575°C/ 1,065°F), often with bornite (p.50), galena (p.54), chalcopyrite, pyrite (p.62), baryte (p.134), and quartz (p.168). It is also found in contact metamorphic deposits.

Copper ore
This 9th-century brass Arabic astrolabe is believed to have been made of copper extracted from tetrahedrite.

OXIDES

The minerals in this group have crystal structures in which metals or semimetals occupy spaces between oxygen atoms. The properties of oxides vary: the metallic ores and gemstone varieties tend to be hard and have a high specific gravity.

COMPOSITION

Oxides can be either simple or multiple. Simple oxides, such as cuprite (Cu_2O), contain only one metal or semimetal and oxygen. Multiple oxides have two different metal sites, both of which may be occupied by several different metals or semimetals. The minerals in the spinel ($MgAl_2O_4$) group are examples of multiple oxides.

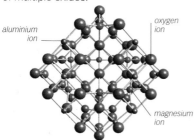

aluminium ion

oxygen ion

magnesium ion

Spinel crystal structure
In spinel, magnesium and aluminium combine with oxygen. Other metals can replace magnesium and aluminium to form the spinel series of minerals.

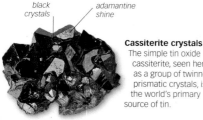

black crystals

adamantine shine

Cassiterite crystals
The simple tin oxide cassiterite, seen here as a group of twinned prismatic crystals, is the world's primary source of tin.

Queensland
The Queensland region of eastern Australia is a treasure trove of minerals. Several deposits of alluvial sapphire (aluminium oxide) are found here.

OCCURRENCE AND USES

Oxides occur as accessory minerals in many igneous rocks, especially as early crystallizing minerals in ultrabasic rocks, in pegmatites, and as decomposition products of sulphide minerals. Many resist weathering and are found concentrated in placers.

Many oxide minerals are important ores of chromium, uranium, tantalum, zinc, tin, cerium, tungsten, manganese, copper, and titanium. Other oxides, such as quartz and corundum, are important gemstone minerals.

Chrome bumper
The large, chrome-plated front bumper of this classic American 1956 Chevrolet is a dramatic example of chromium derived from the oxide chromite.

Iceberg
This small, beached iceberg still shows some of its original depositional layering.

broken edge of glacier

layering

VARIANTS

Frost Crystalline ice in a frost-like form

Hailstone A huge 5 cm x 9 cm (2 in x 3 ½ in) hailstone

♣ H_2O

ICE

Although largely absent at lower latitudes, ice is probably the most abundant mineral exposed on Earth's surface. Liquid water is not classified as a mineral because it has no crystalline form. As snow, ice forms crystals that seldom exceed 7 mm (¼ in) in length, although as massive aggregates in glaciers, individual crystals may be up to 45 cm (17 ½ in) long. Other forms of ice include branching, tree-like frost, skeletal, hopper-shaped, prism-like frost, and hailstones and icicles made up of many randomly oriented crystals.

Ice crystals are generally colourless, but the common white colour of ice is due to gaseous inclusions of air that reflect light. There are at least nine polymorphs – different crystalline forms – of ice, each forming under different pressure and temperature conditions, but only one form exists at Earth's surface. The hardness of ice varies with its crystal structure, purity, and temperature. At temperatures found in the Arctic and high-alpine zones, ice is so hard it can erode stone when windblown.

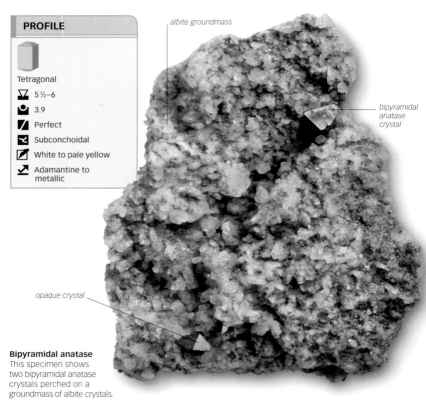

albite groundmass

bipyramidal anatase crystal

opaque crystal

Bipyramidal anatase
This specimen shows two bipyramidal anatase crystals perched on a groundmass of albite crystals.

VARIANTS

rock matrix

Black anatase Schist speckled with tiny black anatase crystals

Octahedral crystal A perfectly formed, modified bipyramidal anatase crystal

TiO_2

ANATASE

Formerly known as octahedrite, anatase is a polymorph of titanium dioxide. Its name comes from the Greek word *anatasis,* which means "extension" – a reference to the elongate octahedral crystals that are the most common habit of anatase. Anatase crystals can also be tabular and, rarely, prismatic. Hard and brilliant, the crystals can be brown, yellow, indigo-blue, green, grey, lilac, or black in colour.

Anatase forms in veins and crevices in metamorphic rocks, such as schists (pp.291–92) and gneisses (p.288), and is derived from the leaching of surrounding rocks by hydrothermal solutions. Anatase also forms in pegmatites (p.260), often in association with the minerals brookite (p.77), ilmenite (p.90), fluorite (p.109), and aegirine (p.209). It is found in sediments and is sometimes concentrated in placer deposits. Much anatase is formed by the weathering of titanite (p.234). Weathered anatase becomes rutile (p.78). Although rutile replaces anatase, it retains the anatase crystal shape.

PROFILE

Orthorhombic

5½–6

4.1

Indistinct

Subconchoidal to uneven

White, greyish, yellowish

Metallic to adamantine

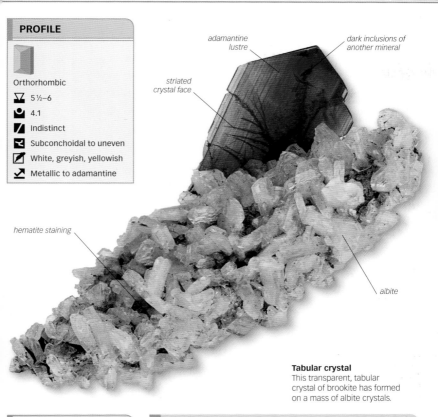

adamantine lustre

dark inclusions of another mineral

striated crystal face

hematite staining

albite

Tabular crystal
This transparent, tabular crystal of brookite has formed on a mass of albite crystals.

VARIANT

Dipyramidal crystal A black brookite specimen with metallic lustre

TiO_2

BROOKITE

Named in 1825 after British crystallographer H.J. Brooke, brookite, like anatase (p.76) and rutile (p.78), is composed of titanium dioxide. However, unlike anatase and rutile, brookite exhibits orthorhombic symmetry. Usually brown and metallic, brookite may also be red, yellow-brown, or black. Crystals can be tabular or, less commonly, pyramidal or pseudohexagonal. They may be thin or thick and up to 5 cm (2 in) long. Iron is almost always present in this mineral's structure to a small degree, and brookite containing niobium is also known.

Brookite occurs in hydrothermal veins, in some contact metamorphic rocks, and as a detrital mineral in sedimentary deposits. Being relatively dense, it is common in areas with natural concentrations of heavy minerals, such as the diamond placer deposits of Brazil. It generally occurs with other minerals, including rutile, anatase, and albite (p.177). Brookite is widespread in mineral veins in the Alps. In the Fronolen locality in northern Wales, UK, it forms crystals on crevice walls in diabase rock.

PROFILE

Tetragonal

⏷ 6–6½

💧 4.2

▧ Good

▨ Conchoidal to uneven

▨ Pale brown to yellowish

⤢ Adamantine to submetallic

Single crystal
This large, semi-transparent, and striated single crystal of rutile originates from Val di Vizze, Trentino-Alto Adige, Italy.

uneven fracture

adamantine sheen

vertical striations along length of crystal

typical prismatic crystal shape

VARIANTS

rutile needle

Rutilated quartz Pale-golden rutile crystals in polished quartz

uneven fracture

Massive rutile Dark-hued crystals in rock groundmass

🜨 TiO₂

RUTILE

A form of titanium oxide, rutile takes its name from the Latin *rutilis*, which means "red" or "glowing". It often appears as pale golden, needle-like crystals inside quartz (p.168). When not enclosed in quartz, it is usually yellowish or reddish brown, dark brown, or black. Crystals are generally prismatic but can also be slender and needle-like. Multiple twinning is common and is either knee-shaped, net- or lattice-like, or radiating, forming wheel-like twins. Rutile may also radiate in star-like sprays from hematite crystals.

Rutile often occurs as a minor constituent of granites (pp.258–59), gneisses (p.288), and schists (p.291), and also in hydrothermal veins and in some clastic sediments. It commonly forms microscopic, oriented inclusions in other minerals, producing an asterism effect.

Quartz rutile cabochon
Slender rutile crystals are clearly visible inside this polished, convex-cut, colourless quartz.

black crystals

twinned crystals

crystals form as short prisms

rock groundmass

PROFILE

Tetragonal

6–7

7.0

Indistinct

Subconchoidal to uneven

White, greyish, brownish

Adamantine to metallic

Prismatic crystals
These twinned cassiterite crystals are short, dark-coloured, and prismatic, occurring on a rocky groundmass.

VARIANT

varlamoffite crystals

Varlamoffite cassiterite A specimen displaying the yellow variety of tin oxide

SnO_2

CASSITERITE

The tin oxide cassiterite takes its name from the Greek word for tin, *kassiteros*. Also called tinstone, it is the only important ore of tin. Colourless when pure, it commonly appears brown or black due to iron impurities. Rarely, it is grey or white. Its crystals are usually heavily striated prisms and pyramids. Twinned crystals are quite common. It can also be massive, occurring as a botryoidal, fibrous variety (wood tin) or as water-worn pebbles (stream tin).

Cassiterite forms in association with igneous rocks in hydrothermal veins at high temperature (575°C/1,065°F or above), with tungsten minerals such as ferberite (p.145), and with topaz (p.234), molybdenite (p.64), and tourmaline (p.224). Durable and relatively dense, it becomes concentrated in placer deposits after erosion from its primary rocks.

Brilliant gemstone
This faceted, golden orange cassiterite gem is transparent with a resinous lustre.

dull lustre

uneven fracture

Massive pyrolusite
This dark grey specimen of
massive pyrolusite has an
even fracture.

PROFILE	
Tetragonal	
◫	6–6½
◖	4.4–5.1
◪	Perfect
◪	Uneven, brittle, splintery
◪	Black or bluish black
◪	Metallic to earthy

♣ MnO_2

PYROLUSITE

Pyrolusite is the primary ore of the element
manganese. Specimens are typically light grey to
black in colour. Pyrolusite usually occurs as massive
aggregates. It also forms metallic coatings, crusts, fibres,
nodules, botryoidal masses, concretions, and coatings
that may be powdery or branching. Crystals are rare;
when found, they are opaque and prismatic.

Pyrolusite forms under highly oxidizing conditions
as an alteration product of manganese minerals, such as
rhodochrosite (p.121). It has been found in bogs, lakes, and
shallow marine environments and as a deposit laid down
by circulating waters. Excellent crystals are found at Horni
Blatna, Czech Republic, and at Bathurst, New Brunswick,
Canada. The mineral is mined extensively in Russia, India,
Georgia, and Ghana. Pyrolusite is used as a decolorizing
agent in glass, as a colouring agent in bricks, and in dry cell
batteries. It is also used in the manufacture of steel and
saltwater-resistant manganese-bronze, which is used to
make ships' propellers.

PROFILE

Orthorhombic

⊻ 8½

⬥ 3.7

◪ Distinct

◩ Uneven to conchoidal

◪ Colourless

⬈ Vitreous

Cyclic twin
The cyclic twinning of chrysoberyl exhibited by this specimen is common in the mineral.

striation on crystal face

greenish yellow twinned crystal

transparent with vitreous lustre

pseudohexagonal twinned crystal

VARIANTS

Siberian alexandrite A group of twinned alexandrite crystals with mica from Russia

Yellow gemstone Cat's eye chrysoberyl in the most desirable honey-yellow colour

$BeAl_2O_4$

CHRYSOBERYL

A beryllium aluminium oxide, chrysoberyl is hard and durable. It is inferior in hardness only to corundum (p.95) and diamond (p.47). Chrysoberyl is typically yellow, green, or brown in colour. It forms tabular or short prismatic crystals and heart-shaped or pseudohexagonal twinned crystals. Alexandrite, one of its gemstone varieties, is one of the rarest and most expensive gems. Another variety, cat's eye, is also prized as a gemstone. It contains parallel fibrous crystals of other minerals that reflect light across the surface of a polished gemstone – an effect known as chatoyancy.

Chrysoberyl occurs in some granite pegmatites (p.260), gneisses (p.288), mica schists, and marbles (p.301). Crystals that weather out of the parent rock are often found in streams and gravel beds.

Colour change
Alexandrite exhibits colour change – from brilliant green in daylight to cherry-red under tungsten light.

PROFILE

Orthorhombic

6–6½

5.2–8.0

Distinct

Subconchoidal or uneven

Red, brown, or black

Submetallic to resinous

Ferro-columbite
This opaque, tabular crystal
of ferro-columbite exhibits a
submetallic to resinous lustre.

metallic lustre

uneven fracture

VARIANT

Yttrotantalite Dark crystals
of the coltan series mineral
yttrotantalite (yttrium-rich
tantalite) in a light matrix

$(Fe,Mn)(Nb,Ta)_2O_6–(Fe,Mn)(Ta,Nb)_2O_6$

COLUMBITE–TANTALITE

Columbite forms the coltan series – a nearly complete
solid-solution series – with the mineral tantalite. Minerals
at the columbite end of this series are niobium-rich, and
those at the tantalite end are tantalum-rich. Tantalite
and columbite have similar crystal structures, but
tantalite is denser, and tantalum atoms replace niobium
atoms in the columbite crystal structure. The name
of the mineral is prefixed with "ferro-" or "mangano-",
depending on the content of iron or manganese.
Ferro-columbite is the most common mineral of the
coltan group. Scandium and tungsten may also be
present as minor constituents.

Coltan minerals are brown or black in colour and are
often iridescent. They are either massive or form tabular
or short, prismatic crystals. They are the most abundant
and widespread of the niobates and tantalates, and
are the most important ores of niobium and tantalum.
Coltan minerals mainly occur in granite pegmatite
rocks (p.260) and in detrital deposits.

Botryoidal uraninite
This uraninite specimen demonstrates the botryoidal habit common in this mineral.

botryoidal habit

yellow uranium oxide

dull to submetallic lustre

UO_2

URANINITE

Discovered by the German chemist M.H. Klaproth in 1789, uraninite is a major ore of uranium. The pioneering work on radioactivity by Pierre and Marie Curie was based on uranium extracted from uraninite ores. It is black to brownish black, dark grey, or greenish. It commonly occurs in massive or botryoidal forms, or in banded or granular habits, and less commonly as opaque octahedral or cubic crystals.

Uraninite crystals occur in granitic pegmatites (p.260). Uraninite forms with cassiterite (p.79) and arsenopyrite in hydrothermal sulphide veins at high temperatures (575°C/1,065°F or above). It also forms at medium temperatures (200–575°C/400–1,065°F) as pitchblende. It also occurs as small grains in sandstones and conglomerates, where it may have weathered into secondary uranium minerals.

Uranium pellets
These ceramic pellets of enriched uranium are ready for use in nuclear reactors.

indistinct cleavage

iridescence

conchoidal fracture

Massive samarskite
This specimen of massive samarskite exhibits an iridescent sheen on some surfaces.

PROFILE

 (Y,Fe,U) (Nb,Ta)O$_4$

Orthorhombic

 5–6

 5.7

 Indistinct

 Conchoidal, brittle

 Dark reddish brown to black

 Vitreous to resinous

SAMARSKITE

Named in 1847 after Vasili Yefrafovich von Samarski-Bykhovets of Russia, samarskite is a complex oxide of yttrium, iron, tantalum, niobium, and uranium. Two types of samarskite are recognized – samarskite-(Y) or yttrium samarskite; and samarskite-(Yb) or ytterbium samarskite. The mineral is usually black and opaque but translucent in thin fragments. Crystals are stubby, opaque, and prismatic with a rectangular cross section – although samarskite is commonly found in the massive form. It is often brown or yellowish brown due to surface alteration. Specimens with high uranium content have a yellow-brown, earthy rind. Samarskite samples are usually radioactive.

Samarskite is usually found in rare, earth-bearing granitic pegmatites (p.260). It forms in similar conditions as columbite (p.82), and so the minerals are closely associated. Samarskite is also associated with monazite (p.150), garnet, and other minerals. Yttrium from samarskite has been used in cathode-ray televisions, optical glass, and special ceramics.

modified octahedra

uneven
fracture

Octahedral pyrochlore
In this specimen of pyrochlore, modified octahedra display multiple twinning.

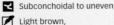
$(Na,Ca)_2Nb_2(O,OH,F)_7$

PYROCHLORE

A major source of the element niobium, pyrochlore is a complex niobium sodium calcium oxide. Its name comes from the Greek *pyr* and *chloros*, which mean "fire" and "green" respectively – a reference to some specimens that turn green after heating. Pyrochlore is orange, brownish red, brown, or black in colour. Crystals are typically well-formed octahedra with modified faces. They are frequently twinned or occur as either granular or massive aggregates. Pyrochlore often contains traces of uranium and thorium, and it may be radioactive. In such cases, its internal structure may be disrupted.

Pyrochlore forms in pegmatite rocks (p.260) and in igneous rocks dominated by carbonate minerals. It is an accessory mineral in silica-poor rocks, often occurring with magnetite (p.92), apatite (p.148), and zircon (p.233). It also accumulates in some detrital deposits. Niobium is a major alloying element in nickel-based superalloys. It has been used either alone or together with zirconium in claddings for nuclear-reactor cores.

Microlite crystals
This specimen of crystalline microlite contains tantalum in place of the niobium typically found in pyrochlore.

vitreous lustre

uneven fracture on surfaces

twinned octahedra

PROFILE

Cubic

5–5 ½

6.4

Distinct to difficult

Subconchoidal to uneven

Yellowish to brownish

Resinous to vitreous

 $(Na,Ca)_2Ta_2O_6(O,OH,F)$

MICROLITE

Named in 1835, microlite takes it name from the Greek word *micros,* which means "small" – a reference to the small size of the crystals found in the locality where the mineral was first discovered. Microlite can, in fact, form excellent octahedral crystals, which can be up to 1 cm (⅜ in) on an edge. It also occurs as irregular grains. Specimens can be yellow, brown, black, green, or reddish. Microlite is related to pyrochlore (p.85), and both minerals are dominated by rare-earth elements: microlite by tantalum and pyrochlore by niobium.

Microlite is found in pegmatites (p.260), especially those rich in lepidolite (p.198) or other lithium-bearing minerals, and in albite (p.177). It is a major ore of tantalum, which is especially useful in high-capacitance electronic devices, particularly those used in miniaturized circuitry. Microlite is also used in corrosion-resistant chemical equipment. Excellent crystals are found at Dixon, New Mexico, USA; Shingus, Gilgit, Pakistan; Mattawa, Ontario, Canada; and at numerous localities in Brazil.

twinned crystal

adamantine lustre on crystal faces

translucent red

Red cuprite
Cuprite crystals are octahedral, cubic, or rarely dodecahedral. They come from Bisbee and other regions in Arizona, USA.

PROFILE

Cubic

 3½–4

 6.1

 Distinct

 Conchoidal, brittle

 Brownish red, shining

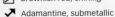 Adamantine, submetallic

VARIANT

Chalcotrichite Bright red, hair-like crystals of the chalcotrichite variety

Cu_2O

CUPRITE

A relatively soft, heavy copper oxide, cuprite is an important ore of copper. Its crystals are either cubic or octahedral in shape and commonly striated. Massive or granular aggregates with the appearance of sugar are common. Cuprite is translucent and bright red when freshly broken but turns to a dull metallic grey colour on exposure to light and pollutants. Cuprite is sometimes known as ruby copper due to its distinctive red colour.

In the variety called chalcotrichite or plush copper ore, the crystals are a rich carmine colour, fibrous, capillary, and silky in appearance. They are found in loosely matted aggregates. Cuprite of the tile ore variety is soft, earthy, brick-red to brownish red in colour, and often contains intermixed hematite (p.91) or goethite (p.102).

Step cut
Rare transparent cuprite is sometimes cut for collectors, as in this rectangular step cut.

Crystalline zincite
This specimen of coarsely crystalline zincite in a white calcite groundmass is from Sterling Hill, New Jersey, USA.

deep red zincite

white calcite groundmass

coarsely crystalline texture

PROFILE

Hexagonal

4–5

5.7

Perfect

Conchoidal

Orange-yellow

Resinous, submetallic

VARIANT

Granular habit Granular zincite with black franklinite

ZnO

ZINCITE

Red oxide of zinc is another name for zincite, which is a minor ore of zinc. Zincite occurs mostly as cleavable or granular masses. Natural crystals are rare, but when they occur they are pyramidal, pointed at one end and flat at the other. These crystals can be orange, red, yellow, or green.

Zincite is found mainly as an accessory mineral in zinc-ore deposits. It is commonly associated with black franklinite and white calcite. Zincite may be a rare constituent of volcanic ash. Crystals are found only in secondary veins or fractures, where zincite forms by the chemical alteration or metamorphism of zinc deposits. Some so-called natural zincite crystals in the collectors' market are, in fact, large crystals that have formed in the chimneys of smelters. Natural crystals are rarely fluorescent; artificial crystals may range from fluorescent green to fluorescent yellow. The classic locality for fine zincite crystals is Franklin, New Jersey, USA. It is also found at Varmland and Nordmark, Sweden.

psuedocubic perovskite crystal

striations on crystal

plagioclase groundmass

Perovskite crystals
In this specimen, two striated, pseudocubic perovskite crystals are set in a groundmass of plagioclase feldspar.

PROFILE

Orthorhombic

 5 ½

 4.0

Imperfect

Subconchoidal to uneven

Grey to colourless

 Adamantine or metallic

$CaTiO_3$

PEROVSKITE

A calcium titanium oxide, perovskite was named after the Russian mineralogist Count Lev Alekseevich Perovski in 1839. The composition of perovskite varies considerably: niobium can substitute for up to 44.9 per cent titanium by weight, and cerium and sodium can substitute for calcium. When specimens are black, they have a metallic lustre; when brown or yellow, they appear adamantine. Although perovskite is an orthorhombic mineral, its crystals are usually pseudocubic. Perovskite crystals can be pseudo-octahedral in varieties where niobium or cerium has replaced a large amount of titanium. The crystals tend to be deeply striated and are frequently twinned.

Perovskite occurs in igneous rocks that are rich in iron and magnesium. It also occurs in contact metamorphic rocks associated with magnesium- and iron-rich intrusive igneous rocks and in some chlorite and talc schists. It is also found in carbonaceous chondrite meteorites (p.337).

PROFILE

Trigonal

⬥ 5–6

⬥ 4.7

⬥ None

⬥ Conchoidal

⬥ Black to reddish brown

⬥ Metallic to submetallic

metallic lustre

lamellar ilmenite

twinned ilmenite crystals

oligoclase feldspar groundmass

Ilmenite crystals
This specimen exhibits opaque, black, lamellar, and twinned crystals of ilmenite.

VARIANT

ilmenite crystal

quartz

Tabular crystals Thin, grey, tabular ilmenite crystals with actinolite and quartz

$FeTiO_3$

ILMENITE

Named after the Il'menski Mountains near Miass, Russia, where it was discovered, ilmenite is a major source of titanium. Usually thick and tabular, its crystals sometimes occur as thin lamellae (fine plates) or rhombohedra. Ilmenite can also be massive, or occur as scattered grains. Intergrowths with hematite (p.91) or magnetite (p.92) are common, and ilmenite can be mistaken for these minerals because of its opaque, metallic, grey-black colour. Unlike magnetite, however, ilmenite is non-magnetic or very weakly magnetic; and it can be distinguished from hematite by its black streak. It may weather to a dull brown colour.

Ilmenite is widely distributed as an accessory mineral in igneous rocks, such as diorite (p.264) and gabbro (p.265). It is a frequent accessory in kimberlite rocks (p.269), associated with diamond (p.47). It is also found in veins, pegmatite rocks (p.260), and black beach sands associated with magnetite, rutile (p.78), zircon (p.233), and other heavy minerals.

Rhombohedral hematite
These superb hematite crystals from Elba, Italy, demonstrate hexagonal or rhombohedral form and metallic lustre.

modified
rhombohedral
crystal

colourful tarnish
on surface

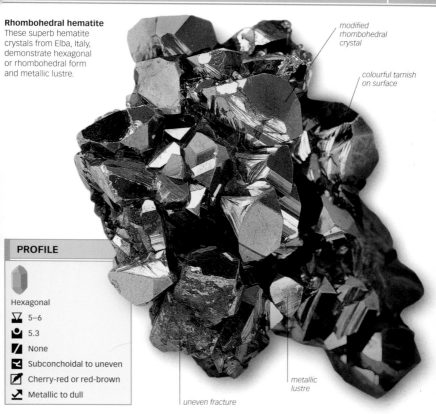

metallic
lustre

uneven fracture

PROFILE

Hexagonal

⬡ 5–6

💧 5.3

▮ None

⬲ Subconchoidal to uneven

▨ Cherry-red or red-brown

⬲ Metallic to dull

VARIANTS

Kidney ore A perfect example of hematite's botryoidal habit

Specular hematite
Brilliant platy crystals of specular hematite

Iridescent hematite
An iridescent crystal on rock

Fe_2O_3

HEMATITE

Dense and hard, hematite is the most important ore of iron (p.39) because of its high iron content and its abundance. The mineral occurs in various habits: steel-grey crystals and coarse-grained varieties with a brilliant metallic lustre are known as specular hematite; thin, scaly forms make up micaceous hematite; and crystals in petal-like arrangements are called iron roses. Hematite also occurs as short, black, rhombohedral crystals and may have an iridescent tarnish. The soft, fine-grained, and earthy form of hematite is used as a pigment.

Important hematite deposits occur in sedimentary beds or in metamorphosed sediments. A compact variety known as kidney ore has a kidney-shaped surface. A form of ground hematite called rouge is used to polish plate glass and jewellery.

Oval cabochon
This oval cabochon of black hematite is faceted on top. Hematite cabochons have been sold as "marcasites".

PROFILE

Cubic

5½–6

5.2

None

Conchoidal to uneven

Black

Metallic to semimetallic

iron fillings attracted by magnetic surface

magnetic field

Magnetic magnetite
Magnetic specimens of magnetite, such as this one covered with iron filings, are known as lodestones.

VARIANTS

Octahedral crystal
A magnetite crystal showing classic octahedral form

Magnetite crystals A cluster of black magnetite crystals

Fe_2O_4

MAGNETITE

An iron oxide, magnetite is named after the Greek shepherd boy Magnes, who noticed that the iron ferrule of his staff and the nails of his shoes clung to a magnetite-bearing rock. All magnetite can be picked up with a magnet, but some magnetite is itself naturally magnetic and attracts iron filings and deflects compass needles. Magnetite usually forms octahedral crystals, although it sometimes occurs as highly modified dodecahedrons. Specimens can also be massive or granular, occurring as disseminated grains and as concentrations in black sand. Magnetite is similar in appearance to hematite (p.91), but hematite is nonmagnetic and has a red streak.

Magnetite occurs in a range of geological environments. It forms at high temperatures (575°C/1,065°F or above) as an accessory mineral in metamorphic and igneous rocks and in sulphide veins. A major ore of iron (p.39), magnetite forms large ore bodies. Economically important deposits occur in silica-poor intrusions of igneous rocks and in banded ironstones (p.329).

vedish fergusonite
this specimen from Ytterby,
veden, fergusonite crystals rest
a groundmass of feldspar.

feldspar

fergusonite crystal

PROFILE

Tetragonal

 5½–6½

 4.2–5.7

Poor

Subconchoidal, brittle

Brown, yellow-brown,
greenish grey

Vitreous to submetallic

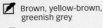 (Ce,Y,La,Nd)NbO$_4$

FERGUSONITE

Named after the Scottish mineralogist Robert Ferguson (1767–1840), the fergusonite group contains several minerals. All fergusonites may be considered as sources of the rare metals they contain. The most common is fergusonite-(Y), which is rich in yttrium. Its crystals are prismatic to pyramidal in shape and black to brownish black. Fergusonite-(Ce) is cerium-rich, dark red to black in colour, and forms prismatic dipyramidal crystals – although these are rare. Fergusonite-(Nd), a neodymium-bearing fergusonite, is usually granular. Another member of the fergusonites, formanite-(Y), is found as tabular crystals and anhedral pebbles. Yet other fergusonites, most of which appear in minor quantities, bear the prefix "beta".

Fergusonites can also have varying amounts of erbium, lanthanum, niobium, dysprosium, uranium, thorium, zirconium, and tungsten. They can be found in granitic pegmatites (p.260) associated with other rare-earth minerals and in placer deposits.

Massive romanèchite
This specimen of massive romanèchite demonstrates its dull lustre.

massive habit

dull lustre

PROFILE

Orthorhombic

5–6

4.7

None

Uneven

Brownish black, shiny

Submetallic to dull

VARIANT

Botryoidal romanèchite
Dense, submetallic, botryoidal romanèchite

$(Ba, H_2O)(Mn_4+Mn_3+)_5O_{10}$

ROMANÈCHITE

A hard, black, barium manganese oxide, romanèchite is named after its occurrence at Romanèche-Thorins, France. It is one of the manganese oxides that were formerly grouped together under the name psilomelane, which has been applied to several distinct minerals. Although the name psilomelane is no longer used to refer to a particular mineral, it continues to be used as a term of convenience for a group of barium-bearing manganese oxides. Romanèchite specimens are usually fine-grained or fibrous. Crystals are rare; when found, they are prismatic.

Romanèchite forms as an alteration product of other manganese minerals and is an ore of manganese. The mineral also forms in bogs, lakes, and shallow seas. Although romanèchite is named after a French locality, it was first identified at Schneeberg, Saxony, Germany. Other important deposits of romanèchite are at Tekrasni, India; Pilbara, Australia; Cornwall, England; and Hidalgo County, New Mexico, USA.

PROFILE

Hexagonal or trigonal

9

4–4.1

None

Conchoidal to uneven

Colourless

Adamantine to vitreous

Sapphire crystal
This water-worn crystal has a pyramidal form and exhibits the colour zoning that is common in sapphire.

colour zoning

blue colouring due to traces of titanium

VARIANTS

vitreous lustre

Ruby in matrix
Prismatic Kashmir rubies embedded in a rock matrix

Common corundum
An opaque, dipyramidal crystal of common corundum

Al_2O_3

CORUNDUM

After diamond, corundum is the hardest mineral on Earth. The name corundum comes from the Sanskrit *kuruvinda*, meaning "ruby" – the name given to red corundum. Ruby and sapphire are gem varieties of corundum. An aluminium oxide, corundum is commonly white, grey, or brown, but gem colours include red ruby and blue, green, yellow, orange, violet, and pink sapphire. Colourless forms also occur. Ruby forms a continuous colour succession with pink sapphire; only stones of the darker hues are considered to be ruby.

Corundum crystals are generally hexagonal, either tabular, tapering barrel-shaped, or dipyramidal. Corundum can also be massive or granular. It forms in syenites (p.262), certain pegmatites (p.260), and in high-grade metamorphic rocks. It is concentrated in placer deposits.

Antique ruby ring
In this ring, a square-cut ruby has been set at right angles to its square setting.

PROFILE

Cubic

7½–8

3.6–4.1

None

Conchoidal to uneven

White

Vitreous

Spinel octahedrons
In this specimen, octahedral crystals of pleonaste, or black spinel, are set in a quartz groundmass.

octahedral spinel crystal

quartz groundmass

VARIANTS

Spinel aggregate Numerous ruby spinel crystals

Black spinel A modified octahedron of black spinel on a rock matrix

$MgAl_2O_4$

SPINEL

Spinel is the name of both an individual mineral and of a group of metal-oxide minerals that share the same crystal structure. Minerals in this group include gahnite (p.97), franklinite, and chromite (p.99). Spinel is found as glassy, hard octahedra, or as grains or masses. Though familiar as a blue, purple, red, or pink gemstone, spinel also occurs in other colours. Red spinel is called ruby spinel; its blood-red colour is due to the presence of chromium.

A minor constituent of peridotites (p.266), kimberlites (p.269), basalts (p.273), and other igneous rocks, spinel also forms in aluminium-rich schists (pp.291–92) and metamorphosed limestones. Water-worn crystals come from stream deposits. The earliest known spinel dates back to 100BCE and was discovered near Kabul, Afghanistan.

Spinel gemstone
This superb faceted spinel shows excellent red-lavender colour and good clarity.

octahedral crystal

rock groundmass

Octahedral gahnite
This blue octahedron of gahnite is from Franklin, New Jersey, USA. Other gahnite localities are Colorado and Maine, USA.

PROFILE

Cubic

 7 ½–8

 4.6

 Indistinct

 Conchoidal, irregular

Greyish

Vitreous

$ZnAl_2O_4$

GAHNITE

A zinc aluminium oxide, gahnite is a member of the spinel group and frequently forms the simple octahedral crystals typical of the group. Crystals usually show good external form. They may be striated on faces and cleavage surfaces. Usually dark green or blue to black in colour, they can reach up to 12 cm (4½ in) on an edge. Crystals can sometimes be grey, yellow, or brown in colour. Gahnite also occurs as irregular grains and masses, and in some lithium pegmatites (p.260) as gem-clear nodules.

Gahnite was named in 1807 after the Swedish chemist and mineralogist John Gottlieb Gahn. It is found in crystalline schists (pp.291–92) and gneisses (p.288), in granites (pp.258–59) and granitic pegmatites, and in contact metamorphosed limestones. It sometimes forms from the low-grade metamorphism of bauxite (p.101) and is also found in placer deposits. Superb crystals occur at Salida and Cotopaxi, Colorado, USA; at Falun, Sweden; and at Minas Gerais, Brazil.

uneven fracture

submetallic lustre

crystal appears octahedral

massive habit

Hausmannite crystals
In this hausmannite specimen, pseudo-octahedral crystals rest on a base of massive hausmannite.

$Mn^{2+}Mn_2^{3+}O_4$

HAUSMANNITE

Named in 1827 after Johann Friedrich Ludwig Hausmann, a German professor of mineralogy, hausmannite is dark brown or black and is usually granular or massive. Well-formed crystals are uncommon yet distinctive. They are pseudo-octahedral in shape but often have additional faces. Small amounts of iron and zinc may substitute for manganese in the hausmannite structure. Hausmannite forms in hydrothermal veins, and it also occurs where manganese-rich rocks have been metamorphosed. It is often found associated with other manganese oxides, such as pyrolusite (p.80), romanéchite (p.94), and the manganese–iron mineral bixbyite. Superb crystals, up to 4 cm (1½ in) long, come from Brazil, South Africa, and Germany.

Hausmannite is an ore of manganese, which is added to aluminium and magnesium alloys to improve corrosion resistance. Manganese oxides are important in the manufacture of steel, where they absorb the sulphur in iron ores and impart strength.

PROFILE

Tetragonal

5½

4.8

Perfect

Uneven

Reddish brown

Submetallic

nodular chromite

Nodular chromite
The metallic lustre of chromite is visible on the broken surfaces of these nodules.

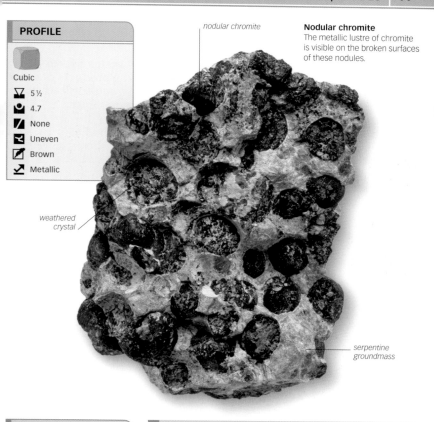

weathered crystal

serpentine groundmass

VARIANT

Massive chromite A glossy black specimen of chromite

$FeCr_2O_4$

CHROMITE

A member of the spinel mineral group, chromite is an iron chromium oxide and the most important ore of chromium. Crystals are uncommon, but when found they are octahedral. Chromite is usually massive or in the form of lenses and tabular bodies, or it may be disseminated as granules. It is sometimes found as a crystalline inclusion in diamond. Chromite is dark brown to black in colour and can contain some magnesium and aluminium.

Chromite is most commonly found as an accessory mineral in iron- and magnesium-rich igneous rocks or concentrated in sediments derived from them. It occurs as layers in a few igneous rocks that are especially rich in iron and magnesium. Almost pure chromite is found in similar layers in sedimentary rocks. The layers are preserved when the sedimentary rocks metamorphose to form serpentinite (p.298). Referred to as chromitites, these rocks are the most important ores of chromium. The weathering of chromite ore bodies can also lead to its concentration in placer deposits.

HYDROXIDES

Hydroxides form when metallic elements combine with a hydroxyl radical. They are found predominantly as weathering products of other minerals. Hydroxide minerals are usually less dense and softer than oxide minerals. Many hydroxides are important ore minerals.

COMPOSITION

Nearly all hydroxides form at low temperatures (up to 200°C/400°F), when water reacts with an oxide. They contain the hydroxyl radical, which is a single chemical unit made up of one atom of hydrogen and one atom of oxygen.

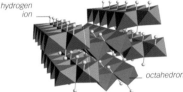

hydrogen ion

octahedron

Crystal structure of diaspore
In the aluminium hydroxide diaspore, aluminium ions are in octahedral coordination with hydroxyl groups, forming strips of octahedra.

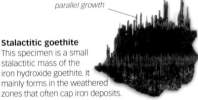

stalactites in parallel growth

Stalactitic goethite
This specimen is a small stalactitic mass of the iron hydroxide goethite. It mainly forms in the weathered zones that often cap iron deposits.

OCCURRENCE AND USES

Hydroxide minerals are found in most places where water has altered primary oxides. Some hydroxides are also precipitated directly. They are often important ore minerals. The aluminium hydroxides diaspore, bohemite, and gibbsite constitute bauxite, the ore of aluminium. Goethite, an iron hydroxide, is an ore of iron.

UMBER

OCHRE

Artists' pigments
Although now mostly replaced by synthetics, goethite (formerly called limonite) has provided the pigment in umbers and ochres for millennia.

Les-Baux-De-Provence
The mixture of aluminium hydroxide minerals called bauxite is named after the village of Les-Baux-de-Provence in southeastern France, where it was first recognized in 1821.

Pisolitic bauxite
This bauxite specimen shows a classic pisolithic habit, meaning that it is made up of numerous pisoliths – grains up to the size of a pea.

pisolitic structure

pisolith

aluminium oxide groundmass

dull to earthy lustre

PROFILE

Crystal system None

 1–3

 2.3–2.7

 None

Uneven

Usually white

Earthy

VARIANT

Bauxite as an ore Primary ore of the metal aluminium

♨ Mixture of hydrous aluminium oxides

BAUXITE

Although bauxite is not a mineral, it is nonetheless one of the most important ores, since it is the sole source of aluminium. The product of weathering of aluminium-rich rocks, it contains several constituent minerals. Bauxite is variably creamy yellow, orange, pink, or red because of the presence of quartz (p.168), clays, and hematite (p.91) and other iron oxides in addition to several hydrated aluminium oxides.

Bauxite forms as extensive, shallow deposits in humid tropical environments. It may be nodular, pisolitic, or earthy. Deposits are soft, easily crushed, and textureless or hard, dense, and pea-like. Bauxite may also be porous but strong and stratified, or it may retain the form of its parent rock.

Versatile aluminium
A key metal of the modern age, aluminium is used to make products ranging from takeaway trays to spacecraft.

Orthorhombic

5–5½

4.3

Perfect

Uneven

Brownish yellow to ochre-red

Adamantine to metallic

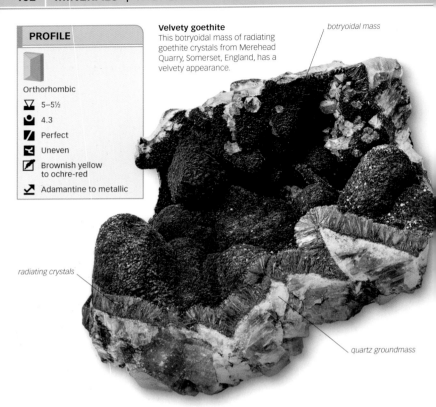

Velvety goethite
This botryoidal mass of radiating goethite crystals from Merehead Quarry, Somerset, England, has a velvety appearance.

botryoidal mass

radiating crystals

quartz groundmass

VARIANTS

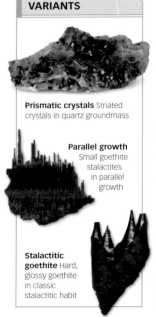

Prismatic crystals Striated crystals in quartz groundmass

Parallel growth Small goethite stalactites in parallel growth

Stalactitic goethite Hard, glossy goethite in classic stalactitic habit

FeO(OH)

GOETHITE

Named after the German mineralogist Johann Wolfgang von Goethe in 1806, goethite is a common mineral. It can be brownish yellow, reddish brown, or dark brown in colour, depending on the size of the crystal in the specimen – small crystals appear lighter, and larger ones darker. It can occur as opaque black, prismatic and vertically striated crystals; velvety, radiating fibrous aggregates; flattened tablets or scales; and reniform or botryoidal masses. Goethite can also occur in stalactitic or massive forms and in tufts and drusy coatings.

Goethite is an iron oxide hydroxide, although manganese can substitute for up to 5 per cent of the iron. It forms as a weathering product in the oxidation zones of veins of iron minerals, such as pyrite (p.62), magnetite (p.92), and siderite (p.123). Goethite may occur with these minerals in the gossan, or iron hat, which is the weathered capping of an iron ore deposit. It also occurs in a form called bog iron ore, which can be produced by living organisms.

PROFILE

Monoclinic

⬙ 4

⬙ 4.3

⬙ Perfect, good

⬙ Uneven

⬙ Reddish brown to black

⬙ Submetallic

Prismatic manganite
This specimen is a mass of pseudo-orthorhombic prisms showing typical deep striations on the crystal faces.

flat termination

submetallic lustre

striation

uneven fracture

VARIANT

bundles of manganite crystals

Crystal bundles Manganite crystals grouped in bundles

👤 MnO(OH)

MANGANITE

A widespread and important ore of manganese, manganite is hydrated manganese oxide. The mineral had been described by a number of different names since 1772, but was finally given its current name, which it owes to its manganese component, in 1827. Opaque and metallic dark grey or black, crystals of manganite are mostly pseudo-orthorhombic prisms, typically with flat or blunt terminations, and are often grouped in bundles and striated lengthways. Multiple twinning is common. Manganite can also be massive or granular; it is then hard to distinguish by eye from other manganese oxides, such as pyrolusite (p.80).

An important ore of manganese, manganite occurs in hydrothermal deposits formed at low temperatures (up to 200°C/400°F) with calcite (p.114), siderite (p.123), and baryte (p.134), and in replacement deposits with goethite (p.102). Manganite also occurs in hot-spring manganese deposits. It alters to pyrolusite and may form by the alteration of other manganese minerals.

Dark red diaspore
In this specimen, a mass of dark red, thin, platy diaspore crystals rests in a groundmass of corundum.

trace chromium gives lilac colour

platy crystal

corundum groundmass

 AlO(OH)

DIASPORE

Diaspore takes its name from the Greek word *diaspora*, which means "scattering" – a reference to the way diaspore crackles and depreciates under high heat. Its crystals are thin and platy, elongated, tabular, prismatic, or needle-like and are often twinned. Diaspore can be massive or can occur as disseminated grains. It may be colourless, white, greyish white, greenish grey, light brown, yellowish, lilac, or pink in colour. The same specimen can appear to have different colours when viewed from different directions.

Diaspore forms in metamorphic rocks, such as schists (p.292) and marbles (p.301), where it is often associated with corundum (p.95), spinel (p.96), and manganite (p.103). It is widespread in bauxite (p.101), laterite (p.326), and aluminous clays.

Faceted gem
Zultanite, which is a rare, transparent type of diaspore crystal from Turkey, is a collector's gem.

Hexagonal or trigonal

2½

2.4

Perfect

Uneven, sectile

White

Waxy to vitreous/pearly

Fibrous brucite
This fibrous mass of brucite with
a vitreous lustre is from Timmins,
Ontario, Canada.

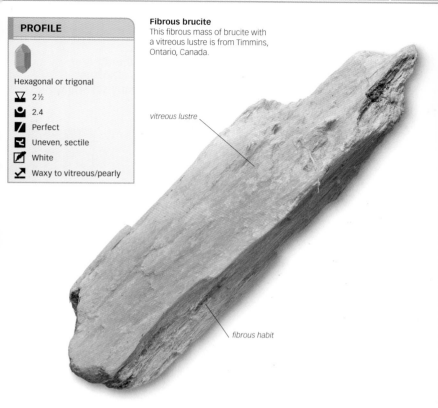

vitreous lustre

fibrous habit

VARIANTS

brucite crystal

Tabular crystals Tabular
brucite in a rock groundmass

Nemalite A fibrous variety
of brucite

$Mg(OH)_2$

BRUCITE

Named after the American mineralogist Archibald
Bruce in 1824, brucite is magnesium hydroxide. Usually
white, it can be pale green, grey, or blue. Manganese may
substitute to some degree for magnesium, producing
yellow to red coloration. Its crystals can be tabular or form
aggregates of plates. They tend to be soft, and range from
waxy to glassy in appearance. Fine large crystals have
been collected from nemalite, a variety of brucite that
occurs in fibres and laths. Brucite may also occur in
massive, foliated, fibrous, or,
more rarely, granular habits.

Brucite is found in metamorphic
rocks, such as schist (p.292), and
in low-temperature hydrothermal
veins (up to 200°C/400°F) in
marbles (p.301) and chlorite
schists. It is used as a primary
source of medical magnesia and
as a fire retardant.

Kiln lining
Because of its high melting
point, brucite is used to line
kilns, such as the potter's kiln
being used here.

HALIDES

Minerals in this group consist of metals combined with one of the four common halogen elements: fluorine, chlorine, iodine, or bromine. Halides tend to be soft and many crystallize in the cubic system.

COMPOSITION

Compositionally and structurally, there are three broad categories of halide mineral: simple halides, halide complexes, and oxyhydroxy-halides. Simple halides form when a metal combines with a halogen. Halite and fluorite are examples of simple halides. In halide complexes, the halide is usually bound to aluminium, creating a molecule that behaves as a single unit, which is in turn bound to a metal. For example, in cryolite, fluorine and aluminium are bound to sodium. Oxyhydroxy-halides are very rare. Atacamite is an example of these halides.

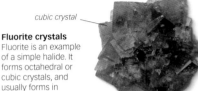

cubic crystal

Fluorite crystals
Fluorite is an example of a simple halide. It forms octahedral or cubic crystals, and usually forms in hydrothermal veins.

OCCURRENCE

Many halides occur in evaporite deposits. Others occur in hydrothermal veins or form when halide-bearing waters act upon the oxidation products of other minerals.

USES

Halides are important industrial minerals. Halite, or table salt, is the classic example. Other halides are used as fertilizers, in glass making and metal refining, and as minor ores.

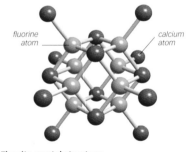

fluorine atom

calcium atom

Fluorite crystal structure
Fluorine is an example of a simple halide. Calcium atoms combine with flourine atoms to form crystals in the cubic system.

Fertilizing crops
The halides sylvite and carnallite are important sources of potash for fertilizers. Potash reduces many diseases, rot, and mildew of food plants.

Salt Lake
Thick, white crusts of the halide mineral halite encrust rocks along the edge of the Great Salt Lake, Utah, USA.

granular carnallite
s granular mass of carnallite
s a red colour due to inclusions
hematite.

granular surface

colour due to
impurities

PROFILE

Orthorhombic

2½

1.6

None

Conchoidal

White

Greasy

$KMgCl_3 \cdot 6H_2O$

CARNALLITE

First discovered in Germany, carnallite was named after Rudolph von Carnall, a Prussian mining engineer, in 1856. It is usually white or colourless but may appear reddish or yellowish depending on the presence of hematite (p.91) or goethite (p.102) impurities. Hydrated potassium and magnesium chloride, carnallite is generally massive to granular in habit. Crystals are rare because they absorb water from the air and dissolve. When found, crystals are thick and tabular, pseudohexagonal, or pyramidal.

Carnallite forms in the upper layers of marine evaporite salt deposits, where it occurs with other potassium and magnesium evaporite minerals. The mineral is Russia's most important source of magnesium. Caustic potash, a potassium hydroxide, is produced from carnallite.

Potash fertilizer
Carnallite is an important source of potash, which is used in fertilizers, and caustic potash.

Cryolite crystals
This mass of translucent cryolite crystals on rock has patches of siderite on it.

greasy lustre

nearly cubic crystal

brown siderite

PROFILE

Monoclinic

2½

3.0

None

Uneven

White

Vitreous to greasy

VARIANT

pseudocubic outline

greasy lustre

Massive cryolite specimen
A close-up of a massive cryolite fragment

Na_3AlF_6

CRYOLITE

Few people have heard of cryolite, but it is one of the most important minerals of our age. Aircraft could not fly without it, and modern engineering of all kinds would be stunted in its absence. Synthetic cryolite is an essential ingredient in aluminium production. The mineral takes its name from the Greek terms *kryos* and *lithos*, which mean "ice" and "stone" – an allusion to its translucent, ice-like appearance. Cryolite is usually colourless or white. Rarely it can be brown, yellow, reddish brown, or black. It occurs commonly as coarse, granular, or massive aggregates and rarely, as pseudocubic crystals.

Cryolite forms mainly in certain granites (pp.258–59) and granitic pegmatites (p.260). The largest deposit of cryolite, at Ivigtut, Greenland, is now exhausted. Lesser amounts are found in Spain, Russia, and the USA.

Cryolite in aviation
Synthetic cryolite is used to separate aluminium – an indispensable metal in aviation – from its ores.

PROFILE

Cubic

4

3.0–3.3

Perfect octahedral

Flat conchoidal

White

Vitreous

Twinned crystals
This group of fine green cubic fluorite crystals exhibits the classic penetration twins, which are typical of this mineral.

zones of purple and green

twinned crystals

cubic habit

iron-stained coating

VARIANTS

Purple octahedron
An octahedral crystal of purple fluorite

Yellow fluorite A group of bright yellow fluorite cubes

Near-white fluorite
A group of unusually colourless cubes

CaF_2

FLUORITE

An important industrial mineral, fluorite used to be known as fluorspar. The name fluorite comes from the Latin word *fluere*, which means "to flow" – a reference to its use in iron smelting to improve the fluidity of slags and the refining of metals. Fluorite commonly occurs as vibrant, well-formed crystals. A single crystal may have zones of different colours that follow the contour of the crystal faces. Fluorite crystals are widely found in cubes, while fluorite octahedra – which are often twinned – are much less common. The mineral can also be massive, granular, or compact.

Fluorite occurs in hydrothermal deposits and as an accessory mineral in intermediate intrusive and silica-rich rocks. It is used in the manufacture of high-octane fuels and steel and in the production of hydrofluoric acid.

Blue John
Veins of banded purple, white, and yellow fluorite, known as Blue John, are visible in this vessel.

PROFILE

Cubic

⊻ 2½

◖ 2.1–2.6

◰ Perfect cubic

◰ Conchoidal

◰ White

⬦ Vitreous

cubic crystal

vitreous lustre

rock groundmass

Halite crystals
In this specimen from Inowroclaw, Poland, cubic crystals of halite cover a rock groundmass.

VARIANTS

Cubic halite Twinned, cubic crystals on rock groundmass

Massive halite A specimen of massive, pink halite

Blue halite Unusual blue cubic halite on rock

⚛ NaCl

HALITE

Culinary rock salt is actually halite. Its name is derived from the Greek word *hals*, which means "salt". Most halite is colourless, white, grey, orange, or brown, but it can also be bright blue or purple. The orange colour comes from inclusions of hematite (p.91), while the blue and purple colours indicate defects in the crystal structure. Halite is commonly found in massive and bedded aggregates as rock salt. It also occurs in coarse, crystalline masses or in granular and compact forms.

Halite crystals are usually cubic. Sometimes, halite may form "hopper" crystals – in which the outer edges of the cube faces have grown more rapidly than their centres, leaving cavernous faces. It is widespread in saline evaporite deposits.

Table salt
Mined since ancient times and also used as a currency, common table salt is the mineral halite.

PROFILE

Cubic

⊻ 2½

⊻ 2.0

⊿ Perfect cubic

⊠ Uneven

⊡ White

⊿ Vitreous

interlocking cubic crystal

transparent at crystal margin

vitreous lustre

Sylvite crystals
The pinkish, interlocking, cubic crystals in this specimen are typical of sylvite.

VARIANT

Sylvite in potash A specimen of massive potash containing the mineral sylvite

⚛ KCl

SYLVITE

Millions of tons of sylvite are mined annually for the manufacture of potassium compounds, such as potash fertilizers. Sylvite is also used to manufacture metallic potassium. The mineral was first discovered in 1823 on Mount Vesuvius, Italy, where it occurs as encrustations on lava. The name sylvite comes from its Latin medicinal name, *sal digestivus Sylvii*, which means "digestive salt". Sylvite is also known as sylvine. Usually colourless to white or greyish, sylvite can be tinged blue, yellow, purple, or red. Sylvite crystals are cubic, octahedral, or both. It commonly occurs as crusts and as columnar, granular, or massive aggregates.

Sylvite is found in thick beds either mixed or interbedded with halite (p.110), gypsum (p.136), and other evaporite minerals, although it is rarer than halite.

Sylvite fertilizer
Crushed potash, as seen here, is used as a fertilizer and comes from the mineral sylvite.

PROFILE

Tetragonal

1–2

6.5

Distinct

Conchoidal

Pale yellow-white

Adamantine

rock groundmass

yellowish crust of calomel

Calomel encrustations
A thin crust of yellowish calomel crystals coats a rock groundmass in this specimen.

VARIANT

black calomel crystal

Calomel in groundmass
Crystals of black calomel in a rock groundmass

♣ HgCl

CALOMEL

A mercury chloride, calomel takes its name from two Greek words: *ómorfi*, which means "beautiful", and *méli*, which means "honey" – an allusion to its sweet taste, although it is, in fact, toxic. Calomel is also referred to as horn quicksilver and horn mercury. Specimens are soft, heavy, and plastic-like, with crystals that are pyramidal, tabular, or prismatic, often with complex twinning. Calomel is also found as crusts and can be massive and earthy. It fluoresces brick red.

Calomel occurs as a secondary mineral in the oxidized zones of mercury-bearing deposits, together with native mercury, cinnabar (p.56), goethite (p.102), and calcite (p.114). It was used as a laxative and a disinfectant as well as in the treatment of syphilis from the 16th century until the early 20th century, when the toxic effect of its mercury component was discovered. Following widespread poisoning, calomel's use as a teething powder in Britain was suspended only in 1954. It is still used as an ore of mercury and in insecticides and fungicides.

CARBONATES

There are approximately 80 known carbonate minerals. Most of them are rare, but the common carbonates calcite and dolomite are major rock-forming minerals. Carbonates form rhombohedral crystals and are soft, soluble in hydrochloric acid, and often vividly coloured.

COMPOSITION

All carbonates contain the carbonate group CO_3 as the basic compositional and structural unit. This group has a carbon atom in the centre of an equilateral triangle of oxygen atoms, giving rise to the trigonal symmetry of many carbonate minerals. This basic unit is joined by one or more metals or semimetals such as calcium, sodium, aluminium, manganese, barium, zinc, and copper.

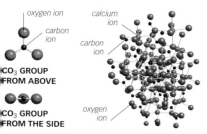

oxygen ion

carbon ion

calcium ion

carbon ion

oxygen ion

CO_3 GROUP FROM ABOVE

CO_3 GROUP FROM THE SIDE

Calcite crystal sructure
In calcite, three oxygen ions surround each carbon ion in a CO_3 group. Each calcium ion combines with six oxygen ions to form an octahedron.

lenticular crystal

Crystalline calcite
Calcite is the most common carbonate and occurs in a wide range of crystalline forms. Lenticular and scalenohedral crystals are seen in this specimen.

OCCURRENCE

Calcite and dolomite are found in sediments such as chalk and limestone. They also occur in sea shells and coral reefs, in evaporate deposits, and in metamorphic rocks, such as marble. Other carbonates, such as rhodochrosite, azurite, and malachite, are principally secondary minerals.

USES

The carbonate minerals calcite and dolomite are important in the manufacture of cement and building stone. Other carbonates find uses as ores of metals: witherite of barium; strontianite of strontium; siderite of iron; rhodochrosite of manganese; smithsonite of zinc; and cerussite of lead.

intricate growth pattern

Malachite jewel box
The copper carbonate malachite has been a favourite carving stone for three millennia.

Mining at Trona
Trona in the Panamint Valley, California, USA, is named after the large evaporite deposit of the carbonate mineral trona, which was discovered there.

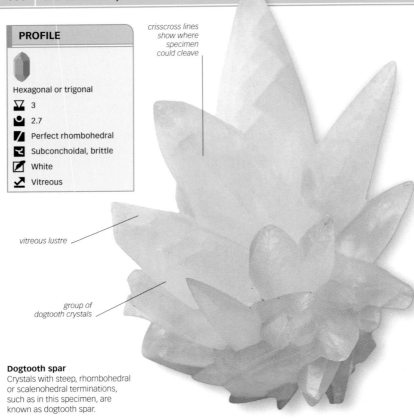

crisscross lines show where specimen could cleave

vitreous lustre

group of dogtooth crystals

Dogtooth spar
Crystals with steep, rhombohedral or scalenohedral terminations, such as in this specimen, are known as dogtooth spar.

VARIANTS

Butterfly twin A twinned, pink crystal of calcite

Nailhead spar
A rhombohedral calcite crystal on galena

Scalenohedron
A single, scalenohedral calcite crystal

♦ $CaCO_3$

CALCITE

The most common form of calcium carbonate, calcite is known for the variety and beautiful development of its crystals. These occur most often as scalenohedra and are commonly twinned, sometimes forming heart-shaped, butterfly twins. Crystals with rhombohedral terminations are also common; those with shallow rhombohedral terminations are called nailhead spar. Highly transparent calcite is called optical spar.

Although calcite can form spectacular crystals, it is usually massive, occurring either as marble (p.301) or as limestone (p.319). It is also found as fibres, nodules, stalactites, and earthy aggregates. Calcite specimens can occur in metamorphic deposits, igneous rocks, and hydrothermal veins.

Alabaster sphinx
Virtually all ancient Egyptian "alabaster", such as that used to make this small sphinx, was actually calcite.

semi-transparent crystal

prismatic crystal

radiating habit

PROFILE

Orthorhombic

3½–4

2.9

Distinct

Subconchoidal, brittle

White

Vitreous inclining to resinous

Pseudohexagonal crystals
This specimen consists of a radiating group of prismatic, semi-transparent, pseudohexagonal, twinned aragonite crystals.

VARIANTS

Intergrown crystals
A mass of pseudohexagonal crystals of aragonite

Flos ferri
Coral-like aragonite crystals on rock matrix

Cyclic twin
A classic aragonite cyclic twin from Spain

$CaCo_3$

ARAGONITE

Although aragonite has the same chemical composition as calcite (p.114), its crystals are different. They are tabular, prismatic, or needle-like, often with steep pyramidal or chisel-shaped ends, and can form columnar or radiating aggregates. Multiple twinned crystals are common, appearing hexagonal in shape. Although aragonite sometimes looks similar to calcite, it is easily distinguished by the absence of rhombohedral cleavage. Specimens can be white, colourless, grey, yellowish, green, blue, reddish, violet, or brown.

Aragonite is found in the oxidized zones of ore deposits and in evaporites, hot spring deposits, and caves. It is also found in some metamorphic and igneous rocks. Banded, stalactitic aragonite can be polished as an ornamental stone.

Mother of pearl
Aragonite is also produced by some living animals. It is seen here forming the inner layer of a marine mollusc shell.

twinned crystals

galena

rock groundmass

Witherite crystals
This specimen contains a group
of witherite crystals and galena
on a rock groundmass.

PROFILE

Orthorhombic

 3–3½

4.3

Distinct, imperfect

Uneven, brittle

White

Vitreous

 $BaCo_3$

WITHERITE

This barium carbonate was named in 1790 after the English mineralogist William Withering. Witherite is white, colourless, or tinged yellow, brown, or green. Its crystals are always twinned, either as prisms which appear hexagonal in shape, or as pyramids, which are frequently paired. They can also be short to long prismatic or tabular and may have striations running across the prism faces. Witherite can also be fibrous, botryoidal, spherular, columnar, granular, or massive.

Most witherite comes from hydrothermal veins formed at low temperatures (up to 200°C/400°F), usually resulting from the alteration of baryte (p.134). Specimens feel relatively heavy for their size due to the presence of the high-density element barium. Witherite is preferred over the commonly found barium mineral baryte for the preparation of other barium compounds because it is more soluble in acids. These compounds are used in case-hardening steel, in copper refining, in sugar refining, in vacuum tubes, and in many other applications.

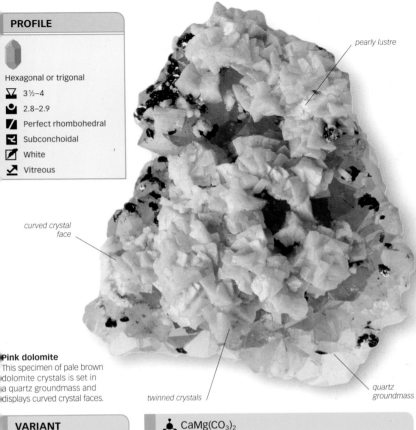

PROFILE

Hexagonal or trigonal

⬙	3½–4
⬖	2.8–2.9
◩	Perfect rhombohedral
◩	Subconchoidal
◩	White
⬈	Vitreous

pearly lustre

curved crystal face

Pink dolomite
This specimen of pale brown dolomite crystals is set in a quartz groundmass and displays curved crystal faces.

twinned crystals

quartz groundmass

VARIANT

saddle-shaped crystal

Tabular crystals Pink, saddle-shaped, tabular crystals of dolomite in a crust-like form

 CaMg(CO$_3$)$_2$

DOLOMITE

An important rock-forming mineral, dolomite is named after the French mineralogist Déodat Gratet de Dolomieu. It is a colourless to white, pale brown, greyish, reddish, or pink mineral. Its crystals are commonly rhombohedral or tabular, often have curved faces, and sometimes cluster in saddle-shaped aggregates. Dolomite may be striated horizontally and twinned. Some crystals may be up to 5 cm (2 in) long. It can also be coarse to fine granular, massive, and, rarely, fibrous.

Dolomite is the main constituent in dolomite rocks and dolomitic marbles. It occurs as a replacement deposit in limestone (p.319) affected by magnesium-bearing solutions, in talc schists, and in other magnesium-rich metamorphic rocks. Dolomite is found in hydrothermal veins associated with lead, zinc, and copper ores. It is also found in altered, silica-poor igneous rocks, in some carbonatites (p.272), and in serpentinites (p.298). Crystals of dolomite frequently form in cavities in limestone and marble (p.301).

coarse crystalline habit

Magnesite crystals
This crystalline mass of magnesite is on a rock groundmass.

perfect rhombohedral cleavage

VARIANT

Rhombohedral magnesite
Rare, rhombohedral crystals of the colourless form of magnesite

$MgCO_3$

MAGNESITE

This carbonate of magnesium takes its name from its magnesium component. It is generally massive, lamellar, fibrous, chalky, or granular. Distinct crystals are rare, but when found they are either rhombohedral or prismatic. Most commonly white or light grey, magnesite can be yellow or brownish when iron substitutes for some of the magnesium.

Magnesite forms mainly as an alteration product in magnesium-rich rocks, such as peridotites (p.266). It can occur as a primary mineral in limestones (p.319) and talc or chlorite schists, in cavities in volcanic rocks, and in oceanic salt deposits. It is also found in some meteorites (pp.335–37). An important source of magnesium, magnesite is used as a refractory material, as a catalyst and filler in the production of synthetic rubber, and in the manufacture of chemicals and fertilizers. Magnesium derived from magnesite is alloyed with aluminium, zinc, or manganese for use in aircraft, spacecraft, road vehicles, and household appliances.

Tabular crystals
In this specimen, a mass of tabular cerussite crystals covers a rock groundmass.

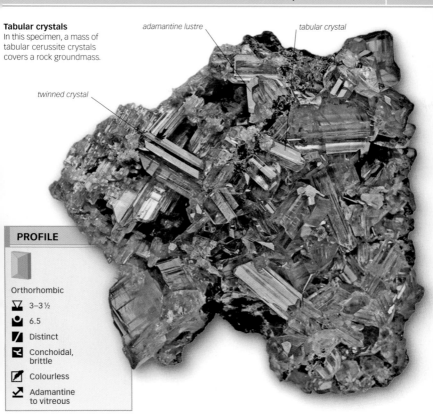

adamantine lustre

tabular crystal

twinned crystal

VARIANTS

Cyclic twin A star-shaped, crystalline specimen of cerussite from Zambia

Jack-straw cerussite Delicate, needle-like crystals of jack-straw cerussite

Prismatic crystal A striated, colourless, prismatic crystal of cerussite

$PbCO_3$

CERUSSITE

Known since antiquity, cerussite is named after the Latin word *cerussa*, which describes a white lead pigment. After galena (p.54), it is the most common ore of lead. Cerussite is generally colourless or white to grey, but may be blue to green due to copper impurities. Its crystal habits are highly varied. Cerrusite forms tabular or pyramidal crystals or, sometimes, twins that may be star-shaped or reticulated (net-like) masses. Fragile aggregates of randomly grown prismatic crystals known as jack-straw cerussite are also common. The adamantine lustre of cerussite crystals is particularly bright.

A widespread secondary mineral that occurs in the oxidation zones of lead veins, cerussite is formed by the action of carbonated water on other lead minerals, particularly galena and anglesite (p.132).

Collector's gem Faceted cerussite stones, such as this rare gem, are brilliant but too soft to be worn.

PROFILE

Monoclinic

⊻ 3½–4

◔ 3.8

▨ Perfect

◪ Conchoidal, brittle

◪ Blue

⤢ Vitreous to dull earthy

Large crystals
In this specimen of azurite, large, well-formed crystals rest on a goethite groundmass.

vitreous lustre

goethite groundmass

blocky, azure-blue crystal

VARIANTS

Bladed crystal A single, bladed azurite crystal

Tabular crystals Thin, parallel azurite crystals on a rock groundmass

Radiating crystals
A spherical concretion of azurite

🜨 $Cu_3(CO_3)_2(OH)_2$

AZURITE

A deep blue copper carbonate hydroxide, azurite was used as a blue pigment in 15th- to 17th-century European art and probably in the production of blue glaze in ancient Egypt. It takes its name from the Persian word *lazhuward*, which means "blue". Azurite forms either tabular or prismatic crystals with a wide variety of habits. Tabular crystals commonly have wedge-shaped terminations. Azurite forms rosette-shaped crystalline aggregates or occurs in massive, stalactitic, or botryoidal forms. Well-developed crystals are dark azure blue in colour, but massive or earthy aggregates may be paler.

Azurite is a secondary mineral formed in the oxidized portions of copper deposits. Massive azurite used for ornamental purposes is sometimes called chessylite, after Chessy, France.

Cabochon gemstone
This cabochon exhibits the vivid blue colour of azurite and the green colour of malachite.

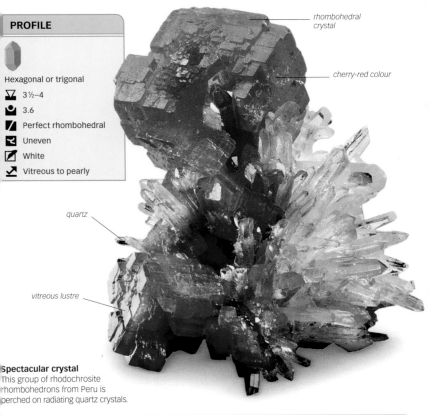

PROFILE

Hexagonal or trigonal

- ⚡ 3½–4
- ⬤ 3.6
- ▰ Perfect rhombohedral
- ▰ Uneven
- ▰ White
- ⤢ Vitreous to pearly

rhombohedral crystal

cherry-red colour

quartz

vitreous lustre

Spectacular crystal
This group of rhodochrosite rhombohedrons from Peru is perched on radiating quartz crystals.

VARIANTS

Classic crystals
Rhombohedral rhodochrosite in classic rose-pink colour

Red rhodochrosite Bright, cherry-red colour typical of many manganese minerals

👤 $MnCO_3$

RHODOCHROSITE

A prized collectors' mineral, rhodochrosite is a manganese carbonate. It was given its name – derived from the Greek *rhodokhros*, which means "of rosy colour" – in 1800. Rhodochrosite has a classic rose-pink colour, but specimens can also be brown or grey. It forms dogtooth or rhombohedral crystals like calcite (p.114), but it may also occur in stalactitic, granular, nodular, botryoidal, and massive habits.

Rhodochrosite is found in hydrothermal ore veins with sphalerite (p.53), galena (p.54), fluorite (p.109), and manganese oxides. It also occurs in metamorphic deposits and as a secondary mineral in sedimentary manganese deposits. Abundant at Butte, Montana, USA, and other localities, rhodochrosite is sometimes mined as an ore of manganese.

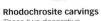

Rhodochrosite carvings
These two decorative ducks were carved from banded rhodochrosite and white calcite.

Ankerite rhombohedra
This group of ankerite rhombohedra is set in a rock groundmass.

twinned crystals

rock groundmass

rhombohedral crystal

perfect cleavage

PROFILE

Hexagonal or trigonal

3 ½–4

2.9

Perfect

Subconchoidal

White

Vitreous to pearly

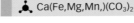 $Ca(Fe,Mg,Mn,)(CO_3)_2$

ANKERITE

Considered a rock-forming mineral, ankerite is calcium carbonate with varying amounts of iron, magnesium, and manganese in its structure. It was named in 1825 after the Austrian mineralogist M.J. Anker. Though usually pale buff coloured, ankerite can be colourless, white, grey, or brownish. Much ankerite becomes dark on weathering, and many specimens are fluorescent. Ankerite forms rhombohedral crystals similar to those of dolomite (p.117), often with similarly curved faces forming saddle-shaped groups; it can also form prismatic crystals. However, ankerite is more commonly massive or coarsely granular.

Ankerite forms as a secondary mineral from the action of iron- and magnesium-bearing fluids on limestone (p.319) or dolomite rock (p.320). It is a waste mineral in hydrothermal ore deposits and also occurs in carbonatites (p.272), low-grade metamorphosed ironstones, and banded ironstone formations (p.329). Ankerite is also found in iron ore deposits with siderite (p.123).

PROFILE

Hexagonal or trigonal

- 3 ½–4
- 3.9
- Perfect rhombohedral
- Uneven or subconchoidal
- White
- Vitreous to pearly

Rhombohedral crystals
This group of well-formed siderite rhombohedra with many twinned crystals rests on a rock groundmass.

rhombohedral crystal

pearly lustre

twinned crystals

quartz

VARIANTS

Botryoidal siderite Grape-like siderite bunches on a base of massive siderite

Single crystal A large, rhombohedral, single crystal of siderite

$FeCO_3$

SIDERITE

An ore of iron, siderite takes its name from the Greek word *sideros*, which means "iron". Formerly known as chalybite, siderite can form rhombohedral crystals, often with curved surfaces. The mineral can also form scalenohedral, tabular, or prismatic crystals. Single crystals up to 15 cm (6 in) long are found in Quebec, Canada. However, siderite is more commonly massive or granular and sometimes botryoidal or globular in habit.

A widespread mineral, siderite occurs in igneous, sedimentary, and metamorphic rocks. In sedimentary rocks, siderite occurs in concretions (p.333) and in thin beds with coal (p.253) seams, shale (p.313), and clay. Well-formed crystals are found in hydrothermal metallic veins and in some granitic and syenitic pegmatites (p.260). An outcrop of siderite originally mined for iron by American colonists is still visible at Roxbury, Connecticut, USA. Rare transparent siderite is sometimes cut as gemstones for collectors.

PROFILE

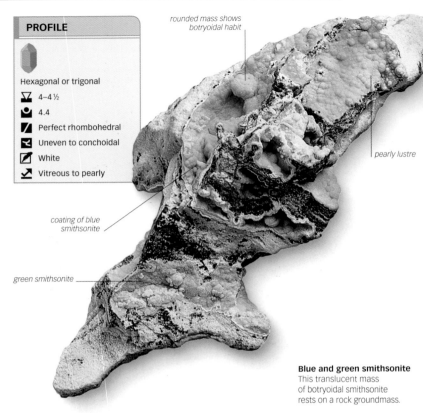

Hexagonal or trigonal

◢ 4–4½

◢ 4.4

◢ Perfect rhombohedral

◢ Uneven to conchoidal

◢ White

◢ Vitreous to pearly

rounded mass shows botryoidal habit

pearly lustre

coating of blue smithsonite

green smithsonite

Blue and green smithsonite
This translucent mass of botryoidal smithsonite rests on a rock groundmass.

VARIANT

White smithsonite A mass of earthy smithsonite on a rock groundmass

$ZnCo_3$

SMITHSONITE

An ore of zinc that continues to be frequently mined, smithsonite may have provided the zinc component of brass in ancient metallurgy. Specimens can be of various colours, such as yellow, orange, brown, pink, lilac, white, grey, green, and blue. Although smithsonite rarely forms crystals, when found, they are prismatic, rhombohedral, or scalenohedral and often have curved faces. A zinc carbonate, smithsonite commonly occurs as massive, botryoidal, spherular, or stalactitic masses, or sometimes, as honeycombed aggregates called dry-bone ore.

Smithsonite is a common mineral, found in the oxidation zones of many zinc ore deposits and in adjacent calcareous rocks. It is often found with cerussite (p.119), azurite (p.120), malachite (p.125), pyromorphite (p.151), and hemimorphite (p.227).

Cabochon
Soft smithsonite is occasionally cut into cabochon gemstones for collectors.

Monoclinic

3½–4

3.9–4.0

Perfect

Subconchoidal to uneven, brittle

Pale green

Adamantine to silky

Botryoidal malachite
This specimen of malachite on chrysocolla is from Etoile du Congo Mine in Katanga province, Congo.

rock groundmass

botryoidal habit

chrysocolla

VARIANTS

Fibrous malachite
A radiating group of fibrous malachite crystals

Stalactitic malachite
A group of radiating, fibrous malachite crystals

Malachite section
A section cut through a malachite stalactite

$Cu_2CO_3(OH)_2$

MALACHITE

Possibly the earliest ore of copper, malachite is believed to have been mined in the Sinai and eastern deserts of ancient Egypt from as early as 3000 BCE. Single crystals are uncommon; when found, they are short to long prisms. Malachite is usually found as botryoidal or encrusting masses, often with a radiating fibrous structure and banded in various shades of green. It also occurs as delicate fibrous aggregates and as concentrically banded stalactites.

Malachite occurs in the altered zones of copper deposits, where it is usually accompanied by lesser amounts of azurite (p.120). It is mainly valued as an ornamental material and gemstone. Single masses weighing up to 51 tonnes (50 tons) were found in the Ural Mountains of Russia in the 19th century.

Polished malachite
This specimen of the mineral malachite has been polished to show dark and light colour bands.

BORATES

Borate minerals are compounds containing boron and oxygen. Most borate minerals are rare, but a few, such as borax, ulexite, colemanite, and kernite, form large, commercially mined deposits. Borates tend to be soft and either white or colourless.

COMPOSITION

Structurally, boron and oxygen may form a triangle (BO_3) or a tetrahedron (BO_4), each with a central boron atom. These structures act as a single chemical unit. Every unit is bonded to a metal, such as sodium in borax and calcium in colemanite. Borates tend to be hydrous or contain a hydroxyl (OH) group, which acts as a chemical unit bonded into their structure. Some borates contain both.

silky lustre

crystals have translucent ends

Ulexite
This is a classic evaporite borate. A hydrous sodium calcium borate, ulexite can form parallel, fibrous crystals that act as optic fibres when viewed from an end.

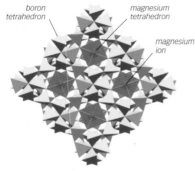

boron tetrahedron

magnesium tetrahedron

magnesium ion

Crystal structure of boracite
In boracite, densely packed boron tetrahedra combine with the metals magnesium and iron (not shown). The borate radical is in the form of tetrahedra.

OCCURRENCE AND USES

Borates appear in two geological environments. In the first, borate-bearing solutions that result from volcanic activity flow into a closed basin, where evaporation takes place. Basin deposits usually occur in desert regions, such as the Mojave Desert and Death Valley in California. Borax, ulexite, and colemanite occur in these evaporate deposits. In the second environment, borate minerals are formed as a result of rocks being altered by heat and pressure at relatively high temperatures (575°C/1,065°F or above).

Borates are used as pottery glazes, solvents for metal-oxide slags in metallurgy, welding fluxes, fertilizer additives, soap supplements, and water softeners.

Fireworks
Boron carbide is used to give a green colour to fireworks, in place of the toxic barium compounds that were once used.

Borax crust
This crust formed at the edge of Searles Lake in southern California, USA, is principally composed of borax, a borate produced by evaporation.

Borax crystals
This group of prismatic borax crystals coated with an opaque layer of tincalconite is set on a rock groundmass.

prismatic crystal

coating of white tincalconite

rock groundmass

PROFILE

Monoclinic

 2–2½

 1.7

 Perfect, imperfect

 Conchoidal

White

Vitreous to earthy

$Na_2B_4O_5(OH)_4 \cdot 8H_2O$

BORAX

An important source of boron, borax has been mined since ancient times. A hydrated sodium borate, borax's colourless crystals dehydrate in air to become the chalky mineral tincalconite. Specimens can also be white, grey, pale green, or pale blue. Borax has short prismatic to tabular crystals, although in commercial deposits it is predominantly massive.

Borax is an evaporite formed in dry lake beds with halite (p.110) and other borates and evaporite sulphates and carbonates. It is used in metal-casting and steel-making. Molten borax beads were historically used to test the composition of other minerals – powdered minerals were fused with the beads, and colour change in the beads revealed what the minerals contained.

Boron soap
Compounds derived from borax and, to a lesser extent, ulexite, are key components of many soaps.

Ulexite slice
This ulexite specimen has a fibrous structure and has been sliced and polished to show its fibre-optic effect.

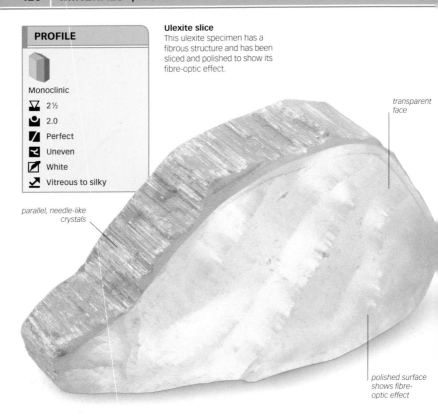

transparent face

parallel, needle-like crystals

polished surface shows fibre-optic effect

VARIANT

Fibrous crystals Parallel, fibrous ulexite crystals with a silky lustre

 $NaCaB_5O_6(OH)_6 \cdot H_2O$

ULEXITE

An important economic borate mineral, ulexite is named after the German chemist George Ludwig Ulex, who determined its composition in 1850. It is either colourless or white and has a number of habits. It is commonly found in nodular, rounded, or lens-like crystal aggregates, which often resemble balls of cotton wool. Less commonly, ulexite is found in dense veins of parallel fibres known as television stone because the fibres transmit light from one end of the crystal to the other. Ulexite also occurs in radiating or compact aggregates of crystals.

Ulexite is found in playa lakes and other evaporite basins in deserts, where it is derived from hot, boron-rich fluids. The mineral commonly occurs with colemanite (p.130), anhydrite (p.133), and glauberite (p.141).

Television stone
An unusual property of the form of ulexite shown above is its ability to "transmit" images.

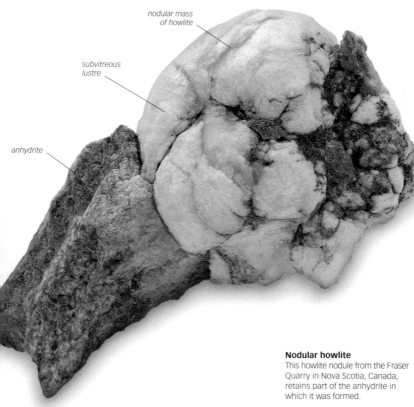

nodular mass
of howlite

subvitreous
lustre

anhydrite

Nodular howlite
This howlite nodule from the Fraser
Quarry in Nova Scotia, Canada,
retains part of the anhydrite in
which it was formed.

PROFILE

Monoclinic

 3½

 2.6

 None

 Conchoidal to uneven

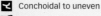 White

 Subvitreous

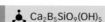 $Ca_2B_5SiO_9(OH)_5$

HOWLITE

Named in 1868 after the Canadian chemist, geologist,
and mineralogist Henry How, howlite is a calcium
borosilicate hydroxide. It generally forms cauliflower-like
nodular masses. The nodules are white, with fine grey or
black veins of other minerals running across in an erratic,
often web-like pattern. Crystals are rare, but when
found they are tabular and seldom exceed
1 cm (⅜ in) in length. When dyed, howlite
specimens resemble and are sometimes
sold as turquoise (p.154), although they
are easily distinguished by their inferior
hardness and lighter colour.

Howlite usually occurs
associated with other boron
minerals, such as kernite and
borax (p.127). It is easily fused
and is used to make carvings,
jewellery components, and other
decorative items.

Stained howlite
This tumble-polished and
dyed or stained piece
of howlite looks similar
to turquoise.

vitreous lustre

prismatic structure

translucent crystal

Complex crystals
Colemanite commonly occurs as colourless, brilliant, and complex crystals, as in this specimen.

PROFILE

Monoclinic

4–4 ½

2.4

Perfect, distinct

Uneven to subconchoidal

White

Vitreous to adamantine

$CaB_3O_4(OH)_3 \cdot H_2O$

COLEMANITE

An important source of boron, colemanite was named in 1884 after William Coleman, the owner of the mine in California, USA, where it was discovered. It is colourless, white, yellowish white, or grey. Colemanite occurs as short prismatic or equant crystals in nodules or as granular or coarse, massive aggregates. It is usually massive in commercial deposits, but individual crystals up to 20 cm (8 in) long have also been found.

Colemanite is found in playas and other evaporite deposits, where it replaces other borate minerals, such as borax (p.127) and ulexite (p.128), which were originally deposited in huge inland lakes. Borosilicates derived from colemanite and other minerals are used to make glass that is resistant to chemicals, electricity, and heat.

Heat-resistant glass
Borosilicate glass is used in car headlights, laboratory glassware, ovenware, and industrial equipment.

SULPHATES, MOLYBDATES, CHROMATES, AND TUNGSTATES

These minerals are grouped together because they have similar structures and chemical behaviour. Sulphates are soft and light, chromates are rare and brightly coloured, and tungstates and molybdates are dense, hard, brittle, and vividly coloured.

COMPOSITION

Sulphate minerals have a tetrahedral crystal structure, with four oxygen atoms at each corner and a sulphur atom in the centre. The sulphate tetrahedron behaves chemically as a single, negatively charged radical or unit. All sulphates contain an SO_4 group.

The basic structural unit of the chromates, molybdates, and tungstates is also a tetrahedron formed from four oxygen atoms, with a central chromium (Cr), molybdenum (Mo), or tungsten (W) atom, respectively. The chromate minerals all contain a CrO_4 group, the molybdates an MoO_4 group, and the tungstates a WO_4 group.

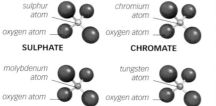

sulphur atom
oxygen atom
SULPHATE

chromium atom
oxygen atom
CHROMATE

molybdenum atom
oxygen atom
MOLYBDATE

tungsten atom
oxygen atom
TUNGSTATE

Crystal structure
Tetrahedra are the structural basis of the sulphates, chromates, tungstates, and molybdates. The central metal atom gives each group its name.

Baryte crystals
This large group of tabular baryte crystals is from the Wet Grooves mine, Yorkshire, England. Baryte has important industrial and medicinal uses.

vitreous lustre

tabular crystal

OCCURRENCE

Sulphates, such as gypsum, occur in evaporite deposits; others, such as baryte, mainly occur in hydrothermal veins. Many tungstates are found in hydrothermal veins and pegmatites. Chromates and molybdates are often found as secondary minerals.

USES

The sulphates gypsum and baryte are major industrial minerals. Chromates, tungstates, and molybdates are rare but when found concentrated are important ores of the metals they contain.

Plaster cast
About 75 per cent of the calcium sulphate gypsum that is mined is used to make plaster of Paris. Most is used for wallboards, but some finds medical uses, such as making plaster casts.

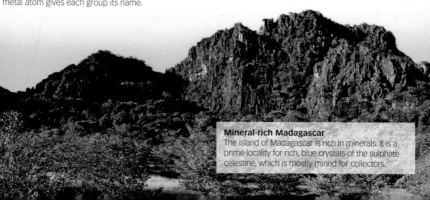

Mineral-rich Madagascar
The island of Madagascar is rich in minerals. It is a prime locality for rich, blue crystals of the sulphate celestine, which is mostly mined for collectors.

Orthorhombic

⛏ 2½–3

🔨 6.4

🗡 Good, distinct

✂ Conchoidal, brittle

▱ Colourless

⚡ Adamantine to resinous, vitreous

Anglesite crystals
These striated prismatic crystals of anglesite are on a rock groundmass with galena.

prismatic crystal

rock groundmass

galena

VARIANTS

Pyramidal crystal A pointed crystal of anglesite with galena

adamantine lustre

Single crystal A crystal of anglesite that has an adamantine lustre

🔬 PbSO$_4$

ANGLESITE

Named in 1832 after the large deposit of this mineral found on the island of Anglesey in Wales, anglesite is colourless to white, greyish, yellow, green, or blue and often fluoresces yellow under ultraviolet light. It commonly occurs in massive, granular, or compact forms. It has a number of crystal habits: thin to thick tabular, prismatic, pseudorhombohedral, and pyramidal with striations along the length. Exceptionally large crystals – up to 80cm (31in) long – have been found.

Used since ancient times as an ore of lead, anglesite forms in the oxidation zones of lead deposits. It is an alteration product of galena (p.54), formed when galena comes into contact with sulphate solutions. Anglesite is sometimes found in concentric layers with a core of unaltered galena.

Oval-cut anglesite
Anglesite is soft and easily cleaved. It is one of the stones used to test the skills of master gem cutters.

German anhydrite
This reddish specimen of anhydrite is from Germany. It shows perfect, nearly cubic, cleavage.

perfect cleavage

transluscent crystal

vitreous lustre

PROFILE

Orthorhombic

 3½

 3.0

 Perfect, good

 Uneven to splintery

 White

 Vitreous to pearly

$CaSO_4$

ANHYDRITE

An important rock-forming mineral, anhydrite is a calcium sulphate. It takes its name from the Greek word *anhydrous*, which means "without water". Anhydrite is usually colourless to white. Specimens can also be brownish, reddish, or greyish or pale shades of pink, blue, or violet. Individual crystals are uncommon, but when found they are blocky or thick tabular. Crystals up to 10 cm (4 in) long come from Swiss deposits. Anhydrite is usually massive, granular, or coarsely crystalline.

Anhydrite is one of the major minerals in evaporite deposits and commonly occurs in salt deposits associated with halite (p.110) and gypsum (p.136). It alters to gypsum in humid conditions. Anhydrite is often a constituent of cap rocks above salt domes that act as reservoirs for natural oil. It also occurs in volcanic fumaroles and in seafloor hydrothermal "chimneys". Anhydrite is used in fertilizers and as a drying agent in plasters, cement, paints, and varnishes.

Baryte crystals
This large group of tabular baryte crystals is from the Wet Grooves Mine in Yorkshire, England.

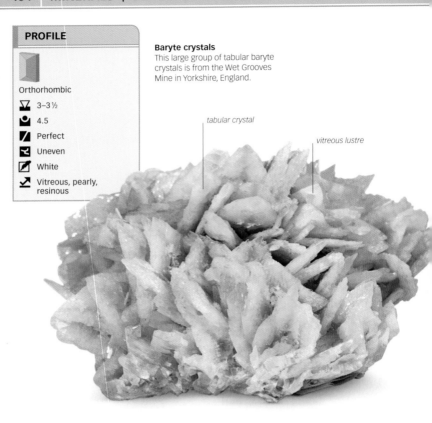

tabular crystal

vitreous lustre

VARIANTS

Cockscomb White cockscomb baryte resting on sphalerite

cockscomb

Prismatic crystals
A group of yellow prismatic baryte crystals

Stalagmite section
Baryte in a stalagmitic form

♣ BaSO₄

BARYTE

The barium sulphate baryte takes its name from the Greek word *barys*, which means "heavy" – a reference to its high specific gravity. It has also been called heavy spar. Baryte crystals are sometimes tinged yellow, blue, or brown. Golden baryte comes from South Dakota, USA. Crystals are well-formed, usually either prismatic or tabular. Cockscomb (crested aggregates) and desert roses (rosette aggregates) of crystals are common. Transparent, blue baryte crystals may resemble aquamarine but are distinguished by their softness, heaviness, and crystal shape. Baryte can also be stalactitic, stalagmitic, fibrous, concretionary, or massive.

Baryte is a common accessory mineral in lead and zinc veins. It is also found in sedimentary rocks, clay deposits, marine deposits, and cavities in igneous rocks.

Baryte gemstone
Although transparent baryte is soft and difficult to cut, it is sometimes faceted for collectors.

Orthorhombic

3–3½

4.0

Perfect

Uneven

White

Vitreous, pearly on cleavage

Celestine crystals
This superbly crystallized specimen of blue celestine crystals is from Madagascar. The largest crystal is more than 3.5cm (1½in) long.

vitreous lustre

large, tabular crystal

blue coloration

small celestine crystals

granular celestine

VARIANTS

Colourless celestine
Prismatic, colourless crystals on a sulphur groundmass

Single crystal A light blue prismatic crystal of celestine

$SrSO_4$

CELESTINE

Often light blue in colour, celestine takes its name from the Latin word *coelestis*, which means "heavenly"– an allusion to the colour of the sky. Specimens can also be colourless, white, light red, green, medium to dark blue, or brown. Celestine crystals are commonly more than 10cm (4in) long. Well-formed, transparent, light- to medium-blue, tabular crystals are common, and some have been known to reach more than 75cm (30in) in length. Crystals can also be blocky, bladed, or form elongate pyramids. Celestine may also be massive, fibrous, granular, or nodular in habit.

Celestine forms in cavities in sedimentary rocks (pp.306–33). It commonly occurs in evaporite deposits and can be precipitated directly from sea water. It can occasionally form in hydrothermal deposits. Celestine is an ore of strontium.

Collector's gem
Celestine is too soft to wear. Faceted celestine demonstrates the skills of master cutters.

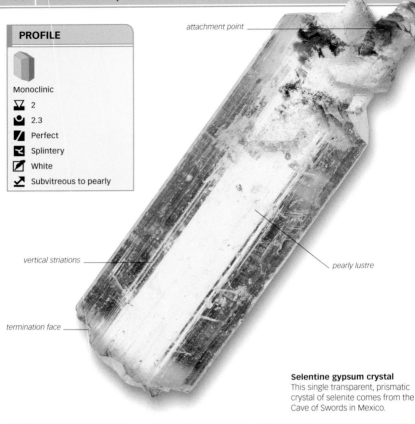

attachment point

vertical striations

pearly lustre

termination face

Selentine gypsum crystal
This single transparent, prismatic crystal of selenite comes from the Cave of Swords in Mexico.

VARIANTS

silky sheen

Gypsum satin spar Fibrous gypsum crystals

bladed crystal

Desert rose Spherical clusters of bladed selenite

Fishtail twin Colourless, translucent selenite gypsum with fishtail twinning

$CaSO_4 \cdot 2H_2O$

GYPSUM

A widespread calcium sulphate hydrate, gypsum is found in a number of forms and is of great economic importance. It is colourless or white but can be tinted light brown, grey, yellow, green, or orange due to the presence of impurities. Single, well-developed crystals can be blocky with a slanted parallelogram outline, tabular, or bladed. Twinned crystals are common and frequently form characteristic "fishtails". Numerous transparent, sword-like selenite gypsum crystals 2 m (6½ ft) or more long can be found at the Cave of Swords, Chihuahua, Mexico, one of the world's most spectacular mineral deposits.

Gypsum occurs in extensive beds formed by the evaporation of ocean brine. It also occurs as an alteration product of sulphides in ore deposits and as volcanic deposits.

Cat's eye sheen
Satin spar, a fibrous variety of gypsum, can be cut into a cabochon gem with a cat's eye sheen.

massive habit

Massive melanterite
This nodule of melanterite shows typical massive form and some minor crystallization.

blue indicates
presence of copper

PROFILE

Monoclinic

 2

 1.9

Perfect

Conchoidal, brittle

White

Vitreous

 $FeSO_4 \cdot 7H_2O$

MELANTERITE

A hydrous iron sulphate, melanterite takes its name from the Greek word *melas*, which means "sulphate of iron". Melanterite is the iron analogue of the copper sulphate chalcanthite, the two minerals having similar molecular structures. Most specimens of melanterite are colourless to white but can become green to blue as copper increasingly substitutes for iron. Melanterite is generally found in stalactitic or concretionary masses and rarely forms crystals. When crystals occur, they are short prisms or pseudo-octahedrons.

Melanterite is a secondary mineral formed by the oxidation of pyrite (p.62), marcasite (p.63), and other iron sulphides. It is frequently deposited on the timbers of old mine workings. Melanterite also occurs in the altered zones of pyrite-bearing rocks, especially in arid climates and in coal (p.253) deposits, where it is an alteration product of marcasite. Iron sulphate is used in water purification as a coagulant and also as a fertilizer.

kaolinite

crystalline chalcanthite

rock groundmass

Massive and crystalline chalcanthite
This specimen of chalcanthite occurs with patches of kaolinite. It exhibits both massive and crystalline forms of the mineral.

granular chalcanthite

PROFILE

Triclinic

2½

2.3

Not distinct

Conchoidal

Colourless

Vitreous

VARIANT

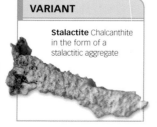

Stalactite Chalcanthite in the form of a stalactitic aggregate

$CuSO_4 \cdot 5H_2O$

CHALCANTHITE

A hydrated copper sulphate, chalcanthite takes its name from the Greek words *khalkos*, which means "copper", and *anthos*, which means "flower". It used to be known as blue vitriol. It is commonly peacock blue, although some specimens are greenish. Natural crystals are relatively rare. Chalcanthite usually occurs in veinlets and as massive and stalactitic aggregates.

This widespread, naturally occurring mineral forms through the oxidation of chalcopyrite (p.57) and other copper sulphates that occur in the oxidized zones of copper deposits. Being a water-soluble mineral, it is often found forming crusts and stalactites on the walls and timbers of mine workings, where it crystallizes from mine waters. In arid areas, such as Chile, chalcanthite concentrates in sufficient quantities without being dissolved away to constitute an important ore of copper. Although chalcanthite is a sought-after collectors' mineral, its crystal structure disintegrates over time as it readily absorbs water.

Monoclinic

3½–4

4.0

Perfect

Uneven to subconchoidal

Pale green

Vitreous

Acicular brochantite
This brochantite specimen from
Chile has needle-like crystals on
a groundmass of iron oxides.

iron-oxide
groundmass

mass of needle-like
brochantite crystals

VARIANT

blue
azurite

Brochantite on azurite
Green brochantite with
blue azurite

$Cu_4SO_4(OH)_6$

BROCHANTITE

A hydrous copper sulphate, brochantite is emerald
green, blue-green, or blackish green in colour. It was
named in 1824 after the French geologist and mineralogist
A.J.M. Brochant de Villiers, who was the first pupil admitted
to the École des Mines, Paris, and who later became its
Professor of Geology and Mines. Brochantite usually forms
prismatic or needle-like crystals, which rarely exceed
more than a few millimetres in length. Twinning is common
in crystals. Brochantite is also found in tufts and druse
crusts and as fine-grained masses.

Brochantite forms in the oxidation zones of copper
deposits, especially those that occur in the arid regions
of the world. In these regions, brochantite is usually
associated with azurite (p.120), malachite (p.125), and
other copper minerals. In Arizona, USA, and Chile,
the mineral is abundant enough to be an ore of copper.
Splendid specimens of brochantite come from Namibia,
and Bisbee, Arizona, where prismatic crystals may
exceed 1cm (⅜in) in length.

vitreous to silky lustre

PROFILE

Orthorhombic

2–2 ½

1.7

Perfect

Conchoidal

White

Vitreous to silky

fibrous strand

vitreous to silky lustre

Fibrous epsomite
This epsomite specimen occurs in a fibrous habit and shows a vitreous to silky lustre.

VARIANT

Powdery mass Epsomite coating on a rocky groundmass

$MgSO_4 \cdot 7H_2O$

EPSOMITE

Epsom salts is the common name for this hydrated magnesium sulphate mineral. It was first found around springs near the town of Epsom in Surrey, England, and was named after that locality in 1805. It is colourless, white, pale pink, or green. Epsomite crystals are rare. When found, they are either prismatic or fibrous. Epsomite usually occurs as crusts, powdery or woolly coatings, or sometimes as botryoidal or reniform masses.

Magnesium sulphate occurs in solution in sea water, saline lake water, and spring water. When the water evaporates, epsomite precipitates, forming deposits. It is also found with coal (p.253), in weathered magnesium-rich rocks, sulphide ore deposits, and dolomite (p.320) and limestone caves.

Refined epsom salt
This widely used medication is derived from epsomite. One common use is as a natural laxative.

PROFILE

Monoclinic

⊻ 2½–3

◔ 2.8

◧ Perfect, indistinct

◩ Conchoidal

◪ White

↗ Vitreous to waxy

Glauberite crystals
This group of dipyramidal glauberite crystals is from Ciempozuelos, Madrid, Spain.

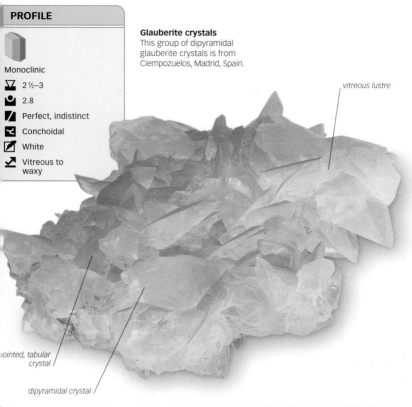

vitreous lustre

jointed, tabular crystal

dipyramidal crystal

VARIANTS

Single crystal A single pyramidal crystal of glauberite

Pseudomorph A specimen with glauberite replaced by calcite

🜋 $Na_2Ca(SO_4)_2$

GLAUBERITE

This mineral was named in 1808 after its similarity to another chemical, Glauber's salt, which in turn was named after the German alchemist Johann Glauber. Glauberite is a sodium calcium sulphate. It can be colourless, pale yellow, reddish, or grey, and its surface may alter to white, powdery sodium sulphate. Crystals can be prismatic, tabular, and dipyramidal, all with combinations of forms and all of which may have rounded edges. Glauberite crystal pseudomorphs form when other minerals, such as calcite (p.114) and gypsum (p.136), replace it. Glauberite has a slightly saline taste, turns white in water, and fuses to a white enamel.

This mineral forms under a variety of conditions. It is primarily an evaporite, forming in both marine and salt-lake environments. It is also found in cavities in basaltic igneous rocks and in volcanic fumaroles. Moulds and casts of quartz (p.168) and prehnite (p.205) formed from glauberite are frequently found in basalt cavities in Patterson, New Jersey, USA.

PROFILE

Monoclinic

- 2½–3
- 6.0
- Distinct in one direction
- Conchoidal to uneven, brittle
- Orange-yellow
- Vitreous

Prismatic crystals
This spectacular specimen of orange crocoite shows partly striated, prismatic crystals.

elongated prismatic crystal

brilliant orange crocoite

VARIANTS

Red crocoite Red, prismatic crystals of crocoite in a rock groundmass

Atypical crocoite
An almost reticulated growth of crocoite

PbCrO₄

CROCOITE

One of the most eye-catching of minerals, crocoite is bright orange to red in colour. It takes its name from the Greek word *krókos*, which means "saffron". Crocoite crystals are prismatic, commonly square-sectioned, slender and elongated, and sometimes cavernous or hollow. They may be striated along the length and may rarely show distinct terminations. Crystals usually occur in radiating or randomly intergrown clusters. Crocoite can also occur in granular or massive forms. On exposure to light, much of the translucence and brilliance of the mineral is lost.

Crocoite is a rare mineral, as specific conditions – an oxidation zone of lead ore and the presence of low-silica igneous rocks that serve as the source of chromium – are required for its formation. It is the official mineral emblem of Tasmania, where exceptional crystals, 7.5–10 cm (3–4 in) long and having a brilliant lustre and colour, are found. Crocoite is identical in composition to the pigment chrome yellow.

PROFILE

Tetragonal

2 ½–3

6.5–7.0

Distinct

Subconchoidal to uneven

White

Subadamantine to greasy

tabular wulfenite crystal

iron-oxide groundmass

Yellow wulfenite
The wulfenite crystals on this iron-oxide groundmass show classic, square, platy development.

VARIANTS

Square crystals Typical thin, tabular crystals of wulfenite

Red cloud wulfenite Crystals found in Red Cloud Mine in Arizona, USA

$PbMoO_4$

WULFENITE

The second most common molybdenum mineral after molybdenite, wulfenite was named after F.X. Wülfen, an Austro-Hungarian mineralogist, in 1841. The colour of specimens varies and can be yellow, orange, red, grey, or brown. Wulfenite usually forms as thin, square plates or square, bevelled, tabular crystals. Crystals sometimes show different terminations on each end, probably due to twinning. Bright, colourful, and sharply formed crystals are popular with collectors. Wulfenite also occurs in massive, earthy, and granular forms.

Wulfenite is a minor source of molybdenum. Tungsten substitutes for the molybdenum, although in most specimens it is present only in trace amounts. Wulfenite is a secondary mineral formed in the oxidized zones of lead and molybdenum deposits, and it occurs with other minerals, including cerussite (p.119), pyromorphite (p.151), and vanadinite (p.155). It is relatively widespread and is often found in superb crystals, occasionally up to 10 cm (4 in) on an edge.

Hübnerite crystals
In this specimen, translucent hübnerite crystals grow on a quartz groundmass with tarnished tetrahedrite.

prismatic hübnerite crystal

adamantine lustre

quartz groundmass

tarnished tetrahedrite

PROFILE

Monoclinic

4–4½

7.3

Perfect

Uneven

Yellow to brown

Submetallic/adamantine to resinous

 $MnWO_4$

HÜBNERITE

Named after the German mineralogist Adolf Hübner, who first described it in 1865, hübnerite is an important ore of tungsten. It is found as prismatic, long prismatic, tabular, or flattened crystals with striations and is commonly twinned. It can also form groups of parallel or subparallel crystals or radiating groups. Hübnerite is generally reddish brown. In transparent crystals, it can change colour when viewed from different directions and show strong internal reflection.

Hübnerite is the manganese end member of a manganese–iron solid-solution series. It occurs in granitic pegmatites (p.260) and in thermal veins at high temperatures (575°C/1,065°F or above). The mineral is also recovered from alluvial gravels, in which it can concentrate.

Bulb filament
Hübnerite is an ore of tungsten, which is mainly used in light bulb filaments.

Ferberite crystal
This ferberite crystal is from Cinovec, Czech Republic. It shows the prismatic habit of the mineral.

submetallic lustre

opaque grey ferberite

 FeWO₄

FERBERITE

The principal ore of tungsten, ferberite is an iron tungstate. It was named in 1863 after Moritz Rudolph Ferber, a German industrialist and mineralogist. Ferberite forms black crystals, which are commonly elongated or flattened with a wedge-shaped appearance. Twinning and striations are common in crystals. Ferberite is also found as granular masses.

Ferberite is the iron end member of a solid-solution series it forms with hübnerite (p.144), the manganese end member. Together, they constitute the mineral formerly called wolframite. Ferberite occurs in hydrothermal veins at high temperatures (575°C/1,065°F or above) and in granitic pegmatites (p.260) with other minerals.

Tungsten steel
Rocket nozzles, such as those used in Saturn V, are made of heat-resistant, hard, and strong tungsten steel.

Bipyramidal scheelite
This group of orange-yellow scheelite crystals clearly shows a tetragonal bipyramidal habit.

magnetite groundmass

bipyramidal scheelite crysta

PROFILE

Tetragonal

 4½–5

 6.1

 Distinct

 Uneven to subconchoidal

 White

 Vitreous to greasy

 CaWO$_4$

SCHEELITE

Named in 1821 after the Swedish chemist C.W. Scheele, scheelite is calcium tungstate. Its crystals are generally bipyramidal and twinned but also form in granular or massive aggregates. Irregular masses of colourless, grey, orange, or pale brown scheelite can be difficult to spot, but they fluoresce vivid bluish white under a short-wave ultraviolet light. Scheelite is sometimes associated with native gold (p.42), and its fluorescence is used by geologists in their search for gold deposits.

Scheelite commonly occurs in contact with metamorphic deposits, in hydrothermal veins formed at high temperatures (575°C/1,065°F or above), and less commonly in granitic pegmatites (p.260). Opaque crystals weighing up to 7 kg (15½ lb) come from Arizona, USA. Scheelite is a major source of tungsten.

Brilliant cut scheelite
Transparent scheelite is relatively rare. Stones faceted from it are only for gem collectors.

PHOSPHATES, VANADATES, AND ARSENATES

The phosphate, arsenate, and vanadate minerals are grouped together because their crystal structures are similar. The phosphates are the most numerous of the three groups, with more than 200 known minerals.

COMPOSITION

Phosphates contain phosphorus and oxygen in a 1:4 ratio, written as PO_4. The combined atoms act as a single unit that in turn combines with other elements to form phosphate minerals. Arsenates have a basic structural unit of arsenic and oxygen, written as AsO_4, which combines with other elements to form arsenate minerals. Most arsenates are rare and many are brilliantly coloured. Vanadates mostly contain the same type of structural tetrahedra as the phosphates and arsenates, written as VO_4. The structures of vanadates are complex, and these minerals are relatively rare.

OCCURRENCE

Primary phosphates usually crystallize from aqueous fluids derived from igneous crystallization; secondary phosphates when primary phosphates are altered in the presence of water; and rock phosphates from phosphorus-bearing organic material.

USES

Phosphates are of major economic importance as fertilizers. Vanadates are minor ores of vanadium and have no other economic importance. The only exception is carnotite, an important source of uranium.

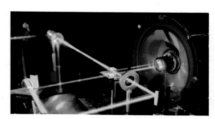

High-speed laser
Garnet containing yttrium, which is derived from the yttrium phosphate xenotime, is used to make lasers. The direction of the laser beams is changed using mirrors.

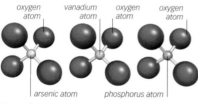

oxygen atom · vanadium atom · oxygen atom · oxygen atom · arsenic atom · phosphorus atom

Crystal structure
The arsenate (AsO_4), vanadate (VO_4), and phosphate (PO_4) ions consist of a metal atom bonded to four oxygen atoms. Each ion acts as a single unit.

Colorado Plateau
Spread across the Colorado Plateau in western Colorado, USA, are extensive deposits of carnotite (a phosphate of uranium, vanadium, and potassium).

PROFILE

Monoclinic

5

3.1–3.2

Indistinct, variable

Conchoidal to uneven

White

Vitreous, waxy

Apatite crystals
These spectacular apatite crystals from Panasqueira Mine, Beira Baixa, Portugal, occur with muscovite and a small amount of arsenopyrite.

colour-zoned crystal

prismatic crystal

hexagonal, transparent crystal

VARIANTS

albite

Chlorapatite crystal
Double-terminated chlorapatite

Brilliant apatite
A single yellow crystal of hydroxylapatite

Hydroxylapatite A specimen with a waxy lustre

$Ca_5(PO_4)_3(F,OH,Cl)$

APATITE

A series of calcium phosphate minerals that differ in composition are known as apatites. The name apatite is derived from the Greek *apate*, which means "deceit" – a reference to its similarity to crystals of aquamarine, amethyst, and olivine (p.232). Apatites can occur as green, blue, violet-blue, purple, colourless, white, yellow, pink, or rose-red specimens. All the apatites are structurally similar and are commonly found as transparent, well-formed, glassy crystals and in masses or nodules. Crystals are short to long prismatic, thick tabular, or prismatic with complex forms.

Apatites occur in marbles (p.301), skarns (p.302), and other metamorphic rocks. Rich deposits of apatite also occur in sedimentary rocks. As an accessory mineral, it occurs in a wide range of igneous rocks and in hydrothermal veins.

Step-cut gemstone
Owing to the brittleness of apatite, an edge of one facet of this blue gemstone has become chipped.

tabular, twinned crystal aggregate

Tabular crystals
Thin, tabular, twinned crystals characteristic of autunite are clearly visible in this lemon-yellow specimen.

vitreous lustre

PROFILE

Tetragonal

 2–2 ½

 3.1–3.2

Perfect basal

Uneven

Pale yellow

 Vitreous to pearly

$Ca(UO_2)_2(PO_4)_2 \cdot 10–12H_2O$

AUTUNITE

A popular collector's mineral, autunite is a calcium uranium phosphate. Greenish or lemon yellow in colour, autunite specimens fluoresce green under ultraviolet light. Crystals of autunite have a rectangular or octagonal outline. Coarse groups are found, but scaly coatings are more common. Autunite is also found as crusts with crystals standing on edge, giving a serrated appearance.

Autunite is named after Autun, the place in France where it was discovered. It is formed in the oxidation zones of uranium ore bodies as an alteration product of uraninite (p.83) and other uranium-bearing minerals. It also occurs in hydrothermal veins and in pegmatites (p.260). Since autunite contains uranium and is radioactive, it must be stored carefully and handled as little as possible. When mildly heated, tetragonal autunite dehydrates into orthorhombic meta-autunite. Most museum and collector specimens of autunite have been converted to meta-autunite. A moist atmosphere helps to prevent dehydration.

PROFILE

Monoclinic

⬛ 5

⬛ 4.6–5.4

⬛ Perfect, good, poor

⬛ Conchoidal to uneven, brittle

⬛ White

⬛ Resinous, waxy, or vitreous

Monazite crystal
This striated crystal of monazite is from Arendal, Aust-Agder, Norway, which is an important monazite locality.

termination

prism face

striation

VARIANT

Monazite fragment A brown crystal fragment showing growth lamellae

$(Ce,La,Th,Nd)PO_4$

MONAZITE

The monazite group consists of three different phosphate minerals, all sharing the same crystal structure. The most widespread is monazite-(Ce), cerium phosphate, which is yellowish or reddish brown to brown, greenish, or nearly white. Monazite-(Ce) forms prismatic, flattened, or elongated crystals, which are occasionally large, coarse, and commonly twinned. Two other species of monazite are monazite-(La), which is lanthanum phosphate, and monazite-(Nd), which is neodymium phosphate.

Monazite is a common accessory mineral in granites (pp.258–59) and gneisses (p.288) and in pegmatites (p.260) and fissure veins. Detrital monazite can accumulate as monazite sands. Lanthanum is used in oil refining. Neodymium is used for colouring glass.

Cerium oxide
Monazite-(Ce) is a source of cerium. Cerium oxide is used for polishing glass, stone, and gemstones.

PROFILE

Hexagonal

3½–4

7.0

Poor

Uneven to subconchoidal, brittle

White

Resinous

goethite groundmass

resinous lustre

barrel-shaped crystal

Barrel-shaped crystals
This mass of pyromorphite on a goethite groundmass shows its typical barrel-shaped crystals.

VARIANTS

Lime-green crystals Crystals showing pyromorphite's intense coloration

prismatic crystal

Yellow-green crystals
A specimen of pyromorphite with yellow-green prismatic crystals

$Pb_5(PO_4)_3Cl$

PYROMORPHITE

A minor ore of lead but a popular collector's mineral, pyromorphite forms a continuous chemical series with mimetite (p.164) in which phosphorus and arsenic replace each other. Pyromorphite gets its name from the Greek words *pyr*, which means "fire", and *morphe*, which means "form" – an allusion to its property of becoming crystalline on cooling after it has been melted to a globule. It is dark green to yellow-green, shades of brown, a waxy yellow, or yellow-orange. Crystals may be either simple hexagonal prisms or rounded and barrel-shaped, spindle-shaped, or cavernous. Some crystals exhibit different colours when viewed from different directions and some produce electricity on application of mechanical stress. The mineral can also be globular, reniform, or granular in habit.

Pyromorphite occurs as a secondary mineral in the oxidized zones of lead deposits with galena (p.54), goethite (p.102), cerussite (p.119), smithsonite (p.124), and vanadinite (p.155). Pseudomorphs of pyromorphite after galena are common.

Torbernite crystals
In this specimen, tabular crystals of torbernite rest on an iron-rich groundmass.

iron-stained rock matrix

tabular torbernite crystal

PROFILE

Tetragonal

2–2½

3.2

Perfect, basal

Uneven

Pale green

Vitreous to subadamantine

VARIANT

Meta-torbernite Green sheaves of meta-torbernite crystals in rock matrix

$Cu(UO_2)_2(PO_4)_2 \cdot 8–12H_2O$

TORBERNITE

Named in 1793 after the Swedish mineralogist Torbern Olaf Bergmann, torbernite is a uranium-bearing mineral and a minor ore of uranium. Torbernite forms thin to thick tabular crystals that are commonly square in outline, foliated mica-like masses, sheaf-like crystal groups, or scaly coatings. Specimens are bright mid green, emerald green, leek green, or grass green in colour. Torbernite is chemically unstable, and with increased hydration it transforms to metatorbernite. In fact, all specimens are probably meta-torbernite. It is also radioactive and needs to be handled with appropriate care.

Torbernite is found as a secondary mineral formed in the oxidation zones of deposits containing uranium and copper and is associated with other phosphate minerals. It forms as an alteration product of uraninite (p.83) or other uranium-bearing minerals. Torbernite is also associated with uraninite, autunite (p.149), and carnotite (p.159). Fine specimens occur in Cornwall, England, in the Flinders Range, Australia, and elsewhere.

quartz

Massive aggregate
This specimen of massive triplite is from Megiliggar Rocks in Cornwall, England.

massive triplite

PROFILE

Monoclinic

 5–5½

 3.5–3.9

 Good in three directions

 Uneven to subconchoidal

 White to brown

Vitreous to resinous

$(Mn,Fe,Mg)_2PO_4(F,OH)$

TRIPLITE

The first occurrence of triplite was described in 1813 in Chanteloube, Limousin, France. Although it is a fluoridated manganese phosphate, in most triplite samples iron partially replaces manganese. Triplite takes its name from the Greek word *triplos,* which means "triple" – a reference to its three cleavages oriented at right angles to each other. Its crystals are typically rough and poorly developed but may have many indistinct forms. Triplite is more commonly nodular or massive. Specimens may be chestnut brown, reddish brown, flesh red, or salmon pink in colour. If altered, they may be brownish black to black. Translucent crystals may also exhibit different colours when viewed from different directions (a phenomenon known as pleochroism), going from yellow-brown to reddish brown.

Triplite is a primary mineral in granite pegmatites (p.260) with complex zones and in some hydrothermal tin veins. It may be accompanied by sphalerite (p.53), pyrite (p.62), apatite (p.148), and tourmaline (p.224).

Blue turquoise
In this specimen, nodular masses of light blue turquoise rest in a groundmass of iron oxide.

turquoise

iron-oxide groundmass

PROFILE

Triclinic

5–6

2.6–2.8

Good

Conchoidal

White to green

Waxy to dull

VARIANTS

Turquoise vein Massive turquoise in a small vein

Green turquoise A hard, green nugget from the USA

Turquoise in rock Blue-green, massive turquoise in rock

 $CuAl_6(PO_4)_4(OH)_8 \cdot 4H_2O$

TURQUOISE

One of the first gemstones to be mined, turquoise is a hydrous copper aluminium phosphate. Beads made of turquoise that date back to c.5000 BCE have been recovered in Mesopotamia (present-day Iraq). This mineral usually occurs in massive or microcrystalline forms, as encrustations or nodules, or in veins. Crystals are rare; when found, they occur as short, often transparent prisms. Turquoise varies in colour from sky blue to green, depending on the amount of iron and copper it contains.

"Turquoise" is derived from the French word for "Turkey", as it was first transported to Europe through Turkey. Turquoise occurs in arid environments as a secondary mineral probably derived from the decomposition of apatite (p.148) and some copper sulphides.

Carved elephant
Turquoise is a favourite of Chinese stone carvers, who produced this charming turquoise elephant.

vanadinite
adinite crystals are often
antly coloured in shades of
and yellow. This specimen has
ooth-faced, prismatic crystals.

adamantine lustre

prismatic crystal

rock groundmass

PROFILE

Hexagonal

 3

 6.9

 None

Uneven, brittle

Whitish yellow

Adamantine

$Pb_5(VO_4)_3Cl$

VANADINITE

A relatively rare mineral, vanadinite is a lead chloro vanadate. The bright red or orange-red colours of vanadinite make it popular among mineral collectors, although it is sometimes brown, red-brown, grey, yellow, or colourless. Crystals are usually in the form of short, hexagonal prisms but can also be found as hexagonal pyramids or as hollow prisms. They can also be needle-like. Small amounts of calcium, zinc, and copper may substitute for lead, and arsenic can completely substitute for vanadium in the crystal structure to form the mineral mimetite (p.164). The mineral is also found as rounded masses or crusts.

Vanadinite forms as a secondary mineral in oxidized ore deposits containing lead, often associated with galena (p.54), goethite (p.102), baryte (p.134), and wulfenite (p.143). Vanadium from vanadinite is used to make strong vanadium steels.

Steel spanner
Vanadium imparts strength and hardness to steel that is used to make high-stress tools, such as this spanner.

Concretionary variscite
Variscite is often found in nodules and concretions like the sliced specimen shown here. It can be sometimes mistaken for turquoise.

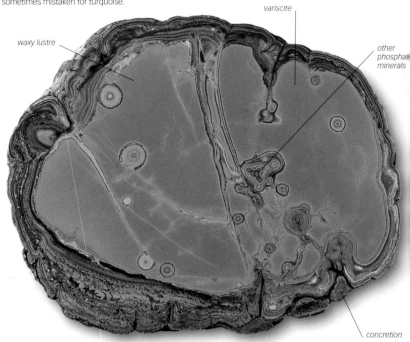

variscite

waxy lustre

other phosphate minerals

concretion

$AlPO_4 \cdot 2H_2O$

VARISCITE

This mineral was named after Variscia, the old name for the German district of Voightland, where it was first discovered, in 1837. Variscite is pale to apple green in colour. It is predominantly found as cryptocrystalline or fine-grained masses and in veins, crusts, or nodules. It rarely forms crystals.

Variscite forms in cavities produced by the action of phosphate-rich waters on aluminous rocks. It commonly occurs in association with apatite (p.148) and wavellite (p.158). It is valued as a semiprecious gemstone and is used for carvings and as an ornamental material. Variscite is porous, and, when worn next to the skin, tends to absorb body oils, which discolour it. A mineral that appears to be turquoise (p.154) but is actually variscite is sometimes marketed by the name variquoise.

Cabochon
Variscite can be polished into inexpensive gems, but their softness makes them vulnerable to wear.

PROFILE

Monoclinic

1½–2

2.7

Perfect

Uneven

Bluish white

Vitreous to earthy

Needle-like vivianite
This specimen of radiating vivianite crystals is set on a rock groundmass.

radiating, bladed crystal

in, transparent crystal

crystals in cavity left by fossil shell

vitreous lustre

VARIANT

Prismatic crystal Blue-black, elongated prismatic crystals of vivianite

$Fe_3(PO_4)_2 \cdot 8H_2O$

VIVIANITE

Named in 1817 after the English mineralogist John Henry Vivian, vivianite occurs as elongated, prismatic, or bladed tabular crystals. Specimens may be rounded, corroded, concretionary, earthy, or powdery in form. Vivianite can also form star-like groups or encrustations or occur in massive or fibrous forms. Sometimes colourless when freshly exposed, vivianite becomes either pale blue to greenish blue or indigo blue on oxidation. Before the development of modern synthetic chemicals, vivianite was the source of the sought-after blue paint pigment blue ochre.

Vivianite is a widespread secondary mineral, forming in the weathered zones of iron ore and phosphate deposits and in complex granite pegmatites (p.260).

Blue ochre
Powdered vivianite was used to make blue ochre, a rare and expensive pigment.

radiating wavellite crystals

unbroken spherule

vitreous lustre

Radiating crystals
Needle-like crystals of wavellite
form radiating aggregates on this
rock groundmass.

PROFILE

Orthorhombic

 3½–4

 2.4

 Good

 Subconchoidal to uneven

 White

Vitreous to resinous

$Al_3(PO_4)_2(OH,F)_3 \cdot 5H_2O$

WAVELLITE

Named in 1805 after the amateur English mineralogist
William Wavell, wavellite is a hydrated aluminium
phosphate. Specimens are usually green but can also
be white, greenish white, green-yellow, yellowish brown,
turquoise blue, brown, or black. They may exhibit colour
zoning. Crystals are uncommon but when found are short
to long prismatic, elongated, and striated parallel to the
prism faces. Wavellite is commonly found as translucent,
greenish, globular aggregates of radiating crystals up to
3 cm (1¼ in) in diameter, as crusts, or as stalactitic deposits.

Wavellite is a secondary mineral that forms in low-grade
aluminous, metamorphic rocks;
goethite (p.102) and phosphate
rock deposits; and, rarely, in
hydrothermal veins. It is also
found in areas where phosphate
minerals have been weathered
in granites (p.258) and granitic
pegmatites (p.260).

Match production
Phosphorous sulphate
derived from wavellite and
other phosphates is a major
component of matches.

Carnotite crust
A crust of vivid yellow, powdery radioactive carnotite coats this fragment of sandstone.

powdery coating

crust of carnotite

PROFILE

Monoclinic

 2

 4.7

 Perfect

 Uneven

Yellow

Pearly to dull

$K_2(UO_2)_2(VO_4)_2 \cdot 3H_2O$

CARNOTITE

A radioactive mineral, carnotite was named in 1899 after the French chemist and mining engineer Marie-Adolphe Carno. It is bright to lemon yellow or greenish yellow. Carnotite is generally found as powdery or microcrystalline masses; tiny, disseminated grains; or crusts. Crystals are platy, rhombohedral, or lath-like.

Carnotite is a secondary mineral formed by the alteration of primary uranium-vanadium minerals. It occurs chiefly in sandstone (p.308), either disseminated or in concentrations around fossil wood or other fossilized vegetable matter. Pure carnotite contains about 53 per cent uranium by weight, which is used to generate nuclear energy and in atomic weapons. It has also been mined for vanadium and radium, from World War II onwards.

Radium dial
Sourced from carnotite, radium has been used to create illuminated watch hands and dials.

vitreous lustre

rounded crystal cluster

Adamite crystals
Rounded, whitish crystal clusters of adamite rest on a rock groundmass in this specimen.

PROFILE

Orthorhombic

3 ½

4.4

Good

Subconchoidal to uneven, brittle

White

Vitreous

VARIANTS

Reddish adamite Adamite crystals on a reddish orange iron-oxide matrix

adamite crystal

Spheroidal adamite
A cluster of yellow, spheroidal adamite crystals on a goethite groundmass

$Zn_2AsO_4(OH)$

ADAMITE

Named in 1866 after the French mineralogist G.J. Adam, who discovered adamite in Chile, this mineral is a zinc arsenate hydroxide. It is rarely colourless or white, and many specimens fluoresce green under ultraviolet light. Adamite is often brightly coloured due to traces of other elements: copper commonly substitutes for zinc to yield yellow or green crystals depending on its concentration; manganese may substitute for zinc to yield crystals that are pink or violet. Adamite crystals are elongated, tabular, or blocky. This mineral also occurs as rosettes and spherical masses of radiating crystals.

Adamite forms as a secondary mineral in the oxidized zones of zinc and arsenic deposits, often associated with goethite (p.102), azurite (p.120), smithsonite (p.124), mimetite (p.164), scorodite (p.165), hemimorphite (p.227), and olivenite. Although adamite has no commercial uses, its bright and lustrous crystals are highly sought after by mineral collectors.

Clinoclase rosettes
In this specimen, rosettes of clinoclase crystals are seen with associated olivenite.

rosette of radiating clinoclase crystals

olivenite

PROFILE

Monoclinic

 2½–3

 4.3

 Perfect

 Uneven, brittle

 Bluish green

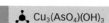 Vitreous to pearly

$Cu_3(AsO_4)(OH)_3$

CLINOCLASE

Discovered in 1830 in the Wheal Gorland mine in Cornwall, England, clinoclase was named in 1868. It takes its name from the Greek *me klísi*, which means "to incline", and *gia na spásei*, which means "to break" – a reference to its oblique basal cleavage. The vitreous crystals of clinoclase are translucent dark blue to dark greenish blue. They can be elongated or tabular or occur as single, isolated crystals that appear rhombohedral. Specimens can also form rosette-like aggregates or occur as crusts or coatings with a fibrous structure.

Clinoclase forms as a secondary mineral in the oxidized zones of deposits containing copper sulphides. Associated minerals include goethite (p.102), azurite (p.120), malachite (p.125), brochantite (p.139), adamite (p.160), quartz (p.168), and olivenite. Specimens come from Broken Hill, New South Wales, Australia; Tintic district, Utah, and Majuba Hill, Nevada, USA; the Vosges, France; and the Tsumeb Mine, Namibia.

Tabular chalcophyllite
A mass of vivid blue, tabular chalcophyllite crystals rests on a rock groundmass.

rock groundmass

tabular chalcophyllite crystal

Hexagonal or trigonal

 2

2.7

Perfect basal

Uneven to subconchoidal

Pale green

Pearly to vitreous

$Cu_{18}Al_2(AsO_4)_2(SO_4)_3(OH)_{27}\cdot33H_2O$

CHALCOPHYLLITE

A vivid blue-green in colour, chalcophyllite takes its name from the Greek words *chalco*, which means "copper" and *phyllon*, which means "leaf" – an allusion to its copper content and its common foliated habit. Chalcophyllite was first described after material collected in Germany and named in 1847. Translucent crystals exhibit a blue-green colour when viewed from one direction and appear almost colourless from another direction. Crystals are platy, six-sided, and flattened and may have triangular striations. Chalcophyllite may also be rosette-like, tabular, drusy, or massive.

This mineral occurs in hydrothermal copper deposits, often accompanied by cuprite (p.87), azurite (p.120), malachite (p.125), brochantite (p.139), and clinoclase (p.161).

Statue of Lamma
Chalcophyllite was used as an ore of copper when this copper statue was made in the period 1800–1600 BCE.

PROFILE

Monoclinic

1½–2½

3.1

Perfect

Uneven, sectile

Pale red

Adamantine to vitreous, pearly

Acicular crystals
These brightly coloured, needle-like crystals of erythrite are from Bou Azzer, Morocco.

rock groundmass

purplish pink erythrite

needle-like crystal

VARIANT

Erythrite crust A thin crust of erythrite on a brown rock base

$CO_3(AsO_4)_2 \cdot 8H_2O$

ERYTHRITE

Although of little commercial value, erythrite is an important tool for prospectors looking for cobalt and related silver deposits. The bright purplish pink colour of erythrite in a rock indicates the presence of cobalt. This explains why miners call erythrite "cobalt bloom". Erythrite is a cobalt arsenate hydrate. It forms a chemical replacement series with annabergite, in which nickel replaces cobalt in the erythrite structure. Its colour may vary from crimson red to peach red, with the lighter colours indicating a higher nickel content. The coloration may also occur in bands. Well-formed crystals are rare, but when found they occur as deeply striated, prismatic to needle-like, commonly radiating, globular tufts of crystals, or as powdery coatings.

Erythrite is a secondary mineral found in the oxidized zones of cobalt-nickel-arsenic deposits. Fine specimens come from Canada and Morocco. Erythrite is also found in Mexico, France, southwestern USA, the Czech Republic, Germany, Australia, and elsewhere.

PROFILE

Hexagonal

3½–4

7.3

Poor

Conchoidal to uneven, brittle

White

Resinous

Mimetite on manganese oxide
This specimen from England contains "campylite" – a rounded variety of mimetite – and baryte on nodules of manganese oxide.

rounded masses of campylite

baryte

resinous lustre

manganese-oxide matrix

VARIANTS

crystalline campylite

Campylite Massive and crystalline varieties of campylite set in a rock groundmass

Prismatic crystals Mimetite in the form of prismatic, barrel-shaped crystals

$Pb_5(AsO_4)_3Cl$

MIMETITE

An arsenate mineral, mimetite is the end member of a solid-solution series with pyromorphite (p.151). It is named after the Greek word *mimetes*, which means "imitator" – a reference to its resemblance to pyromorphite. Although similar in physical characterisitics and crystal form to pyromorphite, mimetite is a less common mineral. It forms heavy, barrel-shaped, hexagonal crystals or rounded masses. It is also found as botryoidal, granular, tabular, and needle-like aggregates. Mimetite specimens may be colourless or occur in shades of yellow, orange, brown, and green.

Mimetite is a secondary mineral, which forms in the oxidized zone of lead deposits and in other localities where the elements lead and arsenic occur together. Excellent specimens come from Chihuahua, Mexico; Saxony, Germany; Attica, Greece; Broken Hill, Australia; and Bisbee and Tombstone, Arizona, USA. A single crystal mined from Tsumeb in Namibia measured 6.4 cm (2½ in) in length.

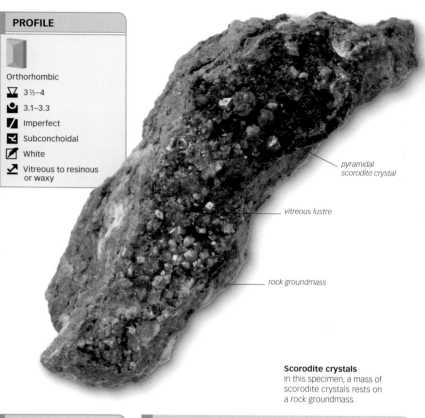

PROFILE

Orthorhombic

3½–4

3.1–3.3

Imperfect

Subconchoidal

White

Vitreous to resinous or waxy

pyramidal scorodite crystal

vitreous lustre

rock groundmass

Scorodite crystals
In this specimen, a mass of scorodite crystals rests on a rock groundmass.

VARIANT

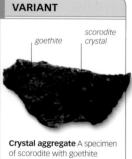

goethite *scorodite crystal*

Crystal aggregate A specimen of scorodite with goethite

$FeAsO_4 \cdot 2H_2O$

SCORODITE

A hydrated iron arsenate mineral, scorodite takes its name from the Greek word *scorodion*, which means "garlic-like" – an allusion to the odour emitted by the arsenic when specimens are heated. Scorodite can vary considerably in colour depending on the light under which it is seen: pale leek green, greyish green, liver brown, pale blue, violet, yellow, pale greyish, or colourless. It may be blue-green in daylight but bluish purple to greyish blue in incandescent light; in transmitted light it may appear colourless to pale shades of green or brown. Crystals are usually dipyramidal, appearing octahedral, and may have a number of modifying faces. They may also be tabular or short prisms. Drusy coatings are common. Scorodite can also be porous and earthy or massive.

Scorodite is found in hydrothermal veins, hot spring deposits, and oxidized zones of arsenic-rich ore bodies. Associated minerals may be pharmacosiderite, vivianite (p.157), adamite (p.160), and various iron oxides.

SILICATES

The silicates constitute around 25 per cent of all known minerals and 40 per cent of the most common ones. All silicates are built around a basic structure of silicon and oxygen. They are a major component of Earth and occur in lunar samples and meteorites.

COMPOSITION

The silicates make up about 95 per cent of the crust and upper mantle of Earth. All silicates contain silicon and oxygen. Silicon is a light, shiny metal that looks like pencil lead; oxygen is a colourless, odourless gas.

In silicates, silicon and oxygen combine to form structural tetrahedra, each with a silicon atom in the centre and oxygen atoms at the corners. Silicate tetrahedra may exist as discrete, independent units and connect only with other silicate tetrahedra (as in quartz), or they may link with other elements such as iron, magnesium, and aluminium. Tetrahedra may also share their oxygen atoms at corners, edges, or, more rarely, faces, creating variations in the structure. The different linkages also create voids of varying sizes, which are occupied by the ions of various metals. These substitutions occur where atoms are of a relatively similar size. Silicates are divided into six

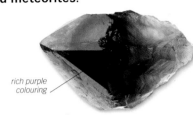

rich purple colouring

Amethyst crystal
The tectosilicate mineral quartz occurs in several differently coloured varieties. These include amethyst (above), rock crystal, smoky quartz, and citrine.

main groups (see panel, below) according to the structural configurations that result from the different ways in which tetrahedra and other elements are linked. Within these main groups are further subdivisions based on chemistry – that is, the type and location of other atoms in the structure. Many groups are solid-solution series, such as the feldspars (see panel, opposite) and the garnets, in which the ions of various metals and semimetals substitute for each other within the silicate structure.

SILICATE GROUPS

The six silicate groups are based on the six different ways in which the basic silica tetrahedra are linked. These differing linkages create voids of different sizes and configurations that allow positively charged atoms of varying sizes to fit into the structure.

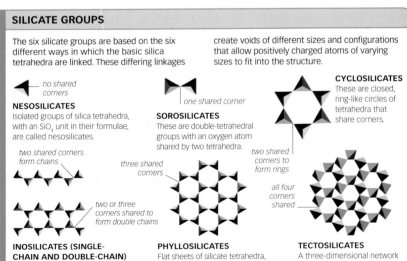

no shared corners

NESOSILICATES
Isolated groups of silica tetrahedra, with an SiO_4 unit in their formulae, are called nesosilicates.

one shared corner

SOROSILICATES
These are double-tetrahedral groups with an oxygen atom shared by two tetrahedra.

CYCLOSILICATES
These are closed, ring-like circles of tetrahedra that share corners.

two shared corners form chains

three shared corners

two shared corners to form rings

all four corners shared

two or three corners shared to form double chains

INOSILICATES (SINGLE-CHAIN AND DOUBLE-CHAIN)
Chains of silica tetrahedra with Si_2O_6 groups are called single-chain inosilicates.

PHYLLOSILICATES
Flat sheets of silicate tetrahedra, with an Si_2O_5 unit in their chemical formulae, are called phyllosilicates.

TECTOSILICATES
A three-dimensional network of silica tetrahedra, linked at each corner makes up a tectosilicate.

THE FELDSPARS

The feldspars are a group of aluminosilicate minerals that contain calcium, sodium, or potassium. As shown here, there are three major solid-solution series within the group. Feldspar is the most abundant mineral in Earth's crust.

ALKALI FELDSPARS

ORTHOCLASE
$KAlSi_3O_8$

SANIDINE
$(K,Na)ALSI_3O_8$

ALBITE (Ab)
$NaAlSI_3O_8$

MICROCLINE
$KAlSi_3O_8$

ANORTHOCLASE
$(Na,K)ALSI_3O_8$

PLAGIOCLASE FELDSPARS

OLIGOCLASE
$(Na,Ca)(Al,Si)$
$AlSi_3O_8$

ANDESINE
$NaAlSi_3O_8...$
$CaAl_2Si_2O_8$

LABRADORITE
$(Ca,Na)Al(Al,Si)$
Si_2O_2

ANORTHITE (An)
$CaAl_2Si_2O_8$

BYTOWNITE
$(NaSi,CaAl)Al_2Si_2O_8$

OCCURRENCE AND USES

The ultimate source of all silicates is igneous rock in which tectosilicate feldspar minerals are the major component. Silicates are found not only on Earth but also on the Moon and in meteorites. After feldspar, quartz is the most abundant mineral in the crust and upper mantle. It occurs in nearly all high-silica igneous, metamorphic, and sedimentary rocks. In silica-poor rocks where quartz does not form, other minerals develop. Since many silicates, especially quartz and its varieties, are resistant to weathering, they form the major component of most detrital sediments. There are numerous uses of silicates. Quartz and its varieties find use as gemstones, in electronic and optical applications, and as abrasives. The feldspars are used in glass and ceramics, as gemstones, and as abrasives. Other silicates are ores, and yet others are important gem, ornamental, and industrial minerals. The tough rocks formed from silicate minerals are used as major building and industrial materials.

Jadeite mask

The single-chain inosilicate jadeite is one of the oldest minerals used. Although difficult to shape, it has been used for tools and ornaments.

The Ural Mountains

Located in west-central Russia, the Ural Mountains are a treasure trove of silicate minerals, which are used in industry and as gemstones.

PROFILE

Hexagonal or trigonal

- 7
- 2.7
- None
- Conchoidal
- White
- Vitreous

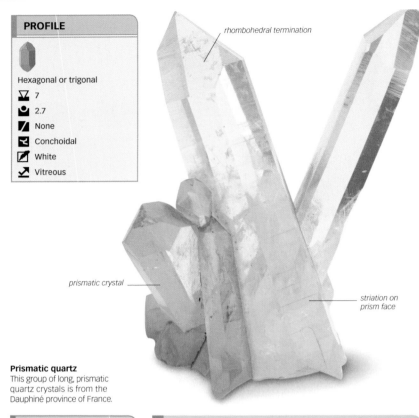

rhombohedral termination

prismatic crystal

striation on prism face

Prismatic quartz
This group of long, prismatic quartz crystals is from the Dauphiné province of France.

VARIANTS

Pyramidal amethyst
An amethyst specimen with pyramidal terminations

milky quartz

termination

smoky quartz

Smoky quartz Double-terminated smoky quartz in milky quartz

termination

Milky quartz
A white, terminated quartz prism

SiO_2

QUARTZ

One of the most common minerals in Earth's crust, quartz has two forms: macrocrystalline (with crystals that can be seen by eye) and cryptocrystalline (formed of microscopic crystals). Macrocrystalline quartz is usually colourless and transparent, as in rock crystal, or white and translucent, as in milky quartz. Coloured varieties include: pink and translucent rose quartz; transparent to translucent lavender or purple amethyst; transparent to translucent black or brown smoky quartz; and transparent to translucent yellow or yellow-brown citrine. All crystalline varieties form hexagonal prisms and pyramids.

Cryptocrystalline varieties of quartz include chalcedony (p.169), agate (p.170), and jasper (p.171). Quartz occurs in nearly all silica-rich sedimentary, igneous, and metamorphic rocks.

Oval citrine
This large, oval-cut citrine is set in a silver brooch. It is encircled by silver leaves and faceted amethysts.

PROFILE

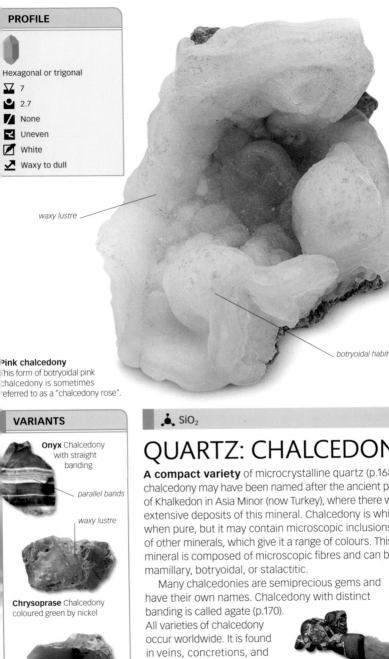

Hexagonal or trigonal

7

2.7

None

Uneven

White

Waxy to dull

waxy lustre

Pink chalcedony
This form of botryoidal pink chalcedony is sometimes referred to as a "chalcedony rose".

botryoidal habit

VARIANTS

Onyx Chalcedony with straight banding

parallel bands

waxy lustre

Chrysoprase Chalcedony coloured green by nickel

Carnelian A piece of red-orange chalcedony

 SiO_2

QUARTZ: CHALCEDONY

A compact variety of microcrystalline quartz (p.168), chalcedony may have been named after the ancient port of Khalkedon in Asia Minor (now Turkey), where there were extensive deposits of this mineral. Chalcedony is white when pure, but it may contain microscopic inclusions of other minerals, which give it a range of colours. This mineral is composed of microscopic fibres and can be mamillary, botryoidal, or stalactitic.

Many chalcedonies are semiprecious gems and have their own names. Chalcedony with distinct banding is called agate (p.170). All varieties of chalcedony occur worldwide. It is found in veins, concretions, and geodes. It forms in cavities, cracks, and when silica-rich waters at low temperatures (up to 200°C/400°F) percolate through existing rocks.

Chalcedony blade
This Aztec sacrificial knife has a finely chipped chalcedony blade and a mosaic handle.

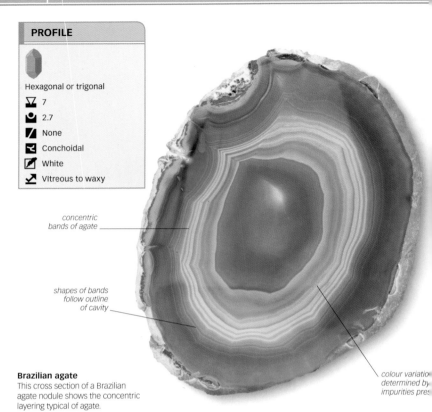

concentric
bands of agate

shapes of bands
follow outline
of cavity

colour variatio
determined by
impurities pres

Brazilian agate
This cross section of a Brazilian
agate nodule shows the concentric
layering typical of agate.

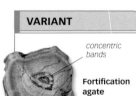
⚛ SiO_2

CHALCEDONY: AGATE

A common, semiprecious chalcedony, agate has
been worked since prehistoric times. It is a compact,
microcrystalline variety of quartz (p.168), and it has the
same physical properties as quartz. Agate is characterized
by concentric colour bands in shades of white, yellow,
grey, pale blue, brown, pink, red, or black.

Other names often precede the word agate to indicate
the mineral's visual characteristics or place of origin.
One of these is fire agate, which
has inclusions of reddish to brown
hematite that give an internal
iridescence to polished stones.
Another is fortification agate,
which has concentric bands of
colour resembling an aerial view
of an ancient fortress. Most
agates are found in cavities in
ancient lavas or other extrusive
igneous rocks.

Snuff bottle
The 19th-century Chinese
snuff bottle seen here has
been carved from agate.
It has a jade stopper.

PROFILE

Hexagonal or trigonal

- 7
- 2.7
- None
- Conchoidal
- White
- Vitreous

Colour variation
Hematite colours this example of jasper brownish red. Threads of white quartz veins make a crisscross pattern on this specimen.

brownish red jasper

white quartz vein

colour variation due to other minerals

VARIANTS

Mammillary jasper Red jasper in mammillary form

Ribboned jasper A specimen of jasper with parallel, reddish bands

SiO_2

QUARTZ: JASPER

An impure variety of cryptocrystalline quartz (p.168), jasper takes its name from the Greek word *iaspis*, which is probably of Semitic origin. It is fine-grained or dense, and it contains various amounts of other materials, which give it opacity and colour. Hematite (p.91) gives jasper a brick-red to brownish red colour; clay a yellowish white or grey colour; and goethite (p.102) a brown or yellow hue.

Jasper forms when silica-rich waters at low temperatures (up to 200°C/400°F) percolate through cracks and fissures in other rocks, incorporating a variety of materials and leaving behind deposits. It is found worldwide wherever cryptocrystalline quartz occurs. The classification and naming of jasper varies greatly and often incorporates place names or colours. Only some of these are formally recognized as varieties of jasper, leaving great latitude in defining which jasper is which. Colour names such as "red" or "green" can apply to a range of shades, while locality names, such as "Bruneau jasper" after a canyon in Idaho, USA, tend to be more specific.

PROFILE

Crystal system Amorphous

🔨	5–6
💧	1.9–2.3
▨	None
◩	Conchoidal
◪	White
⤢	Vitreous

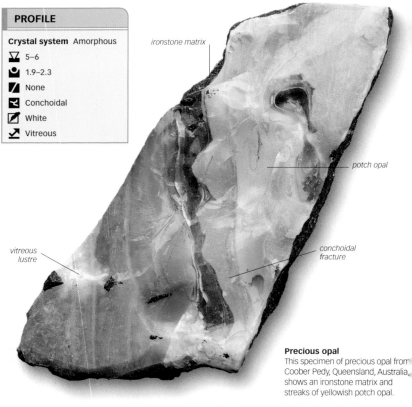

ironstone matrix

potch opal

vitreous lustre

conchoidal fracture

Precious opal
This specimen of precious opal from Coober Pedy, Queensland, Australia, shows an ironstone matrix and streaks of yellowish potch opal.

VARIANTS

Boulder opal
Blue mass of opal in an iron-oxide nodule

Opal pseudomorph Crystals of glauberite replaced by opal

Fire opal Non-iridescent, transparent opal

♣ $SiO_2 \cdot nH_2O$

OPAL

Known since antiquity, opal derives its name from the Roman word *opalus,* which means "precious stone". Although it is colourless when pure, the vast majority of common opal occurs in opaque, dull yellows and reds. It varies from essentially amorphous to partially crystalline. Precious opal is the least crystalline form of the mineral, consisting of a regular arrangement of tiny, transparent, silica spheres. Regularly arranged spheres of a particular size create a diffraction effect called colour play.

Opal is widespread and is deposited at low temperatures (up to 200°C/400°F) from silica-bearing, circulating waters. It is found as nodules, stalactitic masses, veinlets, and encrustations in most kinds of rocks. Opal constitutes important parts of many sedimentary accumulations, such as diatomaceous earth.

Victorian ring
Some cut opal dries and cracks with age and needs to be kept moist. The opal in this ring is well preserved.

Monoclinic

6–6 ½

2.5–2.6

Perfect

Subconchoidal to uneven, brittle

White

Vitreous

Orthoclase prisms
In this specimen, white, blocky prisms of orthoclase are associated with cleavelandite albite and set in pegmatite.

translucent, prismatic orthoclase crystal

cleavelandite albite

VARIANTS

Yellow orthoclase A crystal of yellow orthoclase

Moonstone rough An opalescent variety of orthoclase

twinned crystal

prismatic crystal

Orthoclase crystals Twinned orthoclase with smaller prism

$KAlSi_3O_8$

ORTHOCLASE

An important rock-forming mineral, orthoclase is the potassium-bearing end member of the potassium–sodium feldspar solid-solution series. It is a major component of granite (pp.258–59) – its pink crystals give granite its typical colour. Crystalline orthoclase can also be white, colourless, cream, pale yellow, or brownish red. Orthoclase appears as well-formed, short, prismatic crystals, which are frequently twinned. It may also occur in massive form. Moonstone is a variety of orthoclase that exhibits a schiller effect.

Pure orthoclase is rare, as some sodium is usually present in the structure. Specimens are abundant in igneous rocks rich in potassium or silica, in pegmatites (p.260), and in gneisses (p.288). This mineral is important in ceramics, to make the item itself and as a glaze.

Moonstone-set brooch
Orthoclase exhibits the schiller effect which creates the shimmer seen on the moonstones in this brooch.

Prismatic sanidine
This single, well-formed prismatic crystal of sanidine rests in a groundmass of the volcanic rock trachyte.

square cross section

translucent sanidine crystal

trachyte groundmass

PROFILE

Monoclinic

 6–6½

2.6

Perfect, good

Conchoidal to uneven

White

Vitreous

$(K,Na)AlSi_3O_8$

SANIDINE

A member of the solid-solution series of potassium and sodium feldspars, sanidine is the high-temperature form of potassium feldspar, forming at 575°C (1,065°F) or above. Crystals are usually colourless or white, glassy, and transparent, but they may also be grey, cream, or occur in other pale tints. They are generally short prismatic or tabular, with a square cross section. Twinning is common. Crystals have been known to reach 50cm (19½in) in length. Sanidine is also found as granular or cleavable masses.

A widespread mineral, sanidine occurs in feldspar- and quartz-rich volcanic rocks, such as rhyolite (p.278), phonolite, and trachyte (p.279). It is also found in eclogites (p.299), contact metamorphic rocks, and metamorphic rocks formed at low pressure and high temperature. Sanidine forms spherular masses of needle-like crystals in obsidian (p.280), giving rise to what is called snowflake obsidian. Significant occurrences of sanidine are at the Alban Hills near Rome, Italy; Mont St.-Hilaire, Canada; and Eifel, Germany.

Prismatic microcline
Numerous prismatic crystals of light-coloured microcline sit atop a pegmatite groundmass, along with smoky quartz.

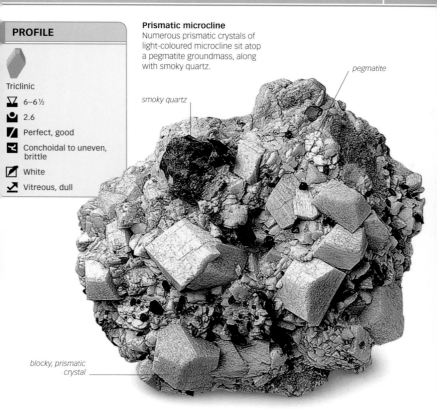

pegmatite

smoky quartz

blocky, prismatic crystal

🜨 KAlSi$_3$O$_8$

MICROCLINE

Used in ceramics and as a mild abrasive, microcline is one of the most common feldspar minerals. It can be colourless, white, cream to pale yellow, salmon pink to red, or bright green to blue-green. Microcline forms short prismatic or tabular crystals that are often of considerable size: single crystals can weigh several tonnes and reach metres in length. Crystals are often multiply twinned, with two sets of fine lines at right angles to each other. This gives a "plaid" effect that is unique to microcline among the feldspars. Microcline can also be massive.

The mineral occurs in feldspar-rich rocks, such as granite (pp.258–59), syenite (p.262), and granodiorite (p.263). It is found in granite pegmatites (p.260) and in metamorphic rocks, such as gneisses (p.288) and schists (p.291–92).

Amazonite cabochon
This Arts and Craft ring exhibits an asymmetrically set cabochon of amazonite in a rose-and-foliage design.

vitreous lustre

single prismatic crystal

Prismatic anorthoclase
This specimen of pink and grey prismatic anorthoclase shows well-developed crystal faces.

PROFILE

Triclinic

 6–6½

 2.6

 Perfect, good

 Conchoidal to uneven, brittle

 White

Vitreous

 (Na,K)AlSi$_3$O$_8$

ANORTHOCLASE

This member of the sodium- and potassium-rich feldspar group takes its name from the Greek word *anorthos*, which means "not straight" – a reference to its oblique cleavage. Anorthoclase is colourless, white, cream, pink, pale yellow, grey, or green. Its crystals are prismatic or tabular and are often multiply twinned. Anorthoclase crystals can show two sets of fine lines at right angles to each other like microcline (p.175), but the lines are much finer. Specimens can also be massive or granular.

Anorthoclase forms in sodium-rich igneous zones. It commonly occurs with ilmenite (p.90), apatite (p.148), and augite (p.211). Much anorthoclase exhibits a gold, bluish, or greenish schiller effect, making it one of several feldspars known as moonstone when cut *en cabochon*. A type of the igneous rock syenite (p.262) called larvikite has large schillerized crystals of anorthoclase and is highly prized as an ornamental stone. Anorthoclase is widespread, but fine examples come from Cripple Creek, Colorado, USA; Larvik, Norway; and Fife, Scotland.

PROFILE

Triclinic

⬙ 6–6½

⬤ 2.6

◩ Perfect, good

⬕ Conchoidal to uneven, brittle

◪ White

⬈ Vitreous to pearly

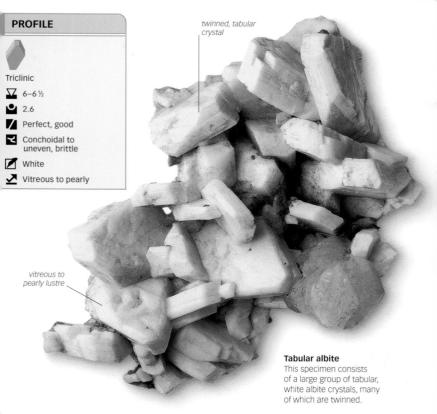

twinned, tabular crystal

vitreous to pearly lustre

Tabular albite
This specimen consists of a large group of tabular, white albite crystals, many of which are twinned.

VARIANT

tourmaline

quartz

albite

Albite base Tourmaline and quartz crystals on albite

🜨 NaAlSi$_3$O$_8$

ALBITE

A rock-forming mineral, albite takes its name from the Latin word *albus*, which means "white" – a reference to its usual colour. Specimens can also be colourless, yellowish, pink, or green. Albite occurs as tabular or platy crystals that are often twinned, glassy, and brittle. It can also be massive or granular. Albite was named in 1707.

This mineral is the solid-solution end member of both the plagioclase and the sodium- and potassium-rich feldspars. It occurs in pegmatites (p.260) and in some feldspar- and quartz-rich igneous rocks. Albite also forms through chemical processes in certain sedimentary environments and occurs in low-grade metamorphic rocks. The cleavelandite variety occurs in complex pegmatites as thin plates or scales.

Facet-grade albite
Faceted albite, although fragile, is sometimes used in jewellery, along with albite's moonstone variety.

PROFILE

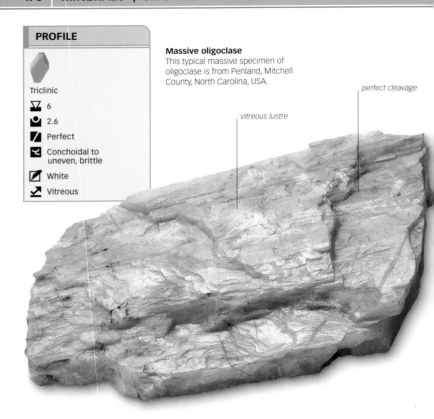

Triclinic

⎓ 6

🔨 2.6

▨ Perfect

✂ Conchoidal to uneven, brittle

◩ White

⬚ Vitreous

Massive oligoclase
This typical massive specimen of oligoclase is from Penland, Mitchell County, North Carolina, USA.

vitreous lustre

perfect cleavage

VARIANTS

Sunstone rough
An uncut specimen of sunstone oligoclase

smoky quartz

Oligoclase crystal A pink crystal accompanied by smoky quartz

🜨 $(Na,Ca)Al_2Si_2O_8$

OLIGOCLASE

In 1826, the German mineralogist August Breithaupt named this mineral after two Greek words: *oligos*, which means "little", and *clasein*, which means "to break" – as it was thought to have a less perfect cleavage than albite (p.177). Oligoclase can be grey, white, red, greenish, yellowish, brown, or colourless. Its usual habit is massive or granular, although it can form tabular crystals that are commonly twinned.

Oligoclase is the most common of the plagioclase feldspars. It occurs in granite (pp.258–59), granitic pegmatites (p.260), diorite (p.264), rhyolite (p.278), and other feldspar- and quartz-rich igneous rocks. It also occurs in high-grade, metamorphosed gneisses (p.288) and schists (pp.291–92).

Semiprecious oligoclase
Sunstone oligoclase, such as the oval example seen here, has hematite or goethite inclusions.

PROFILE

Triclinic

6–6½

2.7

Perfect

Conchoidal to uneven, brittle

White

Vitreous

vitreous lustre

anorthite crystal

augite

Pink anorthite
In this specimen, pink crystals of anorthite occur with augite.

VARIANT

Anorthite aggregate A mass of blue-grey anorthite

$CaAl_2Si_2O_8$

ANORTHITE

The calcium-rich end member of the plagioclase-feldspar solid-solution series, anorthite takes its name from the Greek word *anorthos*, which means "not straight" – a reference to its triclinic form. Its brittle, short, glassy crystals are well-formed prisms that can be coloured white or shades of grey, pink, or red. Specimens are also massive or granular. Anorthite is a calcium aluminosilicate and can contain up to 10 per cent albite (p.177).

Anorthite is a major rock-forming mineral present in many magnesium- and iron-rich igneous rocks, contact metamorphic rocks, and chondroditic meteorites (p.337). Pure anorthite is uncommon; it weathers readily and is rare in rocks exposed at the surface for long periods. Anorthosite (p.261), a rock composed mainly of anorthite, makes up much of the lunar highlands. The so-called Genesis Rock, brought back by Apollo 15, is made of anorthosite and dates back to the formation of the Moon, which occurred about 4.1 billion years ago. Anorthite was also discovered in the comet Wild 2.

PROFILE

Triclinic

⬡ 6–6½

◗ 2.7

▟ Perfect

◩ Uneven to conchoidal

▨ White

⬚ Vitreous

Blue labradorite
This specimen shows polysynthetic twinning typical of plagioclase feldspars. This is evident as a series of parallel lines on the broken faces.

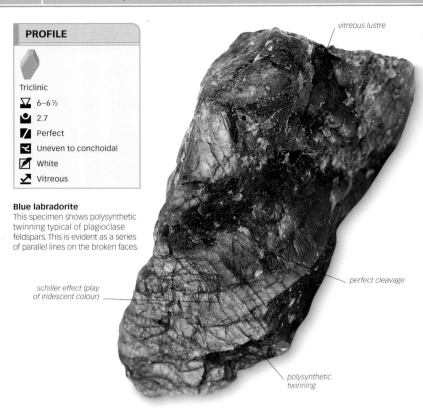

vitreous lustre

perfect cleavage

polysynthetic twinning

schiller effect (play of iridescent colour)

VARIANTS

Schiller effect Orange, purple, and blue flashes visible in a specimen of labradorite

Orange sunstone Labradorite "sunstone" from Oregon, USA

♣ $NaAlSi_3O_8$–$CaAl_2Si_2O_8$

LABRADORITE

The calcium-rich, middle-range member of the plagioclase feldspars, labradorite is characterized by its schiller effect – a rich play of iridescent colours, mainly blue, on cleavage surfaces. Specimens are generally blue or dark grey but can also be colourless or white. When transparent, labradorite is yellow, red, orange, or green. This mineral seldom forms crystals, but when crystals do occur, they are tabular. It most often forms masses with crystals that can be microscopic or up to 1m (3ft) or more wide.

Labradorite is a major constituent of certain medium-silica and silica-poor igneous and metamorphic rocks, including diorite (p.264), gabbro (p.265), basalt (p.273), andesite (p.275), and amphibolite (p.296). Gem-quality labradorite from Finland is known as spectrolite.

Semiprecious gemstone
The polished oval of labradorite in this choker beautifully displays the stone's rainbow iridescence.

blue porphyry

triclinic crystal

andesine crystal

PROFILE

Triclinic

6–6½

2.7

Perfect

Conchoidal to uneven

White

Subvitreous to pearly

Andesine crystals
This specimen has andesine crystals up to 2 cm (¾ in) long in blue porphyry. It was found in Estérel, Var, France.

VARIANT

Andesite porphyry Andesite is a major constituent of this porphyry rock

$NaAlSi_3O_8$–$CaAl_2Si_2O_8$

ANDESINE

The plagioclase feldspar andesine is named after the Andes Mountains in South America, where it is abundant in andesite lavas. A white, grey, or colourless mineral, andesine often forms well-defined crystals that usually exhibit multiple twinning. It can also be massive or occur as rock-bound grains.

A sodium calcium aluminosilicate, andesine is an intermediate member of the plagioclase solid-solution series. It occurs widely in igneous rocks of medium silica content, especially in andesite (p.275). Andesine is also found in other intermediate igneous rocks, such as syenite (p.262) and diorite (p.264). Specimens are commonly associated with magnetite (p.92), quartz (p.168), biotite (p.197), and hornblende (p.218). Andesine typically occurs in metamorphic rocks formed under high pressure and temperatures (575°C/1,065°F or above). It is also found as detrital grains in sedimentary rocks. The accurate identification of individual specimens involves detailed study and analysis.

Massive nepheline
This specimen of nepheline from Arkansas, USA, shows the mineral's most typical massive habit.

translucent with a vitreous lustre

massive habit

VARIANT

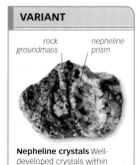

rock groundmass

nepheline prism

Nepheline crystals Well-developed crystals within cavities in a rock groundmass

$(Na,K)AlSiO_4$

NEPHELINE

The most common feldspathoid mineral, nepheline takes its name from the Greek word *nephele*, which means "cloud" – a reference to the fact that the mineral becomes cloudy or milky in strong acids. Specimens are usually white in colour, often with a yellowish or greyish tint. They can also be colourless, grey, yellow, or red-brown. Nepheline is generally massive. Crystals usually occur as hexagonal prisms, though they can exhibit a variety of prism and pyramid shapes. Nepheline also forms large, tabular phenocrysts in igneous rocks.

This rock-forming mineral is found in iron- and magnesium-rich igneous rocks with perovskite (p.89), spinel (p.96), and olivine (p.232). It also occurs in intermediate igneous rocks with aegirine (p.209) and augite (p.211) and in some volcanic and metamorphic rocks.

Ceramic bowl
Nepheline is sometimes used as a substitute for feldspars in ceramics, such as this porcelain bowl.

vitreous lustre

calcite matrix

dodecahedral crystal

Crystalline lazurite
This specimen from Badakhshan,
Afghanistan, shows superbly
developed lazurite crystals that
are up to 1.9 cm (¾ in) long.

VARIANTS

Polished slab A slice of
lazurite showing intense colour

Lapis lazuli
An uncut piece
of lapis lazuli
streaked with calcite

marble

Lazurite in marble Lazurite
dispersed in marble

$Na_3Ca(Al_3Si_3O_{12})S$

LAZURITE

A sodium calcium aluminosilicate, lazurite is the main
component of the gemstone lapis lazuli and accounts for
the stone's intense blue colour, although lapis lazuli also
typically contains pyrite (p.62), calcite (p.114), sodalite
(p.184), and haüyne. Lazurite specimens are always deep or
vibrant blue. Distinct crystals were thought to be rare until
large numbers were brought out of mines in Badakhshan,
Afghanistan, in the 1990s. These are usually dodecahedral
and are much sought after. Most lazurite is either massive
or occurs in disseminated grains.

Lapis lazuli is relatively rare. It
forms in crystalline limestones
(p.319) as a product of contact
metamorphism. The best quality
lapis lazuli is dark blue with minor
patches of calcite and pyrite. In
addition to its use as a gemstone,
lapis lazuli was used as one of the
first eye shadows.

Expensive pigment
Powdered lapis lazuli
was once used to make
ultramarine, one of the
most expensive pigments.

PROFILE

Cubic

5½–6

2.1–2.3

Poor to distinct

Uneven to conchoidal

White to light blue

Vitreous to greasy

Massive sodalite
This sodalite specimen shows intense blue colour, which can sometimes lead to the mineral being mistaken for lapis lazuli.

vitreous lustre

uneven fracture

massive habit

VARIANTS

Polished sodalite A specimen that has been polished to bring out its colour

Indian sodalite A specimen of light blue sodalite found in India

$Na_4Al_3Si_3O_{12}Cl$

SODALITE

Named in 1811 after its high sodium content, sodalite is sodium aluminium silicate chloride. Specimens can be blue, grey, pink, colourless, or other pale shades. They sometimes fluoresce bright orange under ultraviolet light. Sodalite nearly always forms massive aggregates or disseminated grains. Crystals are relatively rare; when found, they are dodecahedral or octahedral.

Sodalite occurs in igneous rocks and associated pegmatites (p.260). It is sometimes found in contact metamorphosed limestones (p.319) and dolomites (p.320) and in rocks ejected from volcanoes. Rare crystals are found on the Mount Vesuvius volcano in Italy. Uncommon transparent specimens from Mont St.-Hilaire, Canada, are faceted for collectors.

Sodalite beads
This unusual modern Egyptian necklace has beads made of blue sodalite and red carnelian.

Leucite crystals
In this specimen formed at a high temperature, fine psuedotrapezohedral crystals of leucite rest in cavities in a rock groundmass.

leucite pseudotrapezohedron

rock groundmass

VARIANTS

Single crystal A single yellowish crystal of leucite

Italian leucite A crystal in pseudotrapezohedral form from Casserta, Italy

$KAlSi_2O_6$

LEUCITE

The name leucite comes from the Greek word *leukos*, which means "matt white" – a reference to the mineral's most common colour. Specimens can also be colourless or grey. Crystals are common and can be up to 9 cm (3½ in) wide. More often, leucite occurs as massive or granular aggregates or as disseminated grains. It is tetragonal at temperatures below 625°C (1,155°F) and cubic with trapezohedral crystals at higher temperatures. The trapezohedral form is preserved as the mineral cools and develops tetragonal symmetry.

Leucite is found in potassium-rich and silica-poor igneous rocks. It is found with nepheline (p.182), sodalite (p.184), natrolite (p.186), analcime (p.190), and sodium- and potassium-rich feldspars, and occurs worldwide.

Potassium fertilizer
Because of leucite's high potassium content, the mineral is used as a fertilizer in some countries.

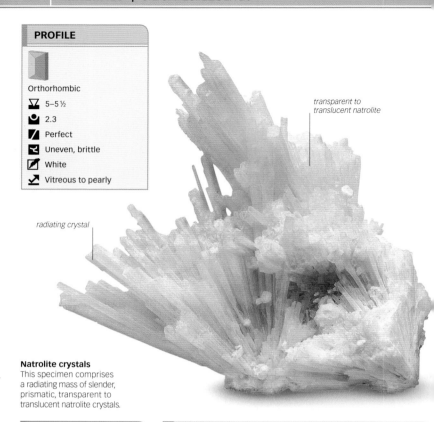

transparent to translucent natrolite

radiating crystal

Natrolite crystals
This specimen comprises a radiating mass of slender, prismatic, transparent to translucent natrolite crystals.

VARIANT

natrolite

calcite

Natrolite and calcite
A specimen including white calcite and light orange natrolite

$Na_2Al_2Si_3O_{10} \cdot 2H_2O$

NATROLITE

A hydrated sodium aluminosilicate, natrolite takes its name from the Greek word *natrium*, which means "soda" – a reference to the sodium content of this mineral. Natrolite can be pale pink, colourless, white, red, grey, yellow, or green. Some specimens fluoresce orange to yellow under ultraviolet light. Natrolite crystals are generally long and slender, with vertical striations and a square cross section. They may appear tetragonal and can grow up to 1 m (3 ft) in length. Natrolite is also found as radiating masses of needle-like crystals and as granular or compact masses. This mineral produces an electric charge in response to both pressure and temperature changes.

Natrolite is found in cavities or fissures in basaltic rocks (p.273), volcanic ash deposits, and veins in granite (pp.258–59), gneiss (p.288), and other rocks. It also occurs in altered syenites (p.262), aplites, and dolerites (p.268). Specimens are often associated with quartz (p.168), heulandite (p.187), apophyllite (p.204), and other zeolites.

PROFILE

Monoclinic

3½–4

2.2

Perfect

Uneven, brittle

Colourless

Vitreous to pearly

red heulandite crystal

basalt groundmass

Red heulandite
In this specimen, tabular crystals of heulandite line a cavity in a basalt groundmass.

VARIANT

Colourless crystals Typical, colourless, coffin-shaped heulandite crystals

$CaAl_2Si_7O_{18} \cdot 6H_2O$

HEULANDITE

The name heulandite is used to refer to a series of five zeolite minerals, all of which look the same but vary in composition. The group was named in 1822 after the British collector and mineral dealer J.H. Heuland. Heulandite is usually colourless or white but can also be red, grey, yellow, pink, green, or brown. When found, crystals are elongated, tabular, and widest at the centre, creating a coffin shape. Occasionally, trapezohedral crystals are found. Heulandite specimens can also be granular or massive.

Heulandite forms at low temperatures (up to 200°C/400°F) in a wide range of environments: with other zeolites filling cavities in granites (pp.258–59), pegmatites (p.260), and basalts (p.273); in metamorphic rocks; and in weathered andesites (p.275) and diabases.

Oil refining
Heulandite and other zeolites are used to filter out unwanted molecules during oil refining.

tuft of acicular crystals

silky lustre

PROFILE

Monoclinic

5

2.3

Perfect

Uneven, brittle

White

Vitreous to silky

Cotton stone
When mesolite forms hair-like tufts, such as in this specimen, it is known as cotton stone.

VARIANTS

White mesolite Needles of mesolite on green apophyllite

Acicular mesolite
A radiating mass of needle-like crystals

$Na_2Ca_2(Al_6Si_9)O_{30} \cdot 8H_2O$

MESOLITE

First described in 1816, mesolite takes its name from two Greek words: *mesos*, which means "middle", and *lithos*, which means "stone" – a reference to the fact that this mineral is chemically intermediate in composition between scolecite and natrolite (p.186). Mesolite is structurally identical and similar in appearance to scolecite and natrolite, which makes it difficult to identify in hand specimens. Specimens can be white, pink, red, yellowish, green, or pale coloured. It occurs as long, slender needles, radiating masses, prisms, and, less commonly, compact masses or fibrous stalactites.

Mesolite is found in cavities in basalts (p.273) and andesites (p.275), where delicate, glassy prisms can occur with stilbite, heulandite (p.187), and green apophyllite (p.204). It is also found in hydrothermal veins. Exceptional specimens occur in Ahmadnagar and Poona, India; Neubauerberg, the Czech Republic; Naalsoy in the Faroe Islands; Victoria Land, Antarctica; and in Washington, Oregon, and Colorado, USA.

pseudocubic chabazite
This group of pseudocubic
chabazite crystals is from the Bay
of Fundy in Nova Scotia, Canada.

pseudocubic
chabazite crystal

basalt

PROFILE

Triclinic

4–5

2.0–2.2

Indistinct

Uneven, brittle

White

Vitreous

VARIANT

basalt

Chabazite in basalt A group
of white chabazite crystals in a
hollow in basalt

$(Na,Ca_{0.5},K)_4(Al_4Si_8O_{24})\cdot12H_2O$

CHABAZITE

This is a group of three common zeolite minerals that
look alike but have distinct properties: chabazite-Ca,
chabazite-K, and chabazite-Na. The name is derived from
the Greek *chabazios* or *chalazios*, both of which mean
"hailstone". Specimens are colourless, white, cream, pink,
red, orange, yellow, or brown. Chabazite crystals occur as
distorted cubes or pseudorhombohedrons consisting of
multiple twins. They may also be prismatic. Twinning is
common in all forms of chabazite.

Chabazite is found in cavities in pegmatites (p.260),
basalt (p.273), andesite (p.275), volcanic ash deposits, and
granitic (pp.258–59) and metamorphic (pp.288–303) rocks.
It is widespread, with crystals that are 2.5–5 cm (1–2 in) long
occurring in several locations. Chabazite and some other
zeolites have an open crystal structure that is sieve-like
and permits small molecules to pass through, while
preventing the passage of larger molecules. This structure,
for example, helps to filter methane from gases emitted
by decaying organic waste matter.

PROFILE

Cubic

5–5½

2.3

None

Subconchoidal, brittle

White

Vitreous

trapezohedral analcime crystal

Analcime trapezohedrons
This group of superbly crystallized analcime trapezohedrons from the Dean Quarry, Cornwall, England, rests on a bed of calcite crystals.

calcite crystal

vitreous lustre

VARIANT

Colourless analcime A single crystal of colourless analcime on a rock groundmass

$Na(AlSi_2)O_6 \cdot H_2O$

ANALCIME

Formerly grouped with the feldspathoids, analcime is now classified as a zeolite. A sodium aluminium silicate, analcime is named after the Greek word *analkimos*, which means "weak" – a reference to the weak electrical charge that this mineral produces when it is heated or rubbed. Specimens are usually colourless or white but can also be yellow, brown, pink, red, or orange. Most analcime crystals are trapezohedral. Variations in the ratio and order of the sodium–aluminium portion in analcime can lead to structural variations and variation in crystal system.

Analcime occurs in seams and cavities in granite (pp.258–59), basalt (p.273), gneiss (p.288), and diabase, associated with calcite (p.114), prehnite (p.205), and other zeolites. It also occurs in extensive beds formed by precipitation from alkaline lakes.

Silica dessicator
Made from analcime, silica gel, such as in this dessicator rapidly absorbs moisture and has many drying uses.

translucent serpentine

no cleavage

greasy lustre

Monoclinic or triclinic

3½–5½

2.5–2.6

Perfect but not visible

Conchoidal to splintery

White

Subvitreous to greasy, resinous, earthy, dull

Precious serpentine
This high-quality specimen is composed of many serpentine minerals. It is the kind often carved and sold as jade.

VARIANTS

Lizardite A specimen of this fine-grained serpentine mineral from Cornwall, UK

platy mass

Antigorite A specimen of this serpentine mineral with characteristic, corrugated plates

$(Mg,Fe,Ni)_3Si_2O_5(OH)_4$

SERPENTINE

Resembling snakeskin in appearance, serpentine is a group of at least 16 white, yellowish, green, or grey-green magnesium silicate minerals. Although they usually form mixtures, individual members of the group can sometimes be distinguished. Four common serpentine minerals include chrysotile (p.192), antigorite, lizardite, and amesite, which occur in platy or pseudohexagonal, columnar crystals. Although their chemistry is complex, these minerals look similar.

Serpentines are secondary minerals derived from the chemical alteration of olivine (p.232), the pyroxenes, and the amphiboles. It is found in areas where highly altered, deep-seated, silica-poor rocks are exposed, such as along the crests and axes of great folds, in island arcs, and in Alpine mountain chains.

Williamsite cabochon
A variety of serpentine, williamsite is an ornamental stone that is sometimes cut as an inexpensive gem.

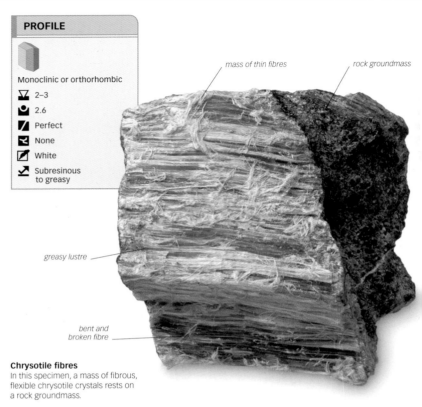

PROFILE

Monoclinic or orthorhombic

▽	2–3
🖤	2.6
⧄	Perfect
◪	None
▨	White
⤴	Subresinous to greasy

mass of thin fibres

rock groundmass

greasy lustre

bent and broken fibre

Chrysotile fibres
In this specimen, a mass of fibrous, flexible chrysotile crystals rests on a rock groundmass.

VARIANT

vein of chrysotile

Asbestos mineral A specimen of fibrous chrysotile

♣ $Mg_3Si_2O_5(OH)_4$

CHRYSOTILE

The fibrous serpentine mineral chrysotile is the most important asbestos mineral. Also known as white asbestos, it accounts for about 95 per cent of all asbestos in commercial use. Chrysotile fibres are tubes in which the structural layers of the mineral are rolled in the form of a spiral. Individual chrysotile fibres are white and silky, while aggregate fibres in veins are green or yellowish. The fibres are generally oriented across the vein and less than 1.3 cm (½ in) in length, but they can be longer. The mineral sometimes appears golden, and its name is derived from the Greek for "hair of gold".

Chrysotile can take three different forms: clinochrysotile, orthochrysotile, and parachrysotile. These are chemically identical, but orthochrysotile and parachrysotile have orthorhombic rather than monoclinic crystals. These forms are indistinguishable in hand specimens, and clinochrysotile and orthochrysotile may occur within the same fibre. Specimens occur as veins in altered peridotite (p.266) with other serpentine minerals.

riclinic or monoclinic

1

2.8

Perfect

Uneven to subconchoidal

White

Pearly to greasy

Foliated talc
This specimen of green, foliated talc exhibits its pearly lustre and mica-like cleavage.

greasy lustre

micaceous cleavage

foliated talc

VARIANT

pearly lustre

Pearly talc A pearly, tooth-like piece of talc

$Mg_3Si_4O_{10}(OH)_2$

TALC

Easily distinguishable by its extreme softness, talc is white, colourless, pale to dark green, or yellowish to brown. Crystals are rare; talc is most commonly found in foliated, fibrous, or massive aggregates. It is often found mixed with other minerals, such as serpentine (p.191) and calcite (p.114). Dense, high-purity talc is called steatite.

Talc is a metamorphic mineral found in veins and magnesium-rich rocks. It is often associated with serpentine, tremolite (p.219), and forsterite (p.232) and occurs as an alteration product of silica-poor igneous rocks. Talc is widespread and is found in most areas of the world where low-grade metamorphism occurs. The name soapstone is given to compact masses of talc and other minerals due to their soapy or greasy feel.

Talcum powder
Talc is the principal mineral used to make talcum powder. It acts as an astringent on the skin.

PROFILE

Triclinic or monoclinic

- 1–2
- 2.7–2.9
- Perfect
- Uneven
- White
- Pearly to dull

Pyrophyllite stars
This aggregate of pyrophyllite displays radiating, star-like groups of laths with associated quartz.

radiating mass of pyrophyllite crystals

quartz crystal

VARIANT

pyrophyllite crystals

Pyrophyllite on rock Groups of pyrophyllite crystals on a rock groundmass

 $Al_2Si_4O_{10}(OH)_2$

PYROPHYLLITE

An aluminium silicate hydroxide, pyrophyllite takes its name from the Greek words *pyr* and *phyllon*, which respectively mean "fire" and "leaf" – a reference to the mineral's tendency to exfoliate when heated. Pyrophyllite can be colourless, white, cream, brownish green, pale blue, or grey. It is usually found in granular masses of flattened lamellae. Pyrophyllite rarely forms distinct crystals, though it is sometimes found in coarse laths and radiating aggregates. Specimens are often so fine-grained that the mineral appears textureless.

Pyrophyllite forms by the metamorphism of aluminium-rich sedimentary rocks, such as bauxite (p.101). It is a good insulator and is used in heat-resistant applications, such as in making fire bricks.

High gloss
Bright, reflective flakes of powdered pyrophyllite are added to lipstick to give it a high sheen.

Colourful fuchsite
Fuchsite is a minor variety of white muscovite. Specimens such as this one are coloured by traces of chromium.

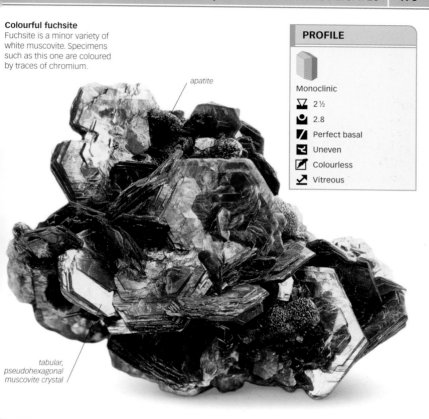

apatite

tabular,
pseudohexagonal
muscovite crystal

VARIANTS

Tabular crystals Silver-brown crystals of tabular muscovite

Platy muscovite Crystals of muscovite in a rock groundmass

Green fuchsite Bright green fuchsite in a rock groundmass

$KAl_2(Si_3Al)O_{10}(OH,F)_2$

MUSCOVITE

Also called common mica, potash mica, or isinglass, muscovite is the most common member of the mica group. Specimens are usually colourless or silvery white but can also be brown, light grey, pale green, or rose red. Muscovite typically occurs as tabular crystals with a hexagonal or pseudohexagonal outline. Crystals can be up to 3m (9¾ft) in diameter. Muscovite can also form thin, flat sheets and fine-grained aggregates. Fine-grained muscovite is called sericite or white mica, while bright green specimens rich in chromium are called fuchsite.

A common rock-forming mineral, muscovite occurs in metamorphic rocks, such as gneisses (p.288) and schists (pp.291–92), and in granites (pp.258–59), veins, and pegmatites (p.260). It is also found in some fine-grained sediments. Muscovite has considerable commercial importance. Its low iron content makes it a good electrical and thermal insulator. In Russia, thin, transparent sheets of muscovite, called muscovy glass, were used as window panes.

PROFILE

Monoclinic

⊽ 2

🔲 2.4–2.9

▨ Perfect basal

◪ Uneven

▨ Green

↗ Dull to earthy

aggregate of small grains

Grainy glauconite
This typically massive specimen of glauconite includes grains and shows a dull lustre.

dull lustre

VARIANTS

Glauconite sandstone
Sandstone with a high percentage of glauconite

Nodular glauconite Light green nodules of glauconite

♣ $(K,Na)(Mg,Al,Fe)_2(Si,Al)_4O_{10}(OH)_2$

GLAUCONITE

A member of the mica group, glauconite was named in 1828 after the Greek word *glaukos*, which means "blue-green" – a reference to the mineral's usual colour. Specimens can also be olive green to black-green. The mineral usually occurs as rounded aggregates or pellets of fine-grained, scaly particles. It weathers readily and easily crumbles to a fine powder.

A widespread silicate, glauconite forms in shallow marine environments, where it is used as a diagnostic mineral to identify continental-shelf deposits with slow rates of accumulation. The sedimentary rock greensand (p.309) is so called because of the green colour imparted by glauconite pellets, which in turn, may incorporate other minerals. Glauconite can also be found in impure limestone (p.319), chalk (p.321), and sand and clay formations. The mineral has long been used as a pigment in artists' oil paint, especially in the paintings of Russian icons. It has also been used in wall paintings dating back to Roman Gaul.

PROFILE

Monoclinic

⬙ 2–3³⁄₁₀

🏺 2.7–3.4

▨ Perfect basal

▨ Uneven

▨ Colourless

⬈ Vitreous to submetallic

rock groundmass

*thin, flexible
sheets of biotite*

Black mica
In this specimen, iron-rich,
tabular, pseudohexagonal crystals
of a biotite-series mica rest on a
rock groundmass.

VARIANT

*pearly
lustre*

*prismatic, twinned
phlogopite
crystals*

Phlogopite Crystals of the
magnesium end member of
the biotite solid-solution series

 $KFe_3,Mg_3(AlSi_3O_{10})(OH,F)_2$

BIOTITE

Once considered a mineral in its own right, biotite
is now recognized as a solid-solution series with the
mineral annite as the iron end member and phlogopite
as the magnesium end member. It was named in honour
of the French physicist Jean-Baptiste Biot in 1847. Micas of
the biotite series usually form large, tabular to short,
prismatic crystals that are often pseudohexagonal in
cross section. They also occur in thin layers or as scaly
aggregates or disseminated grains. Specimens are black
when iron-rich, and brown, pale yellow to tan, or bronze
with increasing magnesium content. They readily cleave
into thin, flexible sheets.

Biotite-series micas are widespread. They are a key
constituent of many igneous and metamorphic rocks,
including granites (pp.258–59), nepheline syenites (p.262),
gneisses (p.288), and schists (pp.291–92). They are also
found in potassium-rich hydrothermal deposits and some
clastic sedimentary rocks. Biotite is used extensively to
date rocks.

PROFILE

Monoclinic

▽ 2½–3½

◉ 3.0

▨ Perfect basal

▧ Uneven

▥ Colourless

↗ Vitreous to pearly

Distinctive colour
Numerous violet pseudohexagonal lepidolite crystals protrude from this pegmatite specimen.

vitreous lustre

granitic pegmatite

tabular lepidolite crystal

VARIANT

Botryoidal lepidolite
Lepidolite in botryoidal habit

$K(Li,Al_3)(AlSi_3)O_{10}(OH,F)_2$

LEPIDOLITE

A light mica, lepidolite is Earth's most common lithium-bearing mineral. Its name is derived from two Greek words: *lepidos*, which means "scale", and *lithos*, which means "stone". Although typically pale lilac, specimens can also be colourless, violet, pale yellow, or grey. Lepidolite crystals may appear pseudohexagonal. The mineral is also found as botryoidal or kidney-like masses and fine- to coarse-grained, interlocking plates. Its perfect cleavage yields thin, flexible sheets.

Lepidolite occurs in granitic pegmatites (p.260), where it is associated with other lithium minerals, such as beryl (p.225) and topaz (p.234). The mineral is economically important as a major source of lithium, which is used to make glass and enamels. It is also a major source of the rare alkali metals rubidium and cesium.

Lithium battery
Extracted from lepidolite, the metal lithium has many industrial uses, such as in lithium batteries.

Vermiculite layers
This specimen of vermiculite, mined in Pennsylvania, USA, shows the mineral's foliated habit.

pseudohexagonal outline

foliated habit

PROFILE

Monoclinic

 1–2

 2.6

 Perfect

 Uneven

White

Oily to earthy

 $(Mg,Fe,Al)_3(Al,Si)_4O_{10}(OH)\cdot 4H_2O$

VERMICULITE

The name vermiculite is applied to a group of mica minerals in which various chemical substitutions occur in the molecular structure. Vermiculite may be completely interlayered with other micas and clay-like minerals. Specimens are green, golden yellow, or brown in colour. Vermiculite usually forms tabular, pseudohexagonal crystals or platy aggregates.

Vermiculite occurs as large pseudomorphs replacing biotite (p.197), as small particles in soils and ancient sediments, and at the interface between feldspar-rich and iron- and magnesium-rich igneous rocks. It also forms by hydrothermal alteration of iron-bearing micas. When heated to nearly 300°C (572°F), vermiculite can expand quickly and strongly to 20 times its original thickness.

Potting soil
Expanded vermiculite is a good growing medium for new plants; it retains water and offers good aeration.

PROFILE

Monoclinic

- 1–2
- 2.1
- Perfect
- Uneven
- White to buff
- Earthy

dull, earthy surface

massive habit

Massive bentonite
Bentonite is always found in massive form, as in the specimen shown here. Under magnification, tiny, hexagonal plates are visible.

VARIANTS

Desert cracking Loss of water from bentonite clays causes shrinkage and cracking

Bentonite sediments Layers of bentonite-rich clay

$(Na,Ca_{0.5})_{0.33}(Al,Mg)_2Si_4O_{10}(OH)_2 \cdot nH_2O$

BENTONITE

This group of minerals are all kinds of clay that expand as they absorb water and shrink as they dry. In regions underlain by bentonites, this property causes immense problems with building foundations. There are three bentonite minerals, each named after the respective dominant element: potassium bentonite, sodium bentonite, and calcium bentonite. The minerals are generally yellow, white, or grey in colour. They occur as microscopic crystals and are earthy and frequently stained.

Although the term bentonite has been used for clay beds of uncertain origin, this mineral group generally forms from volcanic ash that has weathered in the presence of water. Important industrial minerals, bentonites are used as sealants and in oil drilling.

Potting clay
The potting clay used to make this bowl contains bentonite, which is also used in bricks and ceramics.

Powdery kaolinite
In this specimen, powdery kaolinite coats a piece of granite.

powdery kaolinite

earthy lustre

VARIANTS

Blocky kaolinite Blocky, typically white kaolinite

Iron staining A specimen of kaolinite mixed with iron oxides, which gives it an orange colour

$Al_2Si_2O_5(OH)_4$

KAOLINITE

Clay minerals are far removed in their outward appearance from more attractive and glamorous minerals, such as gold and diamond. Yet, by providing the raw material for brick, pottery, and tiles, they have played a vital part in the progress of human civilization. Important among these minerals is kaolinite. Kaolinite forms white, microscopic, pseudohexagonal plates in compact or granular masses and in mica-like piles. Three other minerals – dickite, nacrite, and halloysite – are chemically identical to kaolinite but crystallize in the monoclinic system. All four have been found together and are often visually indistinguishable.

Kaolinite is a natural product of the alteration of mica, plagioclase, and sodium–potassium feldspars under the influence of water, dissolved carbon dioxide, and organic acids. It is used in agriculture; as a filler in food, such as chocolate; mixed with pectin as an anti-diarrhoeal; as a paint extender; as a strengthener in rubber; and as a dusting agent in foundry operations.

pale, earthy mass of illite

Illite mass
One of the major clay minerals, illite is usually found as pale, earthy masses.

VARIANT

Solid illite Solid masses of illite are occasionally found

$K_{0.65}Al_2Al_{0.65}Si_{3.35}O_{10}(OH)_2$

ILLITE

Once regarded as a clay mineral, illite is now classified as a group of mica minerals that bear many structural similarities to the white mica muscovite (p.195). Illite takes its name from its type location in Illinois, USA. It is white, but impurities may tint it grey and other pale colours. It occurs as fine-grained aggregates. Individual hexagonal crystals can only be seen using an electron microscope. Because of its minute crystals, illite can only be positively identified by x-ray diffraction. The degree of crystallization of illite has been used as an indicator of metamorphic grade in clay-bearing metamorphic rocks.

Illite is found in sedimentary rocks and soils. It is the most abundant clay mineral in shales (pp.313–14) and clays. It appears to be derived from the weathering of muscovite and feldspar (pp.173–81).

Mud bricks
Ancient buildings, such as the Funerary Temple in Egypt, were often made from clays bearing illite.

Chrysocolla with azurite
In this specimen, chrysocolla can be seen with the carbonate mineral azurite in a rock groundmass.

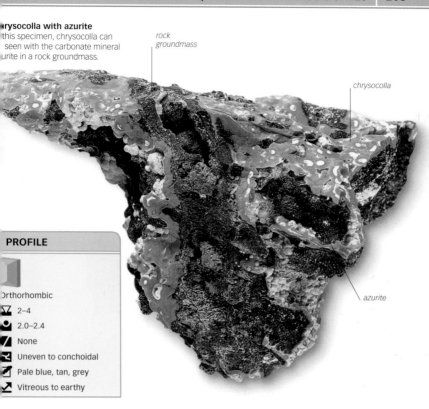

rock groundmass

chrysocolla

azurite

PROFILE

Orthorhombic

2–4

2.0–2.4

None

Uneven to conchoidal

Pale blue, tan, grey

Vitreous to earthy

VARIANTS

Rough chrysocolla
A specimen intergrown with turquoise and malachite

chrysocolla

Cabochon Green chrysocolla within reddish iron oxide

$Cu_2H_2(Si_2O_5)(OH)_4 \cdot nH_2O$

CHRYSOCOLLA

The term chrysocolla was first used by the Greek philosopher Theophrastus in 315 BCE to refer to various materials used in soldering gold. The name is derived from two Greek words: *chrysos*, which means "gold", and *kolla*, which means "glue". A copper aluminium silicate, chrysocolla is generally blue-green in colour. Specimens are commonly fine grained and massive. Crystals are very rare but when found occur as botryoidal, radiating aggregates.

An occasional ore of copper, chrysocolla is a decomposition product of copper minerals, especially in arid regions. It is frequently intergrown with other minerals, such as quartz (p.168), chalcedony (p.169), and opal (p.172), to yield a gemstone variety. Gemstones can weigh more than 2.3 kg (5 lb).

Chrysocolla bracelet
Rich blue-green chrysocolla, such as the cabochon in this antique bracelet, is highly prized as a gemstone.

Green apophyllite
In this specimen, green apophyllite occurs in a basalt groundmass with a white zeolite mineral.

green apophyllite

white zeolite

basalt

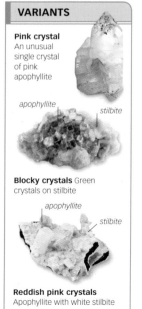

Pink crystal
An unusual single crystal of pink apophyllite

apophyllite

stilbite

Blocky crystals Green crystals on stilbite

apophyllite

stilbite

Reddish pink crystals
Apophyllite with white stilbite

$KCa_4Si_8O_{20}(F,OH) \cdot 8H_2O$ (fluorapophyllite)

APOPHYLLITE

The name apophyllite comes from the Greek words *apo* and *phyllazein*, which mean "to get" and "leaf" respectively – a reference to the way in which the mineral separates into flakes or layers when it is heated. Once considered to be a single mineral, apophyllite is now divided into two distinct species – fluorapophyllite and hydroxyapophyllite. These species form a solid-solution series in which fluorine can predominate over oxygen and hydrogen, and vice versa. Apophyllite specimens are green, pink, colourless, or white. Crystals are transparent or translucent and up to 20 cm (8 in) in length. They occur as square-sided, striated prisms with flat ends and may appear cubic. Apophyllite crystals may also show steep pyramidal terminations.

The mineral frequently occurs with zeolite minerals in basalt (p.273) and less commonly in cavities in granite (pp.258–59). It is also found in metamorphic rocks and in hydrothermal deposits. Colourless and green specimens from India are faceted as collectors' gems.

PROFILE

Orthorhombic

6–6 ½

2.9

Distinct basal

Uneven, brittle

White

Vitreous

Botryoidal prehnite
A group of radiating crystal masses of prehnite resting on a rock groundmass gives a botryoidal form to this specimen.

radiating prehnite crystal

rock groundmass

vitreous lustre

VARIANT

calcite

prehnite

Green prehnite Spherical masses of prehnite occuring with white calcite on a rock groundmass

$Ca_2Al_2Si_3O_{10}(OH)_2$

PREHNITE

A calcium aluminium silicate, prehnite was named in 1789 after its discoverer Hendrik von Prehn, a Dutch military officer. Specimens can be pale to mid green, tan, pale yellow, grey, light blue, or white. Prehnite commonly occurs as globular, spherical, or stalactitic aggregates of fine to coarse crystals. Rare individual crystals are short prismatic to tabular with square cross sections. Many of these have curved faces.

Prehnite is often found lining cavities in volcanic rocks, associated with calcite (p.114) and zeolites (pp.185–90), and in mineral veins in granite (pp.258–59). Crystals up to several centimetres long come from Canada. Transparent specimens from Australia and Scotland are faceted for gem collectors.

White cabochon
Prehnite gems, such as this creamy white cabochon with dark inclusions, are almost too soft to wear.

PROFILE

Orthorhombic

2–2 ½

2.1–2.3

Good but rarely seen

Uneven

White

Dull to earthy

Massive sepiolite
This specimen of massive sepiolite shows a characteristic dull, earthy lustre.

massive habit

dull lustre

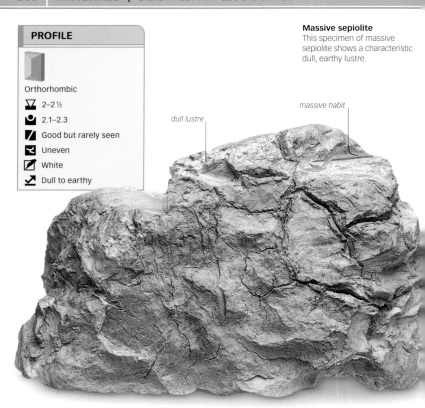

VARIANT

massive habit

Meerschaum A specimen of massive, white sepiolite

$Mg_4Si_6O_{15}(OH)_2.6H_2O$

SEPIOLITE

A compact, clay-like, often porous mineral, sepiolite is best known by its popular name *meerschaum*, which is the German word for "sea-foam". The name sepiolite comes from the mineral's resemblance to the light and porous bone of cuttlefish from the genus Sepia. Sepiolite is usually white or grey and may be tinted yellow, brown, or green. It is usually found in nodular masses of interlocking fibres, which give it a toughness contrary to its mineralogical softness. Sepiolite also occurs in porous aggregates.

Sepiolite is an alteration product of minerals such as magnesite (p.118) and rocks, such as serpentinite (p.298). It is found as irregular nodules in Turkey and elsewhere, and in large sedimentary deposits.

Meerschaum cigar holder
Sepiolite is used in carved tobacco pipes and cigar holders, which develop a brown patina when smoked.

Purple-brown pigeonite
This specimen of pigeonite comes from the Kovdor Pit, Kola Peninsula, Russia.

perfect cleavage

cleavable mass

PROFILE

Monoclinic

 6

 3.2–3.5

 Good

 Uneven to conchoidal, brittle

White to pale brown

Vitreous

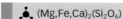 (Mg,Fe,Ca)$_2$(Si$_2$O$_6$)

PIGEONITE

A member of the pyroxene group of minerals, pigeonite is named after Pigeon Point, Minnesota, USA – the locality where it was first identified. Specimens are brown, purplish brown, or greenish brown to black in colour. Pigeonite is generally found as disseminated grains. Well-formed crystals are relatively rare. An iron-rich variety of pigeonite is sometimes called ferropigeonite.

Pigeonite is an important mineral in lunar rocks and also occurs in meteorites (pp.335–37). It is found in lavas and smaller intrusive rock bodies as the dominant pyroxene and as an important component of dolerites (p.268) and andesites (p.275). The temperature limit of pigeonite formation indicates the crystallization temperature of the magma from which it has originated. Maria – the large, dark, flat areas of the Moon once believed to be seas – are in fact basalts (p.273) containing pigeonite. Notable localities on Earth include Skaergaard, Greenland; Mull, Scotland; Labrador, Canada; Mount Wellington, Tasmania; and Goose Creek, Virginia, and New Jersey, USA.

Orthorhombic

⬙ 5–6

📍 3.1–3.9

▨ Good to perfect

▧ Uneven

▧ Grey to white

⬈ Vitreous

Prismatic crystals
This mass of small, prismatic
enstatite crystals rests on
a rock groundmass.

*small, prismatic
crystals*

rock groundmass

VARIANTS

Single crystal A large crystal
from Telemark, Norway

*fibrous
mass*

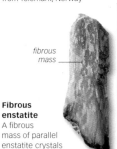

**Fibrous
enstatite**
A fibrous
mass of parallel
enstatite crystals

♣ $Mg_2Si_2O_6$

ENSTATITE

The pyroxene mineral enstatite takes its name from
the Greek word *enstates*, which means "opponent" –
a reference to the use of this mineral as a refractory
"opponent" of heat in the linings of ovens and kilns.
Specimens are colourless, pale yellow, or pale green.
They become darker and turn greenish brown to black
with increasing iron content. Enstatite generally occurs
as massive aggregates or disseminated
grains. Well-formed crystals, when
found, tend to be short prisms, often
with complex terminations. Enstatite
is also found as fibrous masses of
parallel, needle-like crystals.

A widespread mineral, enstatite
forms a solid-solution series with
ferrosilite. The mineral usually
occurs in magnesium- and iron-
rich igneous rocks and in
meteorites (pp.335–37).

Mixed-cut enstatite
Recovered from Myanmar
and Sri Lanka, facet-grade
enstatite, such as this gem,
is mainly cut for collectors.

PROFILE

Monoclinic

▼ 6

◉ 3.5–3.6

◢ Good to perfect

◣ Uneven

◢ Yellow-green to pale green

◿ Vitreous

Terminated crystals
This specimen is composed of a group of prismatic aegirine crystals with feldspar. The crystals have full terminations.

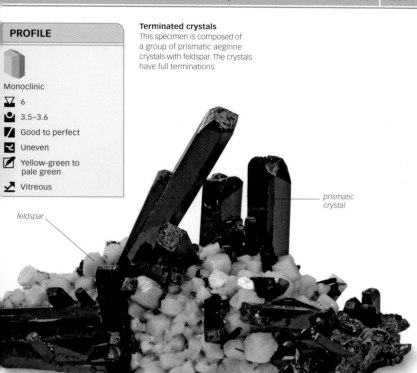

prismatic crystal

feldspar

VARIANTS

Parallel crystals A mass of prismatic aegirine crystals aligned in parallel

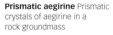

Prismatic aegirine Prismatic crystals of aegirine in a rock groundmass

$NaFe(Si_2O_6)$

AEGIRINE

The sodium iron silicate aegirine was discovered in Norway and named in 1835 after Aegir, the Scandinavian god of the sea. Aegirine is also known as acmite after the Greek word *acme*, which means "point" or "edge" – a reference to the mineral's typically pointed crystals. Specimens are dark green, reddish brown, or black in colour. Aegirine occurs as needle-like or fibrous crystals that form attractive, radiating sprays. The crystals have steep or blunt terminations and are often striated along the length. Prism faces are often lustrous and striated, while the faces of terminations are often etched and dull.

A pyroxene, aegirine forms a solid-solution series with hedenbergite and diopside (p.210). It is found in magnesium- and iron-rich igneous rocks, especially syenitic pegmatites (p.260) and syenites (p.262). It is also found in schists (pp.291–92), metamorphosed iron-rich sediments, and metamorphic rocks altered by circulating fluids. Notable localities include Kongsberg, Norway and Mont St.-Hilaire, Canada.

PROFILE

Monoclinic

◪ 6

🔹 3.3

▨ Distinct in two directions at almost right angles

⬏ Uneven

▨ White to pale green

⬊ Vitreous

Prismatic diopside
This specimen of diopside in a rock groundmass comes from St. Marcel, Valle d'Aosta, Italy.

quartz

prismatic diopside crystal

rock groundmass

VARIANT

Violane A blue, crystalline variant of diopside

🜨 CaMg(Si$_2$O$_6$)

DIOPSIDE

A member of the pyroxene family, diopside takes its name from the Greek for "double" and "appearance", a reference to the variable appearance of the mineral. Specimens can be colourless but are more often bottle green, brownish green, or light green in colour. Diopside occurs in the form of equant to prismatic crystals that are usually nearly square in section. Crystals are less commonly tabular. This mineral can also form columnar, sheet-like, granular, or massive aggregates.

Most diopside is metamorphic and found in metamorphosed silica-rich limestones (p.319) and dolomites (p.320) and in iron-rich contact metamorphic rocks. It also occurs in peridotites (p.266), kimberlites (p.269), and other igneous rocks.

Chrome diopside
Emerald-green diopside, such as the gem shown here, is chromium-rich and is also known as chrome diopside.

PROFILE

Monoclinic

⬙ 5½–6

◆ 3.3

▧ Distinct in two directions at almost right angles

▨ Uneven to subconchoidal

▧ Pale brown to greenish grey

↗ Vitreous to dull

Single crystal
In this specimen, a single, large, dark-coloured augite crystal rests on a groundmass of volcanic tuff.

dark, nearly opaque crystal

good cleavage in two directions nearly at right angles

volcanic tuff

VARIANTS

Greenish black augite
A mass of greenish black, prismatic augite crystals

Prismatic crystal A short prismatic augite crystal from the Czech Republic

♣ $(Ca,Na)(Mg,Fe,Ti,Al)(Al,Si)_2O_6$

AUGITE

The most common pyroxene, augite is named after the Greek word *augites*, which means "brightness" – a reference to its occasional shiny appearance. Most augite has a dull, dark green, brown, or black finish. Augite occurs chiefly as short, thick, prismatic crystals with a square or octagonal cross section and sometimes as large, cleavable masses. It occurs in a solid-solution series in which diopside (p.210) and hedenbergite are the end members.

Augite is common in silica-poor rocks and various other dark-coloured igneous rocks, as well as igneous rocks of intermediate silica content. It also occurs in some metamorphic rocks formed at high temperatures (575°C/1,065°F or above). Augite is a common constituent of lunar basalts and some meteorites (pp.335–37). Notable crystal localities are in Germany, the Czech Republic, Italy, Russia, Japan, Mexico, Canada, and USA. As it is difficult to distinguish between augite, diopside, and hedenbergite in hand specimens, all pyroxenes are often identified as augite.

PROFILE

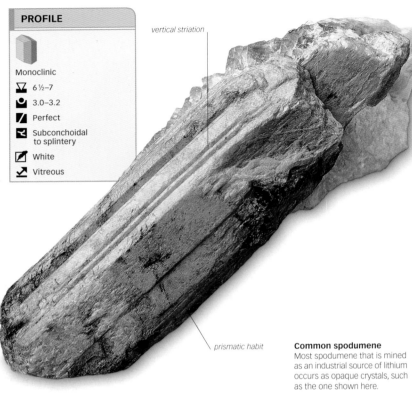

Monoclinic

⬥ 6½–7

⬥ 3.0–3.2

⬥ Perfect

⬥ Subconchoidal to splintery

⬥ White

⬥ Vitreous

vertical striation

prismatic habit

Common spodumene
Most spodumene that is mined as an industrial source of lithium occurs as opaque crystals, such as the one shown here.

VARIANTS

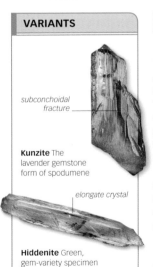

subconchoidal fracture

Kunzite The lavender gemstone form of spodumene

elongate crystal

Hiddenite Green, gem-variety specimen of spodumene

$LiAl(Si_2O_6)$

SPODUMENE

A member of the pyroxene group, spodumene is named after the Greek word *spodumenos*, which means "reduced to ashes" – a reference to the mineral's common ash-grey colour. It can also be pink, lilac, or green. Crystals are prismatic, flattened, and typically striated along their length. Gem varieties of the mineral usually exhibit strong pleochroism.

Spodumene is an important ore of lithium. It occurs in lithium-bearing granite pegmatite dykes, often with other lithium-bearing minerals, such as eucryptite and lepidolite (p.198). One of the largest single crystals of any mineral ever found was a spodumene specimen from South Dakota, USA, 14.3m (47 ft) long and 90 tonnes (88½ tons) in weight.

Strengthened glass
Spodumene is a key source of lithium, which forms lithium fluoride that is used to add strength to glass.

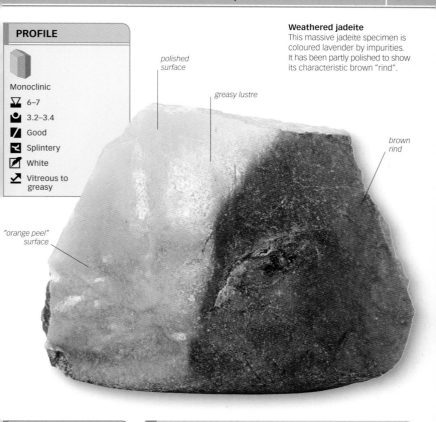

PROFILE

Monoclinic

- 6–7
- 3.2–3.4
- Good
- Splintery
- White
- Vitreous to greasy

"orange peel" surface

polished surface

greasy lustre

Weathered jadeite
This massive jadeite specimen is coloured lavender by impurities. It has been partly polished to show its characteristic brown "rind".

brown rind

VARIANTS

Lilac jadeite A rare and valuable variety of jadeite

polished surface

Imperial jade A rich green specimen of imperial jade

rough, violet mass

Violet jadeite A specimen of rare, valuable, violet jadeite

$Na(Al,Fe)Si_2O_6$

JADEITE

A pyroxene mineral, jadeite is one of the two minerals that are referred to as jade. The other is nephrite (p.217), which is a variety of either tremolite (p.219) or actinolite (p.220). Pure jadeite is white in colour. Specimens can be coloured green by iron, lilac by manganese and iron, or pink, purple, brown, red, blue, black, orange, or yellow by inclusions of other minerals. Jadeite is made up of interlocking, blocky, granular crystals and commonly has a sugary or granular texture. Crystals are short prisms. They are rare but when found are usually in hollows within massive material.

Jadeite occurs in metamorphic rocks formed at high pressure. Although usually recovered as alluvial pebbles and boulders, it is also found in the rocks in which it originally formed.

Jade mask
Jadeite, such as that used in this 18th-century mask, had cultural value for Central and South American Indians.

PROFILE

Triclinic

⚡ 4½–5

🔨 2.9

◪ Perfect

✂ Uneven to splintery

◰ White

⚡ Vitreous to silky

Crystalline wollastonite
The mass of parallel crystals in this specimen are shaped like coarse blades. They show silky lustre and a splintery fracture.

fibrous mass
of crystals

splintery
fracture

VARIANTS

Massive wollastonite
A piece of massive wollastonite

Coarse crytals A mass of coarsely crystalline wollastonite from New York

🜨 $CaSiO_3$

WOLLASTONITE

A valuable industrial mineral, wollastonite is white, grey, or pale green in colour. It occurs as rare, tabular crystals or massive, coarse-bladed, foliated, or fibrous masses. Its crystals are usually triclinic, although its structure has seven variants, one of which is monoclinic. These variations are however, indistinguishable in hand specimens.

Wollastonite forms as a result of the contact metamorphism of limestones (p.319) and in igneous rocks that are contaminated by carbon-rich inclusions. It can be accompanied by other calcium-containing silicates, such as diopside (p.210), tremolite (p.219), epidote (p.230), and grossular garnet (p.245). Wollastonite also appears in regionally metamorphosed rocks in schists (pp.291–92), slates (p.293), and phyllites (p.294).

Ceramic tile
Wollastonite is widely used in ceramics, such as the tile shown here. It is also an ideal base for fluxes and glazes.

Triclinic

6

3.5–3.7

Perfect

Conchoidal to uneven

White

Vitreous

vitreous lustre

Massive rhodonite
This specimen of rough rhodonite shows the intense colouring and fine texture of the best gem-quality material.

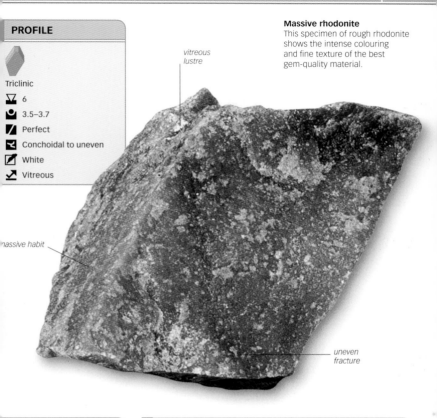

massive habit

uneven fracture

VARIANT

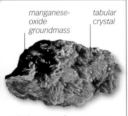

manganese-oxide groundmass

tabular crystal

Tabular crystals Aggregates of tabular crystals

$(Mn,Ca)_5(Si_5O_{15})$

RHODONITE

The semi-precious gemstone rhodonite takes its name from the Greek word *rhodon*, which means "rose" – a reference to the mineral's typical pink colour. Crystals are uncommon but are rounded when found. Rhodonite usually occurs as masses or grains and is often coated or veined with manganese oxides.

Rhodonite is found in various manganese ores, often with rhodochrosite (p.121) or as a product of rhodochrosite that has undergone metamorphism. It has been used as a manganese ore in India but is more often mined as a gem and an ornamental stone. Rhodonite is primarily cut *en cabochon* as beads. Massive rhodonite is relatively tough and is good as a carving medium. Transparent rhodonite is rare. Although extremely fragile, it can be faceted for collectors.

Rhodonite box
Black-veined rhodonite, such as that used here, is relatively tough and is preferred by many carvers.

Radiating crystals
This specimen is a mass of fibrous, radiating crystals of anthophyllite with vitreous lustre.

vitreous lustre

mass of fibrous, radiating crystals

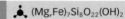
$(Mg,Fe)_7Si_8O_{22}(OH)_2$

ANTHOPHYLLITE

The name anthophyllite comes from the Latin word *anthophyllum*, which means "clove" – a reference to the mineral's clove-brown to dark brown colour. Specimens can also be pale green, grey, or white. Anthophyllite is usually found in columnar to fibrous masses. Single crystals are uncommon; when found, they are prismatic and usually unterminated. The iron and magnesium content in anthophyllite is variable. The mineral is called ferroanthophyllite when it is iron-rich, sodium-anthophyllite when sodium is present, and magnesioanthophyllite when magnesium is dominant. Titanium and manganese may also be present in the anthophyllite structure.

Anthophyllite forms by the regional metamorphism of iron- and magnesium-rich rocks, especially silica-poor igneous rocks. It is an important component of some gneisses (p.288) and crystalline schists (pp.291–92) and is found worldwide. Anthophyllite is one of several minerals referred to as asbestos.

Polished nephrite
This small boulder of nephrite has been sliced and polished to reveal its quality.

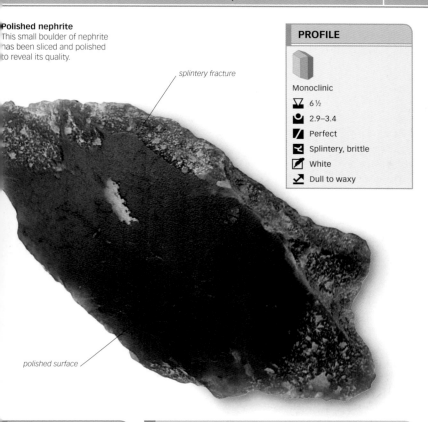

splintery fracture

polished surface

VARIANT

Light green nephrite A mass of light green nephrite

$Ca_2(Mg,Fe)_5(Si_8O_{22})(OH)_2$

NEPHRITE

Not a true mineral name, the term nephrite applies to the tough, compact form of either tremolite (p.219) or actinolite (p.220). Both are calcium magnesium silicate hydroxides and structurally identical, except that in actinolite some of the magnesium is replaced by iron. Nephrite is dark green when iron-rich and creamy white when magnesium-rich. Specimens are composed of a mat of tightly interlocked fibres, creating a stone that is tougher than steel.

Nephrite forms in metamorphic environments, especially in metamorphosed iron- and magnesium-rich rocks, where it is associated with serpentine (p.191) and talc (p.193). It is also found in regionally metamorphosed areas where dolomites (p.320) are intruded by iron- and magnesium-rich igneous rocks.

Nephrite tiki
Hei tikis, such as this one made of nephrite, are worn by the Maori of New Zealand.

PROFILE

Monoclinic

⊻ 5–6

◔ 3.1–3.3

◨ Perfect

◩ Uneven, brittle

◪ White to grey

↗ Vitreous

prismatic hornblende crystal

vitreous lustre

vertical striation

Hornblende crystals
This specimen consists of a group of prismatic hornblende crystals embedded in a rock groundmass.

VARIANTS

white rock groundmass

Prismatic hornblende
Prismatic crystals in a rock groundmass

Massive hornblende
A piece of massive hornblende

six-sided crystal

Single crystal
A single, short prismatic crystal of hornblende

♣ eg: $Ca_2(Fe^2,Mg)_4(Al,Fe^3)(Si_7Al)O_{22}(OH,F)_2$

HORNBLENDE

The name hornblende is applied to a group of minerals that can be distinguished from each other only by detailed chemical analysis. The two end-member hornblendes – iron-rich ferrohornblende and magnesium-rich magnesiohornblende – are both calcium-rich and monoclinic in crystal structure. Other elements, such as chromium, titanium, and nickel, can also appear in the crystal structures of the group. The concentrations of these elements are an indicator of the metamorphic grade of the mineral.

Specimens are green, dark green, or brownish green to black in colour. Hornblende crystals are usually bladed and unterminated, and they often show a pseudohexagonal cross section. Well-formed crystals are short to long prisms. Hornblende also occurs as cleavable masses and radiating groups. The mineral forms in metamorphic rocks, especially gneisses (p.288), hornblende schists, amphibolites (p.296), and magnesium- and iron-rich igneous rocks.

Tremolite crystals
This specimen has plume-like aggregates of white, bladed tremolite crystals.

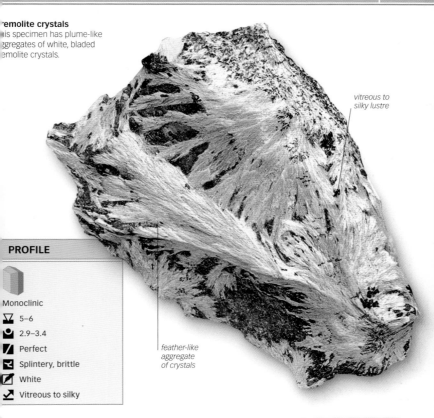

vitreous to silky lustre

feather-like aggregate of crystals

PROFILE

Monoclinic

5–6

2.9–3.4

Perfect

Splintery, brittle

White

Vitreous to silky

VARIANTS

silvery, radiating crystals

Radiating tremolite Radiating crystals of silvery tremolite

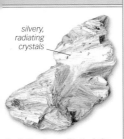

Asbestos fibres Tremolite in fibrous form

$Ca_2(Mg,Fe^2)_5Si_8O_{22}(OH)_2$

TREMOLITE

A calcium magnesium silicate, tremolite forms a solid-solution series with ferroactinolite (p.220), where iron substitutes in increasing amounts for magnesium. The colour of tremolite varies with increasing iron content from colourless to white in pure tremolite to grey, grey-green, green, dark green and nearly black in other specimens. Traces of manganese may tint tremolite pink or violet. When well-formed, crystals are short to long prisms. More commonly, tremolite forms unterminated bladed crystals, parallel aggregates of bladed crystals, or radiating groups. Tremolite and actinolite both form thin, parallel, flexible fibres up to 25 cm (10 in) in length, which are used commercially as asbestos. Tremolite is known as nephrite jade when it is massive and fine-grained.

The mineral is abundant and widespread. It is the product of both thermal and regional metamorphism and is an indicator of metamorphic grade since it converts to diopside (p.210) at high temperatures (575°C/1,065°F or above).

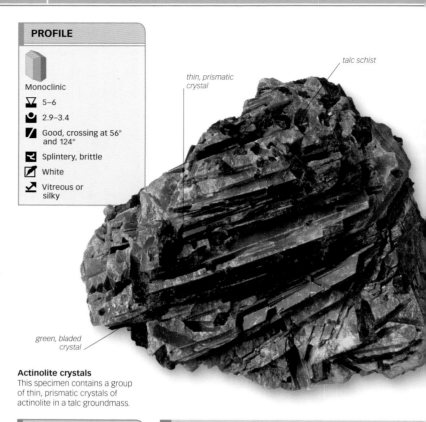

talc schist

thin, prismatic
crystal

green, bladed
crystal

Actinolite crystals
This specimen contains a group
of thin, prismatic crystals of
actinolite in a talc groundmass.

VARIANT

Grey-green actinolite
Crystals of actinolite, some of
which have been powdered

$Ca_2(Mg,Fe^{2+})_5Si_8O_{22}(OH)_2$

ACTINOLITE

Actinolite is an abundant mineral. It is in the middle
of a solid-solution series of calcium, iron, and magnesium
silicates that also includes ferroactinolite and tremolite
(p.219). There is complete substitution in the series
between iron and magnesium, but all have the same
structure. Actinolite was named in 1794 after the Greek
word *aktis*, which means "ray" – an allusion to its radiating
prismatic habit. Specimens range from green to dark green
to black. Well-formed crystals are short to long prisms.
Actinolite usually occurs as unterminated bladed crystals,
parallel aggregates of bladed crystals, or radiating groups.
It is sometimes found as needle-like or fibrous crystals up
to 25 cm (10 in) long. When in this form, it is one of the
minerals that are called asbestos. Massive, fine-grained
actinolite and tremolite are both called nephrite jade.

Actinolite is an amphibole mineral and forms as a
product of low- to medium-grade thermal and regional
metamorphism. Good crystals come from Edwards, New
York, USA, and Kantiwa, Afghanistan.

PROFILE

Monoclinic

6

3.2

Distinct

Uneven to conchoidal

Grey-blue

Vitreous to pearly

dark blue-green glaucophane

fuchsite

pyrite

Italian glaucophane
This specimen from Polloni in Piedmont, Italy, shows glaucophane with fuchsite and pyrite.

VARIANT

prismatic crystal

Glaucophane crystals
Crystals of glaucophane in a rock groundmass

$Na_2(Mg_3Al_2)Si_8O_{22}(OH)_2$

GLAUCOPHANE

The mineral is named after two Greek words: *glaukos*, which means "bluish green"; and *phainesthai*, which means "to appear". Specimens can be grey, lavender blue, or bluish black. Crystals are slender, often lath-like prisms, with lengthwise striations. Twinning is common. Glaucophane can also be massive, fibrous, or granular. When iron replaces the magnesium in its structure, it is known as ferroglaucophane.

Glaucophane occurs in schists (pp.291–92) formed by high-pressure metamorphism of sodium-rich sediments at low temperatures (up to 200°C/400°F) or by the introduction of sodium into the process. Glaucophane is often accompanied by jadeite (p.213), epidote (p.230), almandine (p.243), and chlorite. It is one of the minerals that are referred to as asbestos. Glaucophane and its associated minerals are known as the glaucophane metamorphic facies. The presence of these minerals indicates the range of temperatures and pressures under which metamorphism occurs.

group of prismatic crystals

Riebeckite crystals
The long, striated crystals characteristic of riebeckite are clearly visible in this specimen.

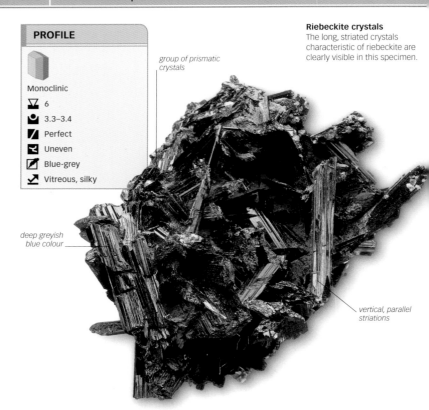

deep greyish blue colour

vertical, parallel striations

VARIANT

blue asbestos

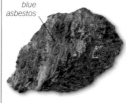

Crocidolite Fibres of blue riebeckite, which constitute blue asbestos

$Na_2(Fe^{2+}_3Fe^{3+}_2)Si_8O_{22}(OH)_2$

RIEBECKITE

A sodium iron silicate, riebeckite is one of the several minerals called asbestos. It was named after Emil Riebeck, a 19th-century German explorer. Though riebeckite specimens are generally greyish blue to dark blue, their colour can vary depending on the concentration of iron in their structure. Riebeckite can occur as prismatic, striated crystals or sometimes as massive or fibrous aggregates.

This mineral occurs in feldspar- and quartz-rich igneous rocks. These include granites (pp.258–59), syenites (p.262) and, feldspar- and quartz-rich volcanic rocks, especially sodium-rich rhyolites (p.278). Riebeckite granite is found on the island of Ailsa Craig in western Scotland and is locally known as ailsite. Ailsite is used to manufacture stones used in the sport of curling.

Tiger's eye ring
Crocidolite, a variant of riebeckite, forms the gemstone tiger's eye when it is silica-saturated.

PROFILE

Orthorhombic

7–7½

2.6

Moderate to poor

Conchoidal to uneven

White

Vitreous to greasy

Cordierite crystals
This group of short prismatic, dark grey cordierite crystals occurs in a rock groundmass.

rock groundmass

cordierite crystal

VARIANTS

Single crystal A large crystal of cordierite in matrix

Iolite A polished gemstone of cordierite called iolite

$(Mg,Fe)_2Al_4Si_5O_{18}$

CORDIERITE

The mineral is named after the French geologist Pierre L.A. Cordier, who first described it in 1813. Specimens can be blue, violet-blue, grey, or blue-green. Gem-quality blue cordierite or iolite is also known as water sapphire because of its colour. Cordierite is pleochroic, exhibiting three different colours when viewed from different angles. Its crystals are prismatic, and the best blue colour is seen along their length.

Cordierite occurs in high-grade, thermally metamorphosed, alumina-rich rocks. It is also found in gneisses (p.288) and schists (pp.291–92) and more rarely in granites (pp.258–59), pegmatites (p.260), and veins of quartz (p.168). Cordierite is important in the production of ceramics used in catalytic converters in cars.

Cordierite jewellery
A variety of cordierite, iolite is used in ornaments because of its colour and brilliance.

PROFILE

Hexagonal or trigonal

7–7 ½

3.0–3.2

Indistinct

Uneven to conchoidal

Colourless

Vitreous

Watermelon tourmaline
Colour can vary either along or across a tourmaline crsytal. This zoning takes its most dramatic form in "watermelon" tourmaline.

green or red crystal rim

crystal sliced across its width

red or pink centre

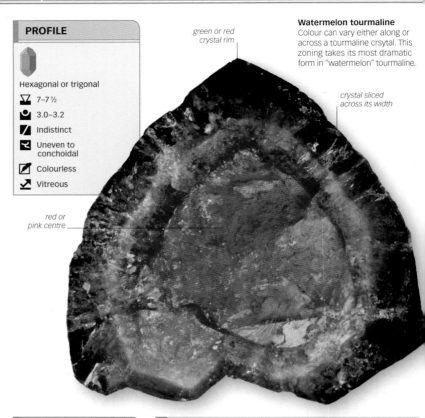

VARIANTS

Schorl Probably the most common tourmaline mineral

Elbaite A gemstone-quality variant of tourmaline

Indicolite A blue-coloured variant of tourmaline

$FeWO_4$

TOURMALINE

Tourmaline is the name given to a family of minerals of complex and variable composition, but all members have the same basic crystal structure. The 11 minerals in the group include elbaite, schorl, dravite, and liddicoatite. Gemstone varieties based on their colour are also recognized, including indicolite (blue), rubellite (pink or red), verdelite (green), and achroite (colourless). These variety names can be applied to more than one mineral. Most tourmaline is dark, opaque, and not particularly attractive, but many of its transparent varieties are valued as gems.

Tourmaline is abundant, and its best formed crystals are usually found in pegmatites (p.260) and metamorphosed limestones (p.319) in contact with granitic magmas. It accumulates in gravel deposits and occurs as an accessory mineral in some sedimentary rocks.

Cut rubellite
This specimen shows the rich red coloration and transparency found in some specimens of rubellite.

PROFILE

Hexagonal or trigonal

7 ½–8

2.6–2.8

Indistinct

Uneven to conchoidal

White

Vitreous

Aquamarine
This mass of prismatic aquamarine crystals is from the Karakoram Range in Pakistan. The name aquamarine means "sea water".

vitreous lustre

transparent sky blue

iron-stained coating

VARIANTS

Heliodor Crystalline heliodor with hexagonal prisms

Emerald An unusually long prismatic crystal of emerald

Morganite A variant with crystals in shades of pink

$MnWO_4$

BERYL

Few people have ever heard of the mineral beryl but almost everyone has heard of its principal gemstone varieties – emerald and aquamarine. Before 1925, beryl's solitary use was as a gemstone but since then many important uses have been found for beryllium. As a result, common beryl, which is usually pale green or white, has become widely sought after as the ore of this rare element. Most beryl is found in granites (pp.258–59), granite pegmatites (p.260), and rhyolites (p.278), but it can also occur in metamorphic rocks, such as schists (pp.291–92).

Emerald owes its grass-green colour to the presence of traces of chromium and sometimes vanadium. Flawless emeralds are rare, but since 1937 the manufacture of synthetic crystals has become possible. Aquamarine is the most common gemstone variety of beryl. Nearly always found in cavities in pegmatites or in alluvial deposits, it forms larger and clearer crystals than emerald. Other gemstone varieties of beryl include heliodor, morganite, and goshenite.

short, prismatic dioptase crystal

vitreous lustre

chrysocolla groundmass

Prismatic dioptase
This spectacular encrustation of dioptase crystals on quartz shows why it is a favourite with collectors.

VARIANTS

Clustered prisms A green dioptase specimen

Lustrous dioptase
A specimen found in Central Africa

🔬 $CuSiO_2(OH_2)$

DIOPTASE

The bright green crystals of dioptase can superficially resemble emerald. Dioptase crystals mined from a rich deposit in Kazakhstan were wrongly identified as emerald when they were sent to Tsar Paul of Russia in 1797. Were it not for its softness and good cleavage, dioptase would make a superb gemstone to rival emerald (p.225) in colour. Its prismatic crystals, often with rhombohedral terminations, can be highly transparent. This explains why the name dioptase is derived from two Greek words: *dia*, which means "through"; and *optazein,* which means "visible" or "to see". Transparent specimens of dioptase appear in different colours depending on the direction from which they are seen, and intensely coloured specimens can be translucent. The mineral can also occur in granular or massive habits.

Dioptase forms in areas where copper veins have been altered by oxidation. Its vibrant colour and its typical occurence as well-formed crystals make it popular with mineral collectors.

PROFILE

Orthorhombic

⚡ 4½–5

🔨 3.4–3.5

▨ Perfect, good, poor

✂ Uneven, brittle

▧ White

⚡ Vitreous

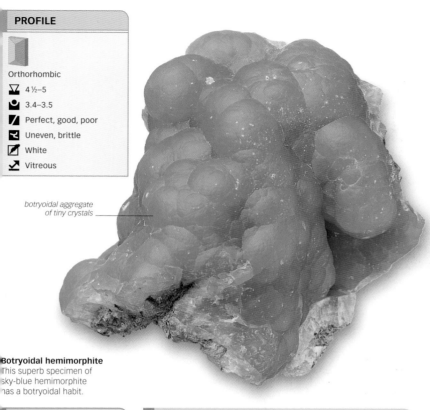

botryoidal aggregate of tiny crystals

Botryoidal hemimorphite
This superb specimen of sky-blue hemimorphite has a botryoidal habit.

VARIANTS

crystal cluster

White hemimorphite Tabular crystals on a rock groundmass

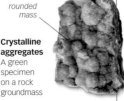

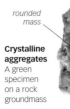

rounded mass

Crystalline aggregates
A green specimen on a rock groundmass

🧪 $Zn_4Si_2O_7(OH)_2 \cdot H_2O$

HEMIMORPHITE

One of two minerals formerly called calamine in the USA, hemimorphite takes its name from the Greek words *hemi*, which means "half", and *morphe*, which means "form" – a reference to its crystalline form. Hemimorphite crystals are double-terminated prisms with a differently shaped termination at each end – pointed at one and flat at the other. Crystals are often grouped in fan-shaped clusters. Hemimorphite can also be botryoidal, chalky, massive, granular, fibrous, or form encrustations. Usually colourless or white, specimens can also be pale yellow, pale green, or sky blue. Some specimens show strong, green fluorescence in shortwave ultraviolet light and weak, light pink fluorescence in longwave ultraviolet light.

Hemimorphite is a secondary mineral formed in the alteration zones of zinc deposits, especially as an alteration product of sphalerite (p.53). It can be half zinc by weight and is an important ore of that metal. Well-crystallized specimens come from Algeria, Namibia, Germany, Mexico, Spain, USA, and China.

PROFILE

Triclinic

⛏ 6½–7

⬤ 3.2–3.3

◨ Good, poor

⬔ Uneven to conchoidal, brittle

▧ Colourless to light brown

⬈ Vitreous

Axinite crystals
This mass of well-formed, transparent, wedge-shaped, tabular axinite crystals rests on a rock groundmass.

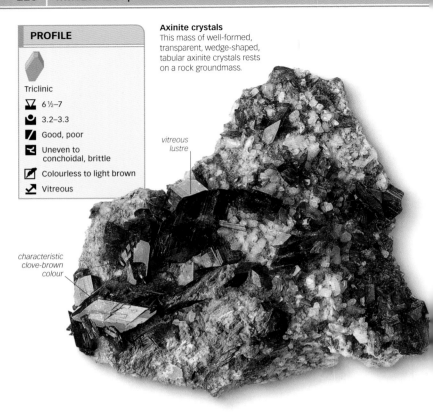

vitreous lustre

characteristic clove-brown colour

VARIANTS

wedge-shaped axinite crystal

Gem quality Wedge-shaped crystals of brown axinite

distinctive axe shape

Unusual growth A small crystal growing on a larger one

⚛ $Ca_2FeAl_2(BSi_4O_{15})(OH)$

AXINITE

This group of minerals takes its name from the axehead shape of its crystals. Axinite minerals also occur as rosettes and in massive and granular forms. The most familiar colour of axinite is clove brown. Varieties can also be grey to bluish grey, honey-, grey-, or golden-brown, violet-blue, pink, yellow, orange, or red. There are four minerals in the group: ferroaxinite, the most common; magnesioaxinite, in which magnesium replaces the iron in ferroaxinite; manganaxinite, in which manganese replaces the iron in ferroaxinite; and tinzenite, which is intermediate in composition between ferroaxinite and manganaxinite.

Axinite is commonly found in contact and low-temperature metamorphic rocks (those formed at up to 200°C/400°F) and in magnesium- and iron-rich igneous rocks.

Axinite gemstone
Brilliant-cut axinite crystals, such as this specimen in an unusual shade of violet, are popular with collectors.

tetragonal crystal

vertical striation

Striated vesuvianite
This superb specimen consists of prismatic, vertically striated vesuvianite crystals.

VARIANTS

Cyprine A specimen of blue vesuvianite, or cyprine

Tetragonal crystal
A single, well-formed crystal of vesuvianite

$Ca_{10}(Mg,Fe)_2Al_4(SiO_4)_5(Si_2O_7)_2(OH,F)_4$

VESUVIANITE

Formerly called idocrase, vesuvianite is named after its place of discovery – Mount Vesuvius in Italy. Usually green or yellow-green, it can also be yellow to brown, red, black, blue, or purple. A greenish blue copper-bearing vesuvianite is called cyprine. An unusual bismuth-bearing vesuvianite from Langben, Sweden, is bright red. The mineral forms pyramidal or prismatic and glassy crystals. Crystals 7 cm (2¾ in) or more long have been found.

Elements such as tin, lead, manganese, chromium, zinc, and sulphur may substitute in the vesuvianite structure. The mineral is formed by the metamorphism of impure limestones (p.319). It is also found in granulites (p.297) and marbles (p.301) accompanied by calcite (p.114), diopside (p.210), wollastonite (p.214), and grossular (p.245).

Vesuvianite gem
Occasionally, vesuvianite is found in translucent to transparent crystals suitable for cutting into gems.

PROFILE

Monoclinic

⬙ 6–7

⬗ 3.4

◧ Good

◩ Uneven to splintery

◪ Colourless or greyish

⬈ Vitreous

Epidote crystals
This superb group of striated epidote crystals, some reaching 2.5 cm (1 in) in length, shows typical prismatic development.

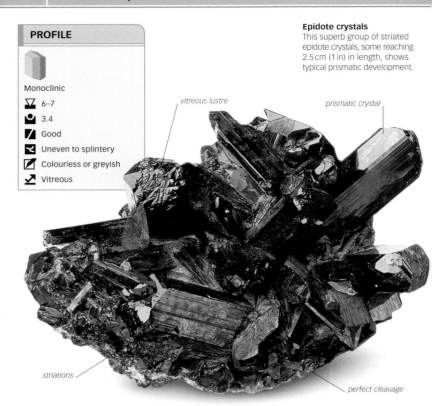

vitreous lustre

prismatic crystal

striations

perfect cleavage

VARIANTS

Pistachio epidote Long, striated crystals from Peru

Acicular epidote Yellowish brown, needle-like crystals

⚛ $Ca_2Al_2(Fe,Al)(SiO_4)(Si_2O_7)O(OH)$

EPIDOTE

An abundant rock-forming mineral, epidote derives its name from the Greek word *epidosis*, which means "increase" – a reference to the fact that one side of the prism is always wider than the others. Epidote is most easily recognized by its characteristic colour – light to dark pistachio green. Grey or yellow specimens are also found. Epidote is pleochroic, exhibiting different colours when viewed from different directions. The mineral frequently forms well-developed crystals. These may be columnar prisms or thick, tabular crystals with faces that are finely striated parallel to the crystal's length. Twinning is common. Specimens can also be needle-like, massive, or granular.

Epidote is found in low-grade, regionally metamorphosed rocks. It also occurs as a product of the alteration of plagioclase feldspars (pp.173–81).

Epidote gemstone
Clear, yellowish green to dark brown epidote gems are rare. Transparent crystals are cut for collectors.

deep vertical
striation

perfect
cleavage

PROFILE

Orthorhombic

6–7

3.2–3.4

Perfect

Conchoidal to
uneven, brittle

White

Vitreous

Zoisite crystals
This specimen of ordinary zoisite
shows a typical prismatic shape
and vertical striations. The crystals
are in a pegmatite groundmass.

VARIANTS

Thulite A pink, manganese-
rich variety of zoisite

Tanzanite A rich purple
gem-quality zoisite variety

$Ca_2Al_3(SiO_4)_3(OH)$

ZOISITE

A calcium aluminium silicate hydroxide, most zoisite
is grey, white, light brown, yellowish green, or pale greenish
grey. A massive, pinkish red variety is called thulite. A lilac-
blue to sapphire-blue variety of zoisite is called tanzanite
and is sometimes mistaken for sapphire (p.95). Zoisite with
inclusions of ruby is called ruby-in-zoisite. Zoisite crystals
exhibit grey, purple, or blue colours depending on the angle
from which they are viewed. Zoisite is found as deeply
striated, prismatic crystals and also as disseminated
grains and columnar or massive aggregates.

The mineral is characteristic of regional metamorphism
and hydrothermal alteration of igneous rocks. It results
from metamorphism of calcium-
rich rocks and typically occurs in
medium-grade schists (pp.291–
92), gneisses (p.288), and
amphibolites (p.296). It is also
found in veins of quartz (p.168)
and pegmatites (p.260).

Ruby in zoisite
Considered a good carving
medium, ruby-in-zoisite has
been used to make this
19th-century desk seal.

PROFILE

Orthorhombic

▽ 6½–7

◔ 3.3–4.3

▧ Imperfect

◪ Conchoidal

▨ White

⬈ Vitreous

rounded, transparent olivine crystal

secondary clay minerals

Peridot crystal
This gem-quality specimen of olivine, or peridot, is from Pakistan. Other important sources include China and Myanmar.

VARIANTS

Forsterite Magnesium-rich olivine is called forsterite

tabular crystal

Fayalite Iron-rich olivine is called fayalite

♣ $(Mg,Fe)_2SiO_4$

OLIVINE

The name olivine may be unfamiliar but most people know of its gemstone variety, peridot, which has been mined for over 3,500 years. The name olivine is applied to any mineral belonging to a solid-solution series in which iron and magnesium substitute freely in the structure. Fayalite is the iron end member of the solid-solution series, and forsterite is the magnesium end member.

Olivine specimens are usually yellowish green, but they can also be yellow, brown, grey, or colourless. Crystals are tabular, often with wedge-shaped terminations, although well-formed crystals of olivine are rare. Olivine may also occur in massive or granular habits. It is a major component of Earth's upper mantle.

Peridot gemstone
Green peridot, such as the one in this brooch, was used by Egyptians since the second millennium BCE.

PROFILE

Tetragonal

⬙ 7 ½

◧ 4.6–4.7

◪ Imperfect

◩ Uneven to conchoidal

◪ White

⬂ Adamantine to oily

twinned zircon crystal

feldspar-and-biotite groundmass

biotite

Afghan zircon
This specimen of zircon crystals in a feldspar-and-biotite matrix is from Afghanistan. The crystals are up to 3 cm (1¼ in) long.

VARIANTS

Purple zircon Crystals of zircon in a rock groundmass

Crystalline cluster Zircon crystals that are embedded in pegmatite

⚛ $ZrSiO_4$

ZIRCON

A superb gem and one of the few stones to approach diamond (p.47) in fire and brilliance, zircon has a high refractive index and colour dispersion. Known since antiquity, zircon takes its name from the Arabic word *zargun*, derived in turn from the Persian words *zar*, which means "gold", and *gun*, which means "colour". Specimens can also be colourless, yellow, grey, green, brown, blue, and red. Brown zircon is frequently heat-treated to turn it blue. The mineral forms prismatic to dipyramidal crystals. Single crystals can reach a considerable size: specimens weighing up to 2 kg (4½ lb) and 4 kg (8¾ lb) have been found in Australia and Russia, respectively.

Zircon is found in metamorphic rocks and silica-rich igneous rocks. It resists weathering and, because of its relatively high specific gravity, concentrates in stream and river gravels and beach deposits.

Zircon bracelet
Gem zircons, such as the colourless, faceted zircons in this bracelet, have been mined for over 2,000 years.

PROFILE

Orthorhombic

8

3.4–3.6

Perfect basal

Subconchoidal to uneven

Colourless

Vitreous

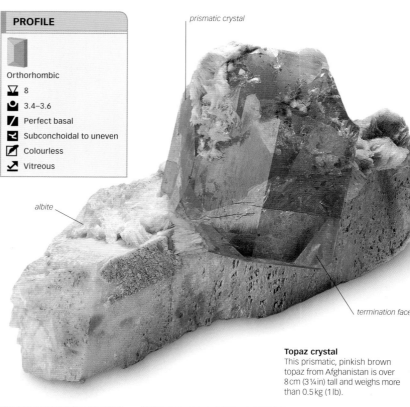

prismatic crystal

albite

termination face

Topaz crystal
This prismatic, pinkish brown topaz from Afghanistan is over 8 cm (3¼ in) tall and weighs more than 0.5 kg (1 lb).

VARIANTS

vitreous lustre

Brown topaz
A fine, natural crystal of brown topaz

line of cleavage

Light blue topaz
A specimen of blue topaz

Imperial topaz
A golden imperial topaz from a deposit in Brazil

$Al_2SiO_4(F,OH)_2$

TOPAZ

The name topaz is thought to have been derived from the Sanskrit *tapaz*, which means "fire". Topaz occurs in a wide range of colours, with sherry-yellow and pink stones being particularly valuable. Colourless topaz has such a high refractive index that brilliant-cut specimens are mistaken for diamond (p.47). Well-formed prismatic crystals have a characteristic lozenge-shaped cross section and striations parallel to their length. The mineral is also found in massive, granular, and columnar habits.

Topaz is formed by fluorine-bearing vapours released in the late stages of crystallization of igneous rocks. It occurs in granites (pp.258–59), rhyolites (p.278), pegmatite dykes, and hydrothermal veins. Rounded pebbles are also found in river deposits. The world's largest faceted topaz weighs over 36,000 carats.

Pink topaz
A clear, octagonal step cut, pink topaz is set here in a gold ring. Natural pink topaz is rare.

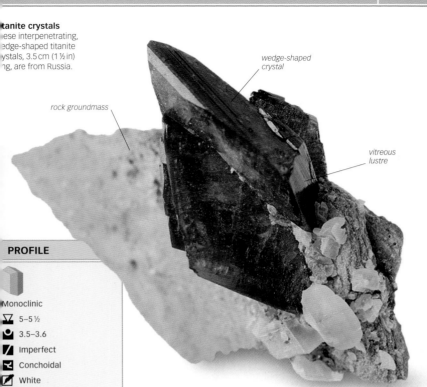

Titanite crystals
These interpenetrating, wedge-shaped titanite crystals, 3.5 cm (1 ½ in) long, are from Russia.

rock groundmass

wedge-shaped crystal

vitreous lustre

PROFILE

Monoclinic

5–5 ½

3.5–3.6

Imperfect

Conchoidal

White

Vitreous to greasy

VARIANT

Crystal group Wedge-shaped titanite crystals

$CaTiSiO_5$

TITANITE

Formerly called sphene, titanite is a calcium titanium silicate. The name sphene originates from the Greek word *sphen*, which means "wedge" – a reference to the typical wedge-shaped crystals of the mineral. Crystals can also be prismatic. Gem-quality crystals occur in yellow, green, or brown colours. Specimens can also be black, pink, red, blue, or colourless. Titanite is strongly pleochroic, exhibiting different colours when seen from different directions. The mineral can also be massive, lamellar, or compact. Faceted titanite is one of the few stones with a colour dispersion higher than that of diamond (p.47).

Titanite is widely distributed as a minor component of silica-rich igneous rocks and associated pegmatites (p.260). It is also found in the metamorphic rocks gneiss (p.288), schist (pp.291–92), and marble (p.301).

Titanite ring
Faceted titanites, such as the brilliant cut set in this gold ring, have superb fire and intense colours.

Orthorhombic

⚡ 6½–7½

💧 3.2

Good to perfect, poor

Conchoidal

White

Vitreous

Andalusite crystals
This group of prismatic andalusite crystals from the Austrian Tyrol is in a groundmass of quartz.

quartz groundmass

prismatic andalusite crystal

VARIANTS

Brown andalusite Prismatic crystals on a rock groundmass

Chiastolite A yellowish brown andalusite crystal with cross-shaped inclusions of carbon

Al_2OSiO_5

ANDALUSITE

Named after the locality in Andalusia, Spain, where it was first described, andalusite is aluminium silicate. It is pink to reddish brown, white, grey, violet, yellow, green, or blue. Gem-quality andalusite exhibits yellow, green, and red colours when viewed from different directions. Andalusite crystals are commonly prismatic with a square cross section. They can also be elongated or tapered. Andalusite can also occur in massive form. A yellowish grey variety called chiastolite occurs as long prisms enclosing symmetrical wedges of carbon-rich material.

Andalusite is found in regional and low-grade metamorphic rocks, where it is associated with corundum (p.95), cordierite (p.223), sillimanite (p.237), and kyanite (p.238). It is rarely found in granites (pp.258–59) and granitic pegmatites (p.260) .

Rectangular step cut Relatively uncommon, transparent andalusite is too brittle to be worn. It is faceted for gem collectors.

PROFILE

Orthorhombic

7

3.2–3.3

Perfect

Uneven

White

Silky

vitreous lustre

elongated, prismatic sillimanite crystal

rock groundmass

Prismatic sillimanite
In this specimen, elongated, prismatic crystals of sillimanite can be seen in a rock groundmass.

VARIANTS

Crystals in rock Sillimanite in a rock groundmass

silky lustre

Fibrous sillimanite A mass of parallel, fibrous crystals

Al_2OSiO_5

SILLIMANITE

Named after the American chemist Benjamin Silliman, sillimanite is one of three polymorphs of aluminium silicate. Commonly colourless to white, sillimanite can also be pale yellow to brown, pale blue, green, or violet. A single specimen may appear yellowish green, dark green, or blue when seen from different angles. The mineral occurs in long, slender, glassy crystals or in blocky, poorly terminated prisms.

Sillimanite is characteristic of clay-rich metamorphic rocks formed at high temperatures (575°C/1,065°F or above). The mineral is often found with corundum (p.95), cordierite (p.223), and kyanite (p.238). Specimens also occur in gneisses (p.288), sillimanite schists, hornfels (p.303), and detrital sediments.

Collectors' gem
Facet-grade sillimanite, such as this specimen, occurs in the gem gravels of Sri Lanka and Myanmar, and in Brazil.

Blady kyanite
This specimen of kyanite with quartz from northern Brazil shows the characteristic elongated, bladed habit of kyanite crystals.

vitreous lustre

long, bladed crystal

rock groundmass

quartz

rock groundmass

staurolite

kyanite

Kyanite in rock Kyanite crystals with staurolite in a rock groundmass

Al_2SiO_5

KYANITE

Named after the Greek word *kyanos*, which means "dark blue", kyanite is blue and blue-grey, the colours generally zoned within a single crystal. Kyanite can also be green, orange, or colourless. Specimens have variable hardness: about 4½ when scratched parallel to the long axis but 6 when scratched perpendicular to the long axis. Kyanite occurs mainly as elongated, flattened blades that are often bent and sometimes as radiating, columnar aggregates.

Kyanite is formed during the regional metamorphism of clay-rich sediments. It occurs in mica schists, gneisses (p.288), and associated hydrothermal quartz veins and pegmatites (p.260). It is used to estimate the temperature, depth, and pressure at which a rock has metamorphosed.

Spark plugs
Kyanite is mined for the aluminium silicate mullite, which is used in spark plugs.

prismatic staurolite crystal

twinned staurolite crystals

vitreous lustre

mica schist groundmass

PROFILE

Monoclinic

⬙ 7–7 ½

⬙ 3.7

⬙ Distinct

⬙ Conchoidal

⬙ Colourless to grey

⬙ Vitreous to resinous

[S]taurolite crystals
[T]his is a specimen of staurolite [i]n a mica schist groundmass. [S]ingle and twinned crystals [c]an be seen here.

VARIANTS

kyanite

staurolite

Staurolite in schist Kyanite and staurolite in schist

Fairy cross A twinned staurolite, or "fairy cross", crystal

$(Fe,Mg)_4Al_{17}(Si,Al)_8O_{45}(OH)_3$

STAUROLITE

A widespread mineral, staurolite takes its name from two Greek words: *stauros*, which means "cross", and *lithos*, which means "stone" – a reference to its typical cross-like twinned form. Cross-shaped penetration twins of the mineral are common and are in great demand as charms. Staurolite specimens are yellowish brown, reddish brown, or nearly black in colour. The mineral normally occurs as prismatic crystals, which are either hexagonal or diamond-shaped in section and often have rough surfaces.

Staurolite occurs in mica schists, gneisses (p.288), and other metamorphosed, aluminium-rich rocks. It forms only under a specific range of pressure and temperature, which helps determine the various conditions under which the metamorphic rock formed.

Trapeze-cut staurolite
Transparent staurolite, as in this stone, is a rare faceting material because of its dark colour and lack of brilliance.

PROFILE

Monoclinic

7 ½

3.0

Perfect

Conchoidal, brittle

White

Vitreous

prismatic euclase crystal

rock groundmass

striated crystal

Blue euclase
This mass of well-developed, prismatic crystals of blue euclase is on a rocky groundmass.

VARIANT

Transparent euclase
A near-transparent, striated euclase crystal

$BeAlSiO_4(OH)$

EUCLASE

Euclase takes its name from two Greek words: *eu*, which means "good", and *klasis*, which means "fracture" – a reference to its perfect cleavage. Generally white or colourless, euclase can also be pale green or pale to deep blue – a colour for which it is particularly noted. It forms striated prisms, often with complex terminations. Massive and fibrous specimens are also found.

Euclase occurs in hydrothermal veins formed at low temperatures (up to 200°C/400°F), granitic pegmatites (p.260), and some metamorphic schists (pp.291–92) and phyllites (p.294). It is also found in stream gravels. Exquisite, colourless, and deep blue colour-zoned crystals come from Karoi in Zimbabwe. Cut euclase resembles certain types of beryl (p.225) and topaz (p.234).

Euclase gemstone
This square-cut euclase gemstone shows small, dark inclusions of another mineral.

PROFILE

Orthorhombic

⚡ 6–6½

🔵 3.2–3.3

◩ Poor

◪ Subconchoidal to uneven

◪ Yellow to orange

◪ Vitreous

Humite crust
In this specimen, a crust of yellowish brown humite crystals covers a rock groundmass that also contains accessory mica.

yellowish brown humite crystal

rock groundmass

VARIANTS

Yellow humite A specimen of massive, yellow humite

Orange humite Massive, orange humite with a brown weathering crust

$(Mg,Fe)_7(SiO_4)_3(F,OH)_2$

HUMITE

Named in 1813 after the English mineral and art collector Sir Abraham Hume (1749–1838), humite is a silicate of iron and magnesium. Manganese substitutes for iron in the structure to form a complete solid-solution series with manganhumite. Specimens are yellow to dark orange or reddish orange in colour, tending towards brown with increasing manganese content. Humite is generally found in granular masses. Well-formed crystals are rare and grow in parallel with one another. Crystals rarely exceed 1 cm (³⁄₈ in) in length and are occasionally twinned.

Humite is found with pyrite (p.62), cassiterite (p.79), hematite (p.91), quartz (p.168), tourmaline (p.224), and mica in contact and regionally metamorphosed limestones (p.319) and dolomites (p.320). Although this mineral occurs worldwide, noteworthy locations include Persberg and elsewhere in Sweden; Isle of Skye, Scotland; Mount Vesuvius, Italy; Valais, Switzerland; and Brewster, New York, USA.

PROFILE

Cubic

7–7 ½

3.6

None

Conchoidal, brittle

White

Vitreous

rock groundmass

pyrope crystal

conchoidal fracture

Pyrope in matrix
This specimen from Mexico includes several pyrope garnets in a matrix. Most pyrope is found as pebbles in placer deposits with other gems.

VARIANT

Gemstone rough Water-rounded pyrope recovered from a placer deposit

$Mg_3Al_2(SiO_4)_3$

PYROPE

The magnesium aluminium garnet pyrope was named in 1803 after the Greek words *pyr* and *ōps*, which mean "fire" and "eye" respectively – a reference to the typical fiery colour of specimens. Manganese, chromium, iron, and titanium substitute in the mineral's structure and act as colouring agents to some degree. Specimens can be rich red, dark red, violet-red, rose red, or reddish orange depending on the composition. Crystals are dodecahedral and trapezohedral, with hexoctahedra sometimes present. The mineral is most often found as rounded grains or pebbles.

Pyrope occurs as a high-pressure mineral in metamorphic rocks. It is also found in high-pressure, silica-poor igneous rocks and in detrital deposits derived from them.

Pyrope gemstones
Beautiful garnet jewellery comes from Bohemia, Czech Republic, where pyropes as big as hens' eggs are found

modified
dodecahedron

schist

well-formed crystal

PROFILE

Cubic

7–7 ½

4.3

None

Subconchoidal, brittle

White

Vitreous

lmandine crystal
his almandine in schist from an area
ear Wrangell, Alaska, USA, shows a
nodified dodecahedral form.

VARIANTS

schist

almandine
crystal

Crystals in schist Numerous
almandine dodecahedrons
rest on schist

almandine
crystal

Almandine in granulite
Crystals of almandine in a
granulite matrix

$Fe_3Al_2(SiO_4)_3$

ALMANDINE

The most common garnet, almandine is named after
Alabanda (now Araphisar) in Turkey, where it has been
cut since antiquity. Almandine is always red, often with
a pink or violet tinge. Specimens can sometimes be nearly
black. This mineral tends to be a pinker red than other
garnets. Crystals often have well-developed faces and
are dodecahedral or trapezohedral or have other more
complex forms. Massive aggregates and rounded grains
are also found. Rutile (p.78) needles
can show as a four-rayed star when
almandine is cut *en cabochon*.

Almandine occurs worldwide.
It is found in gneisses (p.288)
and mica schists, igneous rocks
(pp.256–57), and occasionally as
inclusions in diamond (p.47). When
it occurs in metamorphic rocks,
its presence indicates the grade
of metamorphism.

Faceted almandine
Three faceted almandine
gems and a seed pearl
create a central flower motif
in this antique gold brooch.

Spessartine crystals
In this specimen from Norway, well-formed dodecahedral crystals encrust a rock groundmass.

rock groundmass

uneven fracture

dodecahedral spessartine crystal

VARIANT

Translucent spessartine
An attractive crystal of translucent spessartine

$Mn_3Al_2(SiO_4)_3$

SPESSARTINE

The manganese aluminium silicate spessartine is named after Spessart – the locality in Germany where it was first described. The mineral is pale yellow when nearly pure and orange to deep red, brown, or black in other specimens. A colour change known as the alexandrite effect is occasionally found in spessartine grossular garnet. Crystals are dodecahedral or trapezohedral. Spessartine may also occur as either granular or massive aggregates.

Spessartine almost always contains some amount of iron (p.39). Pure spessartine is relatively rare and is found in manganese-rich metamorphic rocks, granites (pp.258–59), and pegmatite veins (p.260). The heaviest spessartine ever discovered weighs 6,720 carats.

Octagonal step cut
Because of spessartine's ric colour, the liquid inclusions under the edge facets in thi gem are not very noticeable

diopside

grossular crystal

Grossular on diopside
These grossular crystals from
Piedmont, Italy, are set on
a groundmass of diopside.

VARIANTS

Hessonite Reddish brown
dodecahedral grossular crystals

impure
marble

Pink grossular Rounded, pink
grossular crystals in marble

$Ca_3Al_2(SiO_4)_3$

GROSSULAR

The calcium aluminum silicate grossular, a type of
garnet, is named after the Latin word *grossularia*, which
translates into "gooseberry" – a reference to the mineral's
gooseberry-green colour. Specimens can also be pale to
emerald green, white, colourless, cream, orange, red,
honey, brown, or black. When reddish brown or pink,
grossular is called hessonite or cinnamon stone. Grossular
is usually translucent to opaque but can be transparent.

It occurs as rounded dodecahedral or
trapezohedral crystals that are up
to 13 cm (5 in) wide. Specimens can
also be granular or massive.

Grossular forms in impure
calcareous rocks that have
undergone regional or contact
metamorphism, in some schists
(pp.291–92) and serpentinites
(p.298), and occasionally in
meteorites (pp.335–37).

Grossular beads
This strung group is
made up of size-graded,
round, luminescent green
grossular beads.

ORGANICS

Generated by organic (biological) processes, the organics may or may not be crystalline. In some cases, they contain the same mineral matter – such as calcite or aragonite – as that generated through inorganic processes. Organics are widely used as gems.

COMPOSITION

The organics have a highly varied composition. Coral, pearl, and shell form from mineral matter generated by biological processes. Amber is fossilized resin, mainly from extinct coniferous trees, although amber-like substances from even older trees are also known. Copal is a modern equivalent of fossilized amber. Coal is derived from buried organic material, such as peat. Bitumen is a very heavy oil.

Shell
The shells of marine invertebrates capture large amounts of carbon in the form of aragonite. Their remains form extensive beds of carbonate rocks.

OCCURRENCE

The organics are relatively widespread. The shells of freshwater and marine organisms are part of a carbonate cycle that extracts carbon from the environment and returns it as carbonate sediment, either to be reincorporated into other organics or to be lithified. Other organics incorporate carbon in their essential composition.

USES

Coal and bitumen are the organics that find the widest use. Organically derived carbonate rocks are also extensively used as building stone and ballast and in the manufacture of cement. Other organics are used to make ornaments and jewellery.

Coral necklace
This branch-like Native American necklace is made from mall, polished branches and tiny beads of red coral.

red coral

Coral reef
A coral reef forms in shallow ocean areas. Corals are the most important part of the reef and form its main structural framework. Coral skeletons are made of aragonite.

Trigonal   Orthorhombic
Amorphous

⊻ 3 ½

⚒ 2.6–2.7

◪ None

⬔ Hackly

◨ White

⬓ Dull to vitreous

Red coral
The use of red coral dates back to the Iron Age. This specimen from the Mediterranean has a wood-grain pattern on its branches.

wood-grain pattern

coral branch

VARIANTS

Blue coral
A type of coral used in artefacts and jewellery

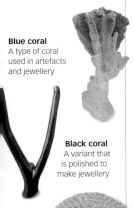

Black coral
A variant that is polished to make jewellery

Brain coral
An elaborate confection of organic aragonite

🜋 Mostly CaCO₃

CORAL

According to Greek legend, coral came from the drops of blood shed when the mythic hero Perseus cut off the head of the monster Medusa. Coral is actually the skeletal material generated by marine animals also known as coral polyps. In most corals, this material is calcium carbonate, but in black and golden corals it is a horn-like substance called conchiolin. Coral has a dull lustre when recovered, but it can be polished and brightened. It is sensitive even to mild acids and can become dull with extensive wear.

Coral is variable in colour. Red and pink precious coral is found in the warm seas around Japan and Malaysia, in African coastal waters, and in the Mediterranean Sea. Black coral comes from the West Indies, Australia, and from around the Pacific Islands.

Coral necklace
This triple-stranded necklace from Morocco is made of coral, silver, and turquoise.

PROFILE

Orthorhombic

▽ 3

📛 2.7

▨ None

⬔ Uneven, brittle

◫ White

⬂ Pearly

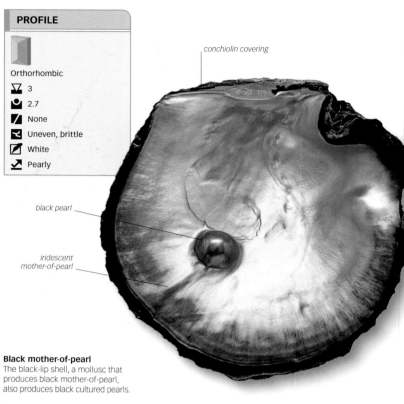

conchiolin covering

black pearl

iridescent mother-of-pearl

Black mother-of-pearl
The black-lip shell, a mollusc that produces black mother-of-pearl, also produces black cultured pearls.

VARIANTS

blister pearl

Blister pearls Attached to the shell, these are flat on one side

Freshwater pearls These have the same lustre as marine pearls

🜨 Mostly CaCO₃

PEARL

A concretion formed by a mollusc, a pearl consists mainly of aragonite (p.115), the same material as the animal's shell (p.249). The shell-secreting cells are located in a layer of the mollusc's body tissue called the mantle. When a foreign particle enters the mantle, the cells build up concentric layers of pearl around it. Colours vary with the mollusc and its environment and can be any delicate shade from black to white, cream, grey, blue, yellow, green, lavender, or mauve.

The finest pearls are produced by limited species of saltwater oysters and freshwater clams. A pearl is valued by its translucence, lustre, colour, and shape. The most valuable pearls are spherical or drop-like, with a deep lustre and good play of colour. Rose-tinted Indian pearls are highly prized.

Pearl bracelet
This Cartier Art Deco bracelet has five strands of cultured pearls with a gold and oxidized-silver clasp.

iridescent mother-of-pearl

inner surface of shell

Abalone shell
Found in warm seas, abalone shells, such as this one from New Zealand, are noted for their multicoloured, iridescent, mother-of-pearl lining.

VARIANTS

Spider conch A type of shell widely used for ornamental purposes

Tortoise shell The shell of a hawksbill turtle

Thorny oyster A shell made up of organic aragonite

 CaCO₃

SHELL

Like coral (p.247), shell is mineral matter generated by biological processes. The mineral component of shell is either calcite (p.114) or aragonite (p.115), both of which are calcium carbonate. Shell forms as the hard outer covering of many molluscs. It is secreted in calcareous layers by cells in the mantle – a skin-like tissue in the mollusc's body wall. Mollusc shells differ in the composition, number, and arrangement of calcareous layers. These layers form as distinct microstructures with different mechanical properties and, in some shells, different colours.

Both marine and freshwater shells are used for ornamentation. Shells with different coloured layers have been carved into cameos since antiquity. Pearly shells were used widely in button making around the 19th century.

Shell perfume bottle
This 19th-century perfume bottle is made of two shells glued together. It has a chain, ring, and pinchbeck stopper.

PROFILE

Crystal system None

 2–2½

About 1.1

None

Conchoidal

White

Resinous

translucent copal

golden-yellow colour

conchoidal fracture

Copal nugget
This specimen of copal closely resembles amber. Some copal is used as an amber substitute in jewellery.

VARIANTS

orange-yellow gum

Kauri gum Resin derived from the Kauri conifer

Copal lumps Lumps of resin from the Protium copal or copal tree

 Various

COPAL

Named after the Nahuatl word _copalli_, which means "resin", copal is a yellow to red-orange resin obtained from various tropical trees. It can be collected from living trees and from accumulations in the soil beneath the trees. It can also be mined if it is buried. Copals from different sources usually have different chemical properties but can have similar physical properties. Copal has approximately the same hardness as amber (p.251) but unlike amber it is wholly or partially soluble in organic solvents.

Buried copal is the nearest to amber in durability and is, in many cases, virtually indistinguishable from it.

Zanzibar in Tanzania is a major source of buried copal. This mineral is also found in China, Brazil, and other South American countries. It is used in varnishes, lacquers, and inks.

Copal beads
In this necklace, beads of a tough and compact form of copal alternate with beads carved from seeds.

PROFILE

Crystal system None

⊿ 2–2½

⬖ 1.1

▮ None

◪ Conchoidal

◪ White

⬈ Resinous

resinous lustre

conchoidal fracture

translucent
mass of amber

Amber nodule
Transparent to translucent, most
amber is golden yellow to golden
orange and occurs as nodules or
small, irregularly shaped masses.

VARIANTS

Wave-rounded amber
A piece of wave-rounded
Baltic amber

Lithuanian amber A group
of amber pieces showing
colour variation

♣ Hydrocarbon (C,H,O)

AMBER

The fossilized resin amber comes mainly from extinct
coniferous trees, although amber-like substances from
earlier trees are also known. It is generally found in
association with lignite coal (p.253). Amber and other
partially fossilized resins are sometimes given mineral-
like names depending on where they are found, their
degree of fossilization, or the presence of other chemical
components. For example, resin that resembles copal
(p.250) and comes from the London clay region is called
copalite. At least 12 other names
are applied to minor variants.

For thousands of years, the
largest source of amber has
been deposits along the Baltic
coast, extending intermittently
from Gdánsk right around to
the coastlines of Denmark and
Sweden. Amber has been traded
since ancient times.

Preserved in amber
As resin dried 40–50 million
years ago, insects were
sometimes fossilized within
the sticky substance.

PROFILE

Crystal system None

⏷ 2 ½

◔ About 1.3

▨ None

◩ Conchoidal

◪ Black to dark brown

↗ Velvety, vitreous, or waxy

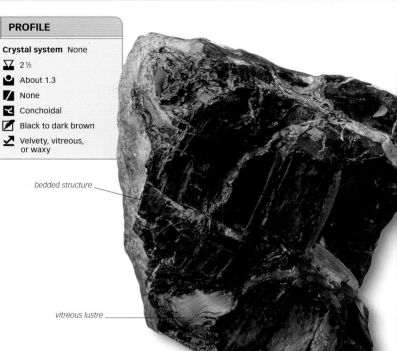

bedded structure

vitreous lustre

Woody structure
This specimen of jet shows the layered, woody structure that is sometimes characteristic of the mineral.

VARIANT

fossil amonite

Jet fossil Jet with fossils of marine origin

♣ Various

JET

Generally classified as a type of coal (p.253), jet has a high carbon content and a layered structure. It is black to dark brown in colour. Specimens sometimes contain tiny inclusions of pyrite (p.62), which have a metallic lustre. Jet is found in rocks of marine origin, perhaps derived from waterlogged driftwood or other plant material. It can occur in distinct beds, such as those at Whitby, England, from where jet has been extracted since the 1st century CE.

Jet has been carved for ornamental purposes since prehistoric times and has been found in prehistoric caves. The Romans carved jet into bangles and beads. In medieval times, powdered jet drunk with water or wine was believed to have medicinal properties.

Jet necklace
This Native American necklace is made of high-quality, fine-grained jet, which shows velvety lustre.

near-metallic lustre

black surface is hard and clean to touch

Anthracite
Hard to the touch, anthracite is naturally shiny. It takes a brilliant polish and is used for decorative as well as practical purposes.

VARIANTS

Lignite A variant having a composition between peat and bituminous coal

Bituminous coal The most common form of coal

Various

COAL

The fossilized remains of plants, coal usually occurs in layered, sedimentary deposits. It is brown or black and made up of an irregular mixture of chemical compounds called macerals, which are analogous to minerals in inorganic rocks. Unlike minerals, macerals have no fixed chemical composition and no definite crystalline structure.

Different varieties of coal are formed depending on the kinds of plant material, varying degrees of coalification (the process by which plant material is converted to coal), and the presence of impurities. Four varieties are recognized. Lignite is the lowest grade and is the softest and least coalified variety. It forms from peat under moderate pressure. Sub-bituminous coal is dark brown to black. Bituminous coal is the most abundant and is commonly burned for heat generation. Anthracite is the highest grade and the most highly metamorphosed form of coal. It contains the highest percentage of low-emission carbon and would be an ideal fuel if it was not relatively scarce.

ROCKS

IGNEOUS ROCKS

Igneous rocks are formed from magma – molten rock. They are classified as extrusive or intrusive depending on whether or not the magma emerged at Earth's surface before crystallizing. Extrusive rocks form on the surface; intrusive rocks form below it.

INTRUSIVE IGNEOUS ROCKS

Intrusive rocks are categorized as plutonic if formed deep inside the crust and hypabyssal if formed at shallow depths. Plutonic intrusive rocks are characterized by their large crystals and generally form geographically large bodies. For example, a batholith is a large igneous body with a surface exposure of at least 100 square km (40 square miles) and a thickness of about 10–15 km (6–9 miles). Batholiths form the cores of great mountain ranges, such as the Rockies and the Sierra Nevada in North America. Granite, diorite, peridotite, syenite, and gabbro are all plutonic igneous rocks.

Hypabyssal intrusive rocks are formed at shallower depths and are characterized by fine crystallization. They occur in sheet-like bodies called dykes and sills, volcanic plugs, and other relatively small formations. Dykes range from less than a centimetre to many metres in thickness and can be hundreds of kilometres in length. Sills are similar to dykes, except that they form parallel to the enclosing rocks and intrude between two strata.

light plagioclase feldspar

dark pyroxene

Gabbro
Most gabbros form as plutonic intrusive rocks. This coarsely crystallized specimen contains light-coloured crystals of plagioclase and dark crystals of pyroxene.

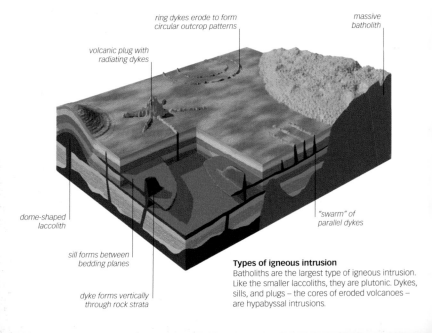

ring dykes erode to form circular outcrop patterns

massive batholith

volcanic plug with radiating dykes

dome-shaped laccolith

sill forms between bedding planes

dyke forms vertically through rock strata

"swarm" of parallel dykes

Types of igneous intrusion
Batholiths are the largest type of igneous intrusion. Like the smaller laccoliths, they are plutonic. Dykes, sills, and plugs – the cores of eroded volcanoes – are hypabyssal intrusions.

XTRUSIVE IGNEOUS ROCKS

xtrusive igneous rocks are also known s volcanic rocks. The principal rock types this category include basalt, obsidian, yolite, trachyte, and andesite. All of these sually form from lava – a magma that as flowed either onto land or underwater. ther extrusive rocks, such as tuff nd pumice, form in explosive volcanic ruptions. These "pyroclastic" rocks are orous because of the frothing expansion f volcanic gases during their formation. asalt is the most common extrusive rock, rming the floor of most oceans and xtensive plateaus on land, such as the eccan plateau of India and the Columbia ver Basalts of Oregon, USA.

COMPOSITION OF IGNEOUS ROCKS

Igneous rocks form from magma, which is essentially a silicate melt. Igneous rocks are classified on the basis of silica content. Felsic rocks have over 65 per cent silica, intermediate rocks 55–65 per cent, mafic rocks 45–55 per cent, and ultramafic rocks less than 45 per cent silica. The silicate minerals that develop from the melt depend on factors such as silica concentration in the melt, the presence and concentration of other elements such as aluminium, iron, magnesium, calcium, sodium, and potassium within the melt, and the temperature and pressure at which crystallization takes place.

vesicle

light colour similar to that of rhyolite

RHYOLITIC PUMICE

pyroxene phenocryst

PORPHYRITIC BASALT

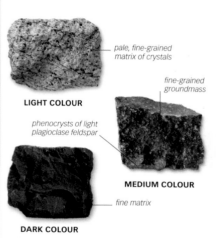

pale, fine-grained matrix of crystals

LIGHT COLOUR

fine-grained groundmass

phenocrysts of light plagioclase feldspar

MEDIUM COLOUR

fine matrix

DARK COLOUR

ain size

e origin of igneous rocks is generally indicated by the ain size of their minerals. Small or microscopic grains e found in extrusives; large grains in intrusives.

Colour

Relatively few igneous rocks are identified by specific colours. Instead, they are generally described as light, intermediate, or dark.

Mount St. Helens
n 1980, Mount St. Helens in the USA erupted, sending thousands of tonnes of pyroclastic debris across northwestern USA. Extensive beds of pumice and tuff form from such eruptions.

PROFILE

- ▲ Silica-rich, plutonic
- ⊕ Crystallization of a silica-rich magma in a major intrusion
- ⌀ 2–5 mm (¹⁄₁₆–³⁄₁₆ in), phenocrysts to 10 cm (4 in)
- ■ Potassium feldspar, quartz, mica
- ▢ Sodium plagioclase, hornblende
- ✸ White, light grey, pink, red

potassium feldspar
crystal

biotite

Dark granite
This specimen of granite
is dominated by large
crystals of potassium
feldspar, quartz, and biotite.

VARIANTS

Pink granite Pink feldspars
give this granite its colour

White granite
A specimen
dominated by
light-coloured
minerals

Hornblende granite Granite
with black hornblende

GRANITE

The most common intrusive rock in Earth's
continental crust, granite is familiar as a mottled pink,
white, grey, and black ornamental stone. It is coarse- to
medium-grained. Its three main minerals are feldspar,
quartz (p.168), and mica, which occur as silvery muscovite
(p.195) or dark biotite (p.197) or both. Of these minerals,
feldspar predominates, and
quartz usually accounts for
more than 10 per cent. The alkali
feldspars are often pink, resulting
in the pink granite often used as
a decorative stone.

Granite crystallizes from
silica-rich magmas that are tens
of kilometres deep in Earth's
crust. Many mineral deposits form
near crystallizing granite bodies
from the hydrothermal solutions
that such bodies release.

Granite staircase
Granite is used as a buildin
stone. This stairway made o
granite ascends to the Bor
Jesus Church in Portugal.

pink orthoclase feldspar

Graphic granite
This specimen of granite shows simultaneous growth of quartz and feldspar, which produces a pattern.

VARIANTS

Porphyritic granite
A specimen in which large feldspar phenocrysts are set in granite

Orbicular granite Granite with spherical phenocrysts of feldspar

TEXTURED GRANITE

Granites with distinct patterns in their crystallization are known as textured granites and in some cases, graphic granites. Graphic granite consists of roughly 30 per cent quartz (p.168) and 70 per cent feldspar, with a few other minerals. These minerals are intergrown in such a way that straight-sided quartz crystals, which look like hieroglyphic characters, are set in a background of feldspar. The texture forms in pegmatites (p.260) when the main minerals crystallize from the magma at the same time.

Orbicular granite is an unusual but spectacular granite containing spheres (orbicules) of concentric layers of granitic minerals. The orbicules are about 5–10 cm (2–4 in) in diameter and often richer than the granite in darker minerals. They are usually restricted to small areas within the larger granite mass. In porphyritic granite, the feldspar crystals are larger and better-formed than the surrounding mineral grains. These granites have been quarried and polished for use as ornamental and building stones.

pink orthoclase feldspar

dark prismatic tourmaline crystal

Tourmaline pegmatite
This specimen contains crystals of black tourmaline in a groundmass of pink feldspar and white quartz.

VARIANTS

Granitic pegmatite
A specimen with feldspar, quartz, biotite, and needle-shaped tourmaline

Blue topaz
A topaz crystal in a pegmatite groundmass

Feldspar pegmatite
A pegmatite dominated by white feldspar, with amphibole

PEGMATITE

Important sources of many gemstones, pegmatites are very coarse-grained igneous rocks, mostly of a granitic composition. Although crystals can be huge – over 10 m (33 ft) in some specimens – individual crystals usually average 8–10 cm (3¼–4 in) in length. The large crystals are due to the considerable amount of water in the magma rather than slow cooling. The most perfect crystals are typically found in openings or pockets. Quartz (p.168) and feldspar dominate, but many other minerals can form large, beautiful crystals. Muscovite (p.195) and other micas commonly occur in pegmatites in large, flat sheets known as books.

Pegmatites are light-coloured rocks and occur in small igneous bodies, such as veins and dykes, or sometimes as patches in larger masses of granite (pp.258–59). Several gemstones – such as tourmaline (p.224) group minerals, aquamarine (p.225), rock crystal, smoky quartz, rose quartz, and topaz (p.234) – are mined from pegmatites.

PROFILE

▲ Ultramafic, plutonic

🌐 Crystallization of a silica-poor magma in a major intrusion

🔎 2–5 mm (¹⁄₁₆–³⁄₁₆ in)

◼ Calcium plagioclase

◻ Olivine, pyroxene, garnet

✳ Light grey to white

plagioclase feldspar crystals

Anorthosite
This specimen of anorthosite is dominated by light-coloured plagioclase feldspars.

VARIANTS

Coarse anorthosite
A specimen with pyroxene and orthopyroxene

Lunar anorthosite Believed to be the first lunar rock to crystallize

ANORTHOSITE

An intrusive igneous rock, anorthosite is composed of at least 90 per cent calcium-rich plagioclase feldspar – principally labradorite (p.180) and bytownite. Olivine (p.232), garnet, pyroxene, and iron oxides make up the remaining 10 per cent. Anorthosite is coarse-grained and either white or grey. Specimens can also be green. Many anorthosites have an interesting "cumulate" texture, where well-formed crystals appear to have settled out of the liquid magma, in a similar way to large grains settling in a sediment.

Anorthosite is not a common rock, but where it does occur, it is found as immense masses, or as layers between iron- and magnesium-rich rocks, such as gabbro (p.265) and peridotite (p.266). Anorthosite is, however, common on the surface of the Moon.

Labradorite relief
Labradorite occurs in anorthosite and is used in carvings, such as this 19th-century relief.

PROFILE

- ▲ Intermediate silica content, plutonic
- 🌐 Crystallization of an alkaline intermediate magma in a major intrusion
- 🔍 2–5 mm (¹⁄₁₆–³⁄₁₆ in)
- ⬛ Potassium feldspar
- ⬜ Sodium plagioclase, biotite, amphibole, pyroxene, hornblende, feldspathoids
- ✳ Grey, pink, or red

Pink syenite
The pink colour of this syenite specimen is due to the presence of alkali feldspar, which predominates in syenite.

amphibole

feldspar

VARIANTS

Nepheline syenite Nepheline crystals with black hornblende

Syenite with zircon Zircon crystals in a syenite groundmass

SYENITE

Visually similar to granite and often confused with it, syenites can be distinguished from granite by the absence or scarcity of quartz. A syenite is any one of a class of rocks essentially composed of: an alkali feldspar or sodium plagioclase (or both); a ferromagnesian mineral, usually biotite (p.197), hornblende (p.218), or pyroxene; and little or no quartz. The alkali feldspars can include orthoclase (p.173), albite (p.177), or less commonly, microcline (p.175). Syenites are attractive, multi-coloured rocks – usually grey, pink, or red. Other minerals that occasionally occur in small amounts in syenite include titanite, apatite (p.148), zircon (p.233), magnetite (p.92), and pyrite (p.62). When syenites contain quartz, they are called quartz syenites.

Nepheline (p.182) and alkali feldspar are essential minerals in nepheline syenite, but this rock can contain other minerals, including unusual and attractive ones, such as eudialyte. If the rock includes a pyroxene, it is usually aegirine (p.209); if an amphibole it is usually arfvedsonite, both of which are rich in sodium.

dark, iron- and magnesium-bearing minerals

coarse texture

speckled granodiorite
This pink granodiorite has a speckled appearance because of the presence of darker minerals, such as mica and hornblende.

VARIANT

Pink granodiorite A specimen of granodiorite with dark mica and hornblende

GRANODIORITE

Among the most abundant of intrusive igneous rocks, granodiorite is a medium- to coarse-grained rock that is similar to granite (p.258) in texture. Granodiorite can be pink or white, with a grain size and texture similar to that of granite, but abundant plagioclase generally makes it appear darker than granite. The biotite (p.197) and hornblende (p.218) give it a speckled appearance. The mica may occur in well-formed hexagonal crystals, and the hornblende may be present in needle-like crystals. Twinned plagioclase crystals are sometimes wholly encased by orthoclase.

The quartz (p.168) present in granodiorite can be grey to white. With increased amounts of quartz and alkali feldspar, granodiorite grades to granite. With less quartz and alkali feldspar, it becomes diorite (p.264). The volcanic equivalent of granodiorite is dacite (p.274). Two historic stones are granodiorite: the Rosetta Stone was carved from it, and the Plymouth Rock is a glacial erratic boulder of granodiorite.

PROFILE

- ▲ Intermediate silica content, plutonic
- 🌐 Crystallization of a magma with intermediate silica content in a major intrusion
- 🔍 2–5mm (¹⁄₁₆–³⁄₁₆ in)
- ⬛ Sodium plagioclase, hornblende
- ⬜ Biotite
- ✹ Black or dark green mottled with grey or white

Two-toned diorite
This diorite specimen gets its two-toned appearance from light-coloured plagioclase feldspar and black hornblende.

plagioclase feldspar

hornblende

VARIANTS

Light-coloured diorite
A specimen of diorite with white plagioclase and a minor amount of hornblende

Fine-grained diorite
A specimen of fine-grained diorite with phenocrysts of hornblende

DIORITE

This medium- to coarse-grained intrusive igneous rock is sometimes sold as "black granite". In general, though, diorite is darker than granite (p.258). It is commonly composed of about two-thirds white plagioclase feldspar and one-third dark-coloured minerals, such as biotite (p.197) and hornblende (p.218). The plagioclases in diorite – oligoclase (p.178) or andesine (p.181) – are rich in sodium. Diorite can be of uniform grain size or have large phenocrysts of plagioclase or hornblende.

The rock can occur as large intrusions or as smaller dykes and sills. Most diorite is intruded along the margins of continents. With small amounts of quartz (p.168) and alkali feldspar, it becomes a granodiorite (p.263); with larger amounts, it is classified as granite.

Neolithic axehead
Diorite can be extremely tough and was used to make ancient tools, such as this neolithic axehead.

Coarse-grained gabbro
This specimen of gabbro has coarse grains, as produced by the formation of large crystals during slow cooling of a magma.

plagioclase feldspar

dark pyroxene

VARIANTS

Layered gabbro Bands of light plagioclase and dark ferromagnesian minerals

Leucogabbro A gabbro with feldspar-rich crystals

Olivine gabbro A gabbro containing olivine

GABBRO

Medium or coarse-grained rocks, gabbros consist principally of dark green pyroxene (augite and lesser amounts of orthopyroxene) plus white- or green-coloured plagioclase and black, millimetre-sized grains of magnetite and/or ilmenite. A gabbro has an intermediate or low silica content and rarely contains quartz (p.168). Gabbro is essentially the intrusive equivalent of basalt (p.273), but unlike basalt gabbro has a highly variable mineral content. It often contains a layering of light and dark minerals (layered gabbro), a significant amount of olivine (olivine gabbro), or a high percentage of coarse crystals of plagioclase feldspar (leucogabbro).

Gabbros are widespread but not common on Earth's surface. They occur as intrusions and as uplifted sections of oceanic crust. Some gabbros are mined for their nickel, chromium, and platinum (p.38). Those containing ilmenite (p.90) and magnetite (p.92) are mined for their iron or titanium.

dark, olivine and pyroxene crystals

Coarse peridotite
This is a specimen of dark, olivine- and pyroxene-rich peridotite from Odenwald, West Germany.

VARIANTS

Green peridotite A specimen containing green olivine

Garnet peridotite Peridotite with red phenocrysts of pyrope garnet

PERIDOTITE

An intrusive igneous rock, peridotite is coarse-grained and dense. It is light to dark green in colour. Peridotite contains at least 40 per cent olivine (p.232) and some pyroxene. Unlike the olivine grains, the pyroxene grains in peridotite have a visible cleavage when viewed under a hand lens. Peridotite forms much of Earth's mantle and can occur as nodules that are brought up from the mantle by kimberlite (p.269) or basalt (p.273) magmas.

The rock is usually found interlayered with iron- and magnesium-rich rocks in the lower parts of layered igneous rock bodies, where its denser crystals first form through selective crystallization and then settle to the bottom of still-fluid or semi-solid crystallizing mushes. A peridotite specimen that has been altered by weathering becomes serpentinite (p.298). Peridotite and pyroxenite (p.267) form in similar environments, but pyroxenite contains a higher percentage of pyroxene. Peridotites are important sources of chromium and nickel.

·roxenite
·oxene, the main component of
·oxenite, can be seen in this specimen,
·ng with smaller amounts of plagioclase
·lspar and accessory sulphide minerals.

plagioclase
feldspar

pyroxene

PROFILE

 Intrusive

 Crystallization of a
silica-poor magma
in a major intrusion

2–5mm (¹⁄₁₆–³⁄₁₆in)

Pyroxene

Biotite, hornblende,
olivine, plagioclase,
nepheline

 Light green, dark green,
or black

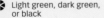

PYROXENITE

This is a coarse-grained, granular igneous rock
that contains at least 90 per cent pyroxene. Pyroxenite
may also contain olivine (p.232) and oxide minerals
when it occurs in layered intrusions or nepheline
(p.182) when it occurs in silica-poor intrusions. A hard
and heavy rock, it is light green, dark green, or black.
Its surface often weathers to rusty brown. Individual
crystals may be 7.5cm (3in) or more in length. Pyroxenites
are usually found with gabbros (p.265) and peridotites
(p.266). Unlike gabbros, pyroxenite contains almost
no feldspars. Also, pyroxenite has less olivine
than peridotites.

The principal minerals usually found accompanying
pyroxenites, in addition to olivine and feldspar, are
chromite (p.99) and other spinels (p.96), garnet, rutile
(p.78), and magnetite (p.92). It has been proposed that
large volumes of pyroxenite form in the upper mantle.
Rare metamorphic pyroxenites are known and are
described as pyroxene hornfels.

PROFILE

- Mafic, plutonic
- Crystallization of a silica-poor magma in a minor intrusion
- 0.1–2 mm (½₂₅₆–¹⁄₁₆ in)
- Calcium plagioclase, pyroxene
- Quartz, magnetite, olivine
- Dark grey to black, often mottled white

Dark grey dolerite
Dolerite's characteristic medium texture and dark colour can be seen in this specimen.

medium texture

plagioclase feldspar

VARIANTS

Weathered dolerite A dolerite specimen showing surface flaking from weathering

Fine-grained dolerite
A specimen of dolerite with fine-grained texture

DOLERITE

A medium-grained rock, dolerite has the same composition as gabbro (p.265): one- to two-thirds is calcium-rich plagioclase feldspar, and the remainder is mainly pyroxene. Specimens can have up to 55 per cent silica and up to 10 per cent quartz (p.168). Plagioclase crystals commonly occur as tiny rectangular crystals within larger pyroxene grains in dolerite. Olivine (p.232) can occur as a constituent in the form of rounded grains that are often weathered orange-brown.

An extremely hard and tough rock, dolerite occurs in dykes and sills intruded into fissures in other rocks. It is a heavy rock that is often polished for use as a decorative stone. Dolerite is also used in its rough state for paving and is crushed for road stone. It is a stone sold under the name "black granite".

Stonehenge, England
The inner circle at Stonehenge in England is made up of about 80 pieces of dolerite "bluestones".

PROFILE

▲ Silica-poor, volcanic

🌐 Extrusion of a fluid part of Earth's mantle

🔎 Wide range

⬛ Olivine, pyroxene, mica, garnet, diopside

⬜ Ilmenite, diamond, serpentine, calcite, rutile, perovskite, magnetite

✳ Dark grey

coarse texture

crystal of ferromagnesian minerals

dark matrix

recciated kimberlite
imberlite is named after Kimberley,
he diamond industry centre in
outh Africa. This is a typically heavy
nd fragmented specimen.

VARIANTS

Weathered kimberlite
Heavily weathered kimberlite
from Kimberley, South Africa

Diamond in kimberlite
An octahedral diamond in
a kimberlite matrix

KIMBERLITE

The major source of diamonds (p.47), kimberlite is a
variety of peridotite (p.266). It is rich in mica, often in the
form of crystals of phlogopite, a type of mica. Other
abundant constituent minerals include chrome-diopside
(p.210), olivine (p.232), and chromium- and pyrope-rich
garnet. Lesser amounts of rutile (p.78), perovskite (p.89),
ilmenite (p.90), magnetite (p.92), calcite (p.114), serpentine
(p.191), pyroxene, and diamond can also be present.

Kimberlite is typically found in
pipes – structures with vertical
sides roughly circular in cross
section. The rock may have been
injected from the mantle into
zones of weakness in the crust.
Fragments of mantle rock are
often brought to the surface
in kimberlites, making them a
valuable source of information
about inner Earth.

Diamond ring
This ring has an emerald-cut
diamond on a gold shank.
Kimberlites are the primary
source rock for diamonds.

PROFILE

- 🔺 Extrusive
- 🌐 Crystallization of an alkaline magma in a minor intrusion
- 🔍 0.1–2 mm (½₅₆–¹⁄₁₆ in)
- ⬛ Orthoclase, plagioclase, biotite, hornblende
- ⬛ Hornblende, magnetite, axinite, amphibole, pyroxene
- ✳️ Dark brown to black

porphyritic texture

brown, weathered surface

Weathered lamprophyre
This weathered, greyish brown specimen of lamprophyre has a porphyritic texture, with large crystals set in a fine matrix.

VARIANTS

Dark brown lamprophyre
A specimen of lamprophyre with mica flakes

Fine-grained lamprophyre
Lamprophyre with fine grains and no phenocrysts

LAMPROPHYRE

The term lamprophyre is used to refer to a group of igneous rocks with high potassium, magnesium, and iron content. Four minerals dominate these rocks: orthoclase (p.173), plagioclase, biotite (p.197), and hornblende (p.218). Amphibole and biotite tend to occur in a groundmass of various combinations of plagioclase and other sodium- and potassium-rich feldspars, pyroxene, and feldspathoids (pp.182–84). Because of their relative rarity and varied composition, lamprophyres do not fit into standard geological classifications. In general, they form at great depth and are enriched in sodium, cesium, rubidium, nickel, and chromium, as well as potassium, iron, and magnesium. Some are also source rocks for diamonds.

The exact origin of lamprophyres is still debated. These rocks occur mainly in dykes, sills, and other small igneous intrusions. They form along the margins of some granites (pp.258–59) and are often associated with large bodies of intrusive granodiorite (p.263).

▲▲ Extrusive

⊕ Two-stage crystallization of an igneous rock

◯ Less than 0.1 mm (½₅₆ in); phenocrysts up to 2 cm (¾ in)

◼ Various

◻ Various

✸ Red, green, purple

Rhomb porphyry
This porphyry has feldspar with rhombic cross sections in a fine-grained groundmass.

fine grains

rhombic feldspar

Quartz porphyry Porphyry with phenocrysts of quartz

fine, dark groundmass

Feldspar porphyry
Phenocrysts of feldspar in a reddish brown groundmass

PORPHYRY

The name porphyry is a general name and textural term for medium- to fine-grained igneous rocks that contain large crystals (phenocrysts) of other minerals, especially if these minerals are found in the smaller crystals of the groundmass. It is most often used for rocks formed in lava flows or minor intrusions. The term porphyry is often prefixed with a reference to the minerals it contains, such as quartz–feldspar porphyry, which contains phenocrysts of the two minerals. Alternatively, the prefix can refer to the composition or texture of the rock. Examples are rhyolite porphyry or rhomb porphyry, respectively.

Porphyries form when crystallization begins deep in Earth's crust and cooling occurs quickly after rapid upward movement of magma. This results in the formation of very small crystals of the groundmass. Historically, the name porphyry was used for the purple-red form of the rock, which has been valued since antiquity as an ornamental stone. Many Egyptian, Roman, and Greek sculptures used this type of porphyry.

carbonate minerals

Carbonatite
This carbonatite specimen contains a mixture of carbonates and other minerals.

VARIANT

Carbonatite with magnetite A specimen of carbonatite with accessory black magnetite

CARBONATITE

An unusual rock type, carbonatite consists of over 50 per cent carbonate minerals – usually calcite (p.114), dolomite (p.117), or siderite (p.123). Most carbonatites also contain some portion of silicate minerals and may contain magnetite (p.92), the brown mica phlogopite, and rare-earth minerals such as pyrochlore (p.85). Specimens are typically cream-coloured, yellow, or brown. Carbonatite looks similar to marble (p.301). It may be coarse-grained if intrusive and fine-grained if volcanic.

The process by which carbonatites form is still a matter of conjecture. They are usually found in areas of continental rifting in veins, dykes, and sills around intrusions of sodium- and potassium-rich igneous rocks. The geochemistry of carbonatites is complex and can vary considerably in specimens. Many contain scarce and valuable ores of rare elements, such as niobium, cesium, tantalum, thorium, and hafnium. Some carbonatites also contain significant amounts of platinum (p.38), gold (p.42), silver (p.43), and nickel.

Fine-grained basalt
This specimen of basalt shows its characteristic fine-grained texture.

fine grains

columnar-jointed, massive basalt

VARIANTS

Vesicular basalt A basalt specimen with holes left by gas bubbles during cooling

Amygdaloidal basalt
A specimen with zeolite crystals in vesicules

Porphyritic basalt
A basalt with phenocrysts of pyroxene

BASALT

Basalt is the most common rock on Earth's surface. Specimens are black in colour and weather to dark green or brown. Basalt is rich in iron and magnesium and is mainly composed of olivine (p.232), pyroxene, and plagioclase. Most specimens are compact, fine-grained, and glassy. They can also be porphyritic, with phenocrysts of olivine, augite (p.211), or plagioclase. Holes left by gas bubbles can give basalt a coarsely porous texture.

Basalt makes up large parts of the ocean floor. It can also form volcanic islands when it is erupted by volcanoes in ocean basins. The rock has also built huge plateaus on land. The dark plains on the Moon, known as maria, and, possibly, the volcanoes on Mars and Venus are made of basalt.

Basalt temple
This magnificent, thousand-pillared temple in Andhra Pradesh, India, is made of grey basalt.

Porphyritic dacite
This dacite specimen has a porphyritic texture, with prominent phenocrysts of plagioclase and biotite.

feldspar phenocryst

hornblende

VARIANTS

Fine-grained dacite A fine-grained specimen of dacite with small phenocrysts

blue-grey dacite

Blue-grey dacite A specimen of dacite with dark phenocrysts

DACITE

An extrusive igneous rock, dacite takes its name from Dacia (modern Romania) – the ancient Roman province where it was first found. The volcanic equivalent of granodiorite (p.263), dacite is usually pink or a shade of grey. It often has flow-like bands. Porphyritic varieties are common, with large crystals usually consisting of blocky plagioclase feldspar or rounded quartz (p.168), or both. Dacite groundmass can be cryptocrystalline or glassy.

Dacite occurs with andesite (p.275) on continental margins, and with rhyolite (p.278) in continental volcanic districts. Along continental margins, dacite magmas form in areas where oceanic crust sinks beneath continental crust. Dacite magmas are chemically altered as they reach the mantle. Dacite lavas are quite viscous because of their moderate silica content. They can thus be quite explosive in eruptions. The explosion of Mount Saint Helens volcano in USA in 1980 was a result of dacite domes formed from previous eruptions. The mineral compositions of dacite lavas tell the history of the magma.

Porphyritic andesite
This specimen of porphyritic andesite
shows light feldspar phenocrysts in a
dark andesite matrix.

fine-grained matrix

*euhedral feldspar
phenocrysts*

VARIANTS

Fine-grained andesite
A specimen from the Solomon
Islands, Pacific Ocean

small phenocrysts

Andesite with plagioclase
A specimen of andesite with
phenocrysts of light plagioclase

**Amygdaloidal
andesite** Vesicles
of andesite filled
with a zeolite

ANDESITE

This volcanic rock is named after the Andes Mountains.
Intermediate in silica content, it is usually grey in colour and
may be fine-grained or porphyritic. Andesite is the volcanic
equivalent of diorite (p.264). It consists of the plagioclase
feldspar minerals andesine (p.181) and oligoclase (p.178),
together with one or more dark, ferromagnesian minerals
such as pyroxene and biotite (p.197).

Amygdaloidal andesite occurs when
the voids left by gas bubbles in the
solidifying magma are later filled
in, often with zeolite minerals
(pp.185–90). Andesite erupts from
volcanoes and is commonly found
interbedded with volcanic ash and
tuff (p.282). Ancient andesites are
used to map ancient subduction
zones as andesitic volcanoes form
on continental or ocean crust
above these zones.

Volcanic andesite
Mount Fujiyama in
Yamanashi Prefecture,
Honshu, Japan, is the cone
of an andesitic volcano.

Vesicular scoria
The large vesicles characteristic of scoria can be seen in this specimen.

brown colour

vesicle

SCORIA

The top of a lava flow is made up of a highly vesicular, rubbly material known as scoria. It has the appearance of vesicular lava. When fresh, scoria is generally dark in colour – dark brown, black, or red. Weathered scoria has a medium-brown colour and forms piles of loose rubble with small pieces. Most scoria is basaltic or andesitic in composition. This rock forms when gases in the magma expand to form bubbles as lava reaches the surface. The bubbles are then retained as the lava solidifies. Scoria is common in areas of recent volcanism, such as the Canary Islands and the Italian volcanoes.

This rock is of relatively low density due to its vesicles, but it is not as light as pumice (p.277), which floats on water. Scoria also differs from pumice in that it has larger vesicles with thicker walls. Scoria finds commercial application as high-temperature insulating material. It also has applications in landscaping and drainage.

round vesicle

Frothy pumice
The hollows (or vesicles) in this pumice clearly show its frothy nature. Vesicles may join together to form hollows or passages.

VARIANTS

Rhyolitic pumice A light-coloured rhyolitic pumice with a frothy structure

Historic pumice A specimen of pumice from the Krakatoa eruption of 1883

PUMICE

A porous and froth-like volcanic glass, pumice is created when gas-saturated liquid magma erupts like a fizzy drink and cools so rapidly that the resulting foam solidifies into a glass full of gas bubbles. Pumices from silica-rich lavas are white, those from lavas with intermediate silica content are often yellow or brown, and rarer silica-poor pumices are black. The hollows in the froth can be rounded, elongated, or tubular, depending on the flow of the solidifying lava. The glassy material that forms pumice can be in threads, fibres, or thin partitions between the hollows.

Although pumice is mainly composed of glass, small crystals of various minerals occur. Pumice has a low density due to its numerous air-filled pores. This means it can easily float in water.

Pumice stone
Pumice is soft and easily shaped. Mildly abrasive, it is often used to remove rough skin.

PROFILE

▲ Feldspar-rich, volcanic

🌐 Extrusion of a silica-rich magma

🔍 Less than 0.1 mm (1⁄256 in)

▪ Quartz, potassium feldspar

▫ Glass, biotite, amphibole, plagioclase, pyroxene

✳ Light to medium grey, light pink

flow banding

hard, flinty appearance

Banded rhyolite
This specimen of rhyolite has visible flow banding across its surface.

VARIANT

Porphyritic rhyolite
Light-coloured rhyolite with phenocrysts of quartz

RHYOLITE

A rare volcanic rock, rhyolite is usually fine-grained. It is often composed largely of volcanic glass (pp.280–81). Individual grains of quartz (p.168), feldspar (pp.173–81), and mica may be present but are too small to be visible. The small size of these grains indicates that crystallization began before the lava flowed to the surface. Rhyolites sometimes have millimetre-scale phenocrysts of quartz, feldspar, or both. Specimens can also include iron- and magnesium-rich minerals, such as biotite (p.197) or pyroxene and amphibole. The granitic magma from which rhyolite crystallizes is very viscous. Therefore, flow banding is often preserved and can be seen on weathered surfaces. Banded rhyolites have few or no phenocrysts. A rhyolite variant with tiny crystals arranged in radiating spheres is called spherulitic rhyolite.

Rhyolite occurs with pumice (p.277), obsidian (p.280), and intermediate volcanic rocks, such as andesite (p.275). Rhyolites are almost exclusively confined to the interiors and margins of continents.

Porhyritic trachyte
This specimen of fine-grained trachyte has phenocrysts of a dark mineral.

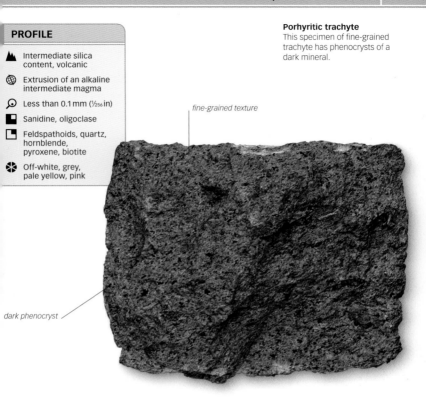

fine-grained texture

dark phenocryst

VARIANTS

Grey trachyte A fine- to medium-grained specimen of trachyte

Porphyritic trachyte Light-coloured trachyte with dark mineral phenocrysts

TRACHYTE

The name trachyte comes from the Greek word *trachys*, which means "rough" – a reference to the rock's typical rough texture. Trachyte's composition is dominated by alkali feldspar – a major component of the fine groundmass and of the abundant phenocrysts that are common in the rock. Dark, iron- and magnesium-rich minerals, such as biotite (p.197), pyroxene, and amphibole, can be present in small quantities. Trachyte is similar to rhyolite (p.278) in colour and occurence, but it contains little or no quartz (p.168).

Trachyte occurs on continents and oceanic islands with other volcanic rocks that are rich in alkali feldspars, have intermediate to high silica content, and are iron- and magnesium-rich.

Trachyte stonework
The cathedral in Morelia, in Mexico's Michoacán state, has ornate stonework of pink trachyte.

Icelandic obsidian
This classic specimen of obsidian from Iceland perfectly demonstrates the rock's conchoidal fracture and vitreous lustre.

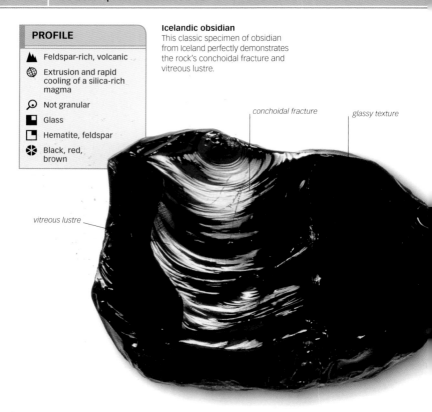

conchoidal fracture

glassy texture

vitreous lustre

VARIANTS

Vesicular obsidian
A specimen with white, silicate-filled vesicles

Snowflake obsidian
A specimen with needle-like crystals in spherical aggregates

Banded obsidian
Obsidian with red hematite

OBSIDIAN

The natural volcanic glass obsidian forms when lava solidifies so quickly that crystals do not have time to form. Specimens are typically jet black, although the presence of hematite (p.90) can produce red and brown variants. The inclusion of tiny gas bubbles can sometimes create a golden sheen. Tiny crystals of feldspar (pp.173–81) and phenocrysts of quartz (p.168) can also be present. Obsidian can show flow banding.

Although obsidian can have any chemical composition, most specimens have a composition similar to rhyolite (p.278) and are found on the outer edges of rhyolite domes and flows. Like rhyolite, obsidian is also found along the rapidly cooled edges of sills and dykes. Most obsidian is relatively young, as the glass gradually crystallizes into minerals over a period of time.

Obsidian tear drop
These polished obsidian nodules are called Apache Tears after the tears of felled Apache warriors.

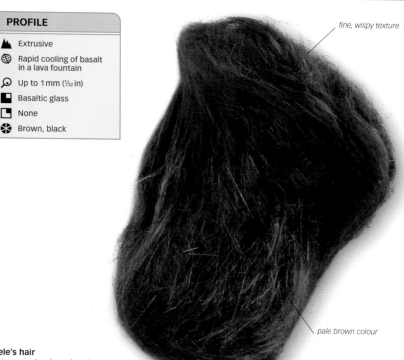

fine, wispy texture

pale brown colour

Pele's hair
This unusual rock produced in volcanic eruptions is made up of hair-like fibres of volcanic glass.

VARIANTS

Pele's tear
A small blob of volcanic glass elongated by airflow

Golden hair A mass of fine, golden volcanic glass

Long strands Particularly long strands of Pele's hair

PELE'S HAIR AND TEARS

Two of the more unusual kinds of extrusive volcanic rock are named after Pele, the Hawaiian goddess of volcanoes. The first of these is Pele's hair, which refers to threads or fibres of volcanic glass (pp.280–81) formed when small droplets of molten basaltic material are blown into the air and spun out by the wind into long, hair-like strands. Specimens are usually emitted from lava fountains, lava cascades, vents, and vigorous lava flows. They are generally deep yellow or golden in colour. A single strand of Pele's hair with a diameter of less than 0.5mm (¹/₁₆in) can be as long as 2m (6½ft). Strands can be blown tens of kilometres away from the vent or fountain where they originated.

The second variety of volcanic extrusive named after Pele is Pele's tears, which are small blobs of volcanic glass formed in much the same way as Pele's hair. Specimens occur as spheres or tear drops that are jet black in colour. They are frequently found on one end of a strand of Pele's hair.

PROFILE

- ▲ Volcanic
- ⊕ Pyroclastic accumulation of fine material
- 🔍 0.1–2 mm (½₂₅₆–⅟₁₆ in)
- ◼ Glassy fragments
- ◻ Crystalline fragments
- ✹ Light to dark brown

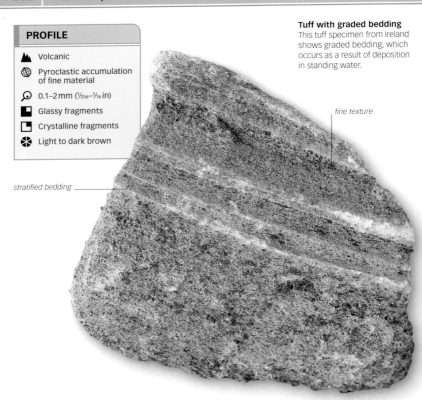

Tuff with graded bedding
This tuff specimen from Ireland shows graded bedding, which occurs as a result of deposition in standing water.

fine texture

stratified bedding

VARIANTS

Lithic tuff A specimen of tuff containing a high percentage of small rock fragments

Crystal tuff A specimen of tuff containing a predominance of crystal fragments

Bedded tuff A specimen of tuff that has fallen in distinct layers

TUFF

Any relatively soft, porous rock made of ash and other sediments ejected from volcanic vents that has solidified into rock is known as tuff. Most tuff formations include a range of fragment sizes and varieties. These range from fine-grained dust and ash (ash tuffs) to medium-sized fragments called lapilli (lapilli tuffs) to large volcanic blocks and bombs (bomb tuffs). Tuffs originate when foaming magma wells to the surface as a mixture of hot gases and incandescent particles and is ejected from a volcano.

The conditions under which the ejected ash solidifies determine the final nature of the tuff. Tuffs can vary both in texture and in chemical and mineralogical composition because of variations in the conditions of their formation and the composition of the ejected material. If the pyroclastic material is hot enough to fuse, a welded tuff (called ignimbrite) forms at once. Other tuffs lithify slowly through compaction and cementation, and can stratify when it accumulates under water.

PROFILE

▲ Extrusive

◉ Mixing of liquid and solid material during crystallization of a basic magma

◎ Less than 0.1 mm (1/256 in), clasts 0.5–20 cm (3/16–8 in)

■ Various

▢ Various

✷ Red, brown, black

Rhyolite breccia
This specimen of volcanic breccia incorporates angular fragments of reddish rhyolite.

vesicular lava

flow banding from original rhyolite deposit

reddish rhyolite fragment

VARIANT

Volcanic breccia A specimen of volcanic breccia that contains large clasts of other volcanics

VOLCANIC BRECCIA

These igneous rocks are formed either by the interaction of lava and scoria (p.276) or by the mixing of cooled lava and flowing lava. Volcanic breccia takes the form of centimetre-scale angular clasts, which may be rocks broken off the side of a magma conduit or rocks picked up off the surface during a pyroclastic or lava flow. In certain types of lavas, especially dacite (p.274) and rhyolite (p.278) lavas, thick and nearly solidified lava is broken into blocks and then reincorporated into the flow of liquid lava. Flowing lavas can also pick up surface rocks and incorporate them into a solidified breccia. In explosive volcanoes, solidified lava may be reshattered numerous times to be reconstituted as breccias.

Flowtop breccia commonly forms at the top of a lava flow where the moving lava picks up loose debris from previous eruptions and flows. It is especially common between basaltic lava flows, which may occur some time apart. Breccias are different from agglomerates (p.284), in which the clasts are rounded.

small, igneous clast

fine-grained ash

PROFILE

- ▲ Extrusive
- ⊕ Pyroclastic accumulation of coarse material
- ⌀ Less than 0.1 mm (¹⁄₂₅₆ in), clasts 0.5–20 cm (³⁄₁₆–8 in)
- ■ Igneous rock fragments
- ▣ None
- ✳ Various

Agglomerate specimen
This specimen of agglomerate contains fine-grained ash and small clasts of other igneous rocks.

VARIANT

red dolomite

Carbonatite agglomerate
A specimen of carbonatite with clasts of red dolomite

AGGLOMERATE

An agglomerate is a pyroclastic rock in which coarse, rounded clasts up to several centimetres long are set in a matrix of lava or ash. The clasts are fragments that may be derived from lava, pyroclastic rock, or country rock (the rock that surrounds or lies beneath a volcano). The rounding of the clasts may have occurred either in the magma during eruption or by later sedimentary reworking. The rounded nature of these clasts is the key to designating the rock as an agglomerate rather than as a volcanic breccia (p.283). In a volcanic breccia, most of the clasts are angular.

A type of agglomerate, vent agglomerate is the rock that plugs either the main vent or a satellite vent of a volcano. The outcrop of this rock is of limited extent and appears circular on a geological map. Like other agglomerates, vent agglomerate contains a variety of clasts of different sizes, shapes, and compositions from the lava, other volcanic rocks, or country rocks. These clasts lie in a matrix of fine-grained igneous rock.

PROFILE

🗻 Extrusive

🌐 Mid-air cooling of masses of silica-poor magma

🔍 2 cm–1 m (¾ in–3¼ ft)

◼ Basalt

◻ None

❇ Dark shades of red, brown, or green

green colour from olivine

Olivine-rich bomb
Volcanoes that emit magnesium- and iron-rich lavas sometimes explosively hurl olivine-rich bombs, such as this one.

VARIANTS

Spindle bomb Lava twisted by aerodynamic forces

cracked outer surface

Breadcrust bomb Bomb with crust that hardened before landing

elongated shape

Spiky spindle A spindle bomb violently spun after ejection

VOLCANIC BOMB

Formed by the cooling of a mass of lava while it flies through the air after eruption, a volcanic bomb is a pyroclastic rock. To be called a bomb, a specimen must be larger than 6.5 cm (2½ in) in diameter; smaller specimens are known as lapilli. Specimens up to 6 m (20 ft) in diameter are known. Volcanic bombs are usually brown or red, weathering to a yellow-brown colour. Specimens can become rounded during transport, though they may also be twisted or pointed. They may have a cracked, fine-grained, or glassy surface.

There are several types of volcanic bomb, which are named according to their outward appearance and structure. Spherical bombs are spheres of fluid magma pulled into shape by surface tension. Spindle bombs are formed by the same process as spherical bombs, except that their rotation in flight leaves them elongated. A breadcrust bomb forms if the outside of the lava bomb solidifies during flight and develops a cracked outer surface while the interior continues to expand.

METAMORPHIC ROCKS

Metamorphism occurs when an existing rock is subjected to pressures or temperatures very different from those under which it formed. This causes its atoms and molecules to rearrange themselves into new minerals in the solid state, without melting.

DYNAMIC METAMORPHISM

There are three different ways in which metamorphic rocks are formed. The first of these is dynamic metamorphism. This occurs as a result of large-scale movements in Earth's crust, especially along fault planes and at continental margins where tectonic plates collide. The resulting mechanical deformation produces angular fragments to fine-grained, granulated, or powdered rocks. These rocks are characterized by a foliated appearance, in which mineral grains align as parallel plates.

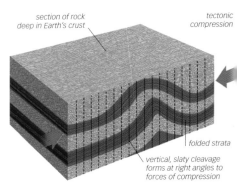

section of rock deep in Earth's crust

tectonic compression

folded strata

vertical, slaty cleavage forms at right angles to forces of compression

Dynamic metamorphism
Tectonic forces transform sedimentary rocks by dynamic metamorphism. Rock strata fold and cleavages develop as minerals align themselves due to the pressure.

REGIONAL METAMORPHISM

The second type of metamorphism is the formation of regional metamorphic rocks. These are associated with mountain building through the collision of tectonic plates. This process increases temperature and pressure over an area of thousands of square kilometres, producing widespread metamorphism. Important regional metamorphic rocks include slates, schists, and gneisses. Which rock forms depends on the temperatures and pressures to which the existing rocks were subjected and the time they spent under those conditions. At the extremes, low temperature and pressure produces slates; high temperature and pressure produces gneisses.

Ancient metamorphic rocks
The Elk Mountains in Colorado, USA, have extensive areas of metamorphic rock, including schists and gneisses thought to have metamorphosed 1.7–1.9 billion years ago.

CONTACT METAMORPHISM

The third type of metamorphism is contact metamorphism or thermal metamorphism. This type occurs mainly as a result of increases in temperature and not in pressure. It is common in rocks near an igneous intrusion. Heat from the intrusion alters rocks to produce an "aureole" of metamorphic rock. The rocks nearest to the intrusion are subjected to higher temperatures than those farther away, resulting in concentric zones of distinctive metamorphic rocks. The minerals of each zone depend on the original composition of the host rocks.

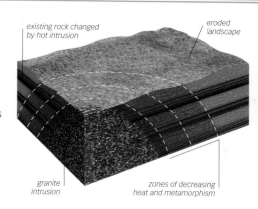

existing rock changed by hot intrusion

eroded landscape

granite intrusion

zones of decreasing heat and metamorphism

Contact metamorphism
A large intrusion of an igneous rock, such as granite, releases heat into the surrounding rocks, altering their mineral content.

CHANGING CHARACTERISTICS

Metamorphism is said to be low grade if it occurs at relatively low temperature and pressure and high grade at the intense end of the temperature and pressure range. The assemblages of minerals in rocks are affected differently depending on the grade of metamorphism and the relative importance of pressure and temperature in the reaction. In some low-grade reactions, the components of existing mineral assemblages are simply redistributed. In other reactions at higher temperatures and pressures, components combine with others present in the rock to form an entirely new set of minerals.

Shale to gneiss
This sequence shows how shale, a sedimentary rock, can be metamorphosed into various other rocks by the application of increasingly high degrees of heat and pressure (from left to right).

SHALE   SLATE   PHYLLITE   SCHIST   GNEISS

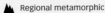

pale feldspar

dark biotite

Banded gneiss
This specimen of classic gneiss shows foliated banding of light and dark minerals.

Folded gneiss A specimen with alternating mineral bands and typical folding

Orthogneiss Gneiss from metamorphosed igneous rocks

Augen gneiss A specimen with large "eyes" of light-coloured feldspar

GNEISS

Distinct bands of minerals of different colours and grain sizes characterize this metamorphic rock. In most gneisses, these bands are folded, although the folds may be too large to see in hand specimens. Gneiss is a medium- to coarse-grained rock. Unlike schist (pp.291–92), its foliation is well developed, but it has little or no tendency to split along planes. Most gneisses contain quartz (p.168) and feldspar (pp.173–81), but neither mineral is necessary for a rock to be called gneiss. Larger crystals of metamorphic minerals, such as garnet, can also be present.

Gneiss makes up the cores of many mountain ranges. It forms from sedimentary or granitic (pp.258–59) rocks at very high pressures and temperatures (575°C/1,065°F or above). A variety called pencil gneiss has rod-shaped individual minerals or mineral aggregates. In augen gneiss, the augens or "eyes" are single-mineral, eye-shaped grains that are larger than other grains in the rock. Orthogneiss is gneiss derived from igneous rock, and paragneiss is gneiss derived from sedimentary rock.

PROFILE

- Dynamic thrust zones
- Stretching of a rock in a large fault
- Low
- Shearing stress
- Streaked out
- Less than 2mm (1/16 in)
- As surrounding rock
- As surrounding rock
- As surrounding rock
- Surrounding rock

foliation

pale mylonite

Deformed mylonite
The folded bands in this mylonite specimen indicate that it has been subjected to extreme deformation.

VARIANT

fine grains

Granular mylonite
A specimen with stretched mineral grains

MYLONITE

The term mylonite refers to fine-grained rocks with streaks or rod-like structures produced by the ductile deformation, or stretching, of mineral grains. This classification is based only on the texture of the rock, and specimens can have different mineral compositions. Mylonite with a large percentage of phyllosilicate minerals, such as chlorite or mica, is known as phyllonite. When mylonite is hard, dark, and so fine that it has the appearance of streaky flint, it is known as ultramylonite. Although generally fine grained, a few mylonites are coarse grained and often sugary in appearance. These are referred to as blastomylonites.

There are many different views on the formation of mylonite. It is typically produced in a zone of thrusts or low-angle faults. Fine-grained mylonites may have been produced by recrystallization under pressure. The fact that mylonite grains are stretched rather than sheared makes it evident that the rock has softened in the metamorphic process.

light quartz
and feldspar

dark gneissose
component

PROFILE

⛰ Regional metamorphic

🌐 Partial melting of rocks
containing quartz and
feldspar

🌡 High

⚖ High

⊞ Foliated, crystalline

🔍 2–5 mm (¹⁄₁₆–³⁄₁₆ in)

◼ Quartz, feldspar, mica

▢ Various

✻ Banded light and dark
grey, pink, white

◀◀ Various, including granite

Mixed migmatite
The mixing of light igneous
and dark metamorphic mineral
elements is evident in this
specimen of migmatite.

VARIANTS

Partial melting Migmatite
with a snake-like vein of
granite, which indicates
partial melting

Migmatite folding
A specimen of migmatite with
distortions produced by
extreme temperatures

MIGMATITE

The term migmatite means "mixed rock" and refers to
rocks that consist of gneiss (p.288) or schist (pp.291–92)
interlayered, streaked, or veined with granite (pp.258–59).
The granitic parts consist of granular patches of quartz
(p.168) and feldspar (pp.173–81), and the gneissic parts
consist of quartz, feldspar, and dark-coloured minerals.
The granite streaks are a result of the partial melting of the
parent rock at temperatures below the melting point
of the schist or gneiss. The layering may be tightly
folded as a result of softening during heating. Migmatites
occur at the borderline between igneous and
metamorphic rocks.

The rock forms near large intrusions of granite when
some of the magma has intruded into the surrounding
metamorphic rocks. Commonly, migmatite occurs
within extremely deformed rocks that once formed the
bases of eroded mountain chains. It forms deep in
the crust at high temperatures (575°C/1,065°F or above)
and pressures.

PROFILE

- Regional metamorphic
- Regional metamorphism of fine-grained sediments
- Low to moderate
- Low to moderate
- Foliated
- 0.1–2 mm (½₅₆–⅛ in)
- Quartz, feldspar, mica
- Garnet, hornblende, actinolite, graphite, kyanite
- Silvery, green, blue
- Mudstone, siltstone, shale, or felsic volcanics

dark biotite _pale muscovite_

wavy folds picked out by mineral bands

Folded schist
The wavy surface of this schist shows the small-scale distortions produced during its formation. It has split along its mica bands.

VARIANTS

Muscovite schist A specimen of schist dominated by white muscovite mica

Blue schist Schist coloured blue by glaucophane

Kyanite schist Small, blue blades of kyanite in schist

SCHIST

This metamorphic rock has a flaky and foliated texture. Specimens have wrinkled, wavy, or irregular sheets as a result of the parallel orientation of the component minerals. Schist shows distinct layering of light- and dark-coloured minerals. The mineral assemblage varies, but mica is usually present. Most schists are composed of platy minerals, such as chlorite, graphite (p.46), talc (p.193), muscovite (p.195), and biotite (p.197). The mineral composition of a schist depends on its protolith or original rock and its metamorphic environment. The mineral assemblage can thus be used to determine the metamorphic history of the rock.

Indian schist carving
Although its texture and composition are often uneven, schist is sometimes used as a carving material.

PROFILE

 Regional metamorphic

 Medium-grade
metamorphism
of silica-rich rocks

 Low to moderate

 Moderate

 Foliated

 2–5 mm (¹⁄₁₆–³⁄₁₆ in)

 Muscovite, biotite, garnet

 Feldspar, staurolite,
sillimanite, kyanite,
cordierite

Light to dark

Silica-rich rocks

wavy foliation

*garnet
porphyroblast*

Garnet porphyroblasts
Garnet is commonly present
in schists, forming large
crystals called porphyroblasts,
as seen here.

VARIANTS

Garnet-chlorite schist
Garnet porphyroblasts in
chlorite schist

**Garnet-muscovite-chlorite
schist** Garnet porphyroblasts
in a specimen of muscovite-
chlorite schist

GARNET SCHIST

Like other schists, garnet schist is a metamorphic rock
with a characteristic texture: wrinkled, irregular, or wavy
as a result of the parallel orientation of its component
minerals, such as chlorite, graphite (p.46), talc (p.193),
muscovite (p.195), and biotite (p.197). In garnet schist,
garnet occurs as porphyroblasts, which are large crystals
set in a metamorphic groundmass with other smaller
crystals. The resulting texture is called porphyroblastic. The
equivalent texture in igneous rocks is called porphyritic.

Garnet schist is widespread and usually forms from
the metamorphism of fine-grained sediments, especially
during the formation of mountains. The mineral assemblage
in garnet schist, like in other schists, helps determine both
the environment in which the original rock formed and
its metamorphic history. Other porphyroblastic schists –
such as staurolite schist, corundum schist, kyanite
schist, muscovite schist, biotite schist, and schists of
other metamorphic minerals – are indicative of other
metamorphic histories.

Welsh slate
This dark grey specimen is from Wales, Britain's principal source of slate. In the USA, slate is quarried in Pennsylvania and Vermont.

fissile splitting

fine grains

foliated structure

VARIANTS

Chiastolite slate High-temperature slate with chiastolite crystals

Spotted slate Slate with small aggregates of carbon

Pyrite Slate with pyrite grains and porphyroblasts

SLATE

A fine-grained metamorphic rock, slate occurs in a number of colours that depend on the minerals in the original sedimentary rock and the oxidation conditions under which that rock formed. Slate has a characteristic cleavage that allows it to be split into relatively thin, flat sheets. This is a result of microscopic mica crystals that have grown oriented in the same plane. True slates split along the foliation planes formed during metamorphism, rather than along the original sedimentary layers.

Slate is common in regionally metamorphosed terrains. It forms when shale (p.313), mudstone (p.316), or volcanic rocks rich in silica are buried as well as subjected to low pressures and temperatures (up to 200°C/400°F). The ability of slate to split into thin sheets makes it ideal as a durable roofing material.

School slate
This child's school slate is from Victorian times. In the past, all school "blackboards" were made from slate.

sheen on surface

dark phyllite

flat surface

Irregular surface
This example of phyllite shows bands of minerals and a cleaved surface that is more irregular than that found in slate.

VARIANTS

Coarse foliation An example of coarsely foliated phyllite

Alternating minerals Phyllite with bands of minerals

Garnet porphyroblasts Small, dark garnets on foliated surface

PHYLLITE

Like slate (p.293), phyllite is a fine-grained metamorphic rock that is usually grey or dark green in colour. It has a shinier sheen than slate because of its larger mica crystals. The rock has a tendency to split in the same manner as slate because of a parallel alignment of mica minerals. However, the split surfaces are more irregular than in slate, and phyllite splits into thick slabs rather than thin sheets. Many phyllite specimens have a scattering of large crystals called porphyroblasts, which grow during metamorphism. The rock is often deformed into folds a few centimetres wide and is veined with quartz (p.168). Biotite (p.197), cordierite (p.223), tourmaline (p.224), andalusite (p.236), and staurolite (p.239) are commonly found in phyllite.

This rock occurs in both young and old eroded mountain belts in regionally metamorphosed terrains. It forms when fine-grained sedimentary rocks, such as shales (p.313) or mudstones (p.316), are buried and subjected to relatively low pressures and temperatures (up to 200°C/400°F) for a long period of time.

PROFILE

🔺 Regional metamorphic

🌐 Regional metamorphism of orthoquartzite

🌡 High

〰 Low to high

▦ Crystalline

🔎 2–5 mm (¹⁄₁₆–³⁄₁₆ in)

◼ Quartz

◻ Mica, kyanite, sillimanite

✳ Almost any

◁◀ Sandstone

interlocking grains

crystalline quartz

Crystalline metaquartzite
The metamorphic variety of quartzite is a crystalline rock with over 90 per cent quartz.

VARIANTS

Pale metaquartzite
A specimen of metaquartzite with a very high percentage of quartz

Grey metaquartzite
A specimen that reflects the colour of the original sandstone

QUARTZITE

This quartz-rich metamorphic rock is usually white to grey when pure. Specimens can be various shades of pink, red, yellow, and orange when mineral impurities are present. Quartzite is very hard and brittle and shows conchoidal fracture. It usually contains at least 90 per cent quartz (p.168).

Metamorphic quartzite, or metaquartzite, forms when sandstone (p.308) is buried, heated, and squeezed into a solid quartz rock. It is found with other regional metamorphic rocks formed during the shifting of Earth's tectonic plates. Quartzite can also refer to sedimentary sandstone converted to a much denser form through the precipitation of silica cement in pore spaces. The two types of quartzite can be distinguished by examining the grains under a microscope: metamorphic quartzite consists of interlocking crystals of quartz, whereas sedimentary quartzite, or orthoquartzite, contains rounded quartz grains. Crushed quartzite is often used as railway ballast and in the construction of roads.

PROFILE

🔺 Regional metamorphic

🌐 High-grade metamorphism of silica-poor igneous rocks

🌡 Low to moderate temperatures (up to 575°C/1,065°F)

〰 Low to moderate

▦ Foliated, crystalline

🔍 2–5 mm (¹⁄₁₆–³⁄₁₆ in)

◼ Hornblende, tremolite, actinolite

▢ Feldspar, calcite, garnet, pyroxene

✳ Grey, black, greenish

◀◀ Basalt, greywacke, dolomite

coarse texture

amphibole crystal

Amphibolite composition
Though it comprises mainly amphibole minerals, amphibolite can also contain feldspar, garnet, pyroxene, and epidote.

VARIANTS

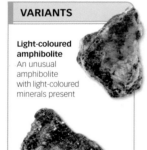

Light-coloured amphibolite
An unusual amphibolite with light-coloured minerals present

Hornblende-rich amphibolite
A hornblende-rich specimen of amphibolite

Green amphibolite
Amphibolite with many garnet porphyroblasts

AMPHIBOLITE

As the name suggests, amphibolites are dark-coloured, coarse-grained rocks that are dominated by amphiboles: the black or dark green hornblende (p.218) and the green tremolite (p.219) or actinolite (p.220). Specimens may contain grains of calcite (p.114), feldspar (pp.173–81), and pyroxene and large crystals of minerals such as garnet. Except for garnet, the mineral grains in amphibolite are usually aligned. The rock can also show banding.

Amphibolites form from the metamorphism of iron- and magnesium-rich igneous rocks, such as gabbros (p.265), and from sedimentary rocks, such as greywacke (p.317). They comprise one of the major divisions of metamorphic rocks as classified by their mineral assemblages. These rocks form under conditions of low to moderate pressures and temperatures (up to 575°C/1,065°F). Amphibolites are used in road building and in other aggregates where high degrees of strength and durability are required.

fine matrix

plagioclase feldspar

Unfoliated rock
Unlike many other regionally metamorphosed rocks, granulite is characterized by a lack of foliation.

VARIANT

porphyroblast

Light-coloured granulite
This specimen of granulite has numerous porphyroblasts

GRANULITE

This metamorphic rock is named after its even-grained, granular texture. Specimens are typically tough and massive. Granulite has a high concentration of pyroxene, with diopside (p.210) or hypersthene, garnet, calcium plagioclase, and quartz (p.168) or olivine (p.232). It has nearly the same minerals as gneiss (p.288) but is finer-grained, less perfectly foliated, and has more garnet.

Formed at high pressures and temperatures (575°C/ 1,065°F or above) deep in Earth's crust, granulites are characteristic of the highest grade of metamorphism. Rocks formed under these conditions belong to a category of metamorphic rocks known as the granulite facies. Mineral groups such as micas and amphiboles cannot survive at the high metamorphic grade under which granulites form and are converted into pyroxenes and garnets. Most granulites date from the Precambrian Age, which ended over 500 million years ago. They are of particular interest to geologists as many of them represent samples of the deep continental crust.

PROFILE

🔺 Regional

🌐 Water-rich, low-grade metamorphism of olivine-rich rocks

🌡 Low temperatures (up to 200°C/400°F)

〰 Low

🏢 Nonfoliated

🔍 Less than 0.1 mm ($\frac{1}{256}$ in)

⬛ Serpentine

⬜ Chromite, magnetite, talc

❇ Medium to dark

◀◀ Olivine-rich igneous rocks

easily seen coarse grain

mottled, patchy texture

Grainy serpentinite
This example of serpentinite clearly shows its fine grains.

VARIANT

Alpine serpentine Red and green serpentinite streaked with calcite from the Alps

SERPENTINITE

An attractive rock, serpentinite is composed of serpentine (p.191) and other serpentine-group minerals. It commonly has flowing bands of various colours, especially green and yellow. Serpentine minerals form by a metamorphic process called serpentinization that alters olivine and pyroxene-rich, silica-poor igneous rocks. This process occurs at low temperatures (up to 200°C/400°F) and in the presence of water. The original minerals are oxidized to produce serpentine, magnetite (p.92), and brucite (p.105). The degree to which a rock undergoes serpentinization depends on the composition of the parent rock and the mineral composition of its components, especially its olivine (p.232). For example, fayalite-rich olivines serpentinize differently than forsterite-rich olivines.

Serpentinite is used as a decorative stone since it can be easily cut and polished. It is also mixed into concrete aggregate and used as a dry filler in the steel shielding jackets of nuclear reactors.

PROFILE

🔺 Regional

🌐 High-pressure metamorphism of silica-poor igneous rocks

🌡 High temperatures (575°C/1,065°F or above)

📶 High

▦ Foliated, crystalline

🔎 2–5 mm (⅟₁₆–³⁄₁₆ in)

⬛ Pyroxene, garnet

⬜ Kyanite, quartz, olivine, diopside

✳ Various colours

◀◀ Silica-poor igneous rocks

Distributed eclogite grains
Eclogites, such as this one with red garnet and green pyroxene, are formed under great pressure, and are thought to originate in the mantle.

red pyrope garnet

green omphacite

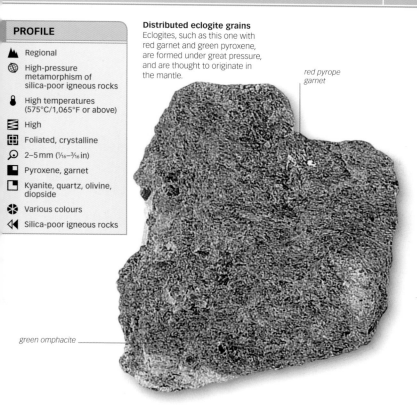

VARIANTS

Mantle rock Eclogite with garnet porphyroblasts

Fine-grained eclogite Garnet- and pyroxene-rich specimen of eclogite

ECLOGITE

A rare but important rock, eclogite is formed only by conditions typically found in the mantle or the lowermost and thickest part of the continental crust. Its overall chemical composition is similar to that of igneous basalt (p.273). It is a beautiful, coarse-grained, dense rock of bright red garnet and contrasting bright green omphacite – a pyroxene characteristic of high-temperature metamorphism. Diopside (p.210) and olivine (p.232) are commonly present as well. Eclogite grains may be evenly distributed or banded.

Eclogite forms at very high temperatures (575°C/1,065°F or above) and pressures from silica-poor igneous rocks. Many investigators believe that eclogite is characteristic of a considerable portion of the upper mantle. When brought upwards into the crust, eclogites are mainly found as xenoliths (foreign inclusions) in igneous rocks and as isolated blocks up to 100 m (330 ft) wide in other metamorphic rocks. Although rare, diamonds (p.47) may occur in eclogites.

Soapstone specimen
This specimen of soapstone shows the foliation of the original talc.

greasy lustre

massive habit

VARIANTS

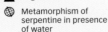

Foliated soapstone
Soapstone with visible foliation

Flaky soapstone Soft soapstone with a flaky surface

Green soapstone
A specimen of soapstone consisting primarily of green talc

SOAPSTONE

Also known as steatite, soapstone is a fine-grained, massive rock. Talc (p.193), one of the softest minerals, is its principal component. Soapstone specimens are easily recognized by their softness: they have a greasy feel and can be scratched with a fingernail. Soapstone may also contain varying amounts of amphiboles, such as anthophyllite (p.216) and tremolite (p.219), and chlorites. Specimens can be green, brown, or black when polished, but they become white when scratched.

Soapstone is found associated with other metamorphosed silica-poor igneous rocks, such as serpentinite (p.298). It is used in fireplace surrounds as it absorbs and distributes heat evenly. It is also carved into moulds for soft-metal casting.

Lion dog seal
Soapstone, such as that used in this Chinese seal, has been used to carve ornaments for millennia.

iron-oxide cement

Marble breccia
This specimen of marble has been cracked and shattered, the veins infilled, and fragments recemented with iron- and calcium-rich cement.

marble fragment

hematite vein

PROFILE

▲	Regional or contact metamorphic
🌐	Contact or regional metamorphism of limestone or dolomite
🌡	High temperatures (575°C/1,065°F or above)
▤	Low to high
▦	Crystalline
🔍	Up to 2 cm (¾ in)
■	Calcite
▥	Diopside, tremolite, actinolite, dolomite
✳	White, pink
◀◀	Limestone, dolomite

VARIANTS

Olivine marble
Marble with small crystals of olivine

Green marble A specimen of marble coloured by green silicate minerals

Grey marble Marble from relatively pure limestone

MARBLE

A granular metamorphic rock, marble is derived from limestone (p.319) or dolomite (p.320). It consists of a mass of interlocking grains of calcite (p.114) or the mineral dolomite (p.117).

Marbles form when limestone buried deep in the older layers of Earth's crust is subjected to heat and pressure from thick layers of overlying sediments. It may also form as a result of contact metamorphism near igneous intrusions. Impurities in the limestone can recrystallize during metamorphism, resulting in mineral impurities in the marble, most commonly graphite (p.46), pyrite (p.62), quartz (p.168), mica, and iron oxides. In sufficient amounts, these can affect the texture and colour of the marble.

Taj Mahal, India
The Taj Mahal is built of Makrana – a white marble that changes hue with the angle of the light.

brown calcite

diopside and tremolite

PROFILE

▲▲ Contact

⊕ Contact metamorphism of limestone

🌡 High temperatures (575°C/1,065°F or above)

⧩ Low

⊞ Crystalline

⌀ 0.1–20mm (1/256–3/4 in)

■ Calcite

▢ Garnet, serpentine, forsterite, vesuvianite

❋ Variegated

◁◀ Limestone, dolomite

Skarn specimen
This specimen of skarn with calcite and dark minerals shows the rock's typical veined and banded appearance.

VARIANT

Garnet in skarn A uvarovite garnet porphyroblast in a skarn matrix

SKARN

This rock is a product of the contact metamorphism of limestone (p.319) or dolomite (p.320) by an igneous intrusion, often granite (pp.258–59), with an intermediate or high silica content. Hot waters derived from the granitic magma are rich in silica, iron, aluminium, sulphur, and magnesium. When limestone or dolomite is invaded by this high-temperature hydrothermal solution, the carbonate minerals calcite (p.114) and dolomite react strongly with the slightly acid solution. The elements carried in the solutions combine with the calcium and magnesium in the parent rock to form silicate minerals, such as diopside (p.210), tremolite (p.219), and andradite. The resulting rock is usually a highly complex combination of calcium-, magnesium-, and carbonate-rich minerals.

Skarn minerals can be fine- to medium-grained. They also occur as coarse, radiating crystals or bands. Some skarns are rich in metallic ores and form valuable deposits of metals, including gold (p.42), copper, iron, tin, lead, molybdenum, and zinc.

PROFILE

- ▲ Contact metamorphic
- ⊕ Contact metamorphism of fine-grained sediment
- 🌡 Moderate to high temperatures (200°C/400°F or above)
- ⊟ Low to high
- ⊞ Crystalline
- 🔍 Less than 0.1 mm (1/256 in)
- ◼ Hornblende, plagioclase, andalusite, cordierite, and others
- ◻ Magnetite, apatite, titanite
- ✳ Dark grey, brown, greenish, reddish
- ◀◀ Almost any rock

dark, pyroxene crystals

Pyroxene hornfels
In this specimen of hornfels, dark porphyroblasts of pyroxene can be seen.

VARIANTS

Garnet hornfels A specimen coloured red by garnet crystals

Cordierite hornfels Hornfels with small grains of cordierite, quartz, and mica

Chiastolite hornfels Hornfels with elongated porphyroblasts of chiastolite (andalusite)

HORNFELS

Formed by contact metamorphism close to igneous intrusions at temperatures as high as 700°–800°C (1,300°–1,450°F), hornfels can form from almost any parent rock and is notoriously difficult to identify. Its composition depends on the parent rock and the exact temperatures and fluids to which the rock is exposed. Specimens are usually dense, hard, and hard to break. They are fine-grained and relatively homogeneous, with a conchoidal, flint-like fracture. The rock may sometimes appear glassy. The colour is usually even throughout, though specimens may also be banded.

Hornfels is often categorized by the mix of minerals present in the specimen. Garnet hornfels, for example, is characterized by large crystals of garnet set into a rock matrix. Cordierite hornfels contains large crystals of cordierite (p.223) that can be up to several centimetres in diameter. An outcrop of hornfels rarely extends more than a few metres from the contact and may pass outwards into spotted slate.

SEDIMENTARY ROCKS

Sedimentary rocks are formed at or near Earth's surface either by accumulation of grains or by precipitation of dissolved material. These rocks make up the majority of the rock exposed at Earth's surface, but are only about 8 per cent of the volume of the entire crust.

LITHIFICATION

The transformation of loose grains of sediment into sedimentary rock is known as lithification. The grains are often bound together by a cementing agent, which is generally precipitated from solutions that filter through the sediment. In some cases, the cementing agent is created at least in part by the breakdown of some rock particles of the sediment itself. The most common cement is silica (usually quartz), but calcite and other carbonates as well as iron oxides, baryte, anhydrite, zeolites, and clay minerals also form cements. The cementing agent becomes an integral and important part of the sedimentary rock once it is formed. In some cases, clastic sedimentary rocks (see opposite) can also be formed by simple compaction – a process in which the grains bind together under extreme pressure.

Lithification can sometimes take place almost immediately after the grains have

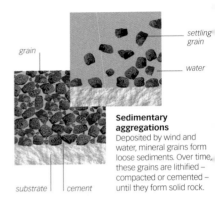

Sedimentary aggregations
Deposited by wind and water, mineral grains form loose sediments. Over time, these grains are lithified – compacted or cemented – until they form solid rock.

been deposited as sediment. In other cases, hundreds or even millions of years may pass by before lithification occurs. At any given time, there are large amounts of rock fragments that have been produced by weathering but have not been lithified and simply exist as a form of sediment.

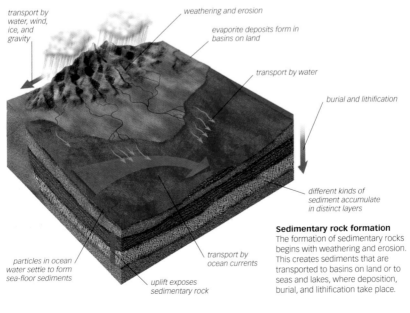

Sedimentary rock formation
The formation of sedimentary rocks begins with weathering and erosion. This creates sediments that are transported to basins on land or to seas and lakes, where deposition, burial, and lithification take place.

CLASTIC ROCKS

Clasts are rock fragments ranging in size from boulders to microscopic particles. Clastic sedimentary rocks are grouped according to the size of the clasts from which they form. Larger clasts such as pebbles, cobbles, and boulder-sized gravels form conglomerate and breccia; sand becomes sandstone; and finer silt and clay particles form siltstone, mudstone, and shale. The mineral composition of clastic rocks can be subject to considerable change over time.

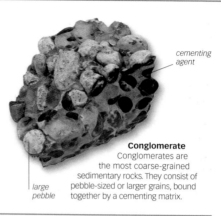

cementing agent

large pebble

Conglomerate
Conglomerates are the most coarse-grained sedimentary rocks. They consist of pebble-sized or larger grains, bound together by a cementing matrix.

CHEMICAL ROCKS

Chemical sedimentary rocks are formed by the precipitation of the transported, dissolved products of chemical weathering. In some cases, the dissolved constituents are directly precipitated as solid rock. Examples include banded iron formations, some limestones, and bedded evaporite deposits – that is, rocks and mineral deposits of soluble salts resulting from the evaporation of water. In other sedimentary rocks, such as limestone and chert, solid material first precipitates into particles, which are then deposited and lithified.

White cliffs of Dover
Located near the town of Dover in Kent, England, the celebrated White cliffs of Dover are spectacular deposits of chalk many metres thick.

FOSSILS

A fossil is a remnant, impression, or trace of an organism that has lived in a past geological age. Fossils are preserved almost exclusively in sedimentary rocks. The most common fossils are of aquatic plants and animals. After an organism dies, the soft parts decompose, leaving behind only the hard parts – the shell, teeth, bones, or wood. Buried in layers of sediment, the hard parts gradually turn to stone. In a process known as permineralization, water seeps through the rock, depositing mineral salts in the pores of the shell or bone, thereby fossilizing the remains. In some cases, the organic matter is completely replaced by minerals as it decays. In other cases, circulating acid solutions dissolve the original shell or bone, leaving a cavity of identical shape, which is filled in as new material is deposited in the cavity, creating a cast.

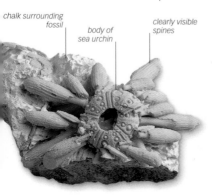

chalk surrounding fossil

body of sea urchin

clearly visible spines

Fossil in chalk
Large sea urchin fossils, such as this well-preserved example, are usually found in chalk, which is itself made up of the fossils of tiny marine organisms.

PROFILE

- ▲ Detrital, from pebbles
- ⊕ Marine, freshwater, glacial
- ⊘ 2mm (¹⁄₁₆in) to several cm (in) in finer matrix
- ■ Any hard mineral can be present
- ◱ Any mineral can be present
- ✹ Varies
- ✹ Very rare

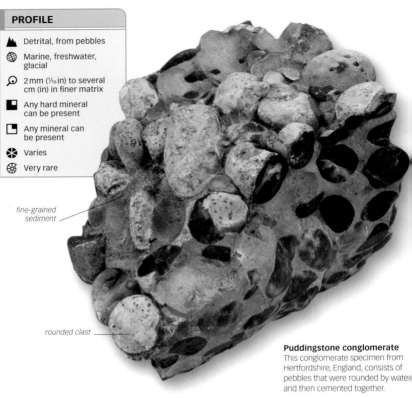

fine-grained sediment

rounded clast

Puddingstone conglomerate
This conglomerate specimen from Hertfordshire, England, consists of pebbles that were rounded by water and then cemented together.

VARIANTS

Quartz conglomerate
A specimen with large clasts of quartz

Polygenetic conglomerate
A specimen with clasts of various rock types

alluvial diamond

Alluvial diamond
A diamond cemented into a conglomerate

CONGLOMERATE

Rocks formed by the lithification of rounded rock fragments that are over 2mm (¹⁄₁₆in) in diameter are known as conglomerates. They can be further classified by the average size of their constituent materials–pebble-conglomerate (fine), cobble-conglomerate (medium), and boulder-conglomerate (coarse). Conglomerate can also be known by the rock or mineral fragments in its composition; for example, a quartz pebble conglomerate.

Depending on the environment in which these fragments are deposited, these rocks may be of two types. Well-sorted conglomerates result from water flow over a long period. These have well-sorted pebbles (with a small size variation) generally of only one rock or mineral type and a few small particles between the pebbles. Poorly sorted conglomerates form from rapid water flow and deposition. They have poorly sorted pebbles (of varying sizes) of mixed rock and mineral types with a number of small particles between the pebbles.

PROFILE

- ▲ Detrital, from coarse sediment
- ⊕ Marine, freshwater, glacial
- ⌀ 2 mm (¹⁄₁₆ in) to several cm (in) in finer matrix
- ■ Any hard mineral can be present
- ▢ Any mineral can be present
- ✺ Varies
- ✸ Very rare

angular fragment

grey, silica-rich fragment

Poorly sorted breccia
This specimen of breccia shows large and small angular fragments with no clear pattern of orientation.

VARIANTS

Limestone breccia
Fragments of limestone in breccia

Polygenetic breccia
A specimen with clasts of different types of rock

Fault breccia Cemented clasts shattered by faulting

BRECCIA

Lithified sediments with rock fragments that are more than ¹⁄₁₆ in (2 mm) in diameter but angular or only slightly rounded are called breccias. The lack of rounding indicates that little or no transportation took place before the fragments became incorporated in the rock.

Breccias can form in several ways. Rocks can shatter – for example, due to frost action or earth movement – and the fragments then become cemented in the new position. Shattered fragments may also move before being cemented – for example, they may accumulate at the base of a cliff or be carried by a flash flood. Breccias can also form in areas of active faulting. In areas where faulting occurs underwater, newly shattered material can also move in underwater landslides and become cemented to form breccia.

Breccia vase
This ancient Egyptian carved vase made of breccia or mottle stone was used to store liquids.

Structure in sandstone
This sandstone from Yorkshire, England, is derived from deposits of wind-blown sand. The bedding planes, which slumped after deposition, are well preserved.

fine-grained texture

evidence of slumping

VARIANTS

Micaceous sandstone
A specimen with flakes of mica and patches of iron oxide

Goethite sandstone Sand grains with red goethite

Red sandstone
A specimen of quartz sandstone coloured red due to the presence of iron oxides

SANDSTONE

The second most abundant sedimentary rock after shale (p.313), sandstone makes up about 10 to 20 per cent of the sedimentary rocks in Earth's crust. Sandstones are classified according to texture and mineralogical properties into micaceous sandstone, orthoquartzite (p.310), and greywacke (p.317). They are usually dominated by quartz (p.168) and have visible sandy grains and other minerals present in varying amounts. Well-rounded grains are typical of desert sandstone, while river sands are usually angular, and beach sands somewhere in between.

Bedding is often visible in sandstones as a series of layers representing successive deposits of grains. Bedding surfaces may show either ripples or the cross bedding typical of dunes. Sandstone is an important indicator of deposition and erosion processes.

Sandstone platform
This platform in the centre of the courtyard pool at Fatehpur Sikri, India, is made from red sandstone.

Marine greensand
This specimen is from the Atlantic coastal plain of North America, where greensand is a common type of rock.

well-sorted sediment

green colouring from glauconite

PROFILE

	Detrital, from glauconite-rich marine sand
	Marine
	0.1–2 mm (¹⁄₂₅₆–¹⁄₁₆ in)
	Quartz, glauconite
	Feldspar, mica
	Green
	Vertebrates, invertebrates, plants

VARIANT

Greensand banding
A band of greensand within a rock outcrop

GREENSAND

A quartz sandstone with a high percentage of the green mica mineral glauconite (p.196) is known as greensand or glauconitic sandstone. The term glauconite is also loosely applied to any glauconitic sediment. Glauconite is believed to form in shallow, oxygen-poor marine environments that are rich in organic detritus. It forms as a result of a slow accumulation of sediments, by the replacement of calcite (p.114), or by primary deposition. It may contain shell fragments and larger fossils. Some glauconite pellets are biogenic, originating as faecal pellets.

Greensand tends to be weak and friable, although relatively hard greensand has been used as building stone. The soil derived from greensand varies, ranging from fertile to sterile. Glauconite is favoured in organic cultivation as a natural source of potassium and phosphorus. Its potassium content is useful in radiometric age-dating. Due to its chemical-exchange properties, the glauconite in greensand is used as a water softener and in water-treatment systems.

quartz grains

Pink orthoquartzite
Though this specimen of pink orthoquartzite is composed almost entirely of quartz, it is coloured by small amounts of iron oxide.

PROFILE

 Detrital

 Terrestrial

0.1–2 mm (¹⁄₂₅₆–¹⁄₁₆ in)

 Quartz

Heavy minerals, such as zircon and rutile

 Light to medium

 Rare, vertebrates

VARIANT

Grey orthoquartzite
A specimen coloured grey by quartz grains

ORTHOQUARTZITE

A pure quartz sandstone, orthoquartzite is usually composed of well-rounded quartz (p.168) grains cemented by silica. The high degree of rounding of the grains indicates that they have travelled some distance, which also accounts for the high degree of sorting. Some orthoquartzites are up to 99 per cent quartz, with only minor amounts of iron oxide and traces of other erosion-resistant minerals, such as rutile (p.78), magnetite (p.92), and zircon (p.233). Lesser amounts of other minerals can colour the generally white or pinkish specimens either grey or red. Orthoquartzites can be differentiated in hand specimens from other sandstones by their lighter colour and absence of other minerals.

Orthoquartzites rarely preserve fossils, although the sedimentary structures are usually preserved. The presence of silica cement makes orthoquartzites durable. They tend to resist weathering and form prominent outcrops. Orthoquartzite is distinct from metamorphic quartzite, also known as metaquartzite (p.295).

Grey arkose
Darker variants of arkose, such as this specimen, tend to be older than pink arkose.

pinkish feldspar

quartz grains

PROFILE

▲ Detrital, from feldspar-rich sand

⊕ Terrestrial, marine, or freshwater

◉ 0.1–2 mm (½₅₆–⅟₁₆ in)

■ Quartz, feldspar

▯ Mica

✳ Pinkish, pale grey

⊛ Rare

VARIANT

Pink arkose A variant of arkose formed more recently than grey arkose

ARKOSE

A pink sandstone, arkose is coloured by an abundance of feldspars (pp.173–81), especially pink alkali feldspars. Its high feldspar content (more than 25 per cent of the sand grains) sets it apart from other sandstones. Arkose specimens are relatively coarse and consist primarily of quartz (p.168) and feldspar grains, with small amounts of mica. The grains tend to be moderately well-sorted and angular or slightly rounded. They are usually cemented with calcite (p.114) or sometimes with iron oxides or silica. The flat cleavage faces and angular grain shape of the feldspars reflect light under a hand lens. Sandstones with a feldspar content of 5–25 per cent are called subarkoses.

Arkose forms from the quick deposition of sand weathered from granites (pp.258–59) and gneisses (p.288). The development of arkoses is thought to indicate either a climatic extreme or a rapid uplift and high relief of the source area. Arkoses are common along the front ranges of the Rocky Mountains.

reddish colour from iron oxides

Quartz gritstone
Specimens of quartz gritstone, such as this, are composed of more than 75 per cent quartz.

VARIANT

Feldspathic gritstone
A variant containing up to 25 per cent feldspar

GRITSTONE

Providing material for grindstones and millstones, gritstone has, in the past, been a commercially important sedimentary rock. It is a porous rock composed of cemented, coarse, often angular sand grains, with occasional small pebbles. Quartz (p.168) is always the greatest component, but specimens often contain iron oxides that give them a yellow, brown, or red colour. In some, the grains can be easily rubbed out; in others, strong cement makes the rock suitable for use as grinding stones.

Gritstones originate in river deposits and frequently show signs of cross bedding or current bedding. The Millstone Grit, a gritstone deposit in northern England, was mined for millstones used in flour mills and for grindstones, which were used to make paper pulp from wood and sharpen tools. Gritstone is still quarried for use as building material worldwide. Large exposures of gritstone are favoured by rock climbers because the rough surface provides outstanding friction, enabling them to grip the smallest features in the rock.

Grey shale
This specimen of shale from Runswick Bay, Yorkshire, England contains fossils of bivalves and ammonites.

fossilized ammonite

fissile sheets

fossilized bivalve

PROFILE

▲ Detrital, from mud, clay, or organic material

🌐 Marine, freshwater, glacial

🔎 Less than 0.1 mm ($\frac{1}{256}$ in)

◼ Clays, quartz, calcite

◻ Pyrite, iron oxides, feldspar

✱ Various

⊛ Invertebrates, vertebrates, plants

VARIANTS

Fossiliferous shale Shale with numerous fossils of brachiopods

alum-rich mineral

Light-coloured shale
A specimen with alum-rich, light-coloured areas

SHALE

The most abundant sedimentary rock, shale makes up about 70 per cent of all sedimentary rocks in Earth's crust. It consists of a high percentage of clay minerals, substantial amounts of quartz (p.168), and smaller amounts of carbonates (pp.114–25), feldspars (pp.173–81), iron oxides, fossils, and organic matter. Shales are coloured reddish and purple by hematite (p.91) and goethite (p.102); blue, green, and black by ferrous iron; and grey or yellowish by calcite (p.114). They split easily into thin layers.

Shales consists of silt- and clay-sized particles deposited by gentle currents on deep ocean floors, shallow sea basins, and river floodplains. They occur thinly interbedded with layers of sandstone (p.308) or limestone (p.319) and in sheets up to several metres thick.

Fossil Trilobite
Preserved in grey shale, this fossil trilobite is more than 400 million years old.

Dark oil shale
This specimen of oil shale shows dark, kerogen-rich layers. When heated, the kerogen gives off a vapour that contains oil.

kerogen-rich rock

PROFILE

- ▲ Detrital
- ⊕ Inland seas
- ○ Less than 0.1 mm (¹⁄₂₅₆ in)
- ■ Quartz, feldspar
- ▢ Alum
- ✳ Grey, black
- ⊕ Invertebrates, vertebrates, plants

VARIANT

Oily surface A specimen with condensed droplets of oil visible on the surface

OIL SHALE

The name oil shale is a general term for organic-rich sedimentary rocks that contain kerogen – a chemically complex mixture of solid hydrocarbons derived from plant and animal matter. When subjected to intense heat, these shales yield oil. Oil shales range from brown to black in colour. They are flammable and burn with a sooty flame. Some oil shales are true shales in which clay minerals are predominant. Others are actually limestones (p.319) and dolomites (p.320). Much of the original organic material in oil shales is unrecognizable, but it is believed to be derived from plankton, algae, and microorganisms that live in fresh sediment.

In previous centuries, small amounts of oil have been successfully recovered from oil shales. During the past century, oil shales have been mined with rock types varying from shale (p.313) to marl (p.322) and other carbonate rocks. Various pilot plants have been built to extract oil from shales, but the commercial results have been modest so far.

Grey siltstone
The tiny grains that make up siltstone are too small to be seen without a microscope.

silt-sized grains

dark colour
from carbon

PROFILE

▲ Detrital, from silt

⊕ Marine, freshwater, glacial

◯ Up to 0.1 mm (¹⁄₂₅₆ in)

◼ Quartz, feldspar

◻ Mica, chlorite, mica-rich clay minerals

✳ Grey to beige

⊛ Invertebrates, vertebrates, plants

VARIANT

Fossiliferous siltstone
A fern fossil enclosed in siltstone

SILTSTONE

Formed from grains whose sizes vary between that of sandstone (p.308) and mudstone (p.316), siltstone is a sedimentary rock. Like sandstone, it can form in different environments and have different colours and textures. Siltstones are typically red and grey with flat bedding planes. Plant fossils and other carbon-rich matter are common in darker-coloured siltstones. Examples tend to be hard and durable and do not easily split into thin layers. However, the presence of mica may produce a siltstone that splits into thicker, flagstone-like sheets. In addition to mica, siltstone may contain abundant chlorite and other mica-rich clay minerals.

Although many shales (p.313) contain more than 50 per cent silt, siltstones are usually chemically cemented and show cross bedding, ripple marks, and internal layering. This indistinct layering tends to weather at oblique angles unrelated to bedding. Siltstone is less common than shale or sandstone and rarely forms thick deposits.

PROFILE

- ▲ Detrital, from mud
- 🌐 Marine, freshwater, glacial
- 🔍 Less than 0.1 mm (¹⁄₂₅₆ in)
- ◼ Clays, quartz
- ▢ Calcite
- ✴ Grey, brown, black
- ❋ Invertebrates, vertebrates, plants

curved fracture

mud-sized grain

Mudstone specimen
Mudstone is somewhat similar in appearance to siltstone, but its grains are smaller and it has a broken surface with a much finer texture.

VARIANTS

Fossiliferous mudstone
A specimen of mudstone with numerous invertebrate fossils

Calcareous mudstone
A mudstone variant with a substantial amount of calcite

MUDSTONE

A grey or black rock formed from mud, mudstone contains carbon-rich matter, clay minerals, and detrital minerals such as quartz (p.168) and feldspar (pp.173–81). Mudstones look like hardened clay and can show the cracks seen in sun-baked clay deposits.

As in shale (p.313), mudstone's individual grains are clay- and silt-sized particles that can only be seen under a hand lens. Mudstone generally has the same colour range as shale, with similar associations between colour and content. Unlike shale, mudstone is not laminated during lithification and is not easily split into thin layers. The lack of layering is either due to the original texture or the disruption of layering. Mudstone deposits may be up to several metres in thickness.

Nautiloid fossil
This fossil nautilus is preserved in mudstone. The iridescence of a part of its shell is still visible.

poorly sorted minerals

fine-grained groundmass

ine-grained greywacke
his specimen shows the
oor sorting characteristic of
reywacke. The angular clasts
re set in a fine-grained matrix.

angular fragment

VARIANTS

Dirty sandstone A specimen from Canada with typical dirty appearance and poor sorting

Turbidite A greywacke formed by undersea avalanches

GREYWACKE

Easily confused with igneous basalt (p.273), greywacke is a turbidite – a rock resulting from rapid deposition in a turbulent marine environment. It gets its name from the German word *grauwacke*, which signifies a grey, earthy rock. Also called dirty sandstone, greywacke is hard, and mostly grey, brown, yellow, or black.

Greywacke is composed of poorly sorted, coarse- to fine-grained quartz (p.168), feldspar (pp.173–81), and dark-coloured minerals such as amphibole and pyroxene, set in a fine-grained matrix of clay, calcite (p.114), or quartz. Greywackes may occur in thick or thin beds along with slates (p.293) and limestones (p.319). In ancient Egypt, this stone was used to make sarcophagi, vessels, and statues.

Greywacke carving
This ancient Egyptian greywacke carving dates from 1370 BCE. It is an offering to the god of writing.

PROFILE

- 🔺 Detrital
- 🌐 Glacial
- 🔍 From less than 0.1 mm (½₅₆ in) to many m (ft)
- ■ Rock fragments
- ▢ Rock fragments
- ❋ Various
- ⊛ None

large clast

grey clay matrix

Tillite specimen
The large variation in clast sizes in tillites is evident in this specimen.

VARIANTS

oversized clast

Large clast Tillite with a large clast in a finer matrix

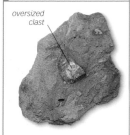

Differing clast sizes
A specimen of tillite with rounded clasts of differing sizes

TILLITE

Unsorted and unstratified rock material deposited by glacial ice that has later been lithified is called tillite. As glaciers move down valleys, they erode and transport rocks. On melting, they deposit this material, which is referred to as till. Glacial tills consist of pre-existing rock fragments pushed forward or sideways by the glacier, newly eroded material ground or broken up by the glacier, or mixtures of the two.

Tillites are typically made of grains with a wide range of sizes. They include fragments ranging from clay-sized particles to large blocks. The largest pieces give rise to the rock's alternative name, "boulder clay". The matrix, which frequently comprises a large percentage of the rock, is often made from rock flour, an unweathered and finely ground rock powder. Matching beds of ancient tillites on opposite sides of the South Atlantic Ocean provided early evidence for continental drift – the idea that continents move relative to one another – which was an important precursor to the theory of plate tectonics.

Fossiliferous limestone
This limestone specimen from Oxfordshire, England, includes several fossil invertebrates.

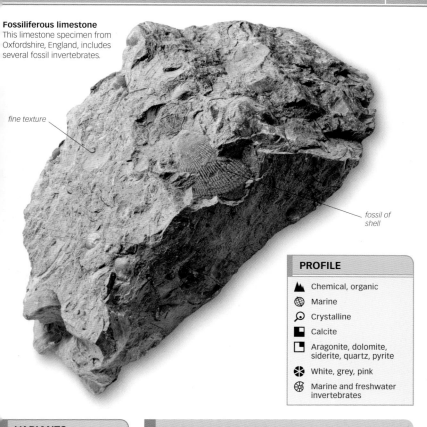

fine texture

fossil of shell

PROFILE

▲	Chemical, organic
🌐	Marine
🔍	Crystalline
■	Calcite
▢	Aragonite, dolomite, siderite, quartz, pyrite
✸	White, grey, pink
❋	Marine and freshwater invertebrates

VARIANTS

Coral limestone Limestone formed from fossil coral

Freshwater limestone Uncommon variant of limestone

Oolitic limestone Round ooliths set in calcite cement

LIMESTONE

Composed mainly of calcite (p.114), this abundant rock forms multiple layers that are thick and extensive. It can be yellow, white, or grey. Specimens can be identified by the rapid release of carbon dioxide and a fizzing sound when they react with dilute hydrochloric acid. Limestones can be compact, grainy, or friable. Many have cross bedding or ripple marks. The texture of limestone ranges from coarse and fossil-rich to fine and microcrystalline.

Limestone generally forms in warm, shallow seas either from calcium carbonate precipitated from sea water or from the shells and skeletons of calcareous marine organisms. It is used in construction, as a raw material in the manufacture of glass, as a flux in metallurgical processes, and in agriculture.

Limestone mask
This face mask dating from the Neolithic Period has been carved out of mottled limestone.

PROFILE

- ▲ Chemical
- ⊕ Marine
- ☉ Crystalline
- ■ Dolomite
- ▢ Calcite
- ✳ Grey to yellowish grey
- ✸ Invertebrates

fine-to-medium texture

compact carbonate rock

Dolomite rock
This specimen of dolomite
has a uniform texture that
is typical of the rock.

VARIANT

Red dolomite A specimen of
dolomite coloured with iron
oxides and hydroxides

DOLOMITE

This rock, formed exclusively from the mineral dolomite
(p.117), is also called dolostone. Most dolomite rocks are
believed to be limestones (p.319) in which dolomite has
replaced the calcite (p.114) in contact with magnesium-
bearing solutions. This process is called dolomitization.
Fresh dolomite looks similar to limestone, while weathered
dolomite is yellowish grey. Dolomites have fewer fossils
than limestones because fossils and other features are
destroyed by the dolomitization process. Dolomite fizzes
less violently than limestone when
in contact with hydrochloric acid.

Dolomite typically occurs as
massive layers. It is also present
as thin layers or pods within
limestone. Dolomite is used as
a flux to make steel. It can also
be used as a lightweight building
aggregate, in breeze blocks, and
in poured concrete.

Environment-friendly flux
In contrast to other steel-
making fluxes, dolomite
produces slag that can
be reused.

Microscopic fossils
This specimen of chalk, which is almost entirely calcite, is made up of tiny fossils of marine organisms.

soft, white, powdery texture

fine, white grain

PROFILE

▲ Chemical, organic

⊕ Marine

◎ Less than 0.1 mm (¹⁄₂₅₆ in)

■ Calcite

▭ Quartz, glauconite, clays

✸ White, grey, buff

⊕ Invertebrates, vertebrates

VARIANTS

Red chalk A specimen of chalk that takes its colour from incorporated hematite

Marine chalk A specimen of chalk pitted by the boring of marine animals

CHALK

A soft, fine-grained, easily pulverized, white to greyish variety of limestone is known as chalk. It is composed of calcite shells of minute marine organisms. Small amounts of other minerals, such as apatite (p.148), glauconite (p.196), and clay minerals, are usually present. Silica from sponge spines, diatom and radiolarian skeletons, and nodules of chert (p.332) and flint can also be present.

Extensive chalk deposits were formed during the Cretaceous Period (142 to 65 million years ago), the name being derived from the Latin word *creta*, which means "chalk". Chalk is used to make lime and cement and as a fertilizer. It is also used as a filler, extender, or pigment in a wide variety of materials, including ceramics and cosmetics.

Blackboard chalk
One of chalk's longstanding uses has been compression into sticks for writing on blackboards.

Green marl
Marls differ in colour depending on their mineral content. Green marls, such as this one, are coloured by either glauconite or chlorite.

green colour

fine grain size

curved fracture

PROFILE

- ▲ Detrital, from lime mud
- 🌐 Marine, freshwater
- 🔍 Less than 0.1 mm (¹⁄₂₅₆ in)
- ◼ Clays, calcite
- ▯ Glauconite, hematite
- ✳ Various
- ✳ Vertebrates, invertebrates, plants

VARIANT

Red marl A specimen coloured red by iron oxides

MARL

Calcareous mudstone or marl is a term applied to a variety of rocks that have a range of compositions but are all earthy mixtures of fine-grained minerals. In some countries, marl is referred to by the German terms *mergel* and *seekreide*, both of which mean "lake chalk". Marls usually consist of clay minerals and calcium carbonate. They form in shallow fresh water or seawater. The calcium carbonate content is frequently made up of shell fragments of marine or freshwater organisms or calcium carbonate precipitated by algae. The high carbonate content of marls makes them react with dilute acid.

Marls are whitish grey or brownish in colour but can also be grey, green, red, or variegated. Greensand marls contain the green mineral glauconite (p.196), and red marls, iron oxides. Marl is much less easily split than shale (p.313) and tends to break in blocks. Specimens are often nodular, and the nodules are usually better cemented than the surrounding rock.

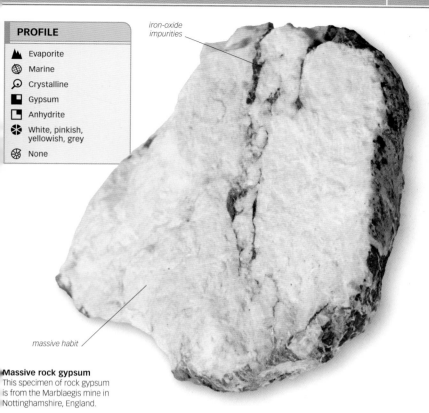

iron-oxide impurities

PROFILE

- ▲ Evaporite
- 🌐 Marine
- ⌀ Crystalline
- ◼ Gypsum
- ◻ Anhydrite
- ✱ White, pinkish, yellowish, grey
- ✤ None

massive habit

Massive rock gypsum
This specimen of rock gypsum is from the Marblaegis mine in Nottinghamshire, England.

VARIANT

boleite crystal

Gypsum with boleite Blue crystals of boleite seen in a groundmass of gypsum

ROCK GYPSUM

Also called gyprock, rock gypsum is the sedimentary rock formed mainly from the mineral gypsum (p.136). Though it is commonly granular, it can also occur as fibrous bands. Rock gypsum occurs in extensive beds formed by the evaporation of ocean water, in saline lakes, and in salt pans. It also occurs in some shales (p.313), limestones (p.319), and dolomitic limestones. Rock gypsum is commonly interlayered with other evaporites, such as rock anhydrite (p.133) and salt (p.324).

Most of the gypsum that is extracted – about three-quarters of the total production – is calcined (heated to drive off some of its water) for use as plaster of Paris. Unaltered rock gypsum is used as a fluxing agent, fertilizer, filler in paper and textiles, and retardant in Portland cement.

Mesopotamian seal
This ancient cylinder seal, with engravings of stags and scorpions, is made of alabaster gypsum.

orange colour from iron-rich clays

crystalline salt

Crystalline rock salt
This specimen of crystalline rock salt is coloured orange by iron-rich clays incorporated during deposition.

PROFILE

▲▲	Evaporite
⊕	Marine
⌀	Crystalline
◼	Halite
▢	Anhydrite
✳	White, pinkish, grey, yellowish
⊛	None

VARIANTS

Pink rock salt A specimen coloured pink by traces of iron oxides

Massive rock salt Rock salt with coarse, white and blue crystals

ROCK SALT

Familiar as common table salt, rock salt is the massive rock form of the mineral halite (p.110). It occurs in beds that range in thickness from a metre or so to more than 300m (990ft). Rock salt forms as a result of the evaporation of saline water in partially enclosed basins. It is commonly interlayered with beds of shale (p.313), limestone (p.319), dolomite (p.320), and other evaporites, such as anhydrite (p.133) and gypsum (p.136).

Rock salt often occurs in salt domes, which consist of a core of salt surrounded by strata of other rock. The domes can be 2km (1 mile) or more thick and up to 10km (6 miles) in diameter. They can occur with petroleum deposits: oil from oil-rich shales migrates up and gets caught on the underside of a salt dome.

Natural salt
Many people prefer natural salt for their cooking. Much of it comes from evaporating brines.

Porous diatomite
This specimen of
diatomite exhibits its
typical porous structure
and rough texture.

loose, porous structure

rough texture

PROFILE

▲	Detrital
🌐	Accumulation of silica-rich organisms
🔎	Less than 0.1 mm (¹⁄₂₅₆ in)
⬛	Opal
⬜	None
✳	White
🌐	Diatoms

DIATOMITE

Also called diatomaceous earth, diatomite consists
of about 90 per cent silica; the remainder is made up of
compounds such as aluminum oxides and iron oxides.
Diatomite is easily crumbled into a fine, white to off-white
powder. It is made of the fossilized remains of organisms
called diatoms. A form of algae, diatoms have hard shells
made of amorphous silica (opal) and containing many
fine pores. Most float on the surface of the sea.
Occasionally, large quantities are deposited in ocean
sediments, eventually forming diatomite. A few significant
deposits of freshwater diatomite are also known. Diatoms
are so small that diatomite specimens may contain
millions of diatom shells per cubic centimetre.

An important industrial rock, diatomite is easily mined.
It is used for the filtration of beverages, liquid chemicals,
industrial oils, cooking oils, fuels, and drinking water. Its
low-abrasive qualities find use in toothpastes, polishes,
and non-abrasive cleaners. It is also used as a filler and
extender in paint and paper.

Red-brown laterite
This specimen shows the intermixture of iron and aluminium oxides with sand or other rock detritus characteristic of laterites.

iron-oxide minerals

sand grains

Desert-varnished laterite
A variant of laterite with a polished surface

LATERITE

Laterite is nodular soil rich in hardened iron and aluminium oxides and resembles bauxite (p.101) in composition. Nodules of laterite are red-brown or yellow and contain grains of sand or hardened clay. The rock forms in hot, wet tropical climates, where it develops by intensive and prolonged chemical weathering of the underlying rock. Evaporation and leaching of minerals from rock, loose sediment, and soil leaves behind insoluble salts. This results in a variety of laterites differing in their thickness, grade, chemistry, and ore mineralogy.

Laterite is a source of bauxite, which is an ore of aluminium and exists largely in clay minerals and various hydroxides. Laterite ores have also been a source of iron and nickel. Many laterites are solid enough to be used as building blocks. An example is the laterite seen at the famous temple in Angkor Wat, Cambodia. Crushed laterite has been widely used to make roads. Laterites are also being increasingly used in water treatment.

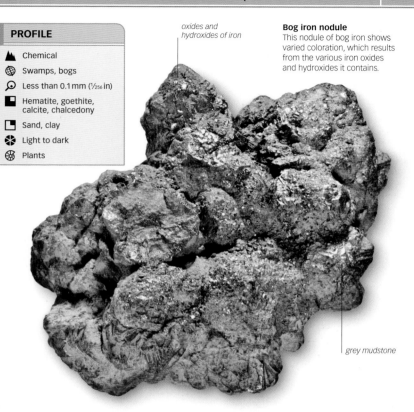

oxides and
hydroxides of iron

Bog iron nodule
This nodule of bog iron shows
varied coloration, which results
from the various iron oxides
and hydroxides it contains.

PROFILE

- ▲ Chemical
- 🌐 Swamps, bogs
- 🔎 Less than 0.1 mm (1/256 in)
- ◼ Hematite, goethite, calcite, chalcedony
- 🔲 Sand, clay
- ✳ Light to dark
- ✳ Plants

grey mudstone

VARIANT

Bog iron ore Grey mudstone
with oxides and hydroxides
of iron

BOG IRON

Impure iron deposits that develop in bogs or
swamps are known as bog iron. Bog iron is typically
a brown-yellow mudstone with yellow, red, brown, or
black concretions of iron oxides and hydroxides. In
general, bog ores consist of iron hydroxides, primarily
goethite (p.102). Bog iron can contain up to 70 per cent
iron oxide. It often contains carbon-rich plant material,
which is sometimes preserved by iron minerals. Bog
iron typically forms in areas where iron-bearing
groundwater emerges as springs. As the iron encounters
the oxygen-rich surface water, it oxidizes, and the iron
oxides precipitate out.

Bog iron was formerly used as an ore and was widely
sought in the preindustrial age. The Romans and the
Vikings made extensive use of bog iron as a source of
iron. Bog iron was also the principal source of iron in
colonial USA. Although it is still forming today, the iron
requirements of modern industry demand much larger
sources of ore.

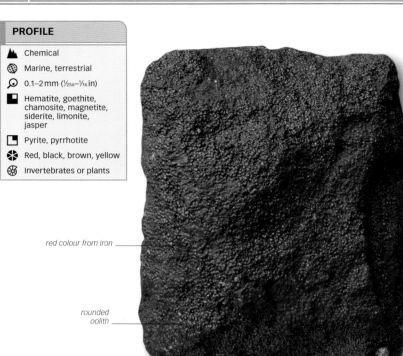

red colour from iron

rounded oolith

Oolitic ironstone
This specimen of ironstone is made up of small, rounded oolites, which are cemented by hematite.

VARIANT

Sandy ironstone A specimen of a leaf fossil beautifully preserved in ironstone

IRONSTONE

The term ironstone is applied to sandstones and limestones that contain more than 15 per cent iron. Ironstones are rich in iron-bearing minerals such as hematite (p.91), goethite (p.102), siderite (p.123), and chamosite. These minerals give ironstones a dark red, brown, or yellow colour.

Ironstone no longer appears to be forming; partly because of this, the process by which it forms is something of a mystery. Some ironstones seem to have formed early in Earth's history when oxygen was not as abundant in the atmosphere as it is now. Precambrian ironstones, which are more than 500 million years old, as well as slightly later ones, formed prior to 240 million years ago, are common. Many of the later ironstones consist of oolites (small spheres) of hematite and contain fossils. Although historically used as an iron ore, ironstone is too limited in quantity to be an economic modern source of iron.

Banded ironstone
This specimen of ironstone shows prominent banding of alternate chert- and iron-rich material.

hematite-rich layer

chert layer

BANDED IRONSTONE

Also known as banded iron formations, banded ironstone is made up of thin layers of alternating red, brown, or black iron oxides, which may be hematite (p.91) or magnetite (p.92), and grey or off-white shale (p.313) or chert (p.332). It is a very fine-grained rock that breaks into smooth, splintery pieces. Particularly abundant in Precambrian rocks, which are more than 500 million years old, banded ironstone can form very thick sequences, such as in the Hammersley Range of Australia, where it is an economically important iron ore.

Banded iron layers are found in some of the oldest known rock formations, dating from more than 3,700 million years ago. These layers are believed to have formed in the seas as a result of dissolved iron combining with oxygen released by the green algae that flourished in the oceans at that time. This was then precipitated into oxygen-poor sea-floor sediments that were forming shale and chert. The banding of ironstone is assumed to result from cyclic variations in the oxygen available.

PROFILE

- Chemical
- Terrestrial
- Less than 1 mm (1/32 in)
- Calcite or silica
- Aragonite
- White
- Rare

Calcareous tufa
This specimen of calcareous tufa is full of holes and irregular shapes. It was formed by the evaporation of water.

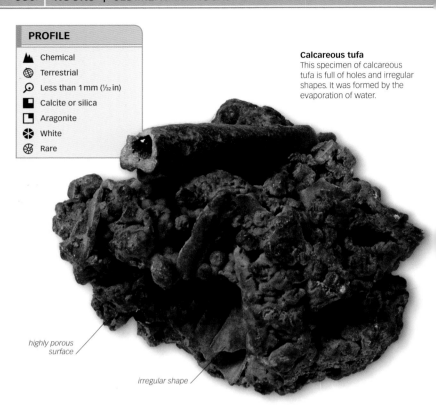

highly porous surface

irregular shape

VARIANTS

Yellow tufa Irregularly shaped tufa that lacks bedding

Fossilized tufa Tufa formed around plant remains

TUFA

Two different sedimentary rocks that precipitate from water are known as tufa. Calcareous tufa, or calc-tufa, is a soft, porous form of limestone deposit composed principally of calcium carbonate (calcite) that precipitates from hot springs, lake water, and ground water. Calc-tufa is often stained red by the presence of iron oxides.

Siliceous tufa, which is also called siliceous sinter, is a deposit of opaline or amorphous silica that forms through the rapid precipitation of fine-grained silica as an encrustation around hot springs and geysers. It is believed to have been partly formed by the action of algae in the heated water. The term "sinter" means that it has several hollow tubes and cavities in its structure, which are often a result of organic matter that has decomposed later.

Stone Wedding
This pink tufa formation is in the Rhodope Mountains, Bulgaria. It is locally called the Stone Wedding.

Flint nodule
This nodule shows a variation in colour due to differences in the extraneous material enclosed while the silica making the rock solidified.

compact silica

sharp edge

conchoidal fracture

VARIANTS

Melanterite A nodule of hydrous iron sulphate

Pyrite nodule A nodule of radiating pyrite crystals

Marine nodule A nodule of manganese oxides

NODULES

A rounded mineral accretion that differs in composition from its surrounding rock is known as a nodule. Nodules are commonly elongated with a knobby irregular surface and are usually oriented parallel to the bedding of their enclosing sediment. Most nodules are formed by the accumulation of silica in sediments and its subsequent solidification. Nodules containing manganese, phosphorous, titanium, chromium, and other valuable metals develop on the sea floor but are uneconomical to mine. Other nodules form around plant and animal remains as part of the fossilization process.

Pyrite (p.62) is commonly found as nodules. It occurs as spheres, rounded cylinders of radiating crystals, and flat, radiating discs, or "suns". Clay ironstone, a mixture of siderite (p.123) and clay, sometimes occurs as layers of dark grey-to-brown nodules overlying coal seams. Chert (p.332) and flint often occur as nodules of nearly pure cryptocrystalline quartz (p.168) within beds of limestone (p.319) or chalk (p.321).

Grainy chert
This specimen of fine-grained chert
shows the way the rock breaks
along flat to rounded surfaces.

*rounded fracture
surface*

fine-grained texture

VARIANT

**Fossiliferous
chert**
A specimen
containing
fossilized
primitive
plants

CHERT

A rock composed of microcrystalline silica is known
as chert. It is commonly grey, white, brown, or black and
may contain small fossils. Traces of iron (p.39) may give
chert a light green to rusty-red colour. Chert occurs as
beds or nodules. It breaks along flat to rounded, smooth
surfaces and has a glassy appearance. The rock
forms by precipitation from silica-rich
fluids and colloids.

Flint is chert that occurs in marly
limestones (p.319) or chalk (p.321). It is
generally grey in colour. Flint is found
as nodules, often in bands parallel to
the bedding planes, and breaks with
a conchoidal fracture. The nodules
are irregular but rounded. Flint
resists weathering, so it can form
thick pebble beds on beaches
and accumulate in soils that are
derived from chalk.

Flint axe
A prized material for tool
making, flint was one of the
earliest rocks to be mined
and extracted.

PROFILE

- ▲ Chemical
- ⊕ Postdepositional
- ⊘ Crystalline
- ▪ Calcite, silica
- ▫ Celestine
- ✷ Grey, brown
- ⊛ Invertebrates, plants

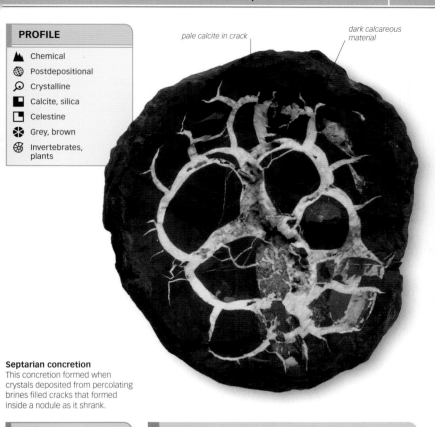

pale calcite in crack

dark calcareous material

Septarian concretion
This concretion formed when crystals deposited from percolating brines filled cracks that formed inside a nodule as it shrank.

VARIANT

Ironstone concretion
Pteridosperm (seed fern) fossilized in an ironstone concretion

CONCRETIONS

Nodules and concretions are distinctly different geologically, although they have some visual similarities. Unlike nodules, which are of different compositions than their hosts, concretions are made of the same material as their host sediment and cemented by other minerals, mainly calcite (p.114), iron oxides, and silica. Concretions are often much harder and more resistant to erosion than their surrounding rock and can be concentrated by weathering. They usually form early in the burial history of the sediment before the rest of the sediment is hardened into rock.

Concretions vary in shape, hardness, and size. They can be so small that they need to be seen under a magnifying lens. Specimens can also be huge bodies 3m (9¾ft) or more in diameter and weighing several tons. In some localities, fossil collectors seek out concretions that have formed around plant and animal remains and perfectly fossilized them. The largest fossil from concretions was an almost complete hadrosaur – a type of dinosaur.

METEORITES

Meteorites are rocks that formed elsewhere in our Solar System and orbited the Sun before colliding with Earth and falling to its surface. The fragments most likely to survive are either very large (weighing 10 g/⅓ oz or more) or very small (1 mg or less).

STRUCTURE

There are three basic types of meteorite: irons, composed mostly of metallic iron and varying amounts of nickel; stony-irons, composed of a mixture of iron and silicate minerals; and stony meteorites, which are further classified into chondrites and achondrites, depending on the presence or absence of small igneous, silicate spheres called chondrules. The most common type of stony-irons are pallasites, which are iron meteorites with centimetre-sized, translucent, olivine or pyroxene crystals scattered throughout.

Pallasite section
The stony-iron meteorites known as pallasites are usually one part olivine crystals to two parts metal. In this specimen, olivine is more abundant.

iron-nickel groundmass

small to medium grains

olivine crystal

Achondrite
This stony meteorite found in Haryana, India, lacks chondrules, the small spheres of igneous minerals that would make it a chondrite.

OCCURRENCE

Meteorites are found on every continent. They are often found in environments where they are highly visible – ice caps and deserts being examples. They range in size from microscopic specimens to masses that weigh many tonnes. Rocks that have been melted by meteorite impacts called tektites, are also widespread.

THE ORIGIN OF THE SOLAR SYSTEM

Meteorites are of particular interest in the study of the origin of the Solar System. Nearly all meteorites are thought to be fragments of asteroids – rocky bodies that formed in the solar nebula at about the same time as Earth. Radiometric dating puts the age of most meteorites at about 4.5 billion years, the same age as Earth.

Lunar discoveries
Over 100 meteorites are now believed to be material dislodged from the Moon, providing a more representative sample of the lunar surface than those brought back by astronauts.

Barringer Crater
This well-preserved impact crater is in the Arizona Desert, USA, and is 1.2 km (¾ mile) in diameter. The meteorite that created it fell about 50,000 years ago and was about 50 m (165 ft) across.

Iron meteorite
The kamacite and taenite crystals in this iron meteorite occur as fine, crosshatched lines, forming what is known as a Widmanstätten pattern.

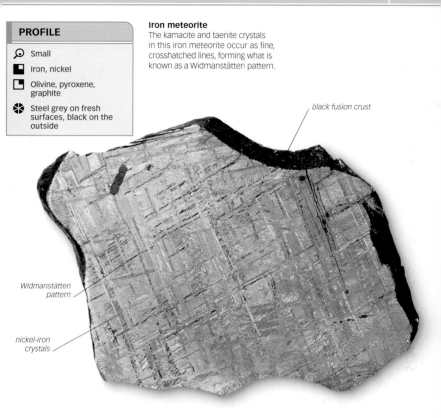

black fusion crust

Widmanstätten pattern

nickel-iron crystals

VARIANT

pointed metal

Fusion surface An iron meteorite with a partially vaporized surface

IRON METEORITE

These meteorites are believed to be the shattered fragments of the formerly molten cores of large, ancient asteroids. As the name suggests, iron meteorites are composed mostly of metallic iron (p.39) and up to 25 per cent nickel, to produce two minerals, kamacite and taenite, which are otherwise rare on Earth. Other minerals present in minor amounts in iron meteorites include troilite, graphite (p.46), phosphides, and some silicates – most commonly olivine (p.232) and pyroxene. Iron meteorites are divided into a number of subgroups based on their chemical makeup.

Since iron meteorites are so different from most terrestrial rocks, they are recognized more often than other kinds of meteorites and tend to be over represented in meteorite collections. It is estimated that only about 6 per cent of meteorites are iron meteorites. Chemical and isotope analysis of a number of iron meteorites indicates that at least 50 distinct parent asteroids were involved in their creation.

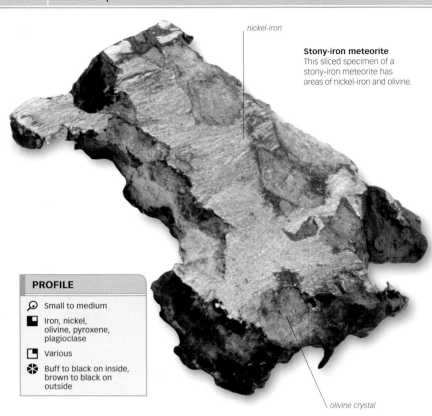

nickel-iron

Stony-iron meteorite
This sliced specimen of a
stony-iron meteorite has
areas of nickel-iron and olivine.

olivine crystal

PROFILE

🔎 Small to medium

⬛ Iron, nickel,
olivine, pyroxene,
plagioclase

⬜ Various

✳ Buff to black on inside,
brown to black on
outside

VARIANTS

Meteorite from Antarctica
Stony-iron meteorite from the
Thiel Mountains, Antarctica

"Thumbprint" surface
Meteorite from Chile with a
melted surface resembling
a thumbprint

STONY-IRON METEORITE

Composed of a mixture of metallic nickel-iron and
silicate minerals, stony-iron meteorites make up about
1 per cent of recovered meteorites. Pallasites, the most
common type of stony-iron meteorites, are iron meteorites
with centimetre-sized, translucent crystals of olivine (p.232),
or sometimes pyroxene, scattered throughout. Pallasites
were believed to have originated along the boundaries of
the iron cores and silicate mantles of large asteroids. But
some experts now believe they are impact-generated
mixtures of core and mantle materials.

The other main group of stony-iron meteorites are
known as the mesosiderites. Relatively rare, these
consist of about equal parts of metallic nickel-iron and
silicate minerals, namely pyroxene, olivine, and calcium-
rich feldspar (pp.173–81). They have an irregular, often
brecciated texture, with the silicates and metal occurring as
lumps, pebbles, or fine-grained intergrowths.

black fusion crust

thumb-shaped depression

stony interior

Stony meteorite
The stony composition of this meteorite is visible on its broken surface. Its outside has melted on its passage through the atmosphere.

VARIANTS

Achondrite A specimen with more varied composition than chondrites

Chondrite Variant of stony meteorites usually composed of olivine and pyroxene

STONY METEORITE

These meteorites can be divided into chondrites and achondrites, which are named after chondrules – small, igneous, silicate spheres that dominate most chondritic meteorites. Chondrules are largely made up of pyroxene and olivine (p.232), with lesser amounts of glass, and may contain calcium-rich feldspar (pp.173–81). They can be up to 1 cm (³⁄₈ in) wide. Chondritic asteroids are some of the oldest and most primitive astronomical bodies in the Solar System. They may have formed by rapid heating in the cloud of dust from which the Solar System originated. More than 80 per cent of the meteorites that fall to Earth are chondrites.

Achondritic meteorites, in which chondrules are absent, are believed to represent the crust or mantle of asteroids that developed separate mineral shells around an iron-nickel core. They are similar to igneous rocks (pp.258–85) and impact breccias on Earth. Although most achondrites appear to come from asteroids, about 20 of those recovered are believed to have originated on Mars and another 20 on the Moon.

GLOSSARY

ACCESSORY MINERAL
A mineral that occurs in a rock in such small amounts that it is disregarded in its definition.

ACICULAR HABIT
A needle-like crystal habit of some minerals. See also *habit*.

ADAMANTINE LUSTRE
A type of bright mineral lustre similar to that of diamond. See also *lustre*.

AGGREGATE
An accumulation of mineral crystals or rock fragments.

ALKALINE ROCK
A class of igneous rocks abundant in potassium- and sodium-rich minerals.

ALTERATION
The chemical, thermal, or pressure process or processes by which one rock or mineral is changed into another.

ALTERATION PRODUCT
A new rock or mineral formed by the alteration of a previous one. See also *alteration*.

ALUM
Any of a group of hydrated double salts, usually consisting of aluminum sulphate, water of hydration, and the sulphate of another element.

AMYGDALE
A secondary in-filling of a void in an igneous rock. Minerals that occur as amygdales include quartz, calcite, and the zeolites.

ASSOCIATED MINERALS
Minerals found growing together but not necessarily intergrown. See also *intergrowth*.

AUREOLE
The area around an igneous intrusion where contact metamorphism has occurred.

BASAL CLEAVAGE
Cleavage that occurs parallel to the basal crystal plane of a mineral. See also *cleavage*.

BATHOLITH
A huge, irregularly shaped mass of igneous rock formed from the intrusion of magma at depth. See also *magma*.

BLADED HABIT
A crystal habit in which wide, flat crystals appear similar to knife blades. See also *habit*.

BOTRYOIDAL HABIT
A mineral habit in which crystals form globular aggregates similar to bunches. See also *aggregate*, *habit*.

BRECCIA
A sedimentary rock made up of angular fragments. See also *igneous breccia*.

CABOCHON
A gemstone cut with a domed upper surface and a flat or domed under surface; gemstones cut in this way are said to be cut *en cabochon*. See also *cut*, *gem*, *gemstone*.

CARAT
A unit of gemstone weight, equivalent to 0.2g (0.007oz). Carat (also spelled "Karat") is also a measure of gold purity, the number of parts of gold in 24 parts of a gold alloy: 24kt is pure gold; 18kt is three quarters gold. See also *gem*, *gemstone*.

CHATOYANCY
The cat's-eye effect shown by some stones cut *en cabochon*. See also *cabochon*.

CLAST
A fragment of rock, especially when incorporated into a sedimentary rock.

CLASTIC ROCK
A sedimentary rock composed of cemented clasts. See also *clast*.

CLAY
Mineral particles smaller than about 0.002mm (0.00008in).

CLEAVAGE
The way certain minerals break along planes dictated by their atomic structure.

COLLOID
Any substance that consists of particles substantially larger than atoms or molecules but too small to be visible to the unaided eye.

COLOUR DISPERSION
The separation of white light into its constituent colours.

CONCHOIDAL FRACTURE
A curved or shell-like fracture in many minerals and some rocks. See also *fracture*.

CONCRETION
A rounded, nodular mass of rock formed from its enclosing rock and commonly found in beds of sandstone, shale, or clay.

CONTACT TWINNING
The phenomenon of two or more crystals growing in parallel contact with each other and sharing a common face. See also *twinned crystals*.

CRYPTOCRYSTALLINE HABIT
A mineral habit that is crystalline but very fine-grained. Individual crystallized components can be seen only under a microscope. See also *habit*.

CUT
The final shape of a ground and polished gem, as in emerald cut. See also *gem*, *gemstone*, *gem cutting*.

DENDRITIC HABIT
A type of habit in which crystals form branching, tree-like shapes. See also *habit*.

DETRITAL ROCKS
Sedimentary rocks formed essentially of fragments and grains derived from existing rocks. See also *sedimentary rock*.

DIATOMACEOUS EARTH
A sedimentary rock composed of the siliceous shells of microscopic aquatic plants known as diatoms.

DIFFRACTION
The splitting of light into its component colours. See also *x-ray diffraction*.

DISCOVERY/TYPE LOCALITY
The site where a mineral was first recognized as a new mineral.

DOUBLE REFRACTION
The splitting of light into two separate rays as it enters a stone.

DRUSY COATING
A sheet of numerous, often well-formed, small crystals covering a mineral.

DULL LUSTRE
A type of lustre in which little or no light is reflected. See also *lustre*.

DYKE
A sheet-shaped igneous intrusion that cuts across existing rock structures.

EARTHY LUSTRE
A non-reflective mineral lustre. See also *lustre*.

EQUANT
A mineral habit that refers to a crystal that is of equal size in all directions; a rock composed of grains of equal size.

EUHEDRAL
A term describing crystals with well-formed faces.

EVAPORITE
A mineral or rock formed by the evaporation of saline water.

EXTRUSIVE ROCK
A rock formed from lava that either flowed onto Earth's surface or was ejected as pyroclastic material. See also *intrusive rock*, *lava*.

FACES
The external flat surfaces that make up a crystal's shape.

FELDSPATHOIDS
Minerals similar in chemistry and structure to the feldspars but with less silica.

FELSIC ROCK
An igneous rock with more than 65 per cent silica and more than 20 per cent quartz. It is also known as acidic rock.

FISSILE TEXTURE
A rock texture that allows the rock to be split into sheets. See also *texture*.

FLOW BANDING
Layering in a rock that originated when the rock was in a fluid, molten state.

FOLIATION
The laminated, parallel orientation or segregation of minerals.

FOSSIL
Any record of past life preserved in the crustal rocks. Apart from bones and shells, fossils can include footprints, excrement, and borings.

FRACTURE
Mineral breakage that occurs at locations other than along cleavage planes. See also *cleavage*.

FUMAROLE
In volcanic regions, an opening in the ground through which hot gases are emitted.

GARNET
A member of a group of silicates with the general formula $A_3B_2(SiO_4)_3$ in which A can be Ca, Fe^{2+}, Mg, or Mn^{2+}; and B can be Al, Cr, Fe^{3+}, Mn^{3+}, Si, Ti, V, or Zr.

GEODE
A hollow, generally rounded nodule lined with crystals. See also *nodule*.

GEM, GEMSTONE
A cut stone worn in jewellery, valued for its colour, rarity, texture, or clarity. It may even be an unset stone cut for use as jewellery. See also *cut*, *rough gemstone*.

GEM CUTTING
The process of shaping a gemstone by grinding and polishing. See also *cut*, *gem*, *gemstone*.

GLASS
A solid substance showing no crystalline structure – in effect, a very thick liquid. See also *glassy texture*.

GLASSY TEXTURE
The smooth consistency of an igneous rock in which glass formed due to rapid solidification. See also *glass*, *texture*.

GRANULAR TEXTURE
A rock or mineral texture that either includes grains or is in the form of grains. See also *texture*.

GRAPHIC TEXTURE
The surface appearance of some igneous rocks in which quartz and feldspar have intergrown to produce an effect resembling a written script. See also *texture*.

GROUNDMASS
A fine-grained rock into or on top of which larger crystals appear to be set. It is also known as a matrix.

HABIT
The mode of growth and appearance of a mineral. The habit of a mineral results from its molecular structure.

HACKLY FRACTURE
A mineral fracture that has a rough surface with small protuberances, as on a piece of broken cast iron. See also *fracture*.

HEMIMORPHIC FORM
A crystalline form with a different facial development at each end.

HOPPER CRYSTAL
A crystal whose growth has created a hopper-shaped concavity on one or more faces.

HYDROTHERMAL DEPOSIT
A mineral deposit formed by hot water ejected from deep within Earth's crust.

HYDROTHERMAL MINERAL
A mineral derived from hydrothermal deposition. See also *hydrothermal deposit*.

HYDROTHERMAL VEIN
A rock fracture in which minerals have been deposited by fluids from deep within Earth's crust. See also *hydrothermal deposit*, *pegmatite*, *vein*.

HYPABYSSAL
A term describing minor igneous intrusions at relatively shallow depths within Earth's crust.

IGNEOUS BRECCIA
An igneous rock made up of angular fragments. See also *breccia*.

IGNEOUS ROCK
A rock that is formed through the solidification of molten rock.

INCLUSION
A crystal or fragment of another substance within a crystal or rock.

INTERGROWTH
Two or more minerals growing together and interpenetrating each other. See also *associated minerals*.

INTERMEDIATE ROCK
An igneous rock that is intermediate in composition between silica-rich and silica-poor rocks.

INTRUSIVE ROCK
A body of igneous rock that invades older rock. See also *extrusive rock*.

IRIDESCENCE
The reflection of light from the internal elements of a stone, yielding a rainbow-like play of colours.

LAMELLAR HABIT
A type of crystal habit in which plates or flakes occur in thin layers or scales. See also *habit*.

LAVA
Molten rock extruded on to Earth's surface. See also *magma*.

LITHIFICATION
The process by which unconsolidated sediment turns to stone. See also *recrystallization*.

LUSTRE
The shine of a mineral caused by reflected light.

MAFIC ROCK
An igneous rock with 45–55 per cent silica. Such rocks have less than 10 per cent quartz and are rich in iron-magnesium minerals. They are also known as basic rocks. See also *ultramafic rock*.

MAGMA
Molten rock that may crystallize beneath Earth's surface or be erupted as lava. See also *lava*.

MAMILLARY HABIT
A mineral habit in which crystals form rounded aggregates. See also *aggregate, habit*.

MASSIVE
A mineral form having no definite shape.

MATRIX
See *groundmass*.

METAL
A substance characterized by high electrical and thermal conductivity as well as by malleability, ductility, and high reflectivity of light.

METALLIC LUSTRE
A shine similar to the typical shine of polished metal. See also *lustre*.

METAMORPHIC ROCK
A rock that has been transformed by heat or pressure (or both) into another rock.

METEOR
A rock from space that completely vaporizes while passing through Earth's atmosphere.

METEORITE
A rock from space that reaches Earth's surface.

MICA
Any of a group of hydrous potassium or aluminium silicate minerals. These minerals exhibit a two-dimensional sheet- or layer-like structure.

MICROCRYSTALLINE HABIT
A mineral habit in which crystals are so minuscule that they can be detected only with the aid of a microscope. See also *habit*.

MINERAL GROUP
Two or more minerals that share common structural and/ or chemical properties.

MOONSTONE
A gem-quality feldspar mineral that exhibits a silvery or bluish iridescence. Several feldspars, especially some plagioclases, are called moonstone.

NATIVE ELEMENT
A chemical element that is found in nature uncombined with other elements.

NODULE
A generally rounded accretion of sedimentary material that differs from its enclosing sedimentary rock.

NONMETAL
An element, such as sulphur, which lacks some or all of the properties of metals. See also *metal*.

OOLITHS
Individual spherical sedimentary grains from which oolitic rocks are formed. Most ooliths comprise concentric layers of calcite.

ORE
A rock or mineral from which a metal can be profitably extracted.

OXIDATION
The process of combining with oxygen. In minerals, the oxygen can come from the air or water.

PEGMATITE
A hydrothermal vein composed of large crystals. See also *hydrothermal vein*.

PENETRATION TWINNING
The phenomenon of two or more crystals forming from a common centre and appearing to penetrate each other. See also *twinned crystals*.

PHENOCRYST
A large crystal set in an igneous rock groundmass, creating a porphyritic texture. See also *porphyritic texture*.

PISOLITIC HABIT
A mineral habit characterized by pea-sized grains with a concentric inner structure. See also *habit*.

PLACER, PLACER DEPOSIT
A deposit of minerals derived by weathering and concentrated in streams or beaches because of the mineral's high specific gravity.

PLASTIC ROCK
A type of rock that is easily folded when subjected to high temperature and pressure.

PLATY HABIT
The growth habit shown by flat, thin crystals. See also *habit*.

PLAYA DEPOSIT
A mineral deposit formed in a desert basin that is intermittently filled with a lake.

PLEOCHROIC, PLEOCHROISM
The phenomenon of a mineral or gem presenting different colours to the eye when viewed from different directions.

PLUTON
A mass of igneous (plutonic) rock that has formed beneath Earth's surface by the solidification of magma.

POLYMORPH
A substance that can exist in two or more crystalline forms; one crystalline form of such a substance. See also *pseudomorph*.

PORPHYRITIC TEXTURE
An igneous rock texture in which large crystals are set in a finer matrix. See also *phenocryst*, *texture*.

PORPHYROBLAST
A relatively large crystal set in a fine-grained matrix in a metamorphic rock.

PORPHYROBLASTIC TEXTURE
A texture characterized by relatively large crystals in a fine-grained matrix. See also *texture*.

PRECIPITATION
The condensation of a solid from a liquid or gas.

PRIMARY MINERAL
A mineral that has crystallized directly from an igneous magma and is unaltered by rain, groundwater, or other agents. See also *secondary mineral*.

PRISMATIC HABIT
A mineral habit in which parallel rectangular crystal faces form prisms. See also *habit*.

PROTOLITH
A rock that existed prior to undergoing metamorphic transformation into a different rock type.

PSEUDOMORPH
A crystal with the outward form of another species of mineral. See also *polymorph*.

PYRAMIDAL HABIT
A crystal habit in which the principal faces join at a point. When two such pyramids are placed base to base, the crystal is said to be di- or bi-pyramidal. See also *habit*.

PYROCLASTIC ROCK
A rock consisting of airborne material ejected from a volcanic vent.

PYROXENE
A member of a group of 21 rock-forming silicate minerals that typically form elongate crystals.

RADIOMETRIC DATING
The determination of absolute ages of minerals and rocks by measuring certain radioactive and radiogenic atoms in them.

RARE-EARTH MINERAL
A mineral containing a significant portion of one or more of the 17 rare-earth elements, principally ytterbium, gadolinium, neodymium, praseodymium, cerium, lanthanum, yttrium, and scandium.

RECRYSTALLIZATION
The redistribution of components to form new minerals or mineral crystals; in some cases new rocks form. It occurs during lithification and metamorphism. See also *lithification*.

REFRACTIVE INDEX
A measure of the slowing down and bending of light as it enters a stone. It is used to identify cut gemstones and some minerals. See also *cut*, *gem*, *gemstone*.

RENIFORM HABIT
A mineral habit with a kidney-like appearance. See also *habit*.

REPLACEMENT DEPOSIT
A deposit formed from minerals that have been altered. See also *alteration product*.

RESINOUS LUSTRE
A shine having the reflectivity of resin. See also *lustre*.

RETICULATED
Having a network or a net-like mode of crystallization.

ROCK FLOUR
Very fine-grained rock dust, often the product of glacial action.

ROUGH GEMSTONE
An uncut gemstone. See also *cut*, *gem*, *gemstone*.

SALT DOME
A large, intrusive mass of salt, sometimes with petroleum trapped beneath.

SCHILLER EFFECT
The brilliant play of bright colours in a crystal, often due to minute, rod-like inclusions.

SCHISTOSITY
A foliation that occurs in coarse-grained metamorphic rocks. It is the result of platy mineral grains. See also *foliation*.

SCORIACEOUS
A term for lava or other volcanic material that is heavily pitted with hollows and cavities. See also *lava*.

SECONDARY MINERAL
A mineral that replaces another mineral as a result of weathering or alteration. See also *alteration*, *primary mineral*.

SECTILE
The property of a mineral that allows it to be cut smoothly with a knife. See also *fracture*.

SEDIMENTARY ROCK
A rock that either originates on Earth's surface as an accumulation of sediments or precipitates from water.

SEMIMETAL
A metal, such as arsenic or bismuth, that is not malleable. See also *metal*.

SILICA-POOR ROCKS
Rocks containing less than 50 per cent silica. See also *silica-rich rocks*.

SILICA-RICH ROCKS
Rocks containing more than 50 per cent silica. See also *silica-poor rocks*.

SLATY CLEAVAGE
The tendency of a rock, such as slate, to break along flat planes into thin, flat sheets. See also *cleavage*.

SOLID-SOLUTION SERIES
A series of minerals in which certain chemical components are variable between two end members with fixed composition.

SPECIFIC GRAVITY
The ratio of the mass of a mineral to the mass of an equal volume of water. Specific gravity is numerically equivalent to density (mass divided by volume) in grams per cubic centimetre.

SPHEROIDAL HABIT
A crystal habit in which numerous crystals radiate outwards to form a spherical mass. See also *habit*.

STALACTITIC HABIT
A mineral habit in which the crystalline components are arranged in radiating groups of diminishing size, giving the appearance of icicles. See also *habit*.

STRIATION
A parallel groove or line appearing on a crystal.

SUBLIMATION, SUBLIMATE
The process by which a substance moves directly from a gaseous state to a solid state. A sublimate is the solid product of sublimation.

SUNSTONE
A gemstone variety of feldspar with minute, plate-like inclusions of iron oxide oriented parallel to one another throughout. See also *gem*, *gemstone*.

TABULAR HABIT
A crystal habit in which crystals take the shape of a cereal box. See also *habit*.

TERMINATION
Faces that make up the ends of a crystal.

TEXTURE
The size, shape, and relationships between rock grains or crystals.

TWINNED CRYSTALS
Crystals that grow together as mirror images with a common face (contact twins) or grow at angles up to 90 degrees to each other and appear to penetrate each other (penetration twins).

ULTRAMAFIC ROCK
An igneous rock with less than 45 per cent silica. It is also known as an ultrabasic rock. See also *mafic rock*.

VEIN
A thin, sheet-like mass of rock that fills fractures in other rocks.

VESICLE
A small, spherical or oval cavity produced by a bubble of gas or vapour in lava, left after the lava has solidified. See also *lava*.

VITREOUS LUSTRE
A shine resembling that of glass. See also *lustre*.

VOLCANIC PIPE
A fissure through which lava flows. See also *lava*.

WELL-SORTED ROCK
A sediment or sedimentary rock with grains or clasts that are roughly of the same size.

X-RAY DIFFRACTION
The passing of x-rays through a crystal to determine its internal structure by the way in which the x-rays are scattered. See also *diffraction*.

ZEOLITE
A group of hydrous aluminium silicates characterized by their easy and reversible loss of water.

INDEX

Page numbers in **bold** indicate main entries.

ACKNOWLEDGMENTS

Produced in collaboration with the **Smithsonian Institution**, in Washington, DC, USA, the world's largest museum and research complex. This renowned research centre is dedicated to public education, national service, and scholarship in the arts, sciences, and history.

Smithsonian Enterprises
Carol LeBlanc, Vice President; Brigid Ferraro, Director of Licensing; Ellen Nanney, Licensing Manager; Kealy Wilson, Product Development Coordinator.

The publisher would like to thank the following people: Frances Green for helping to plan the profile sections; Janet Mohun, Miezan van Zyl, Lizzie Munsey, and Martyn Page for editorial work; Steve Setford for proof reading; Jane Parker for the index; David Roberts for database work; and Sophia Tampakopoulos, Jacket Design Development Manager.

DK India would like to thank Neha Chaudhary, Jubbi Francis, and Suefa Lee for editorial assistance; Vaibhav Rastogi for design assistance; and Mahima Barrow, Nidhilekha Mathur, Swati Mittal, and Neha Samuel for picture selection assistance.

The publisher would like to thank the following for their kind permission to reproduce their photographs:

(Key: a-above; b-below/bottom; c-centre; f-far; l-left; r-right; t-top)

6-7 Corbis: William James Warren/ Science Faction. **8 Corbis:** Roger Wood (tr). **8-9 Corbis:** Ludovic Maisant (b). **9 Corbis:** Kevin Schafer (t). **14 Science Photo Library:** Steve Gschmeissner (b). **24 The Bridgeman Art Library:** Ashmolean Museum, University of Oxford, UK (cr); Egyptian National Museum, Cairo, Egypt/Giraudon (cl). **Corbis:** Jack Fields (bl); Bernard Bisson/Sygma (br). **26 Corbis:** WildCountry (br). **Dorling Kindersley:** Neil Fletcher (cl). **27 Corbis:** Momatiuk - Eastcott (t). **28 Dorling Kindersley:** Neil Fletcher (b). **Getty Images:** Keith Douglas (t). 29 Getty Images: John Elk III (t). **32 Corbis:** Jim Sugar (cr). **Getty Images:** American Images Inc (cl). **33 Corbis:** Philippe Eranian (t). **34-35 Getty Images:** National Geographic. **36 Corbis:** Ricki Rosen/SABA (cl). **FLPA:** Silvestris Fotoservice (b). **39 Dorling Kindersley:** Peter Anderson © Dorling Kindersley, Courtesy of the Danish National Museum (br). **40 Dorling Kindersley:** Colin Keates, Courtesy of the Natural History Museum, London (br). **41 Dorling Kindersley:** Clive Streeter, Courtesy of The Science Museum, London (cl). **42 Dorling Kindersley:** Harry Taylor, Courtesy of the Natural History Museum, London (cl). 43 Dorling Kindersley: Judith Miller/Woolley and Wallis (br). **44 Dorling Kindersley:** Colin Keates, Courtesy of the Natural History Museum, London (cl). **45 Dorling Kindersley:** Colin Keates, Courtesy of the Natural History Museum, London (br). **47 Smithsonian Institution, Washington, DC, USA:** (br). **48 Corbis:** Eric and David Hosking (t). **Science Photo Library:** Ben Johnson (b). **60 Smithsonian Institution, Washington, DC, USA:** (cl). 61 Smithsonian Institution, Washington, DC, USA: (bl). **65 Dorling Kindersley:** Alan Hills and Barbara Winter © The British Museum (cr). **Tony Waltham Geophotos:** (b). 69 Corbis: Heritage Images (br). **72 Dorling Kindersley:** Neil Fletcher (bl). **73 akg-images:** Rabatti – Domingie (br). **74 Corbis:** Steve Parish/Steve Parish Publishing (t). **Dorling Kindersley:** Courtesy of Dream Cars (br). **75 Corbis:** Klaus Lang/All Canada Photos (t); WIN-Images (cl); Jim Reed (br). **77 Dorling Kindersley:** Neil Fletcher (bl). **81 Smithsonian Institution, Washington, DC, USA:** (br). **83 Corbis:** Bettmann (br). **88 Dorling Kindersley:** Neil Fletcher (bl). **100 Corbis:** Vince Streano (b). **105 Corbis:** Michael S. Yamashita (cl). **106 Corbis:** Stevens Fremont/ Sygma (cr). **Tony Waltham Geophotos:** (b). **109 Dorling Kindersley:** Courtesy of the Oxford University Museum of Natural History (br). **113 Dorling Kindersley:** Judith Miller/333 Auctions LLC (cr). **Tony Waltham Geophotos:** (b). **114 Corbis:** (br). **118 Getty Images:** (bl). **119 Dorling Kindersley:** Neil Fletcher (clb). **121 Smithsonian Institution, Washington, DC, USA:** (t). **126 Tony Waltham Geophotos:** (b). **131 Corbis:** Gallo Images (b); Larry Mulvehill (cr). **134 Smithsonian Institution, Washington, DC, USA:** (clb). **140 Dorling Kindersley:** Neil Fletcher (clb). **141 Dorling Kindersley:** Neil Fletcher (bl). **145 NASA:** Marshall Space Flight Center (br). **147 Corbis:** David Muench (b). **Science Photo Library:** Hank Morgan/University of Massachusetts at Amherst (cr). **151 Smithsonian Institution, Washington, DC, USA:** (clb, bl). 159 Dorling Kindersley: Judith Miller/Mark Laino (br). 162 Dorling Kindersley: British Museum Images (br). **167 Alamy Images:** Pavel Filatov (b). **Dorling Kindersley:** Michel Zabe © CONACULTA-INAH-MEX (cr). **168 Dorling Kindersley:** Judith Miller/Private Collection (br). **169 Dorling Kindersley:** British Museum Images (br). **170 Dorling Kindersley:** Judith Miller/Wallis and Wallis (br). **173 Dorling Kindersley:** Judith Miller/Sylvie Spectrum (br). **175 Dorling Kindersley:** Judith Miller/Dreweatt Neate (br). **178 Dorling Kindersley:** Colin Keates, Courtesy of the Natural History Museum, London (br). **179 Alamy Images:** Piotr & Irena Kolasa (b). **181 Science Photo Library:** Joel Arem (b). **182 Dorling Kindersley:** British Museum Images - DK Images (br). **184 Dorling Kindersley:** Judith Miller/N. Bloom & Son Ltd. (br). **185 Alamy Images:** RF Company (cl). **Science Photo Library:** Joel Arem (bl). **190 Dorling Kindersley:** Neil Fletcher (cl); Clive Streeter, Courtesy of The Science Museum, London (br). **191 Dorling Kindersley:** Neil Fletcher (bl). **193 Dorling Kindersley:** Judith Miller/ Cooper Owen (b). **194 Corbis:** Scientifica/Visuals Unlimited (bl). **196 U.S. Geological Survey:** G.R. Mansfield (bl); E. D. McKee (cl). **198 Dorling Kindersley:** Neil Fletcher (cl). **200 Dorling Kindersley:** Judith Miller/David Rago Auctions (br). **Dreamstime.com:** Gelyngfjell (bl, cl). **206 Dorling Kindersley:** Judith Miller/Dreweatt Neate (br). **209 Alamy Images:** Andre Joubert (t); RF Company (bl). **214 Getty Images:** DEA/C. Bevilacqua (cl). **Science Photo Library:** Scientifica, Visuals Unlimited (bl). **215 Smithsonian Institution, Washington, DC, USA:** (clb). **217 Dorling Kindersley:** Judith Miller/Blanchet et Associes (br). **Getty Images:** DEA/Photo 1 (cl). **218 Getty Images:** Mark Schneider (clb); Scientifica (cla). **222 Dorling Kindersley:** John Chase, Courtesy of The Museum of London (br). **223 Dorling Kindersley:** Judith Miller/Lesley Craze Gallery (br). **226 Alamy Images:** Alan Curtis (bl); Greg C Grace (cl). **230 Getty Images:** Mark Schneider (cl); Visuals Unlimited/Scientifica (bl). **231 Dorling Kindersley:** Judith Miller/Woolley and Wallis (br). **232 Dorling Kindersley:** Judith Miller/HY Duke and Son (br). **241 shutterstone.com:** (cl, bl). **243 Dorling Kindersley:** Judith Miller/Joseph H Bonnar (br). **246 Dorling Kindersley:** Martin Strmiska (c) Alamy (b). **248 Dorling Kindersley:** Judith Miller/Beaussant Lefevre (br). **249 Dorling Kindersley:** Judith Miller/Wallis and Wallis (br). **252 Dorling Kindersley:** Colin Keates, Courtesy of the Natural History Museum, London (cl). **Corbis:** Chris Harris/All Canada Photos. **257 Corbis:** Gary Braasch (b). **259 Dorling Kindersley:** Neil Fletcher (bl). **261 Dorling Kindersley:** Judith Miller/N. Bloom & Son Ltd. (br). **Smithsonian**

Institution, Washington, DC, USA: (bl). **264 Corbis:** Visuals Unlimited (bl). **Getty Images:** Mark Schneider/Visuals Unlimited (cl). **269 Dorling Kindersley:** Judith Miller/HY Duke and Son (br). **270 Dorling Kindersley:** Neil Fletcher (cl). **Getty Images:** DEA/A. Dagli Orti (bl). **272 Alamy Images:** RF Company (t). **274 Alamy Images:** Susan E. Degginger (bl). **Getty Images:** DEA/R. Appiani (cl). **275 Dorling Kindersley:** Image Plan (c) Corbis (br). **276 Alamy Images:** Phil Degginger (t); Susan E. Degginger (b). **281 Alamy Images:** Photo resource Hawaii (clb). **Corbis:** (bl). **283 Dorling Kindersley:** Neil Fletcher (cl). **shutterstone.com:** (t). **286-287 Alamy Images:** Daniel Dempster Photography (b). **291 Dorling Kindersley:** Judith Miller/Ormonde Gallery (br). **293 Dorling Kindersley:** Courtesy of the Blists Hill Museum, Ironbridge, Shropshire (br). **294 Alamy Images:** Susan E. Degginger (clb); RF Company (cla); geoz (bl). **296 Alamy Images:** geoz (cl); RF Company (bl); Fabrizio Troiani (clb). **297 Alamy Images:** The Art Archive (b). **300 Alamy Images:** Leslie Garland Picture Library (cl). **Corbis:** Scientifica/Visuals Unlimited (t, bl). **Dorling Kindersley:** Neil Fletcher (clb). **305 Corbis:** Ric Ergenbright (cr). **307 Dorling Kindersley:** Peter

Hayman/The Trustees of the British Museum (br). **309 fotoLibra :** Brian G Burgess (b). **316 Dorling Kindersley:** Colin Keates, Courtesy of the Natural History Museum, London (cl). **317 The Bridgeman Art Library:** Detroit Institute of Arts, USA/Gift of Lillian Henkel Haass and Constance Haass (br). **319 Dorling Kindersley:** The Trustees of the British Museum (br). **320 shutterstone.com:** (bl). **323 Dorling Kindersley:** The Trustees of the British Museum (br). **326 Dorling Kindersley:** Neil Fletcher (bl, t). **327 fotoLibra :** John Cleare (t). **332 Dorling Kindersley:** Courtesy of the Pitt Rivers Museum, University of Oxford (br). **333 Dorling Kindersley:** Colin Keates, Courtesy of the Natural History Museum, London (cl). **334 Corbis:** (cr). **Smithsonian Institution, Washington, DC, USA:** (c). **335 Dorling Kindersley:** Neil Fletcher (b). **336 Dorling Kindersley:** Colin Keates, Courtesy of the Natural History Museum, London (cl); Courtesy of the Oxford University Museum of Natural History (t). **337 Dorling Kindersley:** Neil Fletcher (bl)

All other images
© Dorling Kindersley
For further information see:
www.dkimages.com